THE OXFORD BOOK OF
JAPANESE SHORT STORIES

Theodore William Goossen is a translator, broadcaster, and critic who teaches Japanese literature and culture at York University in Toronto, Canada. A frequent visitor to Japan since 1968, his interests include Japanese baseball and sumo wrestling.

T0068652

THE
OXFORD BOOK OF
JAPANESE
SHORT STORIES

Edited by

Theodore W. Goossen

OXFORD
UNIVERSITY PRESS

OXFORD
UNIVERSITY PRESS

Great Clarendon Street, Oxford OX2 6DP

Oxford University Press is a department of the University of Oxford.
It furthers the University's objective of excellence in research, scholarship,
and education by publishing worldwide in

Oxford New York

Auckland Cape Town Dar es Salaam Hong Kong Karachi
Kuala Lumpur Madrid Melbourne Mexico City Nairobi
New Delhi Shanghai Taipei Toronto

With offices in

Argentina Austria Brazil Chile Czech Republic France Greece
Guatemala Hungary Italy Japan Poland Portugal Singapore
South Korea Switzerland Thailand Turkey Ukraine Vietnam

Oxford is a registered trade mark of Oxford University Press
in the UK and in certain other countries

Published in the United States
by Oxford University Press Inc., New York

© Introduction and selection Theodore W. Goossen 1997

The moral rights of the author have been asserted
Database right Oxford University Press (maker)

First published 1997
Reissued 2010

All rights reserved. No part of this publication may be reproduced,
stored in a retrieval system, or transmitted, in any form or by any means,
without the prior permission in writing of Oxford University Press,
or as expressly permitted by law, or under terms agreed with the appropriate
reprographics rights organization. Enquiries concerning reproduction
outside the scope of the above should be sent to the Rights Department,
Oxford University Press, at the address above

You must not circulate this book in any other binding or cover
and you must impose this same condition on any acquirer

British Library Cataloguing in Publication Data

Data available

Library of Congress Cataloging in Publication Data

Data available

Printed in Great Britain
on acid free paper by
Clays Ltd, Elcograf S.p.A.

ISBN 978-0-19-958319-5

15

For my parents,
Eugene C. Goossen and Jean Griffin Goossen

Oxford University Press gratefully
acknowledges the financial support of the
Japan Foundation in the publication
of this work.

ACKNOWLEDGEMENTS

A great many people have helped me during the several years I have been working on this project. I have benefited tremendously from the comments and suggestions of Kawamoto Koji, Kinya Tsuruta, and Jay Rubin, my triumvirate of advisors, whose knowledge and experience were a constant source of inspiration. My students at York University played an important role by providing me with the feedback I needed to move forward. Miya Narushima patiently read through the originals with me, contributing her linguistic and literary sensitivity to the painstaking editing process. My editor at Oxford, George Miller, was a constant companion and friend despite the ocean that separated us, and the anthology bears the mark of his incisive mind and generous spirit. Finally, Meg Taylor shared the burdens and joys of the book's conception and preparation with a boundless store of skill, enthusiasm, and warmth.

Needless to say, a project of this scope required the support of my family and friends. To my wife, Tam, our daughters, Jeananne and Carolyn, my mother-in-law Tam Kwai Lan, and to David and Melanie, I give my heartfelt thanks for putting up with me during a long and often hectic process. My gratitude also goes out to my first *sensei*, Antony V. Liman and Akiyama Shun, who guided me through my first awkward steps in the field. There have been many others as well who contributed to the book, suggesting stories and helping me keep my eye on the 'big picture'. In the end, however, I alone must bear the responsibility for the selections, as well as for any errors or oversights that may be contained in these pages.

CONTENTS

[Surnames appear as the first part of Japanese names]

Contents

Contents

Contents

INTRODUCTION

As a child, I devoured short stories. The shorter the better, in fact. I can recall coming across collections of them in my father's library, and happily working my way through the volumes, selecting only those pieces of twenty pages or less. Anything longer was too much to get through in one sitting, which was the way I liked to read. I loved legends and fables as well, not only for their brevity, but because I could understand all the words. I was especially attached to a slender, tattered book of Japanese fairy tales, translated and illustrated around the turn of the century. None of these stories—of miniature heroes born from peaches, badgers who turned into tea kettles, sparrows with severed tongues, and so forth—struck me as strange in the least. A good story is just a good story when we are very young.

As I grew older, things grew more complicated. In the classroom, I learned how to distinguish 'short stories' from the other kinds, and why the ones in my textbook were examples of 'good writing'. It was the early 1960s, and, in my school at least, the guidelines were still pretty strict; a proper short story was to present a 'slice of life', replete with a conflict and its resolution, a clear ending, and so forth. Over the past few decades, however, the short story has changed: like so many modern genres, its seams have burst, loosing a wide variety of 'misshapen' offspring which lack conflicts, resolutions, clear endings, sometimes even recognizable characters.

Introducing the Japanese short story in this uncertain and un-bounded world is much easier than it would have been in the old days, when the hard-and-fast rules were still in play, and the Western image of Japan wrapped in layers of exoticism. Japanese short stories do differ from their Western counterparts, to be sure, but these differences are hardly mystical—they can be understood, and used to expand our idea of what forms good writing can take. For example, Japanese literature has lyrical roots, and thus places more stress on atmosphere and beauty, and less on structured plot, than its Western cousins. The tradition also tends to favor shorter works—the novel may rule the West, but not Japan, where short stories have been regarded as 'purer' than longer, ostensibly more commercial efforts. In fact, this anthology contains many of the best-loved works of

Japanese modern literature, one of the world's great artistic traditions, which can now stand on its own, free of the weight of the Oriental mystique.

It is thus with a sense of confidence that I offer you this selection of short stories spanning the whole of Japan's modern era. For readers who would like to have some background and context, I have appended the following brief Introduction, which is divided into two sections: Generations, which gives a brief overview of the authors and their times, and Legacies, a look at some of the traditions of Japanese stories as they have developed over the past century. For those of you who want only to enjoy the stories, I can say with assurance: Don't worry. You will.

Generations

In modern Japan, where change has been swift, it has been claimed that five years makes a generation. I have no reason to argue with this; any figure I might set is bound to be arbitrary. Still, given that the birth-dates of the youngest and oldest authors in this anthology are roughly a century apart, and that, in reproductive terms at least, twenty years is a reasonable length of time, I have divided this section into five 'generations': trail-blazers, settlers, wanderers, survivors, and entertainers. Please keep in mind, however, that these are broad categories, and that any writer, regardless of age, is shaped by the events of his or her times.

Trail-Blazers

> As a child I enjoyed studying the Chinese classics. Although the time I spent in this kind of study was not long, it was from the Chinese classics that I learned, however vaguely and obscurely, what literature was. In my heart, I hoped that it would be the same way when I read English literature . . . But what I resent is that despite my study I never mastered it. When I graduated I was plagued by the fear that I had somehow been cheated by English literature.
>
> (*A Theory of Literature* by Natsume Soseki, 1906)[1]

It is hard to imagine the extent of the impact that Western literature had on the first Japanese to encounter it in the late nineteenth

---

[1] Karatani Kojin (ed.), *Origins of Modern Japanese Literature* (Chapel Hill, NC: Duke University Press, 1993), 17–18. Trans. Brett de Bary. (All quotations are translated by the editor if not otherwise indicated.)

century. Only a few decades had passed since Admiral Perry had arrived aboard his black ships, unannounced and uninvited, to lay down like a Mafia godfather the offer that could not be refused: Japan must end over two centuries of isolation and start trading with the outside world, or face the consequences. Confronted with this ultimatum, Japan revamped its entire political system, abolishing the four feudal classes, establishing an elected government, and 'restoring' the young Meiji emperor to a position of symbolic importance.

The Meiji era (1868–1912) was half over, and the modernizing of the nation well under way, by the time literature started to catch up. The sons of the disenfranchised samurai—the highly educated warrior caste which had ruled Japan for centuries—were hunched over their books, absorbed in deciphering the intricacies of English grammar and Western science. They were eager students, idealistic and ambitious, and full of dreams about what the future might hold for them and their country. Yet, when they turned to study literature, their texts were the same Chinese and Japanese classics that their fathers had used. Who would pioneer a new literature, at once Japanese and 'modern', that could speak to the change and transformation going on around them?

Mori Ogai and Natsume Soseki, the authors of the two opening stories, were among the first of those who stepped forward to take up this challenge. Certainly no one could have been better equipped for the task: gifted in European languages, they excelled in classical Chinese as well, and had a deep knowledge of Japan's literary traditions. Yet the task they faced was daunting. Writers of fiction were dismissed as frivolous and vulgar by traditional society, which was still influenced by Confucian views on the subject. A new language for literature, which would reflect how people actually spoke, and which could be used to express exciting new concepts like 'love' and 'individualism', had to be created from scratch. Finally, it was necessary to grapple with the literary forms—the novel, the short story, the poem—that had been developed in the West.

This did not mean, however, that the trail blazed by Ogai, Soseki, and their contemporaries ran parallel to that of Western literature. These were no blind admirers of what the West had to offer— Soseki, for one, felt that he had been somehow 'cheated' by English literature. Ogai had studied in Germany, Soseki in England, and both were acutely aware that the features of foreign culture—the language, the customs, the sense of beauty and form—were altogether different from Japan's. To create a new, modern Japanese literature, they had to carve new trails, not follow old ones. They had to be experimental writers. This meant that, once they felt they had taken what they could use from Western literature, they moved on. Ogai eventually turned to traditional materials—legends like 'Sansho the Steward', the first story in this anthology, and the lives of historical figures—while Soseki, a brilliant theoretician, was able to anticipate developments yet to occur in the West. Through their efforts, and those of the other trail-blazers, by 1910 the Japanese short story was already established as a genre linked with, but not identical to, its counterpart in the West.

Settlers

> I discovered the value of the printed word as a youth living in a remote corner of Japan. I had yet to set foot in a big city, but I could order books and magazines from Tokyo, and thus learn that, in the West, Homer, Dante, Shakespeare, and Goethe were admired as the greatest poets of all time. In the same fashion, I came to know of the three great Kabuki actors of the day—Danjuro, Kikugoro, and Sadanji . . . When I go to Tokyo, I thought, I must see them perform with my own eyes. When I go to Tokyo, I must learn enough English to read the four masters on my own. As I sat there in my shabby second-floor room, I could feel the future stretching brightly out before me.
>
> (*On Dante* by Masamune Hakucho, 1927)

Trail-blazers lead the way through uncharted land, settlers farm and build upon it. So it was with the second generation of modern Japanese writers. In their hands, the short story flourished, taking on a wide variety of colors and shapes, some of which are easy for us to recognize, and some less so. This group of writers could read almost all the short-story masters—Maupassant and Chekhov, Poe and Turgenev, Flaubert and Hans Christian Andersen—in Japanese translation, and had access to recent films and books from abroad. Thus, like Masamune Hakucho, most did not find it necessary or natural to draw a hard line between the foreign and the native, whether in their writing or their personal lives, a way of thinking that reflected the cosmopolitan atmosphere of the Taisho era (1912–26).

An architectural expression of this is the dream house of Shiga

Naoya, who was considered the 'god of autobiographical literature'. From the outside, it looks quite traditional, but the wealthy Shiga wanted a bright, sunlit home, so he installed a number of large glass windows and raised the ceilings to add a sense of spaciousness. The walls and alcoves were filled with his collection of Western and Japanese art, and the kitchen and dining area were arranged so that men and women were encouraged to mingle together freely instead of breaking up into separate groups, as was normally the case. This type of architectural concept was out of keeping with the traditional ideal as championed by Tanizaki Jun'ichiro in his famous essay, 'In Praise of Shadows'. Tanizaki, who was to fiction what Shiga was to autobiographical literature, lauded the traditional out-house as an example of the old aesthetic—it was to be dim and shadowy, without a trace of the shiny porcelain that represented the crassness of sanitized modern culture. Yet, when Tanizaki built his own house, and the architect crowed that he knew just what the great man wanted, having read his essay, Tanizaki and his family drew the line—under no conditions were they willing to sacrifice the convenience of modern plumbing for an aesthetic ideal.

The youngest settlers, like the Nobel Prize-winning Kawabata Yasunari, came of age at the very end of the era of Taisho cosmo-politanism, in the mid-1920s. This was both a good and a bad time to be a writer. On the positive side, opportunities had never been more plentiful. A publishing boom was under way, and all the mass-circulation literary magazines were looking for manuscripts to fill their pages. As the number of readers multiplied, the fees increased, and suddenly parents no longer objected to their children becoming writers. Even small journals flourished. The down side, however, was that in the aftermath of the great Tokyo earthquake of 1923 these journals, and the literary world in general, were fracturing along political lines. Proletarian literature, riding the crest of the wave unleashed by the Russian Revolution, was all the rage, and those like Kawabata who were interested in pursuing other, non-socialist objectives soon found themselves a distinct minority. Social commitment, not literary quality, became the ticket to success. Yet, within a few years, an increasingly conservative and militaristic government had stamped out the proletarian movement, and was turning its attentions to the rest of the literary community. The settlers and their children were being driven from their homes, and the dark and dreary years of wandering were beginning.

Introduction

Wanderers

> We who choose suicide seldom know what our true reasons
> are ... The decision to take one's life (like the decision to
> commit any act) is bound to stem from complex motives. Yet,
> in my case, I can pinpoint the cause as a feeling of vague
> uneasiness. A vague uneasiness over what the future may hold
> in store for me.
>
> (*Letter to an Old Friend* by Akutagawa Ryunosuke, 1927)

In the West, World War Two swept in like a sudden tempest, as
mass invasions in Europe and the surprise attack on Pearl Harbor
were quickly followed by all-out warfare. For the citizenry of
Japan, however, the Pacific War came as does a distant storm, with
flashes of light on the horizon, and the occasional, almost inaudible
rumble. It began in 1931 with the invasion of Manchuria, and
ended shortly after atomic bombs were dropped on Hiroshima and
Nagasaki in 1945, by which time most Japanese cities had been
burned to the ground in devastating air raids. Yet, since information
was strictly controlled, most Japanese had few facts to go on, just
a 'vague uneasiness', the phrase Akutagawa Ryunosuke had used
to explain his suicide on the eve of the country's descent into
militarism.

Literary censorship was stepped up in this process: writers could
be subjected to imprisonment and ideological 'reorientation' if they
displeased the authorities by voicing socialist ideas. Indeed, during
the last years of the war, works that did not directly support the
national effort were banned from publication. Even after Japan's
surrender, the American-led Occupation imposed its own equally
strict code, to the dismay of those who had dared dream that, finally,
censorship would be abolished. To come of age as a writer in the
1930s and '40s, then, was to enter into a shifting world where
personal and artistic survival meant keeping one's head down, and
staying on the move. Japanese writers had become refugees in their
own land.

Nevertheless, the new generation, which I call the wanderers,
managed to broaden and enrich Japanese literature, not just by
what they wrote, but by who they were. For while almost all the
trail-blazers and settlers had come from Japan's university-educated
élite, the wanderers often hailed from working-class backgrounds.
Hayashi Fumiko and Hirabayashi Taiko, for example, probably

would have spent their lives as factory workers or café hostesses had it not been for the proletarian movement, which actively recruited working-class talent. Hayashi had literally grown up a wanderer, as we can see in her autobiographical story, 'The Accordion and the Fish Town'. After supporting herself through school by working nights, she made her way to Tokyo, where she met Hirabayashi, as well as a string of feckless lovers who seem to have spent all of their time talking revolution and borrowing money. Once she found she could support herself as a writer, however, she never looked back, turning out books at a phenomenal rate, to an ever-expanding audience. In fact, together with authors like Hirabayashi, Enchi Fumiko, and Okamoto Kanoko, Hayashi helped dispel once and for all the assumption that, apart from the brief and early flowering of Higuchi Ichiyo, all good modern writers were male.

Settlers write from established homes, wanderers from the margins. Hayashi, as a woman raised in poverty, had that marginality from birth: others, like Dazai Osamu, the son of a wealthy and powerful family from north-east Japan, had to go out and earn it. This he did by engaging in a life of rebellious dissolution that included a number of suicide attempts, three of them suicide pacts with women. The third, in 1948, was a success, if you can call it that. For several years, I lived not far from where this took place, an unthreatening, tree-lined channel called the Tamagawa Canal. It seemed hard to believe that Dazai, Japan's most popular writer at the time, could have drowned in what amounted to a large drainage ditch. His readers understood the darkness that had sucked him down, though, for it was everywhere—in his self-mocking literature, in the charred ruins of the cities, and in the straggling lines of returning, defeated soldiers. The challenge now was to rebuild, but for the weary Dazai, who had carried the burden of hopelessness so jauntily for so long, even the thought of rebuilding must have been overwhelming. The storms had passed, but for the wanderers the physical and spiritual damage remained.

Survivors

> My father buried all his Western books in the garden during the War—they were just too dangerous to keep around. After Japan surrendered, we dug them up, and I started trying to read them. Baudelaire's poetry made the biggest impression on me.

It was so fresh and free of the old poetic clichés. This, I
thought, is the way I must learn to write!

(Interview with the poet Ooka Makoto, 1992)

From the rubble, a fresh generation of writers took wing. I call
them the survivors, for they had come through a catastrophe, and
were driven by the sense of urgency often found in people who
have had a brush with death. They wanted to get moving, and
fast. There was no need to defer to their teachers—how could
you respect someone who preached patriotic fascism one year and
liberal democracy the next?—or their fathers, whose loss of authority
was underlined by the presence of the swaggering GI occupiers,
who enticed Japanese women with nylon stockings, chocolate
bars, and dreams of American prosperity. Paternalism was dead, at
least for the time being, and a new literature which would fit
the post-war era was waiting to be constructed. There was another
more tangible reason behind their hurry, however—economic survival. Jobs were hard to find, and money scarce. People were so
starved for entertainment, though, that writers could eke out a
decent living despite the minuscule rates being paid by the war-
ravaged publishing houses. As the economy recovered, the rates
went up, but the frenetic creativity remained, making the survivors
a prolific and well-paid group.

Mishima Yukio personified this trend. He was full of ideas about
Japanese culture, which he claimed was rotting under the weight of
American-style materialism, and he was extremely productive: although known abroad for his novels, his reputation in Japan is based
more on the brilliance of his essays, plays, and short stories. Mishima
never pretended to stand naked before his readers, as Dazai and
Hayashi Fumiko often did. Instead, he tantalized them with flashes
of what might lie beneath his many costumes. His images could be
bloody and disturbing, or they could be delicate and nuanced, as
we find in 'Onnagata', which represents Japanese tradition in the
willowy form of a Kabuki actor who specializes in female roles.

In the end no one was really sure where to draw the line between
Mishima and his various personas. His final act was the most flam-
boyant of all. Flanked by the smartly uniformed young men of his
private 'army', Mishima drove to Self-Defense Force headquarters in
downtown Tokyo, took the commanding officer hostage, and then
harangued the assembled troops on their duty to emperor and

country from a balcony. Amidst a chorus of hoots and taunts, he retired to an inside room to commit ritual suicide, an act he had rehearsed for years in his fiction and in one particularly gory self-produced film. There are many theories about why he did this, but one fact remains: through his death, Mishima Yukio imprinted himself upon the memory of the world at large. In historical terms, as he planned, Mishima turned out to be the ultimate survivor.

The world at large was important to Mishima, the first Japanese author to cultivate a foreign audience, yet he was passed over for the Nobel Prize for literature in favor of his own mentor, Kawabata Yasunari, in 1968. The second winner, in 1994, was Oe Kenzaburo. A decade younger than Mishima, Oe was just 10 when the war ended, living in the mountains of the isolated island of Shikoku in a village much like the one in 'Prize Stock'. When he grew older, he went to Tokyo University, and was right in the middle of the huge student protests against Japan's military treaty with the United States, which used Japan as a base in the Korean and Vietnam wars. Whereas Mishima had defended the glories of Japanese martial values and the emperor, Oe became their implacable foe.

The birth of a brain-damaged son shifted Oe's focus, but he never abandoned the ideals of his youth, which had been forged in war-time and sharpened in an age of political struggle. Yet, as in the United States and Europe, the student protest movement lost its steam in the early 1970s, when its leaders grew out of touch with the less radical rank and file. After one of the most militant and violent groups, the Japanese Red Army, horrified the country by murdering a number of its own members at a secret mountain retreat, the break was complete. One era had ended, and another was under way.

Entertainers

> Japan—the world's only post-atomic-bomb society. If you think of our country that way, it's easy to see why Kawabata and Mishima lost hope . . . Some think you can counter-balance American popular culture with something that is solidly and uniquely Japanese. When you try to pin that something down though, you realize there's nothing there . . .
>
> (Novelist/filmmaker, Murakami Ryu, in conversation with Sakamoto Ryuichi, 1985)[2]

---

[2] Murakami Ryu and Sakamoto Ryuichi, *E V Café* (Tokyo: Kodansha, 1989), 354 (abridged and paraphrased).

Just as the experience of the war unites the survivors, so does the growth of middle-class society provide common ground for the following generation. Once again, Japanese writers had to adapt to survive, this time in a market crammed with other forms of faster-paced entertainment. To lure a new audience away from their TV screens and *manga* (a dynamic and versatile form of comics), lighter fare was needed which could speak to them in ways that fitted their comfortable, yet often stifling lives.

Enter the entertainers. Their motives are no less serious than those of the generations that preceded them, but they are confronting a literary landscape in which a great many things have changed. The walls dividing pure and popular fiction have collapsed: autobiographical works, so long a staple of serious writing, are no longer in vogue, while popular forms such as science fiction and mysteries are taken up by many of the best writers. The gulf between Japanese and 'global' culture has narrowed to the extent that American films and books tend to be better known than Japanese ones. The cheap apartment houses and bars that were the writer's traditional places of refuge have been demolished to make way for shiny, up-scale establishments. Finally, the figure of the writer, which once loomed so large, has shrunk to more normal, human proportions.

In a challenging landscape such as this, entertainers have had to develop fresh acts to attract new audiences. Given their youth, it is hard to summarize the impact they will have on Japanese literature, but they are certainly after something more than 'mere entertainment': indeed, they use their mesmerizing tunes to lead their readers beneath the surface of things, exploring the pitfalls and paradoxes of modern life. This need not be an unremittingly dark and troubling journey, however—it can be light and playful, and leavened with a good deal of postmodern pastiche. Just the title of Murakami Haruki's bewitching novel *The Hard-Boiled Wonderland and the End of the World*, for example, calls up three types of popular literature—hard-boiled detective, fantasy, and apocalyptic—while the story itself takes the reader from the superficiality of downtown Tokyo, to an eerie walled town ('the end of the world'), to a subterranean realm populated by grotesque monsters, a mad scientist, and his fat, sexy daughter. Tolkien, Lewis Carroll, Raymond Chandler, Bob Dylan, the Beatles, the film *Blade Runner*—there is almost no end to the play of popular references. Yet Haruki's novel seems to question, as does 'The Elephant Vanishes', the very existence of Japanese culture in the present day.

Could 'Japanese culture' be vanishing? The question is likely to strike us as strange. After all, we have been trained to regard Japan as a most separate place. Depending on the book or the movie we are viewing, it has been displayed as exotic and charming, or as the embodiment of danger. It is always enigmatic, never 'like us'. In a similar way, the Japanese have tended, throughout their entire modern period, to stress what makes them different from the West. The result has been a dance of mutual convenience, whose steps are synchronized to allow each partner to feel totally distinct from the other. Now, however, the music is ending, and we are walking off the floor into a real world where the boundaries between cultures are blurring. Identity, whether national or personal, has become an open question, to be grappled with, and enjoyed, by writers and readers everywhere.

Legacies

Like all modern literary forms in Japan, the short story draws from native traditions as well as those of the West. Since these legacies have helped shape the genre, I offer them to you here, once again in a very general five-part grouping: stories of the self, the water trade, love and obsession, legends and fairy tales, and political and social comment. Keep in mind, however, that a given story is likely to be closely related to several of these legacies.

Stories of the Self

> These times have passed, and there was one who drifted uncertainly through them, scarcely knowing where she was . . . Yet, as the days went by in monotonous succession, she had occasion to look at the old romances, and found them masses of the rankest fabrication. Perhaps, she said to herself, even the story of her own dreary life, set down in a journal, might be of interest . . .

(*The Gossamer Years* by 'the mother of Michizane', 974)[3]

Slightly over a millennium has passed since a lonely Japanese noblewoman, frustrated by her husband's neglect, took up her brush and

---

[3] Edward Seidensticker, trans., *The Gossamer Years* (Tokyo: Charles E. Tuttle, 1964), 33.

began to fashion a record of her joys and sufferings with these now-famous opening lines. This journal, or diary, was filled with poems for, like all members of the aristocracy, she was trained in the art of poetic composition, and expressed her feelings through references to the world of flowers and trees, animals and insects, chilling rains and fragrant breezes. As a diary, *The Gossamer Years* has no actual plot; instead, the author's observations are linked by the passage of the seasons, and the movements of her own heart. Did she find solace in recording her life in this fashion? Perhaps, but we will never know for sure, for all we have is her written record, and that was shaped by her conscious and unconscious motives, and the literary forms she used. Stories of the self are never as transparent as they appear.

This lyric, 'autobiographical' legacy—which includes, besides the diary, the personal essay and poetic travelogue—has had a profound influence on the development of the Japanese short story. In many cases, and to varying degrees, we are encouraged to assume that the author and the central character are one and the same person, and that the events described actually happened. The form of the story, therefore, is meant to follow the form of the experience itself; in this genre, cleverly constructed plots are a hindrance, for they distance readers from the sense of 'real life' and intimacy that they are seeking to attain.

Yet it would be a mistake to assume that these 'plotless stories', as they are sometimes called, are simple reminiscences. Take, for example, 'Night Fires', which is based on a trip to the mountains by Shiga Naoya, his wife, and a close friend. On the surface, not much happens—they stroll on the mountainside, enjoy a leisurely boat-ride on the lake, and build a bonfire. There are no accidents or quarrels, nor is there any tension between them and the young innkeeper who guides them around.

If one turns from the characters to their surroundings, however, it is clear that a great deal is going on. In 'Night Fires', nature is not a backdrop for human events, but a vibrant, active force that dwarfs the protagonists, drawing them into its rhythms and mysteries. This is what is often termed a 'Shinto landscape', for all of its elements—the ancient trees, the lake, the mountains, the animals, birds, and insects, the people—are filled with a sacred force, and thus can be seen as gods, or *kami*. The landscape in Shiga's story brings apparent opposites together, then extinguishes their boundaries like flaming branches hitting the water's surface. Lights and their reflections are everywhere, in the sky, on the shore, on the lake, and within the darkest recesses of the forest. The boundaries between individuals are also obliterated, sometimes miraculously, as we see in the story of the innkeeper's brush with death in the snow. In the same vein, emotions, which we normally think of as being highly personal, are presented as a shared experience, binding the members of the group to each other, and to their vast surroundings. For Shiga Naoya, paradoxically, the story of the self reaches its ultimate goal when the 'self' disappears within a greater natural reality.

There are many other autobiographical stories in this anthology: some, like 'Lemon' and 'The Accordion and the Fish Town', are assumed to be a fairly factual recounting of events; others, like 'Merry Christmas' and 'A Very Strange Enchanted Boy', seem to be more fictional. Ultimately, however, such distinctions fail to mean very much, since any person's view of reality, like the testimonies of the witnesses in 'In a Grove', is bound to diverge sharply from that of another. What matters more is the heightened sense of intimacy that the autobiographical, often lyrical legacy of Japanese literature has endowed to the short-story form.

Stories of Love and Obsession

> Ninefold mists have risen and come between us.
> I am left to imagine the moon beyond the clouds.
>
> The autumn moon is the autumn moon of old.
> How cruel the mists that will not let me see it.
>
> (*The Tale of* Genji by Murasaki Shikibu, *c.*1010)[4]

Love poems are among the most ancient of Japanese literary forms, one of the pillars of the lyrical tradition. Although love was on everyone's lips, however, it could never be spoken of in a crude and direct manner—instead, it had to be evoked through natural images, like the moon and the mists in the verses above, exchanged by pining lovers in the eleventh-century masterpiece, *The Tale of Genji*. As a result, when Western literature was introduced to Japan, its translators were perplexed by the simple words, 'I love you', for they did not exist in Japanese. In fact, despite its attractions, Western-style romantic love proved to be an elusive dream for most Japanese of the pre-war era.

After the war, the cultural gulf gradually narrowed as Japan be-

[4] Edward Seidensticker, trans., *The Tale of Genji* (New York: Knopf, 1976), ii. 203.

came more industrialized and middle class, and American values spread. Today, 'love marriages' are more common than the arranged kind, and the words 'I love you' no longer sound so awkward and foreign. Writers like Yoshimoto Banana have a huge following of young readers who understand love quite differently than their grandparents did. Yet, despite these changes, modern Japanese expressions of love still tend to be less direct and more lyrical than those of Western cultures.

This helps explain why there are two 'carp stories' in this anthology, Ibuse Masuji's 'Carp' and Mukoda Kuniko's 'Mr Carp', for the Japanese word for carp is *koi*, which, when written with a different character, is one of Japan's oldest and most frequently used words for love. Ibuse's depiction of love between friends is poetic and suggestive, Mukoda's, of a love forsaken, detached and ironic, yet in each case the carp is a major player in the story, imbibing the complex passions of its owners as it moves from one watery home to the next. To gain some insight into the feelings of the lovers, in other words, we have to look at the fish!

If indirection and lyricism form the warp of Japanese literary expressions of love, then obsession and the breaking of taboos are the weft. The pining lovers of *The Tale of Genji*, for example, are actually Prince Genji and his stepmother, Fujitsubo, who is the image of his late mother. Their illicit affair produces a child, ostensibly Genji's brother, who later becomes emperor. This means that Genji's obsession with Fujitsubo has led him to break two taboos—not only has he slept with his father's wife, he has undermined the legitimacy of the country's high priest and unifying symbol. Yet Genji is regarded as Japan's archetypal romantic hero, for his sins stem, not from wickedness, but from pure, uncontrollable passion.

Stories like 'Aguri', 'The Flower-Eating Crone', and 'Toddler-hunting' deal directly with this theme of passion and obsession. As in the case of Prince Genji, however, it is not moral issues that predominate, but aesthetic and psychological ones. Is Aguri the beauty that her hilariously besotted lover believes her to be, or is she ugly, with her white skin and Western clothes? (It is no coincidence that the English word *ugly* is pronounced *a-gu-ri* in Japan.) Who is the flower-eating crone, and why does she appear, lips stained with blossoms, at the end of the protagonist's life? What is the link between the heroine's obsession with little boys in

'Toddler-hunting', and her sadomasochistic sexual life? The line between what society defines as 'normal' and 'perverted' is intentionally blurred in all these stories, leaving us to ponder the nature of beauty, and its impact upon the innermost reaches of the human psyche. Stories of obsession, in short, lead us away from the black-and-white world of rights and wrongs, and into the mysteries of the life force itself.

Stories of the Water Trade

> The breezes of love are all-pervasive
> By Shijimi River, where love-drowned guests
> Like empty shells, bereft of their senses,
> Wander the dark ways of love
> Lit each night by burning lanterns,
> Fireflies that glow in the four seasons,
> Stars that shine on rainy nights.
> By Plum Bridge, blossoms show even in summer.
> Rustics on a visit, city connoisseurs,
> All journey the varied roads of love . . .
>
> (*The Love Suicides at Sonezaki* by Chikamatsu
> Monzaemon, 1703)[5]

The days of blossom-like geisha are long past, but their fragrance remains in old stories and plays, and in colorful *ukiyoe* prints. Three hundred years ago, in the days of Chikamatsu, geisha and the dashing Kabuki actors were the royalty of Japanese popular culture, models of style in a society where glamour and refined sensuality meant everything. Geisha of the highest rank were known by name throughout Japan: men wishing to court them had to be not only very wealthy, but adept at the intricate protocol of seduction, which was made all the more challenging by the courtesans' skill at poetry and witty repartee. Female entertainers of the lower ranks, on the other hand, were little more than prostitutes; yet they too could be elevated on stage as epitomes of pure love and devotion if their lives ended in double suicides with young and penniless lovers.

Times changed, and as lanterns gave way to neon signs, the geisha lost much of their mystique. Nevertheless, they and the others who work in the 'water trade' of Japan's huge entertainment industry

[5] Donald Keene, trans., *Four Major Plays of Chikamatsu* (New York: Columbia University Press, 1961), 47.

have continued to figure prominently in the world of fiction. An early writer like Nagai Kafu, for example, treated the geisha as a poignant symbol of a dying tradition, while Kawabata Yasunari's classic 'The Izu Dancer' transformed a young and impoverished traveling entertainer—one of the outcaste groups of Japanese society—into a vision of virginal purity. Later, in the post-war era, when sexual matters could be written about more freely, the kinkier side of life in the water trade came to predominate. Yet even at its most debased, the image of the young entertainer-prostitute has retained some of that erotic blend of innocence and carnality, constraint and self-abandonment, that attracted prior generations of readers.

Okamoto Kanoko concocts a very different sort of mixture in 'Portrait of an Old Geisha'. Her old geisha is certainly no fragile blossom, nor is she the projection of some male fantasy. After wandering the 'varied roads of love' for most of her professional life, she has retired to a simpler, healthier form of existence, secure in her cultural achievements and the sizable fortune her charms and business acumen have helped her to accumulate. Yet her vitality makes it hard for her to be satisfied with such a quiet life, so she brings a source of stimulation—a young man—into the house, ostensibly to pair with her adopted daughter. In reality, however, his comings and goings serve to keep her own passions churning.

There is an autobiographical aspect to this story, since Okamoto Kanoko was known for her young boyfriends, who often lived and traveled with her and her husband. Looked at from another angle, however, 'Portrait of an Old Geisha' is a testimony to the robustness of traditional culture, and the women who have kept it alive. The aging geisha does not shrink from the machines of modern life, she embraces them and their inventors. Electricity turns her on, for she links it to the principle of sexual energy, which she has spent a lifetime learning how to master. She is an embodiment of the positive side of the world of the water trade, the only place where independent women have historically been able to flourish by using, not just their bodies, but also their wits.

Legends and Fairy Tales

The virtue of a legend like Sansho the Steward is that there is enough of a fixed story to prevent the writer from completely losing himself as he goes along . . . Without examining the legend in too much detail, I let myself be taken by a dreamlike image of this story that seems itself a dream.

('History As It Is and History Ignored' by Mori Ogai, 1915)[6]

Since their inception, in the eighth-century story of a heavenly girl born from a bamboo stalk, Japanese tales have drawn from the rich store of legends and fairy tales of East Asia. Many of these stories originated in China and India, and were spread with the teachings of Buddhism, and by other less religious story-tellers. They could be performed at temple fairs, sometimes by traveling blind monks, who sang them to the accompaniment of a lute-like instrument called the *biwa*. Eventually, these and the many other kinds of popular folk-tales—about ghosts and gods, warriors and beautiful women—found their way into written collections, which in turn became valuable sources for short-story writers seeking to construct new tales for modern times.

Mori Ogai's 'Sansho the Steward', for example, is a recounting of one of Japan's most beloved legends. Although it changes some basic features while embellishing others, its portrait of two children ripped from the safe haven of family and exiled to a life of slavery is true to the original. Most of all, the figure of the self-sacrificing sister, Anju, is refined and elevated to the status of a true culture hero: in Ogai's dream-like scenario, she stands as the embodiment of all that is noble and inspiring in Japanese traditional culture.

One person's dream can be another's nightmare, of course, and for other writers, dreams of the past were often populated by demons. 'The Third Night', written by Natsume Soseki as part of his collection, *Ten Nights of Dream*, is a good case in point. As in 'Sansho', ancient images seem to have risen unbidden into the author's consciousness; yet here they convey the past as a guilt-ridden nightmare, filled with inchoate memories of murder and betrayal, instead of a purified ideal. Even the figure of the child is transformed from a symbol of hope into a harbinger of doom, a representation of the crushing weight of Japan's betrayal of its own past.

'In the Forest, Under Cherries in Full Bloom', by Sakaguchi Ango, bears a certain similarity to 'The Third Night'. Yet the post-war context raises a new set of issues. Here, the back-riding demon

---

[6] David Dilworth and J. Thomas Rimer (eds.), *The Historical Fiction of Mori Ogai* (Honolulu; Hawaii University Press, 1991), 182. Trans. J. Thomas Rimer.

(a familiar figure in Japanese legend) appears as a beautiful woman, this time representing the burden, not of the past betrayed, but of the pretense of Japan's traditional culture, with its refined, cherry-blossom aesthetic. Better to be an honest barbarian, Sakaguchi implies in his blackly humorous way, than to cover one's moral decay in the garb of refinement and breeding.

Stories of the past, whether dreams or nightmares, may reflect the age in which they were written, but they can also speak to timeless issues. 'In a Grove', by Akutagawa Ryunosuke, for example, raises the existential dilemma presented by the essential unknowability of 'truth'. Among the stories in this anthology, this has had the most impact on the West, since it provides the central structure for Kurosawa Akira's classic film *Rashomon*. Loosely based on a selection from the twelfth-century collection, *Tales of Times Now Past*, 'In a Grove' is arranged as seven testimonies in a trial for murder. In effect, the reader is asked to play the role of judge, logically sifting through the evidence, and assessing guilt. Yet, in the wake of the trauma caused by the crime, a rape-murder (or suicide), each participant remembers events so differently that, gradually, the issue of guilt and innocence fades, and one is left to contemplate the writhings of the human soul in extremity.

Stories of Political and Social Comment

> We are told that the sage Emperors of old ruled with compassion. They roofed their palaces with thatch, neglecting even to trim the eaves; they remitted the already modest taxes when they saw the commoners' cooking-fires emit less smoke than before. The reason was simply that they cherished their subjects and wished to help them. To compare the present to the past is to see what kind of government we have today.
>
> (*An Account of My Hermitage* by Kamo no Chomei, 1212)[7]

If poetic evocations of love and nature are the original ancestors of Japanese literature, and the worlds of the *demi-monde* and the storytellers two of their most welcome guests, then the work of social or political comment is the unwanted stepchild languishing at the door. In a lyrical tradition, after all, beauty and feeling take precedence over more worldly matters, a perspective that in Japan's case was

---

[7] Helen McCullough (ed.), *Classical Japanese Prose* (Palo Alto, Cal.: Stanford University Press, 1990), 384. Trans. Helen McCullough.

reinforced by the traditions of Buddhism, which stressed the benefits of the contemplative life, and Confucianism, which viewed the 'serious' business of social criticism as its exclusive domain.

Yet, despite the inhospitable surroundings, such commentary did find its way into Japanese literature: Kamo no Chomei, for example, was a recluse priest living during a period of political change and natural disaster, who lamented the indifference of the authorities to the suffering of the common people. To point out these short-comings, Chomei naturally referred back to idealized ancient times, when emperors were said to rule with wisdom and compassion, and shunned the trappings of power. For writers in traditional East Asia, the past could be used to provide models for the future, or converse-ly, to warn of mistakes which were in danger of being repeated.

This pattern did not disappear with the advent of the modern age, when social criticism became a fully fledged member of Japan's literary family. Ogai's 'dream' of 'Sansho the Steward', for example, was not just a fairy tale—it also had contemporary political rele-vance, for it elevated a vision of pure self-sacrifice at a time when that most central of all samurai virtues was being manipulated and transformed in the interests of the expanding Japanese empire. After the collapse of that empire, however, self-sacrifice tended to be seen very differently. The reluctant priest's one-way trip to sea in Inoue Yasushi's 'Passage to Fudaraku', for example, parallels the experience of the *kamikaze* suicide bombers who celebrated their funerals on the runway before they took off, thereby becoming 'living gods'. Were they noble heroes, or trapped victims? Who had driven them to their fates? By setting his story in medieval times, Inoue established a distance to help people confront these difficult questions, and shed the remnants of an outworn dream.

Not all critics of the war, however, spared their readers in this way. Kojima Nobuo's 'The Rifle' is brutally frank in describing the atrocities that Kojima's comrades wreaked upon the Chinese popu-lation, while Oe Kenzaburo's 'Prize Stock' evokes the nightmare of wartime by viewing it through the eyes of a young boy in an isolated mountain village. 'Prize Stock' is a particularly complex work, all the more difficult for its portrait of the captured black airman, the 'pet' of the village children. In fact, however, like Jim in *The Adventures of Huckleberry Finn* (one of Oe's favorite works, and a strong influence on this story), the black soldier in 'Prize Stock' is the key to the young boy's enlightenment, for he brings him face-to-face with the cruelty and hypocrisy of a war-riven adult world. Whereas Huck Finn finally frees Jim and heads off for a more natural life in the American west, however, Oe's hero awakens from his initiation to the smell of rot, and a land where no frontier seems to beckon.

Today, of course, the frontier is little more than a nostalgic memory, even for Americans: Huck Finn's dreaded 'civilization' has spread everywhere, and with it the prejudices and conservative values of middle-class consumerism. To attack these, young Japanese writers have devised new types of stories, which are lighter and more ironic in tone than the darkly impassioned 'Prize Stock'. Shimada Masahiko's 'Desert Dolphin', for example, is a teasing parable which also revolves around a stranger fallen from the sky, an angel with limpid eyes and hypnotic voice who lands in the middle of a drab futuristic metropolis. 'Dolphin' lampoons the materialistic concerns of the repressed 'straight' world, and celebrates the joys of music, drugs, and homoeroticism. It also draws liberally on a number of popular genres—fantasy, science fiction, romantic comic books, even rock videos. In short, it dresses its social commentary in the playful garb of the postmodern, one of the most recent, but certainly not the last, of the trends that have helped shape Japanese literature.

Back when I was living near the Tamagawa Canal, the site of Dazai Osamu's final plunge, I attended a weekly literary discussion group led by a noted Japanese critic. I remember once when we were discussing '*L'Étranger*' (a particularly poignant title for me, since I was the only foreigner in the room) a fellow member threw up her hands in despair, turned to me, and said, quite out of the blue, 'If we can't understand this, then how can you understand Japanese literature?' I thought this was somewhat unfair—Camus's novel was rather a mystery to me as well—but her question echoed in my mind long afterwards. Was I doomed to failure in my attempts to understand a foreign tradition; would I be 'cheated', as Natsume Soseki felt he had been by English literature?

These questions no longer trouble me as they once did. No one, I have learned, has a monopoly on literary sensibility. The 'objective' pronouncements of experts are inevitably shaped by personal likes and dislikes and the tides of academic discourse, while students often come up with insights that elude their teachers. This anthology is no exception to the rule. I have tried to provide a cross-section of modern stories, selecting what seemed to me to be the best works by the best translators, and avoiding any overlap with existing anthologies. There have been many writers I wanted to include but couldn't, while popular forms like historical romance and detective fiction have been almost entirely omitted. Treat this anthology, then not as the last word but as a first step into a living tradition which you can appreciate, and interpret, on your own.

MORI OGAI (1862–1922)

SANSHO THE STEWARD

Translated by J. Thomas Rimer

An unusual band of travelers walked along the little-used road that led from Kasuga in Echigo to the province of Imazu. The little group was led by a mother, barely thirty, followed by her two children. The girl was fourteen, the boy twelve. With them was a servant woman of about forty, who urged on the two weary children. 'We'll soon be at the inn where we will spend the night,' she told them. Of the two children, the girl showed particular fortitude: although she dragged her feet as she walked, she kept up her spirits and tried as best she could not to show her mother or brother how tired she was, and occasionally she would remind herself to maintain a more resilient step. If the four had been making a pilgrimage to some nearby temple, their appearance would not have been extraordinary, but with their walking sticks and bamboo hats, which added a certain gallant note to their appearance, the group drew every passerby's curiosity and even sympathy.

The road now skirted a group of farmers' houses and continued along beside them. The road had many stones and pebbles, but since it was dry from the crisp autumn air and mixed with clay, it formed a hard surface easy for walking, unlike the sandy roads near the sea, where travelers were always buried up to their ankles.

As they walked along, a sudden burst of the setting sun illuminated a long row of thatched huts, roofs jumbled together, surrounded by a grove of oaks.

'Look at the beautiful maple leaves!' the mother called back to her children.

The two glanced in the direction where she pointed but did not reply, so the servant woman said, 'The leaves here have turned completely. No wonder that the mornings and evenings have become so cold ...'

The girl suddenly looked at her brother, then said, 'If we could only hurry to where father is waiting for us . . .'

The boy replied in the wise fashion that children adopt, 'We haven't yet gone very far.'

The mother spoke in an admonishing tone. 'That's right. We must cross many mountains like the ones we have crossed until now, and we must also cross many rivers and seas by boat. Every day you must exert all your energies and be very good as we walk.'

'Well, I want to go as fast as we can,' the girl said.

Now everyone fell silent as they went along.

From the opposite direction came a woman carrying an empty pail. She was a worker who gathered seawater for the salt farm at the beach.

The serving woman called to her. 'Is there anywhere nearby where travelers can spend the night?'

The woman stopped and examined the four of them. Then she spoke. 'I'm sorry for you. You've gotten yourselves in a bad place to be when the sun goes down. There's not a house here that will put up travelers. Not a one.'

'How could that be?' continued the servant woman. 'Why are people so inhospitable in these parts?'

Taking notice of the increasingly lively conversation, the children walked over to the woman; now the servant woman and the children seemed to surround her.

'That's not it. There are many religious and kind-hearted people here. But there are the orders from the governor of the province. There is nothing we can do about it. Look over that way,' she said, pointing in the direction from which she had come. 'If you go as far as that bridge, you will see there is a signboard put up. All the details are written there, they say. There have been some terrible men, slave dealers, roaming around near here, and so there is a prohibition against giving shelter to travelers. Seven nearby families have been implicated, I hear.'

'How difficult for us. We have the children, and I don't think we'll be able to go on much farther. Isn't there anything we can do at all?'

'If you continue on as far as the beach where I came from, it will be completely dark, and you will have no recourse but to find a good place to sleep around there. What I would do if I were you would be to sleep over there under the bridge. There are many large logs stacked up very close to the stone wall along the shore of the river. They are logs that have been floated down from higher up the Arakawa River. Children play under them during the day. There are places deep inside where it's always dark and the wind doesn't penetrate. I sleep in the quarters of the owner of the salt fields where I work every day, just over there in the midst of that grove of oaks. After night falls, I'll bring you straw and some mats.'

The mother, who had been standing apart and listening to the discussion, now came over to the woman. 'We have truly met with a kind person and we thank you for your suggestion. Let's go there and stay for the night. We would be most grateful if you could lend us some straw or some matting. At least enough for me to put down a bed for the children.'

The woman agreed and started home toward the grove of oak trees. The four travelers hurried off in the direction of the bridge.

The little group arrived at the foot of the Oge bridge that crossed the Arakawa. Just as the woman had told them, a new signpost had been placed there. She had been correct as well about the orders from the governor of the province.

If there were slave traders, why was no investigation made of them in the area? Why did the governor issue orders prohibiting the lodging of strangers and thus cause great hardship to travelers arriving late in the day? This order seemed to be no real solution to the problem. Yet for the people of that time, it was the governor's decree. Indeed, the mother herself did not dispute the regulation but only lamented the family's fate at having come to a place where there were such rules.

By the base of the bridge there was a road used by people who did their laundry by the river. Using this path they climbed down to the riverbed itself. They found the logs piled up against the stone fence. Following along the wall they managed to pass underneath the logs. The boy, full of curiosity, bravely made his way first.

Crawling deep inside, they found a place where the logs formed a kind of cave. Below their feet a huge log had fallen sideways, making a floor.

The boy climbed up on the log, crawled back into the farthest corner, and called to his sister to hurry up and come inside. She timidly followed him.

'Please wait a moment,' said the servant woman, and, making the children stand aside, she took down a bundle she was carrying on her back, pulled out some extra clothing, and spread it out in one corner for all of them to sit on. When their mother was seated, the children clung to her, one on each side. Since leaving their home in Shinobugōri in Iwashiro, they had slept in places more exposed than this one, even when under a roof. Of necessity they had become accustomed to difficult conditions, and what they found here was by no means the worst they had experienced.

Along with the extra clothing, the servant woman took out some food that had been carefully saved. She put it down in front of the children and said, 'We can't make a fire here. We must not be found by those awful men. I will go to the home of the owner of that salt beach and see if I can bring us some hot water. And perhaps I can ask for straw or mats as well.'

The servant woman hurried off in her diligent fashion. The children began to eat their dried fruits and rice with great appetite.

A moment later they heard someone's footsteps entering the hollow space under the logs. The mother called out, 'Ubatake!' the name of the serving woman. However she suspected that it might be someone else, since the oak forest was too far to permit a trip back and forth in such a short time.

The person who entered was a man about forty years old. He was so lean that every muscle could be seen and counted from outside his skin; he had a smile on his face like that of an ivory doll and held a Buddhist rosary in his hands. He walked over to where the children were sitting in a nonchalant manner, as if he were in his own home, then sat down on the log beside them.

The children could only look at him in astonishment. They did not find him frightening, as he did not seem at all what they expected a dangerous man to look like.

'I am a sailor named Yamaoka Tayu. There have been some slave traders around here recently, and the governor has forbidden anyone to stop over in these parts. But he doesn't seem to be able to catch the criminals. I feel sorry for travelers in these parts, and so I try to help them. Fortunately my house is a bit removed from the road. If you stay there secretly, nobody will bother you. I sometimes walk around in places where travelers might be sleeping outside, in the woods or under the bridge, and I've already taken quite a few to stay with me. I see the children are eating sweets. That won't fill them up. And it's bad for their teeth. I've nothing special at my place, but I could fix you some rice porridge with yams. Come along and let

4

me take care of you.' The man did not try to tempt them; indeed he spoke half as though to himself.

Listening carefully, the mother was moved by the laudable intentions of this man who would go so far as to break the law to help others. She told him, 'I am very grateful for your kind offer. But I am concerned that we will cause great difficulties to anyone who took us in. Yet if you could somehow manage to feed the children a bit of something hot, some rice gruel perhaps, and give us a roof to sleep under, we will all be eternally grateful to you.'

Yamaoka nodded. 'You are a woman who knows how to make a wise decision. Let me show you the way,' he said, rising to go.

The mother added, in a tone of regret, 'Please wait here just a bit more. As you have already promised to take care of the three of us, I hesitate to ask anything more of you, but there is another person traveling with us.'

Yamaoka scrutinized them more carefully. 'You have another companion? A man or a woman?'

'A serving woman I brought with me to look after the children. She went back down the road a bit to find us some hot water. She should be back very soon.'

'A serving woman. Then I'll be glad to wait.' Yamaoka's impassive face relaxed, then seemed touched with a shadow of joy.

The sun was still hidden behind the mountains of Yone, and mist hung over the deep blue water on the bay of Naoe.

A boatman helped a small group into his boat and cast off from the shore. It was Yamaoka and the four travelers who had spent the night in his house.

The evening before, they had all waited for Ubatake, who finally returned with some hot water in a cracked wine jug, before going on to stay the night with Yamaoka. Ubatake herself had been quite apprehensive but had gone with them as well. Yamaoka had put up the travelers in a thatched hut in the midst of a pine grove to the south of the main road and had given them some yams and rice porridge. Then he asked them about their itinerary. After putting the exhausted children to sleep, their mother, beneath the dim lamp, told Yamaoka something of her own situation.

She said she was from Iwashiro. Her husband had gone to Tsukushi and had not returned, so now she was taking the two children there to inquire as to his whereabouts. Ubatake, she continued, had been with the family since she served as a nurse when her daughter was born; since the serving woman had no relatives, she had made her a companion for the long and doubtful journey. They had managed to come this far, she concluded, yet in relation to the distance to the western provinces, it seemed they had hardly left home. Would it be better to go from here by land? By sea? Since Yamaoka was a sailor, he must know about even the most remote areas. She asked him to advise her as best he could.

At though he considered this the simplest of questions, Yamaoka Tayu told her without any hesitation that they should go by sea. If they continued on by land, he said, they would soon reach a dangerous place on the borders of Etchu province, where rough waves dashed against sharp rocks. Travelers waited in caves for the tide to recede so they could run along a narrow path underneath the rocks. The waves fell back for such short periods of time that children and parents alike had no time to look back at each other. If, on the other hand, they went by the mountain road, they would have to cross over a path so dangerous that if they took one false step, if even one stone loosened under their feet, they would risk plunging to the bottom of the deep valley below. There was no telling how many such difficult places they would encounter before they reached the western provinces and Tsukushi. On the other hand, the sea route was quite safe. If they found a reliable sailor, he could pilot them, with no effort on their part, a hundred *ri*, even a thousand. While he could by no means go as far as Tsukushi himself, Yamaoka said, he knew sailors from various provinces, and he could arrange to take the family by boat to a place where they could locate a boatman who would be able to take them that far. Tomorrow morning, he suggested, as though it were no trouble at all, he would take them there in his own boat.

Early the next morning Yamaoka hurried the travelers out of the house. At that moment, the mother took a bit of money from a small bag, thinking to pay him for their lodgings. He stopped her and said that he would take nothing, but suggested that he guard the small bag of money for her. Such valuable things, he told her, should always be given to the landlord when they stayed in an inn, or to the master of the ship when they traveled by sea.

Ever since she first allowed Yamaoka to give them lodgings, the mother had shown a tendency to accept his word. However, although she was grateful to him for having helped them, even to the extent of breaking the law, she did not necessarily trust him in every particular. Rather she kept consenting to the certain autocratic tone in his voice to which she was able to put up no resistance. There was clearly something unsettling about this situation, yet she did not have any reason to fear Yamaoka. She had not fully comprehended her own feelings.

She boarded the boat with a certain feeling that there was nothing else that she could do. When the children themselves saw the calm water, spread out like a blue carpet before them, they joined her, full of excitement over the beauty of what they saw. Only the face of Ubatake retained a trace of the uneasiness she had felt when she had returned the evening before to meet Yamaoka for the first time.

Yamaoka cast off. As he pushed away from shore with a pole, the boat began to roll gently in the water.

For a certain interval, Yamaoka rowed south close to the bank in the direction of the border of Etchu province. The mist suddenly vanished and the waves sparkled in the sun.

The party now came to a spot hidden by rocks, away from any sign of human habitation, where the waves washed the sand and cast up seaweed. Two boats were anchored there. When the two boatmen saw Yamaoka, they called to him.

'Anything to offer?'

Yamaoka lifted his right hand and showed them his folded thumb. Then he moored his boat beside theirs. The four upright fingers was a sign that he had four persons.

One of the boatmen was named Miyazaki no Saburo, from Miyazaki in Etchū. He showed Yamaoka his open left hand. According to the signals, the right hand meant the number of items, the left meant money. His gesture indicated a price of five *kanmon*.

'Try me!' said the second boatman, and he quickly raised his arm, showed an open hand, then held up his index finger. His name was Sado no Jiro and he bid six *kanmon*.

'How dare you!' screamed out Miyazaki. 'Don't try to outbid me!' Sado braced himself for a fight. The two boats tilted, splashing water onto the decks.

Yamaoka looked calmly at the faces of the two boatmen. 'You're all excited, aren't you? Neither one of you will go home empty-handed. I'll divide my guests between you, so that they won't be overcrowded. Sado's price will serve.'

Yamaoka turned to the travelers. 'Go in these boats, two of you in each. Both are going to the western provinces. These boats are hard to move if they're overloaded.'

Yamaoka helped the two children to enter Miyazaki's boat, and the mother and Ubatake to enter Sado's. As he did so, both Miyazaki and Sado quietly pressed some money in his hand.

Ubatake pulled on her lady's sleeve and was just saying, 'What about the bag that was put in Yamaoka's charge . . . ?' when Yamaoka suddenly pushed his empty boat away.

'Now I take my leave of you. I'm supposed to turn you over to another responsible person. My job is now done. Good luck to you.'

They heard the sound of oars moving busily, and Yamaoka's boat was soon far away.

The mother said to Sado, 'I suppose you will be rowing along the same route, for the same harbor? . . .'

Sado and Miyazaki looked at each other and laughed loudly. Then Sado replied, 'I hear the Chief Priest of the Rengebuji says that any boat you board is the ship of the Buddha, bound for the same Other Shore!'

From then on the two boatmen rowed on in silence. Sado went north, Miyazaki to the south. The passengers called desperately to each other, but the boats merely drew farther apart.

The mother, mad with grief, pulled herself up as far as she could on the gunwales of the boat. She called to the children, 'The worst fate has befallen us. We may never see each other again. Anju, always take care of your guardian amulet, the image of Jizo, your guardian god. Zushio always keep with you the sword your father gave you. And always do your best to keep together!' Anju was her daughter, Zushio the younger son.

The children could do nothing more than call hopelessly for their mother.

The boats drew farther and farther apart. The children's mouths seemed to stay open like young birds waiting for their food, but their cries no longer could traverse the widening distance.

Ubatake raised her voice to speak to Sado no Jiro, but as he did not turn to listen, she clung to his legs, brown and tough like the trunks of red pines. 'What are you doing? How can I go on living without those dear children? Their mother feels the same. She will feel her life is worthless without them. Turn around and row after the other boat, please. Please, be merciful!'

'Quiet down!' cried Sado, as he aimed a backward kick at her. Ubatake fell to the deck. Her hair came loose and spilled over the side into the water.

She rose. 'I cannot bear it. Forgive me, my lady,' she said, and with this, she leapt into the sea head first.

The boatman cried out and tried to catch her, but he was too late.

The mother now removed her outer robe and passed it over to Sado. 'This garment has little value, but I want you to have it. Goodbye.' She put her hand on the gunwale, ready to follow Ubatake.

'You fool,' cried Sado, and pulled her down by her hair. 'Do you think I am going to let you die? You are much too valuable for that.'

Sado dragged out the boat's hawser and tied her securely with it. He went on rowing due north.

Miyazaki rowed southward along the bank with the two children still calling for their mother.

'Are you still at it?' Miyazaki scolded them. 'Maybe the fish at the bottom of the sea can hear you, but not her. Those two have probably reached Sado by now and are already chasing the birds away in the millet fields.'

The two children held tight to each other and wept. Although they had left their home village and traveled great distances, they had at least been with their mother; now, unexpectedly separated from her, they had no idea what they ought to do. Overwhelmed with grief, they were unable to grasp how this separation might affect their own destinies.

When noon came, Miyazaki took out some rice cakes and ate them. Then he gave one to Anju and one to Zushio. They took the cakes in their hands and held them, as if they did not want to eat; then looking at each other, they burst into tears again. At night, still sobbing, they slept under rush mats with which Miyazaki covered them.

The children passed several days like this on the boat. Miyazaki made the rounds of one bay and inlet after another in Etchu, Noto, Echizen, and Wakasa, looking for a good buyer for his charge.

Although they were young, no one offered to buy them, perhaps because they seemed frail. On the few occasions when someone seemed interested, there were always difficulties in fixing on a suitable price. Eventually Miyazaki began to grow ill-tempered and would strike them, complaining about their habitual weeping.

Miyazaki traveled from one place to another and finally arrived at the harbor of Yura in the province of Tango. Here, at a place named Ishiura, lived a man named Sansho the Steward. He had a large house and lands. His retainers planted grains in his fields, hunted in the mountains, fished the seas, raised silkworms, wove fabrics, and manufactured everything imaginable in metal goods, pottery, and wooden utensils. Sansho would buy up any kind of person offered. When Miyazaki could not manage to sell his victims elsewhere, he always brought them here.

Sansho's overseer came out to the harbor and quickly bought the two children, for seven *kanmon*.

Putting the money away in his purse, Miyazaki told the overseer, 'Now that I've finished with the little brats, I feel much better.' He went inside the wine shop on the pier.

A fire of blazing coals filled a huge middle space in one room of the gigantic residence built on pillars that were thicker than the span of a man's arms. Facing the fire sat Sansho, leaning on an arm rest and resting on three piled cushions spread on the floor. On his right and left, like guardian statues at a temple, sat his two sons Jiro and Saburo. Sansho once had three sons; but after Taro, the oldest, then sixteen, had witnessed his father brand one of the captives caught after attempting to escape, he had, without a word, wandered out of the house and was never seen again. The incident took place nineteen years before.

The overseer brought Anju and Zushio forward and commanded them to bow to Sansho.

The children did not seem to hear but only stared in astonishment. Just sixty that year, Sansho's face seemed painted with vermilion. He had a wide forehead and full chin, and his hair and beard glittered with silver. The children were more surprised than frightened, and they continued to stare at his face.

Sansho finally spoke. 'So these are the children you bought? They aren't like the others. I'm not quite sure what to do with them. You said they were quite unusual children, but now that you've brought them to me, I think they look sick and pale. I don't see how we can make use of them . . .'

Saburo spoke. While he was the younger of Sansho's sons, he was nearly thirty. 'From what I just saw, they refused to bow after they were told to. And they didn't even identify themselves like the others. They may look frail, but they must be a stubborn pair. Men who serve here begin by cutting firewood and women by drawing saltwater. It should be the same for them.'

'That's right,' the overseer seconded. 'They wouldn't tell me their names either.'

Sansho laughed derisively. 'Perhaps they are too stupid. I'll name them myself. I'll call the older girl Fern and her younger brother Lily. Fern, you go to the seaside and scoop up three measures of water a day. Lily, you go to the mountains and gather three loads of firewood a day. I realize that neither of you is very strong, so I won't demand that your loads be too big.'

Saburo now spoke. 'I think you've been too generous. Take them along,' he told the overseer, 'and give them the things they need for their work.'

The overseer led the children to the hut where the new workers slept. He gave Anju a bucket and a scoop, and Zushio a basket and a sickle. He also gave each of them a container for carrying their noon meal. The hut for the newer slaves was in a different place from where the other captives lived.

By the time the overseer left, it had gotten dark. There was no lamp in the hut.

It was bitter cold the next morning. The bedding the children had found in the hut the night before had been too dirty to use, so Zushio had gone off somewhere and found some matting. They covered themselves as they had on the boat and slept together.

Zushio now took their food containers to the kitchen to obtain their provisions, as he had been told to do the day before by the overseer. Both the roof of the kitchen building and the straw scattered on the ground were covered with frost. The kitchen had a large earthen floor, already filling up with a great many workers waiting for food. As provisions for men and women were given out in different places, Zushio was scolded once because he tried to obtain both his own and his sister's portions, but when he promised that each would come separately the next morning, his two containers were filled and he received two portions of rice gruel in a food box and some hot water in a wooden bowl. The rice gruel was cooked with salt.

As Anju and Zushio ate their morning meal, they bravely came to the conclusion that, subjected to such terrible misfortunes as they were, their only recourse was to bow their heads to fate. Then Anju headed toward the seashore and Zushio toward the mountains. They went together across the frosty grounds through the three gates that encircled Sansho's grounds, then went their separate ways, looking back at each other many times.

The hill where Zushio was sent lay near Yura peak, a little to the south of Ishiura. The place where he was to cut brushwood was not far from the base of the mountain. Passing through an area of outcroppings of purple rock, he came to a fairly wide stretch of land where there was a thick growth of trees.

Zushio went into the grove and looked around him. When he realized that he did not know how to cut firewood, he hesitated to begin and sat vacantly on the fallen leaves, piled like frosty cushions. Eventually he came to himself and tried to cut a branch, then another, only to hurt his finger. He sat down on the leaves again, thinking that if the mountain was this cold, his sister must be all the colder from the wind by the sea. He burst into tears.

When the sun had about reached its height, another woodcutter came along, with a load of firewood on his back. He called out to Zushio. 'So you too work for Sansho the Steward? How much wood are you supposed to cut in a day?'

'I'm supposed to bring back three bundles, but so far I've hardly cut any at all,' Zushio told him quite honestly.

'If you're supposed to cut three, then it's better to finish two of them in the morning. Let me show you the way to cut the branches.' The woodcutter put down his own load and quickly cut one bundle for Zushio.

At this, the boy's spirits rose and he cut a bundle himself by noon and another afterwards.

Anju went north along the riverbank on the way to the beach. She came to the place where saltwater was being scooped up, but she did not know how to do it herself. Gathering her courage, she finally managed to put her ladle in the water, but the waves instantly pulled it out of her hand.

Another girl ladling saltwater nearby retrieved the scoop and returned it to her. 'You can't ladle the water that way,' she told Anju. 'Let me show you how. Put the ladle in your right hand and dip like this. And put the water in the pail; you can hold that with your left hand.' She quickly filled up a pailful for Anju.

'Thank you so much,' Anju told her. 'I wanted to do the work, and it's thanks to you that I've got the idea. Let me try myself now.' Anju had now understood the proper method.

The girl took a liking to the simple-hearted Anju. The two ate their noon meal together, told each other about themselves, and swore to treat each other as sisters. The girl told Anju her name was Ise no Kohagi and that she had been sold into slavery at Futamigaura and brought to Sansho's estates.

So passed the children's first day: by sunset Anju brought back her three loads of saltwater, and Zushio his three bundles of firewood, both achieved through the kindness of others.

Anju scooped her saltwater and her brother cut his wood; she passed her time thinking of her brother, and Zushio on his mountain thought only of his sister. They would wait for evening when they could return to their little hut; then the two of them would take each other's hands and repeat to each other how they longed for their father in Tsukushi and their mother in Sado. They wept as they spoke, spoke as they wept.

Ten days passed. The time now came when they were required to leave the hut set aside for newcomers. They were to join their respective groups of male and female workers.

The children insisted they would rather die than be separated. The overseer conveyed this to Sansho.

'What a lot of nonsense,' he replied. 'Take the girl to the women's quarters and the boy to the men's.'

As the overseer rose to go, Jiro, sitting at the side of his father, called for him to wait. Jiro then said, 'Father, as you say, it might be just as well to separate the two. Still, they did say they would rather die than be separated. Fools that they are, they might just manage to kill themselves. Even though they don't bring in much wood or saltwater, we don't want to lose any hands. If you'll permit me, I'd like to work on a scheme that I think would succeed.'

'Is that so? I don't want any losses either, of course. Do whatever you think best,' Sansho said and turned away.

Jiro had a hut built by the third gate and let the two children live in it.

One evening, the two children were as usual talking about their parents when Jiro happened to come by and overhear them. Jiro always walked around the property to see that there was no quarreling, thieving, or bullying of the weaker workers by the strong.

Jiro entered the hut and spoke to the children. 'Even if you miss your father and mother, Sado is far away. And Tsukushi is even farther. They are not places that children like you could ever get to. If you want to see your parents again, then the best thing to do is to wait until you're grown up.' Without another word, he left them.

On another evening, sometime afterward, the two children were again speaking of their parents. This time, Saburo happened to come by and hear what they said. Saburo liked to hunt birds in their nests and so he used to walk around with a bow and arrow in his hands, looking in all the trees.

Every time the children spoke of their parents, they were so eager to see them that they would act out a fantasy together, pretending to decide what steps to take. On this evening Anju said, 'I suppose we can't make a long voyage until we are grown up. We want to do something impossible. As I think about it, I realize it's no good for both of us to run away from here. Don't worry about me. You must escape and go on ahead to Tsukushi, meet father, and ask him what to do. And then you must go to Sado and find mother.'

Unfortunately, Saburo heard these last words of Anju. Bow and arrow in hand, he abruptly entered the hut. 'So. You two are figuring out some scheme to escape from here. Anyone who tries that is branded. That's the rule of this house. And that red iron is hot, let me tell you.'

The two children turned pale. Anju came forward and spoke to Saburo. 'It was all made up, what I said, sir. Even if my younger brother could escape, how far do you think he could get? I only said such a thing because we are so anxious to see our parents. Before, we were wishing we could turn into birds, so that we could fly to them. We're just making believe.'

Zushio added, 'What my sister says is true. We always talk about things we can never do. It's only to distract ourselves because we want to see our parents so much.'

Saburo studied their faces for a certain time and said nothing. 'Well. If it's make-believe, let it be make-believe. But I heard you talking together, and I know what you said.' With these words, Saburo left them.

That evening the children went to sleep with uneasy thoughts. Then—how long did they sleep?—they could not be sure, but both were awakened by a noise. Ever since coming to the hut they were permitted a light. In its dim glow they saw Saburo standing by their beds. He suddenly came over and grasped the children's hands. He pulled them up and out the door. They were being dragged along the wide road they had followed while looking up at the pale moon the first time they were taken to meet Sansho. They climbed three steps. They passed along a corridor. After winding around and around, they arrived in the great hall where they had been taken the day they arrived. Many people now stood there, in silence. Saburo dragged the two of them before the fire, where the coals were red with heat. They had been apologizing to him since he first dragged them from their hut, but as Saburo said nothing and continued to drag them along, the pair finally fell silent. There were three cushions piled opposite the fire, and Sansho was sitting on them. His face, reflecting the lamps at his sides, seemed to be on fire. Saburo drew out of the fire a pair of glowing hot tongs. He stood staring at them for some time. The iron, at first so hot that it seemed almost transparent, slowly turned black. Suddenly Saburo pulled Anju to him and began to bring the hot iron to her forehead. Zushio tried to pull at his elbow. Saburo kicked him down and held the boy still with his right knee. He finally managed to press the cross-shaped hot iron onto Anju's forehead.

Anju's screams pierced the stillness of the room. Saburo now pushed her aside, pulled up Zushio, and pressed the hot iron into his forehead as well. Zushio's cries now mixed with the slackening sobs of his sister. Saburo then threw down the iron and grabbed the children in the same fashion as before. After looking around the room, he dragged them from the main building as far as the third step, then threw them down on the frozen ground. The children, almost unconscious from pain and fear, somehow sustained themselves and managed without quite knowing how to make their way back to the hut. They fell down on top of their bedding and for a time remained as motionless as two corpses. Then Zushio called to his sister, 'Take out your statue of Jizo.' Anju rose at once and took out the amulet case she kept inside her robe. With a trembling hand she untied the string and took out the little image, which she set up beside their beds. They prostrated themselves before it. Suddenly the unbearable pain seemed to melt away, to vanish. Rubbing their foreheads with their hands, they found no traces of the wounds. With a shock of surprise, the two children woke up.

Anju and Zushio sat up and talked over the experience: they both had had the same dream at the same time. Anju took out her Jizo amulet, looked at it and placed it by her bedside, as she had done in her dream. After they knelt and worshiped, they looked at the forehead of the statue in the dim light. On either side of the sacred white curl of the forehead of the statue, as if carved with a chisel, was a scar in the shape of a cross.

Since the night the children were overheard by Saburo and suffered their terrible dream, Anju's whole being seemed altogether changed. Her expression became tight and drawn; her forehead was pinched and her eyes seemed always to be staring at something far away. And she said nothing. When she came home from the seaside in the evenings, she spoke very little, although before she had eagerly awaited her brother and they would talk over things for hours. Zushio, worried, asked her what was wrong, but she turned aside his questions with an almost imperceptible smile.

Otherwise Anju did not seem changed. When she did speak it was in the same manner as before, and her behavior also remained the same. Yet Zushio, so used to comforting his sister and being comforted by her, now watched her undergo a change that upset him beyond measure. He now had no one in whom to confide. Their world seemed even more dreary and barren than before.

The end of the year brought fitful snowfalls. The male and female workers alike stopped their outside work and were assigned to indoor tasks. Anju was to spin thread. Zushio pounded straw, which needed no special training, but Anju found the spinning difficult. In the evenings, Ise no Kohagi came to teach and help her. Anju said no more to her friend than to her brother; indeed she was often uncivil. Yet Ise no Kohagi took no offense and continued to treat her with sympathy.

The New Year's pine decorations were placed at the gates. But this year there were no ostentatious celebrations. The woman of Sansho's family always remained in the inner rooms of the mansion and rarely came out, so there was little activity to make things lively. There were only the quarrels that broke out in the men's quarters as they drank sake to toast the New Year. Usually any quarreling was severely punished, but at this time of year, the overseer overlooked any incidents. There were occasions when he failed to notice that blood had been spilled in a fight, and even a murder might go unnoticed.

From time to time Ise no Kohagi would come to visit the children in their lonely hut. She seemed to carry some of the warm atmosphere of the women's quarters with her, and while she chatted gaily, she seemed to bring spring into the winter's darkness, producing even the rare shadow of a smile on the face of Anju.

When the three-day holiday passed, the work of the household began again. Anju spun her thread, Zushio beat his straw. Anju had become sufficiently accustomed to her spindle so that, when even Kohagi came in the evening to help, there was little for her to do. Although Anju had changed, this quiet, repetitious work was quite satisfactory for her; indeed it relaxed her and somehow helped disperse her one obsession. Zushio, who could not talk with his sister as he had before, felt reassured when he saw Kohagi come and chat with Anju as she sat spinning.

The water became warmer and grass began to sprout. On the morning of the day before the outside work was to begin again, Jiro made the rounds of the whole mansion and came to the hut. 'How is it going? Will you be able to go off to your duties tomorrow? There are evidently some workers who are sick. When the overseer told me, I thought I would go from hut to hut and see for myself.'

Zushio, who had been beating straw, looked up to answer; but before he could speak, Anju stopped her spinning and, in a most unaccustomed fashion, jumped up and spoke to Jiro.

'Concerning our outside work, I have a request to make, sir. I would like to work in the same place as my brother. Perhaps you could be good enough to arrange for us to work on the mountain together.' There was a flush of red on her pale face, and her eyes were sparkling.

Zushio was profoundly surprised to see again such a change come over his sister, and he found it strange that she suddenly expressed a wish to cut wood without mentioning it to him first. He could only stare at her.

Jiro said nothing but regarded Anju's manner very closely. Anju told him, 'I want nothing more. This is the only thing I ask. Please let me go to the mountain with him.' She repeated her request again and again.

Jiro finally spoke. 'The question of who is permitted to do what kinds of work around here is very important. My father makes all the decisions himself. But it seems to me, Fern, that you have made your request after a good deal of careful thought. I'll take it on myself to arrange things for you. I'm sure you'll be able to go to the mountain. Don't worry about anything. I'm glad you two young ones got through the winter safely.' With this, he left the hut.

Zushio put down his pounding stick and came over to his sister. 'What was all that about? I would be so happy if you could come with me to the mountain. But why did you ask him all of a sudden like that? Why didn't you say anything to me about it?'

Anju's face shone with happiness. 'You are quite right to be surprised. But actually, until I saw his face I had no idea of asking him anything. I just thought of it, all of a sudden.'

'Is that so? How strange,' said Zushio, staring at her face as if he had never seen her before.

The overseer came to the hut with a sickle and basket. 'Fern,' he called, 'I understand you're not going to scoop seawater anymore. You're going to cut firewood. I've brought what you need and I'm going to take back the ladle and the bucket.'

'I'm sorry to cause you so much trouble,' said Anju, getting up quickly. She returned the pail and ladle to him.

The overseer took them but lingered on, as if his business in the hut were not yet finished. He seemed to smile, but in his expression was a trace of embarrassment. He was a man who listened to orders from the whole family of Sansho as if from the gods themselves, and he would carry them out without hesitation, no matter how cruel and rigorous they might be. Yet by nature he was reluctant to see others suffer, or in agony. He felt things were best when they went smoothly, with nothing distasteful involved. The forced smile on his face was a habitual sign that he realized he would have to say or cause someone else trouble.

The overseer spoke to Anju. 'I've still got something to do. You see, Jiro asked the Master about this business of your cutting firewood and tried to make him agree. Saburo was there too, and he said that if you wanted to go up to the mountain, you should be made to look like a boy. The Master laughed and said it was a good idea. So now I've got to cut off your hair and take it back with me.'

Zushio heard this as if he had been pierced to the heart. His eyes filled with tears as he looked at his sister.

Surprisingly, the flush of happiness did not fade from Anju's face. 'Of course. If I'm going to cut firewood, I have to be a man. Cut it off with the sickle.' She bared her neck to the overseer.

Her long glossy hair was quickly cut with one stroke of the sharp instrument.

The next morning the two children, with their baskets on their backs and their sickles tied to their waists, walked hand in hand out of the gate. This was their first occasion to walk together since they came to Sansho's estates.

Zushio could not fathom his sister's motivations; he felt lonely and sad. The day before, after the overseer left, he had tried by various means to coax an explanation from her, but she seemed lost in her own thoughts and never made them clear to him.

When they arrived at the foot of the mountain, Zushio could bear it no longer. 'I just can't believe we're walking together like this after such a long time. I should feel so happy, but I really feel sad. Even when I hold your hand, I can't bear to look at your bald head. I am sure you are thinking about something, hiding it from me. Why can't you tell me about it?'

Anju wore the same joyful expression she showed the day before, and her large eyes were sparkling. She did not answer her brother but grasped his hand all the harder.

There was a marshy spot where the path to the mountain began. Along the shore, last year's withered rushes remained, in bunched confusion, but small green shoots were now appearing in the yellowed grass at the side of the road. Moving to the right and climbing up, the children came to a crevice in the rock where a spring of clear water came gushing out. Passing the spring, they wound up a steep path with a wall of rock on the right.

Just then the morning sun shone onto the surface of the rocks. Anju found a spot where a tiny violet was blooming, its roots sunk down in a crevice weathered between the overlapping rocks. She pointed it out to Zushio. 'Look! It's spring!'

Zushio nodded but said nothing. The girl kept her secret to herself and the boy nursed his sorrow, and so their conversation was broken and their words sifted away like water into sand.

When they arrived at the spot where Zushio had worked the year before, he stopped. 'This is where we have to cut wood,' he said.

'Let's go on and climb a bit higher,' Anju told him. She immediately began to continue upward. Puzzled, Zushio followed her. After a while they reached a relatively high place that seemed the peak of the lower mountain.

Anju stood there staring intently toward the south. Her eyes followed the upper reaches of the Okumo River as it passed Ishiura and flowed into the harbor at Yura; they stopped at a pagoda thrusting from the dense foliage on Nakayama, a mountain about two miles from the other side of the riverbank. 'Look Zushio!' she called out. 'I know you must think it strange that I have been thinking about things for such a long time and I haven't been talking with you the way I always have. I know it. But today, you don't have to cut any wood. And you must listen very carefully to what I tell you. Kohagi was brought here from near Ise. She explained to me the way the road runs from her home to this place. She told me that if you cross over Nakayama mountain there, then Kyoto, the capital, is very close. It's very hard to go directly to Tsukushi from here, and to go back to Sado is also too difficult. But you can certainly get to the capital. Ever since we left Iwashiro with mother, we have only fallen on terrible people, but if fortune turns for the better, there's no telling that you won't meet some kind people as well. So I want you to gather your courage and escape from this place. You must go to Kyoto. If through the protection of the gods and buddhas, you are fortunate enough to meet some good-hearted person, you may be able to get to Tsukushi and find father. And perhaps you can find our mother in Sado, too. Throw away your sickle and basket. Take only your box of food with you.'

Zushio said nothing, but as he listened to his sister, tears ran down his cheeks. 'But then Anju, what will happen to you?'

'Don't worry about me. Do what you have to do as if we were doing it together. When you find father and bring mother back from the island the way I told you, then come back and try to help me.'

'But after I'm gone, I'm afraid you'll be treated in some terrible way,' Zushio said. He remembered the frightening dream in which he and his sister were branded.

'I suppose it will be hard for me, but don't worry. I'll be able to put up with it. They would never kill a slave they paid good money for. If you're not here, I suppose they'll make me do the work of two. But don't worry. I'll cut lots of firewood there where you showed me. Maybe I couldn't manage six bundles, but I'm sure I could cut four, or even five. Let's climb down over there and leave our baskets and sickles. I'll go with you to the foot of the mountain.' She started off ahead of him.

Without making any conscious decision, Zushio followed her instinctively. Anju was now fifteen, Zushio thirteen; already adopting an adult's manner she seemed now as wise as if possessed by some higher power. Zushio simply could not go against her wishes.

When they got down as far as the grove of trees, the two put down their sickles and baskets on the fallen leaves. Anju took out her amulet and pressed it in her brother's hand. 'You know how much I prize this. I want you to keep it for me until we meet again. Think that the image is me and take good care of it, just like your guardian sword.'

'But Anju, what will you do without it?'

'I want you to have it. You will face greater dangers than I. When you don't come back this evening, they will send a party to search you out. No matter how fast you go, if you simply run off without a plan, you're sure to be caught. Go along the upper reaches of the river we saw just now, until you get to Wae. If you are lucky enough not to be seen and can manage to get to the opposite bank, Nakayama can't be much farther. Go there, to the temple—we saw the pagoda sticking up through the trees—and ask for asylum. Stay there for awhile, until your pursuers have given up and gone away. Then run away from the temple.'

'But do you think the priest in the temple will give me shelter?'

'It's all a question of chance. If your luck is good, the priest will hide you.'

'I understand. What you've said seems to have come from the gods or Buddha himself. I've made up my mind. I will do exactly what you say.'

'I'm so happy. You've understood everything I told you. The priest is surely a fine man. I know he will take care of you.'

'Yes. I've come to believe that myself. I'll get away and go to the capital. I'll find father and mother too. And I'll come back for you.' Zushio's eyes took on the same sparkle as his sister's.

'I'll go down to the bottom with you, so let's hurry.' The pair quickly clambered down the hillside. Their whole manner of walking now changed, for Anju's intensity had been transferred to Zushio as well.

They passed the spot where the spring gushed up from the rocks.

Anju took out the wooden bowl in her provision box and dipped into the cool water. 'Let us drink this together to celebrate your departure,' she said, as she took a draught and passed the bowl to her brother.

Zushio emptied the bowl completely. 'Goodbye then, my dear sister. Please take care of yourself. I will get to the temple at Nakayama without being seen by anyone.'

Zushio rushed down the bit of path remaining on the hillside and took the main road running along the swampy area. He hurried off in the direction of the Okumo River.

Anju stood by the spring and watched the figure of her brother grow smaller as he appeared then disappeared behind rows of pine trees. The sun was almost at its highest point, yet she made no effort to climb the mountain again. Fortunately there seemed no other woodcutters at work nearby, so no one questioned Anju, who stood idling away her time at the foot of the mountain path.

Later the search party sent out by Sansho to catch the pair picked up a pair of small straw sandals at the edge of the swamp at the bottom of the hill. They belonged to Anju.

Shadows of pine torches threw wild reflections on the gate of the provincial temple at Nakayama. A throng of people pressed at the gate, led by Sansho's son Saburo, who grasped a white-handled halberd in his hand.

Standing in front of the main building he called out, 'I'm from the family of Sansho the Steward, over at Ishiura. We know for sure one of our workers escaped into the mountains. There's nowhere he could be but here. Hurry up. Hand him over.' Saburo's men called out in a similar fashion.

A stone pavement ran from the front of the main temple building out past the gate. Now it was crowded with Saburo's companions, pine torches in their hand, pushing and shoving. Thronging in on either side of them were almost all the monks from the cloisters. Awakened by the clamor outside the gates, they had come out from the inner sanctuaries and the kitchens alike, wondering what was happening.

When the crowd outside first shouted for the gates to be opened, most of the priests wanted them kept shut, afraid that if the men came in there would be disorder and violence. The Chief Priest, Donmyo Risshi, insisted that the gates be opened. But, the door of the main hall remained shut and silent, even after Saburo called for the return of his fugitive.

Saburo stamped his feet and repeated his demand two or three times. Several of his followers called out to the priest; laughter mixed with their shouts.

Finally the door of the main hall opened quietly. The Chief Priest opened it himself. He wore only a simple stole and took on no air of false majesty as he stood at the top of the steps. From behind him came the dim light of a taper burning in perpetual offering. The light flickered over his tall strong frame and illuminated his even face and black eyebrows, not yet touched by age. He was just over fifty.

The Chief Priest began to speak quietly. The unruly search party fell completely silent at the sight of him, and his quiet voice could be heard in every corner.

'So you are looking for some servant who escaped. In this temple, no one would conceal a person without telling me about it. Since I know nothing about it, the person is not here. However I would like to tell you something else. All of you came here in the dead of night, weapons in hand, pushing at the gate and demanding that it be opened. Thinking some insurrection had broken out, or that you were a group supporting some rebellion, I permitted the gate to be opened. Then what do I find? A search for some menial in your household! This is a temple designated by the Imperial family for prayer. The emperor himself has presented us with an inscribed tablet. And copies of the sutras in gold written by the emperor are among the treasures stored in the pagoda. If any kind of violence is caused here, the governor of the province will surely be reprimanded by the officials who oversee the shrines and temples. And if we should report this to the central temple of Todaiji, there is no telling what kind of action will be taken by the capital. If you consider the situation, I am sure you will agree it would be best to withdraw quickly. I am not being unpleasant, but I wish to tell you this for your own good.' When the Chief Priest finished speaking, he quietly shut the door.

Saburo scowled and grimaced at the closed door. But he did not have the courage to break it down and force his way in. His followers only whispered noisily together, like a wind in the leaves.

Suddenly, a voice called out to them. 'Was the one who escaped a little fellow, about twelve or thirteen? If so, I know something about it.'

Surprised, Saburo turned to study the speaker. He was an older man who bore more than a passing resemblance to Saburo's own father Sansho. He was the keeper of the temple bell. The old man went on talking, 'If it's that little fellow, I saw him at noon from the bell tower. He was hurrying along outside the temple wall, going south. Didn't look strong, but then he's probably that much more light of foot. He must have gotten pretty far by now.'

'So that's it. I can guess how far a boy can get in half a day. Come on!' Saburo hurried away.

The line of pine torches left the temple gate and followed along the outer walls, going south. Watching this from the bell tower, the old man laughed out loud. Startled, two or three crows, asleep in a nearby grove of trees, flew up.

The next day a number of persons were sent out from the temple in all directions. Those who went to Ishiura came back to report that Anju had evidently drowned herself. Those who went south heard that Saburo and his followers went as far as Tanabe, then turned back.

Three days later, the Chief Priest himself left the temple, going in the direction of Tanabe. He took with him a begging bowl as big as a basin and a staff as thick as a man's arm. Zushio followed him, his hair shaved and wearing a Buddhist robe.

The two walked the roads during the days and stopped in various temples along their way to pass their nights. When they arrived at Shujakuno in Yamashiro, the Chief Priest went to rest in the Gongodo temple. Then he took his leave of Zushio. 'Always keep your amulet with you, guard it carefully, and you will surely be able to learn something about your parents,' he said as a final admonition, then turned and left. Zushio realized that the priest had told him the same thing as his dead sister.

When Zushio reached Kyoto, still dressed as a Buddhist priest, he spent the night in Kiyomizu temple.

He slept in a special hall set aside for those who wished to retire for religious devotions. When he awoke the next morning, he saw by his bedside an elderly man, dressed in an old-style court costume. 'Whose son are you?' said the old man. 'If you have anything precious with you, kindly show it to me. I have been in seclusion

24

here since yesterday evening, praying for the recovery of my daughter, who is ill. In a dream I was granted a revelation. I was told that the boy sleeping behind the lattice at my left possessed a wonderful amulet. I was to borrow it and pray to the image. When I came to look this morning, I found you. Please tell me who you are and lend me the amulet. I am Morozane, the Chief Adviser to the Emperor.'

'Sir, I am the son of Mutsu no jo Masauji,' Zushio told him. 'Twelve years ago my father went to the temple of Anrakuji in Tsukushi and never seems to have returned. My mother took me who was born in that year and my sister, who was three, to live in Shinobugōri in the province of Iwashiro. I grew to be a big boy there, and then my mother decided that it was time to take my sister and me on a visit to western Japan to see if we could find my father. When we got as far as Echigo, we were seized by some terrible slave traders. My mother was taken to Sado, and my sister and I were sold at Ura in Tango. My sister died there. The precious amulet I carry with me is this image of Jizo.' He took it out and handed it to Morozane.

Morozane took the little statue in his hand and, holding it close to his forehead, said a prayer. Next he examined the amulet front and back several times, looking at it with the utmost care. Finally, he spoke. 'I have heard of this amulet before. It is a figure in gold of Jizo Bodhisattva, Ruler of Light. This statue was originally brought from Kudara and was paid special reverence by Prince Takami. Since you are in possession of the statue, your noble descent is clear. In the early part of the era of Eiho [1081–1083], when the Retired Emperor was still on the throne, Taira no Masauji was demoted and sent to Tsukushi because he was implicated in a misdemeanor for which the governor of his province was convicted. You are his son. There is no doubt about it. If you have any desire to leave the priesthood, there is a good chance you may later be given an important rank yourself. For the moment, please come to my home as a guest. Let us return there together now.'

The woman referred to as Morozane's daughter was actually an adopted niece of his wife who served as an attendant to the Retired Emperor. Her mother was a sister of the empress. Although this lady had been ill for some time, she quickly recovered after praying with the amulet of Zushio.

Morozane himself had Zushio returned to secular life and with his own hands placed on the boy's head the cap appropriate to his new rank. At the same time he sent a messenger with a letter of pardon to Masauji's place of exile. But when the messenger reached Tsukushi, he learned that Masauji was already dead. Zushio (who had now taken his adult name of Masamichi) was so grieved by the news that he wasted away to nothing.

In the fall of the same year, Masamichi's name was included on the appointment list as governor of Tango. The appointment was an honorary one; Masamichi was not required to go to the province and an adjutant was sent in his place to handle the day-to-day affairs there. However, the first action Masamichi took was to strictly forbid slavery of any kind throughout the province. Sansho the Steward now had to free every last one of his slaves and he began to pay them wages for their work. Sansho and his family expected to face a tremendous loss, yet the farmers and the artisans greatly increased the amount of work they did, and so his family flourished and prospered more than ever before. The Chief Priest who had helped Zushio was greatly elevated in rank, and Kohagi, who had befriended Anju, was able to return to her home village. A pious ceremony of mourning was held in Anju's memory, and a nunnery was built on the shore where she drowned herself.

Having done this much for the province, Masamichi asked for a leave of absence from his duties and crossed over to Sado, disguising his real identity.

The government authorities on Sado were located at Sawata. Masamichi went there and requested the officials to search the entire island for his mother, but her whereabouts was not so simple to discover.

One day Masamichi, lost in his thoughts, left his lodgings and walked through the town. At some point he found he had strayed away from the houses and was on a path running through the fields. The sky was clear and the sun was shining brightly. Masamichi worried to himself over the fact that he could find no trace of his mother. Perhaps, he pondered, the buddhas and gods would not help him because he had simply turned his duties over to others rather than going around to make the search himself. By chance he noticed a rather large farm house. Looking through the sparse hedge that grew on the south side of the building, he saw an open area where the earth had been pounded flat. Straw mats were spread there on which cut grains of millet had been spread to dry. In the midst of the drying grain sat a woman dressed in rags, who carried a long pole in her hand to chase the sparrows coming to peck at the grain. She seemed to murmur what sounded like a song.

Without knowing precisely why, Masamichi was attracted to something in the woman. He stopped and looked inside the hedge. The woman's unkempt hair was clotted with dust. When he looked at her face, he saw she was blind, and a strong surge of pity for her went through him. As the moments passed, he began to understand the words of the little song she was muttering to herself. His body trembled as if he had a fever, and tears welled up in his eyes. For these were the words the woman was repeating over and over to herself:

> Anju koishiya, hoyare ho
> Zushio koishiya, hoyare ho
> Tori mo sho aru mono nareba
> To to nigeo, awazu to mo.

> My Anju, I yearn for you.
> Fly away!
> My Zushio, I yearn for you.
> Fly away!
> Little birds, if you are living still,
> Fly, fly far away!
> I will not chase you.

Masamichi stood transfixed, enraptured by her words. Suddenly his whole body seemed on fire: he had to grit his teeth to hold back the animal scream welling up within him. As though freed from invisible chains, Masamichi rushed through the hedge. Tramping on the millet grains, he threw himself at the feet of the woman. The amulet, which he had been holding up in his right hand, pushed against his forehead when he threw himself on the ground.

The woman realized that something bigger than a sparrow had come storming into the millet. She stopped her endless song and stared ahead of her with her blind eyes. Then, like dried seashells swelling open in water, her eyes began to moisten and to open.

'Zushio!' she called out. They rushed into each other's arms.

NATSUME SOSEKI (1867–1916)

THE THIRD NIGHT

Translated by Aiko Ito and Graeme Wilson

⌐

I dreamt.

There's a six-year-old on my back. And it's certainly my child. But, oddly enough, without my knowing how or why I know it, I know that the child is blind and that his head is blue; clean-shaven blue.

I asked him when he became blind, and he answered 'Oh, from time immemorial.' The voice was that of a child all right but the diction seemed adult; the words, as it were, spoken between equals.

To left and right the paddy-fields lie blue. The path is narrow. Every now and again the shape of a heron lightens the growing darkness.

'I see we've come to the paddies,' said the creature on my back.

'How can you tell?' I asked him turning my head to speak back over my shoulder.

'Because of the creaking of the herons,' came the reply. And indeed, just then, the herons cried twice.

Though the child is my own, I feel a trifle awed. One cannot tell, carrying such an object on one's back, what will happen next. As I peered ahead, wondering where perhaps I might off-load my burden, I saw an enormous forest looming up through the dark. And in the very second when I began to wonder how I might dump my burden there, I heard a jeer from my back.

'Why do you laugh like that?'

The child made no reply, but asked me simply 'Father, am I heavy?'

'No, not heavy.'

'Wait. I'll be heavy soon.'

I said nothing but kept on trudging toward the forest. It was hard going, for the pathway between the paddies twisted irregularly. After

28

a while I came to a point where the pathway split; and, briefly, I rested there.

'There ought to be a signpost somewhere here,' the brat remarked. Sure enough, a stone roughly eight inches square and up to the height of my hip was standing there. On the stone was written 'To the left, Higakubo: to the right, Hottawara.' Though it was dark as dark, the characters, written in red, could be clearly seen. Their red was the red of a newt's belly.

'Fork to the left,' my incubus ordered. Away to the left the forest seemed to be casting down upon our heads dark shadows fallen from high above the sky. So I hesitated. 'Needn't be shy,' the brat remarked. Resigned, I started off again toward the forest. As I plodded along the path and came closer to the forest, wondering how this thing, this mere blind brat, could know so much, the voice on my back observed 'Being blind is certainly inconvenient.'

'That's why I'm carrying you on my back; so that you'll be all right.'

'I ought, I know, to be grateful that you carry me; but people tend to slight me. Which is bad. Even my parent slights me. Which is very bad.'

I felt I'd had about enough. So I hurried on thinking I would get to the forest quickly and throw my hump away.

'Go on a little more, and then you'll see. It was just such an evening,' said the voice as though to itself.

'What was?' I asked in tones that betrayed the feeling that something had only just failed to strike home.

'What was? But you know well enough,' the child answered scornfully. And then I began to feel that I had some idea of what it was all about. I was still quite clear-headed; but I did begin to have a vague feeling that, yes, it was just such an evening. And I felt, as the child had said, that if I trudged a little further I would indeed understand yet more. I felt that I simply must ease my mind by getting rid of this burden on my back before I discovered what the whole thing was about. For to understand would be disastrous. I quickened my pace, and hurried along faster and yet faster.

Rain had started some time back. The path grew darker and darker. I moved as though delirious. The only thing of which I felt quite certain was that a small brat clung to my back and that the brat was shining like a mirror; like a mirror that revealed my past, my present and my future, no smallest fact unblazoned. Besides, the brat was my very own child. And blind. I couldn't stand it any longer.

'Here it is, here it is, Just at the root of that cedar tree.'

The brat's voice rang distinctly through the rain. I stopped before I knew what I was doing. I was deep in the forest and had not known it. A black object perhaps two yards beyond me seemed indeed to be a cedar tree. Just as the brat had said.

'Father, it was at the cedar's root, wasn't it?'

'Yes,' I replied in spite of myself, 'it was.'

'I think in the fifth year of Bunka?'

Now that he mentioned it, it seemed to me that it had indeed been in the fifth year of Bunka.

'It was exactly one hundred years ago that you murdered me.'

As soon as I heard these words, the realization burst upon me that I had killed a blind man, at the root of this cedar tree, on just so dark a night, in the fifth year of Bunka, one hundred years ago. And at that moment, when I knew that I had murdered, the child on my back became as heavy as a god of stone.

THE BONFIRE

Translated by Jay Rubin

A child of the seashore waits alone. The north wind at his back, he sits on the white, withered grass of a sandy slope, watching the dim glow of the sun sinking behind the Izu mountains. His father's ship is long overdue.

Dead reeds bristle thick on the river bank, rustling in the salt wind. The ice that formed unseen at the base of their stalks with the full night tide, shattered by the morning ebb, remains unmelted through the day. Long cracks reach toward the bank like white threads stretching through the twilight. Could a traveler stop by this stream to rest, look around him unaware, unfeeling, and pass on? For this is the grove of Holy Rokudai that even now, after seven centuries, calls forth pity. The cold wind tears through its branches.

Against the gentle current and the drifting fallen leaves, a boat advances. At another time a spirited boatman's song might have echoed along the marshy stream, telling of a frosty night to come. But no, he only looks, says not a word, nor laughs, nor sings, this man, this fisherman or farmer who plies his oar in loneliness.

In the gloom, the reflection of a bridge, a farmer shouldering his hoe: soundlessly the boat scatters them and disappears among the reeds.

And here one sees at times, as in a picture, a pair of young men astride bareback horses, walking them quietly through the shallows of the river mouth as the last rays of the setting sun linger on the slope above. At such an hour the expanse of the beach is deserted. A crow, perched on the prow of a boat on the shore, soundlessly stirs its wings and flies off toward Kamakura.

It was late in December, the last busy days of the year. But the seven or eight boys on the windy beach were as lighthearted and free as ever. The eldest twelve, the youngest nine, they were gathered at the foot of a dune in lively discussion. Some stood. Others sat. One rested his chin in his hands, elbows deep in the sand. As they talked, the sun set in the west.

Their talking done, the boys galloped off along the water's edge. From inlet to inlet each ran as he pleased. The group quickly dispersed. One by one they retrieved what the storm had brought two nights before and the ebb tide had left behind: rotted boards, a chipped bowl, bamboo slivers, chunks of wood, an old ladle with the handle torn off. The boys heaped them up on a dry patch of sand away from the lapping waves. All that they gathered was soaking wet.

What could they be doing in the twilight chill? The sun had long since gone down. The clouds that seemed to enfold the peak of Hakone's Mount Ashigara were dyed a golden hue. The wind had dropped. Fishing boats headed back for the village, sails down and oars working as they neared the shore.

A round-faced boy, dark-skinned but handsome, had found an old mirror frame, the glass long since gone. What a shame it would be, he said, to burn this. But an older boy said, That will burn best of all. He was just then unloading a stout-looking pole that was almost too heavy for him. That won't burn, said the other. Yes it will, said the older boy, turning angrily away. Standing by them another boy shouted happily that today's was the best find they had ever made.

The spoils of their hunt they had gathered for burning. With the red flames, wild joy would be theirs. Running and leaping across, they would prove their courage. And now from the dunes they gathered dry grass. The eldest stepped forward and touched it with fire. They stood in a circle and waited to hear the crack of bamboo split by the flames. But only the grass burned. It caught and died, caught and died. A few puffs of smoke floated up, nothing more. The wood, the bamboo were untouched. The mirror frame alone was charred here and there. With a weird hiss, steam shot out from the end of the pole. One after another the boys dropped to the sand and blew at the pile as hard as they could. But instead of flames, smoke arose, stinging their eyes. Their cheeks were stained with tears.

The sea was dark. The nearby island of Enoshima could no longer be seen. A string of sandpipers swooped along the beach, their cries echoing sadly first near and then far, invisible one moment, appearing the next, dull white shapes in the evening gloom. An excited rush of wings from the reeds: a flock of snipes must have taken to the air.

Look, look, one boy shouted, the Izu hill fires! If their fires burn, then why shouldn't ours? All leaped to their feet, looking out toward the water. Far across the great bay of Sagami, first one fire, then another would flicker and tremble, hardly more than will-o'-the-wisps. Now that the harvest was over, the farmers of Izu must have been burning the chaff off the fields in the hills. Surely these were the fires that brought tears to the eyes of winter travelers, their distant glow telling only of the long, dark road ahead.

The boys danced wildly and clapped and sang, The hills are burning, the hills are burning. Their innocent voices rang through the dusk, down the long, lonely beach, blending with the whispering of the waves which rushed in from the southern tip of the inlet in foaming white lines. The tide was beginning to rise.

A voice called from beyond the sand dunes, How long can you keep playing on that cold, dark beach? Not one of them heard, so transfixed were they by the distant Izu fires. Come home, come home, the voice called again, and this time a small boy heard. My mother is calling, I'm going home, he shouted and ran from the beach. The others behind him shouted and rushed to be first to the top of the dune.

Still vexed by their failure, the eldest boy looked back at the pile as he ran. One last time he looked back from the top of the dune before running down the far side. It has caught, he shouted, Our fire has caught, when he saw the flames on the beach. The others, amazed, climbed back to the top. They stood in a row and looked down.

It was true. The stubborn bits of wood, fanned by the wind, had caught fire. Smoke billowed up and red tongues of flame shot out, disappeared, and shot out again. The sharp crack of bamboo joints splitting in the fire, the shower of sparks with each report. Yes, the fire had caught. But the boys stood their ground, clapped and shouted with joy, then turned and raced down the hill for home.

Now the ocean was dark, and from the beach, too, the sun had faded. All that remained was the winter night's loneliness. And on the desolate beach the fire burned alone, untended.

Then from nowhere appeared a black silhouette, moving along the water's edge toward the fire. It was an aged wanderer. He had just crossed the river and come out to the beach, making his way toward the highway beyond. Sighting the fire, he quickened his pace. His footsteps were labored.

A wonderful fire, he cried. His voice was hoarse and feeble. Casting his staff away, he set down his pack and held his trembling hands over the flames. His knees shook. And his teeth chattered as he said, How cold the night is. His face shone red in the glow of the flames. Deep wrinkles. Sunken eyes, their gleam long since muddied and dull.

His beard and hair were flecked with gray, and powdered with the dust of the road. Only the tip of his nose shone red, his cheeks an earthen color. Who was he, this old man, and where was he from? Where was he bound for—if indeed he himself knew?

The night is so cold, he said to himself. He shivered with the words. In pleasure he pressed his warm palms to his face. His old coat was so tattered the cotton padding showed through. From its skirts near the fire steam arose. Drenched perhaps in the rain of the morning, he had found no way to dry it till now.

The fire is so pleasant, he said as he lifted his staff from the sand. Bracing himself against it he held one leg over the flames. The heavy blue cloth of his traveler's leggings was faded and torn. A bloodless small toe showed through. With the loud crack of splitting bamboo, the flames leaped up to his foot. The old man did not move.

Ah, this wonderful fire. I wish I could thank the person who built it, he said, then paused to shift to the other foot. In the ten long years since I left that happy fireside I have yet to find one so pleasant as this. As he spoke, gazing into the depths of the flames, it seemed he could make out something far, far away. Could it be that in this fire was the image of another as it burned long ago, and with it sons and grandsons long unseen?

The old fireside was joyful indeed. This fire is one of sorrow. No, no. Past is past. And now is now. How pleasantly this fire burns. The old man's voice was trembling. He hurled his staff away, turned his back to the fire, and stood erect, facing the sea. With his fists, he pounded his lower back. He looked up at the clear, black sky. It seemed to envelop the frosty stream of the Milky Way and dip down to the Izu headland in the distance.

The old man was warm now, his sodden cloak dry. Who had built this fire? For whom had it been made? His heart filled with thanks and he felt the tears come. He heard no wind, no waves as he closed his eyes, only the sound of the incoming tide seeping into the sand. In that moment he forgot the sorrow of his endless wandering. The old man's heart returned once more to the days when he was a boy.

At length, the fire began to die. The bamboo, the wood, had all turned to ash. Only the stout pole continued to burn. But the old man was unperturbed—until it was time to walk on. He raised his arms above the fire, as if in a parting embrace. His eyes fluttered once, but he straightened, resolute, turned and strode away. Two steps, three, and he turned back again. He swept up the unburnt splinters and twigs and added them to the fire. Once more it blazed up, and the sight brought a smile to his face.

When the old man had gone the fire burned on, casting its feeble glow into the desolate gloom of night. The night wore on. The tide came in. The boys' fire, the old man's footprints, were erased by the eternal waves.

SEPARATE WAYS

Translated by Robert Danly

≈

There was someone outside, tapping at her window.

'Okyo? Are you home?'

'Who is it? I'm already in bed,' she lied. 'Come back in the morning.'

'I don't care if you are in bed. Open up! It's me—Kichizo, from the umbrella shop.'

'What a bothersome boy you are. Why do you come so late at night? I suppose you want some rice cakes again,' she chuckled. 'Just a minute. I'm coming.'

Okyo, a stylish woman in her early twenties, put her sewing down and hurried into the front hall. Her abundant hair was tied back simply—she was too busy to fuss with it—and over her kimono she wore a long apron and a jacket. She opened the lattice, then the storm door.

'Sorry,' Kichizo said as he barged in.

Dwarf, they called him. He was a pugnacious little one. He was sixteen, and he worked as an apprentice at the umbrella shop, but to look at him one would think he was eleven or twelve. He had spindly shoulders and a small face. He was a bright-looking boy, but so short that people teased him and dubbed him 'Dwarf.'

'Pardon me.' He went right for the brazier.

'You won't find enough fire in there to toast any of your rice cakes. Go get some charcoal from the cinder box in the kitchen. You can heat the cakes yourself. I've got to get this done tonight.' She took up her sewing again. 'The owner of the pawnshop on the corner ordered it to wear on New Year's.'

'Hmm. What a waste, on that old baldie. Why don't I wear it first?'

'Don't be ridiculous. Don't you know what they say? "He who

36

wears another's clothes will never get anywhere in life." You're a hopeless one, you are. You shouldn't say such things.'

'I never did expect to be successful. I'll wear anybody's clothes—it's all the same to me. Remember what you promised once? When your luck changes, you said you'd make me a good kimono. Will you really?' He wasn't joking now.

'If only I could sew you a nice kimono, it would be a happy day. I'd gladly do it. But look at me. I don't have enough money to dress myself properly. I'm sewing to support myself. These aren't gifts I'm making.' She smiled at him. 'It's a dream, that promise.'

'That's all right. I'm not asking for it now. Wait until some good luck comes. At least say you will. Don't you want to make me happy? That would be a sight, though, wouldn't it?' The boy had a wistful smile on his face. 'Me dressed up in a fancy kimono!'

'And if you succeed first, Kichizo, promise me you'll do the same. That's a pledge I'd like to see come true.'

'Don't count on it. I'm not going to succeed.'

'How do you know?'

'I know, that's all. Even if someone came along and insisted on helping me, I'd still rather stay where I am. Oiling umbrellas suits me fine. I was born to wear a plain kimono with workman's sleeves and a short band around my waist. To me, all "good luck" means is squeezing a little money from the change when I'm sent to buy persimmon juice. If I hit the target someday, shooting arrows through a bamboo pole, that's about all the good luck I can hope for. But someone like you, from a good family—why, fortune will come to greet you in a carriage. I don't mean a man's going to come and take you for his mistress, or something. Don't get the wrong idea.' He toyed with the fire in the brazier and sighed over his fate.

'It won't be a fine carriage that comes for me. I'll be going to hell in a handcart.' Okyo leaned against her yardstick and turned to Kichizo. 'I've had so many troubles on my mind, sometimes it feels as if my heart's on fire.'

Kichizo went to fetch the charcoal from the kitchen, as he always did.

'Aren't you going to have any rice cakes?'

Okyo shook her head. 'No thank you.'

'Then I'll go ahead. That old tightwad at the umbrella shop is always complaining. He doesn't know how to treat people properly. I was sorry when the old woman died. *She* was never like that.

These new people! I don't talk to any of them. Okyo, what do you think of Hanji at the shop? He's a mean one, isn't he? He's so stuck-up. He's the owner's son, but, you know, I still can't think of him as a future boss. Whenever I have the chance, I like to pick a fight and cut him down to size.' Kichizo set the rice cakes on the wire net above the brazier. 'Oh, it's hot!' he shouted, blowing on his fingers. 'I wonder why it is—you seem almost like a sister to me, Okyo. Are you sure you never had a younger brother?'

'I was an only child. I never had any brothers or sisters.'

'So there really is no connection between us. Boy, I'd sure be glad if someone like you would come and tell me she was my sister. I'd hug her so tight . . . After that, I wouldn't care if I died. What was I, born from a piece of wood? I've never run into anyone who was a relative of mine. You don't know how many times I've thought about it: if I'm never, ever going to meet anyone from my own family, I'd be better off dying right now. Wouldn't I? But it's odd. I still want to go on living. I have this funny dream. The few people who've been the least bit kind to me all of a sudden turn out to be my mother and father and my brother and sister. And then I think, I want to live a little longer. Maybe if I wait another year, someone will tell me the truth. So I go on oiling umbrellas, even if it doesn't interest me a bit. Do you suppose there's anyone in the world as strange as I am? I don't have a mother or a father, Okyo. How could a child be born without either parent? It makes me pretty odd.' He tapped at the rice cakes and decided they were done.

'Don't you have some kind of proof of your identity? A charm with your name on it, for instance? There must be something you have, some clue to your family's whereabouts.'

'Nothing. My friends used to tease me. They said I was left underneath a bridge when I was born, so I'd be taken for a beggar's baby. It may be true. Who knows? I may be the child of a tramp. One of those men who pass by in rags every day could be a kinsman. That old crippled lady with one eye who comes begging every morning—for all I know, she could be my mother. I used to wear a lion's mask and do acrobatics in the street,' he said dejectedly, 'before I worked at the umbrella shop. Okyo, if I were a beggar's boy, you wouldn't have been so nice to me, would you? You wouldn't have given me a second look.'

'You shouldn't joke like that, Kichizo. I don't know what kind of people your parents were, but it makes no difference to me.

These silly things you're saying—you're not yourself tonight. If I were you, I wouldn't let it bother me. Even if I were the child of an outcast. I'd make something of myself, whether I had any parents or not, no matter who my brothers were. Why are you whining around so?'

'I don't know,' he said, staring at the floor, 'There's something wrong with me. I don't seem to have any get-up-and-go.'

She was dead now, but in the last generation the old woman Omatsu, fat as a sumo wrestler, had made a tidy fortune at the umbrella shop. It was a winter's night six years before that she had picked up Kichizo, performing his tumbler's act along the road, as she was returning from a pilgrimage.

'It's all right,' she had assured him. 'If the master gives us any trouble, we'll worry about it when the time comes. I'll tell him what a poor boy you are, how your companions abandoned you when your feet were too sore to go on walking. Don't worry about it. No one will raise an eyebrow. There's always room for a child or two. Who's going to care if we spread out a few boards for you to sleep on in the kitchen, and give you a little bit to eat? There's no risk in that. Why, even with a formal apprenticeship boys have been known to disappear. It doesn't prevent them from running off with things that don't belong to them. There are all kinds of people in this world. You know what they say: "You don't know a horse till you ride it." How can we tell whether we can use you in the shop if we don't give you a try? But listen, if you don't want to go back to that slum of yours, you're going to have to work hard. And learn how things are done. You'll have to make up your mind: this is where your home is. You're going to have to work, you know.'

And work he did. Today, by himself, Kichizo could treat as many umbrellas as three adults, humming a tune as he went about his business. Seeing this, people would praise the dead lady's foresight: 'Granny knew what she was doing.'

The old woman, to whom he owed so much, had been dead two years now, and the present owners of the shop and their son Hanji were hard for Kichizo to take. But what was he to do? Even if he didn't like them, he had nowhere else to go. Had not his anger and resentment at them caused his very bones and muscles to contract? 'Dwarf! Dwarf!' everybody taunted him. 'Eating fish on the anniversary of your parents' death! It serves you right that you're so short. Round and round we go—look at him! The tiny monk who'll never grow!'

In his work, he could take revenge on the sniveling bullies, and he was perfectly ready to answer them with a clenched fist. But his valor sometimes left him. He didn't even know the date of his parents' death, he had no way to observe the yearly abstinences. It made him miserable, and he would throw himself down underneath the umbrellas drying in the yard and push his face against the ground to stifle his tears.

The boy was a little fireball. He had a violence about him that frightened the entire neighborhood. The sleeves of his plain kimono would swing as he flailed his arms, and the smell of oil from the umbrellas followed him through every season. There was no one to calm his temper, and he suffered all the more. If anyone were to show Kichizo a moment's kindness, he knew that he would cling to him and find it hard ever to let go.

In the spring Okyo the seamstress had moved into the neighborhood. With her quick wit, she was soon friendly with everyone. Her landlord was the owner of the umbrella shop, and so she was especially cordial to the members of the shop. 'Bring over your mending any time, boys. I don't care what condition it's in. There are so many people at your house, the mistress won't have time to tend to it. I'm always sewing anyway, one more stitch is nothing. Come and visit when you have time. I get lonely living by myself. I like people who speak their minds, and that rambunctious Kichizo—he's one of my favorites. Listen, the next time you lose your temper,' she would tell him, 'instead of hitting the little white dog at the rice shop, come over to my place. I'll give you my mallet, and you can take out your anger on the fulling block. That way, people won't be so upset with you. And you'll be helping me—it'll do us both good.'

In no time Kichizo began to make himself at home. It was 'Okyo, this' and 'Okyo, that' until he had given the other workmen at the shop something new to tease him about. 'Why, he's the mirror image of the great Choemon!' they would laugh. 'At the River Katsura, Ohan will have to carry *him*! Can't you see the little runt perched on top of her sash for the ride across the river? What a farce!'

Kichizo was not without retort. 'If you're so manly, why don't you ever visit Okyo? Which one of you can tell me each day what sweets she's put in the cookie jar? Take the pawnbroker with the bald spot. He's head over heels in love with her, always ordering sewing from her and coming round on one pretext or another, sending her aprons and neckpieces and sashes—trying to win her over. But she's never given him the time of day. Let alone treat him the way she does me! Kichizo from the umbrella shop—*I'm* the one who can go there any hour of the night, and when she hears it's me, she'll open the door in her nightgown. "You haven't come to see me all day. Did something happen? I've been worried about you." That's how she greets me. Who else gets treated that way? "Hulking men are like big trees: not always good supports." Size has nothing to do with it. Look at how the tiny peppercorn is prized.'

'Listen to him!' they would yell, pelting Kichizo across the back.

But all he did was smile nonchalantly. 'Thank you very much.' If only he had a little height, no one would dare to tease him. As it was, the disdain, he showed them was dismissed as nothing more than the impertinence of a little fool. He was the butt of all their jokes and the gossip they exchanged over tobacco.

On the night of the thirtieth of December, Kichizo was returning home. He had been up the hill to call on a customer with apologies for the late filling of an order. On his way back now he kept his arms folded across his chest and walked briskly, kicking a stone with the tip of his sandal. It rolled to the left and then to the right, and finally Kichizo kicked it into a ditch, chuckling aloud to himself. There was no one around to hear him. The moon above shone brightly on the white winter roads, but the boy was oblivious to the cold. He felt invigorated. He thought he would stop by Okyo's on the way home. As he crossed over to the back street, he was suddenly startled: someone appeared from behind him and covered his eyes. Whoever it was, the person could not keep from laughing.

'Who is it? Come on, who is it?' When he touched the hands held over his eyes, he knew who it was. 'Ah, Okyo! I can tell by your snaky fingers. You shouldn't scare people.'

Kichizo freed himself and Okyo laughed. 'Oh, too bad! I've been discovered.'

Over her usual jacket she was wearing a hood that came down almost to her eyes. She looked smart tonight, Kichizo thought as he surveyed her appearance. 'Where've you been? I thought you told me you were too busy even to eat the next few days.' The boy did not hide his suspicion. 'Were you taking something to a customer?'

'I went to make some of my New Year's calls early,' she said innocently.

'You're lying. No one receives greetings on the thirtieth. Where did you go? To your relatives?'

'As a matter of fact, I *am* going to a relative's—to live with a relative I hardly know. Tomorrow I'll be moving. It's so sudden, it probably surprises you. It *is* unexpected, even I feel a little startled. Anyway, you should be happy for me. It's not a bad thing that's happened.'

'Really? You're not teasing, are you? You shouldn't scare me like this. If you went away, what would I do for fun? Don't ever joke about such things. You and your nonsense!' He shook his head at her.

'I'm not joking. It's just as you said once—good luck has come riding in a fancy carriage. So I can't very well stay on in a back tenement, can I? Now I'll be able to sew you that kimono, Kichizo.'

'I don't want it. When you say "Good luck has come," you mean you're going off someplace worthless. That's what Hanji said the other day. "You know Okyo the seamstress?" he said. "Her uncle—the one who gives rub-downs over by the vegetable market—he's helped her find a new position. She's going into service with some rich family. Or so they say. But it sounds fishy to me—she's too old to learn sewing from some housewife. Somebody's going to set her up. I'm sure of it. She'll be wearing tasseled coats the next time we see her, la-de-da, and her hair all done up in ringlets, like a kept woman. You wait. With a face like hers, you don't think she's about to spend her whole life sewing, do you?" That's what he said. I told him he was full of it, and we had a big fight. But you *are* going to do it, aren't you? You're going off to be someone's mistress!'

'It's not that I want to. I don't have much choice. I suppose I won't be able to see you any more, Kichizo, will I?'

With these few words, Kichizo withered. 'I don't know, maybe it's a step up for you, but don't do it. It's not as if you can't make a living with your sewing. The only one you have to feed is yourself. When you're good at your work, why give it up for something so stupid? It's disgusting of you. Don't go through with it. It's not too late to change your mind.' The boy was unyielding in his notion of integrity.

'Oh, dear,' Okyo sighed. She stopped walking. 'Kichizo, I'm sick of all this washing and sewing. Anything would be better. I'm tired of these drab clothes. I'd like to wear a crepe kimono, too, for a change—even if it is tainted.'

They were bold words, and yet it didn't sound as if she herself fully comprehended them. 'Anyway,' she laughed, 'come home with me. Hurry up now.'

'What! I'm too disgusted. You go ahead,' he said, but his long, sad shadow followed after her.

Soon they came to their street. Okyo stopped beneath the window where Kichizo always tapped for her. 'Every night you come and knock at this window. After tomorrow night,' she sighed, 'I won't be able to hear your voice calling any more. How terrible the world is.'

'It's not the world. It's you.'

Okyo went in first and lit a lamp. 'Kichizo, come get warm,' she called when she had the fire in the brazier going.

He stood by the pillar. 'No, thanks.'

'Aren't you chilly? It won't do to catch a cold.'

'I don't care.' He looked down at the floor as he spoke. 'Leave me alone.'

'What's the matter with you? You're acting funny. Is it something I said? If it is, please tell me. When you stand around with a long face like that and won't talk to me, it makes me worry.'

'You don't have to worry about anything. This is Kichizo from the umbrella shop you're talking to. I don't need any woman to take care of me.' He rubbed his back against the pillar. 'How pointless everything turns out. What a life! People are friendly, and then they disappear. It's always the ones I like. Granny at the umbrella shop, and Kinu, the one with short hair, at the dyer's shop. First Granny dies of palsy. Then Kinu goes and throws herself into the well behind the dyer's—she didn't want to marry. Now you're going off. I'm always disappointed in the end. Why should I be surprised, I suppose? What am I but a boy who oils umbrellas? So what if I do the work of a hundred men? I'm not going to win any prizes for it. Morning and night, the only title I ever hear is "Dwarf" . . . "Dwarf"! I wonder if I'll ever get any taller. "All things come to him who waits," they say, but I wait and wait, and all I get is more unhappiness. Just the day before yesterday I had a fight with Hanji over you. Ha! I was so sure he was wrong. I told him you were the last person rotten enough to go off and do that kind of thing. Not five days have passed, and I have to eat crow. How could I have thought of you as a sister? You, with all your lies and tricks, and your selfishness. This is the last you'll ever see of me. Ever. Thanks for your kindness. Go on and do what you want. From now on, I won't have anything to do with anyone. It's not worth it. Good-by, Okyo.'

He went to the front door and began to put his sandals on.

'Kichizo! You're wrong, I'm leaving here, but I'm not abandoning *you*. You're like my little brother. How can you turn on me?' From behind, she hugged him with all her might. 'You're too impatient. You jump to conclusions.'

'You mean you're not going to be someone's mistress?' Kichizo turned around.

'It's not the sort of thing anybody wants to do. But it's been decided. You can't change things.'

He stared at her with tears in his eyes.

'Take your hands off me, Okyo.'

NAGAI KAFU (1879–1959)

THE PEONY GARDEN

Translated by Edward Seidensticker

~

Once, on the impulse of the moment, the geisha Koren and I decided to have a look at the peonies in Honjo, and took a fast boat from under Ryogoku Bridge.

It was late in May. Perhaps the peonies would already have fallen. We had run into each other at a play the evening before, and spent the night at a Yanagibashi inn, and rain had kept us from going home, as we had planned, early in the morning. It had not stopped until after noon. Because we had been shut up in a cramped little room all day, the street gave us a feeling of release, and the breeze that blew down the rows of houses from the river was indescribably fresh against faces recovering from overindulgence. We found ourselves leaning against the railing of Yanagibashi Bridge.

It may have been because the rain had stopped that the day seemed far longer than the days before had been. Wisps of cloud from the storm trailed across the sky, like stylized Kano-school clouds on a temple ceiling. The deep, glowing blue of the sky was especially beautiful, and the fading colors of evening. The rich green of the Kanda Canal in the rising tide shone like a freshly polished sheet of glass, catching the sun as it sank into the grove of the Kanda Shrine. At the mouth of the canal where barges and little boats were collecting, the waters of the Sumida spread before us, the more radiant for the depth of the scene. Along the measured lines of the stone embankments, straggly willows waved in the breeze, quiet and languorous beyond description. Samisen practice in the geisha houses near the river had died away. The moving clouds grew brighter by the minute, despite the advance of evening. The faces of passersby and the stripes of their kimonos floated up in the evening light. The whole city, washed of dust by the rain, seemed clean, relaxed, pleasant. Women on the way back from the bath, towels and cosmetics in hand, would strike up conversations as they passed one another, their throats astonishingly white. Bats were already out, and children were already chasing them. Near at hand there was a clanging of streetcars, while in the distance the horns of boats would give forth long blasts and fade away, to be followed by samisens in unison from the second floor of the Kamesei, its great roof thrusting out toward the mouth of the canal. Two newly lacquered rickshaws with red leather steps waited beside the wooden fence of the Ryukotei, not yet dry from the rain. A geisha in a long, sweeping kimono a solid color but for the pattern at the skirt, and her apprentice, in a dazzlingly bright printed kimono, hurried through a gate over which trailed a willow. People in the street turned to look.

'Let's go,' said Koren.

I started down the main street toward Ryogoku Bridge. 'Are you going home right away? Shall I get the rickshaw?'

She shook her head and walked on.

I arched my back as I looked up into the sky, opening from the street to the Sumida. At the approach to the bridge, in the smell of little restaurant kitchens, there was a confusion of streetcars, of people waiting to board them, of carts crossing the bridge. It suddenly seemed to me that, coming from an inn with this woman, I had nothing to do with a world that had gone on moving without me. The world and I were controlled by separate destinies, taking us in separate directions. A sort of quiet always came over me at evening, but this time the quiet was as of a complete loss of strength, and it brought with it a vague, indefinable sadness. I was not especially sorry to say good-bye to the woman. Nor did I regret a day spent in dissipation. Nor was it that the flowing of the waters somehow moved me. I had exhausted the man-made pleasures that a city has only for those born in it, and now, in the wake of the dream, it was as though I were looking back over the whole long series of dreams.

'Be careful.' I took Koren's arm as we crossed the streetcar tracks. She read the sign by the river.

'Express boats to the Fourth Bridge peonies. Four sen.'

'Shall we go?'

'Let's.' Her voice was unusually young and gay. 'I've never been.'

We crossed to an old barge by the plank laid from the embankment, and from the barge to a lighter with thin rush matting on its floor.

The young boatman, perhaps twenty-one or twenty-two, an old-style bib over his frayed undershirt, had been talking to the captain of the empty boat moored to his. Suddenly coming to life as we climbed aboard, he rose to greet us. 'Anyone else for the Honjo peonies?' he called, waving a freshly lighted pipe. 'We're off for the Honjo peonies.'

We could only see legs and feet on the embankment high above us. Fearing that if we had to wait for other passengers we would reach the garden only after dark, I told the man I would rent the whole boat. He took up his oar, and, in fine spirits, threw down a tinder set on the deck, in case we wanted to smoke.

The little boat moved off, swaying in the flood tide of evening, as the sturdy young arms pushed and pulled at the oar. With the swaying came distant, gentle memories, somehow cut of from the present, of how my nurse had rocked me in her arms:

> Rock-a-bye baby, let the boat rock.
> And where will it rock us off to?

By the railing of Ryogoku Bridge, people were watching the ferries as they put in at little boxlike landings by the bridge pilings, and the passengers in the confusion of embarking and disembarking. As the right bank receded into the distance, childish pictures on the signs lining the Mukojima roofs came up sharply. A dark cloud was just then blotting out the evening sun, and beyond the low, crawling form of New Bridge, where the sky descended to cap the mouth of the river, the smoke from the factories spiraled upward. In the middle of the river we brushed prows with the ferry to First Bridge. There were two men on deck. One, apparently a merchant, had a large, square bundle tied to his back in a pale-blue kerchief. The other was a younger man, very handsome, perhaps a gambler, hatless, and with his lined kimono pulled so wide at the chest that his belly band was showing. Our little boat rocked in the wake of a passing steamer, and the flat-bottomed ferry rocked yet more violently. The waves slipped across the water to Hamacho on the right bank, where wonderfully luxuriant spring foliage rose over earthen walls. The spray, threatening to break over the embankment into the street, was clear from across the river. In the wake of the steamer, out sharp-prowed boat moved ahead of the ferry toward the mouth of the Tatekawa Canal. On land jutting out into the river was a line of new two-story houses, perhaps little restaurants. Two young women with chignons were looking down at the water from veranda railings where quilts were airing.

The boatman called up to them: 'Nice weather we're having, ladies.'

They fled in some consternation.

'What are they up to?' I asked.

He smiled contemptuously. 'Whorehouses. Good place for them to set up businesses.'

Koren frowned in distaste and tapped me on the knee. 'Let me have some tobacco.'

With a strong thrust of the oar the boat passed the embankment and headed up the canal. Just beyond the mouth was a bridge with a wooden marker: 'First Bridge.' The canal was a fairly wide one, but wherever there was water, there were barges piled with every imaginable sort of cargo. Work seemed to be over, for a boatman squatted in the prow of each and looked up at the sky as he smoked. Some were washing away sweat with canal water. In the cabins, women with babies strapped to their backs were lighting fires and washing out pots. Their fuel seemed to be coal scrap, which sent up very smelly fumes. Here and there a red cloud of smoke reflected from the canal.

Koren looked curiously at the jumble of barges. 'Do they sleep on them?'

'Of course.'

'How nice.' She looked back at me. 'Away from the world.'

'Don't think about it. It's impossible, and that's that.' So I said, but I, too, was strangely sad. Once we had had a house together in Tsukiji. After about six months, however, we had agreed that she would again become a geisha.

'You wouldn't think of trying to live with me again? You wouldn't like that?'

'Well, I wouldn't exactly dislike it. But it just wouldn't do. Remember how soon you get tired?'

'Yes. But it's no fun being a geisha.'

'It's no fun being anything else either. You wouldn't like being someone's wife and having to do the housework. I said it would be better for us to have our fun while we were young. I'll be thirty-five in a few years, and you'll be thirty. And you agreed, didn't you, when you went back to work?'

48

'That's so. But I'm more trouble to you now than when we were living together. So I think I'd like to struggle along and be your wife.'

'The idea is all right, maybe. But it's one thing to enjoy yourself and not worry about the teahouse bills, and another thing to get down to work. You're sure to pay plenty of attention to who's giving a party and who's having a coming-out and all that sort of thing. But I don't remember that you were much interested in the water bill.'

'So we'll never get married?'

'That's not the point. You'll just have to wait a little while. Till you aren't so worried about falling in love and being fallen in love with, and you don't have any regrets for what you're leaving behind. The days when you worry about whether you're being cheated— those are the days to enjoy. We'll just sort of come together if we don't worry too much about whether we're going to get married or not.'

'What a stupid world it is, though.'

'Very stupid.'

We passed under Second Bridge with its streetcar track, and the canal stretched on ahead, a series of low wooden bridges crossing it, all very much alike. One bridge would pass and another appear. Children swarmed over them like insects. And not only the bridges. Every open space, a landing perhaps, had its crowds of mischievous children. Among them were girls not to be outdone by boys, shouting from both banks:

> Look at the runt on the other bank.
> His head is three inches long.

The shrill voices crossed the canal, and, following the bank, seemed to come down on us from behind, pushing us faster on our way. The breeze stopped and the evening air was suddenly quiet. The white walls of the warehouses reflected clear and fresh from the water, and the fires on the barges were yet redder. The shadows of the kindling wood, in beautiful gabled stacks, were already dark. Sheaves of bamboo standing on end at the approaches to the bridges were sharp, black towers against the evening sky. But the scenery was unchanging, however far we went, and the charm of the boat was vanishing, leaving only the discomfort of the thin rush mats.

'How far do you suppose the canal goes?'

'To Kameido.'

'Is it much farther to the peonies?'

'Not much. That's Third Bridge.' We both bit back yawns. 'Why don't you go find yourself a good-looking actor to keep you amused?'

'You couldn't pay me to. It used to be very exciting when someone would make fun of me, but now it's all such a bore. It isn't even fun when someone starts talking about *you*.'

'No, it's no fun, all this gossip. But it'd be no more fun if we tried living together again.'

'Maybe we should think about committing suicide together.'

'Maybe we should.'

'What would people say, do you suppose?'

'All sorts of things. And we'd be forgotten in three days.'

'That wouldn't be fun.'

'No fun at all.'

We yawned again.

'Maybe you should decide to get along without love and men. That might be cleverer.'

'I'll bet you could get by without women if you decided to. You've had them all.'

'And you? You say you're even tired of actors.'

'Just actors. Actors and husbands are different.'

'Let's say men in general.'

'They've all given me up. I suppose I can get by well enough if no one comes along. But it's no fun, watching other people laugh, and cry. Look—let's go out and live in the country somewhere. Back in the mountains somewhere, away from everyone.'

'It wouldn't last long. You know you can't stand it for even a week. Not in the liveliest mountain resort.'

'So there's nothing for me. Very tiresome.'

The boatman signaled to me as he came up beside a lighter among the barges. There was a landing of sorts between warehouses, and beyond it a rickshaw stand. We climbed ashore. Across the lane, over a gate flanked by a bamboo fence, was the sign of the peony garden.

The low-lying outskirts of town are humid at best, and the lane that day was muddy. Picking our way through the puddles, we went in the gate, and on along flagstones among old dwarfed trees. The evening light was shut off by a low reed awning, shelter against the rain, and the inner garden was dark. Some serving women were setting out lamps. Rows of tree peonies floated up vaguely in the dim, yellow light and what of the evening light came in. The peonies were already falling. Even the blossoms that had not lost all of their petals were faded badly, their hearts black and gaping. Had they been exposed to bright sunlight and fresh breezes, they would have fallen by now. The weariness and boredom of having been made to bloom too long seemed to flow from each blossom. These peonies had something in common with us, I thought. Although there was no wind and not the sound of a footstep as we stood watching, a heavy petal would fall here and a heavy petal would fall there, as if upon some unheard signal. One would fall on dark leaves, another would trail off into the darkness among the leaves, where the light of the lamps did not reach. There were no visitors besides us, for the hour was late and the season past. From time to time the clamor of the children along the canal would increase, as if with a swelling of their ranks.

She turned to me. 'Are these the Honjo peonies? Are these all?'
'Famous places are always disappointments.'
'Let's go back.'
'Yes, let's go back.'

NIGHT FIRES

Translated by Ted Goossen

≈

It had been raining since early morning. Around noon, all of us—my wife and I, the painter S-san, and the young innkeeper K-san and his wife—had gathered in my room to play cards. Now the room was heavy with tobacco smoke, our stomachs stuffed with snacks, the card game a bore. It was about three o'clock.

At last someone got up and slid open a window. The rain had stopped, and crisp mountain air, filled with the scent of fresh green leaves, flooded the room, scattering the stale smoke. We looked around at each other as though we had been brought back to life.

K-san started to jump to his feet, then paused half-way, flexing his hands eagerly in his trouser pockets.

'I'm heading up to work on the cottage.'

'And I guess I'll do some painting,' said S-san, and the two men went out together.

I sat down on the sill of the bay window. The white clouds were lifting, unveiling an expanse of celadon sky. I could see S-san shouldering his paint box and K-san with a jacket draped loosely over his back climbing up the mountain, talking as they went. When they reached the cottage, they chatted a while longer, then S-san headed off into the woods.

I stretched out and began to read. My wife sat beside me sewing. Just when I was growing bored with the book, she suggested we take a stroll up to 'the cottage', actually a small cabin being built for us by K-san and an old charcoal burner named Haru.

When we got there they were just finishing the outhouse.

'It's turning out quite nicely,' K-san said.

I pitched in and every so often my wife gave us a hand. A half-hour or so later S-san emerged from the forest and came tramping across to us over the sodden carpet of leaves from years past.

'What an improvement!' said S-san, admiring K-san's workmanship. 'Extending the roof like that really gives it a house-like shape.'

'The darned thing turned out all right after all, didn't it!' beamed K-san, who'd taken on the whole job himself.

K-san loved to build things. By taking great care with the design and the materials, he had tried to construct not just a 'useful' shack but a complete little house.

A nighthawk sent up its short sharp cry, the sound of wood striking wood. It was getting dark so we quit work.

'We'd better start thinking about building a fence,' old Haru-san said, packing tobacco into his pipe with the palm of his hand. 'Horses and cows come wandering up here sometimes, you know.'

'You're right,' replied K-san. 'We'd feel pretty foolish if our masterpiece got eaten.'

The thought made us all laugh. Since there was no clay on this mountain, houses could not be plastered in the customary way; even the walls of the inn were just boards set together. Our cottage's walls were stuffed with straw matting packed between layers of the kind of burlap used for charcoal sacks.

'Horses and cows could make a feast of it for sure,' said Haru-san seriously. We all broke out laughing again.

Evening on the mountain was always pleasant, especially after rain. As we stood there gazing at the fruits of our day's labor, a gentle elation arose within our breasts, linking us together. It was an invigorating experience.

The weather had been much the same the previous day. It had cleared in the afternoon, and when evening came a beautiful rainbow had arched from Torii Pass all the way across to Mt Kurobi. We lingered around the cottage, just enjoying ourselves. We started climbing the tall oak trees. Even my wife wanted to join in when she heard we could see the rainbow, so K-san and I helped her up to a spot about twenty feet off the ground. Then K-san and S-san, who was in the next tree, tried to out-climb each other. Some forty feet up, K-san found a conveniently forked limb. Stretching out on his back, he rocked the branches up and down in great leafy waves.

'Just like an easy chair,' he called down to us, nonchalantly puffing on his cigarette.

We were still up in the trees when Ichiya, a feeble-minded boy with features too large for his age, appeared with K-san's baby on his back to tell us dinner was ready. By the time we descended, it had grown so dark that we needed a light to search for my wife's comb, which had fallen from the tree. The ground was pitch black.

'Why don't we take a boat ride on the lake tonight?' I suggested, picturing the fun we'd had the night before. Everyone agreed, so after dinner we reassembled around the sunken hearth on the inn's main floor. K-san was mixing condensed milk with hot water from the kettle for his baby.

When we set off for the lake, K-san dropped by the ice-house to pick up a thick oaken plank. Then we cut across the grounds of the adjacent Shinto shrine, which lay shrouded by a stand of fir trees. As we passed by the shrine building, K-san called out to the attendant selling fortunes and charms that the bath was ready. Between the trunks of the great trees, we could see the silver shimmering surface of the lake.

The small boat was pulled halfway up on the sandy shore. S-san, my wife, and I stood on the damp black sand and watched K-san bail out the rainwater that had accumulated earlier in the day. Then he laid the thick plank carefully across the side and invited us aboard. He helped my wife in first, then gave the rest of us a hand. Then we were pushed out into the lake.

The evening was still. A faint afterglow from the setting sun lingered in the western sky, but the mountains surrounding us were as black as the back of some primordial water lizard.

'Doesn't Mt Kurobi look low tonight?' S-san asked K-san from his seat in the bow.

'Mountains always seem lower in the dark,' K-san answered, quietly plying his short oar in the rear of the boat.

'Look, someone's made a bonfire!' cried my wife as we circled around to the far side of Kotori Island. There appeared to be two fires, one burning on the shore, the other in the still water.

'That's strange for this time of year,' said K-san. 'Could be fiddlehead pickers camping out for the night. Maybe they're sleeping in that old charcoal kiln over there. Shall we go take a look?' With a few strong strokes he had changed our course, and we were skimming across the water toward the fire. He kept talking as he paddled, describing how startled he had been once when, swimming back to the shrine from the island, he had bumped into a water snake.

Just as K-san had thought, the fire was burning beside the opening of the kiln.

'Could there really be people in there?' S-san asked him.

'Of course. It wouldn't do to leave a fire unattended like that. Shall we land and have a look?'

'I'd love to take just a peek,' my wife answered.

We reached the shore. Rope in hand, K-san leaped out and pulled the prow up between two rocks. Then he crouched before the kiln and peered intently inside. 'They're sleeping,' he said.

It was a chilly night, and we were all glad to be near a fire. S-san scraped out a live coal with a stick and lit his cigarette. From inside the kiln came a rustling sound, then a groan.

'Must be nice and cozy in there,' said S-san.

'This fire will burn itself out,' said K-san, tossing some stray branches onto the flames. 'When they wake up tomorrow morning they'll be very cold.'

'Couldn't they suffocate with the fire so close?' asked my wife.

'Don't worry, the fire's on the outside,' K-san answered. 'The thing you have to watch out for with these old kilns is that they can collapse on you all of a sudden. They're especially dangerous after a rain.'

'How awful. You must wake them up and warn them!'

'She's right,' S-san chimed in. 'You really should.'

'It's not necessary,' laughed K-san, 'we're talking so loud they can hear everything we say.'

Once more the sound of rustling leaves came from within the kiln, and we all burst out laughing.

'Don't you think we should go?' my wife suggested anxiously.

When we got back to the boat, S-san jumped in first and announced that he would do the rowing this time.

Between the island and the shore, the lake was especially still; one could look over the side of the boat and see below a perfect reflection of the bright, star-filled sky.

'We could make our own bonfire over there,' said K-san.

As was his habit, S-san was whistling 'The Blue Danube' while he rowed.

'Hey, K-san, where's a good place to land?' he asked.

'Just go straight ahead,' K-san replied, glancing back over his shoulder from his seat in the bow.

We all fell silent for some time. Quietly, the boat slipped toward the shore.

'Think you could swim back to shore from here?' I asked my wife, breaking the silence.

'I wonder . . . Yes, I suppose I could make it that far.'

'Can you really swim, ma'am?' K-san asked in a surprised voice.

'When can you start swimming around here?' I asked him.

'Right about now, if we get some warm weather. We were swimming this time last year.'

'Still a bit chilly,' I said, testing the water with my hand. 'All the same, I've taken morning dips up at Lake Ashi during maple-viewing season, and it wasn't as bad as I expected. Why, I've even gone swimming there in early April!'

'You were quite something back in the old days, weren't you!' teased my wife, who knows how much I really hate the cold.

'Shall I put in here?'

'By all means.'

S-san gave three or four strong strokes, and the bow ran up onto the sandy shore with a loud scraping noise. We all got out and stood on the beach.

'How can we make a fire with everything this wet?' asked my wife.

'We'll use birch bark for kindling,' answered K-san. 'It's so oily it'll burn anywhere. I'll go find some firewood, and you can all gather the bark, if you don't mind.'

He disappeared into the black forest, which was overgrown with ferns, butterburs, and other leafy plants. Working separately in the darkness, we could tell where K-san and S-san were by the tips of their cigarettes, which glowed red with each puff. We peeled off strips of the torn and curling bark with our hands. From time to time the silence was split by the crack of K-san breaking deadwood. We gathered all the bark we could carry, took it down to the beach, and piled it in a big heap.

Suddenly, a startled K-san came bounding out of the forest.

'They're in there . . . worms . . . tails all glowing and wriggling like this . . . can't stand the things!' he panted, wriggling his body to show us how they moved. K-san was terrified of all larvae. We went in to take a look, S-san leading the way.

'Around here?' S-san asked K-san, who had dropped a few steps behind.

'There, over there . . . see the light?'

'Yes, here it is,' said S-san, striking a match and holding it down near the ground. A small worm, about an inch in length, was waving its swollen tail slowly about in the air. The tip of the tail glowed a dim blue.

'Worms really scare you, don't they?' said S-san.

'No more walks in the woods for me this year, not with those things around. Let's go build that bonfire.'

We all made our way back to the beach.

With a match, we lit the pile of wet birch bark. A thick column of smoke, black and oily like that from a kerosene lamp, rose into the air—then the bark burst into flames. K-san threw on larger and larger branches, which were quickly consumed by the towering blaze. Now the whole area was illuminated. Across the water, we could see Kotori Island's wooded shore.

K-san brought the oaken plank from the boat and fixed us a place to sit.

'You're so at home on this mountain,' said S-san, 'and yet you're afraid of insect larvae.'

'If I know they're there it's not so bad, but when I come on them all of a sudden it gives me the creeps.'

'Are there any dangerous animals on the mountain?' asked my wife.

'None at all,' replied K-san.

'No big snakes?'

'No.'

'Vipers?' I inquired.

'Sometimes they come across vipers down around Minowa, but nobody's ever seen one up here.'

'I guess there would have been wild dogs in the old days,' said S-san.

'They were around even when I was a boy. I remember how terribly lonely I used to feel when I woke at night and heard them howling in the distance.'

K-san went on to tell us how his father, who loved night fishing, had been surrounded by wild dogs late one night. Only by leaping into the water and wading home through the rocks along the shore had he managed to escape. K-san himself had seen a horse's half-eaten carcass on the mountainside the year it had been opened up as pastureland.

Shiga Naoya

'That same year,' K-san told us, 'dynamite traps baited with meat were set out to destroy the wild dogs. They were wiped out in just a week.'

I mentioned that I had noticed the skull of a small animal several days before in Jigoku Valley.

'Must have been a badger,' said K-san. 'An eagle or something probably got it. Badgers are quite defenseless, you know.'

'So there's really nothing to be scared of on this mountain?' My wife, being a timid sort, just wanted to make sure.

'Well ma'am, if you must know, I saw a giant goblin once,' K-san confessed with a grin.

'I can guess what happened!' crowed my wife, who had seen something similar one misty morning while viewing the 'Sea of Clouds' at Torii Pass. 'It was your own image reflected in the fog, wasn't it!'

'No, that's not quite it,' said K-san.

One night when he was a boy, he was walking home from Maebashi, about five miles from Kogure, when he noticed a dim light in a pine wood a hundred yards or so up the road. A black, misshapen figure at least ten feet tall stood there in the glow. The light would flicker and go out, the monstrous form would melt into the darkness, then reappear as the eerie light returned. A bit farther up the road K-san passed a man with a load on his back resting by the roadside. The 'goblin' had been nothing but the man's reflection as he walked along trying to light a cigarette.

'Supernatural things can usually be explained, can't they?' said S-san.

'Maybe so, but there are exceptions,' my wife spoke out. 'Dreams, for example. I do believe that omens and the like can come to people in their dreams.'

'That's a different matter altogether,' said S-san. Then, as if suddenly remembering something, he turned to K-san. 'Last year, when you were caught in the snow, now that was really strange, wasn't it! Have you heard about that?' he asked, turning to me.

'No.'

'He's right,' said K-san. 'It certainly was unusual.'

This was K-san's story.

The snow on the mountain was already several feet deep when he had hurried off to Tokyo to see his ailing sister, having gotten word that she had taken a turn for the worse. Since she was better than he had feared, though, he headed back home several days ahead of schedule. It was three in the afternoon when he got off the train in Mizunuma. He had planned to spend the night there, but home was just seven miles away, so he decided to press on at least to the foot of the slope, where he had friends who could put him up.

Night was just falling when he reached the second of the two Shinto gates that marked the entrance to the holy mountain. He felt strong and confident he could make the climb. The moon would light his way. But the higher he climbed, the deeper the snow, twice as deep as before. Had there been some kind of packed trail he would have been alright, but there were no footsteps to follow, just soft, deep drifts. He sank nearly to his waist with each step. He had known this mountain all his life, but now, engulfed in a world of white, he was gradually losing his sense of where the path should be.

Torii Pass seemed to be directly above him. Had it been summer, the leaves on the trees would have hidden it from view, but that night, in the moonlight, he felt he could almost reach up and touch it. The snow made it feel even closer. He had no wish to turn back, but as he crawled like an ant up the mountainside, he began to realize how very far it really was. Should he try and retrace his own footsteps back down the slope? If he lost the track, he'd be even worse off. This way, he only had to look up to see where he was going.

K-san struggled on—one breath, one step. He felt neither worry nor fear. He was, however, growing strangely drowsy.

'Later on, when I recalled that feeling,' he told us, 'I knew how close it had been. First you get drowsy, then you fall asleep. Then you die. That's generally how people die in the snow.'

K-san knew his life was at stake, yet, strangely, fear did not overtake him. He was young and strong, he told himself. He was used to the snow. He could make it. For more than two hours he labored up the mountain until at last he reached the Pass. From here on the snow would be deeper, but the path sloped down for a while and then leveled off. He looked at his watch; it was already past one o'clock.

Then he saw two lanterns bobbing in the distance. Who could it be at this hour? Happy to have his solitude broken by anyone, even in passing, he pushed down toward the lights. At Kakumanbuchi, they met.

'Welcome home,' a voice said. 'You must have had a rough climb.' It was his own brother-in-law, accompanied by three ice-cutters who were boarding with his family.

'Where on earth are you going at this time of night?' asked K-san.

'Why, your mother sent us out to meet you.' His brother-in-law saw nothing strange in that. K-san shuddered.

'You see,' K-san told us, 'I'd sent no word that I'd be coming home that day. Apparently, Mother was sleeping with my older child in her arms—well, not exactly sleeping, I guess—when she suddenly got up, roused my brother-in-law, and asked him to go out to welcome me home. Mother said she heard me calling. She sounded so sure, he saw nothing strange either. He woke up the ice-cutters, they all got dressed, then off they went to meet me.

'She heard me call right at the moment I was weakest, when I felt that drowsiness. You know how early we mountain people go to bed, seven or eight o'clock. Everyone was fast asleep. Yet she woke up four men and sent them out in the middle of the night. That's how clearly she had heard me calling.'

'But had you called?' my wife asked.

'No, not once. Why, on that side of the Pass I could have shouted all night and no one would have heard.'

My wife's eyes were filled with tears. 'I see,' she said.

'You don't send four men out in waist-deep snow just because you've had a feeling—she must have actually heard my voice. It takes a while to get ready to go out in snow like that, too, twenty minutes just to wrap on those darned leggings. Make a mistake, they come off and freeze solid as a log before you can get them back on. So while they were making their preparations, Mother built a fire, fixed them rice-balls to eat—you see, there was no doubt in her mind whatsoever.'

This story takes on a deeper meaning if you know how close K-san and his mother were. K-san's late father was not a bad man apparently, just a poor husband. Everybody called him 'Ibsen' after the playwright he supposedly resembled. Usually he lived with his mistress in Maebashi, but each summer up the mountain he would come, always with the girl, to collect the proceeds from the inn. This infuriated young K-san. Time after time the son would clash with his father. And so the son drew closer to the mother, and the mother to the son.

An owl was hooting on Kotori Island. Our bonfire was burning low. K-san took out his pocket watch.

'What time is it?'

'After eleven.'

'Shall we head back?' said my wife.

K-san began to throw sticks from the fire out into the lake. Red sparks scattered like powder as they hurtled through the night. Two identical flaming arcs, one above, one below, converging, meeting with a hiss on the water's face. Then total darkness. Soon we had thrown them all in. K-san took the oar and deftly splashed water on the remaining embers. Now the fire was completely out.

We set off for home. The fiddlehead-pickers' fire was barely flickering. Around Kotori Island, toward the wooded shrine, silently we glided, while the cry of the night owl faded in the distance.

TANIZAKI JUN'ICHIRO (1886–1965)

AGURI

Translated by Howard Hibbett

~

'Getting a bit thinner, aren't you? Is anything wrong? You're not looking well these days. . . .'

That was what his friend T. had said in passing when they happened to meet him along the Ginza a little while ago. It reminded Okada that he had spent last night with Aguri too, and he felt more fatigued than ever. Of course T. could scarcely have been teasing him about *that*—his relations with Aguri were too well known, there was nothing unusual about being seen strolling on the Ginza in downtown Tokyo with her. But to Okada, with his taut-stretched nerves and his vanity, T.'s remark was disturbing. Everyone he met said he was 'getting thinner'—he had worried about it himself for over a year. In the last six months you could almost see the change from one day to the next, as his fine rich flesh slowly melted away. He'd got into the habit of furtively examining his body in the mirror whenever he took a bath, to see how emaciated it was becoming, but by now he was afraid to look. In the past (until a year or two ago), at least people said he had a feminine sort of figure. He had rather prided himself on it. 'The way I'm built makes you think of a woman, doesn't it?' he used to say archly to his friends at the bathhouse. 'Don't get any funny ideas!' But now . . .

It was from the waist down that his body had seemed most feminine. He remembered often standing before a mirror entranced by his own reflection, running his hand lovingly over his plump white buttocks, as well rounded as a young girl's. His thighs and calves were almost *too* bulging, but it had delighted him to see how fat they looked—the legs of a chop-house waitress—alongside Aguri's slim ones. She was only fourteen then, and her legs were as slender and straight as those of any Western girl: stretched out beside his in the bath, they looked more beautiful than ever, which pleased him as much as it did Aguri. She was a tomboy, and used to push

62

him over on his back and sit on him, or walk over him, or trample on his thighs as if she were flattening a lump of dough. . . . But now what miserable skinny legs he had! His knees and ankles had been nicely dimpled, but for some time now the bones had stuck out pathetically, you could see them moving under the skin. The exposed blood vessels looked like earthworms. His buttocks were flattening out too: when he sat on something hard it felt as if a pair of boards had been clapped together. Yet it was only lately that his ribs began to show: one by one they had come into sharp relief, from the bottom up, till now you could see the whole skeleton of his chest so distinctly that it made a somewhat grim anatomy lesson. He was such a heavy eater that his little round belly had seemed safe enough, but even *that* was gradually shriveling—at this rate, you'd soon be able to make out his inner organs! Next to his legs, he had prided himself on his smooth 'feminine' arms; at the slightest excuse he rolled up his sleeves to show them off. Women admired and envied them, and he used to joke with his girl friends about it. Now, even to the fondest eye, they didn't look at all feminine—or masculine either for that matter. They weren't so much human arms as two sticks of wood. Two pencils hanging down beside his body. All the little hollows between one bone and the next were deepening, the flesh dwindling away. How much longer can I go on losing weight like this? he asked himself. It's amazing that I can still get around at all, when I'm so horribly emaciated! He felt grateful to be alive, but also a little terrified. . . .

These thoughts were so unnerving that Okada had a sudden attack of giddiness. There was a heavy, numbing sensation in the back of his head; he felt as if his knees were shaking and his legs buckling under him, as if he were being knocked over backward. No doubt the state of his nerves had something to do with it, but he knew very well that it came from long over-indulgence, sexual and otherwise—as did his diabetes, which caused some of his symptoms. There was no use feeling sorry now, but he *did* regret having to pay for it so soon, and pay, moreover, by the deterioration of his good looks, his proudest possession. I'm still in my thirties, he thought. I don't see why my health has to fail so badly. . . . He wanted to cry and stamp his feet in rage.

'Wait a minute—look at that ring! An aquamarine, isn't it? I wonder how it would look on me.'

Aguri had stopped short and tugged at his sleeve; she was peering into a Ginza show window. As she spoke she waved the back of her hand under Okada's nose, flexing and extending her fingers. Her long slender fingers—so soft they seemed made only for pleasure—gleamed in the bright May afternoon sunlight with an especially seductive charm. Once in Nanking he had looked at a singsong girl's fingers resting gracefully on the table like the petals of some exquisite hothouse flower, and thought there could be no more delicate beauty than a Chinese woman's hands. But Aguri's hands were only a little larger, only a little more like those of an ordinary human being. If the singsong girl's hands were hothouse flowers, hers were fresh young wildflowers: the fact that they were not so artificial only made them more appealing. How pretty a bouquet of flowers with petals like these would be. . . .

'What do you think? Would it look nice?' She poised her fingertips on the railing in front of the window, pressed them back in the half-moon curve of a dancer's gesture, and stared at them as if she had lost all interest in the ring.

Okada mumbled something in reply but forgot it immediately. He was staring at her hands too, at the beautiful hands he knew so well. . . . Several years had passed since he began playing with those delicious morsels of flesh: squeezing them in his palms like clay, putting them inside his clothes like a pocket warmer, or in his mouth, under his arm, under his chin. But while he was steadily aging, her mysterious hands looked younger every year. When Aguri was only fourteen they seemed yellow and dry, with tiny wrinkles, but now at seventeen the skin was white and smooth, and yet even on the coldest day so sleek you'd think the oil would cloud the gold band of her ring. Childish little hands, as tender as a baby's and as voluptuous as a whore's—how fresh and youthful they were, always restlessly seeking pleasure! . . . But why had his health failed like this? Just to look at her hands made him think of all they had provoked him to, all that went on in those secret rooms where they met; and his head ached from the potent stimulus. . . . As he kept his eyes fixed on them, he began to think of the rest of her body. Here in broad daylight on the crowded Ginza he saw her naked shoulders . . . her breasts . . . her belly . . . buttocks . . . legs . . . one by one all the parts of her body came floating up before his eyes with frightening clarity in queer, undulating shapes. And he felt crushed under the solid weight of her hundred and fifteen or twenty

pounds. . . . For a moment Okada thought he was going to faint—
his head was reeling, he seemed on the verge of falling. . . . Idiot!
Suddenly he drove away his fantasies, steadied his tottering legs. . . .

'Well, are we going shopping?'

'All right.'

They began walking toward Shimbashi Station. . . . Now they
were off to Yokohama.

Today Aguri must be happy, he thought, I'll be buying her a
whole new outfit. You'll find the right things for yourself in the
foreign shops of Yokohama, he had told her; in Arthur Bond's and
Lane Crawford, and that Indian jeweler, and the Chinese dress-
maker. . . . You're the exotic type of beauty; Japanese kimonos cost
more than they're worth, and they're not becoming to you. Notice
the Western and the Chinese ladies: they know how to set off their
faces and figures to advantage, and without spending too much
money at it. You ought to do the same from now on. . . . And so
Aguri had been looking forward to today. As she walks along,
breathing a little heavily in the early-summer heat, her white skin
damp with sweat under the heavy flannel kimono that hampers her
long, youthful limbs, she imagines herself shedding these 'unbecoming' clothes, fixing jewels on her ears, hanging a necklace around
her throat, slipping into a near-transparent blouse of rustling silk
or cambric, swaying elegantly on tiptoes in fragile high-heeled
shoes. . . . She sees herself looking like the Western ladies who pass
them on the street. Whenever one of them comes along Aguri
studies her from head to toe, following her with her eyes and
badgering him with questions about how he likes that hat, or that
necklace, or whatever.

But Okada shared her preoccupation. All the smart young foreign
ladies made him think of an Aguri transfigured by Western
clothes. . . . I'd like to buy that for you, he thought; and this
too. . . . Yet why couldn't he be a little more cheerful? Later on
they would play their enchanting game together. It was a clear day
with a refreshing breeze, a fine May afternoon for any kind of
outing . . . for dressing her up in airy new garments, grooming her
like a beloved pet, and then taking her on the train in search of a
delightful hiding place. Somewhere with a balcony overlooking the
blue sea, or a room at a hot-spring resort where the young leaves of
the forest glisten beyond glass doors, or else a gloomy, out-of-the-

way hotel in the foreign quarter. And there the game would begin, the enchanting game that he was always dreaming of, that gave him his only reason for living. . . . Then she would stretch herself out like a leopard. A leopard in necklace and earrings. A leopard brought up as a house pet, knowing exactly how to please its master, but one whose occasional flashes of ferocity made its master cringe. Frisking, scratching, striking, pouncing on him—finally ripping and tearing him to shreds, and trying to suck the marrow out of his bones. . . . A deadly game! The mere thought of it had an ecstatic lure for him. He found himself trembling with excitement. Once again his head was swimming, he thought he was going to faint. . . . He wondered if he might be dying, now at last, aged thirty-four, collapsing here on the street. . . .

'Oh, are you dead? How tiresome!' Aguri glances absent-mindedly at the corpse lying at her feet. The two-o'clock sun beats down on it, casting dark shadows in the hollows of its sunken cheeks. . . . If he *had* to die he might have waited half a day longer, till we finished our shopping. . . . Aguri clicks her tongue in annoyance. I don't want to get mixed up in this if I can help it, she thinks, but I suppose I can't just leave him here. And there are hundreds of yen in his pocket. The money was *mine*—he might at least have willed it to me before he died. The poor fool was so crazy about me he couldn't possibly resent it if I take the money and buy anything I please, or flirt with any man I please. He knew I was fickle—he even seemed to enjoy it, sometimes. . . . As she makes excuses to herself Aguri extracts the money from his pocket. If he tries to haunt me I won't be afraid of *him*—he'll listen to me whether he's alive or dead. I'll have my way. . . .

'Look, Mr Ghost! I bought this wonderful ring with your money. I bought this beautiful lace-trimmed skirt. And see!' (She pulls up her skirt to show her legs.) 'See these legs you're so fond of, these gorgeous legs? I bought a pair of white silk stockings, and pink garters too—all with your money! Don't you think I have good taste? Don't you think I look angelic! Although you're dead I'm wearing the right clothes for me, just the way you wanted, and I'm having a marvelous time! I'm so happy, really happy! You must be happy too, for having given me all this. Your dreams have come true in me, now that I'm so beautiful, so full of life! Well, Mr Ghost, my poor love-struck Mr Ghost who can't rest in peace—how about a smile?'

Then I'll hug that cold corpse as hard as I can, hug it till his bones crack, and he screams: 'Stop! I can't bear any more!' If he doesn't give in, I'll find a way to seduce him. I'll love him till his withered skin is torn to shreds, till his last drop of blood is squeezed out, till his dry bones fall apart. Then even a ghost ought to feel satisfied. . . .

'What's the matter? Is something on your mind?'

'Uh-h . . .' Okada began mumbling under his breath.

They looked as if they were having a pleasant walk together—it ought to have been extremely pleasant—and yet he couldn't share her gaiety. One sad thought after another welled up, and he felt exhausted even before they began their game. It's only nerves, he had told himself; nothing serious, I'll get over it as soon as I go outside. That was how he had talked himself into coming, but he'd been wrong. It wasn't nerves alone: his arms and legs were so tired they were ready to drop off, and his joints creaked as he walked. Sometimes being tired was a mild, rather enjoyable sensation, but when it got this bad it might be a dangerous symptom. At this very moment, all unknown to him, wasn't his system being invaded by some grave disease? Wasn't he staggering along letting the disease take its own course till it overwhelmed him? Better to collapse right away than be so ghastly tired! He'd like to sink down into a soft bed. Maybe his health had demanded it long ago. Any doctor would be alarmed and say: 'Why in heaven's name are you out walking in *your* condition? You belong in bed—it's no wonder you're dizzy!'

The thought left Okada feeling more exhausted than ever; walking became an even greater effort. On the Ginza sidewalk—that dry, stony surface he so much enjoyed striding over when he was well—every step sent a shock of pain vibrating up from his heel to the top of his head. First of all, his feet were cramped by these tan box-calf shoes that compressed them in a narrow mold. Western clothes were intended for healthy, robust men: to anyone in a weakened condition they were quite insupportable. Around the waist, over the shoulders, under the arms, around the neck—every part of the body was pressed and squeezed by clasps and buttons and rubber and leather, layer over layer, as if you were strapped to a cross. And of course you had to put on stockings before the shoes, stretching them carefully up on your legs by garters. Then you put on a shirt, and then trousers, cinching them in with a buckle at the back till they cut into your waist and hanging them from your shoulders with suspenders. Your neck was choked in a close-fitting collar, over which you fastened a nooselike necktie, and stuck a pin in it. If a man is well filled out, the tighter you squeeze him, the more vigorous and bursting with vitality he seems; but a man who is only skin and bones can't stand that. The thought that he was wearing such appalling garments made Okada gasp for breath, made his arms and legs even wearier. It was only because these Western clothes held him together that he was able to keep on walking at all—but to think of stiffening a limp, helpless body, shackling it hand and foot, and driving it ahead with shouts of 'Keep going! Don't you dare collapse!' It was enough to make a man want to cry. . . .

Suddenly Okada imagined his self-control giving way, imagined himself breaking down and sobbing. . . . This sprucely dressed middle-aged gentleman who was strolling along the Ginza until a moment ago, apparently out to enjoy the fine weather with the young lady at his side, a gentleman who looks as if he might be the young lady's uncle—all at once screws up his face into a dreadful shape and begins to bawl like a child! He stops there in the street and pesters her to carry him. '*Please*, Aguri! I can't go another step! Carry me piggyback!'

'What's wrong with you?' says Aguri sharply, glaring at him like a stern auntie. 'Stop acting like that! Everybody's looking at you!' . . . Probably she doesn't notice that he has gone mad: it's not unusual for her to see him in tears. This is the first time it's happened on the street, but when they're alone together he always cries like this. . . . How silly of him! she must be thinking. There's nothing for him to cry about in public—if he wants to cry I'll let him cry his heart out later! 'Shh! Be quiet! You're embarrassing me!'

But Okada won't stop crying. At last he begins to kick and struggle, tearing off his necktie and collar and throwing them down. And then, dog-tired, panting for breath, he falls flat on the pavement. 'I can't walk any more. . . . I'm sick . . . ,' he mutters, half delirious, 'Get me out of these clothes and put me in something soft! Make a bed for me here, I don't care if it *is* in the street!'

Aguri is at her wit's end, so embarrassed her face is as red as fire. There is no escape—a huge crowd of people has swarmed around them under the blazing sun. A policeman turns up. . . . He questions Aguri in front of everyone. ('Who do you suppose she is?' people begin whispering to one another. 'Some rich man's daughter?' 'No, I don't think so.' 'An actress?') 'What's the matter there?' the policeman asks Okada, not unkindly. He regards him as a lunatic. 'How about getting up now, instead of sleeping in a place like this?'

'I won't! I won't! I'm sick, I tell you! How can I ever get up?' Still sobbing weakly, Okada shakes his head. . . .

He could see the spectacle vividly before his eyes. He felt as if he were actually sobbing. . . .

'Papa . . .' A faint voice is calling—a sweet little voice, not Aguri's. It is the voice of a chubby four-year-old girl in a printed muslin kimono, who beckons to him with her tiny hand. Behind her stands a woman whose hair is done up in a chignon; she looks like the child's mother. . . . 'Teruko! Teruko! Here I am! . . . Ah, Osaki! Are you there too?' And then he sees his own mother, who died several years ago. She is gesturing eagerly and trying hard to tell him something, but she is too far away, a veil of mist hangs between them. . . . Yet he realizes that tears of loneliness and sorrow are streaming down her cheeks. . . .

I'm going to stop thinking sad thoughts like that, Okada told himself; thoughts about Mother, about Osaki and the child, about death. . . . Why did they weigh so heavily on him? No doubt because of his poor health. Two or three years ago when he was well they wouldn't have seemed so overpowering, but now they combined with physical exhaustion to thicken and clog all his veins. And when he was sexually excited the clogging became more and more oppressive. . . . As he walked along in the bright May sunshine he felt himself isolated from the world around him: his sight was dimmed, his hearing faded, his mind turned darkly, obstinately in upon itself.

'If you have enough money left,' Aguri was saying, 'how about buying me a wrist watch?' They had just come to Shimbashi Station; perhaps she thought of it when she saw the big clock.

'They have good watches in Shanghai. I should have bought you one when I was there.'

For a moment Okada's fancies flew off to China. . . . At Soochow, abroad a beautiful pleasure boat, being poled along a serene canal toward the soaring Tiger Hill Pagoda . . . Inside the boat two young lovers sit blissfully side by side like turtledoves. . . . He and Aguri transformed into a Chinese gentleman and a singsong girl. . . .

Was he in love with Aguri? If anyone asked, of course he would answer 'Yes.' But at the thought of Aguri his mind became a pitch-dark room hung with black velvet curtains—a room like a conjurer's stage set—in the center of which stood the marble statue of a nude woman. Was that really Aguri? Surely the Aguri he loved was the living, breathing counterpart of that marble figure. This girl walking beside him now through the foreign shopping quarter of Yokohama—he could see the lines of her body through the loose flannel clothing that enveloped it, could picture to himself the statue of the 'woman' under her kimono. He recalled each elegant trace of the chisel. Today he would adorn the statue with jewels—and silks. He would strip off that shapeless, unbecoming kimono, reveal that naked 'woman' for an instant, and then dress her in Western clothes: he would accentuate every curve and hollow, give her body a brilliant surface and lively flowing lines; he would fashion swelling contours, make her wrists, ankles, neck, all strikingly slender and graceful. Really, shopping to enhance the beauty of the woman you love ought to be like a dream come true.

A dream . . . There was indeed something dreamlike about walking along this quiet, almost deserted street lined with massive Western-style buildings, looking into show windows here and there. It wasn't garish, like the Ginza; even in daytime a hush lay over it. Could anyone be alive in these silent buildings, with their thick gray walls where the window glass glittered like fish eyes, reflecting the blue sky? It seemed more like a museum gallery than a street. And the merchandise displayed behind the glass on both sides was bright and colorful, with the fascinating, mysterious luster of a garden at the bottom of the sea.

A curio-shop sign in English caught his eye: ALL KINDS OF JAPANESE FINE ARTS: PAINTINGS, PORCELAINS, BRONZE STATUES. . . . And one that must have been for a Chinese tailor: MAN CHANG DRESS MAKER FOR LADIES AND GENTLEMEN. . . . And also: JAMES BERGMAN JEWELLERY . . . RINGS, EARRINGS, NECKLACES. . . . E & B CO. FOREIGN DRY GOODS AND GROCERIES . . . LADY'S UNDERWEARS . . . DRAPERIES, TAPESTRIES, EMBROIDERIES. . . . Somehow the very ring of these words in his ear had the heavy, solemn beauty of the sound of a piano. . . . Only an hour by streetcar from Tokyo, yet you felt as if you had arrived at some far-off place. And you hesitated to go inside these shops when you saw how lifeless they looked, their doors firmly shut. In these show windows—perhaps because they were meant for foreigners—goods were set out on display in a cold, formal arrangement well behind the glass, quite unlike the ingratiating clutter of the windows along the Ginza. There seemed to be no clerks or shopboys at work; all kinds of luxuries were on display, but these dimly lit rooms were as gloomy as a Buddhist shrine. . . . Still, that made the goods within seem all the more curiously enticing.

Okada and Aguri went up and down the street several times: past a shoeshop, a milliner's shop, a jeweler, a furrier, a textile merchant. . . . If he handed over a little of his money, any of the things in these shops would cling fast to her white skin, coil around her lithe, graceful arms and legs, become a part of her. . . . European women's clothes weren't 'things to wear'—they were a second layer of skin. They weren't merely wrapped over and around the body but dyed into its very surface like a kind of tattooed decoration. When he looked again, all the goods in the show windows seemed to be so many layers of Aguri's skin, flecked with color, with drops of blood. She ought to choose what she likes and make it part of herself. If you buy jade earrings, he wanted to tell her, think of yourself with beautiful green pendants growing from your earlobes. If you put on that squirrel coat, the one in the furrier's window, think of yourself as an animal with a velvety sleek coat of hair. If you buy the celadon-colored stockings hanging over there, the moment you pull them on, your legs will have a silken skin, warmed by your own coursing blood. If you slip into patent-leather shoes, the soft flesh of your heels will turn into glittering lacquer. My darling Aguri! All these were molded to the statue of woman which is you: blue, purple, crimson skins—all were formed to your body. It's *you* they are selling there, your outer skin is waiting to come to life. Why, when you have such superb things of your own, do you wrap yourself up in clothes like that baggy, shapeless kimono?

'Yes, sir. For the young lady? . . . Just what does she have in mind?'

A Japanese clerk had emerged out of the dark back room of the shop and was eying Aguri suspiciously. They had gone into a modest little dress shop because it seemed least forbidding: not a very attractive one, to be sure, but there were glass-covered cases along both sides of the narrow room, and the cases were full of dresses. Blouses and skirts—women's breasts and hips—dangled overhead. There were low glass cases in the middle of the room, too, display-ing petticoats, chemises, hosiery, corsets, and all manner of little lacy things. Nothing but cool, slippery, soft fabrics, literally softer than a woman's skin: delicately crinkled silk crepe, glossy white silk, fine satin. When Aguri realized that she would soon be clothed in these fabrics, like a mannequin, she seemed ashamed at being eyed by the clerk and shrank back shyly, losing all her usual vivaciousness. But her eyes were sparkling as if to say: 'I want this, and that, and that. . . .'

'I don't really know what I'd like. . . .' She seemed puzzled and embarrassed. 'What do *you* think?' she whispered to Okada, hiding behind him to avoid the clerk's gaze.

'Let me see now,' the clerk spoke up briskly. 'I imagine any of these would look good on you.' He spread out a white linen-like dress for her inspection. 'How about this one? Just hold it up to yourself and look at it—you'll find a mirror over there.'

Aguri went before the mirror and tucked the white garment under her chin, letting it hang down loosely. Eyes upturned, she stared at it with the glum look of a fretful child.

'How do you like it?' Okada asked.

'Mmm. Not bad.'

'It doesn't seem to be linen, though. What's the material?'

'That's cotton voile, sir. It's a fresh, crisp kind of fabric, very pleasant to the touch.'

'And the price?'

'Let's see. . . . Now this one . . .' The clerk turned toward the back room and called in a startlingly loud voice: 'Say, how much is this cotton voile—forty-five yen?'

'It'll have to be altered,' Okada said. 'Can you do it today?'

'Today? Are you sailing tomorrow?'

'No, but we *are* rather in a hurry.'

'Hey, how about it?' The clerk turned and shouted toward the back room again. 'He says he wants it today—can you manage it? See if you can, will you?' Though a little rough-spoken, he seemed kind and good-natured. 'We'll start right now, but it'll take at least two hours.'

'That will be fine. We still need to buy shoes and a hat and the rest, and she'll want to change into her new things here. But what is she supposed to wear underneath? It's the first time she's ever had Western clothes.'

'Don't worry, we have all those too—here's what you start with.' He slipped a silk brassière out of a glass case. 'Then you put this on over it, and then step into this and this, below. They come in a different style too, but there's no opening, so you have to take it off if you want to go to the toilet. That's why Westerners hold their water as long as they can. Now, this kind is more convenient: it has a button here, you see? Just unbutton it and you'll have no trouble! . . . The chemise is eight yen, the petticoat is about six yen—they're cheap compared with kimonos, but see what beautiful white silk they're made of! Please step over here and I'll take your measurements.'

Through the flannel cloth the dimensions of the hidden form were measured; around her legs, under her arms, the leather tape was wound to investigate the bulk and shape of her body.

'How much is this woman worth?' Was that what the clerk was calculating? It seemed to Okada that he was having a price set on Aguri, that he was putting her on sale in a slave market.

About six o'clock that evening they came back to the dress shop with their other purchases: shoes, a hat, a pearl necklace, a pair of amethyst earrings. . . .

'Well, come in! Did you find some nice things?' The clerk greeted them in a breezy, familiar tone. 'It's all ready! The fitting room is over here—just go in and change your clothes!'

Okada followed Aguri behind the screen, gently holding over one arm the soft, snowy garments. They came to a full-length mirror, and Aguri, still looking glum, slowly began to undo her sash. . . .

The statue of a woman in Okada's mind stood naked before him. The fine silk snagged on his fingers as he helped apply it to her skin, going round and round the white figure, tying ribbons, fastening buttons and hooks. . . . Suddenly Aguri's face lit up with a radiant smile. Okada felt his head begin to swim. . . .

BLOWFISH

Translated by Ted Goossen

⟨⟩

On his way back from southern Japan, where he had gone to fill in for Nakamura Komanosuke, who had injured his arm in an aerial stunt, the Kabuki star Jitsukawa Endo was stricken with a malady of the brain. It was a snowy day in late December, during a stopover in Hiroshima. He had started drinking around eleven in the morning, and when evening came he was so drunk and had such a bad headache that he could only sprawl on the tatami floor of his small room and listen to the faint hollow rattle of the paper shoji doors. The dizzy spells commenced the following day, and from time to time thereafter his mind would suddenly become hopelessly muddled, or else grow so strangely clear that he felt he could recall each and every event of his life in detail. He also lost the ability to sleep soundly at night.

He returned to Osaka in time to celebrate the New Year's festivities marking the beginning of his twenty-ninth year by the traditional count. On January fourteenth, he spent the night with the widow Masukawa at the Izutoku Inn. The next morning he awoke at nine to an overcast and unseasonably warm day. Stepping out on the balcony, he looked up at the watery sky, searching vainly for a spot on which his eyes might focus. Then, for the first time since Hiroshima, he felt a wave of rapture sweep over him. The sky seemed to collapse in upon itself, pulling his gaze after it. His head swam. Once he was back in his room, however, and had had a few drinks, it grew clear again. The blowfish *sashimi* from the Tamasho Restaurant was delicious too.

'Won't you join me?' he asked the two geisha with him.

'How gracious of you to ask,' they replied, picking up their chopsticks.

The liver of the blowfish contains a deadly poison, but no one felt their lives were in danger, thanks to the consummate skill of the

Tamasho chef, whose motto was, 'If my fish ever gets anyone, may they be reborn as my own son.' Endo had the fleeting premonition that, this time, the fish might indeed 'get' him. Yet he had been experiencing such momentary lapses of nerve since Hiroshima, so he put it out of his mind. Blowfish was his favorite dish, after all, and he dined on it often.

That afternoon he went to the tea-house of a certain theater to rehearse the premiere of the Kyoto season. He was playing Tokubei to Riko's Ofusa, but as they were running through their lines, his tongue grew strangely clumsy.

'My mouth's acting queer for some reason,' he complained, yet he managed to make it through the rehearsal.

On his way home to Sakamachi, he decided to visit the residence of a geisha he was on intimate terms with. He had never stopped there before, although they were practically neighbors. By this time he was feeling terribly dizzy, and so feverish his eyes and nose seemed to be filling with water from the heat.

'My, but you're nice and pink this afternoon,' she teased the moment she laid eyes on him.

'But I haven't touched a drop,' he protested, for in fact the sake had worn off some time before. 'It's just these dizzy spells I've been having since I fell ill in Hiroshima. Can't seem to do a thing for them.'

Yet even as he spoke he thought of the blowfish he had eaten. More precisely, he remembered the strange premonition he had had about it.

'Perhaps the blowfish I ate this morning got me,' he said. She laughed at first, then seemed to recall something.

'Blowfish, you said? I certainly hope you didn't have lucky rice with it. They're a dangerous mix, you know. It's still New Year's, so you might have been served some.'

'No, I've sworn off red-bean rice this season, what with the headaches I've been having.'

But even as he spoke Endo could tell something out of the ordinary was transpiring inside his body. This is what comes of letting one's mind rest on inauspicious things, he thought. All the same, he couldn't rule out the possibility that he was about to bid the world farewell. How ridiculous that seemed, how fantastic! Could someone who had this very morning leaned, hands in pockets, on a veranda railing and gazed with such rapture at the sky, who had last night given himself over so wholly to passion, who even now sat warming himself before the charcoal brazier, die just like that? True, his body had been behaving oddly since morning; true, for the sake of argument, he might have ingested some blow-fish poison. Yet it was still 'unthinkable' (even while recognizing man's mortality) that this entity called himself could cease to exist. 'When we speak of the future, devils laugh,' goes the old saying. Well, he was so incapable of contemplating his own extinction that anything could have laughed and he would have paid no heed. Thus he was able to banter with the geisha about his own demise as if he hadn't a care in the world. 'Blowfish bought me, blowfish got me, blowfish blew me far away,' was one of the ditties he managed to come up with.

Still, he realized that, by slow degrees, the strange feeling in his lips and extremities was spreading. He was happy to note, however, that his mind was even keener than usual. In this state, he felt, he could accomplish anything, on or off the stage.

By about six o'clock, though, he could barely move, and had lost the power to speak. They picked him up and laid him on a bed, still clothed in the black-crested coat he had put on to go out that morning. Nevertheless, despite everything, his complexion was even more beautiful than usual, and when a local doctor tried to slip a foot-warmer underneath the covers, he had enough strength left to kick it away.

Almost imperceptibly, the house was filling with men and women who had heard the news on the street and had come to offer their comfort and assistance. As they moved about, speaking in low tones, the atmosphere of anxiety spread to encompass the entire neighborhood. Endo's youngest brother, Koendo, purified himself with water from the well in the garden and rushed off for Sennichimae, fastening his sash as he went. He was going to pray at the shrine to Kompira, the god he worshipped above all others. Kisho, the middle brother, was burning moxa on the soles of Endo's feet, instructed by the proprietress of the Izutoku Inn, who had hurried to the scene. A woman from Kasaya-machi, aunt to the three men, was sobbing that the mourning period for her sister had not even ended yet. Quickly but heavily, the time for prayers was passing.

When Ebijuro, the greatest actor of the day, arrived it was already late at night. His guide ushered him only as far as the threshold, then tripped back outside to answer an urgent call from one of those in attendance. At this precise moment, Endo's body was being buried in the cool soft earth at the edge of the veranda in a last, desperate attempt to save his life. All that was left uncovered was his head: propped on a gaudy brocaded pillow, bathed in the circle of many-colored lights, his beautiful features stood out vividly. He appeared to be sleeping peacefully, but four or five of his most trusted friends were watching closely for any sign of improvement. The cold night air, heavy with the odor of damp soil, penetrated the heads of the onlookers. One, the venerable Dr Sakai, withdrew from the gathering to stand beside a great stone lantern, whose surface silently trembled with the shadows of the moving people. Perfectly still, hands clasped before him, his demeanour spoke of the modest reserve of a man who has great skills to offer, yet no chance to put them into effect. He was joined by Ebijuro. Removed from the crowd's eyes, the two men exchanged a soft word of greeting.

'Is there nothing that can be done to bring him back?'

'There's not much hope, I'm afraid.'

'What was it? Did a blowfish really get him?'

'Yes, it's blowfish poisoning. And a terrible shame it is,' said the doctor, making it clear that his medical skill was useless in such a situation.

'Humph,' snorted Ebijuro with displeasure, shaking his head several times as if to censure the dying actor.

With that, the two men were swallowed up in the surrounding silence.

Just then, as though awakening from sleep, something began to stir again within Endo's mind.

I must have been unconscious for quite some time, he thought. What on earth is going on! (Here he grew rather anxious.) This can't just be chance—there has to be some sort of explanation. Could it be the illness I caught in Hiroshima? That must be it. But how could anything so minor... (It all began to seem amusing. How could something so trivial possibly threaten his life—the very idea was absurd. Now he was suddenly quite cheerful.) I know I've been through something like this before. (His mind was on the move again.) I remember death seemed as comical then as it does now. (His merriment increased. Having uncovered an experience perfectly matching this one, he searched his memory to try and place it in time.) Ah yes, Father was there, and his reaction was the same as mine is now. (A picture of the burning of the Takeda Theater

77

rose before his eyes.) Izuzuya was playing two roles, Matsuo and Chiyo, using quick costume changes. People were already screaming 'Fire!' when Father calmly set off for the changing room with the wig for Matsuo. Then before we knew it the fire spread to the rooms beneath the stage. (It struck him as strange that he had never been able to recall the event this clearly before, not even the day after it happened.) I rushed back to my room, then made for the emergency exit. On my way, I bumped into Father again, still calmly bearing that hairpiece along in both hands. 'Run for your life!' I cried, unthinkingly raising my voice to him, but he merely gave a quiet chuckle and moved on. He found the idea of his own death amusing, I suppose. Much as I do now.

My life can't really be in danger, can it? Perhaps I should speak to Dr Sakai, just to make sure. After all, there were many who died in the Takeda Theater blaze. Father, for example, was the epitome of calm, yet he was one of those who perished. In which case. . . .

Fear suddenly struck him like a ball of ghostly fire; he had no chance to dodge. He attempted to call out, but it was as if he had never mastered the art of speech. Panic gripped him, yet he had no way of showing it, for his facial muscles had lost their capacity to register feeling.

An hour or so later, Endo's corpse was unearthed and moved back to the bed.

'He'll be missed,' Ebijuro remarked, whereupon Koendo let flow the tears he'd been holding back all night. Tamizo was in attendance. Izumi, the coral merchant's mistress, sat by her dead lover's side, indifferent to public gaze. Many senior geisha were there, women slightly past their prime who might have been Endo's lovers in earlier days. Yet in their midst one could also make out the face of a much younger geisha with tear-swollen eyes.

The following day, the Tamasho Restaurant closed its doors for good.

These events took place in the sixteenth year of the Meiji era, 1883.

OKAMOTO KANOKO (1889–1939)

PORTRAIT OF AN OLD GEISHA

Translated by Cody Poulton

⟫

Hiraide Sonoko was her legal name, but it was not one she was comfortable with. Kosono, which was her professional name, suited her best, rather in the way that Kabuki actors are known by their stage names. But she was gradually trying to wean herself from the business and turn to the simpler pleasures of private life. In any case, she was an old geisha, and perhaps that is what we ought to call her here.

By day one often saw her out shopping, dressed in a matronly kimono of twilled silk, her hair pulled back in a simple Western-style bun. With her maid in tow, she would wander listlessly (a shuffle to her feet, her arms dangling dispiritedly by her sides) up and down the aisles of department stores, always returning to the same spot. But when something in the distance ignited a glimmer of interest in those sullen eyes, she would bolt toward it to investigate, taut as the string on a kite. Aware of nothing but the afternoon's melancholy, she would pass her time in this pointless fashion, scarcely knowing why. Occasionally she would calmly fix her long glinting eyes on some article that caught her fancy as if it were a peony in her dreams and her lips would pout into a faint smile like a young girl's. Then the smile faded, and the melancholy returned to her face.

She carried that pensive expression to work as well, but it would never last long. She was known as a lively raconteur, provided she had the right company. Even the more experienced geisha would forsake their customers and run to hear her, in the hope that they might learn a trick or two about the art of conversation. The witty and eccentric tales she and her friends from the Shimbashi quarter would tell were classics of the world they lived in. Even on her own she often delighted the younger women with stories of her past. Once, for example, when she was still an apprentice geisha, she laughed so hard at some joke that she wet herself and, too humiliated to move, burst into tears. Another time she ran off with a lover and her patron took her own mother hostage until she returned. Or there was the story of how, having just started out on her own and struggling to make ends meet, she was foolish enough to waste twelve yen on a rickshaw fare to Yokohama merely to collect a five yen loan.

Everyone had heard these silly stories before, but she would tell them differently each time, adding a new flourish or two so that she soon had her audience in tears of laughter. There was something eerily unrelenting about her performance: as if possessed, she would draw her audience in, then seize them and not let go until they squirmed and begged to be released. To watch her was to see jealous age using every wile to torment youth.

In her inimitable way she would confide all sorts of secrets about people she had known, though she would never talk about the living. Her circle of acquaintances was surprisingly wide, and included not a few of the famous. For example (whether the story is true or not I cannot say), when the Chinese opera star Mei Lan Fang played at the Imperial Theatre, Kosono went right up to the impresario and demanded to see the actor. 'I don't give a damn what it costs,' she told him, 'give me some time with him.' The wealthy man somehow managed politely to rebuff her.

'Is it true,' one of her listeners insinuated, 'that you slipped your bankbook from the undersash of your obi and showed him the balance just to prove you had the money?'

'What, show him my underthings?' She had a child's quick temper, and sometimes they would goad her just for the fun of it.

'But you know, girls,' she would conclude, 'all said and done, no matter how many men we've known, we're always looking for just one. What's attracted me to this or that one has always been bits and pieces, just fragments of the man I've been looking for all my life. That's why none of them has lasted very long.'

'Who is it you're looking for, then?'

'If I knew that, I'd never have suffered. Maybe it was my first love, or maybe the man I've yet to meet. All said and done, it's the housewives who are luckiest. They don't think twice about marrying the man their parents pick for them, a husband for keeps too. They bear children, have their kids look after them when they grow old, and then they die.'

On such occasions, Kosono would betray something of the sad beauty of her daytime self. The younger geisha would remark that, while they enjoyed Kosono's stories, she always left them feeling rather depressed.

After years of hard work, Kosono had managed to put away a tidy sum. Able for the past ten years or so to pick and choose her engagements, she began to long for a more settled way of life. She divided her living quarters from the geisha house, with a private entrance off the back alley. She adopted a distant relative's child as her daughter and sent her to a finishing school. She also made a point of taking lessons in the more up-to-date arts and pastimes, and perhaps this too was a reflection of her desire to quit the business.

And that is how I first came to know the old lady. A mutual friend had referred her to me for classes in classical waka poetry. 'A geisha's like a penknife,' she told me, 'she needn't be too sharp at any one thing, just handy for a variety of jobs. So just teach me the basics, and I'll be happy.' She added that, perhaps due to her age, she was getting a better class of customer these days. This woman—she was old enough to be my mother—studied with me for about a year, and though she had some flair for waka I felt that the shorter, more uninhibited haiku suited her better, and so I introduced her to another woman poet I knew. In gratitude for whatever I'd managed to teach her, Kosono sent an artisan to put a pond and fountain in my garden. The result is a lovely example of Tokyo-style landscaping.

She was driven by a sense of competition with her peers, I believe. The main wing of her house was remodeled in a blend of Japanese and Western styles, with electrical wiring and lights just like those at the restaurant where she was often engaged. She was both attracted and a little mystified by the conveniences of modern life. Whenever she used one of her new contraptions—her heater that spouted hot water whenever she turned on the tap, or the electric lighter that lit at the touch of her pipe—she experienced a thrill of pleasure.

'You'd think they were alive! Now that's the way things ought to be.' How healthy, how efficient, modern life was! It made her feel as if her generation had been living all these years in a dream, like some old lantern flickering on and off. Every morning she would rise early just to play with her new toys, though she was staggered by the mounting charges on the electric meter. These gadgets often broke down, and she would be obliged to call in the proprietor of the local appliance store, Makita, to have them serviced. Leaning over his shoulder, she watched with fascination as he did his repairs, and was thus able to pick up some technical know-how.

'So, there's positive and negative, and that's what makes the current run, eh? Sounds just like men and women, doesn't it? Electricity's like sex.' She never ceased to be amazed by the wonders of modern civilization.

A house full of women often needs a handyman, which is where Makita proved useful. One day he brought a young man with him and said that from now on this fellow would look after the electrical repairs. The lad's name was Yuki, and his first remark as he stepped inside the door was, 'Where's the shamisen? I thought this was a geisha house.' Yuki's easygoing nature and his knack for cheering people up made him an excellent sparring partner for the old woman.

'Your work's kind of slapdash you know, Yuki,' Kosono said to him one day as he was fixing yet another appliance that had broken down. She had gotten into the habit of kidding him. 'It never lasts more than a week.'

'Can't help it. I'm bored. I just can't get a charge out of this line of work.'

'What do you mean by that?'

'Why, you know—I guess you don't, after all. Folks in your world would say it just isn't sexy enough.'

It occurred to the old geisha then how empty her own life had been. She was reminded of all the parties she had been to, all the men she had known, and not one had really 'charged' her.

'Is that so? What line of work would you find sexy, then?' she asked him.

Yuki replied that he wanted to be an inventor and live off the proceeds from his patents.

'In that case, the sooner you get started the better.'

Yuki looked up at her and clicked his tongue. 'Easier said than done. No wonder folks call your kind playgirls.'

'No, what I mean is, tell me your plan and we'll work out something. Go ahead and do what you really want. I'll see you don't starve.'

And so it was that Yuki left Makita's shop and moved in with Kosono. The old geisha turned a wing of her house into a laboratory, and ordered whatever Yuki required in the way of equipment for his experiments.

Yuki had worked his way through trade school, and since graduation had avoided taking any job that would tie him down, preferring instead to move from one appliance store to another throughout town, living like a day-laborer. That is, until he ran into Makita. An older graduate of the same school, Makita was happy to help out a hometown boy, and for his part Yuki felt obligated to Makita. He had been living over Makita's shop for some time when Kosono made him her offer. Driven to distraction by Makita's many children and the endless round of trivial jobs he had to do, he jumped at what seemed like a heaven-sent opportunity.

Even so, he did not feel particularly grateful. Here was a woman of the *demi-monde* who had lived as she pleased on the easy money she had squeezed out of her men. Was it any wonder, he thought, that she might want to make amends? Since he did not feel overly obligated to her, Kosono's goodwill imposed no burden on him. For the first time in his life, he felt peaceful and happy. Free of the worry of wondering where his next meal would come from, free to do as he pleased, he spent his days engrossed in experiments, carefully comparing his results with the scientific literature, filing away his discoveries, seeking to invent whatever it was the world still lacked but had a need for.

He had changed, that was for sure. Leaning against the back of his chair and puffing on a cigarette, he gazed into the little mirror he had hung on the pillar. In a clean linen shirt, his hair curled with a crimping iron, he cut a manly figure, or so he thought: the very portrait of an inventor. When he tired of working, he would go on to the veranda outside his laboratory, lie on his back, gaze up into the blue, hazy urban sky of the city, and let his fantasies slip easily away into the dreams of an afternoon nap.

Kosono would drop by every few days. She would glance around, taking quick note of whatever he lacked and then have someone bring it over from the main house. 'For a young man, you sure don't put people out, do you? There's never any dirty laundry lying about—your rooms are as neat as a pin,' she remarked.

'That's right. My mother died when I was still a baby, so I had to wash my own diapers.'

'Really!' Kosono laughed. 'But seriously, if a man fills his head with trifles, he'll never amount to much.'

'It's not like I was always this way. Just had to get used to it. It makes me uneasy when I catch myself getting soft.'

'If there's anything you need, anything, don't hesitate to ask.'

Indeed, Kosono was like a mother to Yuki. They celebrated the Day of the First Horse in February snacking on some special sushi she had ordered in.

Kosono's adopted daughter, Michiko, was a capricious girl. Her mother had tried to shelter Michiko from her own society, a world where love is bought and sold like merchandise, but evidently some of it had rubbed off on her. She was precocious, but it was mostly veneer. For Michiko, Yuki was a potential playmate. Once she had overcome her shyness, she took to visiting him virtually every day. Failing to spark his interest (Yuki was not amused by her games), she would retreat, but a few days later she would appear again, loitering at the entrance to his room. She must have thought it a waste not to make the best of having a young man under the same roof. But at the same time it seemed she disapproved of her mother taking this stranger in—what, after all, was he to them?

One day she quite casually parked herself in Yuki's lap and, giving him a winsome but thoroughly artificial wink, asked him to guess how much she weighed. Yuki bounced her up and down a couple of times and said, 'If you're looking for a husband, I'd say you're still a bit lean on the social graces.'

'Hardly. I got an "A" in social studies at school.' Did Michiko really misunderstand Yuki's remark, or was she just pretending?

Yuki's fingers explored the girl's thin body under its covering of clothes. It amused him that she flirted with him like a full-blooded woman but underneath was nothing but an ill-fed child, and he burst out laughing.

'You pig!' Michiko bolted out of his lap.

'Well, with some good food and exercise you'll fill out nicely, just like your mum.'

Michiko didn't know why, but she detested Yuki for that remark.

Yuki's sense of well-being lasted for about half a year, but then he began to feel as if he were losing his edge. He lived in the thrall of his ambitions so long as they remained no more than dreams, but work was another matter altogether. His investigations soon revealed that several of his ideas had already been patented; considerable revision was required if he wanted to avoid a lawsuit. Besides, he began to doubt whether the world really needed his inventions after all. Experts might be impressed with his work, he thought, but while there was a huge market for simple gadgets, society often had no use for more sophisticated discoveries. Yuki had long realized that there was an element of speculation in any enterprise, but only since he had actually thrown himself into this work had he become so keenly aware of how seldom things turned out as one might hope. He began to wonder whether there was any money to be made in this line of work.

Indeed, Yuki had lost interest in his work, but the real reason had more to do with his present frame of mind. While he was still working for others, the dream of devoting himself entirely to his experiments had allowed him to put up with all sorts of trifles and annoyances. But no sooner had he been given all the time in the world than he discovered how tedious and distasteful the whole business was. His new life was quiet, unsettlingly so. He often feared that, preoccupied with his experiments and with no one to consult, some false assumption might lead him astray, and he would fall completely out of step with society.

True, he no longer had any particular concerns about making ends meet—Kosono looked after him well enough. If he needed a break, he could go see a movie or have a few drinks at a bar, then take a taxi home; Kosono was happy to provide him with pocket money for things like that. His old buddies from the shop had invited him out to the brothels a couple of times, but he found it a tawdry business and soon longed for the comforts of his own bed. (His bedding, it should be noted, was on the extravagant side: he had sewn the quilts himself and stuffed them with high-quality down.) He never once stayed out overnight.

In short, he was a man of simple pleasures, easy to please. So why was he not content? It seemed that, try as he might, Yuki could find no burning passion within himself, and the discovery of how strangely indifferent he had become rather chilled him. Surely it was abnormal for a man his age to feel this way, he thought.

Kosono seemed an odd sort of woman to Yuki. There was a toughness in that melancholic face of hers that he hadn't quite figured out. She flew from one thing to another, impelled by a curious cycle of satiation and desire to consume the new, the unknown. When next she came to visit, Yuki asked her if she knew Mistinguett, a popular singer in the Revue Française.

'Yes! That is, I've heard her records. What a voice she's got!' Kosono replied.

'Story has it the old bird's tucked up all her wrinkles in the soles of her feet so they don't show. I must say, it'll be a while before you need to do that.'

She glared at him, but then smiled. 'Me? I've long lost count of the years. I'm not as firm as I used to be, but here, try and pinch me. Go ahead, take some skin between your thumb and finger and squeeze as hard as you can.' She rolled up her sleeve and thrust out her left arm at Yuki.

He did as he was told. With her right hand, Kosono took a pinch of skin on the underside of her arm, then pulled; the flesh between Yuki's fingers slipped away, leaving no impression at all. Yuki tried again, squeezing with all his might, but once more when Kosono pulled the skin the flesh slipped easily through his fingers. Her skin was unforgettable, as white as parchment, and as smooth and weirdly resilient as the belly of an eel.

'Kind of creepy, but I'm impressed.'

With her scarlet crepe under-kimono, Kosono rubbed the spot where Yuki had pinched her. The mark disappeared. 'I owe it all to the beatings I took from my teachers when I was young and learning to dance.' A shadow passed across her face as she recalled the trials of her childhood. There was a pause, and then she fixed her eyes on him and asked, 'What's wrong with you these days? It's not that I'm pushing you to make something of yourself or anything like that, it's just that lately you've been looking like a fish out of water. A man your age should be absorbed in his own life instead of worrying about things like an old lady's vanity. Your cynicism is sapping your strength. You're stagnating.'

Taken aback by her perceptiveness, Yuki confessed, 'It's no use. I don't get a thrill out of anything anymore. Maybe I never did.'

'Rubbish. But it certainly seems like you've got a problem there. You've gained so much weight lately, I could've mistaken you for somebody else.'

Yuki had always prided himself on his good physique, but he had in fact grown quite plump. There was something fleshly and sensual about those sleepy eyelids and that roll of fat he had acquired under his chin. 'I'm too healthy, I guess. If I don't push myself, I'm liable to drown in my own sense of well-being. That's all. Still, I feel kind of uneasy all the time. Never felt like this before.'

'Too much rich food, I'd say.' Kosono knew about the starchy treats Yuki often had delivered. 'Anyway,' she said more seriously this time, 'whatever it takes, find out what it is you're willing to suffer for. You've got to balance pleasure with pain in this life.'

A couple of days later, Kosono arranged an outing for Yuki, accompanied by Michiko and two young geisha, who politely thanked Kosono for the invitation. Yuki had never seen these women before. They were apparently from another establishment, and were dressed up for the occasion. 'I've hired these girls today to make sure you have some fun,' Kosono told Yuki, 'You're our guest, so you'd better enjoy yourself.'

To be sure, the geisha worked hard to amuse him. The younger one made a point of taking Yuki's hand as they boarded the ferry across the river at Takeya, then grabbed him from behind when she pretended to stumble. The scent of her hair filled Yuki's nostrils. As she staggered past him, he caught a glimpse of the nape of her neck, the black hairline fading into the rich flesh, white against the crimson lining of the collar on her kimono. Her face was slightly turned; her finely sculpted nose seemed etched against a cheek so heavily made up that it was as pure white and radiant as enamel.

Kosono sat down in the boat and took out her tobacco pouch and lighter. 'This is a lovely spot,' she said.

The party toured the Arakawa Canal on foot and by taxi, taking in the sights of early summer. The area had been built up with factories and company dormitories, but here and there, in places like Kanegafuchi and Ayase, one could still find vestiges of the old town, like shards among the cinders. A few of the famous silk trees along the Ayase River were left, and among the reeds on the opposite bank there were some boat shops still in business.

'When I was just a young geisha, I had a patron who kept me in a house in Mukojima. He was so jealous he'd never let me out of the quarter, so I'd have to pretend I was going for a walk if I wanted to get away. I'd head straight for the embankment, where my boyfriend had moored his boat under the silk trees, acting as if he was there to fish for carp. And that's where we had what you young folks today call a "rendezvous".'

The daylight was fading, and the blossoms on the silk trees had folded themselves into tight buds. The sound of the shipwrights' hammers had vanished, and a pale mist was clinging to the river surface.

'We even talked about dying together. It would have been so easy—we could have just thrown our legs over the side of the boat and slipped away.'

'How come you didn't?' asked Yuki, imagining the passionate young couple.

'We'd talk about doing it every time we met, but kept putting it off. Then one day two bodies washed up on the riverbank over there, and my boyfriend went to see what the fuss was all about. "Forget it," he told me, "a double suicide is not a stylish way to go." I was ready to die for this man. But I also felt kind of sorry for my patron. He made my skin crawl, still, you can't help but feel something for a man who's so jealous.'

'When I hear how free and easy things were in your time, I feel sick about how cutthroat our job's become,' said the younger geisha.

'Not at all,' Kosono said, waving her hand dismissively. 'Everything today is so brisk and efficient, like electricity. Every age has something going for it, you know—there's still so much you can do.' This was a cue for the two geisha to set to work on Yuki. Throughout the afternoon they turned all their charm on him, with the younger taking the lead and the older one helping out.

Michiko appeared quite put out by it all. At first she stayed aloof and snubbed the other girls, sitting on her own and taking snapshots of the scenery with her pocket Leica. Then she abruptly turned all her attentions on Yuki, shamelessly vying with the two geisha for the young man's favor.

Yuki caught the scent of this headstrong young girl and, without thinking, filled his lungs with it. Faintly acrid with desperation and desire, her smell was both carnal and innocent, like the odor of slightly spoiled chicken. It strangely excited him. But it was no more than a fleeting impression and did not affect him deeply.

The young geisha did not take too well to Michiko's challenge, but she was Kosono's daughter, after all, and they were simply doing what they were being paid for. So they held back whenever Michiko was fawning on Yuki. No sooner had she turned her back on them, however, than they were on him again, flirting for all they were worth. For Michiko, these girls were like flies at a picnic settling on her piece of cake. She tried to vent her frustration on her mother, but Kosono seemed above it all and blithely spent her time gathering chickweed on the embankment for her canaries or drinking beer at the teahouse where they stopped for a snack.

At nightfall the party made its way to the Yaomatsu inn in Suijin for supper. They were about to enter when Michiko gave Yuki a sharp look and said, 'I've had enough Japanese food for one day, thank you. I'm going home.' Surprised, the geisha offered to accompany her, but Kosono laughed and said, 'No problem, fetch her a taxi.' They hailed a cab. Watching Michiko drive off, Kosono remarked, 'She's learning.'

Yuki could no longer make sense of the old woman's actions. Was looking after a young man a way of assuaging her guilt for what she had done to her old lovers? Perhaps not: neighborhood gossip had it that Yuki was her new toy, but if she had heard what was being said, she wasn't letting on. Why was she making such a show of keeping a man who should have been able to look after himself?

He had long since given up his experiments, and he avoided the laboratory altogether. Although Kosono was well aware of this, she never mentioned it to him, which made him suspect all the more that her intentions were not so altruistic after all. The glass doors of the laboratory looked out on the veranda, and beyond, on to the garden. Yuki made a point of turning the other way when he went out there for his regular afternoon nap. Soon it would be summer. The old trees in the garden were green with leaf, and the irises and azaleas beckoned swarms of bluebottles from their nests among the pebbles filling the pond. The sky was a clear and solid blue, across which the occasional cloud, heavy and gray with rain, sailed like a continent. Next door, in the shade of the clothes hanging to dry, a paulownia was in flower.

In his line of work Yuki had been in many kinds of houses: he had spent his days in claustrophobic cupboards, rank with the stench of old vats of soy sauce, fiddling with wires, or at kitchen tables, sitting over lunch with housewives and maids. When he worked on estimates in his room upstairs at Makita's, the children had often come and teased him, tugging at his neck till it was red and swollen. Once, in a fit of generosity, one of the boys took a candy he'd been sucking on, and (with a strand of spittle still dangling from his fingertips) popped it in Yuki's mouth. These memories, so tedious at the time, came flooding back with a pang of nostalgia. A normal life appealed to him now far more than his old vain ambition of becoming an inventor.

And what about Michiko? The old woman watched over the two of them indulgently as if unaware of what was going on, but for all that he had to wonder. Maybe Kosono was grooming him for marriage to Michiko so that she would have someone to look after her in her old age, but there was no way of knowing. He could not imagine that such a proud woman would stoop to such petty machinations. As for Michiko, she'd acquired all the affectations of a woman and more, he thought wryly, but deep down she was still childish and unripe, rather like a boiled chestnut with its tough skin and mealy, tasteless flesh. Michiko was acting quite hostile these days, but still she clung to him in spite of herself. Her visits became more regular and premeditated, every couple of days or so.

One day, Michiko dropped in to see him, entering from the small sitting-room into the twelve-mat room where Yuki had set up his laboratory. She posed there as she would for a photograph, one hand leaning against the pillar, the other tucked into the sleeve of her kimono. She turned, looked at him seductively from the corner of her eye and said, 'It's me.'

Yuki merely grunted. He was lying on the veranda.

Michiko called again, and received the same response: 'Answer me properly, you lazy good-for-nothing, or I won't come see you again,' she said petulantly.

'What a brat,' Yuki muttered. He sat up, crossed his legs, and stared at her. 'Well, well! Japanese hairstyle today, I see.'

'What of it?' Michiko turned away, the line of her back telegraphing signals of a scorned woman. Her kimono collar was pulled down nearly as far as the gaudy bow of her obi, to show off the perfect V of the white nape of her neck; but then her figure trailed off at the hips into the demure line of two stem-like legs. There was something incongruous about the effect, naïve but pretentious, half virgin, half coquette.

Yuki wondered what it would be like if she were his wife, giving her heart and soul to him, fussing over his every need and whim. This prospect of a cozy but thoroughly commonplace life struck him as oddly depressing, and yet, so long as it remained a fantasy, it held the fascination of the unknown. Michiko presented an image of feminine beauty that was almost too perfect: not a single hair was out of place, though her make-up and heavy coiffure made her small face look even smaller. Could he find something there that would make him fall in love with her?

'Look this way again. It really suits you.'

With a little shrug of her shoulder she swung around, nervously touching her collar and hair to see that everything was in place. The baubles of her hairpins jiggled as she did so. 'Fussy, aren't you! How do I look now?' she asked, satisfied that Yuki was taking her seriously. 'I brought you a treat. Guess what it is.'

'I hate guessing. If you've got something for me, you'd better bring it over here.' He began to resent the fact that he had let himself be taken in by this girl.

Michiko looked away, flustered by his reply. 'If you're going to turn your nose up at what people are good enough to offer you, forget it.'

'Give it to me.' Yuki stood up, surprised by the force of his own reaction. He edged toward her. 'Give it here, I tell you!' he ordered. He felt cornered but he liked the feeling, though he knew full well the danger he was in. His desperation inspired a kind of alertness he had never experienced before, and the struggle to overcome his own self-loathing made his forehead break out in a cold sweat.

Thinking Yuki's gruffness was still an act, Michiko continued to look at him scornfully, but something had changed in his manner and she became frightened. Retreating into the sitting room she muttered, 'Come get it yourself.' His eyes on fire, Yuki edged closer and grabbed her shoulders. Michiko cried out, erasing the careful effect of her make-up and distorting her features. Yuki swallowed nervously. 'Give it here!' he repeated, but he no longer sounded so sure of himself.

Michiko could feel his arms trembling uncontrollably. 'Forgive me!' she sobbed, wide-eyed with terror. Yuki continued to stare at her, his face dull, expressionless, and pale. Nervous energy ran down his arms and into Michiko's body.

It suddenly dawned on her what was wrong. 'Men are such cowards,' her mother had often said. The realization that here was a full-grown man struggling to overcome his own fear made Yuki seem somehow lovable to Michiko, like some overgrown and good-natured pet. Composing herself and smiling coyly at him, she said,

'Silly, you don't have to make such a fuss. I'll give it to you.' She wiped the sweat from his forehead with her handkerchief. 'Come on. It's in here.' A sudden rustle of the wind in the leaves startled her. She glanced toward the garden and grasped Yuki's arm as she pulled him into the room after her.

One evening in late spring, Kosono came for a visit, entering by the garden gate with her umbrella raised to shelter her from a rain so fine that it was like smoke. She sat down and smoothed out the hem of the elegant kimono she was wearing. 'I've got an engagement tonight, but I thought I'd drop by,' she told Yuki. 'There's something I wanted to talk to you about.' She took out her tobacco pouch and pulled over an ashtray with the bowl of her pipe. 'I understand you and Michiko have been seeing a lot of each other lately. Don't get me wrong. That's fine by me but, seeing as you're both young and all, what if something were to happen? I've got nothing against *that*, provided you two are a good match and love each other. Don't feel obligated to take Michiko if it's just a passing fancy. Infatuations never last long, and they're hardly worth the trouble in any case. No matter how many affairs I've had they've always ended up the same—I've had nothing but pain from them. Whether it's love or work, you have to throw yourself heart and soul into it. I was never able to, but before I die I'd dearly love to see somebody succeed. No need to rush, just take your time and figure out what it is you really want from life—love, money, what have you. Aim for it and strike when the time's right. That's all I ask.'

Yuki burst out laughing. 'I'm hardly capable of anything so pure as that. Besides, there's fat chance of anything like that in this day and age.'

'It's possible, provided you watch out for it,' she laughed back. 'All I'm saying is, do what you like, eat what you like, but take a gamble on yourself, then sit back and wait. You've got luck and good health on your side and, what's more, the will-power.'

The rickshaw came for her, and she left.

By now, Yuki had a good idea of what the old woman was scheming: she wanted him to accomplish what she herself had failed to do. But surely wasn't what she was asking impossible, for him or for herself, or for anyone? Life lures you on with dreams of your own making, but when all is said and done it hands you only bits and pieces. That he could accept, but she didn't know the meaning of resignation. She seemed insensible to such things.

Perhaps that accounted for her strength. What a formidable old woman! Like a snake that keeps shedding its skin and moving on, all that experience had changed her into something monstrous but also a little tragic. Even so, he resented his own carelessness at getting swept up in her schemes. Given half the chance, he'd get off that ever-ascending escalator she'd put him on and dive into his warm down quilt.

Yuki wandered off that night. He ended up some two hours by train from Tokyo, in a seaside resort where Makita's brother ran an inn. (Yuki had been there once before to do some repairs.) As far as the eye could see there was nothing but ocean, mountains, and passing clouds. Never in his life had he been able to get in touch with nature and gather his thoughts like this. He was young and healthy, the fish was delicious, and the swimming was good. A rare sense of happiness welled up inside him.

His troubles only amused him now. The old geisha was a strange bird for sure: her head was so filled with the trivia of everyday life that she couldn't see how driven she was by her own insatiable ambitions. He couldn't help but laugh at himself too. Life under Kosono's roof was stultifying and oppressive; but free of her, he suddenly felt so lonely. Like an animal who never strays from his prescribed territory, Yuki was still incapable of escaping the old woman's influence, and in spite of himself he'd picked a hiding-place where they would have no trouble finding him. There was something odd, too, about his relationship with Michiko. It was as if, for no reason they would ever understand, the two of them had been touched by lightning.

Yuki had been at the inn for about a week when Makita showed up. Kosono had given him some money and sent him off to find the boy. 'Be sensible,' Makita told him, 'get a decent job and make something of yourself.' He went back with Makita, but running away became something of a habit with him.

Kosono was sitting in the little studio she had built for herself in the storehouse. Her music teacher had just left and she was going over her lessons when Michiko, dressed in her tennis whites, interrupted her with the news that Yuki had disappeared again. 'He wasn't here last night, or the night before either,' Michiko said coolly, as if looking forward to her mother's consternation.

Kosono laid down her shamisen and looked at her daughter innocently, betraying none of the turmoil festering inside her. 'Showing his tail again, is he?' she said. She took a puff on her pipe and carefully straightened the sleeves of her striped Oshima kimono. 'Leave him be. He can't get away with being spoiled forever,' she commented. Brushing away some flecks of ash on her lap, she quietly closed her music. Michiko picked up her tennis-raquet and left, disappointed at her mother's lack of annoyance.

As soon as Michiko had left, Kosono telephoned Makita to ask him to fetch Yuki back. Having nothing to hide from the electrician, she fiercely rebuked the young man for his willfulness, so fiercely in fact that her voice reverberated in the receiver clutched in her hand. But her spite soon gave way to a sadness so intoxicating she felt revived. 'The young have spirit, that's for sure. Good for them!' she muttered as she rang off, dabbing at the corner of her eyes with her sleeve. Every time he ran away, Yuki seemed only to grow in her esteem. But then the thought that Yuki would not come home always left Kosono feeling irrevocably bereft.

I had neither seen nor heard anything from Kosono for some months. One midsummer's day, as I was sitting on my veranda enjoying the sound of water splashing in the fountain she had commissioned, a letter arrived from her. I was no longer her teacher, and to the best of my knowledge she was still taking lessons in haiku from the person I had introduced her to, so I was quite surprised to discover that she had sent some waka to me for correction. I read them eagerly. One of these I feel admirably captures her current state of mind. I have touched it up a bit, but my changes are no more than superficial and have not, I trust, compromised its intent:

> The passing years
> have only compounded my sorrow,
> but the flower of youth
> has no thought for the morrow.

AKUTAGAWA RYUNOSUKE (1892–1927)

IN A GROVE

Translated by Takashi Kojima

The Testimony of a Woodcutter Questioned by a High Police Commissioner

Yes, sir. Certainly, it was I who found the body. This morning, as usual, I went to cut my daily quota of cedars, when I found the body in a grove in a hollow in the mountains. The exact location? About 150 meters off the Yamashina stage road. It's an out-of-the-way grove of bamboo and cedars.

The body was lying flat on its back dressed in a bluish silk kimono and a wrinkled head-dress of the Kyoto style. A single sword-stroke had pierced the breast. The fallen bamboo-blades around it were stained with bloody blossoms. No, the blood was no longer running. The wound had dried up, I believe. And also, a gad-fly was stuck fast there, hardly noticing my footsteps.

You ask me if I saw a sword or any such thing?

No, nothing, sir. I found only a rope at the root of a cedar near by. And . . . well, in addition to a rope, I found a comb. That was all. Apparently he must have made a battle of it before he was murdered, because the grass and fallen bamboo-blades had been trampled down all around.

'A horse was near by?'

No, sir. It's hard enough for a man to enter, let alone a horse.

The Testimony of a Traveling Buddhist Priest Questioned by a High Police Commissioner

The time? Certainly, it was about noon yesterday, sir. The unfortunate man was on the road from Sekiyama to Yamashina. He was walking toward Sekiyama with a woman accompanying him on horseback, who I have since learned was his wife. A scarf hanging

95

from her head hid her face from view. All I saw was the color of her clothes, a lilac-colored suit. Her horse was a sorrel with a fine mane. The lady's height? Oh, about four feet five inches. Since I am a Buddhist priest, I took little notice about her details. Well, the man was armed with a sword as well as a bow and arrows. And I remember that he carried some twenty odd arrows in his quiver.

Little did I expect that he would meet such a fate. Truly human life is as evanescent as the morning dew or a flash of lightning. My words are inadequate to express my sympathy for him.

The Testimony of a Policeman Questioned by a High Police Commissioner

The man that I arrested? He is a notorious brigand called Tajomaru. When I arrested him, he had fallen off his horse. He was groaning on the bridge at Awataguchi. The time? It was in the early hours of last night. For the record, I might say that the other day I tried to arrest him, but unfortunately he escaped. He was wearing a dark blue silk kimono and a large plain sword. And, as you see, he got a bow and arrows somewhere. You say that this bow and these arrows look like the ones owned by the dead man? Then Tajomaru must be the murderer. The bow wound with leather strips, the black lacquered quiver, the seventeen arrows with hawk feathers—these were all in his possession I believe. Yes, sir, the horse is, as you say, a sorrel with a fine mane. A little beyond the stone bridge I found the horse grazing by the roadside, with his long rein dangling. Surely there is some providence in his having been thrown by the horse.

Of all the robbers prowling around Kyoto, this Tajomaru has given the most grief to the women in town. Last autumn a wife who came to the mountain back of the Pindora of the Toribe Temple, presumably to pay a visit, was murdered, along with a girl. It has been suspected that it was his doing. If this criminal murdered the man, you cannot tell what he may have done with the man's wife. May it please your honor to look into this problem as well.

The Testimony of an Old Woman Questioned by a High Police Commissioner

Yes, sir, that corpse is the man who married my daughter. He does not come from Kyoto. He was a samurai in the town of Kokufu in the province of Wakasa. His name was Kanazawa no Takehiko, and his age was twenty-six. He was of a gentle disposition, so I am sure he did nothing to provoke the anger of others.

My daughter? Her name is Masago, and her age is nineteen. She is a spirited, fun-loving girl, but I am sure she has never known any man except Takehiko. She has a small, oval, dark-complected face with a mole at the corner of the left eye.

Yesterday Takehiko left for Wakasa with my daughter. What bad luck it is that things should have come to such a sad end! What has become of my daughter? I am resigned to giving up my son-in-law as lost, but the fate of my daughter worries me sick. For heaven's sake leave no stone unturned to find her. I hate that robber Tajomaru, or whatever his name is. Not only my son-in-law, but my daughter . . . (Her later words were drowned in tears.)

Tajomaru's Confession

I killed him, but not her. Where's she gone? I can't tell. Oh, wait a minute. No torture can make me confess what I don't know. Now things have come to such a head, I won't keep anything from you.

Yesterday a little past noon I met that couple. Just then a puff of wind blew, and raised her hanging scarf, so that I caught a glimpse of her face. Instantly it was again covered from my view. That may have been one reason; she looked like a Bodhisattva. At that moment I made up my mind to capture her even if I had to kill her man.

Why? To me killing isn't a matter of such great consequence as you might think. When a woman is captured, her man has to be killed anyway. In killing, I use the sword I wear at my side. Am I the only one who kills people? You, you don't use your swords. You kill people with your power, with your money. Sometimes you kill them on the pretext of working for their good. It's true they don't bleed. They are in the best of health, but all the same you've killed them. It's hard to say who is a greater sinner, you or me. (An ironical smile.)

But it would be good if I could capture a woman without killing her man. So, I made up my mind to capture her, and do my best not to kill him. But it's out of the question on the Yamashina stage road. So I managed to lure the couple into the mountains.

It was quite easy. I became their traveling companion, and I told

them there was an old mound in the mountain over there, and that
I had dug it open and found many mirrors and swords. I went on to
tell them I'd buried the things in a grove behind the mountain, and
that I'd like to sell them at a low price to anyone who would care
to have them. Then . . . you see, isn't greed terrible? He was beginning to be moved by my talk before he knew it. In less than half an
hour they were driving their horse toward the mountain with me.

When he came in front of the grove, I told them that the treasures
were buried in it, and I asked them to come and see. The man had
no objection—he was blinded by greed. The woman said she would
wait on horseback. It was natural for her to say so, at the sight of a
thick grove. To tell you the truth, my plan worked just as I wished,
so I went into the grove with him, leaving her behind alone.

The grove is only bamboo for some distance. About fifty yards
ahead there's a rather open clump of cedars. It was a convenient spot
for my purpose. Pushing my way through the grove, I told him a
plausible lie that the treasures were buried under the cedars. When
I told him this, he pushed his laborious way toward the slender cedar
visible through the grove. After a while the bamboo thinned out,
and we came to where a number of cedars grew in a row. As soon
as we got there, I seized him from behind. Because he was a trained,
sword-bearing warrior, he was quite strong, but he was taken by
surprise, so there was no help for him. I soon tied him up to the root
of a cedar. Where did I get a rope? Thank heaven, being a robber,
I had a rope with me, since I might have to scale a wall at any
moment. Of course it was easy to stop him from calling out by
gagging his mouth with fallen bamboo leaves.

When I disposed of him, I went to his woman and asked her to
come and see him, because he seemed to have been suddenly taken
sick. It's needless to say that this plan also worked well. The woman,
her sedge hat off, came into the depths of the grove, where I led her
by the hand. The instant she caught sight of her husband, she drew
a small sword. I've never seen a woman of such violent temper. If
I'd been off guard, I'd have got a thrust in my side. I dodged, but
she kept on slashing at me. She might have wounded me deeply or
killed me. But I'm Tajomaru. I managed to strike down her small
sword without drawing my own. The most spirited woman is
defenseless without a weapon. At last I could satisfy my desire for her
without taking her husband's life.

Yes, . . . without taking his life. I had no wish to kill him. I was about to run away from the grove, leaving the woman behind in tears, when she frantically clung to my arm. In broken fragments of words, she asked that either her husband or I die. She said it was more trying than death to have her shame known to two men. She gasped out that she wanted to be the wife of whichever survived. Then a furious desire to kill him seized me. (Gloomy excitement.)

Telling you in this way, no doubt I seem a crueler man than you. But that's because you didn't see her face. Especially her burning eyes at that moment. As I saw her eye to eye, I wanted to make her my wife even if I were to be struck by lightning. I wanted to make her my wife . . . this single desire filled my mind. This was not only lust, as you might think. At that time if I'd had no other desire than lust, I'd surely not have minded knocking her down and running away. Then I wouldn't have stained my sword with his blood. But the moment I gazed at her face in the dark grove, I decided not to leave there without killing him.

But I didn't like to resort to unfair means to kill him. I untied him and told him to cross swords with me. (The rope that was found at the root of the cedar is the rope I dropped at the time.) Furious with anger, he drew his thick sword. And quick as thought, he sprang at me ferociously, without speaking a word. I needn't tell you how our fight turned out. The twenty-third stroke . . . please remember this. I'm impressed with this fact still. Nobody under the sun has ever clashed swords with me twenty strokes. (A cheerful smile.)

When he fell, I turned toward her, lowering my blood-stained sword. But to my great astonishment she was gone. I wondered to where she had run away. I looked for her in the clump of cedars. I listened, but heard only a groaning sound from the throat of the dying man.

As soon as we started to cross swords, she may have run away through the grove to call for help. When I thought of that, I decided it was a matter of life and death to me. So, robbing him of his sword, and bow and arrows, I ran out to the mountain road. There I found her horse still grazing quietly. It would be a mere waste of words to tell you the later details, but before I entered town I had already parted with the sword. That's all my confession. I know that my head will be hung in chains anyway, so put me down for the maximum penalty. (A defiant attitude.)

Akutagawa Ryunosuke

The Confession of a Woman Who Has Come to the Shimizu Temple

That man in the blue silk kimono, after forcing me to yield to him, laughed mockingly as he looked at my bound husband. How horrified my husband must have been! But no matter how hard he struggled in agony, the rope cut into him all the more tightly. In spite of myself I ran stumblingly toward his side. Or rather I tried to run toward him, but the man instantly knocked me down. Just at that moment I saw an indescribable light in my husband's eyes. Something beyond expression . . . his eyes make me shudder even now. That instantaneous look of my husband, who couldn't speak a word, told me all his heart. The flash in his eyes was neither anger nor sorrow . . . only a cold light, a look of loathing. More struck by the look in his eyes than by the blow of the thief, I called out in spite of myself and fell unconscious.

In the course of time I came to, and found that the man in blue silk was gone. I saw only my husband still bound to the root of the cedar. I raised myself from the bamboo-blades with difficulty, and looked into his face; but the expression in his eyes was just the same as before.

Beneath the cold contempt in his eyes, there was hatred. Shame, grief, and anger . . . I don't know how to express my heart at that time. Reeling to my feet, I went up to my husband.

'Takejiro,' I said to him, 'since things have come to this pass, I cannot live with you. I'm determined to die, . . . but you must die, too. You saw my shame. I can't leave you alive as you are.'

This was all I could say. Still he went on gazing at me with loathing and contempt. My heart breaking, I looked for his sword. It must have been taken by the robber. Neither his sword nor his bow and arrows were to be seen in the grove. But fortunately my small sword was lying at my feet. Raising it over head, once more I said, 'Now give me your life. I'll follow you right away.'

When he heard these words, he moved his lips with difficulty. Since his mouth was stuffed with leaves, of course his voice could not be heard at all. But at a glance I understood his words. Despising me, his look said only, 'Kill me.' Neither conscious nor unconscious, I stabbed the small sword through the lilac-colored kimono into his breast.

Again at this time I must have fainted. By the time I managed to look up, he had already breathed his last—still in bonds. A streak of sinking sunlight streamed through the clump of cedars and bamboos, and shone on his pale face. Gulping down my sobs, I untied the rope from his dead body. And . . . and what has become of me since I have no more strength to tell you. Anyway I hadn't the strength to die. I stabbed my own throat with the small sword, I threw myself into a pond at the foot of the mountain, and I tried to kill myself in many ways. Unable to end my life, I am still living in dishonor. (A lonely smile.) Worthless as I am, I must have been forsaken even by the most merciful Kwannon. I killed my own husband. I was violated by the robber. Whatever can I do? Whatever can I . . . I . . . (Gradually, violent sobbing.)

The Story of the Murdered Man, as Told Through a Medium

After violating my wife, the robber, sitting there, began to speak comforting words to her. Of course I couldn't speak. My whole body was tied fast to the root of a cedar. But meanwhile I winked at her many times, as much as to say 'Don't believe the robber'. I wanted to convey some such meaning to her. But my wife, sitting dejectedly on the bamboo leaves, was looking hard at her lap. To all appearance, she was listening to his words. I was agonized by jealousy. In the meantime the robber went on with his clever talk, from one subject to another. The robber finally made his bold brazen proposal. 'Once your virtue is stained, you won't get along well with your husband, so won't you be my wife instead? It's my love for you that made me be violent toward you.'

While the criminal talked, my wife raised her face as if in a trance. She had never looked so beautiful as at that moment. What did my beautiful wife say in answer to him while I was sitting bound there? I am lost in space, but I have never thought of her answer without burning with anger and jealousy. Truly she said, . . . 'Then take me away with you wherever you go.'

This is not the whole of her sin. If that were all, I would not be tormented so much in the dark. When she was going out of the grove as if in a dream, her hand in the robber's, she suddenly turned pale, and pointed at me tied to the root of the cedar, and said, 'Kill him! I cannot marry you as long as he lives.' 'Kill him!' she cried many times, as if she had gone crazy. Even now these words threaten to blow me headlong into the bottomless abyss of darkness.

Has such a hateful thing come out of a human mouth ever before? Have such cursed words ever struck a human ear, even once? Even once such a . . . (A sudden cry of scorn.) At these words the robber himself turned pale. 'Kill him,' she cried, clinging to his arms. Looking hard at her, he answered neither yes nor no . . . but hardly had I thought about his answer before she had been knocked down into the bamboo leaves. (Again a cry of scorn.) Quietly folding his arms, he looked at me and said, 'What will you do with her? Kill her or save her? You have only to nod. Kill her?' For these words alone I would like to pardon his crime.

While I hesitated, she shrieked and ran into the depths of the grove. The robber instantly snatched at her, but he failed even to grasp her sleeve.

After she ran away, he took up my sword, and my bow and arrows. With a single stroke he cut one of my bonds. I remember his mumbling, 'My fate is next.' Then he disappeared from the grove. All was silent after that. No, I heard someone crying. Untying the rest of my bonds, I listened carefully, and I noticed that it was my own crying. (Long silence.)

I raised my exhausted body from the foot of the cedar. In front of me there was shining the small sword which my wife had dropped. I took it up and stabbed it into my breast. A bloody lump rose to my mouth, but I didn't feel any pain. When my breast grew cold, everything was as silent as the dead in their graves. What profound silence! Not a single bird-note was heard in the sky over this grave in the hollow of the mountains. Only a lonely light lingered on the cedars and mountain. By and by the light gradually grew fainter, till the cedars and bamboo were lost to view. Lying there, I was enveloped in deep silence.

Then someone crept up to me. I tried to see who it was. But darkness had already been gathering round me. Someone . . . that someone drew the small sword softly out of my breast in its invisible hand. At the same time once more blood flowed into my mouth. And once and for all I sank down into the darkness of space.

MIYAZAWA KENJI (1896–1933)

THE BEARS OF NAMETOKO

Translated by John Bester

It's interesting, that business of the bears on Mt Nametoko. Nametoko is a large mountain, and the Fuchizawa River starts somewhere inside it. On most days of the year, the mountain breathes in and breathes out cold mists and clouds. The peaks all around it, too, are like blackish green sea slugs or bald sea goblins. Halfway up it there yawns a great cave, from which the river Fuchizawa abruptly drops some three hundred feet in a waterfall that goes thundering down through the thick-growing cypresses and maples.

Nowadays nobody uses the old highway, so it is all grown over with butterbur and knotweed, and there are places where people have put up fences on the track to stop cattle from straying and climbing up the slopes. But if you push your way for about six miles through the rustling undergrowth, you will hear in the distance a sound like the wind on a mountaintop. If you peer carefully in that direction, you might be puzzled to see something long, white, and narrow trailing down the mountain in a flurry of mist: this is the Ozora Falls. And in that area, they say, there used to be any number of bears.

Now, I must confess that I have never actually seen either Mt Nametoko or the liver of a newly killed bear. All this is based on what I've heard from other people or worked out for myself. It may not be entirely true, though I for one believe it.

But I do know that Mt Nametoko is famous for its bear's liver, which is good for stomach-aches and helps wounds heal. At the entrance to the Namari hot spring there is a sign that says 'Bear's Liver from Mt Nametoko.' So there are definitely bears on the mountain. I can almost see them, going across the valleys with their pink tongues lolling out, and the bear cubs wrestling with each other till finally they lose their tempers and box each other's ears. It was bears like these that the famous hunter Kojuro Fuchizawa once killed so freely.

Kojuro was a swarthy, well-knit, middle-aged man with a squint. His body was massive, like a barrel, and his hands were as big and thick as the handprint of the god Bishamon that they use to cure people's illnesses at the Kitajima Shrine. In summer, he wore a cape made of bark to keep off the rain, with leggings, and he carried a woodsman's axe and a gun as big and heavy as an old-fashioned blunderbuss. With his great yellow hound for company, he would tramp across the mountains, from Mt Nametoko to Shidoke Valley, from Mitsumata to Mt Sakkai, from Mamiana Wood to Shira Valley.

When he went up the old, dried-up valleys, the trees grew so thickly that it was like going through a shadowy green tunnel, though sometimes it suddenly became bright with green and gold, and at other times sunlight fell all around as though the whole place had burst into bloom. Kojuro moved at a slow and ponderous pace, as completely at home as though he were in his own living room. The hound ran on ahead, scampering along high banks or plunging into the water. He would swim for all he was worth across the sluggish, faintly sinister backwaters, then, when he finally reached the other side, would shake himself vigorously to dry his coat and stand with wrinkled nose waiting for his master to catch up. Kojuro would come across with his mouth slightly twisted, moving his legs stiffly and cautiously like a pair of compasses, while the water splashed up in a white curl above his knees.

The bears in the area of Mt Nametoko were fond of Kojuro. One proof of this is that they would often gaze down in silence from some high place as he squelched his way up the valleys or passed along the narrow ledges, overgrown with thistles, that bordered the valley. Clinging to a branch at the top of a tree or sitting on a bank with their paws around their knees, they would watch with interest as he went by.

The bears even seemed to like Kojuro's hound.

Yet for all that, they didn't like it much when they really came up against him, and the dog flew at them like a ball of fire, or when Kojuro with a strange glint in his eyes leveled his gun at them. At such times, most of them would wave their paws as though in distress, telling him that they didn't want to be treated in that way.

But there are all kinds of bears, just as there are all kinds of people, and the fiercest of them would rear up on their hind legs with a great roar and advance on Kojuro with both paws stretched out, ignoring the dog as though they could crush him underfoot as easily as that. Kojuro would remain perfectly calm and, taking aim at the center of the bear's forehead from behind a tree, would let fly with his gun.

The whole forest would seem to cry out loud, and the bear would slump to the ground. Dark red blood would gush from his mouth, he would snuffle rapidly, and he would die.

Then Kojuro would stand his gun against a tree, cautiously go up to the bear, and say something like this:

'Don't think I killed you, Bear, because I hated you. I have to make a living, just as you have to be shot. I'd like to do different work, work with no sin attached, but I've got no fields, and they say my trees belong to the authorities, and when I go into the village nobody will have anything to do with me. I'm a hunter because I can't help it. It's fate that made you a bear, and it's fate that makes me do this work. Make sure you're not reborn as a bear next time!'

At times like this the dog, too, would sit by him with narrowed eyes and a dejected air. The dog, you see, was Kojuro's sole companion. In the summer of his fortieth year, his whole family had fallen sick with dysentery, and his son and his son's wife had died. The dog, however, had remained healthy and active.

Next, Kojuro would take out of his pocket a short, razor-sharp knife and in one long stroke slit the bear's skin open from under his chin down to his chest and on to his belly. The scene that followed I don't care to think about. Either way, in the end Kojuro would put the bright red bear's liver in the wooden chest on his back, wash the fur which was all in dripping, bloody tassels in the river, roll it up, put it on his back, and set off down the valley with a heavy heart.

It even seemed to Kojuro that he could understand what the bears were saying to each other. Early one spring, before any of the trees had turned green, Kojuro took the dog with him and went far up the marshy bed of Shira Valley. As dusk drew near, he began to climb up to the pass leading over to Bakkai Valley, where he had built a small hut of bamboo grass to shelter in. But for some reason or other Kojuro, unusually for him, took the wrong trail. Any number of times he started up, then came down and started up again; even the dog was quite exhausted and Kojuro himself was breathing heavily out of one side of his mouth before they finally found the hut he'd built the year before, which was half tumbled down.

Remembering that there had been a spring just below the hut, Kojuro set off down the mountain, but had only gone a little way when to his surprise he came across two bears, a mother and a cub barely a year old, standing in the faint light of the still new moon, staring intently at the far-off valley with their paws up to their foreheads, just as human beings do when gazing into the distance. To Kojuro, the bears looked as if they were surrounded by a kind of halo, and he stopped and stared at them transfixed.

Then the small bear said in a wheedling voice, 'I'm sure it's snow, Mother. Only the near side of the valley is white, isn't it? Yes, I'm sure it's snow!'

The mother bear went on staring for a while before saying, 'It's not snow. It wouldn't fall just in that one place.'

'Then it must have been left there after the rest melted,' said the cub.

'No, I went past there only yesterday on my way to look for thistle buds.'

Kojuro stared hard in the same direction. The moonlight was gliding down the mountainside, which gleamed like silver armor. After a while the cub spoke again.

'If it's not snow then it must be frost. I'm sure it is.'

There really will be a frost tonight, thought Kojuro to himself. A star was shimmering blue, close to the moon; even the color of the moon itself was just like ice.

'I know what it is,' said the mother bear. 'It's cherry blossom.'

'Is that all? Even *I've* seen that.'

'No, you haven't, dear.'

'But I *have*. I went and brought some home myself the other day.'

'No—that wasn't cherry. It was some kind of beech, I think.'

'Really?' the cub said innocently.

For some reason, Kojuro's heart felt full. He gave a last glance at the snowy flowers over in the valley, and at the mother bear and her cub standing bathed in the moonlight, then stealthily, taking care to make no sound, withdrew. As he crept away, praying all the while that the wind wouldn't blow his scent in their direction, the fragrance of spicebush came sharply to him on the moonlight.

When he went to town to sell the bearskins and the bear liver, that same brave Kojuro cut a much humbler figure.

Somewhere near the center of the town there was a large hardware store where winnowing baskets and sugar, whetstones and cheap cigarettes, and even glass fly traps were set out for sale.

Kojuro had only to step over the threshold of the shop with the great bundle of bearskins on his back for the people there to start smiling as though to say, 'Here he is again.' The owner of the place would be seated massively beside a large brazier in a room leading off the shop.

'Thank you for your kindness last time, sir,' Kojuro would say; and the hunter who back in the hills was completely his own master would lay down his bundle of skins and, kneeling on the boards, bow low.

'Well, well. ... And what can I do for you today?'

'I've brought along a few bearskins again.'

'Bearskins? The last ones are still lying around here somewhere. We don't need any more.'

'Come on, sir—give us a chance. I'll let you have them cheap.'

'I don't care how cheap they are, I don't want them,' the shopkeeper would tell him calmly, tapping out the small bowl of his pipe against the palm of his hand.

Whenever he heard this, Kojuro, brave lord of the hills, would feel his face twist with anxiety.

Where Kojuro came from, there were chestnuts to be found in the hills, and millet grew in the apology for a field that lay at the back of the house; but no rice would grow, nor was there any soybean paste for making soup. So he had to have some rice, however little, to take back to the family of seven—his old mother and his grandchildren.

If he had lived down in the village, he would have grown hemp for weaving cloth, but at Kojuro's place there were only a few wisteria vines, which were woven into baskets and the like.

After a while, Kojuro would say in a voice hoarse with distress, 'Please—please buy some, whatever the price.' And he'd bow down low again.

The shopkeeper would puff smoke for a while without saying

anything, then, suppressing a slight grin of satisfaction, would seat himself in front of Kojuro and hand him four large silver coins. Kojuro would accept them with a smile and raise them respectfully to his forehead. Then the owner of the shop would gradually unbend.

'Here—give Kojuro some sake.'

By now Kojuro would be glowing with delight. The shopkeeper would talk to him at leisure about this and that. Deferentially, Kojuro would tell him of things back in the hills. And soon word would come from the kitchen that the meal was ready. Kojuro would rise to go, but in the end would be dragged off to the kitchen, where he would go through his polite greetings once again.

Almost immediately, they would bring a small black lacquered table bearing slices of salted salmon with chopped cuttlefish and a flask of warm sake.

Kojuro would seat himself very correctly at the table, then start to eat, balancing the pieces of cuttlefish on the back of his hand before gulping them down, and reverently pouring the yellowish sake into the tiny cup. . . .

However low prices might be, anyone would have agreed that two yen was too little for a pair of bearskins.

It really was too little, and Kojuro knew it. Why, then, didn't he sell his skins to someone other than that hardware dealer? To most people, it would be a mystery. But in those days there was an order to things: it was a matter of course that Kojuro should get the better of the bears, that the shopkeeper should get the better of Kojuro, and that the bears—but since the shopkeeper lived in the town, the bears couldn't get the better of him, for the moment at least.

Such being the state of affairs, Kojuro killed the bears without feeling any hatred for them. One year, though, a strange thing happened.

Kojuro was squelching his way up a valley and had climbed onto a rock to look about him when he saw a large bear, his back hunched, clambering like a cat up a tree directly in front of him. Immediately, Kojuro leveled his gun. The dog, delighted, was already at the foot of the tree, rushing madly round and round it.

But the bear, who for a while seemed to be debating whether he should come down and attack Kojuro or let himself be shot where he was, suddenly let go with his paws and came crashing to the ground. Instantly on his guard, Kojuro tucked his gun into his shoulder and closed in. But at this point the bear put up his paws and shouted:

'What are you after? Why do you have to shoot me?'

'For nothing but your fur and your liver,' Kojuro replied. 'Not that I'll get anything much for them when I take them to town. I'm sorry for you, but it just can't be helped. Though when I hear you say that kind of thing, I almost feel I'd rather live on chestnuts and ferns and the like, even if it killed me.'

'Can't you wait just two more years? For myself, I don't care whether I die or not, but there are still things I've got to do. When two years are up, you'll find me dead in front of your house, I promise. You can have my fur and my insides too.'

Filled with a stange emotion, Kojuro stood quite still, thinking.

The bear set his four paws firmly on the ground and began, ever so slowly, to move away. But Kojuro went on standing there, staring vacantly in front of him.

Slowly, slowly, the bear walked away without looking back, as though he knew very well that Kojuro would never shoot him from behind. For a moment, his broad, brownish black back shone bright in the sunlight falling through the branches of the trees, and at the same moment Kojuro gave a painful groan, then headed home across the valley.

It was just two years later. One morning, the wind blew so fiercely that Kojuro, sure that it was blowing down trees and hedge and all, went outside to look. The cypress hedge was standing untouched, but at its foot lay something brownish black that seemed familiar. His heart gave a turn, for it was exactly two years since that day, and he had been feeling worried in case the bear should come along. He went up to it, and found the selfsame bear lying there as he had promised, dead, in a great pool of blood that had gushed from his mouth. Almost without thinking, Kojuro pressed his hands together in prayer.

It was one day in January. As Kojuro was leaving home that morning, he said something he had never said before.

'Mother, I must be getting old. This morning, for the first time in my life, I don't feel I want to wade through all those streams.'

Kojuro's mother of ninety, who sat spinning on the veranda in the sun, raised her rheumy eyes and glanced at him with an expression that might have been either tearful or smiling.

Kojuro tied on his straw sandals, heaved himself to his feet, and set off. One after the other the children poked their faces out of the barn and smiling said, 'Come home soon, Grandpa.'

Kojuro looked up at the smooth, bright blue sky, then turned to his grandchildren and said, 'I'll be back later.'

He climbed up through the pure white, close-packed snow in the direction of Shira Valley. The dog was already panting heavily, his pink tongue lolling, as he ran ahead and stopped, ran ahead and stopped again. Soon Kojuro's figure sank out of sight beyond a low hill, and the children returned to their games.

Kojuro followed the bank of the river up Shira Valley. Here the water lay in deep blue pools, there it was frozen into sheets of glass, here the icicles hung in countless numbers like bead curtains, and on both banks the berries of the spindletree peeped out like red and yellow flowers. As he climbed upstream, Kojuro saw his own glittering shadow and the dog's, deep indigo and sharply etched on the snow, mingling as they moved with the shadows of the birch trunks.

On the other side of the mountain from Shira Valley there lived, as he had confirmed during the summer, a large bear.

On he went upstream, fording five small tributaries that came flowing into the valley, crossing the water again and again from right to left and from left to right. He came to a small waterfall, from the foot of which he began to climb up toward the ridge. The snow was so dazzling it seemed to be on fire, and as he toiled upward, Kojuro felt as if he saw everything through purple glasses.

The dog was climbing as though determined that the steepness of the slope would not beat him, clinging grimly to the snow, though he nearly slipped many times. When they finally reached the top, they found themselves on a plateau that sloped gently away, where the snow sparkled like white marble and snow-covered peaks thrust up into the sky all about them.

It happened as Kojuro was taking a rest there at the summit. Suddenly, the dog began to bark frantically. Startled, Kojuro looked behind him and saw the same great bear that he had glimpsed that summer rearing up on his hind legs and lumbering toward him. Without panicking, Kojuro planted his feet firmly in the snow and took aim.

Raising his two massive front paws, the bear charged staight at him. Even Kojuro turned a bit pale at the sight.

Kojuro heard the crack of the gun. Yet the bear showed no sign of falling, but seemed to come swaying on toward him, black and raging like a storm. The dog sank his teeth into his leg. The next moment, a great noise filled Kojuro's head and everything around him went white. Then, far off in the distance, he heard a voice saying, 'Ah, Kojuro, I didn't mean to kill you.'

'This is death,' he thought. All about him he could see lights twinkling incessantly like blue stars. 'Those are the signs that I'm finished,' he thought, 'the fires you see when you die. Forgive me, Bears.' As for what he felt from then on, I have no idea.

It was the evening of the third day after that. A moon hung in the sky like a great ball of ice. The snow was a bright bluish white, and the water gave off a phosphorescent glow. The Pleiades and Orion's belt glimmered now green, now orange, as if they were breathing.

On the plateau on top of the mountain, surrounded by chestnut trees and snowy peaks, many great black shapes were gathered in a ring, each casting its own black shadow, each prostrate in the snow like a Muslim at prayer, never moving. And there at the highest point one might have seen, by the light of the snow and the moon, Kojuro's corpse set in a kneeling position. One might even have imagined that on Kojuro's dead, frozen face one could see a chill smile as though he were still alive. Orion's belt moved to the center of the heavens, then tilted still further to the west, yet the great black shapes stayed quite still, as though they had turned to stone.

YOKOMITSU RIICHI (1898–1947)

SPRING RIDING IN A CARRIAGE

Translated by Dennis Keene

The cold late-autumn wind began to sound among the pine trees on the shore. In a corner of the garden a clump of small dahlias shrank in upon themselves. From the side of the bed where his wife lay he watched a sluggish tortoise moving in the pond. The tortoise swam and the bright shadows that were cast back from the water swayed on the surface of the dry rocks.

'Oh, do look. Isn't the light on the pine trees lovely now.'

'You've been looking at the pine trees?'

'Yes.'

'I've been looking at the tortoise.'

They were returning to silence again.

'You've been lying there all that time and the only thought in your head is that the light on the pine trees is lovely?'

'Yes. But I'm making up my mind not to think about anything.'

'It is not in any way feasible that a human being should be able to lie down and not think.'

'Well, I do think about things, like wanting to get better and then going down to the well and scrubbing and scrubbing away at all the washing. I think about that so much.'

This unforeseen desire on her part made him smile.

'You are certainly a queer one. Making me take all this time and trouble so that you can do the washing. That's great.'

'But I remember when I used to be so well. I want to be like that again. You've been an unlucky person, haven't you?'

'Uh,' he said.

He thought about those years before they'd married, the four or five years' battle with her family. Then he thought about when they were married, the two years of troubles caught in the middle between wife and mother. Then his mother died, leaving them alone together, and then she had immediately become ill and had taken to her bed, and he remembered that long year of suffering also.

'I see what you mean, anyway. I'd rather like to do the washing myself.'

'I wouldn't mind for myself if I died now. But it's you. I want to give you something back for what you've done, then I'd like to die after that. I worry so much nowadays that I won't be able to. It's only that.'

'What are you going to give me, then, if you're going to give me something back?'

'Well, first of all, I'd look after you. . . .'

'And?'

'There're lots of things I'd do.'

But he was aware that she was not going to recover now.

'That sort of thing doesn't matter to me, not a bit. But you know, what I would like, I'd like just once to wander around Munich—Munich in the rain. It would have to be raining. I wouldn't want to go otherwise.'

'I want to go too. I want to.' She started wriggling about on the bed, her stomach plunging and rippling like waves.

'You've been ordered absolute rest and quiet.'

'But I don't want it, I don't. I want to walk. Help me get up, please. Please help me up.'

'I will not.'

'Help me up. I don't care if I do die.'

'Nothing will come of dying.'

'I don't care. Just help me up.'

'Look, keep still, can't you? I'll tell you what you can do. You can spend your whole life over it. Look at the pine trees and that light on them, and think of the one word that describes it perfectly. Just the one, all right?'

She became silent and absorbed. That was one peaceful problem to quiet her with. He stood up trying to think of others.

Out at sea the afternoon waves broke on the rocks and scattered. A boat leaned and rounded the sharp point of the headland. Down on the beach two children sat like scraps of paper, steaming potatoes in their hands, against a background of deep, surging blue.

The waves after waves of suffering that came in upon him had never been something to be evaded. The origin of those waves of suffering, each different in each onslaught, existed in his very flesh, had been there from the beginning. He had decided to taste this suffering as the tongue tastes sugar, to scrutinize it with the total light of his senses. Which would taste best in the end? My body is a scientific flask; the most important thing is absolute clarity.

The dahlias lay tangled and twisted on the ground, pieces of old, dried-up rope. All day the wind blew in from the sea, from the horizon, and it was winter.

Off he went through the swirling sand, twice a day, to buy her the fresh chicken innards that she liked to eat. He would try every poulterer's in the streets on the sea front one after the other, and each time, after an initial glance from the yellow chopping board out into the yard and then back again, he would ask: 'Any innards? Innards?'

When he was in luck and the agatelike innards were brought out from the ice, he would stride off heroically back home and arrange them neatly by her bedside.

'This one like a rounded jewel is a pigeon's kidney. This glossy liver came from a domestic duck. And look at this, just like a piece of lip bitten right off. And this green one is, look, an emerald from the jade mountain in far Tibet.'

His eloquence inflamed her, and she would writhe exotically on the bed in her hunger, like a girl waiting for her first kiss. But he would snatch the innards cruelly away from in front of her, and plop them immediately into the saucepan.

She watched the contents of the saucepan through the cagelike bars of her bedstead, smiling as they boiled away.

'Looking at you from here, you really are a weird animal,' he said.

'An animal, indeed. Let me remind you that I am still a married lady.'

'That's right, a married lady inside a cage who craves for animals' guts. I've always felt that somewhere there's always been this certain amount of cold-bloodedness inside you trying to get out.'

'Speak for yourself. You're the one who's so cold and intellectual, so cold-blooded, thinking all the time about ways of getting away from me.'

'That's your cage mentality again.'

He always had to end things up like that, because she was sensitive to each motion of his face, to every half-shadow that might drift across it, and he needed to baffle and cancel out what she perceived there. Yet also there were times when this kind of response of hers would outwit him, suddenly slip through to where it hurt and completely unbalance him.

'The truth is that, well, I *do* object to sitting here with you. Tuberculosis is hardly a thing to rejoice over, is it?'

There were times when he counterattacked her openly like that.

'Well, is it? Even if I do manage to get away from you, all it consists of is going round and round that garden. There's a rope that always ties me to the bed where you're lying, and all I can do is move along the circumference it draws. What else have I got? What else besides this misery?'

'It's because. . . . It's because you just want to enjoy yourself,' she said bitterly.

'Then you yourself don't want to?'

'But you, you want to enjoy yourself with other women.'

'All right, that's what you say. But suppose it were true, what then?'

She would always burst into tears at this point. That would shake him, so he would have to retreat the way he had come, very gently taking to pieces the argument he had built.

'But obviously I can't like having to sit by your bed from morning till night. I want you to get well as soon as you can, so I go round and round that same garden all the time, don't I? It's not something exactly up my street.'

'But you only do it for yourself. You're not doing it for me, because you don't care a bit about me.'

When she pressed in upon him this far, he had finally to yield to her cage mentality. She had to be right; yet was it only for himself that he refused to give any expression to his own misery?

'All right, have it your way. I put up with everything simply for my own sake. But whose fault is it that I've got to put up with all this for my own sake? If you weren't here, do you think I'd want to give this stupid impersonation of life inside a zoo? It's being done for you. How can you be so damn ridiculous as to say it's all for me, irrespective of you?'

When things reached this point, his wife's temperature would invariably rise to over a hundred. Thus the clarification of an argument obliged him to stay up all night changing the ice in the ice bag for her head, opening it and closing it, over and over.

However, if he were going to make clear to her the reasons why he needed a break from all this, he had to keep up this frustrating remarshalling of his arguments practically day after day. The work that he did to feed himself and look after her he did in a room apart.

When he did so, again she would be after him with another display of her cage mentality.

'I can't think why you have to always want to escape from me like that. All day you've only come to this room three times. Still, what's there to understand? That's just the sort of person you are.'

'What are you trying to tell me you want me to do? In order to make you better, I have to buy food and medicine. If I'm just going to sit about here doing nothing, where's the money to come from? Are you asking me to do conjuring tricks or something?'

'But I don't see why you couldn't do your work here,' she said.

'Well, I couldn't. If I can't forget about you at least for a while, I can't get anything done.'

'That's right. You're the sort of person who thinks about work twenty-four hours a day, and you couldn't care less about me.'

'Yes, your rival is my work. But that rival of yours is, in fact, always on your side.'

'I feel so lonely.'

'Everybody feels lonely. That's the way it is.'

'It's all right for you. You've got your work. I've got nothing.'

'Why don't you try to find something, then?'

'But I don't want anything, except you. And I just lie here, that's all, looking at the ceiling.'

'Look, stop it, will you. We both feel lonely, right? And I've got a deadline. If I don't get the thing written today it'll be making a lot of trouble for somebody else.'

'That's it. That's you. Your precious deadline is more to you than I am.'

'No, it's not. A deadline is a sign telling me I must not trespass upon the affairs of others. As long as I see and accept the validity of that sign, it is not permitted that I think about my own affairs.'

'There you are, so rational, always so rational. God, I loathe rational people.'

'As long as you remain a member of my household, your responsibility with regard to these contractual signs is the same as my own.'

'You'd be better off not accepting things like that, wouldn't you?'

'Right. Then how do we live?'

'If you're going to be so unfeeling I'd rather be dead.'

Whereupon he gave up and went straight out into the garden, where he took a few deep breaths. Then he took his shopping bag again and without saying a word went off to the town to buy the innards.

But there was his mind going round and round in circles tied up to the bars of her cage, and there was her mind inside its mental cage, and this cage mentality of hers with all her physical irritability kept on at him all the time, hardly allowing him a moment to breathe. Because of this, and because of the acuteness of this neurotic set of ideas she had created for herself within her cage, she was destroying the constitution of her own lungs every day at an ever-increasing pace. When he tapped her chest it made a light, papier-mâché sound. And then she lost all interest even in her favourite chicken innards.

In order to give her some appetite, he brought back various fresh fish from the sea, laid them out on the veranda of her room, and gave a little lecture on them.

'This is the frogfish, the pierrot of the sea who has tired himself with dancing. This is the large shrimp, and this is the small—they are the knights of the sea, fallen with their armour on. This is the saurel, or horse mackerel, the leaf of a tree blown off in a storm.'

'I'd much rather you read the Bible to me,' she said.

From that day onward he was obliged to take out the dirty, stained Bible and read it to her.

'Hear my prayer, O Lord, and let my cry come unto thee. Hide not thy face from me in the day when I am in trouble; incline thine ear unto me; in the day when I call, answer me speedily.

For my days are consumed like smoke, and my bones are burned as a hearth.

My heart is smitten, and withered like grass; so that I forget to eat my bread.'

Then another ill portent followed. One day, after a night of storm, they woke to find that the sluggish tortoise had gone away from the pond in the garden.

As her condition became worse, it grew increasingly impossible for him to leave her bedside. She started to cough up phlegm every minute. Since she couldn't wipe her mouth for herself, he was obliged to do it. Then she started to complain about severe pains in her side. Every twenty-four hours she had about five really prolonged and violent attacks of coughing. Each time she would fumble and claw at her chest with the pain. He felt that when she was like this he should try to remain as calm as possible. But this quiet detachment of his only seemed to provoke her into abuse of him, gasped out while these terrible bouts of coughing went on.

'I like the way you just sit there thinking about other things when someone's in pain like this.'

'Look, calm down. If you shout like that now. . . .'

'So very calm and collected. You make me sick.'

'Suppose I got excited now, what. . . .'

'Shut your damned mouth.'

She snatched at the piece of paper he was holding, rubbed it angrily across her mouth to wipe off the phlegm, then threw it back at him.

Like it or not, he had to go on wiping away with one hand the sweat that poured out of her body, and with the other he had to unceasingly wipe away from her mouth the phlegm that she coughed up. His hips went numb with squatting by her side. The unbearable pain caused her to start flailing her fists about, hitting at his chest, as she lay there staring angrily at the ceiling. The towel he wiped her sweat away with got caught up in her nightdress. She kicked off the bedclothes and tried to get up, panting and heaving.

'No. Stop it. You're not to move.'

'But it hurts. It hurts me.'

'Calm down.'

'I can't stand it.'

'You'll injure yourself.'

'Shut up, can't you.'

Her fists beat against him like stones rattling against a shield as he went on stroking and soothing the now coarse skin of her breast.

Yet even this extremity of suffering he found in fact several degrees less than what he had gone through when she was well and caused him to feel such jealousy. He became aware that her sick body with its corrupted lungs bestowed more happiness upon him than her healthy one had.

—There's an original thought for you. I must hold fast to this novel interpretation.

When he thought about this interpretation as he looked out to sea, he would burst into peals of laughter.

That would provoke her into another display of her cage mentality, and she would look at him with an expression of pain on her face, and say: 'All right, I know exactly what you're laughing about.'

'I doubt it. In fact, I was thinking how I am probably much better off as I am now than if you got better and could play about trying on lots of new clothes. For a start, that pale face of yours gives you a sort of dignity. So you stay in bed like that as long as you feel like it.'

'That's just like you.'

'It's because I'm like me that I can enjoy nursing you.'

'You're always on about nursing, nursing. You bring it out every other word.'

'Because it's something for me to be proud of.'

'Well, if that's what your nursing is, I don't want any.'

'However, if I were to go out of this room for three minutes, wouldn't you go on as if I'd abandoned you for three days? Come on, answer.'

'What I ask is to be nursed without all this talk, all this complaining about it. I don't feel grateful for being nursed when it's done with that sour look on your face, as if it's all such a lot of bother to you.'

'Nursing *is* a lot of bother. Essentially it always has been and always will be.'

'I know that. I just want to be nursed without all this moaning.'

'Do you really? Then we'd better get the whole family and dependants over here, collect a million, and hire ten physicians and a hundred nurses.'

'I'm not asking for anything like that. I just want you to do it yourself.'

'Which means that you are telling me to give an impersonation of ten physicians and a hundred nurses and a man with a million?'

'I didn't say anything at all like that. It's only that I want you to stay here with me all the time, and then I'd feel safe.'

'Exactly. In that case, then, the odd twitch of the lip on my part or the occasional moan will not be beyond the limits of your endurance.'

'If I should die it will be through hatred of you. I shall hate and hate and hate, and then I shall die.'

'No doubt I shall be able to live with it.'

She said nothing in reply. But he could feel how feverishly her mind went on turning over in silence, sharpening itself to inflict the wound it was so desperate to give.

Despite her condition's growing worse like this, he still had to think about his work and his living, but all the looking after her and the lack of sleep gradually wore him down. He knew that the more exhausted he became, the less he would be able to work. As he became incapable of working he would also become incapable of earning a living. And then obviously the expense of her illness would rise, and it would rise in proportion to his increasing inability to meet it. Yet this was the one thing that was certain: he was becoming more and more exhausted.

—What am I going to do?

—I'd like to get ill myself. Then I'd show her how to die without one complaint.

He sometimes felt like that. And yet again there was always the hope that somehow they might be able to pull through this crisis in their lives. Then there was the desire to prove himself to himself. At night, woken by his wife, he would massage her stomach where it hurt her, and would mutter to himself as a form of habit: 'Let more misfortunes fall. Let more misfortunes fall.'

As he was saying so, one lone ball seemed to be struck across an enormous felt table, and rolled and drifted before his eyes.

—That's my ball. But who's been knocking it about at random like that?

'Rub harder, can't you? Why can't you do things as if it all wasn't such a nuisance to you? You never used to be like this. You used to be gentler to me when you rubbed me there. And now you.... Oh, that hurts there, that hurts.'

'I am so tired, growing more and more tired. I don't think I can take it much longer. Then we can both lie down together and not bother about anything any more.'

She suddenly became quiet, and then spoke softly in a pitiful voice like that of an insect crying from somewhere beneath her bed: 'I'm sorry I've been so foul to you, always thinking about myself. You're not to be upset. I don't mind dying now. Everything's all right. So you sleep now. I can put up with it all right now.'

Hearing that, he wept despite himself, and his hand went on rubbing her stomach because he did not feel like letting it rest.

The wintry sea wind withered the grass on the lawn. All day the glass windows shook and rattled like the door of a horse-drawn cab. For a long time he had been unaware of the enormous sea waiting there at his door.

One day he went to the doctor's to pick up his wife's medicine.

'Oh, by the way. I have been meaning to tell you for some time. However ...,' the doctor said. 'There's no hope for your wife.'

'Yes.'

He was very clearly aware of his face going pale.

'There is no left lung, and the right one is too far gone.'

Along the seashore, swayed in a carriage like a piece of luggage, he went home. The bright, glittering sea lay loosely before him, a monotonous curtain concealing death. He felt that he didn't want to see his wife after this. If he never saw her again, it would be possible to think of her always as still being alive.

When he got home he went straightaway to his own room. He thought about ways of managing things so that he wouldn't have to look at her face. After that he went into the garden and lay down on the grass. His body was heavy, dead tired. His tears came feebly; he picked up blades of grass with great care from the dead lawn.

—What is death?

He thought it must be just a matter of vanishing from sight. He got his confused mind under control and entered his wife's room.

She said nothing, only looked fixedly at his face.

'Would you like some winter flowers?'

'You've been crying, haven't you?'

'No.'

'You have.'

'I have nothing to cry about, have I?'

'I know what it is. The doctor said something.'

Having made up her own mind about this, she looked silently up at the ceiling with no particular signs of sadness in her face. He lowered himself into the cane chair by her bedside and looked unwaveringly at her face, as if to memorize it all over again for the last time.

—After a while the door will close between us.

—But both she and I have given each other what there was to give. Now nothing remains.

From that day onward he acted in response to everything she said, like a machine. This was to be his final farewell gift to her.

One day, after a particularly bad bout of pain, she said: 'Would you mind, the next time you've out, buying me some morphine?'

'What would that be for?'

'I shall drink it. People say you drink it and then you go to sleep like that and never wake up again.'

'You mean you die?'

'That's it. I'm not afraid at all of death. How good it must be to be dead.'

'So even you have become brave, and I never knew. But when you reach that point it doesn't matter when you die. Any time will do, so not to worry about it.'

'Only I feel so bad about you, causing you nothing but pain. I am sorry, truly. Forgive me.'

'Yes.'

'I've always understood what was in your heart. And all those selfish things I said, it wasn't me who said them. It was the sickness.'

'I know. The sickness.'

'I've written it down, all I have to say. But I'm not going to show you now. It's under the bed, so look at it when I die.'

He made no reply. All this demanded the bitterest sorrow. But now he did not wish to hear her speak of things that demanded bitterness or sorrow.

Next to the stones of the flower bed, dahlia bulbs, being killed by the frosts, lay where someone had dug them up. Instead of the tortoise, there was now a stray cat that had come from somewhere and that nonchalantly walked into his empty study. His wife hardly spoke at all now, keeping silent with the never-ending pain. Unceasingly she looked at the horizon, at the far-off glittering headland which thrust out onto the surface of the sea.

He sat by her side, sometimes reading the Bible as she demanded.

'Oh Lord, rebuke me not in thine anger, neither chasten me in thy hot displeasure.

Have mercy upon me, O Lord, for I wither away: O Lord, heal me; for my bones are vexed.

My soul is also sore vexed: but then, O Lord, how long?

For in death there is no remembrance of Thee.'

He heard that she was sobbing. He stopped reading the Bible and looked at her.

'What were you thinking about then?'

'Where will my bones be laid? I can't help thinking about it.'

—She had reached the point where she was concerned about her remains.—He was unable to reply to her.

—There's no chance now.

He felt his heart sink as if his head were sinking too. She was weeping much more now.

'What's wrong?' he asked.

'There's no place to lay my bones. What am I going to do?'

Instead of replying, he hurriedly started reading the Bible again.

'Save me, O God, for the waters are come into my soul.

I sink in deep mire, where there is no standing: I am come into deep waters, where the floods overflow me.

I am weary of my crying: my throat is dried: mine eyes fail while I wait for my God.'

So they waited together, two linked stems of a flower that is dying, every day in silence. But they had made total preparation for death. Whatever happened now could be no cause of fear. The pure water carried from the hill brimmed over in its water jug like the heart now finally at peace in his dark and quiet house.

Each morning while she still slept, he walked barefoot the shore that had newly raised its head from the sea. Seaweed cast ashore at high tide the previous night wrapped itself coldly about his feet. Sometimes children who wandered the beach as if driven by the wind would clamber up the pointed rocks, slithering on the brilliant green seaweed.

More and more white sails appeared on the surface of the sea. Each day the white road at the sea's border became more thronged with life. One day the unexpected arrived, a bunch of sweet peas— sent by someone he knew—which rounded the headland to reach them.

At their house, so long made desolate by the cold wind, this was the first scent of spring to reach them.

With his hands covered in pollen, he entered her room holding the flowers as an offering.

'Spring has finally come.'

'They are so beautiful. Aren't they beautiful?' she said, smiling and stretching out her thin and wasted hands toward the flowers.

'Really beautiful, aren't they?' he said.

'Where did they come from?'

'They came riding here in a carriage, along the shore of the sea, scattering the first seeds of spring as they came.'

She took the flowers and hugged them full to her breast. Then she buried her pallid face among the bright flowers, and closed her eyes entranced.

CARP

Translated by John Bester

For more than a dozen years past, I have been troubled by a carp. The carp was given to me in my student days by a friend, Nampachi Aoki (deceased some years ago), as a mark of his unbounded good-will. He told me that he had caught it far away, in a pond in the country near his home.

The carp at the time was one foot long and pure white in color. I was hanging handkerchiefs to dry on the railing outside the window of my boardinghouse, when Aoki arrived with an alumi-num bucket containing a large, white carp covered with a mass of waterweed, and made me a present of it. As a sign of gratitude for his goodwill, I swore that I would never kill the white carp. Enthusiastically, I fetched a ruler and measured its length, and dis-cussed with him where I should keep it.

In the back garden of the boardinghouse there was a gourd-shaped pond. Its surface was littered with bits and pieces from the trees and bamboo, and I hesitated to release the carp in it, but after a little thought decided that there was no alternative. The carp disappeared into the depths of the pond and did not show itself for several weeks.

That winter, I moved to private lodgings. I wanted to take the carp with me, but having no net gave up the idea. Accordingly, once the equinox was past, I returned to the boardinghouse to fish for the carp. On the first day, I hooked two small roach, which I showed to the master of the house. He had no particular interest in fishing, it seemed, but was surprised that there should have been roach in the gourd-shaped pond, and the next day took his place beside me fishing.

At last, on the eighth day, I hooked the carp I wanted, using a silkworm grub. The carp was still as white as ever, and no thinner. But there were transparent parasites lodged on the tips of its fins.

Carefully I removed them, then filled a metal basin with cold water and put the carp in it. I covered it with a fig leaf.

My lodgings, of course, had no pond. I thought, therefore, of killing the carp to have done with it, and many times I took the fig leaf in my fingers and tentatively lifted it. Each time, the carp was opening and closing its mouth, breathing easily and peacefully.

I took the basin to Aoki's to confer with him about it.

'I believe your girl has a large pond in her garden, doesn't she? I wonder if she'd take care of the carp?'

Without hesitation, Aoki led me to a place at the edge of the pond that was overhung by a loquat tree. Before releasing the carp in the pond, I stressed that although I was putting the carp in a pond that belonged to his mistress the fish itself was still unquestionably mine. Aoki gave me a look of displeasure; he seemed to take what I said as motivated by a mere desire to please. I had pledged to him earlier that I would always treasure the fish.

The carp sank deep into the pool, together with the water from my basin.

In the summer, six years later, Nampachi Aoki died.

Although I had often visited him on his sickbed, I had had no idea that the illness was serious. In my ignorance, I felt irritated with him when he would not even accompany me on my walks; and I smoked cigarettes by his bed.

I decided I would buy a cactus in the Formosan Pavilion at the exhibition held that year, and take it to Aoki as a present. But he died on the day that I arrived at his home carrying the pot. I stood at the entrance and rang again and again until his mother appeared, but when she saw me she started sobbing uncontrollably, and I could get nothing out of her. Then I saw all the shoes inside the hall, and among them the dainty, feminine shoes that Aoki's mistress always wore, so I placed the potted cactus on a ledge and went home.

At the funeral two or three days later, the potted cactus that I had given him stood on my friend's coffin, alongside the square, brown student's cap he had always worn. I felt a strong urge to get the white carp from the pond at his girl's place and take it home. The only time he had ever shown displeasure with me had been over the carp.

I made up my mind to write a letter to Aoki's girl. (I reproduce it here in full, lest Aoki's spirit should misinterpret my motives.)

Dear Madam,
    May I offer my heartfelt condolences on the passing of Mr Nampachi Aoki? I am writing to request your kindness in returning a carp (white, and originally one foot long) belonging to myself that Mr Aoki, on my behalf, entrusted to your care in the pond of your garden. In this connection, I should be grateful if next Sunday, whatever the weather, you would allow me to use my fishing rod there, and if you would leave your back gate open from early morning on that day.
                                                    Yours respectfully. . . .

    A reply came. (I have set down the full text here, lest Aoki's spirit should misinterpret his girl's motives.)

Dear Sir,
    Thank you for your letter. I find it perhaps a trifle insensitive that you should ask to fish so soon after a funeral, but since you seem to attach extraordinary value to the fish in question, I agree to your request. You will excuse me if I do not meet you or even come out to greet you, but please do not hesitate to do your fishing.
                                                    Yours in haste. . . .

    Early on Sunday morning, I crept into the residence of the late Nampachi Aoki's mistress, carrying a luncheon box, together with my rod, bait, and bowl. I was considerably agitated. I should have brought the reply to my letter with me, just in case someone found me.
    The fruit of the loquat tree had already ripened to a golden yellow that inspired a lively appetite. I realized, moreover, that the plants and shrubs by the side of the pond were covered with such a fine display of foliage that they concealed me from both the upstairs window and from the platform on the roof. With the wrong end of my fishing rod, I knocked down one of the loquats. In fact, since it was getting near dusk when I finally caught the carp, I ended up by helping myself to a considerable number of the fruit.
    I released the carp in the pool of Waseda University.
    Summer came, and the students began to swim in the pool. Every

day, in the afternoon, I would go to watch and to marvel, as I peered through the wire netting that surrounded the pool, at the skill with which they swam. I was out of work by now and the role of spectator suited me particularly well.

As sunset approached, the students would come out of the water and, without dressing, would sprawl beneath the lacquer trees or smoke and chat with each other. Many a deep sigh I heaved as I gazed at their healthy limbs and the cheerful sight they made as they swam.

When the students had ceased diving into the water, the surface of the pool seemed still quieter than before. Soon, several swallows came flying to the pool, where they fluttered and skimmed the surface. But my white carp stayed deep below the water and refused to show itself. For all I knew, it might be lying dead at the bottom.

One warm, oppressive night I lay awake till dawn. Then, thinking to get some fresh early morning air, I went and walked near the pool. At times like this, we are all prone to dwell on our own solitude, or to tell ourselves that we should find some work, or simply to stand for long periods with our hands tucked in our pockets.

And then I saw it.

There it was, my white carp, swimming about in fine fettle near the surface of the pond. Stepping quietly, I went inside the wire netting and got onto the diving board so that I could see every detail.

My carp, making the most of the space at his command, swam about like a king. And in his wake, anxious not to be left behind, swarmed many roach and dozens of dace and killifish, lending the carp that was mine a still more lordly air.

With tears of emotion in my eyes at the splendid sight, I got down from the diving board, taking care to make no noise.

The cold season came, and the surface of the pool was strewn with fallen leaves. Finally it froze. For that reason, I had already given up any idea of looking for the carp, yet still I did not neglect to come to the pool every morning, just in case. And I amused myself by throwing countless small stones onto the flat surface of the ice. When I tossed them lightly, they skidded swiftly, with a cold sound, over the ice. When I flung them straight down, they stuck into the icy surface.

One morning, the ice was covered with a thin layer of snow. I went and picked up a long bamboo pole, and with it drew a picture on the face of the ice. It was a picture of a fish and it must have been close to twenty feet long. In my mind, it was my white carp.

When the picture was completed, I thought of writing something by the fish's mouth, but gave up the idea and added instead a large number of roach and killifish swarming after the carp in fear of being left behind. Yet how stupid and insignificant the roach and killifish looked! Some of them lacked fins; others, even, had neither mouth nor eyes. I was utterly content.

KAWABATA YASUNARI (1899–1971)

THE IZU DANCER

Translated by Edward Seidensticker

⌢

1

With alarming speed, a shower swept toward me from the foot of the
mountain, touching the cedar forests white as the road began to wind
up into the pass. I was nineteen and traveling alone through the Izu
Peninsula. My clothes were of the sort that students wear, dark
kimono, high wooden sandals, a school cap, a book sack over my
shoulder. I had spent three nights at hot springs near the center of the
peninsula, and now, my fourth day out of Tokyo, I was climbing
toward Amagi Pass and South Izu. The autumn scenery was pleasant
enough, mountains rising one upon another, open forests, deep valleys, but I was excited less by the scenery than by a certain hope. Large
drops of rain began to fall. I ran on up the road, now steep and
winding, and at the mouth of the pass I came to a teahouse. I stopped
short in the doorway. It was almost too lucky: the dancers were
resting inside.

The girl turned over the cushion she had been sitting on and
pushed it politely toward me.

'Yes,' I murmured stupidly as I sat down. Surprised and out of
breath, I found that a simple word of thanks caught in my throat.

She sat near me, we were facing each other. I fumbled for tobacco
and she handed me the ashtray in front of one of the other women.
Still I said nothing.

She was perhaps sixteen. Her hair was swept up after an old style I
did not recognize. Her solemn, oval face was dwarfed under it, and
yet the face and the hair went well together, rather as in the pictures
one sees of ancient beauties with their exaggerated rolls of hair. Two
other young women were with her, and a man in his mid-twenties,
wearing the livery of a Nagaoka inn. A woman in her forties presided
over the group.

I had seen the little dancer twice before. Once I passed her and the other women by a long bridge half-way down the peninsula. She was carrying a big drum. I looked back and looked back again, congratulating myself that here, finally, I had caught the flavor of travel. And then on the third night I saw her dance. She danced just inside the entrance to my inn. I sat on the stairs enraptured. On the bridge yesterday, here tonight, I had said to myself; tomorrow over the pass to Yugano, and surely somewhere along those fifteen miles I will meet them again. That was the hope that had sent me hurrying up the mountain road. But the meeting at the teahouse was too sudden. I was taken quite off balance.

A few minutes later the old woman who kept the teahouse led me to another room, one apparently not much used. It was open to a valley so deep that the bottom was out of sight. My teeth were chattering and my arms were covered with goose-flesh. I was a little cold, I said to the woman when she came back with tea.

'But you're soaked! Come in here and dry yourself.' She led me into her living-room.

The heat from the open fire struck me as she opened the door. I hesitated in the doorway. An old man white and bloated as a drowned corpse was sitting cross-legged by the fire. He turned heavy, languid eyes toward me. Even the irises were yellow, as if rotting. Around him was a mountain of old paper bags and bits of paper. I might have said that he was buried in the mountain. I stared at this apparition, which I could not think of as a living creature.

'I'd as soon not have you see him,' said the woman. 'But he belongs here and he won't do you any harm. He can't move. Put up with him, please, even if he may not be very pleasant to look at.'

Then she told me about him. He had long suffered from palsy and was wholly incapacitated. The mountain around him consisted of advice he had received from all over the country on the treatment of palsy, and the bags had contained medicines, these too from all over the country. He would hear about palsy cures from people who came over the pass and he would read advertisements, never failing to give his attention to each piece of advice and to order each medicine. He passed his time among paper bags and advice. So the pile of moldering paper had built up.

Unable to think of anything to say, I sat hunched beside the fire. An automobile climbing the pass shook the teahouse. It was this cold already in autumn, and soon the snows would be coming. I wondered why the old man stayed on. Steam rose from my kimono, and the fire was so warm that my head began to ache. The old woman went out to talk to the travelers.

'Well now. So this is the girl you had with you before, so big already. Why she's practically a grown woman. Isn't that nice. And so pretty, too. Girls do grow up in a hurry, don't they.'

Perhaps an hour later I heard them getting ready to leave. My heart pounded and my chest was tight, and yet I could not find the courage to get up and go off with them. I fretted beside the fire. But they were women, after all; granted that they were used to walking, I ought to have no trouble overtaking them even if I fell a half-mile or a mile behind. My mind danced off after them as though their departure had given it licence.

'Where will they stay tonight?' I asked the woman when she came back.

'People like that, who knows where they'll stay? If they find someone who'll pay them, that's where it will be. Do you think they know ahead of time?'

Her open contempt excited me. If she is right, I said to myself, then the dancing girl will stay with me tonight.

The rain quieted to a sprinkle, the pass cleared. I felt that I could wait no longer, though the woman assured me that the sun would be out in another ten minutes.

'Take care of yourself,' I said to the old man as I got up, and I meant it. 'Soon it will be getting cold.'

The yellow eyes moved heavily toward me and he nodded slightly.

'Young man, young man!' The woman ran up the road after me. 'This is too much. I really can't take it.'

She clutched at my book sack, trying to return the money I had given her, and when I refused she hobbled along after me. She must at least see me off, she insisted. 'It's really too much. I did nothing for you. But I'll remember, and I'll have something for you when you come this way again. You will come again, won't you? I won't forget.'

Her gratitude for one fifty-sen piece was touching. But I was in a fever to overtake the little dancer, and this hobbling held me back. When we came to the tunnel I shook her off.

'Thank you. The old gentleman is alone. You should go back to him.'

She finally released my book sack.

Cold drops of water were falling inside the dark tunnel. The exit to South Izu was small and bright in the distance.

2

Lined on one side by a white fence, the road twisted down from the mouth of the tunnel like a streak of lightning. Near the bottom of the jagged figure were the dancer and her companions. Another half-mile and I had overtaken them. Since it hardly seemed graceful to slow down at once to their pace, I moved on past the women with a show of coolness. The man, walking some ten yards ahead of them, turned as he heard me come up.

'You're quite a walker.' Then, after a pause: 'Aren't we lucky the rain has stopped.'

Rescued, I walked on beside him. He began asking questions, and the women, seeing that we had struck up a conversation, came tripping up behind us. The man had a large wicker trunk strapped to his back. The older woman held a puppy, the two younger women carried large bundles, one wicker, the other wrapped in a kerchief. The girl had her drum and its stand. The older woman presently joined in the conversation.

'He's a high-school boy,' the older of the young women whispered to the little dancer, giggling as I glanced back.

'Really, even I know that much,' the girl retorted. 'Students come to the island.'

They were from Oshima, one of the Izu islands, the man told me. In the spring they left to wander over the peninsula, but now it was getting cold and they had no winter clothes with them. After ten days or so at Shimoda in the south they would turn north again and sail back to the island from Ito. I glanced again at those rich mounds of hair, at the little figure all the more romantic for being from Oshima. I questioned them about the islands.

'Lots of students come to Oshima for the swimming,' the girl remarked to the woman beside her.

'In the summer, I suppose.' I looked back.

'In the winter too,' she answered in an almost inaudible voice.

'Even in the winter?'

She looked at the other woman and laughed uncertainly.

'Can they swim even in the winter?' I asked again.

She flushed and nodded very slightly, a serious expression on her face.

'The child is out of her mind,' the older woman laughed.

From six or seven miles above Yugano the road followed a river. The mountains and even the sky had taken on the look of the south as we came down over the pass. The man and I were now friends. We skirted a village or two, and as the thatched roofs of Yugano came in sight below, I summoned my courage to announce that I would like to go on to Shimoda with them. He was delighted.

In front of a shabby inn the older woman glanced tentatively at me as if to take her leave. 'But the young gentleman would like to go on with us,' the man said.

'Oh, would he,' she answered easily. 'On the road a companion, in life sympathy, they say. I suppose even poor things like us can liven up a trip. Do come in. We'll have a cup of tea and rest ourselves.'

The younger women looked at me silently and a little shyly, as if the matter were no concern of theirs.

We went upstairs and laid our luggage down. The straw matting and the doors were worn and dirty. The little dancer brought tea from below. As she came to me the teacup clattered in its saucer. She set it down sharply in an effort to save herself, but succeeded only in spilling it. I was not prepared for confusion so extreme.

'Dear me. The child's come to a dangerous age,' the older woman said, frowning and tossing a cloth to the girl, who wiped tensely at the tea.

This odd remark gave me pause. I felt the excitement aroused by the comment of the woman at the teahouse subside.

'That's a good piece of material,' said the older woman, examining the splashed pattern of my kimono. 'It's just like Tamiji's, isn't it. Just like Tamiji's.' She said this several times, then addressed me again. 'We left a boy in school. You made me think of him. The same kind of pattern. They're so expensive these days.'

'Where is he in school?'

'The fifth grade.'

'Oh?'

'He's up in Kofu, in the mountains. We've been on Oshima for a long time, but we're originally from Kofu.'

An hour or so later the man took me to another inn. I had thought that I was to stay with them. We climbed down over rocks and stone steps about a hundred yards from the road. There was a public bath on the bank of a small river. Just beyond it a bridge led to the garden of my inn.

We went together for a bath. He was twenty-three, he told me, and his wife had had two miscarriages. Because he wore the Nagaoka livery, I had assumed he was from Nagaoka, in the northern part of the peninsula. His face and way of speaking seemed not unintelligent. I speculated that, from curiosity or a fancy for one of the women, he might have come along to help with their luggage.

I had lunch when we returned from the bath. We had left Yugashima at eight, and it was still not yet three.

On his way out, he called to me from the garden.

I threw down some money in an envelope. 'Get yourself some fruit or something. Excuse me for throwing it.'

He started to go without it, but turned to pick it up.

'You shouldn't,' he said, and threw it back.

It came to rest on the thatch of the roof. I tossed it down again. This time he took it.

A heavy rain began to fall from about sunset. The mountains, gray and white, flattened and lost perspective, and the river grew yellower and muddier and noisier by the minute. I felt sure that the dancers would not be out on such a night, and yet I could not sit still. Two, three times I went down to the bath. My room was dusky. A light hung in a rectangular opening above the sliding doors separating my room from the next, to serve both rooms.

Then, distant in the rain, I heard the beating of a drum. I slid open the shutters, almost wrenching them from their grooves, and leaned out the window. The drum-beat seemed to be coming nearer. The rain, driven by a strong wind, lashed at my head. I closed my eyes and tried to concentrate on the drum, on where it might be, whether it would be coming this way. Presently I heard a shamisen, and now and then a woman's voice calling to someone, or a loud burst of laughter. The dancers had been called to a party in the restaurant across from their inn, it seemed. I could distinguish two or three women's voices and three or four men's. Soon they will be finished there, I told myself, and they will come here. The party seemed to go beyond harmless merriment and to approach the rowdy. Now and again a shrill woman's voice came across the darkness like the crack of a whip. I sat rigid, more and more on edge, staring out through the open shutters. At each drum-beat I felt a surge of relief. 'Ah, she's still there. She's still there and playing the drum.' And each time the drumming stopped, the silence seemed intolerable. It was as though I were being driven under by the beating of the rain.

For a time there was a confusion of footsteps—were they playing tag, were they dancing? And then complete silence. I glared into the darkness, trying to see what the silence might mean. What would she be doing, who would be sullying her through the rest of the night?

I closed the shutters and lay down. My chest was painfully tight. I went down to the bath again and splashed about violently. The rain stopped, the moon came out. The autumn sky, washed by the rain, shone crystalline in the distance. I thought for a moment of running out barefoot to look for her. It was after two.

3

The man came by my inn at nine the next morning. Just out of bed, I invited him along for a bath. Below the bathhouse the river, swollen from the rain, flowed warm in the South Izu autumn sun. My anguish of the night before no longer seemed real. Even so, I wanted to hear what had happened.

'That was a lively party you had last night.'

'You could hear us?'

'I certainly could.'

'Locals. They make a lot of noise, but it's just noise.'

He seemed to consider the matter quite routine. I said no more.

'Look. They've come for a bath, over there across the river. Damned if they haven't seen us. Look at them laugh.' He pointed over to the public bath, where seven or eight naked figures showed through the steam.

One small figure ran out into the sunlight and stood for a moment at the edge of the platform calling something to us, arms raised as though for a plunge into the river. It was the dancer, her nakedness covered by not even a towel. I looked at her, at the young legs, at the sculpted white body, and suddenly a draught of fresh water seemed to wash over my heart. I laughed happily. She was a child, a mere child, a child who could run out naked into the sun and stand there on tiptoes in her delight at seeing a friend. I gave a soft, happy laugh. It was as though a layer of dust had been cleared from my head. I laughed on and on. Because of her abundant hair she had seemed older, and because she was dressed like a girl of sixteen or seventeen. I had made an extraordinary mistake indeed.

We were back in my room when the older of the two young
women came to look at the chrysanthemums in the garden. The little
dancer followed her half-way across the bridge. Her eyes on the two,
the older woman came out of the bath. The dancer shrugged and ran
back, as if to say she would be scolded if she came any nearer. The
older woman came to the bridge.

'Come on over,' she called to me.

'Come on over,' the younger woman echoed, and the two of them
turned back toward their inn.

The man stayed on in my room until evening.

I was playing Go with a traveling paper merchant that night when
I heard the drum in the garden. I started toward the veranda.

'Don't you want to watch them?'

'Stupid stuff. It's your turn. I played here.' Intent upon the game,
the man poked at the board.

I fidgeted, and the performers seemed about to leave.

'Good evening,' the man called up.

I went out to the veranda and beckoned him in. After a whispered
conference they came to the doorway. The man came in first. In
order of age they offered formal greetings from the veranda, like
geisha. It had suddenly become clear I was going to lose the Go
match.

'It's all over. I give up.'

'Oh, come now. I'm doing worse than you are. It's close, either
way.'

Paying no attention at all to the performers, the merchant counted
stones and played with yet greater concentration. Their instruments
put away tidily in a corner, the performers started a game on another
board. It was the simpler game of lining up stones. I quickly lost the
match I had in fact been winning.

'How about another?' said the merchant. 'Let's have another
game.'

But I laughed evasively, and after a time he gave up and departed.
The women came nearer.

'Do you have anywhere else to go tonight?'

'Do we?' the man asked the women.

'How about it? Maybe we could ask to take a holiday.'

'How nice,' said the dancer.

'You won't get scolded?'

'We couldn't find any customers if we tried.'

They stayed until past midnight, taking turns at the Go board.

I felt alert and clear-headed after they left. I would not be able to sleep. I called in to the merchant, a man approaching sixty.

He hurried out, ready for battle.

'It's an all-night match tonight. We'll play the whole night through.' I felt invincible.

4

We were to leave Yugano at eight the next morning. I poked my school cap into my book sack, put on a hunting cap I had bought in a shop not far from the public bath, and went up to the inn by the highway. I walked confidently upstairs—the shutters on the second floor were open—but I stopped short in the hall. They were still in bed.

The dancing girl lay almost at my feet, sharing a quilt with the youngest of the women. She flushed deeply and pressed her hands to her face with a quick flutter. Traces of heavy make-up were left from the evening before, rouge on her lips and dots of rouge at the corners of her eyes. The recumbent figure seemed to flow toward me, a surge of light and color. As if dazzled by the morning light, she rolled over and slipped out of bed, her hands still against her face. Then she knelt on the veranda and thanked me for the evening before. I stood over her uncomfortably.

The man and the older of the young women were sleeping together. They must be married. I had not thought of the possibility before.

'You must excuse us,' said the older woman, sitting up in bed. 'We meant to leave this morning, but it seems there's to be a party tonight, and we thought we'd see what might come of it. Maybe we can meet in Shimoda, if you really must go on ahead. We always stay at the Koshu Inn. You'll have no trouble finding it.'

I felt deserted.

'Or maybe you could wait till tomorrow,' the man suggested. 'She says we have to stay another day. But it's good to have company on the road. Let's go together tomorrow.'

'A very good idea,' agreed the woman. 'It seems a shame, now that we've gotten to know you. Tomorrow we start out even if it's raining pitchforks. Day after tomorrow it will be forty-nine days since the baby died. We've meant all along to have services in Shimoda to show that we remember, and we've been hurrying to get there in time. It would be very kind of you to join us. I can't help but think there's a reason for it, our getting to be friends this way.'

I agreed to wait another day. I went downstairs and sat in the dirty little office talking to a clerk while I waited for them to dress. Presently the man came down and we walked to a pleasant bridge south of the town. He leaned against the railing and talked about himself. In Tokyo he had belonged to a modern theater company. Even now he sometimes appeared in amateur theatricals on Oshima, while at parties on the road he could do imitations of actors if called upon to. The strange arm-like protuberance in one of the bundles was a stage sword, he explained, and the wicker trunk held both household goods and costumes.

'I made a mistake and ruined myself. My brother has taken over the family up in Kofu and I'm not much use there.'

'I thought you were from Nagaoka.'

'I'm afraid not. That's my wife, the older of the two women. She's a year younger than you. She lost her second baby on the road this summer. It only lived a week, and she really isn't well yet. The older woman is her mother, and the girl is my sister.'

'You said you had a sister—thirteen, I think you said?'

'That's the one. I tried to think of some way to keep her out of this business, but it couldn't be helped.'

He said that his name was Eikichi, his wife was Chiyoko, and the dancer, his sister, was Kaoru. The other girl, Yuriko, was a sort of maid. She was sixteen, and the only one among them who was really from Oshima. Eikichi was becoming somewhat sentimental. He gazed down at the river, and for a time I thought he was about to weep.

On the way back, just off the road, we saw the little dancer petting the dog. She had washed away the make-up.

'Come on over,' I called, thinking to go back to my inn.

'I couldn't very well by myself.'

'Bring your brother.'

'Thank you. I'll be right over.'

A short time later Eikichi appeared.

'Where are the others?'

'They couldn't get away from Mother.'

But the three of them came clattering across the bridge and up the stairs while we were at the Go board, playing the simpler game. After elaborate bows they waited hesitantly in the hall.

Chiyoko came in first. 'Please, please,' she called gaily to the others. 'You needn't stand on formality in *my* room!'

An hour or so later they all went down for a bath. I must come along, they insisted, but the idea of a bath with three young women was somewhat daunting. I said I would go later. In a moment the little dancer came back upstairs.

'Chiyoko says she'll wash your back if you come down.'

Instead she stayed with me, and the two of us played at lining up stones. She was surprisingly good. In a series of matches, I had no trouble disposing of Eikichi and the other women. I can beat most people, indeed, but I had trouble with her. It was good not to have to play a deliberately bad game. A model of propriety at first, sitting bolt upright and extending her hand to make a play, she soon forgot herself and leaned intently over the board. Her hair, so rich it seemed unreal, almost brushed against my chest. Suddenly she flushed crimson.

'Excuse me. I'll get a scolding for this,' and she ran from the room with the game half finished. The older woman was standing beside the public bath across the river. Chiyoko and Yuriko clattered out of the bath downstairs at almost the same moment and retreated across the bridge without saying good-bye.

Eikichi spent the day at my inn again, though the manager's wife, a solicitous woman, had given it as her opinion that it was a waste of good food to invite such people in for meals.

The dancer was practising the shamisen when I went up to the inn by the highway that evening. She put it down when she saw me, but at the older woman's command, took it up again. She both played and sang. When her voice rose even a little the woman would scold her. 'How often do I have to tell you to keep it down.'

We could see Eikichi on the second floor of the restaurant across the street. He was bellowing away at something for a dinner party.

'What in the world is that?'

'That? He's reciting a Noh play.'

'An odd sort of thing to be doing.'

'Oh, he has as many wares as a dime store. You never know what he'll be up to next.'

A man of about forty slid open a door. He had a room at the inn and was said to be in the poultry business. If the women would come over he would treat them, he said. The dancer and Yuriko took up chopsticks and went over to help themselves to what was left of a chicken stew. As they came back he laid a hand lightly on the girl's shoulder.

'You're not to touch her,' the older woman said, frowning fiercely. 'No one has touched her.'

Addressing him like an old friend, the girl wanted him to read to her from *Adventures of the Lord of Mito*. He soon made his departure. Shy about asking me directly, she remarked more than once how good it would be if someone could be persuaded to go on. I took up the book happily, a certain hope in my mind. I was not disappointed. Her head was almost on my shoulder as I started to read. She looked up at me with a serious, intent expression, her eyes bright and unblinking. It seemed to be her manner when someone read to her. Her face had been almost touching the face of the poultry man as he read to her. I had made a note of it. Her large eyes, almost black, were easily her best feature. The fold of the eyelids was beyond describing. And her laugh was a flower's laugh—the expression does not seem strained when I think of her.

I had read only a few minutes when the maid from the restaurant came for her. 'I'll be right back,' she said as she got herself ready. 'Don't go away. I want to hear the rest.' She knelt on the veranda to take her leave formally.

'You're not to sing, now,' said the older woman.

Taking up the drum, she nodded slightly.

'She's at a bad age. Her voice is changing.'

We could see the girl as if she were in the next room. She knelt beside the drum, her back toward us. The rhythm filled me with a clean excitement.

'A party always picks up speed when the drumming starts,' the woman said.

Chiyoko and Yuriko also went over to the restaurant. In an hour or so the four of them came back.

'This is all they gave us.' The dancer casually dropped fifty sen from her clenched fist into the woman's hand. I read more of the story, and they talked of the baby that had died. At birth it had been as transparent as water. It did not have the strength to cry, but even so it lived a week.

I was not held by curiosity, and I felt no condescension toward them. Indeed, I was no longer conscious that they belonged to that low order, traveling performers. They seemed to know and be moved. They decided that I must visit them on Oshima.

'We can put him up in the old man's house.' They planned everything out. 'That should be big enough, and if we move the old man out it will be quiet enough for him to study as long as he can stay.'

'We have two little houses, and we can give you the one on the mountain. It's as good as empty.'

It was decided, too, that I would help with a play they were giving on Oshima for the New Year.

I came to see that the life of the traveling performer was not the harsh one I had imagined. Rather it was unworried and relaxed, carrying with it the scent of meadows and mountains. Then too this troupe was held together by close family affection. Only Yuriko, the hired girl—perhaps she was at a shy age—seemed uncomfortable in my presence.

It was past midnight when I left their inn. The three younger ones saw me to the door. The little dancer turned my sandals so that I could step into them without twisting. She leaned from the doorway and gazed up at the clear sky.

'The moon is up. And tomorrow we'll be in Shimoda. I love Shimoda. We'll say prayers for the baby, and Mother will buy me the comb she promised, and there are all sorts of things we can do after that. Will you take me to a movie?'

Something about Shimoda seemed to make it a home along the road for performers wandering the hot springs of Izu and Sagami.

5

The luggage was distributed as on the day we came over Amagi Pass. The puppy, a seasoned traveler, lay with its forepaws on the older woman's arms. From Yugano we entered the mountains again. We looked out over the sea at the morning sun, warming the mountain valley. At the mouth of the river a beach opened wide and white.

'That's Oshima.'

'It's so big! You really will come, won't you?' the dancer said.

For some reason—was it the clearness of the autumn sky that made it seem so?—the sea where the sun rose was veiled in a spring-like mist. It was some ten miles to Shimoda. For a time mountains hid the sea. Chiyoko hummed a song softly, lazily.

The road forked. One way was a little steep, but it was more than a mile shorter than the other. Would I choose the short, steep way, or the long, easy way? I took the short way.

The road wound up through a forest, so steep that climbing it was like scaling a wall. Dead leaves made a slippery coating. Breathing became more difficult. I felt a perverse recklessness, and pushed on faster and faster, pressing a knee down with my fist at each step. The others fell behind; presently I could hear only their voices through the trees. But the little dancer, skirts tucked high, came after me with tiny steps. She stayed always a couple of yards behind, neither trying to come nearer nor letting herself fall farther back. Sometimes I would speak to her, and she would stop and answer with a startled little smile. When she spoke I would pause, hoping that she would come up even with me, but always she waited until I had started off again and followed those same two yards behind. The road grew steeper and more twisted. I pushed myself faster, and on she came, two yards behind, climbing earnestly and intently. The mountains were quiet. I could no longer hear the voices of the others.

'Where do you live in Tokyo?'

'In a dormitory. I don't really live in Tokyo.'

'I've been to Tokyo. I went there to dance, when the cherries were in bloom. But I was so little. I don't remember anything about it.'

'Are your mother and father living?' she took up again. And, 'Have you ever been to Kofu?' She talked of the movies in Shimoda, and of the dead baby.

We came to the summit. Laying her drum on a bench among the dead autumn grasses, she wiped her face with a handkerchief. After that she turned her attention to her feet, but then changed her mind and bent down instead to dust off the skirt of my kimono. I drew back in surprise, and she fell to one knee. When she had brushed me off front and back, bent low before me, she stood up to let down her skirts, which had been tucked up for walking. I was still breathing heavily. She invited me to sit down.

A flock of small birds flew up beside the bench. The dead leaves rustled as they landed, so quiet was the air.

'Why do you walk so fast?' She was looking warm.

I tapped the drum and the birds started up in alarm. 'I'm thirsty.'

'Shall I see if I can find water?' But she came back empty-handed through the yellowing trees.

'What do you do with yourself on Oshima?'

She mentioned two or three girls' names that meant nothing to me, and rambled on with a string of reminiscences. She seemed to be talking not of Oshima but of Kofu, of a grammar-school she had been in for the first two grades. She talked artlessly as the memories of her friends came back to her.

The two younger women and Eikichi arrived about ten minutes later, and the older woman ten minutes later still. On the way down I purposely stayed behind, talking to Eikichi. After a hundred yards or so, the dancer came running back.

'There's a spring down below. They're waiting for you to drink first.'

I ran down with her. Water bubbled clear and clean from the shady rocks. The women were standing around the spring.

'Have a drink,' said the older woman. 'We didn't think you'd want to drink after a bunch of women had stirred it up.'

I drank from my cupped hands. The women were slow to leave. They wet their handkerchiefs and washed perspiration from their faces.

At the foot of the slope we came out on the Shimoda highway. Down the highway, sending up clouds of smoke here and there, were the fires of charcoal-makers. We stopped to rest on a pile of wood. The dancer began combing the puppy's shaggy coat with a pinkish comb.

'You'll break the teeth,' her mother warned.

'That's all right. I'm getting a new one in Shimoda.'

It was the comb she wore in her hair, and even back in Yugano I had planned to ask for it when we got to Shimoda. I was a little upset to see her using it on the dog.

On the far side of the road were bundles of bamboo. Remarking that they would be just right for walking-sticks, Eikichi and I started off ahead. Soon the dancer came running up to us. She had a thick stalk of bamboo that was taller than she was.

'What's that for?' asked Eikichi.

In some confusion, she thrust the bamboo at me.

'For a walking stick. I took the biggest one.'

'You can't do that. They'll spot the biggest one. Take it back.'

She went back to the bamboo, and quickly came running up again. This time she gave me a stalk about the thickness of my middle finger. Then, breathing heavily, she collapsed on a ridge between rice paddies and lay absolutely still, seemingly pinned there, as she waited for the other women. Eikichi and I continued to walk about fifteen or twenty feet ahead of them.

'But all he'd have to do would be to get a gold tooth. Then you'd never notice,' came the dancer's voice.

I looked back. She was walking with Chiyoko. The other two were a short distance behind.

'Yes. Maybe you should tell him so.' It was Chiyoko, apparently unaware that I was looking at them.

They were obviously talking about my crooked teeth. Chiyoko must have brought the matter up, and the dancer suggested a gold tooth. I felt no resentment at being talked about and no need to hear more. The conversation was subdued for a time.

'He's nice, isn't he,' the girl's voice came again.

'He seems very nice.'

'He really is nice. It's nice having someone so nice.'

She had an open way of speaking, a youthful honest way of saying exactly what came to her, which made it possible for me to think of myself as, frankly, 'nice'. I looked anew at the mountains, so bright that they made my eyes ache a little. I had come at nineteen to think myself a misfit, an orphan by nature, and it was depression that had sent me forth on this Izu journey. Now I was able to think of myself as a 'nice' person in the ordinary sense of the expression. I find no way to describe what this meant to me. The mountains grew brighter. We were approaching Shimoda and the sea. I swung at the heads of autumn grasses with my walking-stick.

Now and then, at a road into a village, we would see a sign: 'Performer-beggars keep out.'

6

The Koshu Inn was a shabby place in the northern outskirts of Shimoda. I followed the rest up to an attic-like room on the second floor. There was no ceiling, and the roof sloped down so sharply that at the window overlooking the street one could not sit comfortably upright.

The older woman was fussing over the girl. 'Your shoulder isn't stiff? Your arms aren't sore?'

The girl went through the graceful motions of beating a drum. 'No. I won't have any trouble. They're not sore at all.'

'Good. I was worried.'

I lifted the drum. 'Heavy.'

'It's heavier than you think,' she laughed. 'It's heavier than that pack of yours.'

They exchanged greetings with the other guests. The inn was full of peddlers and wandering performers. Shimoda seemed to be a shelter for migratory species. The dancer handed out pennies to the children who darted about. When I started to leave, she ran to arrange my sandals for me.

'You will take me to a movie, won't you?' she whispered, almost to herself.

Eikichi and I, guided part of the way by a disreputable-looking man from the Koshu, went on to an inn said to belong to a former mayor. We had a bath together and ate lunch, freshly caught fish from the sea.

I handed him a little money as he left. 'Buy some flowers for the service tomorrow,' I said. I had explained that I would have to return to Tokyo on the morning boat. I was, as a matter of fact, out of money, but told them I had to be back in school.

I had dinner a scant three hours after lunch and crossed a bridge to the north of the town. I climbed Shimoda Fuji and looked down at the harbor. On my way back I stopped at the Koshu. The performers were sharing a chicken stew.

'Wouldn't you like a taste? We women have been poking around in it, but you can have a good laugh over it some day.' The older woman took a bowl and chopsticks from a wicker trunk and sent Yuriko to wash them.

They pressed me again to stay one more day and be with them at the services, but I continued to make school my excuse.

'Well anyhow we'll see you in the winter,' the older woman said again. 'We'll all come down to the boat to meet you. You must let us know when you're coming. You're to stay with us, now. We wouldn't think of letting you go to a hotel. We'll be waiting for you, and we'll all be there to meet you.'

When the others had left the room I asked Chiyoko and Yuriko to go to a movie with me. Pale and worn, Chiyoko lay with her hands pressed to her abdomen.

'I couldn't, thank you. I'm not up to so much walking.'

Yuriko stared stiffly at the floor.

The little dancer was downstairs playing with the inn children. When she saw me she ran off and began wheedling the older woman for permission to go to the movies. She came back looking withdrawn and crestfallen.

'I don't see anything wrong,' Eikichi argued. 'Why can't she go with him by herself?'

I too found it hard to understand, but the woman was unbending. The dancer was in the hall petting the dog when I went out. I could not bring myself to speak to her, so chilling was this new formality, and she seemed without the strength to look up.

I went to the movies by myself. A woman read the dialogue by a small light. I left almost immediately and returned to my inn. For a long time I sat looking out, my elbows on the window-sill. The town was dark. I thought I heard a drum in the distance. For no good reason I found myself weeping.

7

Eikichi called up from the street as I was having breakfast at seven the next morning. He had on a formal kimono, in my honor it seemed. The women were not with him. I was suddenly lonesome.

'They all wanted to see you off,' he explained when he came up to my room, 'but we were out so late last night that they couldn't get out of bed. They said to tell you they're very sorry and they'll be waiting for you this winter.'

An autumn wind blew cold through the town. On the way to the ship he bought me fruit and tobacco and a package of mints called 'Kaoru'.

'Because that's her name,' he smiled. 'Oranges are bad on a ship, but you can eat persimmons. They even help if you get a little seasick.'

'Why don't I give you this?'

I put my hunting cap on his head, pulled my school cap out of my pack, and tried to smooth away a few of the wrinkles. We both laughed.

As we came to the pier I saw with a quick jump of the heart that the little dancer was sitting at the water's edge. She did not move as we came up, only nodded a silent greeting. On her face were the traces of make-up that I found so engaging. The rather angry red at the corners of the eyes gave her a fresh young dignity.

'Are the others coming?' Eikichi asked.

She shook her head.

'They're still in bed?'

She nodded.

Eikichi went to buy ship and lighter tickets. I tried to make conversation, but she only stared at the point where the canal ran into the harbor. Now and then she would nod a quick little nod, always before I had finished speaking.

'I'm sure we can ask this young fellow.' A man who had the look of a day-laborer came up to me. 'You're going to Tokyo? I saw you and thought I'd ask. Could you see this old woman to Tokyo? She's a very sad case. Her son was working in the silver mine at Rendaiji, but he caught the flu that's been going around and he and his wife both died of it. She has three grandchildren on her hands. We couldn't think of a thing to do. So we're sending her home. She's from Mito. She doesn't know anything about Tokyo. Maybe when you get to the docks at Reiganjima, you could put her on the streetcar for Ueno Station? I know it'll be a nuisance, but please do it. Please. Just look at her. Don't you agree she's a sad case?'

She was standing dumbly, a baby strapped to her back, a girl of two and a girl of four at either hand. I could see a rough sort of meal through an opening in the dirty kerchief. A half-dozen miners were trying to comfort her. I happily said I would do what I could.

'If you would, please.'

'Thanks. We should see her to Mito ourselves, but we can't.'

They addressed me in turn.

The lighter pitched violently. The dancer stared fixedly ahead, her lips pressed tight together. As I started up the rope ladder to the ship I looked back. I could see that she wanted to say goodbye, but she only nodded again. The lighter started back. Eikichi waved the hunting cap, and as the lighter retreated into the distance she began to wave something white.

I leaned against the railing and gazed off toward Oshima until the southern tip of the Izu Peninsula was out of sight. It seemed a long time ago that I had said goodbye to the little dancer. I looked into a state-room to see how things were with the old woman, but she was surrounded by well-wishers. I went on to the state-room next door. The sea was so rough that it was hard even to sit up. A crewman came around with small metal basins. I lay down with my book sack for a pillow, my mind clear and empty. I was no longer conscious of the passage of time. I wept silently, and when my cheek began to feel chilly I turned the sack over. A young boy lay beside me. He was the son of an Izu factory-owner, he said, and he was going to Tokyo to get ready for high-school entrance examinations. My school cap had attracted him.

'Is something wrong?' he asked after a time.

'No. I've just said goodbye to someone.'

I saw no need to disguise the truth, and I was quite unashamed of my tears. I thought of nothing. It was as if I were slumbering in a sort of quiet fulfillment. I did not know when evening came, but there were lights when we passed Atami. I was hungry and a little chilly. The boy unpacked his dinner and I ate as if it were mine. Then I covered myself with part of his cape. I floated in a beautiful emptiness. It seemed natural that I should take advantage of his kindness. It seemed completely natural that I should see the old woman to Ueno early in the morning and buy her a ticket to Mito. Everything sank back into an enfolding harmony. The lights went out, the smell of the sea and of the fish in the hold grew stronger. In the darkness, warmed by the boy beside me, I gave myself up to tears. It was as if my head had turned to clear water. It was falling pleasantly away, drop by drop. Soon, nothing would remain.

KAJII MOTOJIRO (1901–1932)

LEMON

Translated by Robert Ulmer

An ominous mass weighed upon my spirit. The sensation was unlike irritation or ennui; rather, it was as if I had entered a season of hangovers after nights and nights of hard drinking. The tuberculosis and nervous exhaustion were not to blame. Neither was my bone-chilling debt. It was just this indefinable mass. It drove me from the music and poetry I once loved—if I went out and troubled someone to play a record for me, I found that I would have to leave after just a few notes. All I could do was drift endlessly through the streets.

I was attracted to things that had something of an impoverished beauty about them. Decrepit neighborhoods were the landscapes I favored and within them it was not the impersonal main roads that I found most congenial but the shabby back alleys with their grimy laundry hanging out to dry and paths of scattered trash. Peeking in the windows of the squalid rooms that faced the alleyways gave me pleasure as well. Among these tottering houses with their moldering earthen walls, which wind and rain would soon return to the soil, the vigor of life could be glimpsed only in the vegetation, in the occasional shock of a blossoming sunflower or canna.

Sometimes, as I walked along those streets, I tried to imagine that I had escaped from Kyoto to a faraway city where no one knew me, Sendai perhaps, or Nagasaki. It would have to be a peaceful setting. A room at an inn, large and empty. Spotless bedding, the fragrance of mosquito netting and a freshly starched summer kimono. I could spend a month lying there, thinking of nothing. If I wished hard enough, I felt, I could transform this place to that one....As the images took hold, I began to tint them one by one with the colors of my mind, until they could easily be superimposed on my dilapidated surroundings. Then and only then could I taste the joy of losing sight of my real self.

I also found solace in gazing at packages of cheap fireworks. Some

149

came in garish striped bundles of red, purple, gold, and blue and had names like 'Falling Stars of Chusanji Temple', 'Flower Wars', and 'Withered Pampas'. Others, called 'rat firecrackers', were stacked like pinwheels in a box. Things such as these held a strange appeal.

Bits of colored glass were treasures to me—marbles with embossed designs of fish and flowers, Nanking beads. Rolling these about in my mouth gave me great pleasure, for their taste had a subtle yet unique coolness. As a child, my parents had scolded me for this type of behavior. Now, however, perhaps because my decline had made those sweet memories of youth that much dearer, there was something altogether poetic about the beauty of that faint, fresh sensation in my mouth.

As you may have already gathered, I was utterly destitute. Yet the fact that these small things could touch my heart, however slightly, made their purchase a necessary luxury. A matter of a few pennies— yet an extravagance, a thing of beauty, that could still perk up my enervated antennae. In short, a natural consolation.

When I was in better shape, I loved to spend time in department stores like the Maruzen, with its shelves filled with imported goods. Red and yellow bottles of *eau-de-Cologne* and *eau-de-quinine*. Amber and jade-colored perfume flasks of fanciful cut glass in embossed rococo patterns. Pipes and pocket-knives, soaps and tobacco. After an hour of careful scrutiny, I would extravagantly purchase a single pencil of the finest quality. Now, however, Maruzen had become an oppressive, stifling place. The books, the students, the cashiers—all haunted me like phantom debt-collectors.

One morning—I was staying in the rooming houses of my friends, moving from one to the next—my host of the moment went off to school, abandoning me in his empty lodgings. I had no choice but to resume my wandering. Something drove me on from one back alley to another, brought me to a stop in front of a sweet shop, then pushed me on again to a grocery where I spent some time gazing at the dried fish and preserved bean curd. Then I wandered down Teramachi to Nijo Avenue, finally coming to a halt in front of a greengrocer's.

Perhaps I should introduce this establishment, as it was my favorite shop of all. On the surface, it was quite unremarkable, yet it embodied that special beauty such stores possess more than any other place I have ever seen. Its fruits were laid out on a sharply angled chipped black lacquer stand. They had been arranged in such a way that their volume and color seemed frozen in time and space, like a bright allegro that had seen Medusa's face and turned to stone. Farther back in the store, the green vegetables were piled in ever-higher tiers. The carrot leaves were radiant, the beans and arrowroot glistened with beads of water. . . .

The greengrocer's was especially beautiful at night. Flooded with light from display windows, Teramachi is a lively street, albeit far more serene than its counterparts in big cities like Tokyo and Osaka. Yet the area around this one particular shop was curiously dark. True, it sat on the corner of gloomy Nijo Avenue, but that cannot explain why its immediate neighbor on Teramachi was so poorly lit. Had its environs been brighter, however, I doubt it would have enchanted me so. Its awning jutted out like the visor of a cap pulled down over the eyes. (This is not poetic exaggeration—the place really made you want to cry out, 'Look at that store with the low-slung cap!') With no surrounding lights to vie with, and sheer darkness above, the row of electric bulbs hanging beneath the awning bathed the produce like a brilliant summer shower. Viewed from the street, where the naked bulbs sent spirals of light burrowing into my eyes, or from the second-floor window of the coffee-shop across the way, there were few other sights on Teramachi that inspired me as this one did.

This particular day, I took the unusual step of making a purchase there. For something rare was on sale—lemons. Of course, lemons are not all that uncommon in fancier places, but this store was hardly a cut above your average greengrocer and thus seldom carried such items, at least to my notice. And, oh, how I craved those lemons: their color, like a hardened dollop of pure 'lemon yellow' squeezed from a painter's tube; their shape, a perfectly compressed spindle. . . . I decided to buy one. Then once again I set off roaming the streets of Kyoto. I walked for a long time. I felt unusually happy, for it seemed as if the ominous mass that had been weighing upon me for so long had grown lighter the moment I had grasped my new possession. An incongruous paradox, perhaps, but true—my stubborn melancholia had been diverted by a single piece of fruit. How strange the human spirit!

The lemon's coolness was beyond description. At the time, my tuberculosis had worsened to the point that I was always feverish. In fact, I found that I could show my friends and acquaintances how sick I was merely by grasping their hands, since mine were always so much warmer. Perhaps because of that heat, it felt as if the coolness of the lemon was seeping through my palm, refreshing my entire being.

Time and time again, I brought the fruit up to my nose to capture its scent. An image of California, its likely origin, came to me followed the next moment by a snippet from the Chinese classic *The Fruit Merchant* which I had studied once in school—'assailing the nose' was the phrase I remembered. Indeed, when I filled my lungs with the fragrance, a warm wash of blood seemed to course through my body, awakening me to my own vitality. Not once, I thought, had I ever breathed so deeply before.

The idea that in the simple sensations of coolness, texture, fragrance, and shape I had stumbled across what I had sought for so long seems strange to me now. Yet at the time I wanted to shout it from the rooftops.

My step livelier now, I pushed on in growing excitement and even pride, occasionally picturing myself as an elegantly attired poet strutting along the boulevards. I studied the lemon closely, placed it against my grubby handkerchief, then against my cloak to measure how its color reflected their textures, then hefted it in my hand and cried aloud at its perfection. This is what I had grown weary searching for, the perfect weight, the sum total of all things good and beautiful—the thought struck me as terribly droll. All in all, I was blessedly happy.

How I arrived there I do not know, but suddenly I realized I was standing in front of the Maruzen department store. Although I had been avoiding it, this time I felt no reservations about going inside. Let's give it a try, I thought, and strode boldly through its doors.

Yet, for some reason, the sense of well-being that had filled my heart began to vanish the moment I stepped inside. The rows of perfume and tobacco left me cold. I could feel my depression raising its head again, and wondered if the cause might be exhaustion from my long walk. I made my way to the art-books section. Had I enough strength left to lift even one of those heavy tomes? Nevertheless, one after the other, I managed to lug them down and open them. That was all, though—I had no desire to examine them more carefully. As if bewitched, I compulsively pulled down book after book, gave each a quick glance, then moved on to the next without returning even one to the shelf. The idea of going any further was unbearable. The last book I chose was one of my favorites, a huge gold-colored collection of the work of Ingres. Yet it was the most burdensome of all. Damn this curse! I felt the lingering fatigue in my arms as I surveyed the pile I had created. By now my depression was back in full force.

In the past, I had leisurely leafed through books such as these, savoring the strange contrast between their beautiful illustrations and the dull surroundings. Why did they no longer attract me?

With a start I recalled the lemon tucked in the sleeve of my kimono. If I were to try placing it atop of this jumbled collection of colors, what then?

The faint surge of excitement I had felt earlier returned. I randomly stacked the books in a tower, roughly dismantled it, then threw it together again. New books from the shelves were added to the edifice, removed, then replaced by others, shaping a dream castle, first of red, then of blue.

At last it was finished. Controlling the trembling in my heart, I carefully placed the lemon upon the castle's peak. It was a perfect fit.

As I surveyed my handiwork, silently and serenely, the lemon's clear hue sucked all the clamorous colors into its spindle shape. Amid the musty air of Maruzen, this spot alone seemed to possess a strange tension. I stood there for awhile, just gazing at the tower.

Suddenly I was jolted by another bizarre idea: why not leave the lemon where it sat and innocently walk out?

A ticklish feeling came over me. 'Should I? Why not!' I briskly left the building.

Out on the street, that ticklish sensation drove me to laughter. What a peculiar villain I was, to leave a glittering golden bomb ticking on the shelves of Maruzen. If the bomb did in fact violently explode in ten minutes' time in the heart of the art-book section, how exciting it would be!

'And then,' I went on enthusiastically pursuing my vision, 'nothing would be left of that oppressive place but a heap of sawdust.'

I walked on down the streets of Kyogoku, festooned with their grotesquely colored motion-picture posters.

THE ACCORDION AND THE
FISH TOWN

Translated by Janice Brown

～

1

Father was very good on the accordion, and my first memories of music begin with his playing. Our family was always making long journeys. I remember one such trip when we had been jolting along on the train for hours, completely bored. My father was smoking pipe tobacco which had been crushed into powder. The accordion was wrapped up in a white cloth, and occasionally when my father moved, his hips pressed against it. Mother was crying as she chanted her prayers, and I sat beside her eating a banana. She was probably thinking about how hard her life was with only my father to depend upon. Father spoke to her quietly, saying something like, 'Just you wait and see. I'll do all right.' His eyes were closed.

The train was creeping along a winding track by the water's edge. Reflected brightly in my fourteen-year-old eyes, like the broad expanse of a shining wall, was a vista of calm spring and billowing clouds. A small town, with Japanese flags flying, lay along the shoreline. When Father opened his eyes and saw the rising-sun flags, he hurriedly stood up and put his head out the window.

'Looks like a festival,' he said. 'Let's get off and see.'

Putting her prayer-book away in her cloth bag, Mother, too, stood up. 'It seems to be a really pretty town,' she said. 'The sun's still high. If we get off here, maybe we can make some money for our lunch.' With that, the three of us hoisted our bags on our backs and got off the train at the seaside town bright with the rising-sun flags.

In front of the station was a large willow tree in bud. Opposite the willow, standing in a row, were several grimy-looking inns. Fleecy clouds drifted above the town, and all along the street the shop signboards displayed pictures of fish. As we walked on the road skirting the beach, the sound of whistling came from one of these shops. The whistling seemed to remind Father of the accordion on his back, and he took it out of the white cloth and put it over his shoulder. The accordion was large and terribly old. Father had attached a leather belt to it since it was supposed to be played hanging from the shoulder.

'Don't play yet,' Mother caught at Father's arm. It was a new town for us, so she probably felt a bit shy.

As we drew in front of the shop, we saw that the whistling was coming from some young men covered in fish-scales who were pounding up fish-bones. The fish pictured on the signboard was a sea bream holding fresh bamboo grass in its gills. We stopped to watch, intrigued by the way the fish-meal was being made.

'Hey buddy, why are the flags out today?' Father asked.

Stopping his pounding, a red-eyed fellow lazily turned and said, 'The mayor came.'

'What a fuss!' Father exclaimed.

We began to walk again. The seafront was lined with many small docks. Across from the docks in waters as smooth and sleek as a river lay a delicate little island. I could see many trees that seemed to have scattered their white blossoms, and under the trees animals that looked like cows walked slowly about.

2

It was a very peaceful scene. I bought some tempura lotus root, its holes stuffed full of mustard. Mother and I shared it while gazing at the island.

'Don't be too long,' she said to Father a bit apologetically. 'It doesn't really matter if you sell anything or not.' Mother held my hand tightly and, pulling me along, walked toward the breakwater. Father was wearing an old policeman's uniform; it had yellow stripes on the front, like ribs. He went up the hill playing the accordion.

'*O-ichi-ni*, oh, one two,' he sang.

When Mother heard the accordion, she looked down and blew her nose. I licked grease off my palm absent-mindedly.

'Here, let me clean you up a little bit.' Mother took the towel she carried at her neck, rolled it around the tip of her little finger, and wiped my nose. 'Why, look how black it is!' The part of the towel she had wrapped around the tip of her finger was as black as a dried mushroom.

Above the town was the elementary school. The breeze smelled of wheat.

'What a nice view!' Mother looked at the sea with narrowed eyes and then, with the towel, wiped a thin film of dust from her hair-knot. I had finished the lotus root and was now watching an old woman in a fried-food stall above the pier. She was frying octopus legs that sizzled.

'What a greedy child you are! Your stomach will pop!' Mother said.

'I want some octopus!'

'What?' Mother glared at me. 'Don't you know how poor we are!'

From the distance came the sound of Father's accordion.

'I gave you plenty of good things to eat on the train!'

'I know, but I want some octopus.'

'You're so annoying.' Mother took out her striped, tasseled coin purse and held it in front of my face. 'Look, now do you understand?' She shook it and into her pale palm spilled green powder and several large two-*sen* copper coins.

'Now, do they look like silver? I haven't any silver coins, so you can't buy octopus.'

'Can't we buy it with copper coins?'

'What a child! You keep on saying the same thing. Do you want to fill your own stomach even if your parents can't eat?'

'I can't help it if I'm hungry!'

Mother slapped my face. Some schoolchildren on their way home were waiting for a ferry nearby. When they saw me get hit, they all burst into laughter. Blood flowed into my throat from my nose. I looked at the reflection of the blue sea and held back salty tears.

'I wish I could get away from here!'

'So you say, but with your stubbornness, no one will take care of you.'

'That's fine with me! I want to be on my own.'

'All you care about is yourself! You had a banana, and then some lotus root, too. Even rich children don't get to eat that.'

'Rich kids always eat delicious things. They don't have to be thankful for rotten bananas.'

'You're old enough to be married, and you still talk about nothing but food!'

'Well, you slapped me, and now look, I've got a nosebleed.'

Mother took a plastic comb out of her bag and combed my hair. Every time the teeth of the comb went through my bushy hair, there was a popping sound and my hair stood on end.

'Your hair's so frizzy, it looks like it's ready to catch on fire.' Mother put the comb in her mouth as if it were a harmonica and licked it; then she combed my bangs.

'Let's go and see if your father's had any luck. If he has, I'll buy you whatever you want,' she said.

3

Mother helped me take off my back-pack. In the purple cloth were my books, watercolors, and a sewing kit.

'He was just playing the accordion. Go and see if he's sold anything.'

I ran on to the wooden pier and up the slope. This town was so cramped that even a dog seemed large in it. Higher up the slope, above the roofs, tents fluttered, and girls wearing hairpins of cherry-wood were everywhere. I could hear Father's voice coming from the midst of a crowd of people that had gathered like ants—he sounded as if he was really working up a sweat.

'Yes, yes, this is our first time in the area, and our company has modern, bottled medicines. We're not selling any old frog-oil cure-alls. No, indeed. In fact, a certain member of the royal family is an honored customer of ours. These medicines can't be bought just anywhere . . .'

The wife of a fisherman bought some medicine for syphilis. One of the girls with a cherrywood ornament selected eye medicine in a seashell container. A man carrying packages bought an ointment for bruises. Father pulled the various medicines out of his shiny, hand-polished black bag as if he were a magician. Then he walked about and showed them off among the crowd which now formed a circle.

The accordion lay on a pile of lumber. Children were touching the keys of the strange contraption, and from time to time they shook its side, laughing uproariously at the off-key noises that emerged. I couldn't stand the sound of the captured accordion, so I pushed my way into the group.

'Yes, yes, indeed, there is nothing as effective for hysteria and for the womb as this medicine, *O-ichi-ni.*'

I pushed aside the children gathered on the lumber, pulled the accordion toward me, and put it on my shoulder.

'What do you think you're doing? This is mine!' I said.

When the children saw my bobbed hair, they began to jeer, 'Short hair! Short hair! Looks like a boy!'

Father adjusted his old army hat slightly and looked over at me. His eyes were sad. 'Don't be a nuisance. Go to your mother.'

The children gathered again like flies around the accordion and pressed the white keys. I ran rat-a-tat-tat over one of the pieces in the lumber pile, posing like a tightrope walker. Then I moved my hips the way I once saw a female juggler do in some town or other.

'Your sash is untied!' a boy carrying stilts over his shoulder pointed at me.

'Really?' I tied up the loosened sash on my stomach, and holding the skirt of my kimono between my thighs, turned the sash until the knot was behind me. The boy was laughing.

A mountain of dried fish lay heaped in a large square lined with white-walled fertilizer storehouses. At the udon noodle stalls, which were lined up like birds around the square, longshoremen stood slurping up the thick slippery noodles. Delicious-looking rice crackers and tempura were displayed in a glass showcase. I leaned against the case and gazed fixedly at the food. My breath clouded the glass.

'Where did you come from? Don't lean on the glass!' A bare-breasted woman scolded me while she wiped her baby's nose.

4

Lights came on in the pagoda of the red temple on the mountain, while clouds resembling sardine scales rose from behind the island. I sang as I walked down to the breakwater. There were lights there now, and peddlers were carrying baskets attached to the ends of long poles. They surrounded the cargo area of a white steamship and called out their wares in loud voices. Mother was leaning against some boxes on the pier, looking up at the ferry dock.

'What have you been doing? Did you see your father?' she asked.

'I saw him! He's selling heaps of medicine.'

'Really?'

'Yeah, really!'

Mother helped me arrange the purple cloth bundle on my hips. She looked pleased. 'It's a warm wind.'

'I need to pee,' I said.

'You can do it somewhere around here.'

Garbage and seaweed floated in the water under the pier. Beneath the garbage, fish flitted about, small and indistinct. A boat was just in from fishing, full of the day's catch, like a pigeon with its chest puffed out. By the time the tide reached the boat's water-line, a pale moon had appeared in the sky.

'You pee like a horse,' Mother said.

'I've been holding it back.' I felt disgusted at such a long pee. With an extra effort I bent over further and peered between my legs. Beyond the white mounds of my buttocks, sky and ship were reversed. My body was so contorted that my neck began to hurt. I could see the sparkling mist of urine as it sprayed on to the pier.

'Watch what you're doing! You could fall in! See, here's your father coming back.'

'Really?'

'Yes, really.'

The sea breeze blew pleasantly between my legs.

'Are you tired?' Mother called out.

Father wiped his face with a towel and called back down to us from the pier, 'Shall we go get some noodles or something?'

I grabbed Mother's hands and swung them back and forth. 'I'm so happy! Father's sold a stack of medicine, hasn't he?'

The three of us sat down on a bench at a stall. We ordered udon noodles. In my bowl were three pieces of fried bean curd.

'Why don't either of you have any bean curd?'

'Quiet! Children shouldn't talk while they eat,' Mother said.

I put one piece of the bean curd into Father's bowl and grinned. He ate it with relish.

'You've done surprisingly well here, so maybe we should stay a few more days,' Mother said.

'At first people thought I was just a disabled soldier, but when they heard me play the accordion, they began to say I was really a class act.'

'You should have let them hear one or two of the really lively pieces,' said Mother.

I added more hot water to the rest of the soup and took a long time to drink it down, as if I were a suckling baby.

A circle of lights came on in the town. The market-place must have been nearby. Women passed by, carrying flat wooden tubs of fish on their heads and calling out, '*Banyori!* Don't you want some *banyori*?'

'Well, it's an interesting place. From the train I could see a lot of temples, and there's fishermen, too, so I just know we can sell our medicines here,' Father said.

'Yes, you're right,' Mother replied.

Father counted out a number of silver coins and handed them to Mother.

'Oh, I want to eat some octopus!'

'Not again! Your father will get angry,' Mother snapped. 'And he'll throw that accordion into the sea!'

'What are you making a fuss about now?' Father asked me. He took a pencil from his notebook and began to check the medicine boxes.

5

That evening, people gathered like moths at the top of the mountain to view the cherry blossoms. We stayed in a cheap inn beside the railway tracks near the station, and lay down in our sweaty clothes.

'This town is full of really energetic people,' said Father. 'Have you ever seen such a lively cherry-viewing crowd before?'

'Those people are out of their minds. What's so great about cherry blossoms?' Mother snorted as if she did not particularly approve. She was untying our bundles.

'Hey, stand up! Come here and look. It's really pretty.' Opening the low smoke-grimed paper window, Father called out to me. He was taking off his soiled puttees.

'I don't want to see them. If I do, I'll want some more sushi.' I made no move to stand up.

Mother gave an amused laugh. I lay face down on the soft old tatami mats. I had Mother take out a book for me, and began to read in a loud voice part of a section on 'Protective Coloration.' Mother

seemed proud of my ability to read smoothly and loudly.
'Mmmmm . . . indeed,' she would murmur from time to time.

'Farmers are stupid, aren't they?' she commented at one point.
'Hanging teapots on inchworms!'

'Probably because the worms resemble tree branches,' Father
replied.

'What kind of insects are they?' Mother asked.

'You get them in the countryside.'

'Really? Are they long?'

'Like silkworms.'

'Have you seen one?'

'Sure have.'

My childlike shadow projected darkly on the dirty wall. Every
time the wind blew into the room, the wick of the lamp flared up.
In the street, some passerby said, 'Rain's not far off.'

'Well, just how much was this smelly room?' Mother asked.

'Sixty *sen* just to sleep.'

'Amazing. Travel is so cruel.'

It was so quiet I thought I could feel the sound of the waves
penetrating my stomach. There was only one set of futon, and as
usual I lay down with a book to read, slipping in at the bottom of
the bedding.

'Mother, aren't we going to have dinner?'

'What are you going on about now? You're in bed, why don't
you sleep?'

'You've had noodles, haven't you?' Father asked. 'Now that I've
got lots of silver coins you may think we can buy whatever we want.
But I have to pay the inn, not to mention the medicine suppliers, and
soon all these coins will be gone. So get to sleep early, and get up
early, and tomorrow I'll give you all the fine white rice you can eat!'
He folded a floor cushion in half and put it under my end of the futon
as a pillow. The words 'white rice' brought tears to my eyes.

'She's growing fast, that's why she eats so much,' Mother said.

'I'm going to have to find some way of keeping food on the table.
I wonder if I can get some work around here.'

My parents seemed not to see me crying as I lay there in the
bedding.

'She reads so well, if we could arrange it somewhere, I'd like her
to go to school,' Mother said.

'If I can sell more tomorrow, we can stay on,' Father replied.

'This is a good place. From the time we got off the train, I've felt really good about it. What's it called?' Mother asked.

'Onomichi,' Father replied. 'Try it.'

'O-no-mi-chi?'

'It's got the mountains and the sea. It's a nice spot,' Father said.

Mother stood up and turned off the light.

6

Four or five pomegranate trees stood in the garden of the inn where we were staying. Under these trees was a large, slightly enclosed, shallow well. When the window of our six-mat upstairs room was open, the pomegranate trees and the well could be seen directly below. The well water was brackish, and when I washed my face, I could taste the salt. We kept a two-day supply of water in the pitcher upstairs. There was no closet or *tokonoma* in our room, so in the mornings we spread a white cloth over the rented bedding. On the veranda was an earthenware charcoal brazier, a bucket, a pan with a handle, and an abalone flowerpot. All in all, a relaxing room for the three of us.

Downstairs lived a couple in their fifties. In the earthen floor area of the kitchen they kept two old handcarts. Although the man looked as if he had never pulled either of them, someone must have been borrowing the carts, since from time to time one would disappear for awhile. The kitchen was always dreary and never smelled of cooking. Every day the woman worked on the veranda in view of the pomegranate trees, rolling slips of fortune-telling paper in white kelp. Since the wall around the well was low, cats and dogs would often fall in. Then the woman would shine an old corroded mirror into the interior of the well and peer down inside.

'There's something about Onomichi,' Mother said one day. 'It's good we didn't go to Osaka.'

'If we had gone to Osaka, things would have been tougher,' agreed Father.

At that time my parents looked fairly prosperous in my eyes. I ate my fill of food every day, and the happy days continued.

'Eat till your stomach bursts,' Mother said. 'As long as you can eat, there's nothing to worry about.'

'Oh, Mother! Do the people downstairs ever eat anything?'

'What do you mean? If people don't eat, they can't live.'

'No, really, last night when I went down to the toilet, I heard the man tell his wife they might as well take the other cart, too, and leave him to die. He was crying.'

'Well! So that cart was used as collateral, and now it will be taken by the moneylenders, too.'

'Don't they have any relatives? I've never seen them eating.'

'Now, don't say that. The man downstairs worked on a ship when he was young, but his leg was broken in the machinery. No one comes to see him. The woman only has her kelp to roll up so they can eat. It's all a great pity.'

'Can't they go to the police?'

'No one knows about all this, and if they did, everyone would laugh at them.'

'But if people do something wrong, don't the police get angry?'

'What people?'

'The ones who broke the man's leg. They act like nothing happened.'

'He's no match for those who have money.'

'That man downstairs must be stupid.'

'What a thing to say!'

Taking the accordion and a lunch, Father would spend his days wandering through the town, playing 'o-ichi-ni, oh, one two' and selling his wares. 'I went to the fishermen's part of town, and when they heard that the o-ichi-ni medicine was there, everyone came out to buy,' he told us one day.

'No doubt because you look so strange,' Mother answered.

The days passed clear and bright. On the mountain the cherry blossoms fell, and all at once the whole vicinity began to sport green leaves. In the distance the first frogs were croaking. Small white 'mosquito-repelling' chrysanthemums were blooming, too.

7

'Shall we go to school?' Father asked one day when he came home from selling. I was planting some roses I'd picked from the mountain tea plantations, putting them under the pomegranate trees. Father was washing his face at the well.

'School? I'm over thirteen and still in the fifth grade. I don't want to go.'

'Going to school is a good thing.'

'Do you think they'll let me into the sixth grade?'

'They'll probably let you in if you keep quiet. You can read really well.'

'But won't mathematics be difficult?'

'Well, then, you'll have to study! Tomorrow I'll take you.'

The idea of going to school made me happy if a little uneasy. That night, my heart thumping, I childishly counted the white numbers that floated under my closed eyelids for as long as I could. About midnight, when I was beginning to doze off, a loud splash came from the well, as if something like a large rock had fallen in. Since the well was deep, when a cat or dog fell in, the sound was usually a faint gurgle. Or it had been up until now. I was not used to hearing such a big splash.

'Mother! What was that?'

'Did it wake you? What is it, I wonder?'

While we were talking, the water splashed again, and we heard someone crying out plaintively. The man downstairs was shouting and crawling around.

'Wake up! Someone has fallen into the well!' Mother cried.

'Who?!'

'Hurry and go see! I think it's the woman downstairs!' she said to Father.

My body was shaking, and I couldn't say a word.

'You come with me!' Father shouted to Mother, and then to me, 'You go back to bed!' He went pounding down the stairs, sounding as if he might break right through them.

Alone, I found the air in the room oppressive. Not able to stand it any longer, I slid open the *shoji* and opened the outside shutter. The leaves of the pomegranate trees gleamed like bean leaves, and a red moon, shaped like a round tray, shone above the mountain. A chill ran over my skin. 'Hey, what happened?' Without thinking, I shouted down. My mother appeared holding the mirror and a lamp.

'Okay! Grab hold of this rope as tight as you can!' Father shouted and tied the end of the rope to the trunk of the middle pomegranate tree.

I heard my mother's faltering voice: 'Hold on a little longer. And get a good grip on the rope. My husband's going to come down.'

'Masako, come down here,' Father shouted when he looked up and saw me peeping down. I was cold, so I put on Father's shirt with the yellow stripes and, practically tumbling down the stairs, went out to the well. The old fellow from downstairs was on the veranda, wailing and carrying on something dreadful.

'Good girl. Now run and get the doctor,' Father said. 'Speak politely!'

In the faint glow of the lantern, the paving-stones shone slickly. A warm night wind ruffled our clothes. Several ropes hung down in the well, and the sound of the old woman groaning came up the shaft.

'Hurry and go! What are you waiting for?'

I went out into the dark town, having no clear idea where I was going. I could hear the wind and waves and, in the distance, what sounded like a shamisen. Raw odors filled the air. It felt as if it were the first night of summer. I was still wearing the policeman's shirt Father wore for clowning around. I hadn't realized that I had buttoned it. Perhaps because of this shirt, the rickshaw man who sleepily answered my knock at the doctor's house on the corner bent down and spoke to me politely. I had never heard such courteous phrases before. 'Yes, that's quite all right. Whether it's one or two o'clock, it's the doctor's duty. I'll run and wake him, and he'll be there right away.'

8

The woman who had fallen into the well climbed out clutching a soaking parcel wrapped in a black cloth. It contained a satin obi with a whale-bone pattern and a hat of sea-otter fur her husband had bought when he worked on the ship. She had probably waited until dark and then set out for the pawnshop by the back way. A pawnshop ticket had fallen out of her sash. Mother seemed to share the woman's suffering, for she hid the ticket from the doctor.

'That was a close call,' the doctor said.

'Will she be all right?'

'She hasn't any bruising. If she gets over her shock, she'll be all right.'

Some of the woman's fortune-telling kelp which I had always wanted to try was strewn in a corner of the room. I popped five or six pieces into my mouth. The taste of pepper bit my tongue.

'Since she's alive, we won't have to clean out the well,' Mother said.

In the morning we rinsed our mouths with the well water. One of the woman's clogs was floating in the well. I borrowed the old mirror, shone it into the well, and managed to pull up the clog in a bamboo basket. Mother made small heaps of salt in the four corners of the stone well enclosure and, pressing her hands together, said a prayer.

It was a cloudy day, and the wind felt like rain. Over his kimono, Father put on soiled formal trousers that he had borrowed from the man downstairs and took me to the elementary school on the mountain. On the way to the school was a shrine to the Emperor Jimmu. Behind this shrine was a pedestrian overpass and below that a train passing by.

'Get on that and you can easily go as far as Tokyo,' Father said.

'Have you been past Tokyo?'

'Women and children can't go that far. Just barbarians live there.'

'Then just the sea is beyond Tokyo?'

'Can't tell. Your father hasn't been there himself.'

It was a school with a lot of stone steps. Father stopped to rest several times on the way up. The schoolyard was as wide as a desert. Growing in its four corners in flower-beds were mountain plum, clematis, thistle, lupines, azaleas, and iris. Above the school building rose the top of the mountain. Looking back, I saw a hazy sea, dotted with islands.

'Wait here.' Father folded his hands over the belt that tied up the formal trousers and went in the white gate of the teachers' room.

Willows did seem to agree with this part of the country, for in the middle of the garden area was a large willow tree with soft buds that trembled like a lamb. I touched the rings on the spinning pole and climbed on the log swing and smelled the scents of the new school. But somehow I felt depressed. I turned and ran back through the school gate as if I were going to continue down the stone steps.

'Hey!' Father called out to me. Shivering like a bird stepping out of the water, I turned back and went through the gate of the teachers' room. In this room were two rows of small book boxes which reminded me of canaries' nests. Father stood with the principal in the center of the room near a brazier. When he saw me, he bowed politely. I realized that I, too, must bow, and so I made a polite, deep obeisance. The principal seemed satisfied.

'Let us go to the classroom,' he said.

'Please look after her for us, then,' Father said and took his leave of the principal. As he went out the gate, I felt sad.

The principal was a tall man. From some school somewhere or other I remembered a saying: 'Stay seven steps behind, and do not step on the teacher's shadow,' so I followed behind the principal at some distance.

'Don't loiter! Walk quickly!' the principal ordered when he turned to look back at me.

Outside the window in a puddle by the water-pump some kind of insect was crying: 'Ka-ro, ka-ro.' The principal opened a warped door that resembled a storm shutter, and from inside the room the children's breath seemed to rush out at me. A board hung from the top of the blackboard. 'Sixth-Year Girls, A-Group,' it read. Since I had left my last school in the middle of my fifth year, this made me a little uneasy.

9

The rainy days went on and on. Gradually I began to hate going to school. Once they got used to me, the other children would gather around and call me names. They called me the daughter of Little Lieutenant *O-ichi-ni*. I thought my father didn't look at all like the Chaplin character. I planned to tell Father about this sometime, but in the long rainy season he was feeling too depressed. We continued eating yellow millet. Every time I ate I felt as if I was living in a barn. At school I didn't have lunch. Instead, at lunchtime I would go to the choir room and play the organ. I played rather well, using Father's accordion music.

Since my speech was rough, I was often scolded by the teacher. She was a fat woman over thirty. She always had a ragged hairpiece peeking out at the front.

'You must use standard Japanese!' she ordered. Thereupon everyone began to use the attractive phrase '*uchi wa ne*' for 'I'. Sometimes I forgot and said '*washi wa ne*,' and everyone would laugh at me. At school I was happy when I got to see lithographs and beautiful flowers I had never seen before. However, most of the children, even as time passed, continued to call me Little Lieutenant.

'I don't want to go to school anymore!' I told Mother.

'You must finish elementary school. Look at me, I can't read books, and I can't do anything but sleep.'

'Yeah, and nag!'

'Who's a nag?'

'I won't tell you!'

'Won't tell me?'

'That's what I said.'

The rain continued day after day. I wanted to cut it down with a sword. Every day the woman downstairs put pepper and fortunes into little pieces of kelp and tied them up with string. Our yellow millet was nearly used up. Mother got some work from the woman downstairs—putting wire through tags. When Mother and Father competed at this, Mother was the winner.

I made a pretence of going to school, but went instead to the mountain behind. The smell of the mountain pervaded my flannel clothes. When it rained, I covered my head with a cloth and played, leaning up against the trunk of a pine tree.

A fine day finally came. I climbed the mountain and lay down in the shade of some bush clover. A man with long hair like our gym teacher was there with O-ume, the girl from the rice shop. Embarrassed, I went back down the mountain. The sea shone pearl-white and dazzled my eyes.

Father and Mother often talked about moving to Osaka, but I didn't want to go. Before I realized it, Father's policeman's uniform had disappeared. When I thought that the accordion might be gone one day, too, I felt a salty sadness deep in my heart.

'Maybe I should pull a rickshaw,' Father said unhappily.

In those days there was a boy I liked, and my father pulling a rickshaw would have been extremely embarrassing. The boy was the son of a fish-shop owner. One time, I'm not sure when, I passed their fish shop, and the boy called out to me, even though he didn't know me, 'Some fish? We've caught lots! How about it? What looks good?'

'Black sea-bream,' I answered.

'Oh, is that what you like?' There was no one in the shop. Sniffing continuously, the boy wrapped up the fish for me in newspaper. The fish-scales shone like silver. 'How many layers do you wear?' he asked me.

'Kimono?'

'Yeah.'

'Not so many, it's warm now.'

'Let me count your collars.' With his smelly hand, the boy counted my kimono collars. When he finished, he pointed to a white fish, 'How about this one too?'

'I like all kinds of fish,' I said.

'Living in a fish shop's good 'cause you can eat the fish.' He said he would take me fishing with him sometime on his family's boat. I felt a rush of excitement. Back in school the next day, I saw that the boy was the leader of the fifth-year class.

10

Through someone's introduction, Father began a business selling face lotion at ten *sen* a bottle. There were blue, red, and yellow bottles, all in beautiful shapes. They had a label with a lilac-flower design, and when I shook the bottles hard, a cloud of powder rose up from the bottom.

'Oh, they're beautiful!'

'The girls will buy them for sure since they're only ten *sen*.'

'I want to buy one, too!'

'Listen to you!'

Somewhere, Father had picked up a song for selling the face lotion:

> Use one jar, light pink your skin will glow,
> Use two jars for skin as white as snow.
> Everyone, come buy from me,
> If you don't, a charcoal ball your face will be.

He practiced this ditty for five days, accompanying himself on the accordion.

'You have to sell them as soon as possible, otherwise they'll be no good, they said.'

'Is it okay to sell them if they're no good?' Mother asked.

'Good, bad, we have to eat. It can't be helped.'

There was a village called Yoshiwa outside Onomichi. It had a sailcloth factory with many female workers, and wives of fishermen lived there, too. Father went there often. I liked this new kind of fashionable business. I stole a red bottle and hid it behind the aluminum water-basin.

'Things are really improving,' I thought, 'if we can get fashionable items like this so cheap.'

About that time, a woman came round selling beef from a basket. Perhaps thinking it a bargain, Mother often splurged and bought some. She cooked it with some *konnyaku* noodles, and the meat turned the color of blood. 'Aha, so this is dog meat!' Father proclaimed. The three of us ate this red meat quite often since it was cheap. 'To be sure, it's dog meat,' said the woman downstairs. When she had given some to a dog, it wouldn't eat it. Proof indeed that this was dog meat.

Completely cloudless days came. One day when I came home from the school on the mountain, Mother was trying to hold back her tears.

'What's wrong?'

'Your father—he's been taken to the police station.'

I'll never forget the sadness I felt then. My eyelids felt as heavy as the leaves of an akebia vine.

'I'm going to the police station for just a bit. Be a good child and stay here.'

'I'm going, too! I want to tell them to let Father come home!'

'It'll make them angry for a child to go. Now wait here!'

'No, no, I'll be lonely all by myself!'

'I'll slap you!'

After Mother left, I cried. The woman downstairs came up, and even though she sat beside me, I continued to wail.

'Father said, during the war, people put stones in the canned goods, and got rich, but Father said that what he's done is such a small thing, it amounts to no more than a grain of sand . . .'

'Now, don't cry, your father isn't bad at all. It's the manufacturers who are the bad ones.'

'I can't help crying! Now we can't eat!'

I ran through the town to the police station. It was evening. Leaning against the wrought-iron door with its arabesque design, I waited for Mother and Father to come out. I grasped the ironwork design and, for some reason or other, repeated Mother's prayers to the sky. I felt so lonely. From behind the building I could hear the bell of the harbor police station clanging away. I went round to the back and, climbing up to a bent, light-blue window-frame, I peeped down into the room inside. The lights were blazing. In a corner of the room Mother's crouching figure caught my eye. She looked like a rat. In front of her Father was being slapped repeatedly by a policeman.

'Now try and sing!' the policeman roared.

In a queer voice, Father played the accordion and sang one line of the face-lotion song.

'Louder!'

'Okay, okay . . . use this powder, your skin will be as white as snow. It's cheap, too,' my father sang.

Father was again showered with blows by the policeman.

'Idiot! Fool!' I screamed like a monkey and ran toward the sea.

'Masako!'

I heard my mother's voice, but it seemed so far away. All I could hear was a grating sound deep inside my head, like cog-wheels turning, grinding.

ENCHI FUMIKO (1905–1986)

THE FLOWER-EATING CRONE

Translated by Lucy North

≈

One late fall afternoon I was sitting in the sunshine on my veranda, touching the petals of a cactus plant that was just coming into bloom.

'What a beautiful flower!' I heard someone say. And there on the other side of the pot, crouching down and peering into it, was the old woman. Her hair was white, but her skin still had a glow, and the apprehensive, shy look in her eyes was just like a little girl's.

'My eyes are so bad, I have to get right up close to see anything,' she explained. Indeed, her face was almost touching the flowers.

'I've been troubled by my own eyesight these past months,' I remarked, 'but your eyes must be even worse than mine!'

I felt a touch of satisfaction as I made this remark. Since the summer, an eye illness had affected my vision, and nothing I looked at was clear anymore: I was losing my sight. Perhaps I was glad to have found a fellow sufferer. I must admit, too, that I enjoyed a childish sense of superiority over the woman with her face in the flowers.

'Yes, it's terrible,' she continued. 'Nowadays I can only just make things out if they're in front of my eyes. It's all dim and out of focus, as if I'm walking through a mist.' The expression on her face, however, seemed quite unclouded by misery.

'What's the name of this plant?' she asked. 'I've not seen one like it before.'

'Crab orchid, I was told many years ago in Atami. But nowadays they're called Shakova cacti at florist shops in Tokyo. That's probably the botanical name.'

'I much prefer crab orchid,' the old woman replied.

The plant had dark green leaves, which were long and segmented like feathers each growing out from the other, with soft prickles at each link—and from these, seemingly out of nowhere, the strangest-looking flowers: triple-layered blossoms, shaped rather like lilies, deep crimson in their center, then magenta, and then, at their outer petals, light pink. The curving, jointed leaves did make me think of a crab's claws, and the delicately bunched flowers were like orchid flowers. I myself had always preferred the unorthodox name.

Two years ago, when I first moved to this small apartment, a certain friend gave me the plant as a house-warming gift. I was so delighted by the sight of it, a beautiful mass of new buds all on the verge of bursting forth, that I decided to keep it inside, in the warmth, thinking the blossoms would also add color to my room. But despite my good intentions, for some reason the buds shriveled and dropped off in two or three days. Hardly a single flower came to full bloom in the end.

In my disappointment, I put the plant, now just a clump of jagged green leaves, out of sight on my balcony, and for the following year I hardly gave it a thought. But the next fall I noticed tiny, jewel-like buds forming on its leaf tips, and soon they swelled into flower all over the plant, their heavy splashes of pink and crimson petals weighing down the leaves in voluptuous profusion.

I'd assumed it was dying, but it had managed, all by itself, to come back to life! Thrilled by this turn of events, I started once more to lavish care on it, and I continued even when all the blossoms had fallen. And now, lo and behold, this year too, the crab orchid was going to favor me with blossoms for yet a third time.

'Perhaps it didn't like being indoors after all,' I remarked to the old woman after relating the story.

'That's probably so,' she replied. 'Perhaps all it needed was the natural moisture of the dew and the rain.'

She smiled brightly at me.

Then, quite brazenly, she reached out, tore off one of the multi-layered blossoms that hung helplessly from a leaf, and crammed it into her mouth. In less than a second, the flower had disappeared between her puckered lips.

'What are you doing?' I gasped. It was a bizarre, disturbing sight: somehow the flower being crammed into her mouth was like a living creature.

'Oh, I'm sorry,' she laughed apologetically. 'You know, the older

I get, the less I seem to be able to restrain myself. It's senility, I suppose. . . .'

She tore off another flower, and this time started nibbling on it like a cherry.

'You don't mean to say you actually like the taste of these flowers!'

'Well, I don't do it for the taste. And this plant, in particular, does seem a little bitter. Some blossoms, though, are delicious.'

Then, with a knowing expression on her face, she asked: 'But have you never eaten flowers yourself?'

Now that she mentioned it, I had done something of the sort. I had always loved flowers from childhood, but I did recall having picked azaleas with my friends and trying to suck the sweet honey at the base of the petals.

Even now, whenever I find any object especially beautiful or striking, I feel an irresistible urge to take it into my hands. Of course, I don't go so far as to cram it into my mouth, but I've always found it hard to be satisfied with admiring objects of beauty in a cool, detached kind of way.

I didn't want to admit to this, though, so I deflected the old lady's question.

'You know, there's a scene featured sometimes in the Kabuki play *Plum Calendar*, where Tanjiro makes love to Adakichi—or Yoneh-achi—and she holds a white plum blossom to her lips, and nibbles on it, and they kiss. I think the use of the flower there represents the ultimate in pure, refined eroticism . . .'

I stole a glance at the old lady's mouth: her lips appeared to be stained with blood.

'Oh, that's just an artistic way of suggesting sexual desire,' the old woman replied calmly. 'You find the same thing in wood-block prints. Look at Kiyonaga.' She munched ravenously away on more flowers.

'But,' she continued between mouthfuls, 'who says we should only *look* at flowers, and not eat them? It's natural: you see a flower you consider especially lovely, and you want to get as close to it as possible. But after a while, looking is not enough—you want to touch it with your hands, pluck it off, crush it, force it open. Finally, you become so consumed with desire, you want to fuse with it, make it part of you. That's when you end up cramming it into your mouth.'

'Is it a flower's beauty you're describing, or the way a man loves a woman?' I tried to joke, though I knew exactly what she meant. 'There is a difference between people and plants, you know!'

'Well, there is and there isn't,' she replied. 'I'm convinced that there is some centripetal force in human beings that makes them want to pull everything—other people, plants, even animals—in toward them. It makes itself felt in all sorts of stories—in Greek myth, for example, where human beings turn into flowers. In old Japanese stories too, where the spirits of cherry trees and willows change into beautiful women to have sexual relations with men. These stories are fantasies—they're the expression of a human desire, a need to do something more than merely sit back and admire objects of nature.'

'Fantasies you say? But here you are in reality doing practically the same thing!'

'Well, I suppose this is reality. One can never tell, you know. One's own idea of reality doesn't necessarily coincide with other people's.'

'You're right. To me, seeing you stuff crimson blossoms into your mouth, I'd have to assume you're out of your head.'

'A crazy woman—yes, I know. And maybe so. But you only say that because you're longing to follow my example. You're just too cowardly, too repressed to follow your own desires through.'

The old lady spoke as if she could read my mind.

'But if, as you say, your eyesight is failing,' she continued, 'it won't be long now before all your repressed desires and regrets, all the monsters and demons waiting inside, will want to burst out and express themselves. There'll be a night parade of a hundred goblins.'

I was silent now, unable to reply.

It was true that ever since my eyesight had worsened, those demons and goblins inside me had become restless. Now they constantly disturbed me, feeling no compunction about interfering in every aspect of my life.

I recalled a strange incident that had happened a few evenings before. Past midnight, I became suddenly conscious of a presence in the study by my bedroom, and softly opening the door, I looked in and saw that I'd left my writing box out, its lid off, and packages of old letters I had been sorting during the day strewn over my desk.

'I knew there was something I'd forgotten to do,' I muttered, picking up the lid to replace it. But just at that moment, a package of letters fell out of it, landing straight on my lap. I didn't even have to look inside to know, right down to the last detail, what lay inside that large unmarked brown envelope. I'd been conscious of it lying at the bottom of the box as I sorted the other documents. But how could it have risen to the top? I didn't recall having touched it earlier. Surely it couldn't have risen by itself? And then to have fallen onto my lap...

The letters in the package were ones I had written to a man, a distant relative. We had started corresponding when I was in my teens, a mere schoolgirl, and he was in his mid-twenties. I was only slightly attracted to him, and he was older after all, but before our friendship could blossom into anything more, he left Japan to go abroad, where he lived for many years, and we never met again. Later, I received the occasional letter from him, and I would feel a twinge of nostalgia. But then the war came, and with it the air raids, and all my memorabilia went up in smoke. Gradually, my own memories of him grew faint, and finally he ceased even to come up in conversation.

A few years ago, however, I received news that he'd died. Even after retiring and returning to live in Japan, I heard, he had continued making trips abroad for his company as a consultant. He had collapsed on a golf course in England, never to regain consciousness. The letters in the package lying in my lap had been sent back to me by his wife several months after that.

His widow wrote in an accompanying note that her late husband had often talked of me, well into his later years. He had told her, she wrote, that if only he and I had been slightly closer in age, he would have asked me to be his wife. He had kept every one of my clumsily penned letters, with notes in a separate book about his own reactions and thoughts.

'Fortunately, our house wasn't damaged in the air raids,' she wrote: 'so your letters remained safe in a drawer of my husband's desk. But now he has died, so I hope you don't mind my taking the liberty of returning them. I enclose too the letters and pressed flowers you sent him on summer vacation from Nikko and Kamakura. The flowers' colors have faded, but perhaps you would like to see them again, and think of them as mementos of your youthful feelings.'

Far from indulging in such a trip down memory lane, I felt I'd been forced to gaze at the adolescent I once was—a gawky, immature girl in whom sensual and spiritual concerns competed uncomfortably for attention. The writing paper with its pressed-flower borders, the epitome of schoolgirl taste; the stiff, high-flown phrases with which I tried to express my thoughts and emotions; even the pinks and violets, now so brittle and dried out that 'faded' seemed too mild a term: I couldn't help despising the person I had been, and despising the man too, for his attraction to me.

Naturally, after that, whenever I remembered the way he had treasured my memory, I couldn't help grimacing in embarrassment and disgust. I didn't go so far as to throw those old letters into the fire, but I never reread them: I simply stashed them away at the bottom of the box.

But recently, I have become painfully aware of my failing health, and especially since my eyes, the windows that open out onto the world, have been growing dim, I am often reminded that at some point in time my life will end.

When people no longer have any impact on the world around them, when they can no longer move forward, perhaps the only way they can continue living is to direct their gaze down into their own psyche—either that, or else, digging out old memories, to look back at their past.

I have never wanted to look back. The idea of looking deep inside myself I don't mind at all, but I am determined not to have to grope about in the past to dig out some reason to carry on living. No matter how narrow or indistinct the world around me becomes, I am determined to keep looking ahead. Even if I end up completely blind, the last thing I want to do is to wallow in nostalgia.

But those demons and goblins didn't care what I wanted: they were forcing me to look back and remember. They had caused that package of old letters to fall out of their box in the dead of night, and into my lap.

Now that you're old and gray, surely you're pleased to have the memory of that young man's infatuation. The same goes for all those other incidents which you hated for their lasciviousness: that time a love letter was slipped into your sleeve by an anonymous student in the bus, or the afternoon you were followed home after your lessons by a strange man. Surely you think back on those incidents with pleasure now that you're in your dotage, as proof that once you were as pretty as a pink, that even you were once 'sweet sixteen'.

I should be even more pleased to be reminded of this man's feelings for me. It was only a friendship, and certainly nothing compared to the full-blown passion of later affairs. But to think that, for all those years, I had warmed his memories of youth, holding a place in his thoughts as an innocent girl utterly unbesmirched by the world... Instead of embarrassed and disgusted, why not just admit to feeling grateful?

Those demons, those monsters had waited for just the right moment. They had dragged out my unconscious thoughts, exposing them before my eyes, and forced me to acknowledge them.

'What did I tell you?' the old woman declared. 'There's something about you that doesn't allow you to go ahead and eat flowers, even though you long to. And yet you still fret, uncomfortable with your inhibition. But a flower won't last forever, you know. You have to gobble it up the moment you get the desire.'

She stood up. 'Why don't we go for a walk? The gingko trees in the park must still be a fine sight.'

'I expect so.' I stood up too. 'There may even be chrysanthemums on display.'

The old woman walked along beside me. Strangely, she seemed to know exactly where to go: her steps were much more certain than mine. Whenever we had to cross a road, she put her hand on my shoulder, to guide me.

'Nobody would ever think you couldn't see,' I remarked.

'You don't seem to have any trouble, either,' she replied, teasingly.

We walked up the red brick-walled road leading through the National University of Fine Arts and Music, and eventually found the museums to our left. Turning right, we reached the flat space of ground with the pool and fountains.

Graceful zelkovas reached up toward the sky, their bare branches a lacework behind the gingko trees whose deep gold foliage, yet to fall, showed up like patches against them.

It was late afternoon. The autumn sunshine made the park an intense contrast of light and shadow. Around the fountains, and under the wisteria trellises, flocks of pigeons alighted, then took off again in storms of dust.

A young couple sat side by side on a bench, eating and chatting to each other, and tossing scraps of paper at the pigeons. They seemed relaxed and lively at the same time. Both were in slacks and sweaters, one red, the other yellow, and the boy's hair was as long as the girl's. It was difficult, especially with my poor eyesight, to tell which was the boy and which the girl.

'They look happy,' the old woman remarked as we sat down nearby, 'and yet they're not doing anything special.' She smiled at me. 'In our time, of course, it would have been scandalous for a young girl to be seen alone with a man.'

'I know. It's been like that for so many hundreds of years that even now the sight of a couple together in public seems forced and unnatural. I was shocked in the United States when I saw young couples on California university campuses hugging and kissing on the lawns.'

'Europeans are more reserved. But people bathe naked in the sea in Scandinavia in the summer. It's a beautiful refreshing sight.'

'Young people behave more naturally together everywhere now, even in Japan.'

Just then the old woman raised a hand and waved.

'Look who that is!' she exclaimed, prodding my shoulder. 'Go on. Why don't you go over and talk to him?'

As I stood up, the pigeons pecking for crumbs at our feet scattered in a mass of feathers and dust. When all was settled, a young man in a dark suit stood before me.

'Well, this is a surprise!' he greeted me. 'Where are you going?'

'I'm on my way to the library,' I answered, without even hesitating. 'What about you?'

'Oh, there's a meeting tonight on campus. I thought I'd run over to your house beforehand, and visit your brother.'

'But he's in Zushi, on a fishing trip with friends.'

'I wish I were a painter and could take it so easy!' he commented. He didn't seem bothered that the point of his visit was gone. With a twinkle in his eye, he asked: 'And what have we been reading today?'

'Drama. Plays from abroad. I have to come to the library for the translations.'

'Strindberg? Björnson? Or is it some play from Ireland?'

'Today I was reading *Strife*, by Galsworthy. It's quite interesting.'

'Oh, a political play.' He glanced at me patronizingly. 'I realize it won't do any good telling you to stop studying so hard, but I hope you don't take your obsession too far. Books aren't the key to happiness, you know.'

'I'm not so sure you can find it outside books, either.' I frowned, unable to articulate the powerful, contradictory thoughts disturbing my mind.

'Well, being a lawyer, I can't say much about literature. But one thing I do know is that I hate blue-stocking women. There's nothing attractive about a woman with her nose in a book.'

Petulantly, I looked away. 'I suppose you think they look prettier working in the kitchen!' I wanted to say. But there was too much inhibition, too much of the shy young girl in me to voice my thoughts out loud.

He didn't even seem to notice I was offended. 'My, it's a lovely day!' he remarked, changing the subject.

'Yes, I love the contrast of the fall colors and the blue sky at this time of year.'

'Well, it won't be long now before the winds come and blow all the leaves away,' was his reply.

The next moment he declared he should be on his way. 'I'll be happy to treat you to cake and coffee at the Seiyo-ken, if you'd like,' he said. 'Even though I'm only a struggling young lawyer, I think I can afford that at least ...'

He was smiling as he said this, but I refused, sensing that I should not accept.

'Well, good-bye. Give my best to your brother.'

'I will. Next time, telephone before you visit.'

He turned and hurried away in the direction of Takenodai.

I continued to brood over what he'd said. 'Reading books will only make you unhappy. I hate blue-stocking women ...' The words irritated me: just as I'd got up my nerve to try and achieve something, somebody had dashed cold water in my face.

But perhaps he was right. Maybe I have ended up as he predicted. And now that I'm losing my sight, I'm deprived of the one pleasure I'd assumed I'd always have. To think that books which I used to thumb through every day have been left untouched for over half a year, gathering dust ... And yet, somehow, I've still found it possible to get through the days ...

If he were alive today, that young man would never dare tell me not to study or devote myself to learning. He would know better than to evaluate my life, deprived as it is of sight, as fulfilled or unfulfilled.

The most he can do now is cause a bundle of old letters to drop into my lap in the dead of night.

But those letters, what should I do with them? Even if I burned them, some unassuaged longing, I feel sure, would remain in their ashes to haunt me.

Suddenly, I looked around. The day was over, and the sun was setting, its yellow glow already darkening into night. The couple in animated conversation sitting on the bench was nowhere to be seen.

And where was my companion, the flower-eating crone?

Perhaps she was over by the fountains, looking at the chrysanthemums in the flower beds. Peering down at my feet in the gathering dusk, I started to shuffle in that direction.

HIRABAYASHI TAIKO (1905–1972)

BLIND CHINESE SOLDIERS

Translated by Noriko Mizuta Lippit

On March 9, 1945, a day when by coincidence one of the biggest air raids took place, the sky over Gumma Prefecture was clear. An airplane, which might have taken off from Ota, flew along with the north wind.

Taking the road from Nashiki in the morning, I (a certain intellectual-turned-farmer) came down from Mount Akagi, where the snow in the valleys of the mountain was as hard as ice. From Kamikambara I took the Ashino-line train to Kiryu, transferred to the Ryoge-line, and got off at Takasaki. I was to transfer again to the Shingo-line to go to Ueno.

It was around four-thirty in the afternoon. Although the sky was still so light as to appear white, the dusty roofs of this machinery-producing town and the spaces among the leaves of the evergreen trees were getting dark. The waiting room on the platform was dark and crowded with people who had large bamboo trunks or packages of vegetables on their shoulders or beside them on the floor. It reverberated with noise and commotion.

After taking a look at the large clock hanging in front of me, I was about to leave the waiting room. Just at that moment, a group of policemen with straps around their chins crossed a bridge of the station and came down to the platform. Among them were the police chief and his subordinate, carrying iron helmets on their backs and wearing white gloves. The subordinate was talking about something with the station clerk who accompanied them, but it seemed that the word of the police chief, who interrupted their talk, decided the matter. The clerk crossed the bridge and then returned from the office with a piece of white chalk in his hand. Pushing people aside, he started drawing a white line on the platform.

I was standing in front of the stairway with one leg bent; I had sprained it when someone dropped a bag of nails in the crowded

Ryoge-line train. The clerk came up to me, pushed me back aggressively, and drew a white line. As was usual in those days, the train was delayed considerably. The passengers, quite used to the arrogance of the clerks, stepped aside without much resistance and, to pass the time, watched what was happening with curiosity.

Shortly, a dirty, snow-topped train arrived. Before I noticed it, the policemen, who had been gathered together in a black mass, separated into two groups. They stood at the two entrances of the car that I was planning to board. The white lines had been drawn right there.

The car seemed quite empty, but when I tried to enter I found myself forcibly prevented by a policeman. I then realized that in the center of the car there was a young, gentle-looking officer sitting and facing another young officer who was obviously his attendant. With his characteristic nose, he was immediately recognizable as Prince Takamatsu.

With the strange, deep emotion that one might experience upon recognizing an existence hitherto believed to be fictitious, I gazed at this beautiful young man. My natural urge was to shout and tell everyone out loud, 'The Prince is in there. He's real!' Yet it was not the time, either for myself or for the other passengers, for such an outburst. Unless one managed to get into one of the cars—at the risk of life and limb—one would have to wait additional long hours; how long, no one knew.

I rushed to one of the middle cars immediately. Yet my motion was slowed by the wasteful mental vacuum that the shock of seeing the Prince had created. I stood at the very end of the line of passengers, looking into the center of the car and trying to see whether there was some way I could get in.

After glimpsing the pleasant and elegant atmosphere in the well-cleaned car with blue cushions, I found myself reacting with a particularly strong feeling of disgust to the dirtiness and confusion of this car. Shattered window glass, the door with a rough board nailed to it instead of glass, a crying child, an old woman sitting on her baggage, a chest of drawers wrapped in a large *furoshiki* cloth, an unwrapped broom—a military policeman appeared, shouting that there was still more space left in the middle of the car, but no one responded to his urging.

I gave up trying to get into this car and ran to the last car. There were no passengers standing there. A soldier, possibly a lower-ranking officer, was counting with slight movements of his head the number of the plain soldiers in white clothes who were coming out of the car. An unbearable smell arose from the line of the soldiers who, carrying blankets across their shoulders, had layers of filth on their skin—filth which one could easily have scraped off.

I was looking up at the doorway wondering what this could mean: then my legs began trembling with horror and disgust.

Looking at them carefully, I could see that all of these soldiers were blind; each one stretched a trembling hand forward to touch the back of the soldier ahead. They looked extremely tired and pale; from their blinking eyes tears were falling and their hair had grown long. It was hard to tell how old they were, but I thought they must be between thirty-five and fifty years old. On further examination, I observed that there was one normal person for every five blind men. The normal ones wore military uniforms which, although of the same color as Japanese uniforms, were slightly different from them. They held sticks in their hands.

Judging from the way they scolded the blind soldiers or watched how the line was moving, I guessed they must be caretakers or managers of the blind soldiers.

'*Kuai kuaide! Kuai kuaide!*' [Quickly, quickly] a soldier with a stick shouted, poking the soldier in front of him. I realized then that all the soldiers in this group were Chinese. I understood why, even aside from the feeling evoked by their extreme dirtiness, they looked strange and different.

All the soldiers who were led out of the car were left standing on the platform. There were about five hundred of them. I doubted my own eyes and looked at them again carefully. All of them half-closed their eyes as if it were too bright, and tears were dripping from every eye. It was certain that every one of them was blind.

The supervising soldiers who were not blind saluted suddenly, and a Japanese officer with a saber at his waist appeared from one of the cars.

'What about the others?' he asked, passing by a soldier who was busy counting the number of blind soldiers.

'They will come later, sir, on such and such a train,' the lower officer answered.

'What on earth is this all about?' the sympathetic yet suspicious expressions of the passengers seemed to ask. A middle-aged woman even started crying, holding her hand-towel to her eyes. It was obvious that both the commander and the lower officer wanted to hide the blind soldiers from the passengers, but it took a long time to get the rest off the train, and the number of onlookers gathering behind the fence gradually increased.

At last those at the head of the line began climbing up the stairs of the station, while the train started moving slowly. I was standing on the steps of the car in front of the one which had just been emptied and was holding on with all my might. I could see the policemen who were guarding the soldiers whispering to each other.

'I guess they were used for a poison gas experiment or they are the victims of some sort of explosion,' said a man with an iron helmet on his back, standing four or five persons ahead of me.

'They don't have to carry out poison gas experiments in the motherland,' a man who appeared to be his companion objected. Following up the companion's comment, I asked a woman of about forty who was standing next to me,

'When did those soldiers get on the train?'

'Let's see, I think at around Shinonoi.'

'Then they must have come from around the Nagoya area,' I said to myself, although it did not give me a clue to understand anything.

Soon the passengers forgot about it and began to converse.

'I came from Echigo. I am on my way to Chiba with my daughter.' The woman whom I had just come to know started talking in a friendly manner. She told me that she was bringing her daughter to report for duty in the women's volunteer army and that her departure had been delayed for a week because her daughter had had an ugly growth on her neck. Since they could not get through tickets to Chiba, they would go as far as they could, then stay in the place they had reached, standing in line until they could buy tickets to continue their journey. They had come this far, she said, but the hardships they had been through were beyond description.

I had been offended a moment ago by the unconcerned way in which this woman had answered my question about the Chinese soldiers, but I now thought I could understand it. The Japanese were too involved in their own affairs to be moved by such an incident.

When the train left a station some time later, I went into the car which had been occupied by the Chinese soldiers, hoping to sit down and rest. I returned soon, however, because the smell there was intolerable.

The conductor came from the end of the train, announcing

'Jimbobara next, Jimbobara next,' as he passed among the passengers. By that time, the windows on the west side were burning with the rays of the setting sun, and the huge red sun was setting with the sanctity of the apocalypse. I realized that the car occupied by the Chinese had been taken away and that my car had become the last of the train.

Yes, there was the Prince, still in the car ahead of us, I remembered. But I was too tired to tell anyone.

After the war was over, I asked the merchants who had their shops in front of the Takasaki station whether they had seen the group of Chinese soldiers boarding the train again. They all said they had never seen them again. Perhaps they never returned from that place.

IN THE FOREST, UNDER CHERRIES
IN FULL BLOOM

Translated by Jay Rubin

≈

Nowadays, when the cherries bloom, people think it's time for a party. They go under the trees and eat and drink and mouth the old sayings about spring and pretty blossoms, but it's all one big lie. I mean, it wasn't until Edo, maybe a couple of hundred years ago, that people started crowding under the cherry blossoms to drink and puke and fight. In the old days—the *really* old days—nobody gave a damn about the view. They were *scared* to go under the blossoms. People today think they can have a wild time under the trees, but take the people out of the picture and it's just plain scary. Look at the old Noh play, the one about the mother who goes crazy trying to find her little boy who was kidnapped. She thinks she can see his ghost there, in the shade of the blossoms that stretch off into the distance. She dies crazy, buried in petals (all right, I made that part up). Without people, a forest of cherries in full bloom is not pretty, just something to be afraid of.

When they crossed Suzuka Pass in the old days, travelers had to take the road that ran through a forest of cherry trees. They were all right when the trees were not in bloom, but under the blossoms they'd lose their minds. They'd race for green trees or dead trees, trying to get out from under the blossoms as fast as they could. When a traveler was alone, all he had to do was run out of there to find relief under ordinary trees, but it was harder for those traveling in pairs. No two people run at the same speed, so one would always fall behind. He'd scream for the other to wait, but the first one, crazed with fear, would leave his friend behind. Passing beneath the flowering forest of Suzuka Pass marked the end of many a friendship: the one who had fallen behind would never trust the other again. And so, to avoid passing beneath the blossoms, travelers quite naturally began to take a less direct route through the mountains, until the cherry forest was left in stillness.

Years went by, and then a robber—a cruel mountain bandit— took to living in the hills. He'd swoop down on the highway, strip the clothes from travelers, and sometimes, if he had to, take their lives. But even he went crazy with fear when he stepped into the blossoming cherry forest. He hated cherry blossoms after that. They scared him. Underneath the blossoms, the wind wouldn't blow, but he still seemed to hear it howling. No, there was no wind, no sound of anything, just himself and his footsteps, wrapped in a cold, silent wind that never moved. He'd feel the life inside him scattering like so many soft, silent cherry blossoms, and he'd want to run out of there, screaming, with his eyes shut tight. Of course, if he actually shut his eyes he'd just crash into a tree, so he couldn't do that, which drove him even crazier.

He was an easygoing fellow, though, the kind that never regrets anything, so he just felt sort of strange that this would happen to him. Oh, well, I'll think about it next year, he told himself. He didn't feel like it this year. Next year, when the trees bloomed again, he'd really think about it. He had been telling himself the same thing every year now for over ten years: I'll think about it next year. And another year would pass.

As he went on making excuses for himself, the number of his wives grew from one to seven. The eighth he got from the highway as he had all the rest: by stripping her husband of his wife and his clothes. Then he killed the husband.

From the moment he killed the husband, the bandit felt there was something weird going on. This time wasn't like the others: something was strange, though he couldn't tell what. But he was not one to dwell on things.

He hadn't planned to kill the man at first. He thought he'd strip him like the others and send him off with a good kick, but the woman was too beautiful. He had to kill her man. This took him by surprise—and he could see it had taken her by surprise as well. He turned around to find her on the ground. Her legs had buckled, and she was staring at him with out-of-focus eyes. 'You're my wife now,' he said to her, and she nodded. He took her hand and tried to pull her up. 'I can't walk. Carry me on your back,' she said. 'Sure, sure,' he said, and swung her up. He started walking, but when he came to a steep rise he told her to get down. She would have to walk—it was too dangerous here.

'No, no,' she said, and clung to his back. 'If this trail is hard for a mountain man like you, how am I supposed to walk it? Just think about that.'

'All right, never mind,' he said with a chuckle, exhausted though he was. 'But anyhow, get down for a minute. It's not that I need a rest or anything—I'm too strong for that. But I don't have eyes in the back of my head. I can't see your pretty face. So get down for a minute and let me take a look.'

'No! No!' she cried, tightening her grip on his neck. 'Not here! This place is too deserted, I hate it! Hurry and take me to your house as fast as you can. Otherwise, I won't be your wife. I'll bite off my tongue and die!'

'Never mind, never mind,' he said. 'I'll do whatever you want.'

Melting with happiness, the bandit dreamed of the life that he would share with this beautiful wife of his. He squared his shoulders and turned slowly to show the woman the mountains all around them: front, back, right, left.

'See these mountains? Every single one of them belongs to me,' he said, but she paid him no heed. Disappointed, he said, 'Do you hear what I'm telling you? Every mountain you see here, every tree, every valley, every cloud rising out of every valley—they all belong to me.'

'Will you *please* hurry up?' she said. 'I don't want to stay here a minute longer. Look at all the rocks on the cliff up there.'

'Never mind, never mind,' he said. 'We'll be getting to my house soon, and I'll make you the best meal you've ever tasted.'

'Can't you go faster? I want you to run!'

'It's too steep. I can't run here, even when I'm alone.'

'So you're a weakling, eh? I wouldn't have guessed it to look at you. I can't believe I've let myself become the wife of such a helpless man! Oh, no, what's to become of me?'

'What are you talking about? A little hill like this...'

'Then hurry up, will you? Don't tell me you're tired already?'

'Just watch. When I get past this stretch, I'll run faster than a deer.'

'But you're breathing so hard. And I think your face is pale.'

'Things are always like that at first. Just wait. When I really get going, I'll run so fast it'll make your head spin.'

But in fact the bandit was so tired he felt he was coming apart at the joints. By the time he reached his house his eyes were swimming, his ears were ringing, and he didn't have the strength to groan. His seven wives came out to greet him, but he had all he could do to work the kinks out of his body and lower the woman to the ground.

The seven wives were stunned at the sight of the most beautiful woman they had ever seen, and she in turn was stunned at the sight of the seven wives' filthiness. Some had been beauties long before, but there was no way to tell that now. Sickened at the sight of them, the woman cringed behind the man.

'What are these mountain women?' she demanded.

'They used to be my wives,' he said, which wasn't bad for an answer made up on the spot. 'Used to be.' But the woman was relentless.

'So *these* are your wives?' she pressed him.

'Well, I mean, you know, that's because I never saw anyone as pretty as you before.'

'Kill that one!' she screamed, pointing at the woman with the best features.

'Oh, come on, I really don't have to kill her. Just think of her as your maid.'

'You killed my husband, didn't you? And now you tell me you can't kill your own wife? What makes you think I'd become the wife of a man like that?'

A moan slipped through the man's tight lips. He leaped at the wife in a single bound and cut her down where she stood. But he had no time to catch his breath.

'Now this one!' screamed the woman. 'Kill this one next!'

The man hung back for a moment, then he strode up to the next wife and sunk his sword into her throat. The head was still rolling on the ground when the woman's clear, lovely voice named her next victim.

'Now this one!' she cried.

The next wife hid her face in her hands and screamed aloud, but the sword shot up in the direction of the scream, then came flashing down. The remaining wives leaped to their feet and scattered in all directions.

'Get them all!' cried the woman. 'Look! There's one in the bushes! And there goes another one behind you!'

The man raised his bloody sword and raced through the woods in mad pursuit. One of the wives was sprawled on the ground, unable to flee. She was the ugliest of them all, and a cripple to boot. After the man had cut down the other wives, he came back to finish her off, but when he raised his sword again, the woman commanded him: 'Don't kill that one. She can be my maid.'

'I might as well kill her while I'm at it.'

'Don't be stupid! I'm telling you not to kill her.'

'Oh, yeah, I guess you're right.'

He threw his sword away and plopped down on the spot. Fatigue welled up within him. His eyes swam, and he felt heavy, as if rooted to the earth. Then he heard the silence and felt a sudden rush of fear. He turned in horror to find the woman standing behind him, looking lost. The man felt as if he had just wakened from a nightmare. The woman's beauty swallowed him: his eyes, his soul ceased to move. But he felt uneasy. He did not know how or why this wave of uneasiness was coursing through his chest, but he could almost ignore it because her beauty had sucked the soul right out of him.

I know this feeling, he thought. Something like this has happened to me before. He thought again, and then it hit him.

In the forest, under cherries in full bloom. It's like that. How was it like that? He didn't know. But it *was* like that, he was sure. This was as much as he ever understood anything. He was the kind of man who didn't mind if he only got the first part.

The long mountain winter had ended, and patches of snow remained on the peaks and in the shade of trees in the valleys, but the time of blossoms was approaching, and signs of spring glittered all across the sky.

This year when the cherries bloom, I'll do it, he thought. It wasn't so bad when he first went under the blossoms. He would push on and walk beneath them. But, a step at a time, his head would get crazier. Ahead, behind, to the right, to the left, he would see only cherry blossoms bearing down upon him until, as he neared the middle of the forest, a blind fear would overtake him. I'll do it this year, he told himself. I'll stand—no, I'll *sit* in the middle of the forest when the cherries are in full bloom. And then it came to him: I'll take *her* with me this time. He glanced at the woman, felt a flutter in his chest, and averted his gaze.

The charred shred of an idea stayed within him: She mustn't find out what I am thinking.

She was impossible to please. He would prepare her meals with all the care he knew how to give, but still she would complain about the food. He ran through the hills, hunting birds and deer for her, hunting wild boar and bear for her. The crippled woman wandered all day through the forest, searching for tender buds and roots for her, but never once did she give any sign of satisfaction.

'You mean I'm supposed to eat this stuff every day?'

'Hey, we're giving you special treats,' said the man. 'Until you got here, we ate these things maybe once in ten days.'

'Well, you're a mountain man. This may be good enough for you, but it sticks in my throat. There's nothing up here in the mountains. All night long, the only thing I hear is owls hooting. The least you can do is give me food as good as what I'm used to in the capital, don't you think? A man like you can't imagine what it's like to breathe the air of the capital. You can't know how terrible it is for me to be shut off from the air of the capital. You've taken it away from me, and in its place you give me only the cawing of crows and the hooting of owls. And you're not even ashamed of yourself! You don't see how cruel you are!'

The man did not know what to make of the woman's spiteful words. He had no idea what she meant by 'the air of the capital'. What could possibly be missing from this happy life in the mountains? He was at a loss to deal with the misery of the woman as she poured out her resentment. He knew of nothing that could guide him in such a task, and so his frustration mounted.

He had killed more travelers from the capital than he could remember. They all had money, and they all carried fancy things. They were easy marks, but sometimes he would open a bag and be disappointed with its contents. Then he would curse his victim: 'So you're from the capital, huh? Farmers have better stuff than this!' For him, the capital was just a place with people who carried fancy things—things he could rob from them. It never crossed his mind to think about where this 'capital' might be.

The woman took great care of her combs, her ornamental hairpins, her rouge. And she would scream at him if he so much as touched her kimono with his hands caked in mud or dripping with the blood of animals. Her kimonos were her life, it seemed, and protecting them her mission. The space around her had to be spotless, and the house kept in order. Nor could she be satisfied, like the others, with a simple robe and narrow sash. She wanted lots of kimonos and many sashes—sashes she could tie in strangely shaped knots, with the ends dangling down for no good reason She would add one pretty thing after another until they all came together as one perfect outfit. The man would stare at her, wide-eyed, and then let out a sigh. Now he saw it: this was how a thing of beauty took shape. And that beauty made him full. Of that there could be no doubt. Meaningless bits and pieces came together to form a whole, but if you took the thing apart again, it would just go back to being meaningless bits and pieces. In his own way, he understood this as a kind of wonderful magic.

The woman ordered him to bring wood from the hills and set him to making things. He himself had no idea what he was making or what it was good for. One of the things she called a 'kosho', which turned out to be a kind of chair. On nice days she would have him take it outside for her and sit in the sun or under a tree with her eyes closed. The other thing she had him make was an armrest. Reclining on the floor indoors, she would lean against it and lose herself in thought. All of this seemed so exotic to him, so enchanting and seductive. It was real magic, and though he himself was helping to make it work, it still brought forth cries of surprise and admiration.

Every morning, the crippled woman would comb the woman's long black hair. The water she used was hauled by the man from a far-off spring that fed the river in the valley. He himself was moved to see the special effort that he was willing to expend for her. What he wanted most of all was to be part of the magic—to be allowed to touch that hair as the comb passed through it. 'No! Not with those hands!' the woman snapped, sweeping him away. The man drew his hands back like a child, ashamed, and watched what was left of his shattered dream. The hair reached its full glossiness, the crippled woman tied it back to expose the face beneath, and a thing of beauty came into being.

'I never thought these could be so...' the man murmured as he toyed with the elaborate hairpins that lay nearby. Such things had never seemed to have any meaning or value to him before, and even

---

now he had no idea what to say about decoration—the harmony and connection between things. Magic, though, was something that he did understand. Magic was what gave things life. Everything had its own life.

'Stop playing with those!' the woman cried. 'Why do you have to do that every morning?'

'It's so strange...'

'What is so strange?'

'Oh, I don't know...' the man mumbled, at a loss.

He had found something truly amazing, but he did not know what it was.

And so the man conceived a fear for the capital. This fear was not an actual terror, but more like the embarrassment and nervousness felt by a know-it-all toward something he doesn't understand. Every time the woman spoke of 'the capital', his heart felt a shudder, but because he had never known a sense of fear toward anything he could see in this world, he was not familiar with that feeling, nor was he accustomed to shame. Toward the capital he felt only the hatred he might hold for an enemy.

He had swooped down on thousands of travelers from the capital, but not one had been able to fight him off, he thought with satisfaction. Nothing in the past gave him any reason to fear being betrayed or wounded, a thought that always made him feel pleased and proud. He measured his own strength against the woman's beauty. A wild boar was the one thing strong enough to give him a little trouble, but even the boar was not an enemy to fear. He did not have to be afraid of anything.

'Are there people in the capital with fangs?'

'There are samurai with bows and arrows.'

He laughed. 'With my bow, I could bring down a little sparrow all the way across the valley. I'm sure there's no one in the capital with skin so hard it would break my sword.'

'There are samurai with armor.'

'Would a sword break against armor?'

'It would.'

'I can wrestle down a bear or a boar.'

'If you're really so strong, take me to the capital. Use your strength to surround me with anything I want. Dress me in the best the capital has to offer. If you can make me feel that kind of deep-down pleasure, then you really are a strong man.'

'That's easy.'

The man set his heart on going to the capital. Before three days and nights had passed, he would surround the woman with piles of combs and ornamental hairpins and kimonos and mirrors and rouge. Of this he had no doubt. The one thing that did concern him, though, was something that had nothing to do with the capital.

And that was the cherry forest.

In another two or three days, the cherry forest would be in full bloom. This was the year, he had decided. He would prove that he could sit still in the middle of the cherry forest at the height of the blossoms. Each day he would slip off to the forest to check on the progress of the buds. 'In three days,' he told the woman when she pressed him to take her to the capital.

'Don't tell me you have preparations to make,' she said with a frown. 'Don't tease me. The capital is calling out to me.'

'But still, I have a promise to keep.'

'*You* have to keep a promise? *Here*? Who is here, in these mountains, for you to make a promise to?'

'Nobody is here. But still, I have a promise I must keep.'

'How very unusual! There's no one here, but still you have a promise to keep. To whom?'

The man could not lie to her.

'The cherries are going to bloom.'

'So you made a promise to see the cherry blossoms?'

'I have to see the cherry blossoms before I leave.'

'And why is that?'

'Because I have to see about going under the blossoms.'

'That's what I am asking you about. *Why* do you have to see about going under the blossoms?'

'Because the cherries are going to bloom.'

'*Why* because the cherries are going to bloom?'

'Because a cold wind fills the place under the blossoms.'

'The place under the blossoms?'

'The place without end. Under the blossoms.'

'The place without end under the blossoms?'

The man got confused and upset.

'Take me with you under the blossoms.'

'I can't do that,' the man insisted. 'I have to be alone.'

The woman gave him a bitter smile.

The man had never seen a bitter smile before, a smile so malicious. He did not think of it as 'malicious', though. He thought of it as something he could never cut through with his sword. He knew this because the woman's smile engraved itself on his brain. Each time he thought of it, it stabbed his mind like a sword blade, and there was no way he could stab it back.

The third day came.

He left without telling the woman. The cherry forest was in full bloom. With his first step into the forest, he thought of the woman's bitter smile. It sliced into his brain with a whole new sharpness. Now he was confused. The cold beneath the blossoms pressed in upon him from the four endless directions. The wind tore through him, turning his flesh transparent, roaring in from all four directions at once, filling the entire space beneath the blossoms. His voice began to howl, and he ran. What utter emptiness! He cried, he prayed, he writhed in agony, he wanted only to get away from this place. The moment he knew he had escaped from beneath the blossoms, he felt as if he were waking from a dream. The only difference was the pain he felt with each labored breath.

The man, the woman, and the crippled maid began to live in the capital.

Each night the man would creep into a mansion under orders from the woman, taking clothes and jewels and trinkets, but these were not enough to satisfy her. What she wanted most of all were the heads of the people who lived in the mansion.

In their own house were heads from dozens of mansions. The heads were lined up in their own special place, surrounded by screens on all four sides. Some heads hung on cords. There were too many of them now for the man to keep track of, but the woman knew them all, even those whose hair had fallen out and whose flesh had rotted, leaving only a skull. She would fly into a rage if the man or her maid dared to move them. The such-and-such family belonged *here*, and the so-and-so family belonged *there*.

The woman played with the heads every day. One head would go out for a stroll with his retinue of retainers. One head family would go to visit another head family. Some heads would fall in love. A woman head would spurn a man head, or a man head would forsake a woman head and make her cry.

Once a young princess was deceived by a councillor of state. On a dark, moonless night, the councillor head crept into the home of the princess head disguised as her lover. Only after he had managed to sleep with her did the princess head realize what had happened. She could not bring herself to hate the councillor head, though. Instead, shedding tears for her own sad fate, she became a nun. Then the councillor head went to the convent and raped the nun head. She wanted to die, but the councillor persuaded her to run away with him to the village of Yamashina, where the councillor head kept her in hiding for himself and she let her hair grow again.

Both the princess head and the councillor head had long since lost their hair. Their flesh was rotten and crawling with maggots, the bone showing through in places. The two heads would drink through the night and indulge in love play, biting each other, teeth clattering against bone, gobs of rotten flesh squashing and sticking, noses collapsing, eyeballs dropping out.

The woman loved it when the faces would stick together and then fall apart. The sight would send her into peals of uncontrollable laughter.

'Eat that cheek, now. Yum yum! Now let's eat her throat. Oh, what a delicious eyeball! Chew chew chew chew chew. Suck suck suck suck suck. Mmmmm, yummy yummy yummy. Oh! Marvelous! Now take a gooood bite!'

The woman's laughter rang out, clear and lovely, as fresh and clean as the ringing of the most delicate porcelain.

One of her heads was that of a shaven-headed priest. On this head she lavished special hatred. She always gave it terrible roles to play. The priest head had to be hated by the others, to be tortured to death or executed by an official. Its hair actually grew out at first, but eventually, like the others, it lost its hair, the flesh rotted off, and before long the head had been reduced to bone. Once that happened, the woman ordered the man to bring her another one. The new priest head he brought retained a trace of boyish beauty. Thrilled, the woman set it on her table, fed it sake, pressed her cheek to its cheek, and licked and tickled it all over. She quickly tired of this.

'I want a big fat one,' she said. 'Make it really disgusting.'

To get the task over with quickly, the man brought back five priest heads at once. There was the head of a doddering old priest, another with thick eyebrows, heavy jowls, and a nose like a toad stuck to its face, one with a horse's face and pointed ears, and one that oozed piety. But the one that the woman liked most of all was a huge priest in his fifties, a truly ugly man with eyes that drooped at the corners, flabby cheeks, and thick, heavy lips that sagged open. She would press her fingertips against the corners of his drooping eyelids and move the skin up in circles, shove sticks up the nostrils of his snub nose, turn the head upside-down and roll it around, clasp it to her breast and force a nipple between its thick lips, laughing all the while she 'suckled' it. But of this head she quickly tired as well.

Then there was the head of a lovely young girl—a pure, gentle, aristocratic head, still childish but with a strangely grown-up sadness in death. Behind her closed eyelids there seemed to lie hidden a jumble of pleasures, sorrows, and knowledge beyond her years. The woman treated this head with all the tenderness she might lavish on a daughter or a niece, endlessly combing out the long black tresses and applying make-up with the utmost care, until a soft, sweet face emerged, bathed in floral fragrances.

For the young girl head, the woman needed the head of a young nobleman. This she also made up with great care. Then the two became lost in mad, passionate, burning love play full of resentful posturing, anger, hatred, lying, deception, and sorrow. But when their passion flared up, the fire from one caught the other and the two became a roaring inferno. Soon, though, some of the filthiest heads—an evil samurai, a lustful older man, and a dissolute priest—came between them. The young nobleman was kicked and beaten and finally killed. Then, from all sides, the filthy heads went after the young girl head, which soon was smeared in patches of the others' rotting flesh. Their fang-like teeth bit into her, tearing off her nose, ripping out her hair. Once this happened, the woman punched holes in the girl head with a needle, cut it with a knife, and gouged out chunks of flesh until it was more filthy and disgusting than all the rest. Then she flung it away.

The man hated the capital. Once it had lost its strangeness for him, all that remained was a feeling that he could never be at home there. He wore the same flowing robes as everyone else in the capital, but his were short, exposing his hairy shanks. He couldn't carry a sword in daylight hours. He had to go out shopping for what he needed. He actually had to pay for drinks at the sake sellers where the whores gathered. The city merchants ridiculed him. The women who came in from the country to sell their piles of vegetables made fun of him, and so did the children. Even the whores laughed at him.

In the capital the nobles rode in ox-carts down the middle of the avenues surrounded by barefoot retainers swaggering in robes and red-faced with the master's sake. The man would be cursed wherever he went—in the market, on the road, in the temple gardens of the city. 'Idiot,' they would call him. 'Dim-wit.' 'Moron.' But none of this bothered him anymore.

The man suffered from boredom more than anything else. People were boring: there was no way around it. They annoyed him in every way. They were just little dogs yapping at the heels of the big dog walking down the street. He could not be bothered to feel anything about them, not resentment or envy or anger. Nothing in the mountains had annoyed him in this way, not the animals, the birds, the trees, the rivers.

'It's so boring here in the capital,' he said to the crippled woman. 'Don't you want to go back to the mountains?'

'The capital's not boring to *me*,' she said. The crippled woman spent each day cooking and doing laundry and gabbing with the neighbors. 'I've got people to talk to here. I'm not bored. The mountains are where it's boring. I don't ever want to go back there.'

'You don't think it's boring talking to people?'

'Of course not. You can't get bored if you're talking all the time.'

'That's funny. The more I talk to people, the more bored I get.'

'You're bored because you *don't* talk to people.'

'You're crazy. I get bored talking to people, so I don't talk.'

'You ought to give it a try. Talk to people. You won't be bored anymore.'

'Talk about what?'

'Anything you want.'

'I don't want to talk about anything.'

Now he was getting annoyed. He gave a big yawn.

The capital had mountains, too. But every mountain had some kind of temple or hermitage on top, and instead of being quiet they were full of people. From up on the mountain, you could see the whole capital. What a lot of houses! he thought. And what a filthy view!

During the day he practically forgot that he spent his nights killing. Now even that was boring. You swung your sword and a head fell off: that was all. And the heads were soft, squishy things.

You couldn't feel the bone. It was like slicing through a radish. Though it always surprised him how heavy they were.

He felt he was beginning to understand the woman. A monk was ringing a temple bell like crazy. It was so damned stupid. You never knew what people were going to do next. If he had to live with them all the time, he'd probably want to do what the woman did and live with them as heads.

But the woman's desire was endless, and so now he was bored with that, too. Her desire was like a bird flying straight across the sky with no end in sight: flying on and on without a rest, never tiring, slicing cleanly through the wind.

The man himself was but an ordinary bird—perhaps an owl that hopped from branch to branch, stopping to doze now and then, maybe crossing a valley if it had to. Physically, he was quick and athletic. He moved well, he walked well, with great vitality. But his heart was a lumbering bird. Flying in an infinite straight line was out of the question for him.

From the mountain-top he watched the sky of the capital. A single bird was flying in a straight line across the sky, this sky that changed from day to night, from night to day, in an endless cycle of light and darkness. At the edges of the sky was nothing, just the infinite repetition of light and darkness, but infinitude was something the man found impossible to comprehend. When he thought about the next day and the next day and the next, and the infinite repetition of light and darkness, it felt as if his head would split in two—not from the effort but the pain of thinking.

At home, he found the woman immersed in playing with her heads. As soon as she saw him come in, she gave the command she had prepared for him: 'Bring me a dancer's head tonight. The head of a beautiful dancer. I want to have her dance for me. I myself will sing the accompaniment.'

The man tried to recall the infinite repetition of light and darkness that he had witnessed from the mountain-top. He then might have seen this room as that sky, with its infinite, endless repetition of light and darkness, but he could no longer bring the sky to mind. And the woman was not a bird. She was just the beautiful woman who was always here. But he answered her: 'I won't do it.'

This came to her as a shock, but once it had sunk in, she laughed.

'So now you've lost your nerve! You're a weakling, like all the others.'

'I am not a weakling.'

'Then what are you?'

'I'm just sick of it. There's no end to it.'

'So what? There's no end to anything. You eat your meals every day. There's no end to that, is there? You sleep every day. There's no end to that, is there?'

'But this is different.'

'Different? How different?'

The man did not know how to answer her, but he knew it was different. To escape the pain of having her out-talk him, he went outside.

'Bring me the head of a dancer,' the woman's voice came after him, but he made no reply.

He tried to think about how it was different, but he could find no answer. Little by little, the day turned into night. He climbed the mountain once again, but the sky could no longer be seen.

When his head cleared, he found himself thinking that the sky would fall. The sky would fall. He felt terrible pain, as if someone were choking him. That was it: he would kill the woman.

By killing her, he could stop the endless repetition of light and darkness. And the sky would fall. Then he could breathe easy. But there would be a hole in his heart. The image of the bird would have flown from his breast and disappeared.

Is she me? he wondered. Was I the bird that flew straight across the sky without end? If I kill her, will I be killing myself? What am I thinking?

Why did he have to bring the sky down? He no longer understood the answer to that, either. All thoughts were hard to grasp. And after thoughts went away, the only thing left behind was pain. Dawn broke. He had lost the courage to go back to the house where the woman was. Instead, he wandered through the mountains for several days.

One morning he woke up to find that he had been sleeping beneath cherry blossoms. The tree stood alone. It was in full bloom. He leaped up with a start—but not to flee. It was only one cherry tree, after all. No, he had leaped up with the thought of the cherry forest on Suzuka Mountain. It must also be in full bloom. He sank into a deep, nostalgic reverie.

Back to the mountains. He would go back to the mountains.

How could he have forgotten such a simple thing? How could he have thought so long and hard about bringing the sky down? His nightmare had ended. He was saved. He had lost the feel of early spring in the mountains, but now its fragrance pressed in upon him, and he had it again, strong and cold.

The man went back to his house in the capital.

The woman seemed overjoyed to see him.

'Where *were* you?' she pleaded. 'I'm sorry I tormented you with such impossible demands. But please try to realize how lonely I've been without you!'

The woman had never spoken to him so tenderly before. Her words stabbed him in the chest, and his resolve was on the verge of melting away. But he had made up his mind.

'I'm going back to the mountains.'

'Without *me*?' she said. 'How could such a cruel thought have taken root inside you?'

Her eyes burned with anger. Her face showed the sharp pain of betrayal.

'When did you turn into such a hard-hearted man?'

'That's what I mean. I hate it here in the capital.'

'Even with *me* here?'

'I just don't want to live here anymore.'

'But *I'm* here, aren't I? Don't you love me any more? While you were gone, all I could think of was you.'

For the first time since he had known her, the woman's eyes filled with tears. The anger had vanished from her face, leaving only her pain at his coldness.

'I thought you could only live in the capital,' he said. 'And I can only live in the mountains.'

'I can only go on living if I have you. Don't you know how I feel?'

'But I can only live in the mountains.'

'I'll go with you, then, if you're going back to the mountains. I can't live a day without you.' She pressed her face to his chest, and he could feel the heat of the tears pouring from her eyes. It was true, then—she couldn't live without him anymore. New heads were her life, and he was the only one who could supply her with them. He was a part of her. She could not let him go. But she was also sure she could lure him back to the capital once he had satisfied his longing for the hills.

202

'Can you live in the mountains?' he asked.

'I can live anywhere if I have you.'

'You can't get the kind of heads you want in the mountains.'

'If I have to choose between you and the heads, I'll forget about the heads.'

The man wondered if he was dreaming. He was too happy. He couldn't believe it. Not even in a dream would he have been able to imagine something like this.

His breast was filled with new hope. Its arrival had been sudden and violent, and the painful thoughts that had been with him only moments before were now somewhere far away, out of reach. He forgot about his yesterdays with the woman, when she had never been so tender. He saw only now and tomorrow.

The two prepared to leave immediately. The crippled maid would remain in the capital. 'Wait here,' the woman whispered to her as they were leaving. 'We'll be back soon enough.'

Now his old mountains opened up before him. They looked as if they would answer if he called out to them. He took the old road. No one ever went that way anymore, and without people to tramp it down, all visible sign of the road had disappeared, leaving only woods and hills. This route would take them through the cherry forest.

'Carry me on your back,' said the woman. 'I can't climb these hills without a road.'

'I don't mind,' said the man.

He swung her up to his back without effort.

He thought about the day he first took the woman. That day, too, he had carried her on his back and climbed up the other side where the road crossed the pass. That day, too, he had been full of happiness, a feeling that today was all the richer.

The woman said, 'The day I met you, I asked you to carry me.'

'I was just thinking the same thing,' said the man with joy in his voice. 'Look,' he said. 'All those mountains are mine. The valleys, the trees, the birds, even the clouds—these mountains are mine. They're so good, I feel like running, don't you? This never happened in the capital.'

'That first day, I made you run with me on your back, remember?'

'Sure I do. I got so tired, I almost fainted.'

The man was not forgetting about the cherry forest in full bloom. But on such a happy day as this, what difference could it make that they would pass beneath it? He was not afraid.

And then the cherry forest appeared before his eyes, a mass of blossoms at their height. Here and there a petal fluttered down in the breeze. A layer of petals covered the earth beneath his feet. But where could they have come from? For, spread out above him, as far as he could see, were clouds of fully opened blossoms, from which it was impossible to imagine that a single petal had been lost.

The man stepped beneath the blossoms. It was utterly still in there, and seemed to be growing colder. Then he noticed that the woman's hands were freezing cold. Now he was afraid, and with the fear came certainty: she was a demon. Suddenly a cold wind began to blow from all four sides of the space beneath the blossoms.

The man saw that clinging to his back was a huge-faced old woman with purple skin. Her mouth gaped open from ear to ear, and her hair was a frizzled mass of green. The man began to run. He tried to knock the demon from his back, but the strength of her grip increased. Her hands dug into his neck; his eyes were growing dim. He was wild now. He pulled the demon's hands apart with all the strength he had, and as his neck slipped out of her grasp, he felt her slide down his back and tumble to the ground. Now it was his turn to attack. He locked his hands on the demon's throat until he realized that he was using all his strength to strangle a young woman, and that she was no longer breathing.

His eyes had clouded over. He tried to open them wider, but that didn't seem to bring his vision back. For all that lay before him, dead, was the woman, the same woman, whom he had strangled with his own hands.

His breathing stopped. At an end, too, were his strength and his thinking. On the woman's body, a few cherry petals had already fallen. He shook her. He cried out to her. He clutched her to him. But all in vain. He threw himself down in tears. Not once in all the years since he had come to live in the mountains had he cried until this day. By the time he was himself again, white cherry petals had begun to pile up on his back.

He was in the very center of the cherry forest. The four edges of the forest were hidden from him by blossoms. Yet his fear had vanished. Gone, too, was the wind that always blew from the edges of the forest in full bloom. Now there was only the hush of blossoms, falling, falling. Here he sat, for the first time, beneath the cherry forest in full bloom. He could go on sitting here forever. Because now he had no place to call home.

Even now, no one knows the secret of the cherry forest in full bloom. Perhaps it was loneliness. For the man no longer had to fear loneliness. He was loneliness itself.

Now, for the first time, he looked all around. Above him were the blossoms. Beneath them was the silent, infinite emptiness, the stillness of the rain of blossoms. That was all. Beyond that, there was no secret.

Some time went by before he felt something inside himself, faintly warm. And this, he found, was his sadness. Little by little, he began to sense the swelling warmth, wrapped as it was in the coldness of the blossoms and the emptiness.

He reached out to pluck the petals from the woman's cheek. But just as his hand reached her face, something strange happened. Beneath his hand lay only drifted petals. The woman had vanished, leaving petals in her place. And as he reached out to part the mound of petals, his hand, his arm, his body vanished. The space filled with petals and with frigid emptiness, nothing more.

INOUE YASUSHI (1907–1992)

PASSAGE TO FUDARAKU

Translated by James T. Araki

~

Not until the spring of 1565, the year in which he must himself put out to sea, did Konko, Abbot of the Fudaraku-ji, meditate earnestly on the Buddhists who had set sail for the island of Fudaraku. True, he had occasionally thought of his predecessors whose sailings he had witnessed, but his musings now were pervaded with an unusual sense of urgency.

Konko had in fact never before given serious thought to the possibility of his embarking on such a voyage. His immediate predecessor as abbot had left these shores of Hama-no-miya in 1560, when he was sixty-one-years old, and the two abbots before him had done so when they were sixty-one, in November of 1545 and November of 1541. Although the three had set sail from Hama-no-miya on the south Kumano coast in November of their sixty-first year, with the Pure Land known as Fudaraku as their destination, there was no rule requiring the abbot of the monastery to do so.

The Fudaraku-ji, as its name suggests, was the fountainhead of the worship of Fudaraku. The monastery had long been known as a counterpart of Fudaraku Island—a realm in the southern region, the Pure Land of the deity of mercy, Kannon—and it had become a custom for devout worshippers to set sail from the Kumano coast for the mythical isle in the hope of being received by Kannon incarnate, in whose Pure Land they would be reborn. Hama-no-miya in time became the customary site for departure, and the Fudaraku-ji the monastery responsible for overseeing the ritual sailing. Persons bound for the mythical isle customarily took lodging at this monastery because of its deep-rooted associations with the belief in Fudaraku. Moreover, several former abbots of the monastery were included among the nine revered as sages for having sailed to Fudaraku—the youngest, according to records kept at the monastery, at the age of eighteen, and the eldest at the age of eighty.

Because the three who had preceded Konko as abbot had put out to sea when they were sixty-one, people came to assume that every abbot of the Fudaraku-ji would embark upon a like voyage in November of his sixty-first year. The tradition associated with the monastery served rather naturally to reinforce the assumption, and Konko, now sixty-one, would have to submit to the dictates of popular expectation. That he had not fully understood the necessity was doubtless due to his innocence of worldly affairs, for he had known only the clergy since his youth.

Konko had at times reflected on the meaning of his role as abbot of the Fudaraku-ji, on the possibility of his presently feeling compelled to attempt the voyage; he regarded the prospect not wholly without anticipation. He was aware of a vague, self-imposed obligation. Dedicated to serving the Buddha, he regarded the eventual voyage with some fascination, yearning perhaps. He still recalled very vividly the dignity of Shokei at the time of his departure, and had long wished he might some day emulate this monk, who had been his teacher. Shokei had attained enlightenment when he was sixty-one, but Konko, aware of his own inadequacies, had never believed he could go so far without devoting himself to spiritual austerities over a long period of time—surely many more years than had been required of his teacher. He had been immersed in the traditions of the Fudaraku-ji for the better part of his life, and he longed desperately for a spiritual insight that would inspire him to embark upon the voyage.

The year 1565 was to be an unexpectedly baneful one for Konko. No sooner did the new year dawn than visitors began to ask him 'When in November do you mean to sail?' or, solicitously, 'Now that the long-awaited year has come, won't you tell me how I might be of assistance?'—questions they earlier would have considered indelicate. Now, however, all visitors seemed to feel obliged to touch on this matter—as if not to do so would be a discourtesy—and well-meant concern was reflected on their faces and in their voices as well.

No one would have addressed the abbot with malice. Since his youth Konko had disciplined himself severely. He had not achieved any great distinction, but he had an unassuming, pleasing manner. And in due course, after he was past his middle age, he came to be accorded a remarkable degree of trust and respect by the faithful. Over the past few years he had not once failed to notice the suggestion of reverence and affection in the eyes of whomever he chanced to meet—villager, Buddhist parishioner, even the ascetic Shinto priests of Nachi Falls. There was no questioning the respect and fondness he now inspired in everyone who knew him.

Konko was disconcerted by the growing expectations. He hoped to dispel them at an early opportunity: he would have it understood that his sailing would not take place until some future year when he was spiritually prepared for it, and that a voyage to Fudaraku undertaken without conviction or faith would likely be a failure. By spring, however, he came to despair of making his intentions known. Had there been only a few to convince, he might have prevailed. But he had to contend not with a mere dozen or even one or two hundred people, but the collective expectations of the whole region.

Whenever Konko ventured out from the monastery he would be showered with coins—offerings to His Reverence. Children, too, ran after him and threw coins. Beggars began to follow him through the streets to pick up the offerings for themselves. The monastery began receiving cenotaphs, customarily kept in homes, together with requests that they be taken by Konko and delivered to the Pure Land of Kannon. There were some who went so far as to entrust him with cenotaphs made for themselves.

In these circumstances Konko seemed to have little choice. Had he mentioned his reluctance to set sail or suggested a postponement until some future year, his words would have fallen on unsympathetic ears, and he might have provoked great disquiet and even violence.

The personal disgrace would not have mattered to Konko, but he could not have endured doing injury to the religion of Kannon. Insignificant though he might be, he was a member of the clergy. If by word or action he were to do injury to the faith, he could not possibly expect divine forgiveness even in death.

On the day of the vernal equinox, Konko announced formally that he would put out to sea in November. The announcement was accompanied by ancient rites at the Kumano Shrine. Having been a participant on seven previous occasions, he was best acquainted with the proceedings and gave instructions on the proper order of events, as well as all the details of the floral offerings and ritual music. Whatever he recited from memory was recorded dutifully by his disciple, a seventeen-year-old monk named Seigen.

At the sight of the youth, Konko thought of himself at twenty-seven, seated beside Yushin, then preparing to make his departure, and noting down Yushin's instructions. If Seigen was to remain at the Fudaraku-ji, then he, too, several decades hence must embark for Fudaraku. The young monk with freshly shaven head, Konko thought, was as pitiful as himself.

The date of the first sailing for Fudaraku is not known. The old chronicles which Konko consulted state that the first to embark was Keiryo, who left the Kumano coast on November 3 in the eleventh year of the Jogan Era, some six centuries before the Eiroku Era of Konko's time. The second was Ushin, who set sail fifty years later, in February of 919. A brief note suggests that he most likely was a monk who had left the far north in the hope of embarking upon the voyage, and had sojourned for some months or years at the Fudaraku-ji prior to his departure. The third was Kogan, in November of 1130, following an interval of more than two hundred years. Some three centuries later, in November of 1443, Yūson became the fourth to set sail for Fudaraku. In November of 1498, seven years before Konko was born, Seiyu put out to sea. Seiyu's exemplary erudition and virtuous attainments were yet well remembered when Konko first came to the Fudaraku-ji. A thirty-three year interval preceded the next sailing, of Yūshin, whom Konko had known well—a monk with eccentric ways, better remembered as the blessed Ashida, a sobriquet he acquired because he habitually wore *ashida*, the common wooden clogs, instead of the sandals appropriate to his vocation.

The belief was commonly held that the Fudaraku-ji existed as a convenience for voyagers to the isle of Fudaraku; and that since early times all Buddhists with good sense had come there, had the appropriate rites conducted, and promptly put out to sea. But Konko knew well that such was not the case. Excluding the first four voyagers and the former abbots of Fudaraku-ji mentioned in early documents, only two or three among the many believed to have made the voyage seemed actually to have set sail. Notices of voyages undertaken by a warrior named Shimokobe Yukihide in 1233 and the priestly courtier Gido in 1475 appear also in records of other monasteries, and so these doubtless were authentic cases. As for the others, there was little or no evidence.

Though sailings for Fudaraku had come to be accepted as

commonplace, over a period of six hundred years no more than nine or ten persons had actually put out to sea. And this was only reasonable. Rarely would a man become prepared spiritually to covet dying at sea as the culmination of his faith. The ones who did were most uncommon monks, a scattering among thousands or myriads, unlikely to appear any oftener than once in decades, even hundreds of years.

There had all the same been an unaccountable increase in the number of voyagers; including Seishin, who had departed five years before, in all seven had left these shores during the sixty years of Konko's lifetime. Among the seven were two young men of twenty-one and eighteen. The zeal for discarding life in the hope of being reborn in the Pure Land was itself the ultimate consummation—this was the essential teaching of the writ, in all its countless scrolls.

Never before, until the beginning of the stir in 1565, had Konko doubted the meaning of the ritual voyage. The voyager would be confined in a doorless wooden box nailed securely to the bottom of a boat; his only provisions would be an oil lamp that would burn out in a matter of days and a small quantity of food. To be cast off thus from the Kumano coast meant certain death at sea. The instant the voyager drew his last breath, the boat would begin carrying his body speedily southward, like a bamboo leaf skimming rapids, toward the isle of Fudaraku. There he would acquire new life, that he might live eternally in the service of Kannon.

A sailing from the shores of Kumano held the promise of an end to mortal life and the beginning of spiritual life. Not doubting this, Konko had noticed in the faces of past voyagers only the unusual serenity and composure that radiate from the hearts of those who have attained to absolute faith. He had seen joy in anticipation of new life, never sadness or fear. The voyagers had seemed tranquil and yet jubilant, and the onlookers, though understandably curious, had seemed wholly intent on glorifying them.

After he had announced his departure, Konko began to think differently of voyagers of the past. Waking and sleeping, he saw the several he had known, their faces somehow different.

Konko secluded himself in his cell through the spring and summer. Should he have stepped outside the monastery, people would have continued to throw coins his way, bow and pray to him as if he were a Buddha, and ask him, among other things, to take this or that to the Pure Land or lay his healing hand on the forehead of a dying man. This was so much bother for Konko, who was now preoccupied with somehow cultivating a genuine willingness to sail for Fudaraku when the time came, three or four months hence. Faced rather suddenly with the inevitability of putting out to sea, he was forced to acknowledge the utter inadequacy of his spiritual preparations. Now he spent his waking hours reciting the scriptures. Whenever an attendant went to his room, there he would be, facing a wall, reading from the scriptures.

Occasionally he would stop, and he would be staring blankly at some object in his room; seldom did he turn to face the attendant, who, when asked, had this same ready description: 'They say that the saints are *yorori* the minute they put out to sea, but His Reverence already looks every inch a *yorori*.'

There was indeed a saying that a saint at sea becomes the fish called the *yorori*. *Yorori* dwell only in the coastal waters between Cape Miki and the Cape of Shio. Fishermen of the region always release *yorori* caught in their nets; they never eat them.

Konko was tall and thin, as the *yorori* is long and slender. But it was not the physical resemblance that prompted the comparison. It was Konko's eyes, small and remote, dull and vacant, as if benumbed, the eyes of the *yorori*.

Konko spent his time either in recitation, his eyes closed, or in silence, staring blankly and vacantly. When his eyes resembled those of the *yorori*, he was thinking about one or another of the past voyagers. A few times in the course of a day, his eyes would regain, if briefly, their normal luster—moments when he suddenly became aware that he had been musing upon some voyager—and he would tell himself that he must not reminisce, that he must dispel whatever notion he had been dwelling upon, that he must instead be reciting the sutras, that all would end well if he continued to recite the sutras. And he would resume his reciting as if possessed.

No sooner had Konko finished another recitation, however, than his eyes were lifeless—a sign that in thought he was again dwelling upon some voyager of the past. He turned to pious recitation in order to keep his eyes from becoming those of a *yorori*, to banish from his vision the faces of past voyagers which appeared and reappeared. He devoted himself to this one purpose, and the effort took its toll of him.

The first time Konko witnessed a sailing for Fudaraku was on the occasion of the departure of Yushin, who was forty-three years old at the time. Konko, who only a half year earlier had moved to the monastery from a temple in his native village of Tanabe, was then twenty-seven. Yushin had been regarded as something of an oddity because of eccentric behavior—his insistence on wearing *ashida* instead of sandals, for instance. Suddenly he seemed to become a man possessed and, to everyone's surprise, declared that he would set sail for Fudaraku. And he embarked on the voyage three months later. Because his sailing was the first in thirty-three years, it attracted considerable notice. On the appointed day, the beach at Hama-no-miya was thronged with people who had come from places as far distant as Ise and Tsu to witness the inspiring event.

Konko and Yushin were both from Tanabe, and this association led to an acquaintance between them and opportunities for Konko to speak informally with him. Konko recalled how he often would remark that he could see Fudaraku Island. When asked its location, Yushin replied that on any clear day the island appeared distinctly on the horizon. Anyone, he added, who had freed himself of delusions and acquired faith in the Buddha could see it. Konko too would see it if he gave himself up wholly to faith in Fudaraku.

'It is level and high,' said Yushin of this island, 'rising on boulders that are pounded incessantly on all sides by the stormy sea. I can hear the pounding of the waves. This tableland with the sea all round it is an infinite expanse, calm, of untold beauty, covered with verdure that can never wither, abounding in springs that can never run dry. Great flocks of vermilion birds, their tails long and flowing, make their nests there. And I see people disporting themselves there—these people do not age as they serve the Buddha.'

Yushin completed the customary ritual and boarded his boat near the first of several sacred gates in a line from the shore. He was oblivious to the presence of well-wishers who crowded the beach, and he spoke only to Konko, who attended him up to the moment of boarding. 'Fudaraku is exceptionally clear today,' Yushin said to him. 'You must join me there someday.' And he laughed softly. Konko, though he did not know why, was startled at Yushin's smile.

Yushin's eyes, ever steady in their gaze, were suddenly piercing, and covered over by a kind of iridescence.

Yushin's boat was escorted as far as Tsunakiri Island, some seven miles from shore, by men on several vessels and there was sent off on its solitary voyage to distant waters.

Those who had escorted Yushin saw the boat moving directly south through the dark waves, speeding away as if it were being pulled in on a line. Perhaps the Buddha was leading it to the island that had dwelt so constantly in his vision. Monks at the Fudaraku-ji who earlier had treated him as an eccentric spoke ill of him no more. The curious actions of the monk who had worn *ashida* were seen in a new light, and each became an episode to be recounted as a legacy of his high attainment.

Konko had been urged by Yushin to make the same voyage one day, and now, thirty-four years later, he was about to sail for Fudaraku. Whenever Konko thought of Yushin, he remembered the strange greenish iridescence in his eyes. There was no doubting Yushin's having seen the Pure Land. Were his eyes, as he studied the isle on the horizon, no different from the eyes of others? His voyage did not carry with it any promise of death. Quite probably he never thought about death. As he had failed to contemplate death, so had he failed to contemplate the renewal of life—these were not his concerns. His strangely glowing eyes had actually envisioned Fudaraku. The island became an obsession with him, and he simply decided to go there.

The sailing of Shokei took place ten years later. When Shokei first announced his intention to put out to sea, no one thought it remarkable. Had he lived his lifetime at the monastery, never associating himself with the belief in Fudaraku, he would have been revered no less. His decision, once it became known, was regarded by all as quite in accord with his character. This response attested to the great admiration with which people regarded this diminutive monk—so small that a child might easily pick him up—face wrinkled ten years beyond his age, eyes brimming with compassion.

Konko was filled with sadness when he learned of Shokei's decision, but only because he hated to say goodbye. When he remembered that he would not again hear those kind words of encouragement, those thoughtful and deeply felt admonitions, the sorrow became torment. Not even separation from the parents who had brought him into this world, he thought, could be sadder.

All through summer of that year, on now-forgotten occasions when Konko had gone to him, Shokei would say: 'Meeting death on the blue expanse of the sea might be rather pleasant.'

'Will you die?' Konko asked, for he had never before associated these sailings with death at sea. There would be death, to be sure, but was not the purpose of it all to acquire eternal life at the end of the voyage?

'Of course I shall die,' Shokei replied. 'I shall die at sea and sink to the bottom, which, by the way, is every bit as expansive as the surface, and I shall make friends with all the fishes.' And he laughed merrily as if the thought gave him considerable pleasure.

When he boarded his vessel and when he sailed away from Tsunakiri Island—at all times, indeed—Shokei was smiling as always. Earlier voyagers had had themselves shut in a box which was then fastened to the bottom of the boat. A similar box-like compartment was placed on his boat, but he did not go inside. He sat at the stern and the onlookers saw him waving goodbye. He shed no tears, but everyone else, young and old, was weeping.

Shokei envisioned drowning at sea, not passage to Fudaraku. Why, then, did he set out on a voyage to the mythical isle?

Konko could think of only one reason. Shokei must have believed that he would serve Kannon best by doing so. In the decade preceding his voyage, Kumano was beset with a succession of disasters—a great earthquake in January of 1538, a landslide in August of that year and, coinciding with it, the inexplicable splintering of every rafter in the main Kumano Shrine, the typhoon of August, 1540, which swept down to the sea every river boat of the commercial guilds and caused countless deaths all along the sea coast, and a destructive flood in August of 1541. To make matters worse, the civil war raging about the capital bred violence in outlying districts. At night the region was the province of brigands, and brutality and killing were the most common of occurrences. Religion was as good as forgotten to Shokei's unhappiness. He must be an inspiration and bring people back to religion.

Konko was disturbed by the thought that a monk as wise as Shokei believed in nothing about the voyage to Fudaraku save only dying at sea. That was not enough for him. The eventuality of reaching Fudaraku Island might not have been of concern to one such as Shokei, who had attained enlightenment. Konko knew, however, that he could not be content with a voyage that carried no promise other than that of sinking to the floor of the sea.

Nichiyo put out to sea four years after Shokei, whom he had succeeded as abbot of the Fudaraku-ji. Nichiyo, sickly and short-tempered, was a contrast to his predecessor. Konko felt as though he had not had a moment's rest during the four years of his service to Nichiyo, who was feared by everyone in the monastery. When he announced his intention to set sail for Fudaraku—it was wholly unexpected—Konko was not alone in breathing a sigh of relief. Life was very precious to Nichiyo; he would have the monastery in an uproar if he so much as caught a cold. In January of his final year his asthma was worse. Because medical treatment had no effect whatever, he concluded that he had not much longer to live. Already sixty-one, he no doubt decided that a voyage to Fudaraku was preferable to dying in a sickbed.

Surely Nichiyo was influenced very strongly by the hope of reaching the Pure Land alive. Since autumn of the year before, he had talked more frequently, and to anyone who would listen, about extraordinary accounts in books he had read—typically, about a monk from such and such province having set sail from Tosa in January of 1142 and having lived to reach Fudaraku Island and to return to Japan with a knowledge of the Pure Land. In arriving at his decision Nichiyo was encouraged immeasurably by these confused accounts. Nevertheless from the time he made the decision until the scheduled day of departure his deportment was consistent with his exalted role. He seemed to acquire unusual confidence at the time the title of sage was conferred upon him and throughout the summer and autumn months he was serene. To all appearances he had no doubts about life and death.

On the day before his departure, Nichiyo walked down to the shore to inspect his boat. He seemed displeased and asked Konko, who was with him, 'Did Shokei ride out in a boat as small as this?' Konko replied that it had been an even smaller one.

The next day as Nichiyo was boarding the boat one foot slid into the water. He seemed very unhappy, indeed wretched. His expression was one of such despair as Konko had not known before. He stood motionless for a time, his dry foot on the boat and his wet foot on the gangplank, and then stepped aboard as if resigning himself to fate. The five who had accompanied him as far as Tsunakiri Island said later that he spoke not one word to them.

Though twenty years had passed, Konko could still see Nichiyo's expression clearly. It reflected, though he did not like to think so, his own feelings of the moment.

Bankei, who embarked upon the voyage when he was forty-two, had like Yushin often remarked that he could see Fudaraku Island. He was a tall, stout man, with a somewhat unruly disposition. Though Konko had never liked him, he was strangely moved when Bankei, ten years younger than he, announced that he would embark for Fudaraku. Bankei was a giant compared to the frail, diminutive voyagers of the past—much too large, it seemed, to be accommodated by the customary boat. His was not the image one could readily associate with the ritual voyage.

Bankei believed that he would live to see Fudaraku Island. 'I don't want to die,' he often said. 'I'll get to the island safely because it beckons me. I can actually see it, and that most certainly means it beckons me there.' He was inclined to ramble on in this vein.

No one gave Bankei the reassurance he sought—with the single exception of Nichiyo's successor, the abbot Seishin, who invariably responded with kind and reassuring words.

Seishin also embarked for Fudaraku when he was sixty-one, and, Konko knew, for a reason distinctly different from the other voyagers. Seishin, who had no kin, was a lonely man. During the time he was abbot he was victim of a series of unhappy deceptions and betrayals. His feelings, like his frail body, were easily injured. He became hopelessly misanthropic, weary of society and of people and life.

Konko and Seishin got along well with each other, perhaps because they were so near the same age. The weariness that possessed Seishin in his old age was complete, and he longed for death above all else. He was not a man of firm religious conviction even though he had been a member of the order since his youth. He veiled his true thoughts, of course, and managed to complete the customary rites and earn the respect and reverence due a monk embarking upon the ritual voyage. Only Konko knew how he really felt.

Not long before the appointed day Seishin said that he would rather walk into the sea striking a bell, and continue walking until he sank beneath the deep waters; but he was dissuaded by his disciples. He departed with dignity as Shokei had.

'I want to reach Fudaraku as quickly as possible,' he said. 'Therefore I need no food or fuel. All I need is a boat with a mast and a sail that bears the inscription "Praise to the Lord Amida."' That was precisely as he had it.

Seishin carried a rosary, but in other respects he bore few of the marks of a Buddhist. He did not intone prayers or finger his beads as his predecessors had.

'At last,' he said, as his boat was being cast off from Tsunakiri Island. 'A man is a trial to others whether he's trying to live or die. But I suppose it must be so.' He seemed happy to be finally alone, free of the many well-wishers.

There were yet two other voyagers: twenty-one-year-old Korin and eighteen-year-old Zenko, who put out to sea when Konko was in his thirties, the former in 1530 and the latter in 1533. The youths were sick and to all appearances on the verge of death when they came to the monastery, accompanied by their parents, to request passage to Fudaraku. Korin had been urged to do so by his parents, who believed that he might by some miracle live to see the island paradise. He apparently knew little about the ritual voyage. He knew, however, that his illness was mortal, and had chosen to abide by his parents' wishes. Zenko was carrying out his own wish. His parents had wanted him to live on and he sought to persuade them that he would die at sea and be carried by the currents to the Pure Land of Fudaraku; they were sadly troubled when they brought him to the monastery.

The youths were accompanied to Tsunakiri Island by large groups of well-wishers, and on both occasions the beach was crowded. Konko had been moved to tears at the sight of the emaciated Zenko putting out to sea, and at the recollection all the sorrow returned.

Summer was speeding by. Konko each day would ask someone to tell him what day of the month it was, and each time doubt his ears. He continued to spend his waking hours reciting from the scriptures. After the autumnal equinox the days passed with astonishing speed. The light of dawn seemed instantly to fade into dusk.

Konko knew well that he was no better prepared spiritually than before. The faces of past voyagers continued to appear and reappear. However fondly he might regard them, they now seemed unrelated to Fudaraku. The grandeur that had fascinated him was gone.

The faces of Yushin and Bankei—both had often said they could see Fudaraku Island—now seemed somehow aberrant. The voyage of Seishin, obviously undertaken in desperation by a thoroughly weary old man, could have had nothing to do with belief in Kannon or the Pure Land. He had only watched the dark waves running in turbulent succession upon the Kumano coast. In this respect he was no different from Konko's teacher, Shokei, who had displayed such remarkable dignity on his departure. Shokei had been certain of imminent death and had noticed only the surging sea on which his mortal remains would rest. He must not have been concerned with reaching Fudaraku and acquiring new life. His serene eyes were those of one who left such concerns behind.

Nichiyo was a man with a set purpose. At his departure, as he sailed, and days or even weeks later with no more than a plank to keep him afloat, perhaps he clung to life, still hoping to be rescued, to have Kannon reach out for him. He hoped for a miracle. He had, in the deepest sense, had no part of faith or of belief in Kannon or Fudaraku. He had seemed to believe, but had not believed.

Though both Korin and Zenko had moved the onlookers profoundly with an appearance of serenity, their voyages had in fact had nothing whatsoever to do with faith. Wasted from illness, they were able to resign themselves to death with less hesitation than most others.

When Konko became aware that he had been gazing at their several faces, he would hastily dismiss them. They were utterly dreary. He would not wish to resemble them, and yet he felt that his face would be any one of theirs the moment he slackened his hold upon himself.

If he was to embark on the voyage, Konko thought, he would not want to look like any of his predecessors. What would his expression be then? He did not quite know, but it must be one that would be appropriate to a truly devout monk setting sail for Fudaraku. If he must put out to sea, he would do so wearing an expression appropriate to his role.

In October, with the date of sailing just one month away, Konko began to think differently of the faces of past voyagers. He underwent another change. He would give anything to be like one of them—it did not matter which one. He had felt as if he could at will resemble any one of the faces, even though the thought was repugnant to him. Now that he longed to be like them, however, he knew that he had been indulging in wishfulness. He had set himself a hard task.

If only he might see the Pure Land! He recalled with envy the extraordinary glow in the eyes of Yushin and Bankei. He envied Seishin's expression of complete relief on gaining the solitude he had long sought. He regarded enviously even Nichiyo's expression, usually sullen as if to reflect some inner turmoil but capable of anger when he was disturbed, as when his foot slid into the water. There was little likelihood of attaining the calmness and dignity of Shokei. Konko even doubted that he could resemble either of the two youths. How were they able at such a tender age to assume expressions of such utter tranquillity and resignation?

Kenko received callers, who were suddenly numerous. He did not know who they were or why they had come. He had neither the will nor the ability to remember. In the morning an attendant would lead him to the Thousand-armed Kannon in the main hall, and there he would sit until noon. Callers would come one after another into the hall. Konko did not speak to them. Having come to say good-bye, they seemed relieved that he did not. They seemed to conclude that in these circumstances words were an inappropriate means of farewell, and Konko's silence seemed not at all strange.

If a visitor spoke to him, Konko did not answer. He recited a holy text softly or sat in silence, his eyes like those of a *yorori*, fixed vacantly upon a darkened corner of the hall.

By November he had lost all awareness of time. When he awoke he would call Seigen. 'Isn't this the day for my voyage?' he would ask. Told that it was not, he would lift his head in apparent relief, and look upon the white sands of the garden. He would gaze at the bright green plantings and listen to the lapping of waves on the beach of Hama-no-miya, which was like an extension of the garden. Only recently had he begun to notice trees and the sound of waves. He perceived things which he had not in many years.

On one of those bright, clear autumn days, Konko asked again if it was not the day for his voyage.

'You will be leaving this afternoon at four,' Seigen replied. Konko stood up and sat down again. His strength seemed to have been drained quite away. He was perfectly still, quite incapable of motion.

An attendant came to say that a group of well-wishing Shinto priests had come from Nachi Falls. Another announced the arrival of a Zen abbot.

Konko at last seemed aware of the stir. With the assistance of several attendants he changed clothes. With several monks in the lead he went to the main hall, where he had sat in meditation every morning since first coming to the monastery. He glanced calmly at the Thousand-armed Kannon, Taishaku, Bonten, and other deities. Soon he was staring at them intently.

Every activity was now dictated by his attendants. He sat before the central image and recited from the scriptures, then returned to his assigned position and sat, gazing intently at the images. The air was thick with incense. The assemblage of monks flowed out of the small hall over the corridors to the garden. The hall itself seemed enfolded in the fullness of the chorus of prayer.

Shortly past noon, Konko retired from the main hall to the cloister, where he had tea with several monks. A sack containing one hundred and eight pebbles, each inscribed with one word from the scriptures, was brought to the veranda. Several sacred scrolls, a statuette of the Buddha, clothing, and a few other items—all to be placed in Konko's boat—were also gathered on the veranda and inspected by the attendants. And, finally, a wooden palanquin to carry these items was brought in and deposited in a manner which one might have thought unnecessarily casual. Though somewhat annoyed by the rough casualness, he did not feel inclined to protest.

The monks left the monastery shortly before the appointed hour. Unseasonably brilliant sunlight filled Konko's eyes. The strand was thronged with people. The party of monks, Konko at its center, moved along with the excited crowd, passed through the sacred gate, and came to the white sand along the shore.

As had Nichiyo years before him, Konko thought that his boat was the smallest of them all. He wondered why they had given him such a tiny boat. There was no boat landing. His boat and three others for those who would see him off lay at the water's edge, as if they had been washed ashore. The three were much larger than Konko's.

He was led aboard his boat at once. Workmen came aboard with a large wooden box which they placed over him. He was suddenly angry. The boat should have had a compartment which he could enter. Instead one had been brought afterwards.

There was a pounding as it was nailed to the boat. Presently the pounding stopped. It was dark inside the box. A door was opened, and various articles were pushed inside. Konko was asked to come out of the box and greet the onlookers, and he did so. The crowd stirred. Coins fell like rain on to the boat and along the shoreline and children fought to collect them. Konko fled back inside. He sat for

some time in the dark while a mast and a sail bearing the formula
'Praise to the Lord Amida' were put up. Everything seemed clumsy
and slow.

Almost two hours passed. With not a word of warning to him, the
boat began to move. He felt it grinding against the pebble-strewn
shore, and then there was the smoothness of the sea. He wanted to
look out, but he could not open the box. It had been tightly sealed.
However hard he pushed, he could not loosen a single one of the
boards.

Then he heard the sound of an oar. He was not alone, then. The
boatman would steer the vessel as far as Tsunakiri Island. There he
would be cast off, alone.

He began to hear an intermittent chiming of bells through the
sound of waves. Straining his ears, he heard a chanting of sacred
words to the accompaniment of the chimes. But the chanting
would be interrupted by the waves. Though at times it would
assume a festive gaiety, it was soon obliterated by the roar of
the sea.

As the boats made land at Tsunakiri Island, Konko found a slit and
pressed his face to it. Night was approaching and the dark billowing
sea seemed infinite.

'It's goodbye, Your Reverence!' the boatman called from above.
Konko was confused. It was customary for voyagers to spend the
night on Tsunakiri Island with the rest of the party and set sail in the
morning.

'I'm to stay here tonight!' Konko shouted, so loudly in fact that he
was surprised by his own voice.

'We're sending you off right now instead of waiting until tomorrow,' the boatman answered. 'The weather is bad, and we don't
want to be stranded here.'

Konko again cried out, but there was no answer. The boatman
had already leapt ashore.

The boat was now pitching and rolling. Konko saw that the sea
was much darker now, a broad expanse of turbulence.

At last he was alone. He sank to the floor. He felt the full
weariness of the day and drifted helplessly into sleep.

Some hours later he awoke. In pitch darkness, he felt the boards
beneath him rising and falling. He heard the crashing of waves
below him, then overhead.

He quickly raised himself and with all his might threw himself against the side of the box. Never before had he resorted to such violence.

He repeated it in desperation five and six times. A board flew loose, and into the compartment came a blast of wind and spray. The box catching the wind sent the boat into a lurch. The next instant Konko felt himself being flung into the sea.

He clung to a plank and stayed afloat through the night. At daybreak he saw Tsunakiri Island close at hand. As a child he had swum often in the coastal waters, and so he was able to save himself.

Around noon he was washed ashore, plank and all. He lay there until evening, when he was noticed by one of the monks who had accompanied him to the island the day before. The party of well-wishers had been detained there because of the high seas.

Konko was given a meal there on the bleak shore. The monks, meanwhile, were huddled together discussing at length what to do. They asked a fisherman for a boat and put Konko in it. Konko by then had regained some of his strength. 'Spare me,' he said, in a barely audible voice. Some of the monks must have heard him, but no one seemed to understand.

The boat was left on the beach for a while, and several men stood around it, regarding it in silence.

The young monk Seigen saw his teacher's lips apparently forming words, though surely not from the scriptures. He leaned close, but he heard nothing. He took out paper and brush and ink. With trembling hand, Konko strung together these words:

> Of mythical isles, of Horai,
> I have known two and ten.
> Believe only in the Pure Land.
> I shall believe in Lord Amida.

The words were barely legible. Again Konko wrote:

> Should you seek Kannon,
> Believe not in Fudaraku.
> Should you seek Fudaraku,
> Believe not in the sea.

Konko put down the brush and immediately closed his eyes. Seigen wondered if his teacher was dead, but he detected a pulse. He studied the words. Their meaning escaped him. They might perhaps

Passage to Fudaraku

be evidence of enlightenment and again they might indicate anger and frustration, no more.

A hastily made box was lowered over Konko and attached securely to the bottom of the boat. Then Konko and the boat were pushed out to sea.

Thereafter the abbots of the Fudaraku-ji were no longer expected to put out to sea when they reached sixty-one. There had been no such rule to begin with. As the account of Konko's voyage became known, it seems, people changed their minds about the role of the abbot of the Fudaraku-ji. Thereafter, when an abbot died, his body was sent out to sea from Hama-no-miya. The ritual voyage was called 'passage to Fudaraku'. There were seven such voyages over the next one hundred and fifty years. Because the sailing took place during the month in which the abbot died, it could be at any time of the year.

There was one more instance of a living embarkation for Fudaraku: Seigen's, thirteen years after Konko's, in November of 1578. Seigen was thirty at the time and the records of the Fudaraku-ji inform us that he put out to sea for the sake of his parents. As for the thoughts of this young monk, who had accompanied Konko to Tsunakiri Island, we have no means of knowing them.

DAZAI OSAMU (1909–1948)

MERRY CHRISTMAS

Translated by Ralph McCarthy

Tokyo presented a picture of effervescent gloom. Though I imagined as I
traveled back to the city that something like this might serve as the
first line of my next story, I found on my return that, as far as I
could see, 'life in Tokyo' was the same as ever. I'd spent the
previous year and three months at my childhood home in Tsugaru,
returning with the wife and children in mid-November of this year,
but when I got back it was as if we'd merely been away on a little
trip of, say, two or three weeks.

'Tokyo after a prolonged absence seems neither better nor worse;
the character of the city hasn't changed at all,' I wrote to someone
back home. 'There are physical differences, of course, but on the
metaphysical level the place is as always. It reminds one of the old
saying: Only death can cure a fool. A little change wouldn't hurt; in
fact, one even feels justified in expecting it.'

Not that I'd changed much myself. I spent a lot of time aimlessly
walking the streets in a plain kimono and inverness.

In early December I entered a movie theater in the suburbs
(perhaps the term 'moving picture house' would be more appropriate—it was an appealingly run-down little shack) and watched an
American film. When I came out it was already six o'clock and the
streets were covered with a smoky white evening mist, through
which darkly clad people hurried about, already thoroughly caught
up in the year-end bustle. No, life in Tokyo hadn't changed at all.

I went into a bookstore and bought a volume by a famous
Jewish playwright. Stuffing the book in my pocket, I turned toward
the entrance, and there, standing on her tiptoes and looking like
a bird about to take flight, was a young woman who was staring
at me.

Blessing or curse?

To meet up with a woman you once pursued but no longer feel

224

any affection for is the worst of misfortunes. And, in my case, most of the ladies I know fit that bill. Most? *All*, is more like it.

The one from Shinjuku? God, not that one...It could be, though.

'Kasai-san?'

The girl said my name in a voice no louder than a murmur, lowered her heels, and gave a short bow. She was wearing a green hat, with the ribbon tied below her chin, and a bright red rain-coat. As I studied her she seemed to grow younger, until her face matched the image of a certain twelve or thirteen-year-old girl in my memory.

'Shizueko.'

A blessing.

'Let's get out of here. Or did you want to buy a magazine or something?'

'No. I came to look for a book called *Ariel*, but that's all right.'

We stepped out onto the crowded street.

'You've grown up. I didn't recognize you.'

That's Tokyo for you. This sort of thing happens.

I bought two ten-yen bags of peanuts from a street stall, put away my wallet, thought for a moment, then pulled out the wallet again and bought another bag. In the old days I'd always brought this girl a gift whenever I went to visit her mother.

Her mother was the same age as I. And she was one of the very few women from my past—no, make that the *only* one—whom, even now, I could have bumped into unexpectedly without becom-ing panic-stricken or nonplussed. Why? Well, she was of what they call 'aristocratic birth', she was lovely, and she was frail of health... but, no, such a set of criteria is merely vain and captious and hardly qualifies her as 'the only one'. She had divorced her tremendously wealthy husband, had suffered a downturn of fortunes, and lived in an apartment with her daughter, surviving on her modest assets. But, no. I haven't even a smidgen of interest in women's life histories, and in fact I have no idea why she parted with her wealthy husband or what exactly is meant by 'modest assets'. And if I were told, I'm sure I would promptly forget. Perhaps it's because I've been so consistently made a fool of by women, but I assume even the most pathetic female life story to be a pack of arbitrary lies and am no longer capable of shedding a single tear in response. In other words, such criteria as being well born, being beautiful, having fallen on hard times—such romantic conditions as these have nothing to do with the reason I single her out as 'the only one'.

The real reasons, four in number, are as follows. One: She was a stickler for cleanliness. Whenever she returned home after being out, she never failed to wash her hands and feet at the front door. I mentioned that she'd suffered a downturn of fortunes, but her tidy two-room apartment was always spic and span from one end to the other, and the kitchen and all the cooking and eating utensils, in particular, were spotless. Two: She wasn't the least bit infatuated with me. There was no need to get into the chasm-like rut of the dreary war of the sexes that accompanies lust, none of the agitated, lecherous confusion of 'Is she attracted to me? Or is it just my vanity speaking? Shall I feel her out? Or is it all in my mind?' As far as I could tell, this woman was still in love with the husband she'd divorced, and deep in her heart she clung firmly to a sense of pride at having once been his wife. Three: She was sensitive to my moods and feelings. When everything in this world is getting me down, to the point that I feel I can't bear it any longer, it's no fun being told things like, 'Well, you certainly seem to be prospering these days.' Whenever I went to this woman's apartment, we were always able to converse about topics that perfectly matched my immediate circumstances and state of mind. 'It's always been like that, in every age, hasn't it?' I remember her saying once. 'If you tell the truth, they kill you. Saint John, Jesus Christ himself...and for John, of course, there was no resurrection....' And she never once uttered a word about a single living Japanese writer. Four, and this is perhaps the most important of all the reasons: There was always an abundance of liquor at her apartment. I don't think of myself as especially stingy, but at those depressing times when I find myself with outstanding bills at all the bars I know, my feet just naturally lead me to places where I can drink all I like for free. Even as the war dragged on, and liquor became harder and harder to come by in Japan, there was always something to drink at that person's apartment. I would show up bearing some cheap gift for the daughter, then drink myself into a stupor before leaving.

These four reasons, then, are my answer to the question of why that person was 'the only one'. If someone were to reply to the effect that what I have just described is in fact one form of love, I would be able to do nothing but gaze back blankly and say, 'Well, maybe so.' If all male-female friendships are a form of love, then perhaps this, too, was love, but I never underwent any sort of anguish in regard to this person, and neither of us was fond of histrionics or complications.

'How's your mother? Same as ever?'

'Oh, yes.'

'Not sick or anything?'

'No.'

'You're still living with her, aren't you?'

'Yes.'

'Is your place near here?'

'But it's a mess.'

'No matter. Let's go get your mother, drag her out to a restaurant, and do some serious drinking.'

'All right.'

As we spoke, the girl seemed to grow less and less chipper. At the same time, though, with every step she took, she looked more and more grown-up to me. She was born when her mother was eighteen, and her mother, like me, was thirty-eight, which would make this girl...

My ego ballooned. It is possible, certainly, to be jealous of one's own mother. I changed the subject.

'*Ariel?*'

'It's really the strangest thing!' Just as I'd planned, she now became quite animated. 'Before, when I'd just entered girls' school, you came to our apartment, it was summer, and you and mother were talking, and the word "*Ariel*" kept coming up, and I didn't have any idea what it might mean, but for some reason I just couldn't forget that word, and...' Suddenly, as if she'd grown tired of her own chatter, her voice trailed off and she fell silent. After we'd walked a bit further, she said, 'It's the name of a book, isn't it,' and fell silent again.

My head swelled even more. That clinches it, I thought. The mother wasn't in love with me, nor had I ever felt lust for her, but as for the daughter, well, I thought, you never know.

Her mother was a person who, reduced to poverty or not, could not live without delicious food, and even before the war against America and England began, she and her daughter had already evacuated to a place near Hiroshima where good food was plentiful. Shortly after the move I'd received a postcard from her, but I was having my share of difficulties at the time and didn't feel much of a need to write back immediately to someone who was taking it easy in the country. Before I ever did get around to writing, my own circumstances had begun to change radically, and now it had been five years since I'd had any contact with them.

Tonight, seeing me after five years, completely unexpectedly, which would be more pleased—the mother or the daughter? I, for some reason, suspected that the girl's pleasure would prove to be deeper and purer than that of her mother. If so, it was necessary for me to make my own affiliation clear. It would not be possible to affiliate myself equally with both. Tonight I would betray the mother and join forces with the girl. It wouldn't matter if, for example, the mother were to scowl with disapproval. It couldn't be helped. It was love.

'When did you come back to Tokyo?'

'October of last year.'

'Right after the war ended, then. It figures. No way a selfish person like your mother could put up with living in the sticks any longer than she had to.'

If there was a rough edge to my voice as I badmouthed the mother, it was only to ingratiate myself with the daughter. Women—no, *people*—have a strong sense of rivalry with one another. Even parents and children.

The girl didn't smile, however. It appeared that to bring up the subject of her mother at all, whether in praise or derision, was taboo. I could only conclude that hers was a particularly bad case of jealousy.

'What great luck, running into you like this.' I changed the subject without missing a beat. 'It was as if we'd agreed to meet at the bookstore at a certain time.'

'I know,' she said, falling easily this time for a little sugary sentiment. I was on to something now.

'Watching a movie to kill the time, then going to that bookstore five minutes before we were to meet...'

'A movie?'

'Yeah, I like to see a film once in a while. This one was about a tightrope walker in the circus. It's interesting to see a performer portray a performer. It brings out the best in even a lousy actor, because he's a performer himself. The sadness of entertainers just oozes out of him, whether he realizes it or not.'

As a topic for conversation between lovers, you can't beat movies. They're perfect.

'I saw that movie, too.'

'Just at the moment the two of them meet, a wave comes rushing between them, and they're separated once more. That part was good. Things like that can happen in life, you know—some little mishap, and you never see each other again.'

Unless you can say treacly things like this without hesitation, you'll never make it as a young woman's lover.

'If I had left that bookstore a minute earlier, we might never have met again, or at least not for another ten years or so.' I was trying to make our chance meeting seem as romantic as possible.

The street became narrow and dark, and there were muddy spots as well, so we could no longer walk side by side. The girl walked in front and I followed with my hands stuffed in the pockets of my inverness.

'How much farther?' I asked. 'Half a *cho*? One *cho*?'

'Well, I never really know how far a *cho* is supposed to be.'

I, too, actually, am pretty hopeless when it comes to judging distances. But to show one's stupidity is taboo in love.

'Are we within a hundred meters?' I said with a cool, scientific air.

'Well...'

'Meters are easier to grasp, right? A hundred meters is half a *cho*,' I told her, but felt a bit uneasy about it. I did some calculating in my head and realized that a hundred meters was about one *cho*. But I didn't correct myself. Clownishness is taboo in love.

'Anyway, it's right over there.'

It was a terribly shabby, barrack-like apartment. We entered and walked down a dim hallway to the fifth or sixth door, where I saw the aristocratic family name: Jinba.

'Jinba-san!' I called through the closed door. I was sure I heard a reply. Then a shadow moved across the glass.

'Ha! She's home!'

The girl stood bolt upright, all the color went out of her face, and she twisted her lips in a grotesque way. Then, suddenly, she burst into tears.

Her mother had been killed during the air raids on Hiroshima, she told me. She also said that, in the delirium of her death throes, her mother had called out my name.

The girl had returned to Tokyo alone and was now working in the legal office of a Progressive Party Dietman, a relative on her mother's side.

She was going to tell me all this, but hadn't been able to get the words out, so she'd gone ahead and led me to the apartment, not knowing what else to do.

Now I realized why it was that she'd looked so downcast whenever I mentioned her mother. It wasn't jealousy, and it wasn't love.

We didn't go in the room, but headed back out to the busy area near the station.

Her mother had always loved broiled eel.

We ducked under the curtain of an eel stall.

'Yes, sir! What'll it be?'

We stood at the counter. There was one other customer, a gentleman sitting on the far side of the stall, drinking.

'Large servings? Or small ones?'

'Small ones. Three of them.'

'Yes, sir!' the young stallkeeper said in a hearty growl. He seemed a genuine 'old Tokyo' type.

As he vigorously fanned the coals in his clay stove, I said, 'Put them on three separate plates.'

'Yes, sir! And the third person? Coming afterwards?'

'There are three of us here now,' I said without smiling.

'H'm?'

'There's this person, and me, and standing between us there's a beautiful woman with a worried look on her face. Don't you see her?' I smiled a bit now.

I don't know what he made of this, but the young stallkeeper grinned, lifted a hand to his forehead, and said, 'I can't top that!'

'Do you have any of this?' I said, raising an imaginary cup to my lips with my left hand.

'The very finest there is! Well, not that good, I guess.'

'Three cups,' I said.

Three plates of eel were set out before us. We left the one in the middle alone, and began eating from the other two. Soon three brimming cups of sake arrived.

I drank mine down in a gulp.

'Let me help,' I said in a voice loud enough for only Shizueko to hear. I lifted her mother's cup and gulped it down, then took from my pocket the three bags of peanuts I'd bought earlier. 'I'm going to drink a bit tonight. Stick with me. You can eat these while I'm drinking,' I said, still keeping my voice down.

Shizueko nodded, and neither of us spoke for some time.

As I silently drained four or five cups in a row, the gentleman on the other side began boisterously joking with the stallkeeper. His jokes were truly inane, amazingly inept, and absolutely devoid of wit, but they struck the gentleman himself as hilarious. The stall-keeper laughed courteously, but the gentleman was in stitches.

'... That's what he said, and of course that bowled me over, then he started singing, "Apples are so pretty, I know just how you feel..." Ha, ha, ha, ha! He's sharp, that fellow, I'll tell you, he said, "Tokyo Station is my home." That killed me, so I said, "My mistress lives in the Maru Building," and now it was his turn to be bowled over...'

He just kept rattling off his utterly unfunny jokes, and I found myself feeling more disgusted than ever with the hopeless lack of any concept of what constitutes a sense of humor that you witness wherever Japanese are drinking. However raucously the gentleman and the stallkeeper laughed, I didn't so much as crack a smile, but merely continued drinking and absently eying the year-end crowds that bustled past the stall.

The gentleman turned to see what I was looking at. After watching the flow of people for a while, he suddenly shouted 'Ha-ro-o! Me-ri-i ku-ri-su-ma-su!' at an American soldier who was walking down the street.

For some reason I burst out laughing this time.

The soldier scowled and shook his head as if to show how silly he thought the gentleman's jest, then strode off and disappeared.

'Shall we eat this, too?' I said, applying my chopsticks to the plate in the middle.

'Yes.'

'Half for you and half for me.'

Tokyo is still the same. It hasn't changed a bit.

NAKAJIMA ATSUSHI (1909–1942)

THE EXPERT

Translated by Ivan Morris

There lived in the city of Hantan, the capital of the ancient Chinese state of Chao, a man called Chi Ch'ang who aspired to be the greatest archer in the world. After many enquiries, he ascertained that the best teacher in the country was one Wei Fei. So great was this Master's skill in archery that he was able, by repute, to shoot a quiverful of arrows into a single willow-leaf at the distance of a hundred paces. Chi Ch'ang journeyed to the far-away province where Wei Fei lived and became his pupil.

First Wei Fei ordered him to learn not to blink. Chi Ch'ang returned home and as soon as he entered his house, crept under his wife's loom and lay there on his back. It was his plan to stare without blinking at the treadle as it rushed up and down directly before his eyes. His wife was amazed to see him in this posture and said that she could not weave with a man, albeit her husband, watching from this strange angle. She was, however, constrained to work the treadle despite her embarrassment.

Day after day Chi Ch'ang took up his peculiar station under the loom and practised staring. After two years he had reached the point of not blinking even if one of his eye-lashes was caught in the treadle. When Chi Ch'ang finally crawled out for the last time from under the machine, he realised that his lengthy discipline had been effective. Nothing now could make him blink—not a blow on the eyelid, nor a spark from the fire, nor a cloud of dust raised suddenly before his eyes. So thoroughly had he trained his eye-muscles to inactivity that even when he slept his eyes remained wide open. One day as he sat staring ahead of him, a small spider wove its web between his eye-lashes. Now at last he felt sufficiently confident to report to his teacher.

'To know how not to blink is only the first step,' said Wei Fei when Chi Ch'ang had eagerly recounted the story of his progress.

'Next you must learn to look. Practise looking at things, and if the time comes when what is minute seems conspicuous, and what is small seems huge, visit me once more.'

Again Chi Ch'ang returned home. This time he went to the garden and searched for a tiny insect. When he had found one barely visible to the naked eye, he placed it on a blade of grass and hung this by the window of his study. Now he took up his post at the end of the room and sat there day after day staring at the insect. At first he could barely see it, but after ten days, he began to fancy that it was slightly bigger. At the end of the third month it seemed to have grown to the size of a silk-worm and he could now clearly make out the details of its body.

As Chi Ch'ang sat staring at the insect, he scarcely noticed the changing of the seasons—how the glittering spring sun changed to the fierce glare of summer; how before long the geese were flying through a limpid autumn sky; and how autumn in turn gave way to the sleety grey winter. Nothing seemed to exist now but the little animal on the blade of grass. As each insect died or disappeared, he had his servant replace it by another one equally minute. But in his eyes they were constantly becoming larger.

For three years he hardly left his study. Then one day he perceived that the insect by the window was as big as a horse. 'I've done it!' he exclaimed, striking his knee, and so saying he hurried out of the house. He could scarcely believe his eyes. Horses seemed as big as mountains; pigs looked like great hills, and chicken like castle-towers. Bounding with joy, he ran back to his house and immediately notched a slender Shuo P'êng arrow on a Swallow bow. He took aim and shot the insect straight through the heart without so much as touching the blade of grass on which it rested.

He lost no time in reporting to Wei Fei. This time his teacher was sufficiently impressed to say, 'Well done!'

It was five years since Chi Ch'ang had embarked on the mysteries of archery and he felt that his rigorous training had indeed borne fruit. No feat of bowmanship now seemed beyond his powers. To confirm this, he set himself a series of exacting tests before returning home.

First he decided to emulate Wei Fei's own accomplishment, and at the distance of a hundred yards he succeeded in shooting every arrow through a willow-leaf. A few days later he undertook the same task, using his heaviest bow and balancing on his right elbow a cup filled to the brim with water; not a drop was spilt and again every arrow found its mark.

The following week he took a hundred light arrows and shot them in rapid succession at a distant target. The first one hit the bull's-eye; the second one pierced the first arrow straight in the notch; the third arrow lodged itself in the notch of the second; and so it continued until in a twinkling all hundred arrows were joined in a single straight line extending from the target to the bow itself. So true had he aimed that even after he had finished, the long line of arrows did not fall to the ground but remained quivering in mid-air. At this, even the Master Wei Fei, who had watched from the side, could not help clapping and shouting, 'Bravo!'

When after two months Chi Ch'ang finally returned home, his wife, chafing at his long neglect, started to rail at him. Thinking to correct her shrewishness, Chi Ch'ang quickly notched a Ch'i Wei arrow on a Raven bow, drew the string to its fullest extension and fired just above her eye. The arrow removed three of her lashes, but so great was its speed and so sure the aim that she was not even aware that anything had happened, and, without so much as blinking, continued to nag at her husband.

There was nothing more for Chi Ch'ang to learn from his teacher Wei Fei. He seemed close to the achievement of his ambition. Yet one obstacle remained, he realised with an unpleasant jolt: that obstacle was Wei Fei himself. So long as the Master lived, Chi Ch'ang could never call himself the greatest archer in the world. Though he now equalled Wei Fei in bowmanship, he felt sure that he could never excel him. The man's life was a constant denial of his own great purpose.

Walking through the fields one day, Chi Ch'ang caught sight of Wei Fei far in the distance. Without a moment's hesitation, he raised his bow, fixed an arrow and took aim. His old master, however, had sensed what was happening and in a flash had also notched an arrow on his bow. Both men fired at the same moment. Their arrows collided half-way and fell together to the ground. Chi Ch'ang immediately shot another arrow, but this was stopped in mid-air by a second unerring arrow from Wei Fei's bow. So the strange duel continued until the Master's quiver was empty but one arrow still remained to the pupil. 'Now's my chance!' muttered Chi Ch'ang and at once aimed the final arrow. Seeing this, Wei Fei broke off a twig from the thorn-bush beside him. As the arrow whistled towards his heart, he flicked the point sharply with the tip of one of the thorns and brought it to the ground at his feet.

Realising that his evil design had been thwarted, Chi Ch'ang was filled with a fine sense of remorse, which, to be sure, he would have been far from feeling had any of his arrows lodged where he intended. Wei Fei, on his side, was so relieved at his escape and so satisfied with this latest example of his own virtuosity that he could feel no anger for his would-be assassin. The two men ran up to each other and embraced with tears of devotion. (Strange indeed were the ways of ancient times! Would not such conduct be unthinkable to-day? The hearts of the men of old must have differed utterly from our own. How else explain that when the Duke Huan one evening demanded a new delicacy, the Director of the Imperial Kitchen, by name I Ya, baked his own son and begged the Duke to sample it; or that the fifteen-year-old youth, who was to be the first Emperor of the Shin Dynasty, did not scruple on the very night his father died to make love three times to the old man's favourite concubine?)

Even as he embraced his headstrong pupil in forgiveness, Wei Fei was aware that his life might any day be threatened again. The only way to rid himself of this constant menace was to divert Chi Ch'ang's mind to some new goal.

'My friend,' he said, standing aside, 'I have now, as you realise, transmitted to you all the knowledge of archery that I possess. If you wish to delve further into these mysteries, cross the lofty Ta Hsing Pass in the western country and climb to the summit of Mount Ho. There you may find the aged Master Kan Ying, who in the art of archery knows no equal in this or any age. Compared to his skill, our bowmanship is as the puny fumbling of children. There is no man in the world but the Master Kan Ying to whom you can now look for instruction. Seek him out, if indeed he be still alive, and become his pupil.'

Chi Ch'ang immediately set out for the West. To hear his achievements described as child's play had pricked his pride and made him fear that he might still be far from realising his great ambition. He must lose no time in climbing Mount Ho and matching his own achievements against those of this old Master.

He crossed the Ta Hsing Pass and made his way up the rugged mountain. His shoes were soon worn out and his feet and legs were cut and bleeding. Quite undaunted, he clambered up perilous precipices and traversed narrow planks set over huge chasms. After a month he reached the summit of Mount Ho and burst impetuously into the cave where dwelt Kan Ying. He proved to be an aged man with eyes as gentle as a sheep's. He was, indeed, quite frighteningly old—far older than anyone Chi Ch'ang had ever seen. His back was bent, and as he walked his white hair trailed along the ground.

Thinking that anyone of such an age must needs be deaf, Chi Ch'ang announced in a loud voice, 'I have come to find out if I am indeed as great an archer as I believe.' Without waiting for Kan Ying's reply, he took the great poplar bow, which he was carrying on his back, notched a Tsu Chieh arrow and aimed at a flock of migrating birds which were passing by high overhead. Instantly five birds came hurtling down through the clear blue sky.

The old man smiled tolerantly and said, 'But my dear Sir, this is mere shooting with bow and arrow. Have you not yet learned to shoot without shooting? Come with me.'

Ruffled by his failure to impress the old hermit, Chi Ch'ang followed him in silence to the edge of a great precipice some two hundred paces from the cave. When he glanced down, he thought that he must indeed have come into the presence of 'the great screen three thousand cubits high' described of old by Chang Tsai. Far below he saw a mountain-stream winding its way like a shining thread over the rocks. His eyes became blurred and his head began to spin. Meanwhile the Master Kan Ying ran lightly on to a narrow ledge which jutted straight out over the precipice and, turning round, said, 'Now show me your real skill. Come where I am standing and let me see your bowmanship.'

Chi Ch'ang was too proud to decline the challenge, and without hesitation changed places with the old man. No sooner had he stepped on to the ledge, however, than it began to sway slightly to and fro. Assuming a boldness that he was far from feeling, Chi Ch'ang took his bow and with trembling fingers tried to notch an arrow. Just then a pebble rolled off the ledge and began to fall thousands of feet through space. Following it with his eye, Chi

Ch'ang felt that he was going to lose his balance. He lay down on the ledge, clutching its edges firmly with his fingers. His legs shook and the perspiration flowed from his whole body.

The old man laughed, reached out his hand and helped Chi Ch'ang down off the ledge. Jumping on to it himself, he said, 'Allow me, Sir, to show you what archery really is.'

Though Chi Ch'ang's heart was pounding and his face was deadly white, he still had sufficient presence of mind to notice that the Master was empty-handed.

'What about your bow?' he asked in a sepulchral voice.

'My bow?' said the old man. 'My bow?' he repeated laughing. 'So long as one requires bow and arrow, one is still at the periphery of the art. Real archery dispenses with both bow and arrow!'

Directly above their heads a single kite was wheeling in the sky. The hermit looked up at it and Chi Ch'ang followed his gaze. So high was the bird that even to his sharp eyes it looked like a tiny sesame seed. Kan Ying notched an invisible arrow on an incorporeal bow, drew the string to its full extension and released it. Chi Ch'ang seemed to hear a swishing sound; the next moment the kite stopped flapping its wings and fell like a stone to the ground.

Chi Ch'ang was aghast. He felt that now for the first time he had glimpsed the limit of the art which he had so glibly undertaken to master.

For nine years he stayed in the mountains with the old hermit. What disciplines he underwent during this time, none ever knew. When in the tenth year he descended from the mountains and returned home, all were amazed at the change in him. His former resolute and arrogant countenance had disappeared; in its place had come the expressionless, wooden look of a simpleton. His old teacher, Wei Fei, come to visit him, said after a single glance, 'Now I can see that you have indeed become an expert! Such as I are no longer worthy ever to touch your feet.'

The inhabitants of Hantan hailed Chi Ch'ang as the greatest archer in the land and impatiently awaited the wonderful feats which he no doubt would soon display. But Chi Ch'ang did nothing to satisfy their expectations. Not once did he put his hands to a bow or arrow. The great poplar bow which he had taken with him on his journey he evidently had left behind. When someone asked him to explain, he answered in a languid tone, 'The ultimate stage of activity is inactivity; the ultimate stage of speaking is to refrain from speech; the ultimate in shooting is not to shoot.'

The more perceptive citizens of Hantan at once understood his meaning and stood in awe before this great expert archer who declined to touch a bow. It was his very refusal to shoot that now caused his reputation to grow.

All sorts of rumours and tales were bruited abroad about Chi Ch'ang. It was reported that always after midnight one could hear the sound of someone pulling an invisible bow-string on the roof of his house. Some said that this was the god of archery, who dwelt each day within the Master's soul and at night escaped to protect him from all evil spirits. A merchant who lived nearby circulated a rumour that one night he had clearly seen Chi Ch'ang riding on a cloud directly above his own house; for once he was carrying his bow, and he was matching his accomplishments against those of Hou I and Yang Yu-chi, the famous archers of legendary times. According to the merchant's story, the arrows fired by the three Masters disappeared in the distance between Orion and Sirius, trailing bright blue lights in the black sky.

There was also a thief who confessed that, as he had been about to climb into Chi Ch'ang's house, a sudden blast of air had rushed through the window and struck him so forcefully on the forehead that he had been knocked off the wall. Thenceforth all those who harboured evil designs avoided the precincts of Chi Ch'ang's house, and it was said that even flocks of migrating birds kept clear of the air above his roof.

As his renown spread through the land, reaching to the very clouds, Chi Ch'ang grew old. More and more he seemed to have entered the state in which both mind and body look no longer to things outside but exist by themselves in restful and elegant simplicity. His stolid face divested itself of every vestige of expression; no outside force could disturb his complete impassiveness. It was rare now for him to speak, and presently one could no longer tell whether or not he still breathed. Often his limbs seemed stark and lifeless as a withered tree. So attuned had he become to the underlying laws of the universe, so far removed from the insecurities and contradictions of things apparent, that in the evening of his life he no longer knew the difference between 'I' and 'he', between 'this' and 'that'. The kaleidoscope of sensory impressions no longer concerned him; for all he cared, his eye might have been an ear, his ear a nose, his nose a mouth.

Forty years after he had come down from the mountains, Chi Ch'ang peacefully left the world, like smoke disappearing in the sky. During these forty years he had never once mentioned the subject of archery, let alone taken up a bow and arrow.

Of his last year, the story is told that one day he visited a friend's house and saw lying on a table a vaguely familiar utensil whose name and use he could, however, not recall. After vainly searching his memory, he turned to his friend and said, 'Pray tell me: that object on your table—what is it called and for what is it used?' His host laughed as if Chi Ch'ang was joking. The old man pressed his question but his friend laughed again, though this time somewhat uncertainly. When he was questioned seriously for a third time, a look of consternation appeared on the friend's face. He gazed intently at Chi Ch'ang and, having made sure that he had heard correctly and also that the old man was neither mad nor speaking in jest, he stammered out in an awe-struck tone, 'Oh, Master. You must indeed be the greatest Master of all times. Only so can you have forgotten the bow—both its name and its use!'

It was said that for some time after this in the city of Hantan painters threw away their brushes, musicians broke the strings of their instruments, and carpenters were ashamed to be seen with their rules.

THE RIFLE

Translated by Lawrence Rogers

~

1

I used to enjoy watching my shadow as I marched with my rifle on my shoulder. I would catch sight of it again and again in the forest of rifle shadows visible through the clouds of dust our gaitered brogans raised in the sun. The forest moved on with the tramp of our feet. The ground that my shadow-rifle crawled over seemed as precious as home to me.

In early spring in northwest China and neighboring Mongolia whirlwinds of dust blow up and come racing across the sky. When one of these swept over us, a fine sand would settle on the surface of our rifles like a bloom of spore dust, no matter that we bundled ourselves in blankets, and when we ran our fingers over the top of the domed cover on the firing chamber, the mark traced was sharp and clear. And indoors, of course, a thick layer built up on our pieces, so that keeping them clean was all the more a challenge.

I felt almost giddy whenever I peered up the barrel of my rifle as it corkscrewed dizzily about a point it fancied in the bright sky. Then I would take out the magazine—the treasure vault—polish what might be likened to a woman's secret place, and firmly grasping the grip, dig out the dirt in the straight-line crack in the butt-plate's 'corn'—that's what I called the butt-plate screw; then I'd oil and swab the bore. That done, I would breathe a profound sigh of relief and wipe clean the forestock. I cannot tell you how much satisfaction the act of wiping it gave me. I could detail from memory its old wounds, each with its own history: the ill-defined circular cut here on the bottom toward the right side; and a little above that, the barren, pinched wound like a scar from an operation; the narrow, Buddha-eye gash on the left near the grip; and the strangest of all, a bump on the underside puffed up like a mole. Maybe during a fire fight some apricot candy got stuck to it and became part of the wood's grain in the sweat and heat under my tightly clenched hand. Again and again in the space of a day I would thus touch my rifle in one place, then another. And each time I did, I remembered her. I touched the gun in order to remember her.

At the age of 21, when I was about to leave the home islands of Japan, I wanted from an older woman of 26—a married woman whose husband had gone off to war—the most generous gift she could give me. I was escorting this woman, pregnant with her husband's child, back to her parent's home, and found myself stroking her swollen white belly, seven months along, in an old, run-down country inn we happened on. I then bade her farewell, having done no more than bury my face in her body's hollows and undulations. To my pleas to let me touch her more, that this was our last time together, she closed her eyes and kept them closed, as though in atonement, and refused to let me have my way, cautiously holding tight to my hands. Smell, things undefined to the touch, and a mole guided me.

I confirmed my very existence whenever I grasped my rifle. It was as though life flowed to me from it. The grip made me think of what her waist had been like before she got pregnant. I would grasp the slender waist of that Meiji model rifle with sadness in my heart.

That hurts, Shin! Stop! It won't work! I was sure I heard it saying that. I turned upon my rifle the brute force I could not direct at her. I was pretty strong then, and it was nothing for me to take hold of the grip, lift the gun up until it was perpendicular to the ground, and hold it in that position a good while.

The rifle had become my woman. And she was an older woman. Deep-down scars, a filled-out stock, an indisputably mature woman. A rifle shiny from the touch of other men's hands.

I didn't want to turn in my rifle, serial number A62377, for a new one. And they let me keep it. That was because when it came to marksmanship, no one who came in when I did could best me. I'm the son of a cabinet-maker and used to play with my father's rulers, so I had a good eye. When I took aim at the target, her lips would begin saying things to me.

Shin, I'll bet the women really go for you, don't they. You're the sort women like. That's a relief. I'm not the only one, am I. That's a big relief, I'll tell you. I don't feel guilty about him. I haven't told anyone, but I don't think it's his baby. I hope it's not. If it's a boy, he'll have your name. I was afraid, to tell you the truth. I almost forget I'm older than you. And if I did that, it would be all over. If I found that you had fallen in love with me. I want you to understand that. But I'll always be with you. I know! I'll be your gun.

I would shoot at the target with complete concentration. And when I fired, five bullet holes would open in tight overlap.

2

The seasoned troopers returned from a campaign, their blood up, about the time we recruits were finishing our basic training. The next day, as usual, we set off on the double for the training grounds outside the city. White opium poppies, blooming as profusely as rapeseed, encircled the collapsed city walls. In street stalls at the side of the road, pots of boiled pigs' feet bubbled in the billowing dust. The forest of guns was on the move. And once again I was absorbed in my own private pleasure. From my shoulder my rifle shouted for joy.

Squad Leader Oya drew a circle with a stick, looked at us, and gave his order.

'You will dig a pit! About this big. Two meters deep. Time allotted: two hours.'

I'll dig the pit, I told my rifle. *Wait for me. I'll be finished in no time. I'm faster than anyone else.* I started shoveling. I enjoyed all kinds of hard work then, whatever it was.

About the time we were finishing our task a curious group made its appearance. Men in Chinese clothes and shoes, and wearing leggings, and an ordinary Chinese woman. Their hands were tied behind them and two had poles on their shoulders. Ah! Chinese soldiers! Soldiers just like me! Immediately a sense of kinship welled within me and I was seized with the urge to say something to them. And how much stronger were my feelings for the woman! I could see my woman in her. I abruptly stopped digging in the pit and stared at her, devouring her with my eyes. I was stunned, speechless. I wondered if they were simply a work detail.

When the group came to a halt, they stood stock-still. Nobody moved.

'Tie them to the stakes!'

I looked up at the squad leader's smile with a feeling of uneasiness. It seemed to me no different from the amiable smile on his face when he used to turn my rifle upside down, slap the stock, pale as a fish's belly, and look it over as he held it upright before him.

'You're really good,' he would say. 'It's like there's a demon in your rifle, know what I mean? Let me have a look at that baby. It's damn near alive, this sucker.'

The seven prisoners made no move toward the pit. They were loath to go over to it, like sulking children set against moving an inch. Bayonets affixed to the ends of rifles prodded them along. Those prodding bayonets would not kill them, but once they stood in front of the hole, they were as good as dead. Several of them stood with their backs arched and were saying something in Chinese. I must have been the only one who was watching the woman. She looked at me, a hint of entreaty in her face. Inadvertently I nodded. Once I had done that I was no longer able to avert my face. She looked only at me; she would not take her eyes off me. A curtain of bangs overhung her dirt-smudged forehead. For whom had she so prettily trimmed her hair? Her face, yes, it was the face of my woman back home. If the chin had been a little longer, she would have looked just like her. But it was not only the face. She was pregnant. This woman, who had been driven like an animal for dozens of miles without adequate rations and brought here at the same fast gait as the soldiers, wore a pair of grimy trousers, and they were slightly distended in front. It seemed to me that she was not a soldier, but rather might have been a member of the resistance.

'Squad Leader, sir!'

My overabundant strength had turned, at a stroke, into a storm of agitation. The squad leader turned, picked up a stone, and tossed it at me.

'Get out of the hole, idiot!' he laughed. 'You're the only one still in it. You want us to bury you?'

He was right. I was still in the hole. The squad leader probably knew exactly what I wanted to say, and besides, what could I say beyond that? He was pleased with me, but not with any sign of weakness.

'Well? Spit it out! Come over here and tell everyone! What is it you want to say? Everyone listen now! What have you got to say to me?'

I loved Squad Leader Oya. He was the perfect soldier. As a soldier there was nothing he couldn't do. I had reached the second degree in kendo when I was in business school and had been captain of the school team, but I was no match for his sword work, all of which he had learned in the military. Even when it came to the abacus, which I considered my forte, I could not hold a candle to him.

'Can't say a thing, can you. You can't say a thing. All right then, *you* will kill her!'

I turned and looked at her in spite of myself.

'Shoot her from 100 meters. After you've shot her, fix bayonet, move out, and charge from a distance of 50 meters. You will then bayonet her. Double time, march!'

I did an about-face and broke into a run. The scorching sand gave way under my brogans. Unripened fruit lay scattered about the devastated melon field. As I ran, trampling the fruit underfoot, I wished that 100 meters would extend forever.

'Halt!'

His voice rode the hot wind in pursuit of me. I did another about-face.

'Ready in a standing position! Aim!'

Instinctively I held my breath. It was then I actually realized I was leveling my rifle, not at a target, but at a woman tied to a stake. I took aim. His command was the tripwire that would compel action. The gun was impatient to catch the target in its sights. As the front sight moved into the rear-sight notch, the woman's lips parted, her voice a whisper.

I wish this baby were yours. I do. But this has to be the end of it. I know I'll start wanting you to love me. If that happened it'd be all over. I'd be finished. Can you understand that, Shin?

My head was swimming. As the dizziness came, it suddenly seemed to me my only connection to this woman was the path the bullet would travel. A path its flat trajectory would undeviatingly follow, a path leading deep into her breast, deep into her soul. And into her belly.

'Fire!'

My piece, A62377, jumped at my shoulder. Immediately I attached my bayonet and started running. As I ran I could see that her head was drooping and that blood colored her chest. Her figure grew larger before me. As I continued to run I became a tool, part of the rifle, a mere tool that gave weight and force and direction to the rifle. As I had learned in training, I took a step forward, my arms extending themselves of their own accord. My mission and my drill were over.

'Well done!'

'Fantastic! With one shot!'

Squad Leader Oya patted my shoulder with obvious pride. 'Now you are a man!'

It was the rifle that sighed with relief and accepted the praise that was forthcoming. A62377, covered with its victim's blood, tried to humor its owner as he held it. A seething rage welled up within me. It was not directed at Squad Leader Oya, but against the tool that had deceived me, which had surreptitiously changed target practice into butchery. I had not become a man—far from it. Moved to wrath that turned my blood flow back upon itself, I fell unconscious on the spot.

3

The days went by in a flurry of activity. In the daytime we ran from one place to another, eating as we ran, practiced kendo, and went on marches, but at night my excess energy was now transformed from affection for my woman into terror of the eyes of the nameless Chinese woman. Far from becoming a man, I was now scarcely half a man. No matter how much I tried to reawaken feeling for my rifle, nothing of the passion I had known theretofore stirred within me, and when no one was around I would ram the cleaning rod into its muzzle and roughly churn it about. I let the butt plate rust and left the rear sight up. Having trampled underfoot the wooden stock that I had so loved out of hatred and the lingering attachment I still felt for the woman who had not stayed with me, I would then fling it down on the rush-mat floor. You're like a blood-sucking whore, I thought, though the fact was I had yet to really know any woman. My rifle, asprawl on the floor.

'Look at yourself!' I screamed. 'What a mess you are!'

I flew at the rifle and shook it, but all I got for my troubles was a mocking smile flitting for an instant across its gas port. OK, I thought, if that's how it is, and I smeared oil all over it, a thick coat of makeup.

Before long, the woman back home died within me. The woman in Chinese dress no longer tormented me. I was numb. And thanks, no doubt, to the whimsicalities to be found in my 21-year-old heart, I took to wenching on my days in town. I began to devote myself to giving pleasure to a Korean woman, limited only by my stamina.

The upshot was I picked up a disreputable disease, and, recruit though I was, was sent to a hospital miles away in the town of Tatong. Rifle A62377 was taken away from me, and I was given a new one of slapdash manufacture whose coarseness anyone could see at a glance. As soon as I took this 16-pound rifle in my hand, I knew that the center of gravity was in the wrong place, and when I supported that part I knew best in the palm of my hand, the bias was obvious. It may have been new, but the muzzle was abraded, and as I peered down the bore I saw that the pattern of light and shadow was irregular. This rifle did not even merit the lingering sense of abhorrence I still harbored.

I returned to my unit with my misshapen rifle and my misshapen mind and body.

4

One day, as I was coming back from the mess kitchen on the food distribution detail, one of the cooks told me to take the squad leader his meal. I had done this before on my own initiative. I had enjoyed doing it. To outwork everyone else, to be always on top of things, and to be thought the better for it, this made the 21-year-old soldier I then was content. As was the custom in the military then, the squad leader would read out loud for everyone to hear letters sent to me by the woman back in Japan. He would also have some fun at my expense.

'When I go back to Japan to get recruits I'm going to visit her for you,' he said once. 'Have her introduce me to a nice girl. Doesn't she have a younger sister?'

Of course, I was no longer getting letters from her by then. And that, too, was probably the squad leader's doing, but I could not bring myself to hate him for it.

'I have brought your food, sir.'

The squad leader's response to my voice was to close the door from the inside and shut me out. I thought this was because my voice had become unmilitary, and I shouted out my message several times in a high-spirited delivery. The door abruptly opened and the squad leader's face, almost expressionless, appeared. He grabbed the tray and flung it down on the stone paving of the quadrangle. Bewildered, I stooped down and started cleaning the mess up. A soldier from the barracks duty squad came running over and pushed me away. If a guy like that had tried that before, I wouldn't have let him get away with it, my serious nature notwithstanding, for I had confidence in my strength. Now, however, I simply stood there, dumbstruck. Because of the squad leader's refusal to eat, mess for all personnel was canceled, and I had to take back by myself the big serving pail, its food untouched, exposed all the while to the hate-filled stares of my comrades. I found out later the reason for this treatment was that the original bolt for my rifle was missing, apparently mixed up with someone else's. I had absolutely no recollection of exchanging it with anyone. Maybe it had been done before I ever got the weapon. When I had my old A62377 I could tell the difference between my base plug or firing-pin point and someone else's just by touch, I hadn't a leg to stand on now because Squad Leader Oya, who I had assumed would come to my defense, stood in the vanguard of those who admonished me for my want of spirit. That was why I ended up in the stockade. The bill of indictment was read out and I brought my rifle—bereft of any bolt now—to present arms. A piece of red cloth hung from its muzzle. They told me in basic training my present arms was excellent, and it had served as a model for everyone else's. And now, too, I gave them a punctilious present arms. It was my sole expression of protest. The red cloth signified the wearing of the convict's red kimono, but in my angry eyes it was the girl's red blood.

Everything receded. My weapon, my clothes, the other soldiers, even thoughts of home. That's how confused I was. I was hassled for anything and everything. A needle turned up missing or lice were found on someone, and immediately suspicion fell on me. The bunch that had earlier delighted in me because of my marksmanship now delighted in my inferiority. The examination for leadership school came and went. Even if it hadn't, I couldn't have taken it, nor had I any desire to. I was left in everyone's dust, a buck private.

About that time they decided to enter me in the division's marksmanship competition, and I was taken from the ranks for the honor of the regiment. I suppose this was the last time the squad leader expected anything of me. I asked him to get back my old rifle, A62377. A master sergeant, an old-timer, had it. The squad leader went and borrowed it and handed it over with a lighthearted smile.

'Get a high score this time and you're on your way up. Listen, remember how you were in training? You were a fine trooper then. I've asked the CO to do what he can for you. Do your best!'

The squad leader was overcome with emotion and wept manfully. I heard all this with my back to him. I was carefully inspecting the rifle. It had changed somehow as it had passed through other men's hands. The mole-bump on its side that I had taken such pleasure in remembering had been taken clean off and the wood was now sleek and smooth. While superficially it appeared to have been well taken care of, its cleaning had apparently been assigned to men who had only a perfunctory interest in maintaining it, and so I could see—to put it one way—earwax in the ears, bits of food between the teeth, flecks of dirt on hair backlit in the sunlight.

Indifferent to the squad leader's emotional speech, I suddenly burst out laughing and flung A62377 to the ground. I had got into the habit of throwing guns about.

'You idiot! Are you out of your mind!? Having been gracious enough to bestow this weapon upon you . . .'

What followed referred of course to His Majesty, the Emperor.

'The bolt, Squad Leader, sir!' I shouted as his brogan pressed down upon my cheek, 'it is the bolt the other man lost! It is not A62377's bolt!'

'Damn you! What of it!?'

'Nothing, sir. I was at fault. But I cannot represent the unit in the competition.'

'You "cannot"? That's not for you to decide! You *will* take part. You're telling me you won't?'

'I will do it, sir. I will do it.'

'You're damn right you will. Your rank insignia, take a good look at it. If I were you, I'd kill myself. Even here we have a suicide a year.'

I took part in the marksmanship competition. I was the only one to score close to zero. I shot my rounds off without even aiming.

5

Well into autumn that year we went out on extended patrol. I walked along thinking to myself that this was just a walking tour on which we were taking along guns, that I ought to ask what the purpose of each man carrying one was, that I simply wanted to eat and rest. Along the way we might run into walkers from the other side carrying *their* guns; then our walking tour would turn into war. This was what it was, this patrol of ours. The forest of rifles, seemingly unaware of this, wound its way upward along a mountain stream, a clear-water river called the Hutuo that flowed from deep within the Wutai Mountains, became the Bai River, and emptied into the sea at Tianjin. Within this silent forest I wanted to shriek my lungs out. Something unreal seemed to emanate from within my 16-pound burden.

I heard the unexpected voice of Oya coming from amid the forest of weapons.

'I'd really feel helpless in this Godforsaken place without my rifle. It's my sacred protector.'

But for me it was precisely because of my rifle that I was intolerably alone. I looked down at my reflection in the river and started. I saw an ashen-faced girl, a stake lashed to her back, entreating me.

The fever was already upon me by that time. My legs had turned to rubber, and getting face down at the river's edge to drink was almost beyond me. I was filled with despair when I saw a mountain of rock rising black before us like something out of a Sung landscape painting. The rifles with their brass muzzle caps filed upward, each affecting its own special look. Some were shod in stockings, some were bandaged, others completely enveloped in bags, and all gamboled about as though at a village festival. As I stood at the foot of the cliff my heart shouted. *Soon they will be consumed by flames, destroyed!*

I had broken ranks and was now bringing up the rear. Self-encouraging chants from halfway up the mountain fell full force upon me in keen reproach. To me, they were the voices of the rifles' malevolent spirits bent on tormenting me. Beside myself, I tried to shout out curses against those voices, but my own voice failed me.

I suddenly realized that someone was boosting me upward. I looked back and almost lost consciousness. The butt of my rifle was pushing me up, and Squad Leader Oya was pushing the gun. My rifle was behind me boosting me up. I spoke in both fear and indignation.

'Sir! Please kill me!'

The squad leader's face was expressionless and offered me no deliverance, only a message. *Some people kill themselves.*

After that I was put on a donkey. When I heard its bray I knew that I was high up off the ground and that it was the donkey, not me, that was doing the walking. And I could feel yet again, as though ordained by fate, the rifle biting into my back.

As dusk approached and the red glow of the setting sun blazed forebodingly on the treeless mountain of rock, a village, half fallen into ruin, appeared dreamlike before us. Our expedition was greeted by house walls across which were painted giant strings of anti-Japanese slogans. Suddenly the report of Czech-made machine guns arose at the summit and reverberated through the gorge.

Instantly the forest of rifles collapsed and started to clamber up the bullet-swallowing mountain of rock. *The festivities have begun! Well now, let's hear the pipes! This is the real thing. Dance! Dance!* Without warning I was dragged down off the donkey I had been riding.

6

There are breaks in my memory after that. When the war ended, I had 17 years left on my sentence to military prison.

They say I tried to burn up my rifle that night by setting fire to some straw. When the squad leader, who had been keeping an eye on me, came running over to cut me down, I picked up the rifle to protect myself. As it happened, the safety catch was off and my finger apparently engaged the trigger accidentally. A round shot out and hit him in the belly. I was cut on the shoulder.

The year after the war ended, I was in a freight depot in Tianjin, waiting for the day I would sail back to Japan. In the army prison I had been forced to squat in solitary for so long my knees had got used to it and now it pained me when I stood. When I had left the prison I had stuffed my rucksack with the personal effects of the warden, who had been sent off to an internment center for war criminals in Nanjing, and had finally made my way to Tianjin, escorted by a master sergeant from the Judge Advocate's Office, and now, day after day, I did forced labor for the Chinese.

Every day truckloads of old Meiji model rifles taken in the disarming of Japanese troops arrived. Presumably these were to be turned over directly to the Chinese military. Each day I would stand on the ground and mechanically catch the weapons as they were thrown down from the trucks, chanting to the rhythm of the work as I apathetically maintained the hurried pace. Then one day as I grabbed one, it seemed to be throbbing with life. I knew without even looking that it was A62377. *I* had forgotten, but my hands remembered. A fortuitous reunion it was, after having long ago gone our separate ways.

As I looked it over I saw that its steel parts, from barrel to butt—bolt included, of course—were all rusted. The stock had dried out and the fitting on the butt plate rattled loosely.

What has happened to that woman? Is she embracing her husband, finally back in Japan? Or is she as moribund as this gun? I talked to myself under my breath as I caught the weapons dropped down to me one after the other. *Shin, I don't want you to love me. I want to love you. Please understand.*

The Chinese soldier's unaccountably hate-filled eyes advanced on me and his whip flashed through the air.

UNZEN

Translated by Van Gessel

～

As he sat on the bus for Unzen, he drank a bottle of milk and gazed blankly at the rain-swept sea. The frosty waves washed languidly against the shore just beneath the coastal highway.

The bus had not yet left the station. The scheduled hour of departure had long since passed, but a connecting bus from Nagasaki still had not arrived, and their driver was chatting idly with the woman conductor and displaying no inclination to switch on the engine. Even so the tolerant passengers uttered no word of complaint, but merely pressed their faces against the window glass. A group of bathers from the hot springs walked by, dressed in large, thickly-padded kimonos. They shielded themselves from the rain with umbrellas borrowed from their inn. The counters of the gift shops were lined with all sorts of decorative shells and souvenir bean-jellies from the local hot springs, but there were no customers around to buy their wares.

'This place reminds me of Atagawa in Izu,' Suguro grumbled to himself as he snapped the cardboard top back onto the milk bottle. 'What a disgusting landscape.'

He had to chuckle a bit at himself for coming all the way to this humdrum spot at the western edge of Kyushu. In Tokyo he had not had the slightest notion that this village of Obama, home of many of the Christian martyrs and some of the participants in the Shimabara Rebellion, would be so commonplace a town.

From his studies of the Christian era in Japan, Suguro knew that around 1630 many of the faithful had made the climb from Obama towards Unzen, which a Jesuit of the day had called 'one of the tallest mountains in Japan'. The Valley of Hell high up on Unzen was an ideal place for torturing Christians. According to the records, after 1629, when the Nagasaki Magistrate Takenaka Shigetsugu hit upon the idea of abusing the Christians in this hot spring inferno, sixty or seventy prisoners a day were roped together and herded from Obama to the top of this mountain.

Now tourists strolled the streets of the village, and popular songs blared out from loudspeakers. Nothing remained to remind one of that sanguinary history. But precisely three centuries before the present month of January, on a day of misty rain, the man whose footsteps Suguro now hoped to retrace had undoubtedly climbed up this mountain from Obama.

Finally the engine started up, and the bus made its way through the village. They passed through a district of two- and three-storey Japanese inns, where men leaned with both hands on the railings of the balconies and peered down into the bus. Even those windows which were deserted were draped with pink and white washcloths and towels. When the bus finally passed beyond the hotel district, both sides of the mountain road were lined with old stone walls and squat farmhouses with thatched roofs.

Suguro had no way of knowing whether these walls and farmhouses had existed in the Christian century. Nor could he be sure that this road was the one travelled by the Christians, the officers, and the man he was pursuing. The only certain thing was that, during their fitful stops along the path, they had looked up at this same Mount Unzen wrapped in grey mist.

He had brought a number of books with him from Tokyo, but he now regretted not including a collection of letters from Jesuits of the day who had reported on the Unzen martyrdoms to their superiors in Rome. He had thoughtlessly tossed into his bag one book that would be of no use to him on this journey—Collado's *Christian Confessions*.

The air cooled as the bus climbed into the hills, and the passengers, peeling skins from the *mikan* they had bought at Obama, listened half-heartedly to the sing-song travelogue provided by the conductor.

'Please look over this way,' she said with a waxy smile. 'There are two large pine trees on top of the hill we are about to circle. It's said that at about this spot, the Christians of olden days would turn around and look longingly back at the village of Obama. These trees later became known as the Looking-Back Pines.'

Collado's *Christian Confessions* was published in Rome in 1632, just five years before the outbreak of the Shimabara Rebellion. By that time the shogunate's persecution of the Christians had grown fierce, but a few Portuguese and Italian missionaries had still managed to steal into Japan from Macao or Manila. The *Christian Confessions* were printed as a practical guide to Japanese grammar for the benefit of these missionaries. But what Suguro found hard to understand was why Collado had made public the confessions of these Japanese Christians, when a Catholic priest was under no circumstances permitted to reveal the innermost secrets of the soul shared with him by members of his flock.

Yet the night he read the *Confessions*, Suguro felt as though a more responsive chord had been struck within him than with any other history of the Christian era he had encountered. Every study he had read was little more than a string of paeans to the noble acts of priests and martyrs and common believers inspired by faith. They were without exception chronicles of those who had sustained their beliefs and their testimonies no matter what sufferings or tortures they had to endure. And each time he read them, Suguro had to sigh, 'There's no way I can emulate people like this.'

He had been baptized as a child, along with the rest of his family. Since then he had passed through many vicissitudes and somehow managed to arrive in his forties without rejecting his religion. But that was not due to firm resolve or unshakeable faith. He was more than adequately aware of his own spiritual slovenliness and pusillanimity. He was certain that an unspannable gulf separated him from the ancient martyrs of Nagasaki, Edo, and Unzen who had effected glorious martyrdoms. Why had they all been so indomitable?

Suguro diligently searched the Christian histories for someone like himself. But there was no one to be found. Finally he had stumbled across the *Christian Confessions* one day in a second-hand bookshop, and as he flipped indifferently through the pages of the book, he had been moved by the account of a man whose name Collado had concealed. The man had the same feeble will and tattered integrity as Suguro. Gradually he had formed in his mind an image of this man—genuflecting like a camel before the priest nearly three hundred years earlier, relishing the almost desperate experience of exposing his own filthiness to the eyes of another.

'I stayed for a long time with some heathens. I didn't want the innkeeper to realize I was a Christian, so I went with him often to the heathen temples and chanted along with them. Many times when they praised the gods and buddhas, I sinned greatly by nodding and agreeing with them. I don't remember how many times I did that. Maybe twenty or thirty times—more than twenty, anyway.

'And when the heathens and the apostates got together to slander us Christians and blaspheme against God, I was there with them. I didn't try to stop them talking or to refute them.

'Just recently, at the Shogun's orders the Magistrate came to our fief from the capital, determined to make all the Christians here apostatize. Everyone was interrogated and pressed to reject the Christian codes, or at least to apostatize in form only. Finally, in order to save the lives of my wife and children, I told them I would abandon my beliefs.'

Suguro did not know where this man had been born, or what he had looked like. He had the impression he was a samurai, but there was no way to determine who his master might have been. The man would have had no inkling that his private confession would one day be published in a foreign land, and eventually fall into the hands of one of his own countrymen again, to be read by a person like Suguro. Though he did not have a clear picture of how the man looked, Suguro had some idea of the assortment of facial expressions he would have had to employ in order to evade detection. If he had been born in that age, Suguro would have had no qualms about going along with the Buddhist laymen to worship at their temples, if that meant he would not be exposed as a Christian. When someone mocked the Christian faith, he would have lowered his eyes and tried to look unconcerned. If so ordered, he might even have written out an oath of apostasy, if that would mean saving the lives of his family as well as his own.

A faint ray of light tentatively penetrated the clouds that had gathered over the summit of Unzen. Maybe it will clear up, he thought. In summer this paved road would no doubt be choked by a stream of cars out for a drive, but now there was only the bus struggling up the mountain with intermittent groans. Groves of withered trees shivered all around. A cluster of rain-soaked bungalows huddled silently among the trees, their doors tightly shut.

'Listen, martyrdom is no more than a matter of pride.'

He had had this conversation in the corner of a bar in Shinjuku. A pot of Akita salted-fish broth simmered in the centre of the sake-stained table. Seated around the pot, Suguro's elders in the literary establishment had been discussing the hero of a novel he had recently published. The work dealt with some Christian martyrs in the 1870s. The writers at the gathering claimed that they could not swallow the motivations behind those martyrdoms the way Suguro had.

'At the very core of this desire to be a martyr you'll find pride, pure and simple.'

'I'm sure pride plays a part in it. Along with the desire to become a hero, and even a touch of insanity, perhaps. But—'

Suguro fell silent and clutched his glass. It was a simple task to pinpoint elements of heroism and pride among the motives for martyrdom. But when those elements were obliterated residual motives still remained. Those residual motives were of vital importance.

'Well, if you're going to look at it that way, you can find pride and selfishness underlying virtually every human endeavour, every single act of good faith.'

In the ten years he had been writing fiction, Suguro had grown increasingly impatient with those modern novelists who tried to single out the egotism and pride in every act of man. To Suguro's mind, such a view of humanity entailed the loss of something of consummate value, like water poured through a sieve.

The road wound its way to the summit through dead grass and barren woods. In days past, lines of human beings had struggled up this path. Both pride and madness had certainly been part of their make-up, but there must have been something more to it.

'The right wing during the war, for instance, had a certain martyr mentality. I can't help thinking there's something impure going on when people are intoxicated by something like that. But perhaps I feel that way because I experienced the war myself,' one of his elders snorted as he drank down his cup of tepid sake. Sensing an irreconcilable misunderstanding between himself and this man, Suguro could only grin acquiescently.

Before long he caught sight of a column of white smoke rising like steam from the belly of the mountain. Though the windows of the bus were closed, he smelled a faintly sulphuric odour. Milky white crags and sand came into clear focus.

'Is that the Valley of Hell?'

'No.' The conductor shook her head. 'It's a little further up.'

A tiny crack in the clouds afforded a glimpse of blue sky. The bus, which up until now had panted along, grinding its gears, suddenly seemed to catch its breath and picked up speed. The road had levelled off, then begun to drop. A series of arrows tacked to the leafless trees, apparently to guide hikers, read 'Valley of Hell'. Just ahead was the red roof of the rest-house.

Suguro did not know whether the man mentioned in the *Confessions* had come here to the Valley of Hell. But, as if before Suguro's eyes, the image of another individual had overlapped with that of the first man and now stumbled along with his head bowed. There was a little more detailed information about this second man. His name was Kichijiro, and he first appeared in the historical records on the fifth day of December, 1631, when seven priests and Christians were tortured at the Valley of Hell. Kichijiro came here to witness the fate of the fathers who had cared for him. He had apostatized much earlier, so he had been able to blend in with the crowd of spectators. Standing on tiptoe, he had witnessed the cruel punishments which the officers inflicted on his spiritual mentors.

Father Christovao Ferreira, who later broke under torture and left a filthy smudge on the pages of Japanese Christian history, sent to his homeland a letter vividly describing the events of that day. The seven Christians arrived at Obama on the evening of December the second, and were driven up the mountain all the following day. There were several look-out huts on the slope, and that evening the seven captives were forced into one of them, their feet and hands still shackled. There they awaited the coming of dawn.

'The tortures commenced on the fifth of December in the following manner. One by one each of the seven was taken to the brink of the seething pond. There they were shown the frothy spray from the boiling water, and ordered to renounce their faith. The air was chilly and the hot water of the pond churned so furiously that, had God not sustained them, a single look would have caused them to faint away. They all shouted, "Torture us! We will not recant!" At this response, the guards stripped the garments from the prisoners' bodies and bound their hands and feet. Four of them held down a single captive as a ladle holding about a quarter of a litre was filled with the boiling water. Three ladlesful were slowly pored over each body. One of the seven, a young girl called Maria, fainted from the excruciating pain and fell to the ground. In the space of thirty-three days, each of them was subjected to this torture a total of six times.'

Suguro was the last one off when the bus came to a stop. The cold, taut mountain air blew a putrid odour into his nostrils. White steam poured onto the highway from the tree-ringed valley.

'How about a photograph? Photographs, anyone?' a young man standing beside a large camera on a tripod called out to Suguro. 'I'll pay the postage wherever you want to send it.'

At various spots along the road stood women proffering eggs in baskets and waving clumsily-lettered signs that read 'Boiled Eggs'. They too touted loudly for business.

Weaving their way among these hawkers, Suguro and the rest of the group from the bus walked towards the valley. The earth, overgrown with shrubbery, was virtually white, almost the colour of flesh stripped clean of its layer of skin. The rotten-smelling steam gushed ceaselessly from amid the trees. The narrow path stitched its way back and forth between springs of hot, bubbling water. Some parts of the white-speckled pools lay as calm and flat as a wall of plaster; others eerily spewed up slender sprays of gurgling water. Here and there on the hillocks formed from sulphur flows stood pine trees scorched red by the heat.

The bus passengers extracted boiled eggs from their paper sacks and stuffed them into their mouths. They moved forward like a column of ants.

'Come and look over here. There's a dead bird.'

'So there is. I suppose the gas fumes must have asphyxiated it.'

All he knew for certain was that Kichijiro had been a witness to those tortures. Why had he come? There was no way of knowing whether he had joined the crowd of Buddhist spectators in the hope of rescuing the priests and the faithful who were being tormented. The only tangible piece of information he had about Kichijiro was that he had forsworn his religion to the officers, 'so that his wife and children might live'. Nevertheless, he had followed in the footsteps of those seven Christians, walking all the way from Nagasaki to Obama, then trudging to the top of the bitterly cold peak of Unzen.

Suguro could almost see the look on Kichijiro's face as he stood at the back of the crowd, furtively watching his former companions with the tremulous gaze of a dog, then lowering his eyes in humiliation. That look was very like Suguro's own. In any case, there was no way Suguro could stand in chains before these loathsomely bubbling pools and make any show of courage.

A momentary flash of white lit up the entire landscape; then a fierce eruption burst forth with the smell of noxious gas. A mother standing near the surge quickly picked up her crouching child and retreated. A placard reading 'Dangerous Beyond This Point' was thrust firmly into the clay. Around it the carcasses of three dead swallows were stretched out like mummies.

This must be the spot where the Christians were tortured, he thought. Through a crack in the misty, shifting steam, Suguro saw the black outlines of a cross. Covering his nose and mouth with a handkerchief and balancing precariously near the warning sign, he peered below him. The mottled water churned and sloshed before his eyes. The Christians must have stood just where he was standing now when they were tortured. And Kichijiro would have stayed behind, standing about where the mother and her child now stood at a cautious distance, watching the spectacle with the rest of the crowd. Inwardly, did he ask them to forgive him? Had Suguro been in his shoes, he would have had no recourse but to repeat over and over again, 'Forgive me! I'm not strong enough to be a martyr like you. My heart melts just to think about this dreadful torture.'

Of course, Kichijiro could justify his attitude. If he had lived in a time of religious freedom, he would never have become an apostate. He might not have qualified for sainthood, but he could have been a man who tamely maintained his faith. But to his regret, he had been born in an age of persecution, and out of fear he had tossed away his beliefs. Not everyone can become a saint or a martyr. Yet must those who do not qualify as saints be branded forever with the mark of the traitor?—Perhaps he had made such a plea to the Christians who vilified him. Yet, despite the logic of his argument, he surely suffered pangs of remorse and cursed his own faint resolve.

'The apostate endures a pain none of you can comprehend.'

Over the span of three centuries this cry, like the shriek of a wounded bird, reached Suguro's ears. That single line recorded in the *Christian Confessions* cut at Suguro's chest like a sharp sword. Surely those were the words Kichijiro must have shouted to himself here at Unzen as he looked upon his tormented friends.

They reboarded the bus. The ride from Unzen to Shimabara took less than an hour. A fistful of blue finally appeared in the sky, but the air remained cold. The same conductor forced her usual smile and commented on the surroundings in a sing-song voice.

The seven Christians, refusing to bend to the tortures at Unzen, had been taken down the mountain to Shimabara, along the same route Suguro was now following. He could almost see them dragging their scalded legs, leaning on walking-sticks and enduring lashes from the officers.

Leaving some distance between them Kichijiro had timorously followed behind. When the weary Christians stopped to catch their breath, Kichijiro also halted, a safe distance behind. He hurriedly crouched down like a rabbit in the overgrowth, lest the officers suspect him, and did not rise again until the group had resumed their trek. He was like a jilted woman plodding along in pursuit of her lover.

Half-way down the mountain he had a glimpse of the dark sea. Milky clouds veiled the horizon; several wan beams of sunlight filtered through the cracks, Suguro thought how blue the ocean would appear on a clear day.

'Look—you can see a blur out there that looks like an island. Unfortunately, you can't see it very well today. This is Dango Island, where Amakusa Shiro, the commander of the Christian forces, planned the Shimabara Rebellion with his men.'

At this the passengers took a brief, apathetic glance towards the island. Before long the view of the distant sea was blocked by a forest of trees.

What must those seven Christians have felt as they looked at this ocean? They knew they would soon be executed at Shimabara. The corpses of martyrs were swiftly reduced to ashes and cast upon the seas. If that were not done, the remaining Christians would surreptitiously worship the clothing and even locks of hair from the martyrs as though they were holy objects. And so the seven, getting their first distant view of the ocean from this spot, must have realized that it would be their grave. Kichijiro too would have looked at the sea, but with a different kind of sorrow—with the knowledge that the strong ones in the world of faith were crowned with glory, while the cowards had to carry their burdens with them throughout their lives.

When the group reached Shimabara, four of them were placed in a cell barely three feet tall and only wide enough to accommodate one tatami. The other three were jammed into another room equally cramped. As they awaited their punishment, they persistently encouraged one another and went on praying. There is no record of where Kichijiro stayed during this time.

The village of Shimabara was dark and silent. The bus came to a stop by a tiny wharf where the rickety ferry-boat to Amakusa was moored forlornly. Wood chips and flotsam bobbed on the small waves that lapped at the breakwater. Among the debris floated an object that resembled a rolled-up newspaper; it was the corpse of a cat.

The town extended in a thin band along the seafront. The fences of local factories stretched far into the distance, while the odour of chemicals wafted all the way to the highway.

Suguro set out towards the reconstructed Shimabara Castle. The only signs of life he encountered along the way were a couple of high-school girls riding bicycles.

'Where is the execution ground where the Christians were killed?' he asked them.

'I didn't know there was such a place,' said one of them, blushing. She turned to her friend. 'Have you heard of anything like that? You don't know, do you?' Her friend shook her head.

He came to a neighbourhood identified as a former samurai residence. It had stood behind the castle, where several narrow paths intersected. A crumbling mud wall wound its way between the paths. The drainage ditch was as it had been in those days. Summer mikans poked their heads above the mud wall, which had already blocked out the evening sun. All the buildings were old, dark and musty. They had probably been the residence of a low-ranking samurai, built at the end of the Tokugawa period. Many Christians had been executed at the Shimabara grounds, but Suguro had not come across any historical documents identifying the location of the prison.

He retraced his steps, and after a short walk came out on a street of shops where popular songs were playing. The narrow street was packed with a variety of stores, including gift shops. The water in the drainage ditch was as limpid as water from a spring.

'The execution ground? I know where that is.' The owner of a tobacco shop directed Suguro to a pond just down the road. 'If you go straight on past the pond, you'll come to a nursery school. The execution ground was just to the side of the school.'

Though they say nothing of how he was able to do it, the records indicate that Kichijiro was allowed to visit the seven prisoners on the day before their execution. Possibly he put some money into the hands of the officers.

Kichijiro offered a meagre plate of food to the prisoners, who were prostrate from their ordeal.

'Kichijiro, did you retract your oath?' one of the captives asked compassionately. He was eager to know if the apostate had finally informed the officials that he could not deny his faith. 'Have you come here to see us because you have retracted?'

Kichijiro looked up at them timidly and shook his head.

'In any case, Kichijiro, we can't accept this food.'

'Why not?'

'Why not?' The prisoners were mournfully silent for a moment. 'Because we have already accepted the fact that we will die.'

Kichijiro could only lower his eyes and say nothing. He knew that he himself could never endure the sort of agony he had witnessed at the Valley of Hell on Unzen.

Through his tears he whimpered, 'If I can't suffer the same pain as you, will I be unable to enter Paradise? Will God forsake someone like me?'

He walked along the street of shops as he had been instructed and came to the pond. A floodgate blocked the overflow from the pond, and the water poured underground and into the drainage ditch in the village. Suguro read a sign declaring that the purity of the water in Shimabara village was due to the presence of this pond.

He heard the sounds of children at play. Four or five young children were tossing a ball back and forth in the nursery school playground. The setting sun shone feebly on the swings and sandbox in the yard. He walked around behind a drooping hedge of rose bushes and located the remains of the execution ground, now the only barren patch within a grove of trees.

It was a deserted plot some three hundred square yards in size, grown rank with brown weeds; pines towered over a heap of refuse. Suguro had come all way from Tokyo to have a look at this place. Or had he made the journey out of a desire to understand better Kichijiro's emotions as he stood in this spot?

The following morning the seven prisoners were hoisted onto the unsaddled horses and dragged through the streets of Shimabara to this execution ground.

One of the witnesses to the scene has recorded the events of the day: 'After they were paraded about, they arrived at the execution ground, which was surrounded by a palisade. They were taken off their horses and made to stand in front of stakes set three metres apart. Firewood was already piled at the base of the stakes, and straw roofs soaked in sea water had been placed on top of them to prevent the flames from raging too quickly and allowing the martyrs to die with little agony. The ropes that bound them to the stakes were tied as loosely as possible, to permit them, up to the very moment of death, to twist their bodies and cry out that they would abandon their faith.

'When the officers began setting fire to the wood, a solitary man broke through the line of guards and dashed towards the stakes. He was shouting something, but I could not hear what he said over the roar of the fires. The fierce flames and smoke prevented the man from approaching the prisoners. The guards swiftly apprehended him and asked if he was a Christian. At that, the man froze in fear, and jabbering, "I am no Christian. I have nothing to do with these people! I just lost my head in all the excitement," he skulked away. But some in the crowd had seen him at the rear of the assemblage, his hands pressed together as he repeated over and over, "Forgive me! Forgive me!"

'The seven victims sang a hymn until the flames enveloped their stakes. Their voices were exuberant, totally out of keeping with the cruel punishment they were even then enduring. When those voices suddenly ceased, the only sound was the dull crackling of wood. The man who had darted forward could be seen walking lifelessly away from the execution ground. Rumours spread through the crowd that he too had been a Christian.'

Suguro noticed a dark patch at the very centre of the execution ground. On closer inspection he discovered several charred stones half buried beneath the black earth. Although he had no way of knowing whether these stones had been used here three hundred years before, when seven Christians had been burned at the stake, he hurriedly snatched up one of the stones and put it in his pocket. Then, his spine bent like Kichijiro's, he walked back towards the road.

ABE KOBO (1924–1993)

THE BET

Translated by Juliet Winters Carpenter

❦

1

Seated at my drawing board, I looked across at the director of general affairs at AB Company. I held myself perfectly straight, my spine a full two inches from the back of the chair, unable to relax until I heard the man's reply. He showed no sign of answering.

In the strong light from the draftsman's lamp over my desk, a thick bundle of blueprints gleamed brightly where the pages had been freshly cut. The director's face was in shadow, partially obscured by the lampshade. I looked at my watch. It was 6:15. Everyone had gone home but my assistant. Fluorescent lights flickered with a noise like the beating of insect wings.

'Well? Is there some problem with my proposal?' I asked.

The man shifted, his chair squeaking as he did so, and probed his jaw with the balls of his fingers as if pushing stray whiskers back into the flesh. At last he spoke. 'Not in the least. We are perfectly content to leave everything in your hands. It's just that this time, the alteration we want done is rather substantial, you might even say drastic.'

'I realize that. It's a great change. This wall, right here, the wall of Room 17 adjacent to Room 18—you want this juxtaposed to the president's office.'

'Yes, yes.' Chuckling, the man took the unlit cigarette he'd been fingering and rubbed its tip over the plans.

'But the president's office, you see, is on the third floor. And Room 17 is on the second floor.'

'Ah, yes. I suppose the technical aspects involved in putting two rooms on different floors next to each other would be quite difficult.'

'That's putting it mildly.'

'But you've solved any number of equally difficult problems before.'

'Well, all I want to know is, is this change really worth the trouble?'

'Well, of course, if we didn't think it necessary then we'd never—'

'Wait. Let's not worry about that now.' I slid forward, leaning back in my chair. The man's beige tie was reflected in the shiny blade of my letter-opener. But then I had to sit up again quickly to begin an explanation of the blueprints. 'As you know, this makes the thirty-sixth time I've had to revise the blueprints.'

'I apologize for all the trouble we've caused you.'

'The number of times doesn't bother me. This is my job, after all. It's only fair that I redo the work as often as necessary, until you're satisfied. All I'm concerned about is . . . well . . . the results. What do you say? Will you look these blueprints over and tell me exactly what you think?'

'But I'm not sure what I—'

'Let me be specific. Here, on this page, will you take a look at this?'

'Uh huh.'

'You see?'

'I'm afraid maps and drawings are not my forte.'

'This is a lateral cross-section.'

'So . . . This would be a stairway. . . . This line is an extension of this line, and . . . wait a minute. There's something peculiar going on. How does this line? . . .'

'It connects here.'

'Then what's this? There seems to be another stairway, right behind the other one.'

'There most certainly is. That was the only way I could connect the first mezzanine with the second, without going through the second floor.'

'Why on earth would you want to do that?'

'There, you see? Even you think it's strange. But that's the sort of thing that happens when I have to put in changes haphazardly, one after another.'

'There's nothing haphazard about any of this.' For the first time, his expression revealed a hint of strain. 'All of the changes we have requested are the result of laborious surveys and meticulous planning.'

'If that's the case, fine. Then I assume you are satisfied with these results?'

'Yes, very interesting. I must say I'm intrigued.'

'Good. You've set my mind at ease. Then you're willing to sign this provisional consent form?'

'I beg your pardon?'

'You see, I need evidence that you agree, in principle, that the blueprints are finished as they are.'

'But what about the new alteration?'

'Yes, yes, I know. But apart from that, in order to wind up the work I've done so far—'

'I fail to see what you're driving at.'

'Surely you realize that this design is totally lacking in common sense.'

'Maybe.'

'Yes, and so I'd like to make it perfectly clear that you're entrusting this work to me in full awareness of these anomalies. Otherwise you might come along later and say, "Well, if you knew it was going to turn out strangely, you didn't have to stick so slavishly to our requests. It's your job to listen to our requests, and make sense out of them." If that happened, all my hard work would go right down the drain.'

'Naturally, you are expected to follow all instructions to the letter.'

'But just because you had a hundred people, you wouldn't need a hundred hallways! However many hundreds of staff you had, one or two hallways would be enough! Just because you might need a detailed street map, there'd be no reason to record the number of branches in every tree along the road! Architectural design is more than numbers.'

'Somehow you seem to have gotten the wrong impression. Every one of our requests is the product of careful study. There's nothing hit-or-miss, and any apparent duplication is deliberate.'

'Then you'll sign?'

'No, I'm afraid I couldn't.'

'Why not?'

'As long as everything has been left to you, I've got to have some sign of assurance from you. Otherwise that puts me in a very

266

awkward position. Don't you see that? But in fact, the more I listen to you, the more it seems to me you have no self-confidence at all and are just trying to escape responsibility.'

'Wait—now you're getting the wrong idea.'

'Then you do have confidence that you know what you're about? Well, in that case—'

'Wait, wait. This job is something everyone in the business has his eye on. I mean after all, the chance to design the new annex for the showcase AB Building—it can't help attracting attention. And I'm as ambitious as the next guy. If this succeeds, it will be great publicity. But if it doesn't . . .'

'Leave the publicity angle to us. That's our specialty.'

'Yes—yes, of course.'

'Or do you expect to fail?'

'No, of course not. But frankly, I am a bit worried. What we've got here goes completely against conventional theories of modern building design.'

'But theory and function are surely not the same.'

'Of course not. But you can't equate architectural function with mechanical function, either. Especially in a large-scale project like this, rather than analyzing every last little detail, a better way to improve function is to maximize the efficient use of space overall. For that reason it works best to begin by dividing the whole into large, simple blocks—'

'Look, who cares about modern theories of design?'

'This happens to be my theory.'

'Then you regret having taken on the project?'

'No, no. Well, there may have been times I felt that way. Sometimes I'd think, I can't show these plans to anybody, my client has made some kind of horrible mistake. And then I'd wonder whatever possessed me to take all your specifications at face value. I spent a lot of time worrying. But I never could get you to see it my way.'

'So you gave up trying?'

'There definitely were times when I felt like it. But as time went by, I don't know, gradually I became intrigued.'

'Intrigued?'

'Yes. These plans definitely fly in the face of all previous architectural theory, especially theories of space utility. But the more I toy with them, the more I sense new, unforeseen possibilities. This just might be the wave of the future. And yet, unable to back it up with any known theory, I wind up confused, at a total loss. I guess you could say I'm starting to lose my bearings.'

'Ah.'

'So you see, in order to shore up my confusion from some outside source, I'd like very much to have you sign here.'

'Good, now I think I understand your position.'

'Then you'll do it?'

'But listening to your account has convinced me more than ever that such a step is totally unnecessary.'

'It has?'

'All you have to do is build up your confidence. That's the only way. Don't you see? It would be easy for me to sign the paper, but that would only underscore your lack of confidence. For your own sake, I have to refuse.'

'But do you people have any idea just how extraordinary these plans are?'

'Don't worry. Look, I have an idea. Why don't you stop by our office some day and see how we operate?'

'I've been by before . . .'

'Yes, but looking in from the outside doesn't give you the real picture. The advertising business is as complicated as a living organism. Once you understand how it operates, I'm sure your doubts will evaporate.'

'Really?'

'Absolutely. Your lack of confidence just goes to show how much you don't understand. So you'll come? When?'

'Any time, as far as I'm concerned.'

'The sooner the better. Tomorrow morning?'

'Fine with me.'

'Good. Then I'll see you tomorrow, say at 8:30.'

'That's just when everyone gets to work, isn't it?'

'Right. I'd like to have you spend the day with us. As a sort of temporary employee, if you don't mind.'

'Fine.'

He nodded, smiling with satisfaction, and started to get up. 'Well, I managed to get by without smoking a single cigarette the whole time I was here,' he said, brushing bits of crushed cigarette from his hands into the ashtray. 'Whenever I feel like a smoke, I crush one in my hands this way. I recommend the technique.

Somehow, feeling the tobacco between your fingers drives home what poison it is, and before you know it you've lost all desire to light up.'

'Yeah ... well ... thanks for everything.' I stood up to see him out, switching off the desk light.

2

The following morning, at 8:30 sharp, I arrived in front of the AB Building. The taxi driver wiped the windshield with his glove, waiting for me to count out the exact change. A utility pole stood among the trees by the side of the street.

Three young women came along, walking in step, and entered the building with a sidelong glance at me. One of them removed her earrings and stuffed them quickly into an overcoat pocket. I followed them up the stone steps.

A cleaning woman by the entrance plunged a rag into a bucket and sloshed it around with red hands as she called out to the young women. 'Welcome home!'

I couldn't believe my ears. But then the trio responded in unison, 'Hi, we're back!' Evidently I had heard correctly.

Did they live here? Maybe they had only gone out for breakfast. This might be one sign of what that fellow last night had spoken of—the hidden complexity of the advertising business.

'Welcome home,' called out another female voice. Certain she couldn't mean me, I went by without replying. 'Yoo-hoo,' she called again, so I turned to find it was the receptionist. Apparently she did mean me.

'Pardon me, are you a visitor?' She was a young thing with a timid, artless expression. 'Could you sign in, please?'

'I guess you almost mistook me for an employee, didn't you?' I said, smiling cheerfully as I accepted a freshly sharpened pencil. Suddenly my glasses fogged up on the inside, and the receptionist disappeared. There was a vague smell of cosmetics and singed paper.

'No, sir.'

'But you said "Welcome home."' Swiftly rubbing the insides of my lenses with the balls of my thumbs, I added, 'You must have a lot of live-in employees in this building.'

'No, it's our custom to greet each other that way.'

'Strange.' I finished filling out the form and said, 'Is this okay?'

'Wait a moment.' Without the slightest hint of a smile, she dialed a number and after a short consultation announced 'You can go on in,' as if letting down her guard for the first time. 'Take the elevator in front to the reception room on the second floor, and wait there.'

The hall was dark, the color of used cooking oil. A group of employees passed swiftly by me, filling up the elevator. The doors closed. Looking around, I caught sight of a stairway on my left. Next to it was a green light. There seemed no point in waiting for the elevator, so I decided to take the stairs.

Wisps of steam rose toward the walls from the radiator in the hallway. Across from the stairway was a door with a wooden sign marked 'Supplies Department', silhouetted with white light from within. As I set foot on the stairs, I spotted a sign beneath the green light on the wall.

DON'T DEFEND—ATTACK

Halfway up, I passed a man who stuck his index finger through his black bow tie and scratched his chin as if performing some rite. Then he paused and said, 'Say, on that card, was there a fire engine siren?'

'Card? What card?' I said.

'Right. Well, you've got me there,' he said, and hurried on by. This time, apparently, I really had been taken for an employee. On the landing I came to another sign.

GIVE FORM TO DESIRE

I kept going up, and came to another landing. Judging from the height of the ceiling on the first floor, there couldn't possibly be two landings on the way up. This had to be the second floor. A wall must be blocking the way. That explained why the receptionist had gone out of her way to tell me to take the elevator. It looked as if I had no choice but to go back down and start over.

Unless by chance there was a secret door somewhere in the wall. I went over to the wall and examined it carefully. Sure enough, I found a small, half-size door. After making sure no one was around, I pulled the latch.

Suddenly, from the other side of the door I heard a low moaning, followed by shrieks that sounded like cries for help. The voice was lifeless, hoarse, and male. Hastily I closed the door and stood stock still. I wanted nothing to do with this. Just as I was turning to head back down the stairs, footsteps came clattering toward me from above.

'Goodness, did you have a red light?!'

In front of me stood a thin woman, her hair chocolate-brown in the dim light, her kneecaps livid, like peeled hard-boiled eggs. Rather than try to make sense of her words, I hesitated, unable to decide whether I should pretend I was on my way up or down. Which would arouse less suspicion? Unless I knew the meaning of this secret door, there was no way of telling. I ended up standing there, waiting for her.

'It was a red light, wasn't it? Wasn't it?'

'Gee I—I really don't know what you mean—'

'But you just came out of there, didn't you?'

'Out of there?'

'Yes, of course!'

'No, I—'

'Don't be mean.'

'I'm telling you I didn't!'

'Hmm . . . then you're just on your way up?'

Apparently, if you had no business here, it was assumed you were heading up, not down.

'Yeah . . . I guess so.'

And so I had no choice but to continue on up the stairs. The woman sniffed, lowered her eyelashes tantalizingly, and passed on by, leaving in her wake a fragrance of lemon drops.

Oh well. Might as well take a peek at the third floor, and then pretend I'd just caught on to my error. On the way down I'd be sure to take the elevator. A pebble was embedded in the sole of my right shoe. I tried to scrape it off on the edge of a step, but I seemed only to have driven it in deeper. Leaning against the banister, I bent over and examined the underside of my heel. It turned out to be an old-fashioned anti-abrasion metal guard. Must have fallen off someone else's shoe and worked its way into mine. I tried prying it off with a fingernail, but it wouldn't budge. I gave up and walked on up the stairs, my right and left shoes making different noises as I went, distracting me.

Third floor.

Once again, my expectations were betrayed. This time there was no wall blocking the way, as on the second floor, but again no corridor. Instead, a room opened up in front of me.

The entrance was open, with no doors. Coughing, sounds of typing, pages being turned—typical office sounds came floating out in a shapeless mélange. Posted over the entranceway was another sign:

KEEP YOUR MIND ALWAYS IN FULL GEAR

As long as there was no hallway, I had no business here. If I couldn't get to the elevator, there was nothing to do but retrace my steps. Just as I was turning, pivoting on that irksome piece of metal stuck in my shoe, a man stepped out from the shadow behind the entrance and beckoned to me, leaning forward with a friendly smile. If he hadn't had such a reassuring, trustworthy sort of expression, I probably would have ignored him and continued on my way downstairs.

3

'Somehow I got turned around. Which way would the elevator be?' I asked.

The man nodded, put a finger to his lips, and threw a meaningful look over his shoulder. Apparently it was forbidden to talk in a loud voice here. Then, in a low, disarming voice, he said, 'There's nothing to be afraid of. You're new, aren't you?'

'No, you see I was told to take the elevator up, and then I managed to get totally lost, and somehow—'

'Don't worry about a thing,' he said soothingly, shaking his head back and forth. 'It's hard on everybody in the beginning. You feel as if you're being pulled apart, right? Just relax. Tensing up is the worst thing you can do. Just leave everything to us and go ahead and let yourself go, freeing yourself from the bonds of consciousness . . . then, spontaneously—' As he spoke, he grabbed my hand and began slowly to massage my palm with his fingertips.

Taken by surprise, I flung him off and cried, 'You don't understand! You've got the wrong idea!'

'Do I?' he said, his affable smile never fading. 'With that attitude, you're only going to cause yourself greater distress. Think carefully. What is it you're afraid of?'

'I'm not afraid of anything!'

'That's the spirit! You haven't got a thing to fear. Why should a publicity man, supervisor of the fourth estate of democracy, be afraid of any fixed ideas?'

'Huh?'

'What is it, you're worried about the poverty of your subconscious, is that it? Well, relax. The subconscious is an inexhaustible vein. The deeper you dig, the more jewels you find. Or tell me, could it be—' He broke off, gave me a searching look, and said, 'Have you by any chance got an Oedipus complex?'

In an effort to recover my poise, I forced myself to smile. 'No, you see, I wandered in here purely by chance, and—'

'You did? Good. You seem to have relaxed, finally.' With an air of relief he nodded, stepped aside, and motioned me inside.

'No, you still don't understand, I'm here by mistake.'

'Mistake?'

'Yeah, the girl told me to take the elevator, but it was full, so here I am.' Having at last found a chance to defend myself, I raced along, scarcely pausing for breath. 'You see, I'm just a visitor. I came here to see the director of the general affairs department. I signed in at the receptionist's desk, and she told me to wait on the second floor, and then I missed the elevator, so I took the stairs on the spur of the moment, not knowing where they went.'

'On the spur of the moment ... not knowing?'

'I'm terribly sorry.'

'Now I get it.' The man moaned, paused, and then mumbled again, 'Now I get it.'

'This building seems to have a very unusual design.'

'I've made a terrible mistake!' Suddenly his face lit up. 'But you know, you've discovered a new rule. I didn't realize it at first. "Just empty your head, and enter into a realm of detachment." This is the first time you've tried it this way, isn't it? You know, it just might work. I can't wait to see your results.'

'No, no, everything I'm saying is the truth. I'm just telling you what happened.'

'Even the way you talk is precious. It's a shame to let it all go to waste out here. Come on in and let's get it down on tape.'

He grabbed my shoulder in absolute faith and pushed me in the direction of the room. How could I relieve him of his misunderstanding? Either I should go along with him and do whatever he asked, or I should run back the way I had come. There were no other options. A young man walked toward us, hands thrust into his pockets, and passed in front of me, mumbling to himself. I caught fragments: 'Dragonfly, peppermint, autumn sky.' The young man's shoulders were broad. Looking at them, I sensed the futility of running. First Smiley would cry out and then this young fellow would catch me, which would only make things worse. It might be smarter just to play along for awhile.

The room was a long rectangle, extending off to my left. What met my eyes was quite different from the usual office setup. Down the middle of the room stretched a long aisle, and on either side of it were rows of cubicles lined up like stalls at a festival. The cubicles were partitioned off from one another, as in a visiting room in a prison, and each faced a counter beyond which everything appeared normal. A dozen or so female employees were absorbed in their work. On closer inspection, I saw they were each dextrously shuffling a pile of cards about as thick as three decks of playing cards. Cards . . . cards . . . hadn't the man on the stairs said something about cards? And about a siren?

On the counter in front of each booth were paper, pens, and a typewriter. A full set of ordinary office implements. There were also a few things whose use I couldn't guess. A black cylindrical tube hung over every cubicle and was evidently a small microphone. Virtually every booth was occupied. Some people were typing, others writing, others muttering into their microphone. What surprised me, however, were the people who would reach out to select a certain number of cards held out in a fan by a girl across the counter, then turn them over eagerly, and study them with a mixture of expectation and uncertainty, as if playing some sort of game. They couldn't really be playing games, and yet it certainly did look that way.

'All right, this will do.' The man's soft hand took hold of my elbow and guided me to a booth, well back on the right side. There was a mat on the floor, and an old-fashioned, high-backed chair. I was afraid I was about to make a total fool of myself. Why hadn't I run away when I had the chance? The man leaned over the counter and motioned to the young women. One of them noticed, nodded, and walked over, fingering the cards with such skill that they danced between her slender fingers like living things.

4

Before my eyes was an array of cards spread out in a large half circle.

None of this had anything to do with me. It was insulting.

'Go ahead, take three cards, any three.'

Failure to state your intentions meant resigning yourself to this sort of misunderstanding.

'Don't think about anything. . . . Just relax.'

Cards . . . games . . . games with no rules . . . Slowly I reached out my hand. . . . The tips of my fingers felt feverish.

'Well, so this is where you were!'

All at once I heard a familiar voice. It was like a spot of color suddenly appearing in a strip of black and white film. For a moment, time stopped, and then my blood began to flow again. Hastily I withdrew my hand and turned around, already rising from my chair. It was the director, my negotiating partner over the plans for the new building. A man like a well-bound antique book, angular and musty.

'Hello! I've been looking all over for you.'

'I got lost. The elevator—'

But suddenly I was too embarrassed to say more. The man who had hauled me in here looked back and forth at us in amazement.

'Well, if the professor's been showing you around, that's fine. He's in charge of this room; he's a great authority on psychology.'

'Well, actually it wasn't quite like that.' The professor inclined his head until it seemed about to settle permanently on his shoulder, and stared at something in the vicinity of my ear.

'I was going to show you this room eventually, anyway,' said the director. 'But it might not be a bad idea to start here. This, you see, is what you might call the heart of our company's operations. Well, what do you think?'

'I haven't actually heard the explanation yet.'

'How far did you get, professor?'

'How far?' Coming back to himself, he rubbed his temples with the fingers of both hands. 'I hadn't actually begun. So you really are a visitor?' he said, looking directly at me. 'Ah, what a surprise. Inexplicable truth. What a rare experience I've had. I might just be able to discover some new law because of it.' His genial smile returned. 'Well, you must have been rather startled yourself!'

'I'll tell you, I didn't have the faintest notion what to do.'

'I can well imagine. But this experience will have wide application. I've got to make a note of it.' No sooner were the words out of his mouth than he spun around and returned to his own desk, at the end of the row of booths.

'Interesting fellow.' The director looked fondly after the retreating figure, adding 'He's really quite the scholar, you know. We're very lucky to have him.'

'Yes. Sorry for all the trouble I caused.'

—This room has no particular designation. We usually just call it the System. All of our employees are required to come here for testing once each morning. A sort of psychoanalytical test. Those cards are printed with all sorts of pictures and symbols. Each person has to choose three cards, immediately derive some connection between them, and come up with a meaningful statement based on that connection. The typewriter is used in much the same way. Without thinking, you type out a random assortment of three letters, and then free associate with whatever you come up with. Here, listen for a moment to the sounds coming from this booth.

—Nails . . . clock . . . penguin. Nails . . . dirt under fingernails . . . boil . . . penguin medicine . . . clock. Medicine for a clock is winding it up. Nails . . . light fire under nails . . . fire clock . . . thermometer . . . thermometer and penguin. A penguin has a thermometer under its wing. An ad for cold medicine . . .

—And next door here, we have free association using the typewriter.

—A, C, M. A is for America, C is for commercial, M is for . . . M . . . is for *manju*, bean-jam buns. America, commercial, manju. Manju with America as commerical base. X-brand manju, exported to America with great success . . .

—That's roughly the way it goes. Everything these people say is recorded by the overhead microphones. The tapes are sent to the consolidation department, where they are screened, and anything that sounds promising is picked up. The ideas are then sorted by division—design, draft, radio, TV, outdoor advertising—and preserved. This system also works as an aptitude test for employees. We strive scientifically to increase productivity by transferring people to new sections according to the nature and trend of their associations. Besides, this is excellent mental training aimed at strengthening the power of association. Three birds with one stone. Shall we move along?

'It seems kind of like milking cows,' I commented.

'Yes. You see, advertising that works on the subconscious has the most powerful effect of all. But the ideas must be arrived at unconsciously, or they lack conviction.'

'Then this staircase also has a sort of psychological function?'

'Yes, yes, it does. Well, it sounds as if you've started to catch on.'

'Yes, I think I have. Now that I see how it works, it all makes perfect sense. I think I did the right thing by coming.'

'I'll show you around the rest of the place and then you can attend to that new alteration I proposed yesterday.'

'No, I think I've seen enough. After all, even the greeting "Welcome home" which surprised me so much at first now seems perfectly natural.'

'Oh? How so?'

'Well, I'm still kind of excited by everything I've seen, so this may be somewhat of an exaggeration, but it seems to me that the employees have all already entrusted their souls to the System. The System is them, even more than their physical selves. That's why the greeting is—has to be—"Welcome home," and the only response can be "I'm back."'

'It looks as if we should have hired you as one of our regular employees, not just our architect. A terrible oversight. Why, you're one of us!'

And so, for a little while, I was able to forget the metal guard wedged in the sole of my shoe.

5

Just then, we came to the second-floor landing, with the secret door.

'By the way,' I said, 'what does the red light mean?'

'Red light?' He turned around and came to a stop. 'You mean the green light, at the foot of the stairs. That's a sign that there are still empty booths in the System room.'

'No, the red light.' I wasn't sure why I was so insistent, but I remembered shining kneecaps . . . a thin woman . . . 'Oh, but you just came out of there, didn't you?' . . . 'Out of there?' . . . the secret door and its handle . . . yes, and then a scream for help . . . Suddenly, I became conscious of the metal guard in my shoe.

'Are you sure it's a red light you mean?'

'Positive.'

'Well, well. You've got sharp eyes. It's a little dark here and hard to make out, but I suspect what you are referring to is that light just overhead.'

As if waiting for something to happen, we looked up together at a dark corner of the ceiling where nothing could be seen. Naturally, nothing happened.

'I just happened to notice it.'

'Ah. Hmm. Let me think. All right, I suppose it wouldn't be a bad idea to stop in here next. Yes, why don't we do that?' The director of general affairs bent over, grabbed the handle on the secret door, and pulled.

'What is that?' I asked sharply.

'Surprised? A passageway.'

'Leading where?'

'It's a shortcut to the president's office.'

The explanation was so simple that I blurted out, 'What, that's all?'

'What do you mean by that?' There was something stiff in his manner, as if he was offended by my response. I was forced to go on.

'As a matter of fact, I opened that door before. I had a feeling it might lead onto the second-floor corridor.'

'And what happened?'

'It was probably my imagination, but I could have sworn I heard a strange voice.'

'A voice?'

'Yes. It sounded like the screams of an old man.'

'Are you sure?'

'Yes. At least, that's how it sounded to me.'

The director opened the door quietly, looking tense, reached around behind the wall and pushed a switch. A light came on, revealing a narrow passageway barely wide enough for one. It was painted bright white, making it impossible to judge how far back it went.

'I don't hear anything.'

'Neither do I.'

'Are you sure it couldn't have been a radio or a tape recording?'

'Well, maybe. Yeah, I suppose it could have been.'

'Don't scare me like that. Well, let's go have a look.'

'Has this all got some connection with the red light?'

'Oh, yes. Very much so. You'll see.'

The director led the way. I followed close behind. The click of metal embedded in my shoe echoed down the narrow, high-ceilinged passageway. It was shorter than I had thought. At the end it curved left and we came to a heavy-looking white door. He rapped on it three times, twice in succession, and we waited until a shrill, lifeless, asthmatic voice replied, 'Who is it?'

'It's me, sir.' The director stepped back and whispered in my ear, 'The president of AB.'

A bell rang and the door opened. There stood a little man covered with wrinkles, as if someone had scribbled all over him. Behind him, an incongruously large room. A flood of colorful posters plastered on the walls.

'Sir, may we have a few moments of your time?'

'What?'

'I brought the architect.'

Behind the director's back, I bowed my head respectfully.

'Ah. But I can only give you five minutes.'

'Thank you very much.'

'What is it, the red light?'

'Yes, sir.'

'Come this way.'

Over in a corner of the room was something like a telephone switchboard. The president, whose gestures were as angular as his appearance, stood in front of the device and looked around with an air of triumph, for all the world like a ship's captain at the helm.

'Tell me,' he said to me, 'do you know who the real politicians are, the ones moving our age? No, you don't. Everyone still thinks that the elected representatives and the ministers of state are the politicians. Well, nothing could be further from the truth. We advertising men are the ones holding the reins. We're the only ones who know how to get the stallion of public opinion and the stallion of capitalism to run in tandem.'

'That's right!' chimed in the director.

'Shall I tell you how? First we plant a seed of desire in the belly of public opinion. A seed so tiny it seems insignificant—the product of our best brains. Once that seed takes hold, it never lets go. It grows like a weed, crying out for fertilizer. We bide our time and just at the right juncture we let people know where to get premium manure. Then they set happily off to buy it, ready to turn their pockets inside out if need be.'

'And the "manure"-producing companies are happy, too,' added the director.

'True.'

'And you, Mr President, are the overseer of production of those secret seeds.'

'It's a heavy responsibility, believe me. I have to oversee the whole process from the word go. Look at this.'

With a solemn, ritualistic air, he pulled a lever toward him. At once a low murmur emerged from the bowels of the machine.

'This is coming from one of the System booths,' he explained. 'The System is set up so I can listen in directly from here. Let's see, this is number B-8.'

B-8 was mumbling:

—Robinson Crusoe and bet. Robinson Crusoe and bet. Robinson Crusoe is naked, he's got nothing to bet with.

'I listen in like this, as necessary. And as necessary, I can summon people straight here.'

'He waits for the person to approach,' added the director, 'then switches on the red light. So the red light is a handy way of sending a private signal to anyone he wants to see.'

'Whoever sees the light goes through the small door and comes in here. I then announce that he or she is being transferred, or getting a raise or cut in pay. Sometimes I encourage them to dig deeper, if they've come up with a promising idea.'

'Keep your mind always in full gear!' cried the director.

'Don't defend, attack!' returned the president.

'Yes, I think now I have a pretty good idea,' I said, at last managing to get a word in. 'So the average construction of space utilization—'

But the president was no longer listening to me. The very wrinkles on his face seemed to be intent on B-8's mutterings.

—Robinson Crusoe and bet. Robinson Crusoe made a bet. He bet that he could go to an uninhabited island and come back within one year wearing modern, civilized clothes. Three million yen prize. He lost. Stupid Robinson.'

'Director, the red light!'

'This Robinson Crusoe thing?' said the director. He immediately picked up the wall receiver and relayed the message to the switchboard.

'Get me through to System. I want B-8, and hurry!'

'What happens if two people come down the stairs together?' I asked the president.

'Of course, we try to arrange it so that won't happen. The present System is still flawed. That's why we want the new annex to be perfect.'

Before I knew it the muttering had stopped. The director was calling into the receiver. 'B-8 left, did he? Anyone else? Is he alone? Good. Over.'

'This button turns on the red light.'

Was it my imagination or was the president's finger shaking with anticipation as he placed it on the white, round protuberance in the center of the machine? 'Light's on.'

'Does it stay on indefinitely?' I asked.

'It goes off the moment he turns that handle.'

'You're calling that man in here to demonstrate to our guest exactly how the System operates, is that it, sir?'

'Don't be an idiot!' bellowed the company president, his chest stuck out, arms akimbo. 'Didn't you realize the genius of that idea we just heard? My calling B-8 in here has nothing to do with either of you! Robinson Crusoe's bet—what an idea! Pure genius. If you can't see that, then there's not much hope for you.'

'Yes, but—'

'But what?'

'The idea's impossible, isn't it?'

'You are an idiot!'

There was the sound of a knock. The president bounded over and opened the door. There stood B-8, stoop-shouldered, looking rather dazed. He wore a blue suit sagging at the shoulders, the pants too short. Small jaw; high, balding forehead.

'Come in, come in! I'm going to use your idea!'

There was a short, compressed silence, about the space of two heartbeats.

'Well, come on in! Your idea is dynamite!'

B-8 did nothing but scrape his feet nervously on the floor.

'Aren't you going to thank me?' cried the president. 'I'm going to use your Robinson Crusoe idea!'

'My Robinson Crusoe idea?'

'Yes—that bet about going naked to an uninhabited island and coming back fully dressed, in civilized clothes!'

'Oh, but that was just a game. Free association. It would never work in real life.'

'We'll offer a grand prize for succeeding in less than a month—ten million yen!'

'It won't work. However much you offer, you won't find any takers.'

'Why not?'

'Because it's impossible.'

'What makes you so sure?'

'Take this shabby old suit of mine. To make it, you'd need special machinery. To make the machinery, you'd need copper and steel. To make that, you'd need ore and coal and a blast furnace.'

'What else?'

'Workers to supply all that, food to feed them, farmers to grow the food.'

'Excellent! You've got the makings of a great slogan there—"To make this shabby suit takes the sweat of the nation." Well, maybe that's a little weak. But the idea is great: countless people you don't even know are working together for your benefit.' He turned to the director. 'I want you to get on this right away!'

'Yes, sir.'

'But, sir,' B-8 put in defensively, 'it's a foregone conclusion that it couldn't be done, so there's really no bet.'

'Of course! That's exactly why it's such a brilliant idea! Everybody's going to think it's impossible. But then a daring challenger comes along and captures the nation's imagination!'

'Is there any such person?'

'Certainly!'

'I can't really imagine anybody—'

'Why, he's standing right here in front of me!'

'Who?'

'You!'

'But—'

'Don't defend, attack! Why, what greater honor could there be than for you, the originator of the idea, to become the challenger!'

'But I—'

'Believe! Believe you can do it! Whether you actually can or not isn't the issue. You've simply got to believe that you can. Now, where shall we promote this?' He turned to the director. 'Where do you think?'

'Well, let me see. Uh, what sort of place did you have in mind?'

'You numbskull! You still haven't begun to grasp the beauty of this plan, have you? The possibilities are infinite. The pitiful figure of Robinson Crusoe, struggling all alone on his uninhabited island, will make a vivid impression on everybody's mind. And they'll start to think "Gee, it's pretty wonderful to be able to go to the store and buy things with money; I don't just throw away my money, I'm able to exchange it for things I need." Then that slogan we were talking about before will come home to them. For example, while they're washing their hands with soap, they'll think, "Through this one little bar of soap, thousands upon thousands of people are waiting on me." Watching the lather, they'll start to feel like royalty. Imagine— thanks to Robinson Crusoe, people's purse strings will loosen like worn-out elastic bands!'

'And the soap companies who didn't take us up on the bet will disappear without a bubble,' added the director of general affairs.

'Well, finally you're starting to catch on.'

'But what if this modern-day Crusoe should win, by some fluke?' the director queried. 'Wouldn't it have exactly the opposite effect? People would start to feel like fools for spending money.'

'He doesn't have a prayer,' said the president flatly.

'Right! That's exactly what I—' began B-8, but the president swiftly cut him off, waving his hand in the air like a fan.

'You keep out of this! I told you before, you've got to be sure of winning! Who's going to give a damn about a fixed deal, a bet they know you're going to lose? I'm convinced you'll lose, you insist you're determined to win. Only then does the outcome become interesting.'

'But however much I personally might subjectively feel I was going to win—'

'Don't throw in the towel! Get out there and try to win! Of course, we'll do what we can to make it easier for you. For example, at regular intervals we'll lower the prize money and lengthen the time span. Ten million if you succeed within a month, nine million for two months, and so on, down to one million yen for the tenth month. That will build up the excitement. We can have people guess what month they think you'll succeed in and heighten the suspense. Don't worry, as long as you project confidence and authority you'll attract your share of believers.'

He shifted his attention back to the director of general affairs, and began issuing orders. 'I want you to round up some big-name sponsors, doesn't matter who. Raise all the money you can. Tell them if they pass this up, it's suicide. Oh, and you'll have to scout around for some uninhabited Pacific island, and charter a boat.'

'Are you really serious?' B-8's face suddenly shriveled, as if it had dehydrated.

'Good Lord, how many times do you have to be told? You mean you still won't believe it? All right, we happen to have a third party here, so let's have him serve as witness.'

The third party he referred to was of course me. Needless to say, I was unable to refuse. To B-8 this little man was his boss—someone not to trifle with—and to me he was someone just as important: a valuable client.

And so the Robinson Crusoe bet between the company president in AB Building and his employee, B-8, was officially on. (But that same day, B-8 was dismissed. This was of course owing to the president's determination to eliminate any conflict of interest, and thus any concern that the outcome might be fixed.)

6

Now, it surely goes without saying that this peculiar experience was extremely fruitful in terms of helping me to understand my client's wishes. As a result, I no longer minded in the slightest if a room on the third floor shared a wall with one on the sixth floor, or you came down a flight of stairs to find yourself on the next floor up. Even if I had been ordered to put in all the ceilings and floors upside down, I probably would have done so without giving it a second thought. It was as if I understood even better than my client just what was wanted in this building.

So in the end I was able to complete the job without any further qualms, and if I do say so myself it came out gratifyingly well. The

president apparently liked it too, because at the ceremony he personally handed me a special gift, in a very moving scene.

So it's about time to draw these notes to an end—although of
course the Robinson Crusoe bet is left hanging in the air. Since by
now it's become famous, I probably should say a word or two more
about it, even if it does have little relevancy to my main topic.

But don't expect too much. Frankly, I haven't got anything of
any great interest or importance to share. Still, compared to more
ignorant third parties, I may be slightly better informed, so for what
it's worth, I'll go ahead and set down what I know.

Officially, of course, B-8 is supposed to be on some uninhabited
island surrounded by a coral reef, working away at his challenge.
Maybe he is. According to the report of the First Interim Investigating Team, the helicopter which took them from the mother ship
was able to touch down on the island only briefly, due to an
approaching typhoon, so they had to leave before establishing contact; but just before lifting off, they apparently heard a loud screech-
ing that sounded like a gigantic bird in its death throes. Later they
decided that it must have been the sound of a seabird known as the
wajiwaji caught in a trap, which they declared proof that 'Robinson'
is alive and well. Certainly it's not impossible. I half think they may
be right.

But there's another plausible theory making the rounds. Some
people say the moment reporters stopped following the chartered
boat, it swung around and headed in the opposite direction. And
another theory claims that while the boat did indeed reach the
island, instead of B-8, what went ashore was a skeleton once used for
experiments at some university hospital. Of course, I don't think we
need pretend surprise at such shenanigans in this day and age; in fact
anyone who believed in the legitimacy of the bet might well risk
being labeled not only naive but a dunce.

The next rumor, however, strikes me as a little too dramatic to be
real. According to this, B-8 was so stricken by the magnitude of the
problems he faced that he committed suicide shortly after setting sail
and arrived on the island a dead man. This, it seems to me, involves
an entirely too romantic view of the monstrosity we call modern
life. Of course, if I hadn't accepted the job of designing that new
building and subsequently encountered the inner workings of the
System, I might very well have been taken in. But fortunately,
having gained the opportunity to design certain aspects of the Sys-

tem with my own hands, I know better. The monstrosity of modern life is far more prosaic, consisting simply in the fact that the wires connecting all the separate elements have gotten hopelessly entangled. That's why I can't help suspecting that there is more truth in the rumor that B-8, disguised in sunglasses, was spotted one day timidly waiting in line in a department store supermarket for economy-size packages of meat.

Then what was it that the investigating team heard? I haven't the slightest assurance that this is true, but as I heard that story I recalled the shrieks I heard through the wall outside the president's office when I visited the old building. Had someone told me those despairing, agonized cries were made by a bird, I probably would have believed it.

Besides, there was one other disturbing coincidence. I have no solid proof and it's probably no more meaningful than, say, the similarity in shape between a starfish and a star, but the fact is that after the opening ceremony, the company president dropped out of sight. Of course, no one ever said so in so many words, but there must have been good reason for him to do so. He was a figure of such commanding authority that his employees, unaccustomed to doubting him, could well have overlooked the significance of his absence. But I, for one, being thoroughly acquainted with the structure of his new office, couldn't help experiencing an ominous twinge of presentiment.

From the time I first set to work on the plans for the president's office, I was given one supreme order: it had to be located at all times squarely in the center of the System. But the System itself was by no means stable, so the only solution was to design a building as fluid and fluctuating as an amoeba. Inhabitants of such a building would suffer from a kind of motion sickness many times worse than seasickness, and no work would get done at all. Well, I wracked my brains and finally hit on a solution: I worked out the path of the president's office as a mathematical function of the System and constructed a maze of twisting tunnels winding through the building, leaving it to an electronic brain to determine the location and direction of the office based on current conditions. I have a certain amount of confidence in the mechanism and am justifiably proud of it, so I hold myself fully accountable for how it functions. But, of course, I can bear no responsibility for how it may have been used. If someone altered the conditions—conditions that in themselves, taken separately, would have meant nothing—to overlap in such a way that the set path of the office was diverted, by however little, then even if the door of the president's office should have opened one day on something totally beyond the scope of my design, I could hardly be blamed. Not even if the president himself ended up smack in the middle of an uninhabited desert island.

YOSHIYUKI JUNNOSUKE (1924–1994)

THREE POLICEMEN

Translated by Hugh Clarke

~

I started the best argument I have had for years in a bar with a man a good twenty years my junior.

Miki was with me at the time. An hour before we had been in another bar. The club was virtually filled with customers. Miki is small with a slight squint, but has long shoulder-length hair and a coquettish face which stand out in a crowd. We were sitting together with our backs to the wall. In front of us sat one of the girls from the bar. Miki gave me a wink, a signal that we should begin. I nodded. Then brushing up Miki's long hair I began, one by one, to undo the buttons running down the back of Miki's dress from neck to waist. I undid them all. Then still sitting alongside Miki, I touched the collar of the dress with my hand. The garment immediately slipped down over Miki's bare shoulders and fell forward. Unrestrained by any bra, the curves of Miki's breasts were revealed for all to see. They were quite large with beautiful pale pink nipples.

'Uh? Hey!'

The girl in front of us just gasped and sat there looking as flustered as if she had been laid bare herself. Soon the customers realized what had happened and for a moment a hush fell over the room. Miki took a deep breath and arched forward, giving a seductive smile.

The manager, in black evening dress, came rushing over.

'If you don't mind! This is no joking matter!'

'Why not?'

'What do you mean, "Why not?" We can't have young ladies suddenly doing this sort of thing.'

'Young ladies?'

So saying I stroked Miki's breasts, at which Miki wriggled and gave a squeal of delight.

'Come now. We can't stand for this!' said the manager.

'Can't stand for it, eh? Well, I suppose not.'

I pulled up Miki's dress again and slowly did up the buttons. A rustle of talk ran through the bar and sighs could be heard from some of the customers.

'Nice breasts, don't you think?'

'Y . . . yes, but . . .'

The girl in front of us looked as if she was trying to fathom the meaning of our extraordinary behaviour.

I said, 'I suppose you'd disapprove, would you, if a man with breasts like a woman exposed his chest like that?'

And Miki chimed in, 'What a thing to say! Don't make things so complicated. I'm a woman all right!'

As soon as Miki spoke the game was up. It was a typical gay-boy voice.

'Uh? . . .'

Once again the girl looked surprised. Later, no doubt the truth would have spread through the bar.

Miki stood up and urged me on, 'Let's go to another place.'

Miki was something of a drinking mate of mine and it had become a kind of ritual for him to expose his breasts at every place we went to.

We were just about to go downstairs into a little basement bar, when Miki said with obvious dissatisfaction, 'Oh, we goin' in here?'

The bar was tiny. Just the mama-san and a bar-tender. We were well known there, so Miki's little show would just be for the customers and there were precious few of them anyhow.

'You've had enough, haven't you? I'm tired tonight. Let's just have a quiet drink.'

When I opened the door, there, right in front of me, was this young friend of mine. He was with two other fellows of the same age whom I knew vaguely by sight.

We got into a discussion with these young men. When your mind is fuddled with drink you can't think clearly. The point of the argument wanders all over the place and it takes you ages to make any headway at all. You suddenly realize that an hour has gone past, but the discussion is still revolving around more or less the same point. It's ridiculous.

It was ridiculous, too, how we got into an argument over whether or not you could bend a spoon with psychic powers.

When I said it was only a trick, the other three combined to attack me, saying that my views were a clear indication of senility.

It transpired that my young friend had recently got himself sandwiched in an entanglement between two girls. Apparently when he was in his cups he would sometimes break down and cry about it. I was surprised to hear that. Worry about women is a concomitant part of all men's lives. Lots of men are crying inside. But they don't let things rest there. They go out and try to deal with the problem. It vexed me to have this fellow, who was obviously still just a child, accuse me of being senile.

'There are human powers which haven't been developed yet.'

'I'm not denying that. But that's not what happens with the spoon. You can't use willpower to make a clock turn backwards, can you?'

'But the spoon actually does bend, doesn't it?'

'That's because force is applied somewhere.'

I demonstrated by bending two or three of the bar's spoons.

'That's what I mean by senility. Life is richer if you believe they bend through supernatural force.'

'If you think life can be made richer by spoons bending, you're pretty pathetic!'

Beside me Miki yawned.

I tried to change the tack of the conversation.

'I'm glad we've only been talking about spoons. If we'd been talking about something else things might have been a lot worse. Do you want to go back to the war years and put us all in uniform?'

But the others weren't going to fall for that. Suddenly Miki said, 'I adore uniforms.'

'Why?'

'They turn me on.'

'That's not what I mean. Would you like having to wear one yourself?'

'I'd hate that.'

'But why do uniforms turn you on, anyway?'

'They look so impressive.'

'What about police uniforms? Do they look impressive? And sailors' uniforms? They're pretty miserable.'

'But they still turn me on.'

I thought he must sense the group behind the uniform. The sweaty masculinity of a group composed entirely of men. Miki was drunk too. There would have been no point in explaining this idea to him. Anyway, no matter what we talked about, nothing fitted properly into place and the argument followed no logical course. Only the time flowed along unimpeded.

It was already almost 3.00 a.m. and everything had been cleared off the tables. The conversation was becoming increasingly fragmented. One of the three young men inadvertently came out with the hackneyed old line.

'The oldies were pretty slack during the war.'

'You think so? You guys believe in spoons bending. If you'd been around during the war, I'm sure you'd've believed the *kamikaze* divine wind would blow you victory.'

As soon as I'd made this reply it occurred to me that during the war I was only a boy myself.

'I was only a kid at the time, but I don't think you can necessarily say that.'

I was not angry so my words were not as barbed as they might have been, but I felt irritated. When one of the boys said, 'It was no big deal being in the war,' my sense of irritation increased.

'Perhaps you're right. But life in wartime is lousy, I can tell you. Every night you have air raid sirens blaring away. Even if you don't go into the shelters every time, the sirens wake you up all right. And you might end up waiting an hour or more for a train.'

As I was defending in this vein, the door burst open. There appeared before us a strapping young policeman. Actually, there were three policemen, but in the narrow doorway they were standing one behind the other. They just stood there in the doorway without coming in.

'What are you doing?'

The mama-san went trotting up to the door and said, 'They're just leaving. Having a chat.'

The policemen cast a glance over the tables.

'No alcohol, eh? It's late. You'd better be getting home.'

Whereupon they simply vanished. All the three policemen cared about was whether the bar was trading out of hours.

'They sure let us off easily. They've got their own lives to lead too. They prefer not to have to investigate complaints either. But, if this had been wartime we'd have been in for it. We'd have been whisked off to the police station for holding an unauthorized meeting and plotting in a secret underground room. We might even have been tortured.'

The three young men were not in the least moved at my words.

Miki, holding a cigarette burnt down low between his fingers, said, 'Uniforms have oomph. They really turn me on.'

He then sank back immobile into the depths of the sofa.

ONNAGATA

Translated by Donald Keene

≈

1

Masuyama had been overwhelmed by Mangiku's artistry; that was how it happened that, after getting a degree in classical Japanese literature, he had chosen to join the kabuki theater staff. He had been entranced by seeing Mangiku Sanokawa perform.

Masuyama's addiction to kabuki began when he was a high-school student. At the time, Mangiku, still a fledgling *onnagata*, was appearing in such minor roles as the ghost butterfly in *Kagami Jishi* or, at best, the waiting maid Chidori in *The Disowning of Genta*. Mangiku's acting was unassertive and orthodox; nobody suspected he would achieve his present eminence. But even in those days Masuyama sensed the icy flames given off by this actor's aloof beauty. The general public, needless to say, noticed nothing. For that matter, none of the drama critics had ever called attention to the peculiar quality of Mangiku, like shoots of flame visible through the snow, which illuminated his performances from very early in his career. Now everyone spoke as if Mangiku had been a personal discovery.

Mangiku Sanokawa was a true *onnagata*, a species seldom encountered nowadays. Unlike most contemporary *onnagata*, he was quite incapable of performing successfully in male roles. His stage presence was colorful, but with dark overtones; his every gesture was the essence of delicacy. Mangiku never expressed anything—not even strength, authority, endurance, or courage—except through the single medium open to him, feminine expression, but through this medium he could filter every variety of human emotion. That is the way of the true *onnagata*, but in recent years this breed has become rare indeed. Their tonal coloring, produced by a particular, exquisitely refined musical instrument, cannot be achieved by playing a normal instrument in a minor key, nor, for that matter, is it produced by a mere slavish imitation of real women.

Yukihime, the Snow Princess, in *Kinkakuji* was one of Mangiku's most successful roles. Masuyama remembered having seen Mangiku perform Yukihime ten times during a single month, but no matter how often he repeated this experience, his intoxication did not diminish. Everything symbolizing Mangiku Sanokawa may be found in this play, the elements entwined, beginning with the opening words of the narrator: 'The Golden Pavilion, the mountain retreat of Lord Yoshimitsu, Prime Minister and Monk of the Deer Park, stands three stories high, its garden graced with lovely sights: the night-lodging stone, the water trickling below the rocks, the flow of the cascade heavy with spring, the willows and cherry trees planted together; the capital now is a vast, many-hued brocade.' The dazzling brilliance of the set, depicting cherry trees in blossom, a waterfall, and the glittering Golden Pavilion; the drums, suggesting the dark sound of the waterfall and contributing a constant agitation to the stage; the pale, sadistic face of the lecherous Daizen Matsunaga, the rebel general; the miracle of the magic sword which shines in morning sunlight with the holy image of Fudo, but shows a dragon's form when pointed at the setting sun; the radiance of the sunset glow on the waterfall and cherry trees; the cherry blossoms scattering down petal by petal—everything in the play exists for the sake of one woman, the beautiful, aristocratic Yukihime. There is nothing unusual about Yukihime's costume, the crimson silk robe customarily worn by young princesses. But a ghostly presence of snow, befitting her name, hovers about this granddaughter of the great painter Sesshu, and the landscapes of Sesshu, permeated with snow, may be sensed across the breadth of the scene; this phantom snow gives Yukihime's crimson robe it dazzling brilliance.

Masuyama loved especially the scene where the princess, bound with ropes to a cherry tree, remembers the legend told of her grandfather, and with her toes draws in the fallen blossoms a rat, which comes to life and gnaws through the ropes binding her. It hardly needs be said that Mangiku Sanokawa did not adopt the puppetlike movements favored by some *onnagata* in this scene. The ropes fastening him to the tree made Mangiku look lovelier than ever: all the artificial arabesques of this *onnagata*—the delicate gestures of the body, the play of the fingers, the arch of the hand—contrived though they might appear when employed for the movements of daily life, took on a strange vitality when used by Yukihime, bound to a tree. The intricate, contorted attitudes imposed by the constraint of the rope made of each instant an exquisite crisis, and the crises seemed to flow, one into the next, with the irresistible energy of successive waves.

Mangiku's performances unquestionably possessed moments of diabolic power. He used his lovely eyes so effectively that often with one flash he could create in an entire audience the illusion that the character of a scene had completely altered: when his glance embraced the stage from the *hanamichi* or the *hanamichi* from the stage, or when he darted one upward look at the bell in *Dōjōji*. In the palace scene from *Imoseyama*, Mangiku took the part of Omiwa, whose lover was stolen from her by Princess Tachibana and who has been cruelly mocked by the court ladies. At the end Omiwa rushes out onto the *hanamichi*, all but wild with jealousy and rage; just then she hears the voices of the court ladies at the back of the stage saying, 'A groom without peer has been found for our princess! What joy for us all!' The narrator, seated at the side of the stage, declaims in powerful tones, 'Omiwa, hearing this, at once looks back.' At this moment Omiwa's character is completely transformed, and her face reveals the marks of a possessive attachment.

Masuyama felt a kind of terror every time he witnessed this moment. For an instant a diabolic shadow had swept over both the bright stage with its splendid set and beautiful costumes and over the thousands of intently watching spectators. This force clearly emanated from Mangiku's body, but at the same time transcended his flesh. Masuyama sensed in such passages something like a dark spring welling forth from this figure on the stage, this figure so imbued with softness, fragility, grace, delicacy, and feminine charms. He could not identify it, but he thought that a strange evil presence, the final residue of the actor's fascination, a seductive evil which leads men astray and makes them drown in an instant of beauty, was the true nature of the dark spring he had detected. But one explains nothing merely by giving it a name.

Omiwa shakes her head and her hair tumbles in disarray. On the stage, to which she now returns from the *hanamichi*, Funashichi's blade is waiting to kill her.

'The house is full of music, an autumn sadness in its tone,' declaims the narrator.

There is something terrifying about the way Omiwa's feet hurry forward to her doom. The bare white feet, rushing ahead toward disaster and death, kicking the lines of her kimono askew, seem to know precisely when and where on the stage the violent emotions now urging her forward will end, and to be pressing toward the sport, rejoicing and triumphant even amidst the tortures of jealousy. The pain she reveals outwardly is backed with joy like her robe, on the outside dark and shot with gold thread, but bright with variegated silken strands within.

2

Masuyama's original decision to take employment at the theatre had been inspired by his absorption with kabuki, and especially with Mangiku; he realized also he could never escape his bondage unless he became thoroughly familiar with the world behind the scenes. He knew from what others had told him of the disenchantment to be found backstage, and he wanted to plunge into that world and taste for himself genuine disillusion.

But the disenchantment he expected somehow never came. Mankigu himself made this impossible. Mangiku faithfully maintained the injunctions of the eighteenth-century *onnagata*'s manual *Ayamegusa*, 'An *onnagata*, even in the dressing room, must preserve the attitudes of an *onnagata*. He should be careful when he eats to face away from other people, so that they cannot see him.' Whenever Mangiku was obliged to eat in the presence of visitors, not having the time to leave his dressing room, he would turn toward his table with a word of apology and race through his meal, so skillfully that the visitors could not even guess from behind that he was eating.

Undoubtedly, the feminine beauty displayed by Mangiku on the stage had captivated Masuyama as a man. Strangely enough, however, this spell was not broken even by close observation of Mangiku in the dressing room. Mangiku's body, when he had removed his costume, was delicate but unmistakably a man's. Masuyama, as a matter of fact, found it rather unnerving when Mangiku, seated at his dressing table, too scantily clad to be anything but a man, directed polite, feminine greetings toward some visitor, all the while applying a heavy coating of powder to his shoulders. If even Masuyama, long a devotee of kabuki, experienced eerie sensations on his first visits to the dressing room, what would have been the reactions of people who dislike kabuki, because the *onnagata* make them uncomfortable, if shown such a sight?

Masuyama, however, felt relief rather than disenchantment when he saw Mangiku after a performance, naked except for the gauzy underclothes he wore in order to absorb perspiration. The sight in itself may have been grotesque, but the nature of Masuyama's fascination—its intrinsic quality, one might say—did not reside in any surface illusion, and there was accordingly no danger that such a revelation would destroy it. Even after Mangiku had disrobed, it was apparent that he was still wearing several layers of splendid costumes beneath his skin; his nakedness was a passing manifestation. Something which could account for his exquisite appearance on stage surely lay concealed within him.

Masuyama enjoyed seeing Mangiku when he returned to the dressing room after performing a major role. The flush of the emotions of the part he had been enacting still hovered over his entire body, like sunset glow or the moon in the sky at dawn. The grand emotions of classical tragedy—emotions quite unrelated to our mundane lives—may seem to be guided, at least nominally, by historical facts—the world of disputed successions, campaigns of pacification, civil warfare, and the like—but in reality they belong to no period. They are the emotions appropriate to a stylized, grotesquely tragic world, luridly colored in the manner of a late woodblock print. Grief that goes beyond human bounds, superhuman passions, searing love, terrifying joy, the brief cries of people trapped by circumstances too tragic for human beings to endure: such were the emotions which a moment before had lodged in Mangiku's body. It was amazing that Mangiku's slender frame could hold them and that they did not break from that delicate vessel.

Be that as it may, Mangiku a moment before had been living amidst these grandiose feelings, and he had radiated light on the stage precisely because the emotions he portrayed transcended any known to his audience. Perhaps this is true of all characters on the stage, but among present-day actors none seemed to be so honestly living stage emotions so far removed from daily life.

A passage in *Ayamegusa* states, 'Charm is the essence of the *onnagata*. But even the *onnagata* who is naturally beautiful will lose his charm if he strains to impress by his movements. If he consciously attempts to appear graceful, he will seem thoroughly corrupt instead. For this reason, unless the *onnagata* lives as a woman in his daily life, he is unlikely ever to be considered an accomplished *onnagata*. When he appears on stage, the more he concentrates on performing this or that essentially feminine action, the more masculine he will seem. I am convinced that the essential thing is how the actor behaves in real life.'

How the actor behaves in real life . . . yes, Mangiku was utterly feminine in both the speech and bodily movements of his real life. If Mangiku had been more masculine in his daily life, those moments when the flush from the *onnagata* role he had been performing gradually dissolved like the high-water mark on a beach into the femininity of his daily life—itself an extension of the same make-believe—would have become an absolute division between sea and land, a bleak door shut between dream and reality. The make-believe of his daily life supported the make-believe of his stage performances. This, Masuyama was convinced, marked the true *onnagata*. An *onnagata* is the child born of the illicit union between dream and reality.

3

Once the celebrated veteran actors of the previous generation had all passed away, one on the heels of the other, Mangiku's authority backstage became absolute. His *onnagata* disciples waited on him like personal servants; indeed, the order of seniority they observed when following Mangiku on stage as maids in the wake of his princess or great lady was exactly the same as they observed in the dressing room.

Anyone pushing apart the door curtains dyed with the crest of the Sanokawa family and entering Mangiku's dressing room was certain to be struck by a strange sensation: this charming sanctuary contained not a single man. Even members of the same troupe felt inside this room that they were in the presence of the opposite sex. Whenever Masuyama went to Mangiku's dressing room on some errand, he had only to brush apart the door curtains to feel—even before setting foot inside—a curiously vivid, carnal sensation of being a male.

Sometimes Masuyama had gone on company business to the dressing rooms of chorus girls backstage at revues. The rooms were filled with an almost suffocating femininity and the rough-skinned girls, sprawled about like animals in the zoo, threw bored glances at him, but he never felt so distinctly alien as in Mangiku's dressing room; nothing in these real women made Masuyama feel particularly masculine.

The members of Mangiku's entourage exhibited no special friendliness toward Masuyama. On the contrary, he knew that they secretly gossiped about him, accusing him of being disrespectful or of giving himself airs merely because he had gone through some university. He knew too that sometimes they professed irritation at his pedantic insistence on historical facts. In the world of kabuki, academic learning unaccompanied by artistic talent is considered of no value.

Masuyama's work had its compensations too. It would happen when Mangiku had a favor to ask of someone—only, of course, when he was in a good mood—that he twisted his body diagonally from his dressing table and gave a little nod and a smile; the indescribable charm in his eyes at such moments made Masuyama feel that he wished for nothing more than to slave like a dog for this man. Mangiku himself never forgot his dignity: he never failed to maintain a certain distance, though he obviously was aware of his charms. If he had been a real woman, his whole body would have been filled with the allure in his eyes. The allure of an *onnagata* is only a momentary glimmer, but that is enough for it to exist independently and to display the eternal feminine.

Mangiku sat before the mirror after the performance of *The Castle of the Lord Protector of Hachijin*, the first item of the program. He had removed the costume and wig he wore as Lady Hinaginu, and changed to a bathrobe, not being obliged to appear in the middle work of the program. Masuyama, informed that Mangiku wanted to see him, had been waiting in the dressing room for the curtain of *Hachijin*. The mirror suddenly burst into crimson flames as Mangiku returned to the room, filling the entrance with the rustle of his robes. Three disciples and costumers joined to remove what had to be removed and store it away. Those who were to leave departed, and now no one remained except for a few disciples around the hibachi in the next room. The dressing room had all at once fallen still. From a loudspeaker in the corridor issued the sounds of stage assistants hammering as they dismantled the set for the play which had just ended. It was late November, and steam heat clouded the windowpanes, bleak as in a hospital ward. White chrysanthemums bent gracefully in a cloisonné vase placed beside Mangiku's dressing table. Mangiku, perhaps because his stage name meant literally 'ten thousand chrysanthemums', was fond of this flower.

Mangiku sat on a bulky cushion of purple silk, facing his dressing table. 'I wonder if you'd mind telling the gentleman from Sakuragi Street?' (Mangiku, in the old-fashioned manner, referred to his dancing and singing teachers by the names of the streets where they lived.) 'It'd be hard for me to tell him.' He gazed directly into the mirror as he spoke. Masuyama could see from where he sat by the wall the nape of Mangiku's neck and the reflections in the mirror of his face still made up for the part of Hinaginu. The eyes were not on Masuyama; they were squarely contemplating his own face. The flush from his exertions on the stage still glowed through the powder on his cheeks, like the morning sun through a thin sheet of ice. He was looking at Hinaginu.

Indeed, he actually saw her in the mirror—Hinaginu, whom he had just been impersonating, Hinaginu, the daughter of Mori Sanzaemon Yoshinari and the bride of the young Sato Kazuenosuke. Her marriage ties with her husband having been broken because of his feudal loyalty, Hinaginu killed herself so that she might remain faithful to a union 'whose ties were so faint we never shared the same bed'. Hinaginu had died on stage of a despair so extreme she could not bear to live any longer. The Hinaginu in the mirror was a ghost. Even that ghost, Mangiku knew, was at this very moment slipping from his body. His eyes pursued Hinaginu. But as the glow of the ardent passions of the role subsided, Hinaginu's face faded away. He bade it farewell. There were still seven performances before the final day. Tomorrow again Hinaginu's features would no doubt return to the pliant mold of Mangiku's face.

Masuyama, enjoying the sight of Mangiku in this abstracted state, all but smiled with affection. Mangiku suddenly turned toward him. He had been aware all along of Masuyama's gaze, but with the nonchalance of the actor accustomed to the public's stares, he continued with his business. 'It's those instrumental passages. They're simply not long enough. I don't mean I can't get through the part if I hurry, but it makes everything so ugly. Mangiku was referring to the music for the new dance-play which would be presented the following month. 'Mr Masuyama, what do *you* think?'

'I quite agree, I'm sure you mean the passage after "How slow the day ends by the Chinese bridge at Seta."'

'Yes, that's the place. Ho-ow slo-ow the da-ay . . .' Mangiku sang the passage in question, beating time with his delicate fingers.

'I'll tell him. I'm sure that the gentleman from Sakuragi Street will understand.'

'Are you sure you don't mind? I feel so embarrassed about making a nuisance of myself all the time.'

Mangiku was accustomed to terminate a conversation by standing, once his business had been dealt with. 'I'm afraid I must bathe now,' he said. Masuyama drew back from the narrow entrance to the dressing room and let Mangiku pass. Mangiku, with a slight bow of the head, went out into the corridor, accompanied by a disciple. He turned back obliquely toward Masuyama and, smiling, bowed again. The rouge at the corners of his eyes had an indefinable charm. Masuyama sensed that Mangiku was well aware of his affection.

4

The troupe to which Masuyama belonged was to remain at the same theatre through November, December, and January, and the program for January had already become the subject of gossip. A new work by a playwright of the modern theatre was to be staged. The man, whose sense of his own importance accorded poorly with his youth, had imposed innumerable conditions, and Masuyama was kept frantically busy with complicated negotiations intended to bring together not only the dramatist and the actors but the management of the theatre as well. Masuyama was recruited for this job because the others considered him to be an intellectual.

One of the conditions laid down by the playwright was that the direction of the play be confided to a talented young man whom he trusted. The management accepted this condition. Mangiku also agreed, but without enthusiasm. He conveyed his doubts in this manner: 'I don't really know, of course, but if this young man doesn't understand kabuki very well, and makes unreasonable demands on us, it will be so hard explaining.' Mangiku was hoping for an older, more mature—by which he meant a more compliant—director.

The new play was a dramatization in modern language of the twelfth-century novel *If Only I Could Change Them!* The managing director of the company, deciding not to leave the production of this new work to the regular staff, announced it would be in Masuyama's hands. Masuyama grew tense at the thought of the work ahead of him, but convinced that the play was first-rate, he felt that it would be worth the trouble.

As soon as the scripts were ready and the parts assigned, a preliminary meeting was held one mid-December morning in the reception room adjoining the office of the theater owner. The meeting was attended by the executive in charge of production, the playwright, the director, the stage designer, the actors, and Masuyama. The room was warmly heated and sunlight poured through the windows. Masuyama always felt happiest at preliminary meetings. It was like spreading out a map and discussing a projected outing: Where do we board the bus and where do we start walking? Is there drinking water where we're going? Where are we going to eat lunch? Where is the best view? Shall we take the train back? Or would it be better to allow enough time to return by boat?

Kawasaki, the director, was late. Masuyama had never seen a play directed by Kawasaki, but he knew of him by reputation. Kawasaki had been selected, despite his youth, to direct Ibsen and modern American plays for a repertory company, and in the course of a year had done so well, with the latter especially, that he was awarded a newspaper drama prize.

The others (except for Kawasaki) had all assembled. The designer, who could never bear waiting a minute before throwing himself into his work, was already jotting down in a large notebook especially brought for the purpose suggestions made by the others, frequently tapping the end of his pencil on the blank pages, as if bursting with ideas. Eventually the executive began to gossip about the absent director. 'He may be as talented as they say, but he's still young, after all. The actors will have to help out.'

At this moment there was a knock at the door and a secretary showed in Kawasaki. He entered the room with a dazed look, as if the light were too strong for him and, without uttering a word, stiffly bowed toward the others. He was rather tall, almost six feet, with deeply etched, masculine—but highly sensitive—features. It was a cold winter day, but Kawasaki wore a rumpled, thin raincoat. Underneath, as he presently disclosed, he had on a brick-colored corduroy jacket. His long, straight hair hung down so far—to the tip of his nose—that he was frequently obliged to push it back. Masuyama was rather disappointed by his first impression. He had supposed that a man who had been singled out for his abilities would have attempted to distinguish himself somehow from the stereotypes of society, but this man dressed and acted exactly in the way one would expect of the typical young man of the modern theatre.

Kawasaki took the place offered him at the head of the table. He did not make the usual polite protests against the honor. He kept his eyes on the playwright, his close friend, and when introduced to each of the actors he uttered a word of greeting, only to turn back at once to the playwright. Masuyama could remember similar experiences. It is not easy for a man trained in the modern theatre, where most of the actors are young, to establish himself on easy terms with the kabuki actors, who are likely to prove to be imposing old gentlemen when encountered off stage.

The actors assembled for this preliminary meeting managed in fact to convey somehow their contempt for Kawasaki, all with a show of the greatest politeness and without an unfriendly word. Masuyama happened to glance at Mangiku's face. He modestly kept to himself, refraining from any demonstration of self-importance; he displayed no trace of the others' contempt. Masuyama felt greater admiration and affection than ever for Mangiku.

Now that everyone was present, the author described the play in outline. Mangiku, probably for the first time in his career—leaving aside parts he took as a child—was to play a male role. The plot told of a certain Grand Minister with two children, a boy and a girl. By nature they are quite unsuited to their sexes and are therefore reared accordingly: the boy (actually the girl) eventually becomes General of the Left, and the girl (actually the boy) becomes chief lady-in-waiting in the Senyoden, the palace of the Imperial concubines. Later, when the truth is revealed, they revert to lives more appropriate to the sex of their birth: the brother marries the fourth daughter of the Minister of the Right, the sister a Middle Counselor, and all ends happily.

Mangiku's part was that of the girl who is in reality a man. Although this was a male role, Mangiku would appear as a man only in the few moments of the final scene. Up to that point, he was to act throughout as a true *onnagata* in the part of a chief lady-in-waiting at the Senyoden. The author and director were agreed in urging Mangiku not to make any special attempt even in the last scene to suggest that he was in fact a man.

An amusing aspect of the play was that it inevitably had the effect of satirizing the kabuki convention of the *onnagata*. The lady-in-waiting was actually a man; so, in precisely the same manner, was

Mangiku in the role. That was not all. In order for Mangiku, at once an *onnagata* and a man, to perform this part, he would have to unfold on two levels his actions of real life, a far cry from the simple case of the actor who assumes female costume during the course of a play so as to work some deception. The complexities of the part intrigued Mangiku.

Kawasaki's first words to Mangiku were, 'I would be glad if you played the part throughout as a woman. It doesn't make the least difference if you act like a woman even in the last scene.' His voice had a pleasant, clear ring.

'Really? If you don't mind my acting the part that way, it'll make it ever so much easier for me.'

'It won't be easy in any case. Definitely not,' said Kawasaki decisively. When he spoke in this forceful manner his cheeks glowed red as if a lamp had been lit inside. The sharpness of his tone cast something of a pall over the gathering. Masuyama's eyes wandered to Mangiku. He was giggling good-naturedly, the back of his hand pressed to his mouth. The others relaxed to see Mangiku had not been offended.

'Well, then, said the author, I shall read the book.' He lowered his protruding eyes, which looked double behind his thick spectacles, and began to read the script on the table.

5

Two or three days later the rehearsal by parts began, whenever the different actors had free time. Full-scale rehearsals would only be possible during the few days in between the end of this month and the beginning of next month's program. Unless everything that needed tightening were attended to by then, there would be no time to pull the performance together.

Once the rehearsal of the parts began it became apparent to everyone that Kawasaki was like a foreigner strayed among them. He had not the smallest grasp of kabuki, and Masuyama found himself obliged to stand beside him and explain word by word the technical language of the kabuki theater, making Kawasaki extremely dependent on him. The instant the first rehearsal was over Masuyama invited Kawasaki for a drink.

Masuyama knew that for someone in his position it was generally speaking a mistake to ally himself with the director, but he felt he could easily understand what Kawasaki must be experiencing. The young man's views were precisely defined, his mental attitudes were wholesome, and he threw himself into his work with boyish enthusiasm. Masuyama could see why Kawasaki's character should have so appealed to the playwright; he felt as if Kawasaki's genuine youthfulness were a somehow purifying element, a quality unknown in the world of kabuki. Masuyama justified his friendship with Kawasaki in terms of attempting to turn this quality to the advantage of kabuki.

Full-scale rehearsals began at last on the day after the final performances of the December program. It was two days after Christmas. The year-end excitement in the streets could be sensed even through the windows in the theater and the dressing rooms. A battered old desk had been placed by a window in the large rehearsal room. Kawasaki and one of Masuyama's seniors on the staff—the stage manager—sat with their backs to the window. Masuyama was behind Kawasaki. The actors sat on the *tatami* along the wall. Each would go up center when his turn came to recite his lines. The stage manager supplied forgotten lines.

Sparks flew repeatedly between Kawasaki and the actors. 'At this point,' Kawasaki would say, 'I'd like you to stand as you say, "I wish I could go to Kawachi and have done with it." Then you're to walk up to the pillar at stage right.'

'That's one place I simply can't stand up.'

'Please try doing it my way.' Kawasaki forced a smile, but his face visibly paled with wounded pride.

'You can ask me to stand up from now until next Christmas, but I still can't do it. I'm supposed at this place to be mulling over something. How can I walk across stage when I'm thinking?'

Kawasaki did not answer, but he betrayed his extreme irritation at being addressed in such terms.

But things were quite different when it came to Mangiku's turn. If Kawasaki said, 'Sit!' Mangiku would sit, and if he said, 'Stand!' Mangiku stood. He obeyed unresistingly every direction given by Kawasaki. It seemed to Masuyama that Mangiku's fondness for the part did not fully explain why he was so much more obliging than was his custom at rehearsals.

Masuyama was forced to leave this rehearsal on business just as Mangiku, having run through his scene in the first act, was returning to his seat by the wall. When Masuyama got back, he was met by the following sight: Kawasaki, all but sprawled over the desk, was intently following the rehearsal, not bothering even to push back the long hair falling over his eyes. He was leaning on his crossed arms, the shoulders beneath the corduroy jacket shaking with suppressed rage. To Masuyama's right was a white wall interrupted by a window, through which he could see a balloon swaying in the northerly wind, its streamer proclaiming an end-of-the-year sale. Hard, wintry clouds looked as if they had been blocked in with chalk against the pale blue of the sky. He noticed a shrine to Inari and a tiny vermilion torii on the roof of an old building near by. Farther to his right, by the wall, Mangiku sat erect in Japanese style on the *tatami*. The script lay open on his lap, and the lines of his greenish-gray kimono were perfectly straight. From where Masuyama stood at the door he could not see Mangiku's full face; but the eyes, seen in profile, were utterly tranquil, the gentle gaze fixed unwaveringly on Kawasaki.

Masuyama felt a momentary shudder of fear. He had set one foot inside the rehearsal room, but it was now almost impossible to go in.

6

Later in the day Masuyama was summoned to Mangiku's dressing room. He felt an unaccustomed emotional block when he bent his head, as so often before, to pass through the door curtains. Mangiku greeted him, all smiles, from his perch on the purple cushion and offered Masuyama some cakes he had been given by a visitor.

'How do you think the rehearsal went today?'

'Pardon me?' Masuyama was startled by the question. It was not like Mangiku to ask his opinion on such matters.

'How did it seem?'

'If everything continues to go as well as it did today, I think the play'll be a hit.'

'Do you really think so? I feel terribly sorry for Mr Kawasaki. It's so hard for him. The others have been treating him in such a highhanded way that it's made me quite nervous. I'm sure you could tell from the rehearsal that I've made up my mind to play the part exactly as Mr Kawasaki says. That's the way I'd like to play it myself anyway, and I thought it might make things a little easier for Mr Kawasaki, even if nobody else helps. I can't very well tell the others, but I'm sure they'll notice if I do exactly what I'm told. They know how difficult I usually am. That's the least I can do to protect Mr Kawasaki. It'd be a shame, when he's trying so hard, if nobody helped.'

Masuyama felt no particular surge of emotion as he listened to Mangiku. Quite likely, he thought, Mangiku himself was unaware that he was in love: he was so accustomed to portraying love on a more heroic scale. Masuyama, for his part, considered that these sentiments—however they were to be termed—which had formed in Mangiku's heart were most inappropriate. He expected of Mangiku a far more transparent, artificial, aesthetic display of emotions.

Mangiku, most unusually for him, sat rather informally, imparting a kind of languor to his delicate figure. The mirror reflected the cluster of crimson asters arranged in the cloisonné vase and the recently shaved nape of Mangiku's neck.

Kawasaki's exasperation had become pathetic by the day before stage rehearsals began. As soon as the last private rehearsal ended, he invited Masuyama for a drink, looking as if he had reached the end of his tether. Masuyama was busy at the moment, but two hours later he found Kawasaki in the bar where they had arranged to meet, still waiting for him. The bar was crowded, though it was the night before New Year's Eve, when bars are usually deserted. Kawasaki's face looked pale as he sat drinking alone. He was the kind who only gets paler the more he has had to drink. Masuyama, catching sight of Kawasaki's ashen face as soon as he entered the bar, felt that the young man had saddled him with an unfairly heavy spiritual burden. They lived in different worlds; there was no reason why courtesy should demand that Kawasaki's uncertainties and anguish should fall so squarely on his shoulders.

Kawasaki, as he rather expected, immediately engaged him with a good-natured taunt, accusing him of being a double agent. Masuyama took the charge with a smile. He was only five or six years older than Kawasaki, but he possessed the self-confidence of a man who had dwelt among people who 'knew the score'. At the same time, he felt a kind of envy of this man who had never known hardship, or at any rate, enough hardship. It was not exactly a lack of moral integrity which had made Masuyama indifferent to most of the backstage gossip directed against him, now that he was securely placed in the kabuki hierarchy; his indifference demonstrated that he had nothing to do with the kind of sincerity which might destroy him.

Kawasaki spoke. 'I'm fed up with the whole thing. Once the curtain goes up on opening night, I'll be only too glad to disappear from the picture. Stage rehearsals beginning tomorrow! That's more

307

than I can take, when I'm feeling so disgusted. This is the worst
assignment I've ever had. I've reached my limit. Never again will I
barge into a world that's not my own.'

'But isn't that what you more or less expected from the outset?
Kabuki's not the same as the modern theater, after all.' Masuyama's
voice was cold.

Kawasaki's next words came as a surprise. 'Mangiku's the hardest
to take. I really dislike him. I'll never stage another play with him.'
Kawasaki stared at the curling wisps of smoke under the low ceiling,
as if into the face of an invisible enemy.

'I wouldn't have guessed it. It seems to me he's doing his best to
be co-operative.'

'What makes you think so? What's so good about him? It doesn't
bother me too much when the other actors don't listen to me during
rehearsals or try to intimidate me, or even when they sabotage the
whole works, but Mangiku's more than I can figure out. All he does
is stare at me with that sneer on his face. At bottom he's absolutely
uncompromising, and he treats me like an ignorant little squirt.
That's why he does everything exactly as I say. He's the only one of
them who obeys my directions, and that burns me up all the more.
I can tell just what he's thinking: 'If that's the way you want it, that's
the way I'll do it, but don't expect me to take any responsibility for
what happens in the performance.' That's what he keeps flashing at
me, without saying a word, and it's the worst sabotage I know, He's
the nastiest of the lot.'

Masuyama listened in astonishment, but he shrank from revealing
the truth to Kawasaki now. He hesitated even to let Kawasaki know
that Mangiku was intending to be friendly, much less the whole
truth. Kawasaki was baffled as to how he should respond to the
entirely unfamiliar emotions of this world into which he had suddenly plunged; if he were informed of Mangiku's feelings, he might
easily suppose they represented just one more snare laid for him. His
eyes were too clear: for all his grasp of the principles of theatre, he
could not detect the dark, aesthetic presence lurking behind the
texts.

7

The New Year came and with it the first night of the new program.
Mangiku was in love. His sharp-eyed disciples were the first to

gossip about it. Masuyama, a frequent visitor to Mangiku's dressing room, sensed it in the atmosphere almost immediately. Mangiku was wrapped in his love like a silkworm in its cocoon, soon to emerge as a butterfly. His dressing room was the cocoon of his love. Mangiku was of a retiring disposition in any case, but the contrast with the New Year's excitement elsewhere gave his dressing room a peculiarly solemn hush.

Opening night, Masuyama, noticing as he passed Mangiku's dressing room that the door was wide open, decided to take a look inside. He saw Mangiku from behind, seated before the mirror in full costume, waiting for his signal to go on. His eyes took in the pale lavender of Mangiku's robe, the gentle slope of the powdered and half-exposed shoulders, the glossy, lacquer-black wig. Mangiku at such moments in the deserted dressing room looked like a woman absorbed in her spinning; she was spinning her love, and would continue spinning forever, her mind elsewhere.

Masuyama intuitively understood that the mold for this *onnagata*'s love had been provided by the stage alone. The stage was present all day long, the stage where love was incessantly shouting, grieving, shedding blood. Music celebrating the sublime heights of love sounded perpetually in Mangiku's ears, and each exquisite gesture of his body was constantly employed on stage for the purposes of love. To the tips of his fingers, nothing about Mangiku was alien to love. His toes encased in white *tabi*, the seductive colors of his under kimono barely glimpsed through the openings in his sleeves, the long, swanlike nape of his neck were all in the service of love.

Masuyama did not doubt but that Mangiku would obtain guidance in pursuing his love from the grandiose emotions of his stage roles. The ordinary actor is apt to enrich his performances by infusing them with the emotions of his real life, but not Mangiku. The instant that Mangiku fell in love, the loves of Yukihime, Omiwa, Hinaginu, and the other tragic heroines came to his support.

The thought of Mangiku in love took Masuyama aback, however. Those tragic emotions for which he had yearned so fervently since his days as a high-school student, those sublime emotions which Mangiku always evoked through his corporeal presence on stage, encasing his sensual faculties in icy flames, Mangiku was now visibly nurturing in real life. But the object of these emotions—granted that he had some talent—was an ignoramus as far as kabuki was concerned; he was merely a young, commonplace-looking director whose only qualification as the object of Mangiku's love consisted in being a foreigner in this country, a young traveler who would soon depart the world of kabuki and never return.

8

If Only I Could Change Them! was well received. Kawasaki, despite his announced intention of disappearing after opening night, came to the theatre every day to complain of the performance, to rush back and forth incessantly through the subterranean passages under the stage, to finger with curiosity the mechanisms of the trap door or the *hanamichi*. Masuyama thought this man had something childish about him.

The newspaper reviews praised Mangiku. Masuyama made it a point to show them to Kawasaki, but he merely pouted, like an obstinate child, and all but spat out the words, 'They're all good at acting. But there wasn't any *direction*.' Masuyama naturally did not relay to Mangiku these harsh words, and Kawasaki himself was on his best behavior when he actually met Mangiku. It nevertheless irritated Masuyama that Mangiku, who was utterly blind when it came to other people's feelings, should not have questioned that Kawasaki was aware of his good will. But Kawasaki was absolutely insensitive to what other people might feel. This was the one trait that Kawasaki and Mangiku had in common.

A week after the first performance Masuyama was summoned to Mangiku's dressing room. Mangiku displayed on his table amulets and charms from the shrine where he regularly worshipped, as well as some small New Year's cakes. The cakes would no doubt be distributed later among his disciples, Mangiku pressed some sweets on Masuyama, a sign that he was in a good mood. 'Mr Kawasaki was here a little while ago,' he said.

'Yes, I saw him out front.'

'I wonder if he's still in the theater.'

'I imagine he'll stay until *If Only* is over.'

'Did he say anything about being busy afterward?'

'No, nothing particular.'

'Then, I have a little favor I'd like to ask you.'

Masuyama assumed as businesslike an expression as he could muster. 'What might it be?'

'Tonight, you see, when the performance is over . . . I mean, tonight . . .' The color had mounted in Mangiku's cheeks. His voice was clearer and higher-pitched than usual. 'Tonight, when the performance is over, I thought I'd like to have dinner with him. Would you mind asking if he's free?'

'I'll ask him.'

'It's dreadful of me, isn't it, to ask you such a thing.'

'That's quite all right.' Masuyama sensed that Mangiku's eyes at that moment had stopped roving and were trying to read his expression. He seemed to expect—and even to desire—some perturbation on Masuyama's part. 'Very well,' Masuyama said, rising at once, 'I'll inform him.'

Hardly had Masuyama gone into the lobby than he ran into Kawasaki, coming from the opposite direction; this chance meeting amidst the crowd thronging the lobby during intermission seemed like a stroke of fate. Kawasaki's manner poorly accorded with the festive air pervading the lobby. The somehow haughty airs which the young man always adopted seemed rather comic when set amidst a buzzing crowd of solid citizens dressed in holiday finery and attending the theater merely for the pleasure of seeing a play.

Masuyama led Kawasaki to a corner of the lobby and informed him of Mangiku's request.

'I wonder what he wants with me now? Dinner together—that's funny. I have nothing to do tonight, and there's no reason why I can't go, but I don't see why.'

'I suppose there's something he wants to discuss about the play.'

'The play! I've said all I want to on that subject.'

At this moment a gratuitous desire to do evil, an emotion always associated on the stage with minor villains, took seed within Masuyama's heart, though he did not realize it; he was not aware that he himself was now acting like a character in a play. 'Don't you see—being invited to dinner gives you a marvelous opportunity to tell him everything you've got on your mind, this time without mincing words.'

'All the same—'

'I don't suppose you've got the nerve to tell him.'

The remark wounded the young man's pride. 'All right. I'll go. I've known all along that sooner or later I'd have my chance to have it out with him in the open. Please tell him that I'm glad to accept his invitation.'

Mangiku appeared in the last work of the program and was not free until the entire performance was over. Once the show ends, actors normally make a quick change of clothes and rush from the theatre, but Mangiku showed no sign of haste as he completed his dressing by putting a cape and a scarf of a muted color over his outer kimono. He waited for Kawasaki. When Kawasaki at last appeared, he curtly greeted Mangiku, not bothering to take his hands from his overcoat pockets.

The disciple who always waited on Mangiku as his 'lady's maid' rushed up, as if to announce some major calamity. 'It's started to snow,' he reported with a bow.

'A heavy snow?' Mangiku touched his cape to his cheek.

'No, just a flurry.'

'We'll need an umbrella to the car,' Mangiku said. The disciple rushed off for an umbrella.

Masuyama saw them to the stage entrance. The door attendant had politely arranged Mangiku's and Kawasaki's footwear next to each other. Mangiku's disciple stood outside in the thin snow, holding an open umbrella. The snow fell so sparsely that one couldn't be sure one saw it against the dark concrete wall beyond. One or two flakes fluttered onto the doorstep at the stage entrance.

Mangiku bowed to Masuyama. 'We'll be leaving now,' he said. The smile on his lips could be seen indistinctly behind his scarf. He turned to the disciple, 'That's all right, I'll carry the umbrella. I'd like you to go instead and tell the driver we're ready.' Mangiku held the umbrella over Kawasaki's head. As Kawasaki in his overcoat and Mangiku in his cape walked off side by side under the umbrella, a few flakes suddenly flew—all but bounced—from the umbrella.

Masuyama watched them go. He felt as though a big, black, wet umbrella were being noisily opened inside his heart. He could tell that the illusion, first formed when as a boy he saw Mangiku perform, an illusion which he had preserved intact even after he joined the kabuki staff, had shattered that instant in all directions, like a delicate piece of crystal dropped from a height. At last I know what disillusion means, he thought. I might as well give up the theatre.

But Masuyama knew that along with disillusion a new sensation was assaulting him, jealousy. He dreaded where this new emotion might lead him.

TODDLER-HUNTING

Translated by Lucy North

Hayashi Akiko couldn't abide little girls between three and ten years old—she detested them more than any other kind of human being. If Akiko, like most women, had married and had babies, she might by now have a child just that age. And what, she often wondered, if she'd had a girl? What then?

She knew that men often said they hated children, only to turn into doting fathers once they had their own. But Akiko couldn't picture her own abhorrence ever yielding to maternal love, an emotion she scarcely possessed anyway. Foreign little girls, even at that age, were slightly more bearable, perhaps because their race was more glaring than their gender. If she'd married a foreigner, she might have been able to stand having a daughter of mixed blood, but if not, she was sure that she would have been a horribly cruel mother. She wouldn't have been satisfied just being cold and harsh to her daughter: her loathing would have required more extreme measures.

Akiko's dislike of little girls was of an entirely different order than her disdain for happy, attractive, conceited women her own age, or for young men throwing their weight around, or for smug, complacent old people. It was more like a phobia, the repulsion some people feel when confronted with small creatures like snakes or cats or frogs.

Akiko could not bear to remember that she herself had once been a little girl.

But in fact her childhood had been happier than other periods of her life. She couldn't recall a single hardship; she might have been the most fortunate child who ever lived, a cheerful thing when she was young. But beneath the sunny disposition, in the pit of her stomach, she'd been conscious of an inexplicable constriction. Something loathsome and repellent oppressed all her senses—it was as if she were trapped in a long, narrow tunnel; as if a sticky liquid seeped unseen out of her every pore—as if she were under a curse.

Once, in science class, they'd had a lesson about silkworms, and with a scalpel the teacher had sliced open a cocoon. Akiko took one look at the faintly squirming pupa—a filthy dark thing, slowly binding itself up in thread issuing from its own body—and knew she was seeing the embodiment of the feelings that afflicted her.

And then for some reason Akiko became convinced that other girls her age shared her strange inner discomfort. Grown-ups, however, did not feel this way, and neither did little boys and older girls.

And sure enough, once she got past ten, the queasiness left her. As if she had stepped out of a tunnel into the vast free universe, finally she could breathe. It was at this time, however, that she started to feel nauseated by any girl still passing through that stage, and her repulsion grew stronger as the years went by.

The more typical a girl this age, the less Akiko could bear to be near her. The pallid complexion; the rubbery flesh; the bluish shadow at the nape of the neck left by the bobbed haircut; the unnaturally high, insipid way the girl would talk; even the cut and color of her clothes: Akiko saw in all this the filthy closeness she had glimpsed in the pupa. She could hardly bear to look at a little girl, still less touch one. Her horror remained undiminished to the present day.

But little boys, now—Akiko found little boys extremely appealing at that age. She didn't know exactly when her attraction for them first surfaced, but with every passing year she found their company more intoxicating. Lately, her encounters with little boys had been intensely pleasurable.

Sasaki had taken the express to Osaka on business. When Akiko saw him off at the train station, he'd handed her a package, a new shirt. He'd found out it was poorly finished when he got it home, he said.

His local tailor had tried to fix it, but Sasaki wanted Akiko to exchange it for him. So she headed for the department store where he had bought it, in Nihombashi.

She ran her errand. It was nearly five o'clock when she left the store for the subway station, hurrying to get ahead of the evening rush. But her pace slowed as she passed a well-known store specializing in children's wear.

It was late in summer, still very hot: heavy afternoon sunlight flooded the pavement. But in the shady showcase window, autumn had already arrived. Pretty little shirts for boys were out on display, pinned up. The clothes leant in various directions, sticking out their sturdy elbows and gesturing with their arms.

One shirt almost seemed to be doing a headstand: its front with its little button-neck opening was folded so its square little chest puffed out. This was probably the only short-sleeved one, to judge by its lack of bulk, but the material looked heavy enough for autumn: it was probably a light woolen weave. Akiko was enchanted by the intensity of its broad red and blue horizontal stripes, and by the soft-looking, neatly folded collar in the same design.

Nothing in the window was tagged, so Akiko tried guessing its price. The shirt probably cost at least fifteen hundred yen. Things she liked tended to be expensive.

Her rapture made her an easy target. A clerk in a white short-sleeved shirt approached.

'For your son, Madam? How old is he?'

Ignoring the question, Akiko asked the price of the shirt.

'One thousand seven hundred yen.'

'Just what I guessed!' Akiko said, feeling if anything rather pleased.

'Shall I get it out?' The clerk reached toward the glass panels at the back of the showcase.

'Oh, please don't,' Akiko begged, hastily. 'It's all right.'

At that moment, they were interrupted. To Akiko's relief, the clerk was called to the telephone at back of the store: she knew that once she touched that adorably sweet shirt, she'd never be able to get out of the shop without it.

But before going off to take the call, the clerk quickly took out the shirt and pressed it into her hands: 'It doesn't hurt to look.'

Akiko stroked the garment tenderly—she could just see a little boy, about four years old, pulling on this cozy, lightweight shirt, his sunburned head popping up through the neck. When the time came, he would definitely want to take it off all by himself. Crossing his chubby arms over his chest, concentrating with all his might, he would just manage to grasp the shirt-tails. But how difficult to pull it up and extricate himself. Screwing up his face, twisting around and wiggling his little bottom, he would try his hardest. Akiko would glimpse his tight little belly, full to bursting with all the food he stuffed in at every meal. The shirt, though, was not going to come off, however hard he tried.

Drawn by the charm of little boys' clothes, and especially by the scenes to which they gave rise in her mind, Akiko had several times ended up buying something—a pair of reversible shorts with brick-colored cuffs; a deerstalker cap of white terry cloth with a tiny pale maroon check; a miniature pea jacket about a foot and a half high. When she'd purchased something, she would seek out a woman friend with a toddler to dress. Once she'd settled on her prey, she would set out to bestow her gift. It didn't matter that she normally never gave the woman a second thought—sometimes they'd even had a falling out—she would bewilder the recipient or make her cringe in embarrassment.

Indifferent about her own clothing, Akiko was obsessed with garments for little boys—so naturally her taste in these had become extremely refined. The people selected to receive her gifts would be dumbfounded. How could this woman, who wasn't a mother herself, find such wonderfully appropriate clothes? Some thought they could guess the motive behind these fits of generosity: unfulfilled maternal love.

Akiko bought the shirt and left the shop with a box under her arm. In no time at all, she had marked out the recipient of her next gift.

She'd heard that the opera troupe of which she'd once been a member was now performing *Madame Butterfly*, and that the son of one of her old colleagues was playing the part of Madame Butterfly's child. She trained her sights on this little boy.

When Akiko had quit the company, she'd had good reasons. Her prospects weren't improving: she was over thirty; she couldn't be a member of the chorus forever; and besides, a bout of tuberculosis had damaged her health. Rather than having quit, it might be more accurate to say that circumstances had forced her to fade away.

And yet, back when she had graduated from music college, her achievements had been impressive. She had given solo recitals, winning praise from a famous music critic. 'Such a feel for the music,' he had written in a review, 'especially in the last piece, Mozart's "Longing for Spring".' The fact was that she'd been on the diva track but, as things turned out, she had landed in the chorus—a source of anguish for Akiko. Even now, she found it difficult to ignore the opera world—though all news of it brought her terrible fits of distress. She'd made no effort to stay in touch with her one-time colleagues.

But that evening—just as Madame Butterfly and Suzuki were singing their lines, *Is poverty upon us? This money is all we have!*—Akiko appeared backstage, astonishing the company.

'I heard Noguchi Masayo's son is performing,' she remarked, but her business wasn't with these people. She'd timed her arrival to coincide with the end of the opera, when the child was on stage, and she didn't have to wait long before he appeared.

'I saw an article about it in the newspaper,' Akiko said, when Masayo stepped into the dressing room, her little boy in tow. 'How exciting! Your son on stage!' She leant down to look at the boy, who was hiding behind his mother.

Masayo had made her debut several years after Akiko, playing roles like Annina, the lady-in-waiting in *La Traviata*, and the gardener's daughter in *Le Nozze di Figaro*. She was a cut above the chorus: when she sang, her photograph appeared in the program. Today, however, she was there to look after her little boy.

'Is this the star himself? And only four years old! Is everything going well?'

'Oh yes. He's a gutsy little guy, really,' Masayo replied. 'And anyway, he doesn't have to do much. He seems to be managing pretty well.'

'Oh, I'm not surprised. You can see it in his face!' Akiko said, her gaze lingering on the boy's soft, plump earlobes and his cheeks, tawny and smooth like little biscuits.

'Do you sing too?' the child inquired.

'Me?' Akiko was slightly taken aback. 'No. Auntie doesn't. . . .'

'Yes, what *are* you doing now?' Masayo asked, as if sensing Akiko's discomfort.

What was she doing? Well . . . generally people who are asked such a thing aren't expected to give any impressive reply. Akiko was no exception to the rule. She decided to take the question as referring to how she was making ends meet.

'Oh, I manage with my Italian skills,' she replied vaguely.

'Of course, I remember—there aren't many people who speak it as well as you. . . .'

Akiko's Italian was, in fact, splendid. She had shown a remarkable aptitude for the language, now much more than a vehicle for singing opera. In the chorus she'd never had a hope of making a living, and she'd been thrown back on her language skills to survive. She had earned extra money by translating articles for fashion magazines, and tutoring younger company members.

Nowadays, she worked part-time at a compressor factory: she was called in whenever the company had to correspond with Italian clients. The technical language had posed difficulties at first, since no Italian–Japanese dictionary was complete enough. She'd taken the words she couldn't decipher, with their English and German counterparts, to the Engineering Section to ask for help. This was where she'd gotten to know Sasaki, who usually dealt with her queries.

'You've got a good deal,' he remarked when they first chatted at length, 'not having to work nine to five.' But the part-time pay was a pittance. It was impossible to meet expenses with her Italian alone, even with other odd jobs here and there. She'd found extra income as a dictation assistant to one of the translators working on a complete set of opera libretti. This job allowed her to indulge herself by buying little garments for little boys.

But preferring to steer Masayo away from these topics, she cheerfully pressed the parcel into her hands and said: 'This is a present to celebrate his debut.'

'Oh, my goodness! You didn't need to. . . .'

'That's all right—I wanted to,' Akiko said, directing her last words to the boy.

'What is it? What is it?' he asked.

'I wonder now whether I shouldn't have brought a toy,' Akiko said. 'Won't you try it on?'

Masayo was still hesitant to accept, but Akiko, tearing off the wrapping paper, pulled out her gift.

'Oh, it's a lovely . . .' Masayo was getting more and more uncomfortable. Akiko, however, had already removed the boy's costume and was getting him into the shirt she had chosen.

'What do you think? Isn't it cute?' she asked.

'Oh, yes. And it's a perfect fit.'

'What a lucky boy!' a girl who was packing up her costume nearby chimed in.

'Does the little lad have a name?' Akiko asked. 'I remember seeing it in the papers, but I . . .'

'Darling, this lady wants to know your name. You can tell her yourself, can't you? And don't forget to say thank you.'

'My name is Noguchi Shūichi. Thank you.'

Akiko laughed. 'Can you get take it off by yourself, Shūichi?'

The child nodded.

'Go on then, show me.'

The boy in his comfy red-and-blue shirt shrugged petulantly: 'I don't want to.'

'You like it, don't you,' Masayo said. 'Even children know when something's extra special. Will you wear that home, Shūichi?'

The child looked up at his mother and nodded.

Akiko was thrilled: the shirt was a good fit and also a great success with the boy. But she couldn't resist one last shot at getting to watch him try to get himself out of it.

'It's still a little warm for this shirt, you know,' she said. 'You don't want to sweat, Shū. Let's take it off and have Mommy carry it home. We can wear it as much as we like when the weather gets cooler. What a big boy,' she added, before he could object: 'Shū can get undressed all by himself.'

Akiko unbuttoned the neck of the shirt, and placed her hands on the chubby little arms sticking out of the short sleeves. She crossed his arms, one over the other, savoring their softness and perspiration, and made sure that each hand grasped the hem.

'Now lift your arms up over your head. Got it?'

Just as she'd imagined, the child started to twist and turn about, wiggling his bottom. Akiko backed off to get a better look, but to her chagrin, Masayo decided to lend him a hand. Catching the shirt from behind, she pulled it up, and slipped it off over his head in no time.

'Easy, isn't it?' Akiko said, crossing her own arms. 'Like this, then up and over.' The child nodded. He copied her, crossing his arms, bringing them up and letting them fall loosely over his bare belly.

'Perfect!' In an excess of joy, Akiko laughed out loud, showing off her soprano voice for the first time in years. 'You little darling!'

'I thought you didn't like children, Miss Hayashi,' remarked a member of the chorus, standing nearby.

Akiko knew perfectly well what she meant—and Masayo was probably thinking the same thing. Some years ago, when Akiko was still with the company, a woman (now on tour in Europe) had played Madame Butterfly with her own child on stage. Akiko was so blatantly repulsed by that child that it had become something of a scandal. The mother, who had joined the troupe at the same time as Akiko, was the star of the company, and her colleagues had concluded that her loathing sprang from jealousy. 'She doesn't have to take it out on a four-year-old!' she'd heard them mutter.

Only Akiko knew the real reason: that the child was a girl.

But tonight Akiko passed it off as a change of heart. 'The older you get,' she replied, 'the more you appreciate children.'

On the way home from her transcription job, Akiko bought some things in the shops in front of the station and reached her apartment as dusk fell. Her last purchase, the block of ice, had almost completely soaked its newspaper wrappings, and her fingers were frozen numb. Struggling to hold her shopping, the evening paper, and a postcard from her mailbox, she could barely turn her key in the lock.

As she stepped inside her apartment, she felt something underfoot—a telegram had been pushed under her door, from Sasaki. He'd been due to visit her place that night, following his morning return. The telegram had been dispatched from the Osaka central post office. He'd had to go on to Hiroshima, Sasaki said, so he'd be delayed two or three days. 'In touch soon,' the closing words ran.

The delivery time was stamped at 8:30 that morning—she must

have just missed it on her way out. Strange, that that had been the requested delivery time. Sasaki had most likely been instructed to go on to Hiroshima by the Tokyo office, or by a superior who'd joined him on the trip. But however the change of plan had been announced, he was bound to have become aware of it some time yesterday between nine and five. Why had he delayed letting her know until 8:30 this morning?

Taking a second look, she saw that he had actually dispatched the telegram last night at 11:37, after which he would have taken the night train to Hiroshima, with an easy morning arrival. It had no doubt simply slipped his mind to send the telegram earlier. He must have been out on the town, and then wanted to avoid giving her a shock in the middle of the night. Akiko tossed the slip of paper aside. To think she had gone to the trouble of buying ice. 'In touch soon'—what did he mean? 'Forgive me,' he should have said!

'Miss Hayashi!' It was her superintendent's voice: 'Do you have a delivery from the liquor store?'

Akiko went downstairs where a delivery man was depositing three bottles of beer just inside the entrance. Hovering nearby was the superintendent, an old woman whose rimless eyeglasses gave her an officious air: 'You got a telegram, didn't you?'

'Yes.'

'Everything all right?'

'Fine,' Akiko replied shortly, gathering up the bottles.

Back in her room, Akiko set about stabbing the ice block with a pick used to open milk bottles. Putting some of the ice shards in a glass, she topped them up with beer. She didn't usually drink, and she didn't particularly like the taste, but it was pleasantly chilly, and she downed two glasses one after the other. Remembering the potato chips she'd flung down on her way in, she reached for the bag and tore it open. But after one bite, she stopped. Her heart was racing—a rush of heat came over her. She had to lie down. She remembered the ice: she could wrap some in a towel for her forehead: that would make her feel better. But it was too much trouble to get up. She lay where she was, sprawled out on the floor.

When she opened her eyes, the room was dark. The luminous hands of the clock stood at a little past eight o'clock, and crickets were chirping outside. It was September, and while the days were still hot, there was a nip in the evening air. She had perspired and her clothes felt cold and clammy against her skin, now that it was no longer flushed with drink.

An unmarried woman past thirty losing her temper because a man two years her junior didn't keep his date; who got drunk on the beer she'd bought for him and that was far too strong for her; and who came to her senses in a black room—whoever heard of such a thing! After sneezing several times, Akiko forced a bitter smile.

She stood up, turned on the light, pulled a blanket out of the cupboard, and lay down again. A woman is supposed to weep at a time like this, she thought, not smile.

'It won't be a long drawn-out thing when we break up,' Sasaki had once told her. 'One day we'll have a fight, and that'll be that.'

'Well—you chose the right person, didn't you!' she'd retorted, and was immediately angry at herself. Why did she have to be so disagreeable? This sourness of hers was precisely what made him say such things.

Had Sasaki been pointing out her danger in being such a wilful woman? No, that interpretation was too romantic—he'd only meant that he was aware of how little she was committed to him, or, for that matter, to any aspect of her life.

'We both chose the right person,' Sasaki had replied. 'So we should try our best to get along.'

Though they were single and still relatively young, the subject of a future together rarely came up for discussion. They didn't even try living together.

About the sort of marriage he'd want, Sasaki had any number of typical requirements. He would no doubt settle down late in life with a nice little wife able to meet them. Akiko didn't have these qualities, nor did she care to develop them. But she couldn't, on the other hand, tolerate fussy older men, and was bored by ones of high standing in business or society, who would in all likelihood be married anyway.

They understood these things about themselves, and about each other—and were aware of their mutual knowledge. For him, she was a stopgap companion. For her, he filled a superficial role as her partner. And the one thing that kept them together was their compatible sexual tastes.

Akiko remembered the first time she was distinctly attracted to Sasaki was when he'd told her about a night he spent helping a woman in labor. It had happened when he was still a student, right after the war.

'I was getting ready for bed,' Sasaki had told her, 'when my old landlady rushed into my room, all in a panic: 'The baby's coming! The baby's coming!' 'Well, don't you think you'd better lie down?' I asked. Her belly was out to here, you know. 'Don't be an idiot,' she said to me, very offended: 'You know I'm a widow.' It was the woman on the second floor who was having the baby. Her husband was a drunk of a journalist—he never came home, and he wasn't around that night, either. And the baby was already halfway born, so she couldn't be taken to the hospital—the whole second floor was in an uproar. The old lady told me to heat some water on the first floor, and take it up to them.

'I'd put the water on to boil,' Sasaki continued, 'when the old woman came to my room again. Now she made me go find a midwife. The first person they'd sent out hadn't returned. Well, finding a midwife in the middle of the night isn't easy, you know. I finally spotted an advertisement for one pasted to a telegraph pole, and raced over to the address, only to be told the woman had moved away five years back. By this time I was getting pretty fed up, I can tell you. But I had to do something for the poor woman, and I finally found another old woman. But by the time I brought her back, it was all over. Still, it's good to get the umbilical cord cut by someone who knows what they're doing.

'I headed back to my room, and there at my door was the old woman *again*. Now they needed someone to get rid of the afterbirth water, she said. Well, I did what she told me, me and the guy who lived in the next room. She told us to throw it away on some farm patch, as far away as possible, but you weren't going to catch me carrying a tub of water like that any farther than I had to. Sloshing all over the place, scum splashing me right in the mouth. Anywhere will do, we thought—and sluiced it down a drain right there on the corner.'

'Was it a boy or a girl?' Akiko had asked.

'The baby? A healthy little boy.'

Sasaki's story had had the most unexpected effect on Akiko. Why had she felt so attracted to him? Because of some story about an escapade helping a woman in labor, someone he didn't even know? She couldn't figure it out—was it his freshness, his boyishness? No, it couldn't have been just that. What had drawn her had been the ruthless streak she detected beneath that innocent story of helping a woman in trouble. *That* had gotten to her. And her hunch had proven correct: later, she'd found out that Sasaki possessed just the predilections she liked.

From the way he said, 'a healthy little boy', though, Sasaki appeared to also have a paternal streak: how did this fit in?

Akiko remembered the postcard in her mail from Noguchi Masayo. Reaching for it, she started reading: Masayo began with the customary seasonal greetings and some words about the joy at seeing her after so many years.

'. . . Last night was closing night,' she continued. 'Shūichi normally wakes up early in the morning, but today he dozed past nine. He must be relieved now that the opera is over—it's funny to think of children feeling that way. He loves the shirt you gave him. He's always telling me he wants to wear it. We can't wait for this hot weather to cool down. . . .'

Akiko wasn't as annoyed as she'd expected. '*Shūichi normally wakes up early in the morning. . . .*' She enjoyed turning the words over in her mind. But, just as she never bought little garments with a particular child in mind, to arrange another encounter with Shūichi to see him wearing her gift was out of the question.

She wondered how Sasaki would react if she told him she wanted a baby. Most likely, he'd pick a fight, storm off, and never return.

Akiko's period was always regular—except for once, when she'd made Sasaki whip her so violently that she couldn't stand up for two days and it came two weeks late. But there was hardly a month when it didn't arrive on time, the bright red blood floating in the white porcelain bowl before being whirled away with the water. When she'd been younger, Akiko had been amazed by her body—by its strangeness. Every month, over and over, it made a little bed inside for a baby, unaware that none would be born, and then took it apart again. And it had seemed to her a grave matter that not one person on this earth was created yet out of her own blood.

But she would always find herself wondering how, after giving birth to the baby, she could get someone else to take care of it—and whether there wasn't some way she could reserve the right to only occasionally oversee its care. She began to greatly envy men, who could avoid parental tasks so easily. All this surely proved how poorly she was endowed with natural maternal urges.

And then, two or three years ago, there had been her bout of pulmonary TB. Her case had been serious, and though her recovery had been surprisingly rapid, she had been told by her doctors that she should never try to have a child—she would never survive. And by now, even had they told her she could have a baby, Akiko no longer wished for one. Aside from the question of how she would arrange it, her physical and emotional stamina had been quite worn down by the disease. And she was so impatient—the thought of being tied down by such a long commitment was insufferable. This, she thought, was probably what kept her in the relationship with Sasaki.

For all these reasons, she had become a woman for whom maternal love was a totally alien emotion—a woman even less able to think of bringing up children. Akiko now felt at ease knowing that having a baby was out of the question for her body—when this fact came to mind, she felt an emotion close to joy.

It was already nine o'clock. She needed to eat, but she stayed sprawled out on the floor. She had recovered her equanimity. The frustration she'd felt began to change into a different sort of excitement. Often, after surges of emotion, a strange fantasy world would descend and take her in its sway. She chose to stay on the floor in the hope of this happening, and already there were signs of it starting.

As the dream world spread out about her, Akiko would plunge herself into it, her pulse beating faster and faster and her skin all moist, and she would reach ecstasy, losing all self-control.

Two figures always appeared in this strange world: a little boy of seven or eight, and a man in his thirties. The details of their personalities and activities varied slightly each time, but the age gap remained constant, as did their relationship as father and child. Their faces were out of focus, but it was important for Akiko to be able to believe that the child, at least, was very very sweet.

The man would be thrashing the boy, and scolding him in so

325

gentle a tone that it was harrowing. The beating would start out as the kind any father might give his son, but gradually it would reach a level of horrifying atrocity. At the very climax of the scene, however, the thought of the impossibility of such things actually happening in the real world would surface in her mind, and Akiko would return abruptly to herself. Her face would be flushed, but she'd know that she was back in reality.

—*You've been a very bad boy, the father starts. I'm going to have to teach you a lesson.*

A crash as the father whacks the boy across the face, almost knocking his head off. The child staggers under the blow, and then gets back on his feet straightaway, trying to bear the pain. But he is unable to resist touching his cheek furtively.

—*Hasn't Daddy warned you time and again not to do that? I suppose it takes more than one lesson to make you understand.*

The father issues an order to someone, and an alligator belt is placed in front of him.

—*Take off your clothes.*

The child does as he is told, and the father begins whipping his buttocks with the belt.

—*How about using our other instrument? The voice is a woman's. The belt is dropped and he picks up a cane.*

More punishment. With every lash of the cane, there are shrieks and agonized cries. The boy is sent sprawling forward, sometimes flat on his face, but he struggles to get up each time, ready to receive the next stroke, a course of action he carries out without being told.

—*Look. Look at the blood. The woman's voice again. There it is, the red fluid trickling down over the child's buttocks, over his thighs. The blood is smeared over the surface of his flesh by yet more thrashes of the cane.*

Another lash, and more blood spurts out from another spot: the two streams trickle down the boy's thigh, as if racing each other. The flow stops halfway down his leg—the blood has already dried. The scene is, after all, taking place in the full heat of the summer sun.

—*Hit me on my back, Daddy, the boy begs.*

—*I was leaving that till last. There's no hurry.*

The father sets down the cane, and taking the boy over to a tin shack, grabs him by the shoulders and forces him against the scorching metal. The child tries to escape, wriggling around and desperately pushing himself away, but to no avail. He is pinned by the heavy body of his father, pressed flat against the searing hot tin. There follows the hiss of roasting flesh.

Pulled away from the wall, the child totters, dazed by pain, but the father hauls him up. Then the father turns the body around so that the woman can get a good look at the raw flayed flesh on the boy's back, dark red stripes branded into his skin by ridges of hot metal.

There is more to come, but now the boy crumples to the ground when told to stand. More scolding. The father ties the child's hands together and hangs him from the branch of a tree.

—What else should I see to? the man asks.

—You haven't touched his stomach. The woman's voice again, insinuating. The child gets a few lashes on his belly, and suddenly, his stomach splits open. Intestines, an exquisitely colored rope of violet, slither out.

The woman gives the order: the man cuts the cord around the child's hands. The boy drops down from the branch to the ground. Now the man pulls the purple rope until it is tight, and jerks the child's body about as if trying to get a kite to rise into the air. The little body at the end of the purple rope is smashed against the corrugated tin shack repeatedly. Every twitch on the rope brings forth pitiful, horrifying screams.

Akiko saw Sasaki when she went into work at the factory. As they walked down the corridor, he asked: 'Feeling better?'

'Doesn't it look like it?'

'You gave me a scare.'

'Serves you right—sending telegrams in the middle of the night.'

Akiko had spent the previous night with Sasaki, but she hadn't mentioned the telegram.

'But it was delivered the next morning, wasn't it?' he asked.

'Yes, that's what bothers me. What were you doing that you got to the post office so late?'

'Oh, I went to the night baseball game, and . . .'

They were in front of the Accounting Department—Akiko had come in to collect her wages. She disappeared behind the door, leaving him in mid-sentence.

Back at home, Akiko started to clear up. That morning in her hurry to get to work she had left her room just as it was. A few pearls had rolled here and there on the floor.

The night before, Akiko had wanted to add a little variety to their usual routine, and she'd looked round frantically for something to help. Finally, she hit upon a pearl necklace.

'They're not real,' she'd said, handing them to him.

'Hmm. Hey, not bad.' Sasaki dangled the necklace from his fingertips to tantalize her.

Then, gripping it tightly, he circled around her. Akiko was already so aroused she felt as if every nerve in her body was concentrated in the flesh of her back. When he brought the beads down on her skin, however, the sting and the smart cracking were over as soon as they started. The thread of the necklace snapped and with a dull patter pearls scattered across the floor. Sasaki and Akiko laughed, a little uncertainly.

Two strands of thread, a few pearls still clinging to them, hung from Sasaki's fist. Putting them in the lid of a mosquito-coil box, he began crawling around on his hands and knees, hunting up the others. Akiko watched him with growing vexation: 'Just leave them, can't you!' Hearing her own tone of voice, she was disappointed to realize that the mood had left her.

But the next moment, Sasaki caught sight of a vinyl wash-rope hanging in a corner, the type with plastic knobs and metal hooks at either end. As he reached for it and started doubling it up, Akiko was already begging him to use the jagged metal hooks on her— they'd make a clicking sound.

It depended on what they used, but they both enjoyed the sound things made whipped against her skin. The more excited the noises made them, the more they would have to suppress their cries. That night, however, Sasaki had been especially resourceful with that length of rope, and Akiko's screams smothered out the thrashing sound. At first they hadn't realized somebody was knocking on the door.

'What's that?' Sasaki froze in mid-stroke, and by an unfortunate coincidence, a fire-engine siren started wailing through the neighborhood. Akiko's heart gave a leap.

Pulling a shirt over his shoulders, Sasaki put his face round the door.

'I was a little worried.' It was the voice of the old superintendent with rimless eye-glasses. 'I don't want them to have to carry you out of there dead.'

The other tenants of the building were familiar with the goings-on in this room. That night, however, they must have gone a little too far.

'Sorry. We didn't mean to worry you.'

'In any case, keep it down, won't you? Remember there are other people living in this building.'

'Sorry. Really.'

Listening to their voices, Akiko suddenly felt sick. For a moment, she thought she would vomit. She lay down, but already everything before her eyes was black.

'What's wrong?'

'The window . . . ,' Akiko said, pushing back the curtain billowing out over her face like a sail in the breeze. 'I'm very cold.'

The shock thinking that a fire had started: had that sent the blood in her already racing heart into turmoil? A moment before, her body had been a mass of red-hot iron filings leaping around in space. Now she was aware of it cooling down rapidly. She didn't seem to have lost consciousness, though—she could hear Sasaki's voice, at some distance, and herself responding. Or at least, so she had thought. Afterwards, he told her that there had been thirty minutes or so when she'd had no reaction to anything he said, and her pulse had grown steadily weaker.

Akiko brought a hand to her brow and her fingers were stiff with cold. Sasaki released her other wrist, and stood up.

'This is bad.' There was the sound of his belt being buckled.

'Where are you going?'

'To get a doctor.'

'I'm all right,' Akiko said, her eyes closed, and she was beginning to feel a little better. A damp hand-towel had been pushed down between her breasts, she realized, and she was covered by a blanket and quilt.

'I really thought they would have to carry a corpse out of here!' Sasaki said the next morning, recounting the scene to her. 'I want you to prepare a testimonial.'

'What for?'

'Just so there's something about our sexual habits maybe having certain consequences, and if I do end up killing you, to prove it was an accident.'

'All right, don't worry. I'll do it.'

329

It was three in the afternoon when Akiko set out for the public bath. Only seven or eight women were there: a new mother with her baby, some old women with nothing better to do, and young women bathing before going off to work in the evening.

For some reason, perhaps having to do with the design of the bathhouse, clients tended to cluster around the middle of the changing-room, while in the bathroom itself they took up places along the outer wall—hardly anyone could be seen elsewhere. Akiko had purposely chosen a time when the place would be empty, and making sure to conceal her cuts with her wash-towel, she picked her way over the tiles, which were covered with dry grains of scrubbing detergent, to an area where there was nobody at all. Opposite the doors was a tub of water so hot that she didn't dare enter it for a while. It was here, in front of the faucet, that Akiko always took up her position. After splashing warm water over herself, she would immerse herself in another bath next to it, where cold water flowed in to modify the temperature.

As she soaked, Akiko would keep an eye on the changing-room, which she could keep in sight because the separating doors had been drawn back. Were there any cute little boys with their mothers? Wasn't even one going to come over and join her?

If she did see a little boy, darkly tanned from the knees down, playing by the edge of the bath with a little boat or a soapbox lid, Akiko couldn't resist giving him one of her special winks. The child never failed to respond. He would float his boat her way on a reconnaissance trip, and she would then make waves, sending it back on a storm, happy to go on playing in the bath forever—rescuing the boat if it sank, and starting up a conversation. Somewhere the mother would be calling her son, but he wouldn't go. Finally, the mother would come and pull him away. One arm gripped by his mother, the other clasping the boat to his chest, the little boy would turn to look back for an instant at Akiko. Then he would head off, his plump little feet smacking the wet tiles. Akiko would get out of the water, a melancholy smile on her lips.

Today, as a result of last night's wild abandon—closer in fact to an act of self-annihilation—Akiko longed more than ever for a little boy to appear. It was a strange attachment that she had to little boys, one which she preferred to keep Sasaki in the dark about.

The bathing area was filling up, but it didn't look as if Akiko's wish would be granted today. Wanting to escape before it got too crowded, she left after a quick scrub without getting into the tub at all.

Akiko walked home, keeping to the shady side of the street. Then, just as she entered an alley, turning the corner by the vegetable shop, she encountered a little boy.

He was about three years old, a toddler she hadn't seen before. Dressed in a grubby athletic jersey and putty-colored pants, he was standing by a stack of cartons and baskets, struggling with a chunk of watermelon.

Akiko got a little closer.

'Good?' she asked, as an opening gambit.

The child nodded without raising his eyes. Wanting a little more of a reaction, she tried again: 'Is that good?'

"Really good." He gave a clear answer this time.

Pointing the little forefinger of his right hand like a pistol, he was using it to dig out the seeds. But his finger was poking around a little too eagerly, so all the seeds seemed to dive back deeper inside their holes. It was only a small chunk of watermelon, cut from a larger slice, but the chunk appeared quite unwieldy, his arms were so stubby and his fists so small.

The child was totally absorbed, concentrating on digging out one particular seed. Refusing to go on to others nearer the surface, he held the chunk in one hand, turning it this way and that, vainly trying with his other to hook out that one recalcitrant seed.

Akiko watched as he plunged his finger into the watermelon flesh. The juice spurted out, running down his fingers and all over his wrist, changing to the color of vinegar as it mixed with the sweat and grime collected there from the various escapades of his day.

His concentration momentarily broken, the boy looked up and took in Akiko's presence.

'Difficult, isn't it?' she said.

The child grunted.

Akiko knelt, and put her bath bag on her knee.

'Let Auntie see.' She pulled his fingers out of the watermelon. She had wanted to keep the boy's hands in her own, holding the chunk with him, but he gave the fruit up to her, and wiped his dripping fingers on the seat of his pants.

The seed was lodged at the very end of a deep hole.

'Do you want Auntie to get it out?'

The child grunted again, rubbing his fist like a harmonica against his lips. Akiko poked with her little finger, and the seed slipped out.

'Good at it, aren't I?'

'You're a grown-up.'

'Well then, leave it to me,' Akiko laughed, keeping the fruit. She proceeded to pick out every seed in the chunk (now mauled to an oozing red mass), including the ones that poked their heads out of the loose wet pulp.

'Now,' she said, holding it out to him, 'Take a bite.'

Using both hands, the child brought the watermelon to his mouth, and with each bite, juice gushed over his small soft-looking upper lip. While he worked on swallowing a mouthful, he would pull the chunk of fruit down with a sharp jerk, and hold it in front of him. Two bright red streaks were pointing up like flames from either side of his mouth.

'Hey,' Akiko said, unable to resist. 'Won't you give me some of that?'

In silence, the child offered up the watermelon. Akiko took hold of it with her hands over his, pulling the boy up to her. She sank her teeth into the fruit, and the mouthful of watermelon was so pulpy and warm, it was like biting into live flesh.

'Good?' the child asked.

Akiko nodded gravely, squeezing as much flavor as she could out of the mouthful of fruit, savoring the tang of the child's sweat, the grime from his fingers, even his saliva, before letting it slide slowly down her throat.

Little boys inhabited such an infinitely wholesome world—Akiko always had the impression that it restored and purified her. Its simplicity was so all-encompassing that anything out of the ordinary about her could pass without notice there. Little boys went along with her in her games—sometimes they almost seemed to egg her on.

Akiko realized that she was still holding the watermelon and the boy's hands up close to her.

'Thank you,' she said, letting them go. 'That was delicious.'

The child stared intently at the watermelon, and before she knew it, he had given it back.

'You have it,' he said. 'I don't want it anymore.'

He probably no longer wanted to eat it now that somebody else's mouth had touched it. He ran off, wiping his fingers on the seat of his trousers. A little way down the street he stopped, turned, and looked back at Akiko, who stood rooted to the spot, not knowing what to do with the unexpected gift in her hands.

MR CARP

Translated by Tomone Matsumoto

∽

'Someone's here,' whispered Mayumi, Shiomura's daughter. 'The kitchen door just opened. I'm sure of it.'

Shiomura didn't like this side of Mayumi. Her piano teacher had told her she had a good ear, so she had decided to enter a conservatory the year after next. Now she unabashedly flaunted her talent, whether to report on an alarm clock going off inside the house two doors away or on how the voice of a sweet potato vendor had changed. Whenever Shiomura said he didn't hear or couldn't tell the difference, Mayumi was blatantly scornful.

Her attitude made him stubborn. 'No one's here. You're imagining things,' he insisted.

Surprisingly, Shiomura's wife, Miwako, for once sided with him. 'If someone's here, he'll call out,' she said. For Miwako this Sunday was special because Shiomura had stayed home, probably on account of the rain shower; he usually played golf on Sunday. The family— Shiomura, Miwako, Mayumi, and eleven-year-old Mamoru—had just finished brunch. Their conversation was not out of the ordinary, but they all laughed frequently. Perhaps Miwako did not want to interrupt their merriment to go into the kitchen and check.

'Mayumi, your ears are out of tune,' Shiomura said.

'Me? No way. You're the one with the bad ears. You're out of tune even when you laugh,' she retorted.

'So laughter has a tune?'

'Sure, it does,' Mayumi declared. Her plump face had given her the nickname 'Shumai,' after the Chinese-style dumplings. When she was serious her eyes showed more of their whites, just like her mother's. 'If you don't believe me, go ahead and laugh, Daddy. You're the only one out of tune.'

Shiomura began to laugh but then caught himself, saying he wouldn't want to laugh when there was nothing funny. Hearing this lame excuse, the other three burst into laughter. Even quiet Mamoru, who seldom laughed, joined in. The loudest and merriest voice of all belonged to Miwako, Shiomura's wife. Finally Shiomura laughed too. Though he knew very little about music, the laughter of his family on Sunday afternoon sounded better than the most splendid chorus.

There is an old saying in Japan that age forty-two is a man's most crucial year. So far Shiomura had been fortunate: his immediate superior had been promoted to managing director in the annual springtime personnel shifts; he was about to pay off the mortgage on their home; his blood pressure was normal and his stomach condition good; he was a fine golfer. 'The snail's on the thorn: God's in his heaven—All's right with the world!' Was that Browning? Shiomura wondered. But he hadn't seen snails in the backyard for years.

'It's a thief,' Mayumi whispered again, insisting that someone was in the kitchen. 'He's just closed the door and left.'

'You don't give up, do you, Mayumi?' Shiomura said. 'Why not just go and have a look yourself?'

Miwako joined in. 'There's nothing worth stealing in the kitchen. He'll be disappointed.' Laughing, she headed for the kitchen. Peering inside, she uttered a cry of surprise and then looked back, puzzled.

'What's the matter? Anything stolen?' Shiomura asked her.

'Not stolen—added,' she replied. On the earthen floor of the kitchen was a plastic bucket with a six-inch gray crucian carp swimming inside it.

'What is this?' shouted Shiomura. 'Mamoru, did you do this? Did you make a bet or something with a friend?'

Mamoru looked at the fish and shook his head. Miwako and Mayumi had no idea why the fish was there either.

'Isn't this strange? How did it get here when no one knows anything about it? Did it walk up here by itself?' Shiomura's voice rose. Miwako, Mayumi, and Mamoru all looked blank.

'I know!' Miwako cried and turned to Shiomura. 'It's you!'

Shiomura felt he had been hit by a hammer. 'What's that supposed to mean?'

'Now just calm down. Put on your thinking cap a moment,' his wife said.

Shiomura knew he was trembling.

'Have you been picking on someone who likes to fish?' she continued. 'Saying things like he could never catch such a big fish or something? I bet that person got upset and deliberately left this big one he caught without telling you.'

Shiomura was relieved. Good. She hasn't got wind of it. But I shouldn't relax yet, he thought. Making a long face, he said, 'I don't have any friends who fish.'

'No? So, you don't know who did it?'

'How could I know? Don't be silly.' Shiomura's voice grew unusually loud.

'I sometimes hear about 10,000-yen notes being left in mailboxes, but I've never heard of a carp in a bucket,' Miwako said. Looking at Shiomura with an eerie, cautious expression, she asked, 'Don't you think we should report this to the police?'

'What could the police do? It's not money, you know,' Shiomura said. He did not want the matter to go to the police. He doubted it was the sort of thing to be reported in the newspapers, but he certainly didn't want the police involved.

'But Daddy, it's a lost and found case, isn't it? It's not right to keep the fish for ourselves.' Mayumi had been argumentative lately.

'It may be lost, but there's been trespassing here.' Shiomura responded with another argument. No police, for God's sake, he thought.

'It's only a fish. Don't exaggerate, dear,' Miwako laughed.

His wife's laughter gave Shiomura some relief. 'Go get rid of it somewhere,' he said to Mamoru. Just as he was reaching in his pockets to offer him a tiny bribe, the boy, who had had his fingers in the bucket and been playing with the fish, asked if he could keep it. Clinging to the bucket, he promised to give up on the pair of roller skates he had been asking for. Normally a very quiet boy, once Mamoru spoke up he would not back down. Shiomura had never permitted Mamoru to keep dogs, cats, or pigeons because he didn't want the house to get dirty, but he couldn't think of any reason not to keep the fish. Mayumi didn't want it because she didn't like the way it had gotten there. Miwako looked confused, not knowing what to say. Mamoru held the bucket tightly and in the end won: he would keep the fish.

Left alone—the other three had gone to search the shed for a bigger container for the carp—Shiomura heaved a big sigh. No doubt about it. This one is Mr Carp. Not that I remember its face, but I recognize the rear fin, the way it's torn in the center. Has he grown this big and fat in the year I haven't seen him? But why would she do this?

The woman's name was Tsuyuko. Divorced, aged thirty-five, when Shiomura got to know her she was working in the Ikebukuro section of Tokyo at a small Japanese-style restaurant owned by a relative. One night, after drinking too much, Shiomura had vomited on the floor and she had cleaned up after him. To show his thanks he bought her a handbag, and after seeing each other a few times, they became lovers. Gaunt and bony, Tsuyuko was not a beautiful woman. But even small things filled her with pleasure. Her conversation was just chitchat, never touching on sorrow or joy; these she was able to express in bed. Once she scratched Shiomura's back with her fingernails, and since it was summer he had had a hard time hiding the marks from his wife. Before he knew it, Shiomura had begun to visit Tsuyuko's apartment once a week. Around that time she began to keep the carp.

Tsuyuko had come across some children trying to throw a fish they had caught into a ditch full of dirty water. Letting the fish loose in soapsuds would kill it, she told the children, and asked them to give it to her. Then she bought a large tropical fish tank. She'd grown up in Kasumigaura in Chiba Prefecture, a fishing town, so she knew how to look after fish.

'I feel like he is watching us,' Shiomura said. In Tsuyuko's cheap apartment with three- and six-mat rooms, the tank was just above their heads as they lay on their futon.

'Don't you worry. Fish are near-sighted,' Tsuyuko said.

Shiomura was not sure that was true.

'I didn't mind living alone after my divorce,' Tsuyuko said, 'but now you've reminded me of what it is like to be with a man. When you don't come, I can't bear the loneliness unless I have something alive and moving in the room.' Tsuyuko clung to Shiomura, like a morning glory wrapping itself around a bamboo stalk.

She named the fish Mr Carp and fed him grains of cooked rice from time to time.

It wasn't that Shiomura came to dislike Tsuyuko or that even the small amounts of money he gave her seemed too extravagant. The real reason he left her was that he did not want to break up his family. He was not unhappy with his wife. At least, that was not why he had had the affair with Tsuyuko. When he went to Singapore on business for a month and then spent the following month in bed with colitis, he took advantage of this natural interruption to stop seeing her. A year had now passed. Shiomura told himself many times that he had never made Tsuyuko any promises about the future, and that she had no reason to hate him for leaving. Now, just when the memories were receding, Tsuyuko had left him Mr Carp.

What was Tsuyuko's message in this? Was it a sign that she was angry, or a kind of revenge? He knew he could call her to ask, but he lacked the confidence that he would not fall into the abyss again. At any rate, Tsuyuko must have heard them all laughing. A married couple and two children. Merrily laughing together. How had Tsuyuko taken that?

I don't want to keep this fish, Shiomura thought. I should have made some excuse when Mamoru started begging for it. But I can't change my mind now; it will seem strange. It's not good to make them suspicious. Mamoru is just a boy. Boys get bored with things quickly. I'll just wait and then let it go free the first chance I get.

The fish had no facial expression. His round eyes looked as if they had been cut from black vinyl and pasted in, like the eyes on the paper carp pennants used for Boys' Day in May. The profile was dignified but from the front the fish looked exactly like former Prime Minister Shigeru Yoshida. There was guile in the way the face revealed nothing. The fish's mouth gulped and closed. Shiomura stared at the fish from the front and thought he had actually caught its eye, but nowhere in the black vinyl did it register 'Ah, it's you' or 'Oh, it's been a long time.' Perhaps the fish had no memory of Shiomura. There was no way to determine what Tsuyuko's intention was.

That Sunday passed with a great fuss made over the carp. They could not find a container large enough for the fish, so Mamoru got an advance on his allowance from his mother, ran to a goldfish shop in the neighborhood, and bought a large, square water tank for 3,500 yen. The shopkeeper told him he should not use water right out of the tap; either he had to let the tap water sit for at least a half- to a full day in the sun or he should add in some chemical dechlorinator. As instructed, Mamoru ran water into the tank, threw in two bean-size tablets of dechlorinator, stirred, and dropped in the fish. Once in the water, the carp relieved itself, producing a surprisingly large stool—it was about the thickness of a pencil as it emerged.

'Mr Carp, you've got some nerve,' Shiomura muttered, thinking no one was around.

'Oh, you've named it Mr Carp?' his wife asked, standing behind him. Shiomura was horrified.

They put the tank with Mr Carp on top of the shoe shelf in the entryway. The quiet middle-aged woman who collected for the *Asahi* newspaper rang the front bell timidly and spoke in a small voice. In contrast, the collector for the *Yomiuri* newspaper had a booming voice and would press the bell as if to break it. Mr Carp had a bad reaction to the loud *Yomiuri* collector, jumping violently and splashing water all over the entryway. It was easy enough to mop up the water, but spots remained on the teak-paneled door frame and walls, perhaps from the dechlorinator. The contractor had suggested plywood when the house was being built, but Shiomura had insisted on the importance of the entryway and spent quite a lot of money for genuine teak wood. Although he knew this was not Tsuyuko's way of getting her revenge, he still couldn't control his anger. He sensed his blood-pressure rising.

The fish required looking after. An abundance of excrement and left-over particles of rotted fish food quickly made the water murky and turbid. In the dirty water, Mr Carp would pucker its lips and knock against the four corners of the tank, inhaling and exhaling small bubbles, seemingly desperate for oxygen. And it didn't like the convenient ready-made food, preferring the kind you crushed in your fingers, but this soon dispersed and dirtied up the water.

Mamoru studied a book he had bought entitled *All About Carp Fishing*. 'Mr Carp is our relative,' he said, shocking Shiomura. Listening to his son's explanation, Shiomura realized it was so. Fish are vertebrates, with fins instead of legs. From an evolutionary standpoint, humans are closer to fish than to some four-legged land creatures because the roots of mankind lie in the ancestors of the vertebrates on land.

In light of this, the face of Mr Carp seemed that of a very deep thinker. 'I know it all,' it seemed to say. Mr Carp knew, for example, that Shiomura had taken pains so as not to be embarrassed at karaoke bars: he had bought a book of lyrics to popular songs and, with Tsuyuko as his teacher, had practiced Aki Yashiro's famous

'Boat Song'. Mr Carp had also seen Shiomura stark naked after a bath, pretending to do Tai-chi to make Tsuyuko laugh and then grabbing her and moving onto the bed.

What helped Shiomura was that his wife, Miwako, was so unruffled. At first, she had seemed preoccupied with the fish, but after a few days, she didn't talk about it much. She could just as easily have been taking care of a plain goldfish bought at some festival. Mayumi, however, detested Mr Carp. She grumbled that the house had stunk of fish ever since it arrived. Averting her face, she refused even to look at the fish. Instead, she stared insolently at Shiomura.

As long as Shiomura was away at work during the day he was fine, but at home, sitting in the family room, he would succumb to nervous exhaustion. Mealtimes with the family were the worst. Inevitably his eyes would stray to the fish tank, which was now right next to the TV. How could he possibly relax? It wasn't simply like having a pet; it was like having someone new added to the family. No wonder the right side of his neck—on the same side as the tank in the room—had developed a cramp.

Massaging his neck, Miwako asked, 'Shall I move the tank?'

'No. It's got nothing to do with the tank,' Shiomura said.

'Really? But you keep watching it all the time,' she said. She pressed the painful spot on his neck so hard that he screamed and jumped up.

The beer had lost its flavor, and Shiomura didn't much feel like going home. He still couldn't read anything in Mr Carp's black vinyl eyes. Nor was there anything he could tell from Miwako's brown goggle-eyed expression. As for Tsuyuko, watching from God knows where, he had absolutely no way of knowing what she was thinking.

The Sunday after Mr Carp arrived, Shiomura asked Mamoru to go for a walk with him. 'You don't mind just wandering around places you've never been to, do you?'

'No, that's okay,' Mamoru replied.

Shiomura said nothing more, and in silence the two took a bus from Ikebukuro, getting off at Shiinamachi, where Tsuyuko lived. Shiomura could not explain his actions, even to himself. He knew well enough what it meant to take his own son to the neighborhood where his ex-mistress's apartment was, but he couldn't help himself.

Mamoru followed Shiomura, as usual without a word. They

walked past the supermarket, the greengrocer's, and the fish shop. From the tea shop next to the kimono shop, the fragrance of roasting tea leaves floated in the air, just as it had a year ago. Tormented, Shiomura felt the salt being rubbed into his wounds. He moved down the street to the lane where Tsuyuko's apartment was located, the same place he had come some forty or fifty times before. What would he say to Tsuyuko if she came out from the apartment and ran into them?

Some of the residents of Tsuyuko's apartment house had gotten to know Shiomura during the year he had come visiting her. To avoid encountering them now, Shiomura walked around the side of the building. Tsuyuko's apartment was the second window from the end on the second floor. She must have moved out, for the clothes hanging at the window were those of a young couple with a baby. Shiomura noticed that Mamoru too was staring at Tsuyuko's window with him. Realizing he had been caught, Mamoru quickly turned his face away, without saying a word.

This is as far as I should go, Shiomura thought. But still he felt like torturing himself a bit more. He wanted to take his son, who had taken over the care of Mr Carp, to visit all of his and Tsuyuko's old haunts—partly out of a sense of duty to the boy but also to help atone for his poor treatment of Tsuyuko.

Shiomura entered a coffee shop two buildings down from the public bathhouse. He and Tsuyuko always used to drop by the shop on their way back from the bathhouse. The owner of the shop, a man about sixty years old, was sitting in his usual place and wearing his usual expression, a horse-racing newspaper spread in front of him. When he saw Shiomura, he waved in welcome and began to speak, but noticing Mamoru behind he lowered his hand and kept silent. Shiomura sat in the very place he had sat in with Tsuyuko and spoke to Mamoru loudly, so the owner of the coffee shop could hear him: 'I'll have coffee; what do you want, Mamoru?'

'A soda,' Mamoru said.

The startled shop owner looked sharply at Shiomura. This had been Tsuyuko's usual order.

Father and son drank their coffee and soda in silence. Pretending to read his paper, the shop owner shot occasional glances at them.

'I wonder how things are . . . ,' Shiomura said as he paid the bill. He omitted 'with her,' but the shop owner seemed to understand.

'Doing well, I guess,' he said.

How had Tsuyuko spent her days during the year since he had stopped coming to see her? Did she have a man she could go to the bathhouse with, and did she then stop in at the coffee shop and have a soda? Shiomura wanted to know, but the shop owner had lowered his eyes to his paper after returning Shiomura's change. Shiomura could guess from his expression that Tsuyuko didn't hate him too much. So that was that. He couldn't help how things had turned out. When Tsuyuko had moved out of her apartment, she must have had a slight grudge, so she had slipped in and dropped off Mr Carp, the idea being that Shiomura should look after him for her from now on. A self-serving interpretation to be sure, but Shiomura chose to believe it. A person good at keeping herself happy should be good at managing her sorrows as well.

I will take good care of Mr Carp, Shiomura vowed. I'll treat him well so he lives a long long time, but if I can't I'll take him to Kasumigaura and let him go. Kasumigaura was Tsuyuko's hometown, and Shiomura thought that if it did come time to let Mr Carp go, he would just take Mamoru with him and leave his wife and daughter behind.

Mamoru did not speak at all on their way home. Once, when Mamoru was about five, Shiomura had taken him to a baseball game. When they returned home, Miwako had asked, 'Mamoru, where did you go with Daddy?'

'Television,' he had replied.

This had become a family legend, but what would the boy say today? Shiomura wondered. When Mamoru spoke, Shiomura expected his wound to smart again.

Lost in such thoughts Shiomura arrived home to find Mr Carp floating belly up in the fish tank.

'Soon after you two left he stuck his mouth up above the water and started gasping for breath. Then he turned on his side and just stopped moving his mouth,' Miwako said. Not knowing what to do, she had left the fish there until they returned.

Mamoru stared at his mother in disbelief as she explained what had happened. Mr Carp was floating with his big round eyes open— the eyes of a paper carp pennant. He appeared to be doing a casual back float. His fan-shaped scales still held the color of the sunset.

Just then Shiomura noticed that the sound of the piano had stopped. Mayumi was standing beside him. 'Carp don't make any noise when they die, do they?' she said. 'I thought it would suffer a lot, splashing water all over, but it didn't at all.'

'Well, he didn't leave a will either, did he?' Shiomura said, trying to sound calm, and let out a giggle. He felt sorry for Mr Carp, but the feeling that at long last he was freed from Tsuyuko was stronger than his pity. For a moment, he imagined that Tsuyuko had drowned herself and that her body was floating somewhere in the sea off Kasumigaura. But this notion was just the product of his male conceit. He pushed it aside.

'Mom, you didn't put detergent or anything in the tank, did you?' said Mamoru.

'What? What did you say? What makes you think I would do such a thing? Don't be silly!' Miwako's goggle-eyes rolled up, revealing her triangular whites. Immediately her tone of voice returned to normal and she asked, 'Mamoru, where did you go with your dad?'

Mamoru did not reply to that. In silence, he put his hand into the tank and poked at the fish. The fish was no longer a fish; it had become something else, floating and bobbing on its side.

'Mamoru, where did you go with your dad?' Miwako demanded.

Mamoru gently poked at the fish and pushed it down into the water again. 'Bow wow!' he said, barking like a dog.

KAIKO TAKESHI (1930–1989)

THE DUEL

Translated by Cecilia Segawa Seigle

~

At the beach, two men were sitting on the coral reef. Beside them were two open lunch boxes on a spread cloth. The younger man occasionally nibbled a piece of fried chicken, while sipping local sake made from black molasses. The older man hugged his long legs, gazing into the horizon across the sea. He drank tea from the thermos bottle and ate sushi. The sky was filled with the characteristic tropical light that was clear, yet hazy at this hour, and its luminosity spread over the entire sky. The vast expanse of the East China Sea, streaked with blues, aquamarines, indigos, was at low ebb, smoothly sensuous, almost lascivious. The only sound was the water caressing and lapping innumerable tiny pores of the reef below their hips. There was no human shadow, no house on the spacious atoll. No cans, bottles, vinyl trash. No footprints, no fingerprints. The young man had been gently rocked by the lapping sound in his body ever since he reached the edge of the water.

Sea water had settled in pools here and there in the dents of the reef. The young man cautiously bent over the puddle, but the countless, tiny tropical fish fled in all directions, frightened by his shadow. Over the calcified bed of fish and insect debris, some fish emitted gleaming light, some wiggled suggestively, some others disappeared, spreading a tiny curtain of sand dust. The young man deliberately dropped a piece of chicken into the pool, instantly causing a commotion in the water. As the white piece glided down the clear aquamarine water, the yellow, the red, the violet flashed and vanished and the chicken was gone instantaneously. A tiny scorpion fish appeared from behind a rock, swaying lazily, its tentacle fins fully spread like peacock feathers. Finding nothing, the little creature swayed back to its rock, disappointed. The young man chuckled or burst out laughing each time he dropped the chicken pieces. Intermittently he threw a jigger or two of sake after them.

The older had thick eyebrows, a strong jaw, and large eyes. From time to time, he pulled out a letter from his coat pocket and read it in silence. A smile spread on his pale, hollow cheeks. His wife had written him a love poem in ancient Manyo style. As he was leaving home with his visitor that morning, she had handed each man a lacquered lunch box. In each she had enclosed a poem and instructed them not to open their lunch until they reached the beach. It seemed his wife wrote poems in the kitchen, while frying chicken or making sushi. The young man had opened his box as soon as they reached the beach and discovered a sheet of letter paper above the wrapped chicken pieces. The poem was written in antiquated but skillful calligraphy, as if challenging him. It was about the queen of all South Sea fishes welcoming the visitor to the island. The older man's lunch box seemed to have contained a love poem for her husband. 'Don't read it on the way,' his wife had said smiling. 'You must wait until you get to the shore. Then you will want to come straight home in the evening.' She had stood at the gate, waving goodbye to the departing men.

The strong, luxuriant sun began to lose its sharp edge, and a soft haze spread over the late afternoon sky. A harbinger of evening began to flow out of the lingering clouds and to permeate the atmosphere almost audibly like mysterious whispering. The offshore aquamarine grew pale while the blues and indigos deepened. Still constantly washing the reef, the sea was somehow growing desolate. The young man stopped playing with the fish and sipped sake, gazing into the ocean. As the sunlight waned, the alcohol seemed to grow heavy, irritating. It was time to stop. He had been able to maintain his freshness all afternoon, sitting on the ancient reef. If he continued to drink until evening, he would grow stale, troubled by words, sentences. But he rolled yet another drop or two of sake on his already coarsened and swollen tongue as though forcing down bitter medicine.

The older man looked at his watch and said, 'It's about time we went. The snakeman must be waiting. You've got to see it at least once for the experience. The man said he would choose the best, both the snake and the mongoose. It's like a cockfight. The battle is short but ferocious.'

'Does the mongoose always win?'

'Not necessarily. Seven or eight out of ten, yes—but sometimes he loses. This is like a *coup de main*. The duel is settled by the point of the sword. When the swords clash, the fight is already over. The mongoose targets the upper jaw of the snake to make sure of his victory. His instinct tells him that the fangs are there. He's never been taught, but he knows where the right spot is. Once he bites into the jaw, he hangs on for dear life and chews it up until the snake's neck is broken. If he misses the jaw, the mongoose loses. If he bites into the body or tail of the snake, the fangs will get him in a second.'

'It's like the duel of Ganryujima!'

'Even if the mongoose wins, if his mouth is hurt while chewing the snake head, the poison will get to him and he will die within twenty-four hours. So, you don't know whether he is the real winner or not until the day after, so says the snakeman.'

The older man continued his explanation, closing his lunch box. A *habu* snake is believed to be myopic and astigmatic. Waving his tongue, he senses the delicate stir in the air as an enemy approaches, and his unique apparatus detects the enemy's heat radiation. He strikes suddenly. He contracts his body into an S, and, pivoting on the third of his body on the ground, flies with the remaining two thirds. With his mouth open wide and baring scythelike fangs, he whips the air, half blind, yet with a deadly accuracy. He drives his fangs into the enemy, pours out one gram of venom, and instantly backs away. One gram of the deadly poison is said to be sufficient to kill thousands of rabbits. A *habu* can kill human beings and dogs; it can swallow eels, blue jays, frogs, black hares, field rats, long-haired rats, rocks, and occasionally, his own kind.

A *habu*'s parents disappear promptly the minute an egg hatches. The baby snake must find his own food from the day he is born, but he already possesses enough poison to kill a man. A solitary creature, a *habu* acts alone and ubiquitously. He slithers through the night, swims noiselessly across a swamp, traverses a valley, and sneaks into a town, creeps into a toilet, a boot, a kitchen, a charcoal sack, anything. Sometimes he creeps into a public bath and into a wo-man's clothes basket there, because he likes dark, warm, damp places. Once captured and put in a locked box, he will refuse to eat or drink, his blind eyes wide open and gaping. He will ignore a rat thrown into the box, keeping his mouth closed for six months or a year. With his eyes shining gold in the sun, or gleaming like dull copper in the dark, he will hold his head high and die of starvation.

The young man exclaimed, 'What a magnificent creature!'

The older man nodded. 'So, a *habu* is a desperado that can kill men and horses. As the saying goes: If his teacher comes, he will stab the teacher; if his father crosses his path, he will kill his father, too. But the mongoose is just as much of a scamp and kills snakes and rats, chickens and hens. In Okinawa, a mongoose gouged out a sleeping baby's eyes. Whether he is starved or full, he will rip the throat of an opponent. So, you might say they are a good match. The funny thing is that each one uses only one weapon. The mongoose attacks the jaw of a snake, and the snake can, if he wants to, wrap himself around the mongoose and strangle him, but he won't. A snake uses only his fangs. If the mongoose bites first, he just writhes helplessly.'

The two men picked up their lunch boxes and stood. They began to trudge over the large reef toward the beach. The sky and the ocean were utterly tranquil. Only the sound of the lapping water droned. The breeze was tempered now by a few cold streaks of air. The acrid odors of seaweeds, some putrid, some fresh, hung heavily in the lagoon. The two men climbed the slope, crept through a long, low, serpentine wall of dark banyan trees entangled with a clump of pines, and entered the village. Looking back at the edge of the village toward the atoll, they found the field of rocks sparkling green and white in the softening sun. Already everything had been erased. Traces of two men eating, talking, and laughing there all afternoon were gone. The sky, sea, reef, all stood silently as they did two thousand years ago.

Walking through the forest, the older man called, 'Hoot, hoot!'

Soon there was a response. Hoot, hoot! The birdcall followed the man, who continued to hoot while walking. Sometimes the hoots seemed to go astray, probably blocked by trees; still they followed the two men.

The young man stopped and cried out, 'An owl! An owl is crying!'

The older man smiled. 'I have a genius for doing things that bring no money.'

He continued to hoot as he walked.

The owl followed him, calling from tree branches, but it finally stopped at the border of the village and, hooting two or three grudging cries, flew away to the deeper part of the forest.

There was a vacant lot in the midst of closely built matchbox shacks. Boxes with metal screens like chicken coops stood in the center of the lot, and a man in a white coat was waiting beside them, holding a stick in his hand. As soon as the two men walked up to him, he began to talk. He was a man of medium height with a ruddy face and sharp eyes. He spoke in a mellow, experienced voice, showing the differences of genitalia on several male and female snakes preserved in alcohol jars. Then, from one of the boxes, he hooked a snake with the tip of a wire and swiftly caught its narrow neck with his bare hand. The snake opened its wide mouth fully and the white, translucent, sharp fangs jutted out from the sheath folds like hypodermic needles. The man put the snake's head against the edge of the wooden box, and the viper angrily bit into the wood, grating its surface. Instantly, liquid shot from its mouth and trickled down the box. Incongruous with its gigantic, triangular head in the ugly color of dirt, and inconsistent with its ferocious gold eyes, wet flesh like the inside of a little girl's crotch suddenly exposed itself under the sun. The mouth orifice was covered with gleaming pink-white membrane. Delicate red and blue distal blood vessels ran through the virginal flesh folds inside. It was moist, clean, white, tender, and fragile. The young man was fascinated. He felt an urge to caress it with his fingers, feel the tension and wetness of the white flesh, and trace the suction of the soft resilient folds into the deep interior. He wanted to fondle the translucent, strong, sharp fangs, too.

What's wrong with me? Am I exhausted? So run-down?

The box was partitioned with a screen divider. In one section was a snake, in the other a mongoose. The snake was slithering, scraping the wooden floor, ceaselessly forming and untangling the S shape. Her head erect and darting swiftly to left and right, she flickered her black tongue continually. She crawled up the dividing metal screen and groped about the screen mesh with her tongue. Her myopic eyes goggling toward the shining mist, she seemed to wonder what this strange vibration and heat could be that came through the air. Her whiplike forebody quivered, stretching and contracting, while her hind half, swinging aimlessly, stored up energy. Beyond the shiny fog was a small quadruped with the body of a weasel and the face of a rat, making light footstep noises as it scampered to right and left. Small red eyes shining, his soft, buff-colored back undulating, the little animal pivoted on his thick tail and stood on his hind legs. Pulling his forelegs to his breast as if beckoning, he squeaked sharply two, three times as though grinding teeth. The young man bent forward in spite of himself, and the animal's small threatening face looked up. Malevolence and cruelty unimaginable from such a small, lovable body flashed in the red eyes. The single-minded bloodthirstiness made its head something mean and base. The young man involuntarily stepped back and turned away.

'Are you ready?' The snakeman's voice was ominous. 'Let's go!' He pulled up the divider. A buff color flashed into the box. The mongoose had darted to the snake's head, dug into it; already his small, white teeth were crunching. Wearing the mongoose on her head, the snake rolled and wriggled and contracted her long body like a corkscrew, but she never tried to wrap around the mongoose. As the older man had described, her only weapon was the fangs, and her defeat had become decisive at the first moment. Silently, she writhed and thrashed about, trying to free herself from the animal. The mongoose's eyes flared and his small, angular, blood-covered head rolled with the snake, but he hung on fast to the slippery body of the snake with his black claws while continuing chomping.

(Forestall, give all to the first moment. Once into the enemy's vitals, never let go! Hang on to the end! Crush! Chew!) The heavy but sharp crunching noise of breaking bones continued for a while. The triangle head lost its shape and the eyes were smashed. Fresh blood spurted, and long fangs protruded helplessly from the upper jaw. Turning his face sideways, the mongoose bit into the white flesh at the root of the fangs and continued to munch. The fangs broke off and fell to the floor. They shined dully in the blood puddle in the evening sun. The mangled head of the snake gaped like a dark vermilion hole. Her body stirred spasmodically, shrinking and stretching, but finally lay long in the pool of blood. Once she lost her head, she was like a decorative cord with its tassle severed. The mouth hung gaping, crushed shapelessly. The white, voluptuous body continued to bleed slowly. His body shivering, the mongoose jutted out his angular face and began to lap up blood and munch noisily on the delicate female body of the snake. He sipped, licked his paws, tore off a mouthful of flesh, chewed.

The two men left the area in silence, shoulder to shoulder. The poverty-stricken houses, like barnacle clusters, stood in the resounding explosion of the setting subtropical sun, and the perfect moment of the day inflamed the sky and the road. The young man stopped and lit a cigarette. Although he had been drinking all afternoon, he felt no trace of the blue flame of alcohol. A thirst slowly spread throughout his body.

'They don't wrestle,' he commented, his voice a little hoarse.

The older man's eyes were somber, virile. He smiled deeply. 'No mercy allowed.'

Trailing a long shadow on the barren road, the older man hung his head low and spoke again. 'No mercy allowed.'

At last, the young man thought, *I have taken my first step on this island.*

OE KENZABURO (1935–)

PRIZE STOCK

Translated by John Nathan

My kid brother and I were digging with pieces of wood in the loose earth that smelled of fat and ashes at the surface of the crematorium, the makeshift crematorium in the valley that was simply a shallow pit in a clearing in the underbrush. The valley bottom was already wrapped in dusk and fog as cold as the spring water that welled up in the woods, but the side of the hill where we lived, the little village built around a cobblestone road, was bathed in grape light. I straightened out of a crouch and weakly yawned, my mouth stretching open. My brother stood up too, gave a small yawn, and smiled at me.

Giving up on 'collecting', we threw our sticks into the thick summer underbrush and climbed the narrow path shoulder to shoulder. We had come down to the crematorium in search of remains, nicely shaped bones we could use as medals to decorate our chests, but the village children had collected them all and we came away empty-handed. I would have to beat some out of one of my friends at elementary school. I remembered peeking two days earlier, past the waists of the adults darkly grouped around the pit, at the corpse of a village woman lying on her back with her naked belly swollen like a small hill, her expression full of sadness in the light of the flames. I was afraid. I grasped my brother's slender arm and quickened my step. The odor of the corpse, like the sticky fluid certain kinds of beetles leaked when we squeezed them in our calloused fingers, seemed to revive in my nostrils.

Our village had been forced to begin cremating out of doors by an extended rainy season: early summer rains had fallen stubbornly until floods had become an everyday occurrence. When a landslide crushed the suspension bridge that was the shortest route to the *town*, the elementary school annex in our village was closed, mail delivery stopped, and our adults, when a trip was unavoidable, reached the *town* by walking the narrow, crumbly path along the mountain ridge. Transporting the dead to the crematorium in the *town* was out of the question.

But being cut off from the *town* caused our old but undeveloped homesteaders' village no very acute distress. Not only were we treated like dirty animals in the *town*, everything we required from day to day was packed into the small compounds clustered on the slope above the narrow valley. Besides, it was the beginning of summer, the children were happy school was closed.

Harelip was standing at the entrance to the village, where the cobblestone road began, cuddling a dog against his chest. With a hand on my brother's shoulder, I ran through the deep shade of the great gingko tree to peer at the dog in Harelip's arms.

'See!' Harelip shook the dog and made him snarl. 'Look at him!'

The arms Harelip thrust in front of me were covered with bites matted with dog hair and blood. Bites stood out like buds on his chest, too, and his short, thick neck.

'See!' Harelip said grandly.

'You promised to go after mountain dogs with me!' I said, my chest clogged with surprise and chagrin. 'You went alone!'

'I went looking for you,' Harelip said quickly. 'You weren't around . . .'

'You really got bit!' I said, just touching the dog with my fingertips. Its eyes were frenzied, like a wolf's, its nostrils flared. 'Did you crawl into the lair?'

'I wrapped a leather belt around my neck so he couldn't get my throat,' Harelip said proudly.

In the dusking, purple hillside and the cobblestone road I distinctly saw Harelip emerging from a lair of withered grass and shrubs with a leather belt around his throat and the puppy in his arms while a mountain dog bit into him.

'As long as they don't get your throat,' he said, confidence strong in his voice. 'And I waited until there were only puppies inside.'

'I saw them running across the valley,' my brother said excitedly, 'five of them.'

'When?'

'Just after noon.'

'I went after that.'

'He sure is white,' I said, keeping envy out of my voice.

'His mother *mated* with a wolf!' The dialect Harelip used was lewd but very real.

'You swear?' My brother spoke as if in a dream.

'He's used to me now,' Harelip said, accentuating his confidence. 'He won't go back to his friends.'

My brother and I were silent.

'Watch!' Harelip put the dog down on the cobblestones and released him. 'See!'

But instead of looking down at the dog we looked up at the sky covering the narrow valley. An unbelievably large airplane was crossing it at terrific speed. The roar churned the air into waves and briefly drowned us. Like insects trapped in oil we were unable to move in the sound.

'It's an enemy plane!' Harelip screamed. 'The enemy's here!'

Looking up at the sky we shouted ourselves hoarse. 'An enemy plane . . .'

But except for the clouds glowing darkly in the setting sun the sky was already empty. We turned back to Harelip's dog just as it was yowling down the gravel path away from us, its body dancing. Plunging into the underbrush alongside the path it quickly disappeared. Harelip stood there dumbfounded, his body poised for pursuit. My brother and I laughed until our blood seethed like liquor. Chagrined as he was, Harelip had to laugh, too.

We left him, and ran back to the storehouse crouching in the dusk like a giant beast. In the semi-darkness inside, my father was preparing our meal on the dirt floor.

'We saw a plane!' my brother shouted at my father's back. 'A great big enemy plane!'

My father grunted and did not turn around. Intending to clean it, I lifted his heavy hunting gun down from the rack on the wall and climbed the dark stairs, arm in arm with my brother.

'Too bad about that dog,' I said.

'And that plane,' my brother said.

We lived on the second floor of the co-operative storehouse in the middle of the village, in the small room once used for raising silkworms. When my father stretched out on his straw mats and blankets on the floor of thick planks that were beginning to rot and my brother and I lay down on the old door which was our sleeping platform, the former residence of countless silkworms that had left stains on the paper walls still reeking of their bodies and bits of rotten mulberry leaf stuck to the naked beams in the ceiling filled to repletion with human beings.

We had no furniture at all. There was the dull gleam of my father's hunting gun, not only the barrel but even the stock, as if the oiled wood were also steel that would numb your hand if you slapped it, to provide our poor quarters with a certain direction, there were dried weasel pelts hanging in bunches from the exposed beams, there were various traps. My father made his living shooting rabbits, birds, wild boar in winter when the snow was deep, and trapping weasels and delivering the dried pelts to the *town* office.

As my brother and I polished the stock with an oil rag we gazed up through the chinks in the wooden slats at the dark sky outside. As if the roar of an airplane would descend from there again. But it was rare for a plane to cross the sky above the village. When I had put the gun back in the rack on the wall we lay down on the sleeping platform, huddling together, and waited, threatened by the emptiness in our stomachs, for my father to bring the pot of rice and vegetables, upstairs.

My brother and I were small seeds deeply embedded in thick flesh and tough, outer skin, green seeds soft and fresh and encased in membrane that would shiver and slough away at the first exposure to light. And outside the tough, outer skin, near the sea that was visible from the roof as a thin ribbon glittering in the distance, in the city beyond the heaped, rippling mountains, the war, majestic and awkward now like a legend that had survived down the ages, was belching foul air. But to us the war was nothing more than the absence of young men in our village and the announcements the mailman sometimes delivered of soldiers killed in action. The war did not penetrate the tough outer skin and the thick flesh. Even the 'enemy' planes that had begun recently to traverse the sky above the village were nothing more to us than a rare species of bird.

Near dawn I was awakened by the noise of a gigantic impact and a furious ringing in the ground. I saw my father sit up on his blanket on the floor like a beast lurking in the forest night about to spring upon his prey, his eyes bright with desire and his body tense. But instead of springing he dropped back to the floor and appeared to fall asleep again.

For a long time I waited with my ears peeled, but that ringing did not occur again. Breathing quietly the damp air that smelled of mold and small animals I waited patiently in the pale moonlight creeping through the skylight high in the storehouse roof. A long time passed, and my brother, who had been asleep, his sweaty forehead pressed against my side, began to whimper. He too had been waiting for the ground to quiver and ring again, and the prolonged anticipation had been too much for him. Placing my hand on his delicate neck like a slender plant stem I shook him lightly to comfort him, and, lulled by the gentle movement of my own arm, fell asleep.

When I woke up, fecund morning light was slanting through every crack in the slat walls, and it was already hot. My father was gone. So was his gun from the wall. I shook my brother awake and went out to the cobblestone road without a shirt. The road and the stone steps were awash in the morning light. Children squinting and blinking in the glare were standing vacantly or picking fleas out of the dogs or running around and shouting, but there were no adults. My brother and I ran over to the blacksmith's shed in the shade of the lush nettle tree. In the darkness inside, the charcoal fire on the dirt floor spat no tongues of red flame, the bellows did not hiss, the blacksmith lifted no red-hot steel with his lean, sun-blackened arms. Morning and the blacksmith not in his shop—we had never known this to happen. Arm in arm, my brother and I walked back along the cobblestone road in silence. The village was empty of adults. The women were probably waiting at the back of their dark houses. Only the children were drowning in the flood of sunlight. My chest tightened with anxiety.

Harelip spotted us from where he was sprawled at the stone steps that descended to the village fountain and came running over, arms waving. He was working hard at being important, spraying fine white bubbles of sticky saliva from the split in his lip.

'Hey! Have you heard?' he shouted, slamming me on the shoulder.

'Have you?'

'Heard?' I said vaguely.

'That plane yesterday crashed in the hills last night. And they're looking for the enemy soldiers that were in it, the adults have all gone hunting in the hills with their guns!'

'Will they shoot the enemy soldiers?' my brother asked shrilly.

'They won't shoot, they don't have much ammunition,' Harelip explained obligingly, 'They aim to catch them!'

'What do you think happened to the plane?' I said.

'It got stuck in the fir trees and came apart,' Harelip said quickly, his eyes flashing. 'The mailman saw it, you know those trees.'

I did, fir blossoms like grass tassles would be in bloom in those woods now. And at the end of summer, fir cones shaped like wild bird's eggs would replace the tassles, and we would collect them to use as weapons. At dusk then and at dawn, with a sudden rude clatter, the dark brown bullets would be fired into the walls of the storehouse. . . .

'Do you know the woods I mean?'

'Sure I do. Want to go?'

Harelip smiled slyly, countless wrinkles forming around his eyes, and peered at me in silence. I was annoyed.

'If we're going to go I'll get a shirt,' I said, glaring at Harelip. 'And don't try leaving ahead of me because I'll catch up with you right away!'

Harelip's whole face became a smirk and his voice was fat with satisfaction.

'Nobody's going! Kids are forbidden to go into the hills. You'd be mistaken for the foreign soldiers and shot!'

I hung my head and stared at my bare feet on the cobblestones baking in the morning sun, at the sturdy, stubby toes. Disappointment seeped through me like treesap and made my skin flush hot as the innards of a freshly killed chicken.

'What do you think the enemy looks like?' my brother said.

I left Harelip and went back along the cobblestone road, my arm around my brother's shoulders. What *did* the enemy soldiers look like, in what positions were they lurking in the fields and the woods? I could feel foreign soldiers hiding in all the fields and woods that surrounded the valley, the sound of their hushed breathing about to explode into an uproar. Their sweaty skin and harsh body odor covered the valley like a season.

'I just hope they aren't dead,' my brother said dreamily. 'I just hope they catch them and bring them in.'

In the abundant sunlight we were hungry; saliva was sticky in our throats and our stomach muscles were tight. Probably it would be dusk before my father returned, we would have to find our own food. We went down behind the storehouse to the well with the broken bucket and drank, bracing ourselves with both hands against the chilly, sweating stones jutting from the inside wall like the swollen belly of a pupa. When we had drawn water for the shallow iron pot and built a fire, we stuck our arms into the chaff heaped at the rear of the storehouse and stole some potatoes. As we washed them, the potatoes were hard as rocks in our hands.

The meal we began after our brief efforts was simple but plentiful. Eating away like a contented animal at the potato he grasped in both hands, my brother pondered a minute, then said, 'Do you think the soldiers are up in the fir trees? I saw a squirrel on a fir branch!'

'It would be easy to hide in the fir because they're in bloom,' I said.

'The squirrel hid right away, too,' my brother said, smiling.

I pictured fir trees covered with blossoms like grass tassles, and the foreign soldiers lurking in the highest branches and watching my father and the others through the bunched green needles. With fir blossoms stuck to their bulky flying suits, the soldiers would look like fat squirrels ready for hibernation.

'Even if they're hiding in the trees the dogs will find them and bark,' my brother said confidently.

When our stomachs were full we left the pot on the dirt floor with the remaining potatoes and a fistful of salt and sat down on the stone steps at the entrance to the storehouse. For a long time we sat there drowsily, and in the afternoon we went to bathe at the spring that fed the village fountain.

At the spring, Harelip, sprawled naked on the broadest, smoothest stone, was allowing the girls to fondle his rosy penis as if it were a small doll. Every so often, face beet-red, laughing shrilly in a voice like a screaming bird, he slapped one of the girls on her naked rear.

My brother sat down next to Harelip and raptly observed the merry ritual. I splashed water on the ugly children drowsily sunning themselves around the spring, put on my shirt without drying myself, returned to the stone steps at the storehouse entrance, leaving wet footprints on the cobblestones, and sat there without moving for a long time again, hugging my knees. Anticipation that was like madness, a heated, drunken feeling, was crackling up and down beneath my skin. Dreamily I pictured myself absorbed in the odd game to which Harelip seemed abnormally attached. But whenever the girls among the children returning naked from the spring smiled timidly at me, their hips swaying at each step they took and an unstable color like mashed peaches peeking from the folds of their meager, exposed vaginas, I rained pebbles and abuse on them and made them cringe.

I waited in the same position until a passionate sunset covered the valley, clouds the color of a forest fire wheeling in the sky, but still the adults did not return. I felt I would go mad with waiting.

The sunset had paled, a cool wind that felt good on newly burned skin had begun to blow up from the valley, and the first darkness of night had touched the shadows of things when the adults and the barking dogs finally returned to the hushed village, the village whose mind had been affected by uneasy anticipation. With the other children I ran out to greet them, and saw a large black man surrounded by adults. Fear struck me like a fist.

Surrounding the *catch* solemnly as they surrounded the wild boar they hunted in winter, their lips drawn tightly across their teeth, their backs bent forward almost sadly, the adults came walking in. The *catch*, instead of a flying suit of burnt-ocher silk and black leather flying shoes, wore a khaki jacket and pants and, on his feet, ugly, heavy-looking boots. His large, darkly glistening face was tilted up at the sky still streaked with light, and he limped as he dragged himself along. The iron chain of a boar trap was locked around both his ankles, rattling as he moved. We children fell in behind the adults, as silent as they were. The procession slowly advanced to the square in front of the school house and quietly halted. I pushed my way through the children to the front, but the old man who was our village headman loudly ordered us away; we retreated as far as the apricot trees in one corner of the square, halted there determinedly, and from beneath the trees kept watch through the thickening darkness over the adults' meeting. In the dirt floor houses that faced on the square the women hugging themselves beneath their white smocks strained irritably to catch the murmuring of the men who returned from a dangerous hunt with a *catch*. Harelip poked me sharply in the side from behind and pulled me away from the other children into the deep shadow of a camphor tree.

'He's black, you see that! I thought he would be all along.' Harelip's voice trembled with excitement. 'He's a real black man, you see!'

'What are they going to do with him, shoot him?'

'Shoot him!' Harelip shouted, gasping with surprise. 'Shoot a real live black man!'

'Because he's the enemy,' I asserted without confidence.

'Enemy! You call him an enemy!' Harelip seized my shirt and railed at me hoarsely, spraying my face with saliva through his lip.

'He's a black man, he's no enemy!'

'Look! Look at that!' It was my brother's awed voice, coming from the crowd of children. 'Look!'

Harelip and I turned around and peered at the black soldier; standing a little apart from the adults observing him in consternation, his shoulders sagging heavily, he was pissing. His body was beginning to melt into the thickened evening darkness, leaving behind the khaki jacket and pants that were somehow like overalls. His head to one side, the black soldier pissed on and on, and when a cloud of sighs from the children watching rose behind him he mournfully shook his hips.

The adults surrounded the black soldier again and slowly led him off; we followed a short distance behind. The silent procession surrounding the *catch* stopped in front of the loading entrance at the side of the storehouse. There the steps down to the cellar where the best of the autumn chestnuts were stored over the winter after the grubs beneath their hard skin had been killed with carbon disulfide yawned open blackly, like a hole inhabited by animals. Still surrounding the black soldier, the adults descended into the hole solemnly, as if a ceremony were beginning, and the white wavering of an adult arm closed the heavy trapdoor from inside.

Straining to catch a sound, we watched an orange light go on inside the long, narrow skylight window that ran between the floor of the storehouse and the ground. We could not find the courage to peek through the skylight. The short, anxious wait exhausted us. But no gunshot rang out. Instead, the village headman's shadowed face appeared beneath the partly opened trapdoor and we were yelled at and had to abandon even keeping watch at a distance from the skylight; the children, carrying with them expectations that would fill the night hours with bad dreams, ran off down the cobblestone road without a word of disappointment. Fear, awakened by their pounding feet, pursued them from behind.

Leaving Harelip lurking in the darkness of the apricot trees, still determined to observe the adults and the *catch*, my brother and I went around to the front of the storehouse and climbed, supporting ourselves against the railing that was always damp, to our room in the attic. We were to live in the same house as the *catch*, that was how it was to be! No matter how hard we listened in the attic, we would never be able to hear screaming in the cellar, but the luxurious, hazardous, entirely unbelievable fact was that we were sitting on a sleeping platform above the cellar to which the black soldier had been taken. My teeth were chattering with fear and joy, and my brother huddling beneath the blanket was shaking as if he had caught a cold. As we waited for my father to come home dragging his fatigue and his heavy gun we smiled together at the wonderful good fortune that had befallen us.

Not so much to satisfy our hunger as to distract ourselves from the uproar in our chests with raising and lowering of arms and precise chewing, we were beginning to eat the cold, hardened, sweating potatoes that were left over when my father climbed the stairs. Shivering, my brother and I watched him place his hunting gun in the wooden rack on the wall and lower himself to the blanket spread on the dirt floor, but he said nothing, merely looked at the pot of potatoes we were eating. I could tell he was tired to death, and irritated. There was nothing we children could do about that.

'Is the rice gone?' he said, staring at me, the skin of his throat puffing like a sack beneath the stubble of beard.

'Yes. . . .' I said weakly.

'The barley too?' he grunted sourly.

'There's nothing!' I was angry.

'What about the airplane?' my brother said timidly. 'What happened to it?'

'It burned. Almost started a forest fire.'

My brother let out a sigh. 'The whole thing?'

'Just the tail was left.'

'The tail . . .' my brother murmured.

'Were there any others?' I asked. 'Was he flying alone?'

'Two other soldiers were dead. He came down in a parachute.'

'A parachute . . .' My brother was entirely lost in a dream. I summoned up my courage.

'What are you going to do with him?'

'Until we know what the town thinks, rear him.'

'Rear him? Like an animal?'

'He's the same as an animal,' my father said gravely. 'He stinks like an ox.'

'It would sure be nice to see him,' my brother said with an eye on my father, but my father went back down the stairs in grim silence.

We sat down on the wooden frame of our sleeping platform to

wait for my father to come back with borrowed rice and vegetables and cook us a pot of steaming gruel. We were too exhausted to be really hungry. And the skin all over our bodies was twitching and jumping like the genitals of a bitch in heat. We were going to rear the black soldier. I hugged myself with both arms, I wanted to throw off my clothes and shout—we were going to rear the black soldier, like an animal!

The next morning my father shook me awake without a word. Dawn was just breaking. Thick light and heavy fog were seeping through every crack in the wall boards. As I gulped my cold breakfast I gradually woke up. My father, his hunting gun on his shoulder and a lunch basket tied to his waist, watched me as I ate, waiting for me to finish, eyes dull yellow from lack of sleep. When I saw the bundle of weasel skins wrapped in a torn burlap bag at his knee I swallowed hard and thought to myself, so we are going down to the *town!* And surely we would report the black man to the authorities.

A whirlpool of words at the back of my throat was slowing the speed at which I could eat, but I saw my father's strong lower jaw covered in coarse beard moving incessantly as if he were chewing grain and I knew he was nervous and irritated from lack of sleep. Asking about the black soldier was impossible. The night before, after supper, my father had loaded his gun with new bullets and gone out to stand night watch.

My brother was sleeping with his head buried under a blanket that smelled of dank hay. When I was finished eating I moved around the room on tiptoes, careful not to wake him. Wrapping a green shirt of thick cloth around my bare shoulders, I stepped into the cloth sneakers I normally never used, shouldered the bundle that was between my father's knees, and ran down the stairs.

Low fog rolled along just above the wet cobblestones; the village, wrapped in haze, was fast asleep. The chickens were already tired and silent; the dogs did not even bark. I saw an adult with a gun leaning against the apricot tree alongside the storehouse, his head drooping. My father and the guard exchanged a few words in low voices. I stole a look at the cellar skylight yawning blackly open like a wound and I was gripped by terrific fear. The black soldier's arm reaches through the skylight and extends to seize me. I wanted to leave the village quickly. When we began walking in silence, careful not to slip on the cobblestones, the sun penetrated the layers of fog and struck at us with tough, heated light.

To reach the village road along the ridge we climbed the narrow path of red earth into the fir forest, where once again we were at the bottom of dark night. Fog that filled my mouth with a metallic taste slanted down on us in droplets large as rain, making it hard for me to breathe and wetting my hair and forming white, shiny beads on the lint of my grimy, wrinkled shirt. The spring water that seeped up through the rotten leaves so soft beneath our feet to soak our cloth shoes and to freeze our toes was not so bad; we had to be truly careful not to wound our skin against the iron stalks of ferns or to surprise the adders watchfully coiled among their stubborn roots.

When we emerged from the fir forest onto the village road, where it was brightening and the fog was burning off, I brushed the fog out of my shirt and short pants as carefully as if I were removing sticky tickseeds. The sky was clear and violently blue. The distant mountains the color of the copper ore we found in the dangerous abandoned mine in our valley was a sparkling, deep-blue sea rushing at us. And a single, whitish handful of the real sea.

All around us wild birds were singing. The upper branches of the high pines were humming in the wind. Crushed beneath my father's boot, a fieldmouse leaped from the piled leaves like a spurting gray fountain, frightening me for an instant, and ran in a frenzy into the brilliant underbrush alongside the road.

'Are we going to tell about the black man when we get to town?' I asked my father's broad back.

'Umm?' my father said. 'Yes. . . .'

'Will the constable come out from town?'

'There's no telling,' my father grunted. 'Until the report gets to the prefectural office there's no telling what will happen.'

'Couldn't we just go on rearing him in the village? Is he dangerous? You think he is?'

My father rejected me with silence. I felt my surprise and fear of the night before, when the black soldier was led back to the village, reviving in my body. What was he doing in that cellar? The black soldier leaves the cellar, slaughters the people and the hunting dogs in the village and sets fire to the houses. I was so afraid I was trembling, I didn't want to think about it. I passed my father and ran, panting, down the long slope.

By the time we were on level road again the sun was high. The red earth exposed by small landslides on both sides of the road was raw as blood and glistening in the sun. We walked along with our foreheads bared to the fierce light. Sweat bubbled from the skin on my head, soaked through my cropped hair and ran from my forehead down my cheeks.

When we entered the *town* I pressed my shoulder against my father's high hip and marched straight past the provocations of the children in the street. If my father hadn't been there the children would have jeered at me and thrown stones. I hated the children of the *town* as I would have hated a species of beetle with a shape I could never feel comfortable with, and I disdained them. Skinny children in the noonday light flooding the town, with treacherous eyes. If only adult eyes had not been watching me from the rear of dark shops I was confident I could have knocked any one of them down.

The town office was closed for lunch. We worked the pump in the square in front of the office and drank some water, then sat down on wooden chairs beneath a window with hot sun pouring through it and waited a long time. An old official finally finished his lunch and appeared, and when he and my father had spoken together in low voices and stepped into the mayor's office I carried the weasel pelts over to the small scales lined up behind a reception window. There the skins were counted and entered in an account book with my father's name. I watched carefully as a nearsighted lady official with thick glasses wrote down the number of skins.

When this job was finished I had no idea what to do. My father was taking forever. So I went looking, my bare feet squishing down the hall like suction cups, one shoe in each hand, for my only acquaintance in the *town*, a man who frequently carried notices out to our village. We all called this one-legged man 'Clerk', but he did other things as well, such as assisting the doctor when we had our physicals at the school annex in the village.

'Well if it isn't Frog!' Rising from the chair behind his desk, Clerk shouted, making me just a little angry, but I went over anyway. Since we called him 'Clerk', we couldn't very well complain about his calling us, the village children, 'Frog'. I was happy to have found him.

'So you caught yourselves a black man!' Clerk said, rattling his false leg under the desk.

'Yes. . . .' I said, resting my hands on his desk where his lunch was wrapped in yellowed newspaper.

'That's really something!'

I wanted to nod grandly at his bloodless lips, like an adult, and talk about the black soldier, but words to explain the huge negro who had been led through the dusk to the village like captured prey I simply couldn't find.

'Will they shoot him?' I asked.

'I don't know.' Clerk gestured with his chin at the mayor's office. 'They're probably deciding now.'

'Will they bring him to town?' I said.

'You look mighty happy the schoolroom is closed,' Clerk said, evading my important question. 'The schoolmistress is too lazy to make the trip out there, all she does is complain. She says the village children are dirty and smelly.'

I felt ashamed of the dirt creasing my neck, but I shook my head defiantly and made myself laugh. Clerk's artificial leg jutting from beneath his desk was twisted awkwardly. I liked to watch him hopping along the mountain road with his good right leg and the artifical leg and jut one crutch, but here the artificial leg was weird and treacherous, like the children of the *town*.

'But what do you care, as long as school is out you have no complaints, right, Frog!' Clerk laughed, his artificial leg rattling again. 'You and your pals are better off playing outside than being treated like dirt in a schoolroom!'

'They're just as dirty,' I said.

It was true, the women teachers were ugly and dirty, all of them; Clerk laughed. My father had come out of the mayor's office and was calling me quietly. Clerk patted me on the shoulder and I patted him on the arm and ran out.

'Don't let the prisoner escape, Frog!' he shouted at my back.

'What did they decide to do with him?' I said to my father as we returned through the sunwashed *town*.

'You think they're going to take any responsibility!' My father spat out the words as if he were scolding me, and said nothing more. Intimidated by my father's foul humor I walked along in silence, in and out of the shade of the *town's* shriveled, ugly trees. Even the trees in the *town*, like the children in the streets, were treacherous and unfamiliar.

When we came to the bridge at the edge of the *town* we sat down on the low railing and my father unwrapped our lunch in silence. Struggling to keep myself from asking questions, I extended a slightly dirty hand toward the package on his lap. Still in silence we ate our rice balls.

As we were finishing, a young girl with a neck as refreshing as a bird's came walking across the bridge. I swiftly considered my own clothes and features and decided I was finer and tougher than any child in the *town*. I stuck both feet out in front of me, my shoes on, and waited for the girl to pass. Hot blood was singing in my ears. For a brief instant the girl peered at me scowlingly, then she ran off. Suddenly my appetite was gone. I climbed down the narrow stairs at the approach to the bridge and walked to the river for a drink of water. Tall wormwood bushes clustered thickly along the bank. I kicked and tore my way through them to the river's edge, but the water was a stagnant, dirty brown. It struck me I was a miserable and meager creature.

By the time we had left the road along the ridge, cleared the fir forest, and emerged at the entrance to the village, calves stiffened and faces caked with dust and oil and sweat, evening had covered the valley entirely; in our bodies the heat of the sun lingered and the heavy fog was a relief. I left my father on his way to the village headman's house to make his report and climbed to the second floor of the storehouse. My brother was sitting on the sleeping platform, fast asleep. I reached out and shook him, feeling the fragile bones in his naked shoulder against my palm. My brother's skin contracted slightly beneath my hot hand, and from his eyes that suddenly opened fatigue and fear faded.

'How was he?' I said.

'He just slept in the cellar.'

'Were you scared all by yourself?' I said gently.

My brother shook his head, his eyes serious. I opened the wooden shutters just a little and climbed onto the window sill to piss. The fog engulfed me like a living thing and swiftly stole into my nostrils. My urine jumped a great distance, spattering against the cobblestones, and when it struck the bay window that jutted from the first floor it rebounded and warmly wet the tops of my feet and my goosepimpled thighs. My brother, his head pressed against my side like a baby animal, observed intently.

We remained in that position for a while. Small yawns rose from our narrow throats, and with each yawn we cried just a few transparent, meaningless tears.

'Did Harelip get to see him?' I said to my brother as he helped me close the wooden shutters, the slender muscles in his shoulders knotting.

'Kids get yelled at if they go to the square,' he said with chagrin. 'Are they coming from town to take him?'

'I don't know,' I said.

Downstairs, my father and the lady from the general store came in talking in loud voices. The lady from the general store was insisting that she couldn't carry the food for the black soldier down to the cellar. That's no job for a woman, your son should be a help! I finished removing my shoes and straightened up. My brother's soft palm was pressed against my hip. Biting my lip, I waited for my father's voice.

'Come down here!' When I heard my father shout I threw my shoes under the sleeping platform and ran down the stairs.

With the butt of his hunting gun my father pointed to the basket of food the woman had left on the dirt floor. I nodded, and lifted the basket carefully. In silence we left the storehouse and walked through the chill fog. The cobblestones underfoot retained the warmth of day. At the side of the storehouse no adult was standing guard. I saw the pale light leaking through the narrow cellar window and felt fatigue break out all over my body. Yet my teeth were chattering with excitement at this first opportunity to see the black man close up.

The imposing padlock on the cellar door was dripping wet; my father unlocked it and peered inside, then carefully, his gun ready, went down alone. I squatted at the entrance, waiting, and air wet with fog fastened to the back of my neck. In front of the countless eyes hovering behind and peering at me I was ashamed of the trembling in my brown, sturdy legs.

'C'mon,' said my father's muffled voice.

Holding the foodbasket against my chest, I went down the short steps. The *catch* was crouching in the dim light of a naked bulb. The thick chain of a boar-trap connecting his black leg and a pillar drew and locked my gaze.

Arms clasped around his knees and his chin resting even further down on his long legs, the *catch* looked up at me with bloodshot eyes, sticky eyes that wrapped themselves around me. All the blood in my body rushed toward my ears, heating my face. I turned away and looked up at my father, who was leaning against the wall with his gun pointed at the black soldier. My father motioned at me with his chin. With my eyes almost closed I stepped forward and placed the basket of food in front of the black soldier. As I stepped back, my insides shuddered with sudden fear and I had to fight my nausea down. At the basket of food the black soldier stared, my father stared, I stared. A dog barked in the distance. Beyond the narrow skylight window the dark square was hushed.

Suddenly the food basket began to interest me, I was seeing the food through the black soldier's starved eyes. Several large rice balls, dried fish with the fat broiled away, stewed vegetables, goat's milk in a cut-glass bottle. Without unfolding from his crouch, still hugging his knees, the black soldier continued to stare at the food basket for a long time until finally I began to feel hunger pangs myself. It occurred to me the black soldier might disdain the meager supper we provided, and disdain us, and refuse to touch the food. Shame assaulted me. If the black soldier showed no intention of eating, my shame would infect my father, adult's shame would drive my father to desperation and violence, the whole village would be torn apart by adults pale with shame. What a terrible idea it had been to feed the black soldier!

But all of a sudden he extended an unbelievably long arm, lifted the wide-mouthed bottle in thick fingers covered with bristly hair, drew it to himself, and smelled it. Then the bottle was tipped, the black soldier's thick, rubbery lips opened, large white teeth neatly aligned like parts inside a machine were exposed, and I saw milk flowing back into a vast, pink, glistening mouth. The black soldier's throat made a noise like water and air entering a drain, from the corners of his swollen lips like overripe fruit that had been bound with string the thick milk spilled, ran down his bare neck, soaked his open shirt and chest, and coagulated like fat on his tough, darkly, gleaming skin, trembling there. I discovered, my own lips drying with excitement, that goat's milk was a beautiful liquid.

With a harsh clanking the black soldier returned the glass bottle to the basket. Now his original hesitation was gone. The rice balls looked like small cakes as he rolled them in his giant hands; the dried fish, head bones and all, was crushed between his gleaming teeth. Standing alongside my father with my back against the wall, buffeted by admiration, I observed the black soldier's powerful chewing.

Since he was engrossed in his meal and paid no attention to us, I had the opportunity, even as I fought the pangs in my own empty stomach, to observe the adults' *catch* in suffocating detail. And what a wonderful *catch* he was!

The black soldier's short, curly hair tightened into small cowlicks here and there on his well-shaped skull, and just above his ears, which were pointed like a wolf's, turned a smoldering gray. The skin from his throat to his chest was lit from inside with a somber, purple light; every time he turned his head and supple creases appeared in his thick, oily neck, I felt my heart leap. And there was the odor of his body, pervading with the persistence of nausea rising into the throat, permeating all things like a corrosive poison, an odor that flushed my cheeks and flashed before my eyes like madness. . . . As I watched the black soldier feeding ravenously, my eyes hot and watery as though infected, the crude food in the basket was transformed into a fragrant, rich, exotic feast. If even a morsel had remained when I lifted the basket I would have seized it with fingers that trembled with secret pleasure and wolfed it down. But the black soldier finished every bit of food and then wiped the dish of vegetables clean with his fingers.

My father poked me in the side and, trembling with shame and outrage, as if I had been aroused from a lewd daydream, I walked over to the black soldier and lifted the basket. Protected by the muzzle of my father's gun I turned my back to the black soldier and was starting up the steps when I heard his low, rich cough. I stumbled, and felt fear goosepimple the skin all over my body.

At the top of the stairs to the second floor of the storehouse a dark, distorting mirror swayed in the hollow of a pillar; as I climbed the stairs a totally insignificant Japanese boy with twitching cheeks and pale, bloodless lips on which he chewed rose gradually out of the dimness. My arms hung limply and I felt almost ready to cry. I fought a beaten, tearful feeling as I opened the rain shutters that someone had closed at some point in the day.

My brother, eyes flashing, was sitting on the sleeping platform. His eyes were hot, and a little dry with fear.

'You closed the rain shutters, didn't you!' I said, sneering to hide the trembling of my own lips.

'Yes—' Ashamed of his timidity my brother lowered his eyes. 'How was he?'

'He smells terrible,' I said, sinking in fatigue. Truly I was exhausted, and I felt wretched. The trip to the *town*, the black soldier's supper—after the long day's work my body was as heavy as a sponge soaked with fatigue. Taking off my shirt, which was covered with dried leaves and burrs, I bent over to wipe my dirty feet with a rag, a demonstration for my brother's sake that I had no desire to accept further questions. My brother observed me worriedly, his lips pursed. I crawled in next to him and burrowed under our blanket with its smell of sweat and small animals. My brother sat there watching me, his knees together and pressing against my shoulder, not asking any more questions. It was just as he sat when I was sick with fever, and I too, just as when I was sick with fever, longed only to sleep.

When I woke up late the next morning I heard the noise of a crowd coming from the square alongside the storehouse. My brother and father were gone. I looked up at the wall and saw that the hunting gun was not there. As I listened to the clamor and stared at the empty gun rack my heart began to pound. I sprang out of bed, grabbed my shirt, and ran down the stairs.

Adults were crowded into the square, and the dirty faces of the children looking up at them were tight with uneasiness. Apart from everyone, Harelip and my brother were squatting next to the cellar window. They've been watching! I thought to myself angrily, and was running toward them when I saw Clerk emerge, head lowered, lightly supporting himself on his crutch, from the cellar entrance. Violent, dark exhaustion and landsliding disappointment buried me. But what followed Clerk was not the dead body of the black soldier but my father, his gun on his shoulder and the barrel still in its bag, talking quietly with the village headman. I breathed a sigh, and sweat hot as boiling water steamed down my sides and the insides of my thighs.

'Take a look!' Harelip shouted at me as I stood there. 'Go on!'

I got down on all fours on the hot cobblestones and peered in through the narrow skylight window that was just at ground level. At the bottom of the lake of darkness the black soldier lay slumped on the floor like a domestic animal that had been pummeled senseless.

'Did they beat him?' I said to Harelip, my body trembling with anger as I straightened. 'Did they beat him when he had his feet tied and couldn't move?' I shouted.

'What?' In order to repel my anger Harelip had readied himself for a fight, his face taut, his lip thrust out.

'Who?'

'The adults!' I shouted. 'Did they beat him?'

'They didn't have to beat him,' Harelip said regretfully. 'All they did was go in and look, Just looking at him did that!'

Anger faded. I shook my head vaguely. My brother was peering at me.

'It's all right,' I said to my brother.

One of the village children stepped around us and tried to look through the skylight window but Harelip kicked him in the side and he screamed. Harelip had already reserved the right to decide who should look at the black soldier through the skylight. And he was keeping a nervous watch on those who would usurp his right.

I walked over to where Clerk was talking to the adults surrounding him. As if I were a village brat with snot drying on my upper lip he ignored me completely and went right on talking, damaging my self-respect and my feeling of friendship for him. But there are times when you cannot afford to nurse your own pride and self-respect. I thrust my head past the hips of the adults and listened to Clerk and the headman talking.

Clerk was saying that neither the *town* office nor the police station was able to take charge of the black prisoner. Until a report had been made to the prefectural office and a reply received, the village must keep the black soldier, was obliged to keep him. The headman objected, repeating that the village lacked the force to hold the black soldier prisoner. Moreover, delivering the dangerous prisoner under guard by the long mountain route was too much for the villagers to handle unaided. The long rainy season and the floods had made everything complicated, difficult.

But when Clerk assumed a peremptory tone, the arrogant tone of a minor bureaucrat, the adults submitted weakly. When it became clear that the village would keep the black soldier until the prefecture had settled on a policy, I left the perplexed, disgruntled adults and ran back to my brother and Harelip where they sat in front of the skylight, monopolizing it. I was filled with deep relief, anticipation, and anxiety I had contracted from the adults and which moved in me like sluggish worms.

'I told you they weren't going to kill him!' Harelip shouted triumphantly. 'How can a black man be an enemy!'

'It'd be a waste,' said my brother happily. The three of us peered through the skylight, cheeks bumping, and seeing the black soldier stretched out as before, his chest lifting and falling as he breathed, we sighed with satisfaction. There were some children who advanced right to the soles of our feet upturned on the ground and drying under the sun, muttering their displeasure with us, but when Harelip sprang up and shouted they scattered, screaming.

Presently we tired of watching the black soldier lying there, but we did not abandon our privileged position. Harelip allowed the children one by one, when they had promised compensation in dates, apricots, figs, persimmons or whatever, to look through the skylight for a short time. As the children stared through the window even the backs of their necks reddened with their surprise and wonder, and when they stood up they rubbed the dirt from their jaws with their palms. Leaning against the storehouse wall I looked down at the children engrossed in this first real experience of their lives while Harelip yelled at them to hurry and their small butts burned in the sun, and I felt a strange satisfaction and fullness, exhilaration. Harelip turned over on his knees a hunting dog that wandered over from the crowd of adults and began pulling ticks and crushing them between his amber nails as he shouted orders and arrogant abuse at the children. Even after the adults had left with Clerk to see him as far as the ridge road we continued our strange game. From time to time we took long looks ourselves, the children's resentful voices at our backs, but the black soldier lay sprawled there as before and gave no indication of moving. As if he had been beaten and kicked, as if merely looking at him had been enough to wound him!

That night, accompanied once again by my father with his gun, I went down into the cellar carrying a heavy pot of gruel. The black soldier looked up at us with eyes yellowed heavily along the edges with fat, then thrust his hairy fingers directly into the hot pot and ate hungrily. I was able to observe him calmly, and my father, who had stopped pointing his gun, leaned against the wall looking bored.

As I looked down at the black man with his forehead aslant above the pot, watching the trembling of his thick neck and the sudden flexing and relaxing of his muscles, I began to perceive him as a gentle animal, an obedient animal. I looked up at Harelip and my brother peering through the skylight with bated breath and flashed a sly smile at their gleaming eyes. I was growing used to the black soldier—the thought planted a seed of proud happiness that sprouted in me. But when the black soldier moved in such a way that the chain on the boar-trap rattled, fear revived in me with tremendous vigor, rushing into even the most distant blood vessels in my body and making my skin crawl.

From that day on, the job of carrying food to the black soldier, once in the morning and once at night, accompanied by my father, who no longer bothered to remove his rifle from his shoulder, was a special privilege reserved for me. When my father and I appeared at the side of the storehouse early in the morning or as evening was becoming night, the children who had been waiting in the square would release all at once a large sigh that rose spreading, like a cloud, into the sky. Like a specialist who has lost all interest in his work but retains his meticulousness on the job, I crossed the square with brows intently knit, never glancing at the children. My brother and Harelip were satisfied to walk on either side of me, so close our bodies touched, as far as the entrance to the cellar. And when my father and I went down the steps they ran back and peered through the skylight. Even if I had become entirely bored with carrying food to the black soldier, I would have continued the job simply for the pleasure of feeling at my back as I walked along that hot sigh of envy risen to resentment in all the children, Harelip included.

I did ask my father, however, for special permission for Harelip to come to the cellar once a day only, in the afternoon. This was to transfer to Harelip's shoulders part of a burden that was too heavy for me to handle alone. A small, old barrel had been placed next to one of the pillars in the cellar for the black soldier's use. In the afternoon, lifting the barrel between us by the thick, heavy rope that ran through it, Harelip and I carefully climbed the steps and walked to the communal compost heap to empty the stinking, sloshing mixture of the black soldier's shit and piss. Harelip went about his work with excessive zeal: sometimes, before we emptied the barrel into the large tank alongside the compost heap, he would stir the contents with a stick and discourse on the state of the black soldier's digestion, particularly his diarrhea, concluding, among other things, that the trouble was caused by the kernels of corn in his gruel.

When Harelip and I went down to the cellar with my father to get the small barrel and found the black soldier astride it, his pants down around his ankles and his black, shiny rear thrust out in almost exactly the attitude of a copulating dog, we had to wait behind him for a while. Harelip, listening to the furtive clinking of the chain that linked the black soldier's ankles on either side of the barrel, eyes glazed dreamily with surprise and awe, kept a tight grip on my arm.

The children came to be occupied entirely with the black soldier, he filled every smallest corner of our lives. Among the children the black soldier spread like a plague. But the adults had their work. The adults did not catch the children's plague. They could not afford to wait motionlessly for the instructions that were so slow to arrive from the town office. When even my father, who had undertaken supervision of the prisoner, began leaving the village to hunt again, the black soldier began to exist in the cellar for the sole purpose of filling the children's daily lives.

My brother and Harelip and I fell into the habit of spending the daylight hours in the cellar where the black soldier sat, our chests hammering with the excitement of breaking a rule at first but soon enough, as we grew accustomed to being there, with complete casualness, as if supervising the black soldier during the day, while the adults were away in the hills or down in the valley, was a duty we had been entrusted with and must not neglect. The peephole at the skylight, abandoned by Harelip and my brother, was passed on to the village children. Flat on their bellies on the hot, dusty ground, their throats flushed and dry with envy, the children took turns peering in at the three of us sitting around the black soldier on the dirt floor. When occasionally, in an excess of envy, a child forgot himself and tried to follow us into the cellar, he received a pommeling from Harelip for his rebellious act and had to fall to the ground with a bloody nose.

In no time at all we had only to carry the black soldier's 'barrel' to the top of the cellar steps, transporting it to the compost heap in the fierce sun while under attack by its ferocious stench was a task carried out by children we haughtily appointed. The designated children, cheeks shining with pleasure, carried the barrel straight up, careful not to spill a drop of the muddy yellow liquid that seemed so precious to them. And every morning all the children, including ourselves, glanced up at the narrow road that descended through the woods from the ridge with almost a prayer that Clerk would not appear with instructions we dreaded.

The chain from the boar-trap cut into the black man's ankles, the cuts became inflamed, blood trickled onto his feet and shriveled and stuck there like dried blades of grass. We worried constantly about the pinkish infection in the wounds. When he straddled the barrel the pain was so bad it made the black soldier bare his teeth like a laughing child. After looking deep into one another's eyes for a long time and talking together, we resolved to remove the boar-trap. The black soldier, like a dull black beast, his eyes always wet with a thick liquid that might have been tears or mucous, sat in silence hugging his knees on the cellar floor—what harm could he do us when we removed the trap? He was only a single head of black man!

When Harelip tightly grasped the key I brought from my father's tool bag, leaned over so far his shoulder was touching the black soldier's knees, and unlocked the trap, the black soldier suddenly rose with a groan and stamped his feet. Weeping with fear, Harelip threw the trap against the wall and ran up the steps; my brother and I, not even able to stand up, huddled together. The fear of the black soldier that had suddenly revived in us took our breaths away. But instead of dropping upon us like an eagle, the black soldier sat back down just where he was and hugged his knees and gazed with his wet, filmy eyes at the trap lying against the wall. When Harelip returned, head hanging with shame, my brother and I greeted him with kind smiles. The black soldier was as gentle as a domestic animal. . . .

Late that night my father came to lock the giant padlock on the cellar door and saw that the black soldier's ankles had been freed, yet he did not admonish me. Gentle as cattle—the thought, like air itself, had crept into the lungs of everyone in the village, children and adults alike.

The next morning my brother and Harelip and I took breakfast to the black soldier and found him puttering with the boar trap. When Harelip had thrown the trap against the wall the mechanism that snapped it shut had broken. The black soldier was examining the broken part with the same expert assurance as the trap-mender who came to the village every spring. And then abruptly he lifted his darkly glistening forehead and indicated with motions what he wanted. I looked at Harelip, unable to contain the joy that seemed to slacken my cheeks. The black soldier had communicated with us, just as our livestock communicated so had the black soldier!

We ran to the village headman's house, shouldered the tool box that was part of common village property, and carried it back to the cellar. It contained things that could have been used as weapons but we did not hesitate to entrust it to the black soldier. We could not believe that this black man like a domestic animal once had been a soldier fighting in the war, the fact rejected the imagination. The black soldier looked at the tool box, then gazed into our eyes. We watched him with joy that made us flush and shiver.

'He's like a person!' Harelip said to me softly, and as I poked my brother in the rear I was so proud and pleased I felt my body twist with laughter. Sighs of wonder from the children billowed through the skylight like fog.

We took the breakfast basket back, and when we finished our own breakfast and returned to the cellar the black soldier had taken a wrench and a small hammer from the tool box and had placed them neatly on a burlap bag on the floor. We sat next to him and he looked at us, then his large, yellowed teeth were bared and his cheeks slackened and we were jolted by the discovery that he could also smile. We understood then that we had been joined to him by a sudden, deep, passionate bond that was almost 'human'.

Afternoon lengthened, the lady from the blacksmith's dragged Harelip off with angry shouts and our butts began to ache from sitting directly on the dirt floor, but still the black soldier worked on the trap, his fingers soiled with old, dusty grease, the spring making a soft metallic click as he cocked and tried it again and again.

Not bored, I watched his pink palm indent where the teeth of the trap pressed into it and watched the oily grime twist into strands on his thick, sweaty neck. These things produced in me a not unpleasant nausea, a faint repulsion connected to desire. Puffing out his cheeks as if he were softly singing inside his broad mouth, the black soldier worked on intently. My brother, leaning on my knees, observed his fingers moving with eyes that shone with admiration. Flies swarmed around us, and their buzzing entangled the heat and echoed with it deep inside my ears.

When the trap bit into the braided rope with a noticeably sharper, sturdier snap, the black soldier placed it carefully on the floor and smiled at me and my brother through the dull, heavy liquid in his eyes. Beads of sweat trembled on the dark polish of his forehead. For truly a long time we peered, still smiling, just as we did with the goats and the hunting dogs, into the black soldier's gentle eyes. It was hot. We immersed ourselves in the heat, as if it were a shared pleasure connecting us and the black soldier, and continued smiling back and forth. . . .

One morning Clerk was carried in covered in mud and bleeding from his chin. He had stumbled in the woods and fallen from a low cliff, and he had been found, unable to move, by a man from the village on his way to work in the hills. As he received treatment at the village headman's house Clerk stared in dismay at his artificial leg, which had bent where the thick, stiff leather was secured with a metal band and could not be properly reattached. He made no effort to communicate instructions from the *town*. The adults grew irritated; we wished Clerk had lain at the foot of the cliff undiscovered and had starved to death, assuming he had come to take the black soldier away. But he had come to explain that instructions from the prefecture still had not arrived. We regained our happiness, our energy, our sympathy for Clerk. And we took his artificial leg, and the toolbox, to the cellar.

Lying on the sweating cellar floor, the black soldier was singing in a soft, thick voice, a song that gripped us with its raw power, a song concealing regret and screams that threatened to overwhelm us. We showed him the damaged artificial leg. He stood up, peered at the leg for a minute, then swiftly fell to work. Cries of delight burst from the children peeping through the skylight, and the three of us, Harelip and my brother and I, also laughed at the top of our lungs.

When Clerk came to the cellar at dusk the artificial leg was completely restored. He fitted it onto his stump of a thigh and stood up, and we again raised a shout of happiness. Clerk bounded up the stairs and went into the square to try the fit of the leg. We pulled the black soldier to his feet by both arms and, without the slightest hesitation, as if it were an established habit already, took him into the square with us.

The black soldier filled his broad nostrils with the young, buoyant, summer-evening air, his first air above ground since he had been taken prisoner, and observed Clerk closely as he tried his leg. All went well. Clerk came running over, took from his pocket a cigarette made of knotweed leaves, a lopsided cigarette that smelled something like a brush fire and smarted fiercely if the smoke got in your eyes, lit it, and handed it to the tall black soldier. The black soldier inhaled it and doubled over coughing violently and clutching his throat. Clerk, embarrassed, smiled a doleful smile, but we children laughed out loud. The black soldier straightened, wiped his tears with a giant palm, took from the pocket of the linen pants hugging his powerful hips a dark, shiny pipe and held it out to Clerk.

Clerk accepted the gift, the black soldier nodded his satisfaction, and the evening sun flooded them in grape light. We shouted until our throats began to hurt and milled around them, laughing as though touched by madness.

We began taking the black soldier out of the cellar frequently, for walks along the cobblestone road. The adults said nothing. When they encountered the black soldier surrounded by us children they merely looked away and circled around him, just as they stepped into the grass to avoid the bull from the headman's house when it came along the road.

Even when the children were all being kept busy working at home and could not visit the black soldier in his underground quarters, no one, adults or children, was surprised to see him napping in the shade of a tree in the square or walking slowly back and forth along the road. Like the hunting dogs and the children and the trees, the black soldier was becoming a component of village life.

On days when at dawn my father returned carrying at his side a long, narrow trap made of hammered wooden slats and a fat weasel with an unbelievably long body thrashing around inside it, my brother and I had to spend the whole morning on the dirt floor of the storehouse, helping with the skinning. On those days we hoped from the bottom of our hearts that the black soldier would come to watch us work. When he did appear we would kneel on either side of my father as he grasped the bloodstained skinning knife with bits of fat stuck to the handle, and, scarcely breathing, would wish the rebellious, nimble weasel a complete and proper death and a deft skinning, for our guest's sake. A last instant of revenge in its final throes, as the weasel's neck was wrung it farted a horrible, terrific smell, and when the skin was laid back with a soft tearing noise at the dully gleaming tip of my father's knife there remained only muscle with a pearly luster encasing a small body so exposed it was lewd. My brother and I, careful not to let the guts spill out, carried the body to the communal compost heap to throw it away, and when we returned, wiping our soiled fingers on broad leaves, the weasel skin was already turned inside out and being nailed to a plank, fat membranes and thin capillaries glistening in the sun. The black soldier, producing what sounded like birdcalls through his pursed lips, was peering at the folds of the skin being cleaned of fat between my father's thick fingers so it would dry more easily. And when the fur had dried as stiff as claws on the plank and was criss-crossed with stains the color of blood like railroad lines across a map and the black soldier saw and admired it, how proud we were of my father's 'technique.' There were times when even my father, as he blew water on the fur, turned to the black soldier with friendly eyes. At such times my brother and the black soldier and my father and I were united, as if in a single family, around my father's weasel-curing technique.

The black soldier also liked to watch the blacksmith at work. From time to time, especially when Harelip was helping forge something like a hoe, his half-naked body glowing in the fire, we would surround the black soldier and walk over to the blacksmith's shed. When the blacksmith lifted with hands covered in charcoal dust a piece of red-hot steel and plunged it into water, the black soldier would raise a cry of admiration like a scream, and the children would point and laugh. The blacksmith, flattered, frequently repeated this dangerous demonstration of his skill.

Even the women stopped being afraid of the black soldier. At times he received food directly from their hands.

It was the height of summer, and still no instructions arrived from the prefectural office. There was a rumor that the prefectural capitol had been bombed, but that had no effect on our village. Air hotter than the flames that burned a city hung over our village all the day long. And the space around the black soldier began to fill up with an odor that made our heads swim when we sat with him in the airless cellar, a strong, fatty odor like the stink of the weasel meat rotting on the compost heap. We joked about it constantly and laughed until our tears flowed, but when the black soldier began to sweat he stank so badly we could not bear to be at his side.

One hot afternoon Harelip proposed that we take him to the village spring; appalled at ourselves for not having had the thought earlier, we climbed the cellar steps tugging at the black soldier's grimy hands. The children gathered in the square surrounded us with whoops of excitement as we ran down the cobblestone road baking in the sun.

When we were as naked as birds and had stripped the black soldier's clothes we plunged into the spring all together, splashing one another and shouting. We were enraptured with our new idea. The naked black soldier was so large that the water barely reached his hips even when he went to the deepest part of the spring; when we splashed him he would raise a scream like a chicken whose neck was being wrung and plunge his head underwater and remain submerged until he shot up shouting and spouting water from his mouth. Wet and reflecting the strong sunlight, his nakedness shone like the body of a black horse, full and beautiful. We clamored around him splashing and shouting, and by and by the girls left the shade of the oak trees where they had been hesitating and came racing into the spring and hurriedly submerged their own small nakedness. Harelip caught one of the girls and began his lewd ritual, and we brought the black soldier over and from the best position showed him Harelip receiving his pleasure. The sun flooded all of our hard bodies, the water seethed and sparkled. Harelip, bright red and laughing, raised a shout each time he slapped the girl's spray-wet, shining buttocks with his open palm. We roared with laughter, and the girl cried.

Suddenly we discovered that the black soldier possessed a magnificent, heroic, unbelievably beautiful penis. We crowded around him bumping naked hips, pointing and teasing, and the black soldier gripped his penis and planted his feet apart fiercely like a goat about to copulate and bellowed. We laughed until we cried and splashed the black soldier's penis. Then Harelip dashed off naked as he was, and when he returned leading a large nanny-goat from the courtyard at the general store we applauded his idea. The black soldier opened his pink mouth and shouted, then danced out of the water and bore down upon the frightened, bleating goat. We laughed as though mad, Harelip strained to keep the goat's head down, and the black soldier labored mightily, his black, rugged penis glistening in the sun, but it simply would not work the way it did with a billy-goat.

We laughed until we could no longer support ourselves on our legs, so hard that when finally we fell exhausted to the ground, sadness stole into our soft heads. To us the black soldier was a rare and wonderful domestic animal, an animal of genius. How can I describe how much we loved him, or the blazing sun above our wet, heavy skin that distant, splendid summer afternoon, the deep shadows on the cobblestones, the smell of the children and the black soldier, the voices hoarse with happiness, how can I convey the repletion and rhythm of it all?

To us it seemed that the summer that bared those tough, re-splendent muscles, the summer that suddenly and unexpectedly gey-sered like an oil well, spewing happiness and drenching us in black, heavy oil, would continue forever and never end.

Later in the day of our archaic bathing in the spring an evening downpour rudely locked the valley in fog, and the rain continued to fall late into the night. The next morning, Harelip and my brother and I kept close to the storehouse wall with the black soldier's food, to avoid the rain that was still falling. After breakfast, the black soldier, hugging his knees, softly sang a song in the dark cellar. Cooling our outstretched fingers in the rainspray sifting through the skylight, we were washed away by the expanse of the black soldier's voice and the sealike solemnity of his song. When the song was finished there was no more spray coming through the skylight. Taking the black soldier's arm, we led him smiling into the square. The fog had swiftly cleared from the valley; the trees had absorbed so much rainwater that their foliage was plump and swollen as baby chicks. When the wind blew, the trees trembled in fits, scattering wet leaves and drops of rainwater and causing small, momentary rainbows from which cicadas darted. In the heat beginning to revive and the tempest of shrill cicadas we sat down on the flat stone at the cellar entrance and for a long time breathed the air that smelled of wet bark.

Scarcely moving, we sat there until, in the afternoon, Clerk, carrying his rain gear, descended the road from the woods and went into the headman's house. We stood up then, leaned against an old, dripping apricot tree, and waited for Clerk to burst from the dark-ness of the house to wave a signal. But Clerk did not appear; instead, the alarm bell on the roof of the headman's barn began to clang, summoning the adults out working in the valley and the woods, and women and children from the rain-wet houses appeared on the cobblestone road. I looked back at the black soldier and saw that the smile was gone from his face. Anxiety suddenly born in me tight-ened my chest. Leaving the black soldier behind, my brother and Harelip and I ran to the headman's house.

Clerk was standing in silence on the dirt floor in the entranceway; inside, the village headman sat crosslegged on the wooden floor, lost in thought. As we waited impatiently for the adults to gather, we struggled to maintain an expectation that was beginning to feel somehow hopeless. From the fields in the valley and from the woods, dressed in their work clothes, their cheeks puffy with discontent, the adults, including my father, who stepped into the entrance-way with several small birds lashed to the barrel of his gun, gradually returned.

The minute the meeting began Clerk floored the children with an explanation in dialect to the effect that the authorities had decided the black soldier was to be turned over to the prefecture. Originally the army was to have come for him, Clerk continued, but as a result of an apparent misunderstanding and general confusion within the army itself, the village had been ordered to escort the black soldier as far as the *town*. The adults would have to suffer only the minor inconvenience of bringing the black soldier in. But we were submerged in astonishment and disappointment; turn over the black soldier and what would remain in the village? Summer would become an empty husk, a shed skin!

I had to warn the black soldier. Slipping past the adults I ran back to where he was sitting in the square in front of the storehouse. Slowly lifting his dull eyeballs he looked up at me halted in front of him and gasping for breath. I was able to convey nothing to him. I could only stare at him while sadness and irritation shook me. Still hugging his knees, the black soldier was trying to peer into my eyes. His lips as full as the belly of a pregnant river fish slowly opened and shiny white saliva submerged his gums. Looking back, I saw the adults leave the dark entranceway of the headman's house with Clerk in the lead and move toward the storehouse.

I shook the black soldier's shoulder as he sat there, and shouted at him in dialect. I was so agitated I felt I would swoon. What could I do, he merely allowed himself to be shaken by my arm in silence and peered around him, craning his thick neck. I released his shoulder and hung my head.

Suddenly the black soldier rose, soaring in front of me like a tree, and seized my upper arm and pulled me tight up against himself and raced down the cellar steps. In the cellar, dumbfounded, I was transfixed for a brief moment by the flexing of the black soldier's taut thighs and the contraction of his buttocks as he moved around swiftly. Lowering the trap door, he secured it by passing the chain on the boar-trap he had repaired through the ring on the door and fastening it around the metal support protruding from the wall. Then he came back down the steps, his hands clasped and his head drooping, and I looked at his fatty, bloodshot eyes that appeared to have been packed with mud, his expressionless eyes, and realized abruptly that he was once again, as when the adults had taken him prisoner, a black beast that rejected understanding, a dangerously poisonous substance. I looked up at the giant black soldier, looked at the chain wrapped around the trap door, looked down at my own small, bare feet. A wave of fear and amazement broke over my vital organs and eddied around them. Darting away from the black soldier I pressed my back against the wall. The black soldier stood where he was in the middle of the cellar, his head drooping. I bit my lip and tried to withstand the trembling in my legs.

The adults gathered above the trap door and began to tug at it, gently at first and then abruptly with a great cackling as of chickens being pursued. But the thick oak door that had been so useful for locking the black soldier securely in the cellar was locking the adults out now, and the children, the trees, the valley.

A few adults peered frantically through the skylight and were immediately replaced by others, bumping foreheads in the scramble. There was a sudden change in their behavior. At first they shouted. Then they fell silent, and a threatening gun barrel was inserted through the skylight. Like an agile beast the black soldier leaped at me and hugged me tightly to himself, using me as a shield against the rifle, and as I moaned in pain and writhed in his arms I comprehended the cruel truth. I was a prisoner, and a hostage. The black soldier had transformed into the *enemy*, and my side was clamoring beyond the trap door. Anger, and humiliation, and the irritating sadness of betrayal raced through my body like flames, scorching me. And most of all, fear, swelling and eddying in me, clogging my throat and making me sob. In the black soldier's rude arms, aflame with anger, I wept tears. The black soldier had taken me prisoner. . . .

The gun barrel was withdrawn, the clamor increased, and then a long discussion began on the other side of the skylight. Without releasing his numbing grip on my arm the black soldier went into a corner where there was no danger of a sniper's bullet and sat down in silence. He pulled me in close to himself, and, just as I had often done when we had been friends, I kneeled with my bare knees within the circle of his body odor. The adults continued to talk for a long time. Now and then my father peered in through the skylight and nodded to his son who had been taken hostage, and each time, I cried. Dusk rose like a tide, first in the cellar and then in the square beyond the skylight. When it got dark the adults began going home several at a time, shouting a few words of encouragement to me as they left. For a long time after that I heard my father walking back and forth beyond the skylight, and then suddenly he was gone and there was no further indication of life aboveground. Night filled the cellar.

The black soldier released my arm and peered at me as though pained by the thought of the warm, everyday familiarity that had flowed between us until that morning. Trembling with anger, I looked away and remained with my eyes on the floor, my shoulders stubbornly arched, until the black soldier turned his back on me and cradled his head between his knees. I was alone; like a weasel caught in a trap I was abandoned, helpless, sunk in despair. In the darkness the black soldier did not move.

Standing, I went over to the steps and touched the boar-trap, but it was cold and hard and repelled my fingers and the bud of a shapeless hope. I did not know what to do. I could not believe the trap that had captured me; I was a baby field rabbit who weakens and dies as it stares in disbelief at the metal claws biting into its wounded foot. The fact that I had trusted the black soldier as a friend, my incredible foolishness, was an agony to me. But how could I have doubted that black, stinking giant who never did anything but smile! Even now I could not believe that the man whose teeth were chattering in the darkness in front of me was that dumb black man with the large penis.

I was trembling with chill, and my teeth chattered. My stomach had begun to hurt. I squatted, pressing my stomach, and I encountered sudden dismay: I was going to have diarrhea, the strained nerves throughout my body had brought it on. But I could not relieve myself in front of the black soldier. I clenched my teeth and endured, cold sweat beading my forehead. I endured my distress for such a long time that the effort to endure filled the space that had been occupied by fear.

But finally I resigned myself, walked over to the barrel we had laughed and hooted to see the black soldier straddle, and dropped my pants. My exposed, white buttocks felt weak and defenseless, it seemed to me I could feel humiliation dyeing my throat, my esophagus, even the walls of my stomach pitch black. When I was finished

I stood up and returned to the corner. I was beaten and I submitted, sinking to the bottom of despair. Pressing my grimy forehead against the cellar wall, warm with the heat of the ground above, I cried for a long time, stifling my sobs as best I could. The night was long. In the woods mountain dogs in a pack were barking. The air grew chill. Fatigue possessed me heavily and I slumped to the floor and slept.

When I woke up, my arm was again in the numbing grip of the black soldier's hand. Fog and adult voices were blowing in through the skylight. I could also hear the creaking of Clerk's artificial leg as he paced back and forth. Before long the thud of a heavy mallet hammering the trapdoor merged with the other noises. The heavy blows resounded in my empty stomach and made my chest ache.

Suddenly the black soldier was shouting, and then he seized me by the shoulder and pulled me to my feet and dragged me into the middle of the cellar into full view of the adults on the other side of the skylight. I could not understand why he did this. The eyes at the skylight peered in at my shame that dangled there by its ears like a shot rabbit. Had my brother's moist eyes been among them I would have bitten off my tongue in shame. But only adult eyes were clustered at the window, peering in at me.

The noise and tempo of the mallet heightened, and the black soldier screamed and grasped my throat from behind in his large hand. His nails bit into the soft skin and the pressure on my Adam's apple made it impossible to breathe. I flailed with my hands and feet and threw back my head and moaned. How bitter it was to be humiliated in front of the adults! I twisted my body, trying to escape the body of the black soldier glued to my back, and kicked his shins, but his thick, hairy arms were hard and heavy. And his shrill screams rose above my moans. The adults' faces withdrew, and I imagined the black soldier had intimidated them into racing to put a stop to the smashing of the trapdoor. The black soldier stopped screaming and the pressure like a boulder against my throat eased. My love for the adults and my feeling of closeness revived.

But the pounding on the trapdoor grew louder. The adults' faces reappeared at the skylight, and the black soldier, screaming, tightened his fingers around my throat. My head was pulled back and my opened lips uttered a shrill, feeble sound I could do nothing about, like the scream of a small animal. Even the adults had abandoned me. Unmoved by the sight of the black soldier choking me to death they continued to batter the door. When they had broken in they would find me with my neck wrung like a weasel's, my hands and feet stiffened. Burning with hatred, despairing, I writhed and wept and listened to the sound of the mallet, my head wrenched back, moaning without shame.

The sound of countless wheels revolving rang in my ears and blood from my nose ran down my cheeks. Then the trapdoor splintered, muddy bare feet with bristly hair covering even the backs of the toes piled in, and ugly adults inflamed to madness filled the cellar. Screaming, the black soldier clasped me to himself and sank slowly down the wall toward the floor. My back and buttocks tight against his sweating, sticky body, I felt a current hot as rage flowing between us. And like a cat that has been surprised in the act of copulation, in spite of my shame, I laid my hostility bare. It was hostility toward the adults crowded together at the bottom of the steps observing my humiliation, hostility toward the black soldier squeezing my throat in this thick hand, pressing his nails into the soft skin and making it bleed, hostility toward all things mixing together as it twisted upward in me. The black soldier was howling. The noise numbed my eardrums, there in the cellar at the height of summer I was slipping into an absence of all sensation replete as if with pleasure. The black soldier's ragged breathing covered the back of my neck.

From the midst of the bunched adults my father stepped forward dangling a hatchet from his hand. I saw that his eyes were blazing with rage and feverish as a dog's. The black soldier's nails bit into my neck and I moaned. My father bore down on us, and seeing the hatchet being raised I closed my eyes. The black soldier seized my left wrist and lifted it to protect his head. The entire cellar erupted in a scream and I heard the smashing of my left hand and the black soldier's skull. On the oily, shining skin of his arm beneath my jaw thick blood coagulated in shivering drops. The adults surged toward us and I felt the black soldier's arm slacken and pain sear my body.

Inside a sticky black bag my hot eyelids, my burning throat, my searing hand began to knit me and give me shape. But I could not pierce the sticky membrane and break free of the bag. Like a lamb prematurely born I was wrapped in a bag that stuck to my fingers. I could not move my body. It was night, and near me the adults were talking. Then it was morning, and I felt light against my eyelids. From time to time a heavy hand pressed my forehead and I moaned and tried to shake it off but my head would not move.

The first time I succeeded in opening my eyes it was morning again. I was lying on my own sleeping platform in the storehouse. In front of the rain shutters Harelip and my brother were watching me. I opened my eyes all the way, and moved my lips. Harelip and my brother raced down the stairs shouting, and my father and the lady from the general store came up. My stomach was crying for food, but when my father's hand placed a pitcher of goat's milk to my lips nausea shook me and I clamped my mouth shut, yelling, and dribbled the milk on my throat and chest. All adults were unbearable to me, including my father. Adults who bore down on me with teeth bared, brandishing a hatchet, they were uncanny, beyond my understanding, provoking nausea. I continued to yell until my father and the others left the room.

A while later my brother's arm quietly touched my body. In silence, my eyes closed, I listened to his soft voice telling me how he and the others had helped gather firewood for cremating the black soldier, how Clerk had brought an order forbidding the cremation, how the adults, in order to retard the process of decay, had carried the black soldier's corpse into the abandoned mine in the valley and were building a fence to keep mountain dogs away.

In an awed voice my brother told me repeatedly that he had thought I was dead. For two days I had lain here and eaten nothing and so he had thought I was dead. With my brother's hand on me I entered sleep that lured me as irresistibly as death.

I woke up in the afternoon and saw for the first time that my smashed hand was wrapped in cloth. For a long time I lay as I was, not moving, and looking at the arm on my chest, so swollen I could not believe it was mine. There was no one in the room. An unpleasant odor crept through the window. I understood what the odor meant but felt no sadness.

The room had darkened and the air turned chill when I sat up on the sleeping platform. After a long hesitation I tied the ends of the bandage together and put it over my head as a sling, then leaned against the open window and looked down upon the *village*. The odor fountaining furiously from the black soldier's heavy corpse blanketed the cobblestone road and the buildings and the valley supporting them, an inaudible scream from the corpse that encircled us and expanded limitlessly overhead as in a nightmare. It was dusking. The sky, a teary gray with a touch of orange enfolded in it, hovered just above the valley, narrowing it.

Every so often adults would hurry down toward the valley in silence, chests thrown out. Every time they appeared I sensed them making me feel nauseous and afraid and withdrew inside the window. It was as if while I had been in bed the adults had been transformed into entirely inhuman monsters. And my body was as dull and heavy as if it had been packed with wet sand.

Trembling with chill, I bit into my parched lips and watched the cobblestones in the road, in pale golden shadow to begin with, fluidly expand, then turn breathtaking grape, contours continuing to swell until finally they submerged, disappearing, in a weak, purple, opaque light. Now and then salty tears wet my cracked lips and made them sting.

From time to time children's shouts reached me from the back of the storehouse through the odor of the black soldier's corpse. Taking each trembling step with caution, as after a long illness, I went down the dark stairs and walked along the deserted cobblestone road toward the shouting.

The children were gathered on the overgrown slope that descended to the small river at the valley bottom, their dogs racing around them and barking. In the thick underbrush along the river below, the adults were still constructing a sturdy fence to keep wild dogs away from the abandoned mine. The sound of stakes being driven echoed up from the valley. The adults worked in silence, the children ran madly in circles on the slope, shrieking gaily.

I leaned against the trunk of an old paulownia tree and watched the children playing. They were sliding down the grassy slope, using the tail of the black soldier's fallen plane as a sled. Straddling the sharp-edged, wonderfully buoyant sled they went skimming down the slope like young beasts. When the sled seemed in danger of hitting one of the black rocks that jutted from the grass here and there, the rider kicked the ground with his bare feet and changed the sled's direction. By the time one of the children dragged the sled back up the hill, the grass that had been crushed beneath it on the way down was slowly straightening, obscuring the bold voyager's wake. The children and the sled were that light. The children sledded down screaming, the dogs pursued them barking, the children dragged the sled up again. An irrepressible spirit of movement like the fiery dust that precedes a sorcerer crackled and darted among them.

Harelip left the group of children and ran up the slope toward me. Leaning against the trunk of an evergreen oak that resembled a deer leg, a tussled stem of grass between his teeth, he peered into my face. I looked away, pretending to be absorbed in the sledding. Harelip peered closely at my arm in the sling and snorted.

'It smells,' he said. 'Your smashed hand stinks.'

Harelip's eyes were lusting for battle and his feet were planted apart in readiness for my attack; I glared back at him but did not leap at his throat.

'That's not me,' I said in a feeble, hoarse voice, 'That's the nigger's smell.'

Harelip stood there appalled, observing me. I turned away, biting my lip, and looked down at the simmering of the short, fine grass burying his bare ankles. Harelip shrugged his shoulders with undisguised contempt and spat forcefully, then ran shouting back to his friends with the sled.

I was no longer a child—the thought filled me like a revelation. Bloody fights with Harelip, hunting small birds by moonlight, sledding, wild puppies, these things were for children. And that variety of connection to the world had nothing to do with me.

Exhausted and shaking with chill I sat down on the ground that retained the midday warmth. When I lowered myself the lush summer grass hid the silent work of the adults at the valley bottom, but the children playing with the sled suddenly loomed in front of me like darkly silhouetted woodland gods. And amidst these young Pans wheeling in circles with their dogs like victims fleeing before a flood, the night air gradually deepened in color, gathered itself, and became pure.

'Hey Frog, feeling better?'

A dry, hot hand pressed my head from behind but I did not turn or try to stand. Without turning away from the children playing on the slope I glanced with eyes only at Clerk's black artificial limb planted firmly alongside my own bare legs. Even Clerk, simply by standing at my side, made my throat go dry.

'Aren't you going to take a turn, Frog? I thought it must have been your idea!'

I was stubbornly silent. When Clerk sat down with a rattling of his leg he took from his jacket pocket the pipe the black soldier had presented him and filled it with his tobacco. A strong smell that nettled the soft membranes in my nose and ignited animal sentiments, the aroma of a brush fire, enclosed me and Clerk in the same pale blue haze.

'When a war starts smashing kids' fingers it's going too far,' Clerk said.

I breathed deeply, and was silent. The war, a long, bloody battle on a huge scale, must still have been going on. The war that like a flood washing away flocks of sheep and trimmed lawns in some distant country was never in the world supposed to have reached our village. But it had come, to mash my fingers and hand to a pulp, my father swinging a hatchet, his body drunk on the blood of war. And suddenly our village was enveloped in the war, and in the tumult I could not breathe.

'But it can't go on much longer,' Clerk said gravely, as if he were talking to an adult. 'The army is in such a state you can't get a message through, nobody knows what to do.'

The sound of hammers continued. Now the odor of the black soldier's body had settled over the entire valley like the luxuriant lower branches of a giant, invisible tree.

'They're still hard at work,' Clerk said, listening to the thudding of the hammers. 'Your father and the others don't know what to do either, so they're taking their sweet time with those stakes!'

In silence we listened to the heavy thudding that reached us in intervals in the children's shouting and laughter. Presently Clerk began with practiced fingers to detach his artificial leg. I watched him.

'Hey!' he shouted to the children. 'Bring that sled over here.'

Laughing and shouting, the children dragged the sled up. When Clerk hopped over on one leg and pushed through the children surrounding the sled I picked up his leg and ran down the slope. It was heavy; managing it with one hand was difficult and irritating.

The dew beginning to form in the lush grass wet my bare legs and dry leaves stuck to them and itched. At the bottom of the slope I stood waiting, holding the artificial leg. It was already night. Only the children's voices at the top of the slope shook the thickening membrane of dark, nearly opaque air.

A burst of louder shouts and laughter and a soft skimming through the grass, but no sled cleaved the sticky air to appear before me. I thought I heard the dull thud of an impact and stood as I was, peering into the dark air. After a long silence I finally saw the airplane tail sliding toward me down the slope, riderless, spinning as it came. I threw the artificial leg into the grass and ran up the dark slope. Alongside a rock jutting blackly from the grass and wet with dew, both hands limply open, Clerk lay on his back grinning. I leaned over and saw that thick, dark blood was running from the nose and ears of his grinning face. The noise the children made as they came running down the slope rose above the wind blowing up from the valley.

To avoid being surrounded by the children I abandoned Clerk's corpse and stood up on the slope. I had rapidly become familiar with sudden death and the expressions of the dead, sad at times and grinning at times, just as the adults were familiar with them. Clerk would be cremated with the firewood gathered to cremate the black soldier. Glancing up with tears in my eyes at the narrowed sky still white with twilight, I went down the grassy slope to look for my brother.

TSUSHIMA YUKO (1947–)

A VERY STRANGE, ENCHANTED BOY

Translated by Geraldine Harcourt

~

There's a song in English that begins: 'There was a boy, a very strange, enchanted boy.' I have an idea it was Nat King Cole who sang it, though I'm not sure. I heard it once on the radio, catching the beginning because the English was unusually clear; I remember being so startled by the words, and by the slow-flowing melody in a minor key, that I felt a chill. I listened intently, wistful and also afraid, as if something impossible had happened. It was a beautiful tune.

There was a boy, a very strange, enchanted boy. . . .

It was a sound that shouldn't have been humanly possible to convey, that should have gone on echoing in a closed space, yet there it was as an actual song.

Although I only heard it that one time, I still can't forget the beginning.

Now that I come to think of it, there was a book as well: The Mysterious Stranger. Its Japanese title, like the song's, was Strange Boy. I was so shaken when I came across it in a bookstore, you'd have thought I'd seen the ghost of one of my family. There on the spine, printed much too boldly, were words that shouldn't have been out in the open. While strongly drawn to them, I hurried away in spite of myself.

Yes, there was a book like that, too.

'I've found *infinity*.'

Michie was surprised by another announcement from her six-year-old.

'Infinity?' she asked. The boy nodded. 'Where?'

'Come here and I'll show you.'

He ran to the bathroom. When she saw where he was headed, she understood.

'Ah, the mirrors.'

'Come on, quick.'

'I already know.'

'Come *on*.'

Reluctantly, she got up.

The bathroom mirror had side pieces which doubled as the fronts of small cupboards; opening both of these turned it into a winged mirror. As a child, Michie too had looked into the winged mirror on her mother's dressing-table and not been able to take her eyes from the scene reflected endlessly in its narrow panels, left and right.

She peered over the child's head into the mirror. Identical frames with parts of their two faces mounted inside ran back in a never-ending series, a dim corridor to infinity. She grew so anxious she couldn't go on watching.

'Mmm, you're right. Wow!'

She straightened up.

'It's on this side too. You have to look over here!'

Michie dutifully glanced at the mirror on the opposite side.

'Ah, so it is. Kind of scary, isn't it? As if we might get sucked in.'

No longer paying any attention to his mother, the boy was gazing open-mouthed at the infinity in the mirror.

There was something odd about the child—sometimes even Michie didn't know what to make of him. When he was four or five, he'd learned that numbers go up from hundreds to thousands to tens of thousands and wanted to know what came after that. Michie answered, '*Oku* [10^8], *cho* [10^{12}], and *kei* [10^{16}], but then I forget.' This wasn't likely to satisfy him, though for a while he contented himself writing figures followed by long strings of zeros on a piece of paper and making Michie read them out loud. Sure enough, before long he was fretting about where numbers ended. When he asked her with a troubled face, 'Do numbers ever come to an end? Where is the end?' Michie answered, 'Yes, they do, but it works the same way as if they didn't.' As she spoke she was inwardly breathing a sigh of relief: thank goodness she'd remembered that much from school.

'Infinity is where numbers end. But infinity means going on forever, so that isn't really the end, you see. It just says you can't count any higher.'

So the child learned the word 'infinity'. And immediately began to puzzle over exactly what it meant.

Later, while reading the newspaper, Michie realized she'd made a mistake. Right away, she let the child know.

'The other day I was talking about infinity, but that's the way that people who count in millions and billions thought of to describe it. It says here that when you count *oku*, *cho*, *kei*, in the end you come to something called Great Mystery. It's like saying "Oh, how strange," because there's just too many numbers in a row. It's kind of funny, isn't it?'

The child obviously didn't understand the difference between the two terms for infinity, but learned the new word anyway, and seemed slightly reassured.

Once he'd gotten hold of an idea he was unable to let it go. Nothing else would make any impression on him while this lasted, and every time he opened his mouth the same subject would come out. As she was forced to listen to the boy go on like this whenever they were together, day after day, Michie would find herself caught up in whatever was obsessing him. By now she knew only too well that she couldn't snap him out of this state no matter how sharply she reminded him of other things; even slapping his cheek wouldn't have worked, and so she couldn't bring herself to waste any more time trying.

There'd been a phase when he could think of nothing but ghosts and monsters. He was always wheedling her to buy ghost and monster books, and when, every five times or so, she gave in, he wouldn't part with the new book for a moment, pestering her to read it whenever he set eyes on her until he knew each creature by heart, from its place of origin to its identifying characteristics. Slippery Shanks, One Stump, the Giant Red Tongue, the River Baby: the child's mind was a night parade of a hundred goblins, and Michie discovered she'd become an expert herself.

With him inventing his own ghosts and drawing any number of pictures of them in a day, perhaps it was only natural that his interest turned next to the world after death. Paradise, Hell, the Ruler of the Underworld, the needle mountain, the lake of blood . . . the scariest things appealed to him. He began wanting to know when he was going to die—when he turned five? Or six? He probably wouldn't live to be ten, he decided, and when Michie told him, 'Eat your dinner properly,' or, 'Hurry up and get undressed,' he would be sure to murmur, 'I'm only going to die soon anyhow.' He said it too coolly for such a young child, and after several days of this Michie burst out tearfully, 'Will you stop that nonsense! You've grown so big already, I wouldn't let you die, not even if somebody murdered you! So you can't die, you hear me?' Either because he'd seen his mother cry or because he actually believed her far-fetched claim, the child kept quiet about his death after that.

Meanwhile, the disapproval of the staff at his day-care centre was another constant worry. He was never boisterous when he was with Michie—if anything, he was *too* quiet—perhaps because of the way she played along patiently and resignedly with his erratic interests. But the day-care centre was forever reporting that he'd thrown a toy that broke a ceiling light, or bullied a girl and hurt her, and the teachers were continually probing the psychological causes of his behaviour. She disregarded the usual comments about his not having a father and the suggestions that, being single, she left him in day care for too long, but the staff's attitude was depressing, even though she did her best to ignore it.

She'd once been told by another mother from the centre whom she'd got to know a little, 'It's about your child: ours wanted to know if he wasn't right in the head. I asked, "Goodness, whatever makes you say a thing like that?" And can you believe it, the woman in charge of his group had said to the children, "Take no notice of him, he isn't right in the head." I thought I should let you know.' On that occasion, too, Michie's eyes had filled unexpectedly with tears, but she'd tried to persuade herself that this sort of thing wasn't worth worrying about.

Her troubles hadn't ended when he started elementary school, either. It took a long time for him to realize that he was supposed to change into indoor shoes on arriving at school, and in the meantime he had gone barefoot in the building and on the playground. As soon as he'd spotted the goldfish swimming in a little pond in a corner of the yard, he'd splashed right in. He couldn't tell the difference between lessons and playtime, textbooks and notebooks. To his homeroom teacher's dismay, her scoldings had no effect at all. He was given a special place in the front row, both in class and at the morning assemblies. And of course, since he wasn't interested, he still couldn't write even the basic phonetic script halfway decently, and here they were in the third term of first grade. Knowing he would have to master a number of characters as well before the term was through, Michie was very anxious. But the child himself, having learned of the existence of something called infinity, was fascinated with outer space and given to worrying about things which even his mother couldn't explain, such as when the sun would die, the relative sizes of the Earth, the Sun, and Betelgeuse, and the beginning and end of the universe. This led him to find out about atoms, and since he was learning to read he was thrilled to discover on his own, in a book at the library, a unit above *oku*, *cho*, and *kei* called *gai* [10^{20}]. 'It says you can't see any water till 330 *gai* of water molecules come together. This piece of fish is made of atoms too, isn't it? And these clothes, and this tatami, and my body, and you too, Mom. But don't they ever come apart? What are atoms like inside?'

Why must he always bug her with questions about things she didn't really understand, like the universe and atoms? It got on Michie's nerves. Apart from anything else, she was concerned that if he spent all his time pursuing interests so utterly remote from everyday life, he might really go funny in the head. She had visions of the child drifting off into the vastness of space, his body a mass of globular atoms like salmon roe. Besides, never mind how familiar he was with figures on the order of billions and sextillions, he was simply hopeless at his arithmetic and couldn't add numbers greater than five. Michie would eventually give up in exasperation.

Yet when she'd come home after a day's work, and they'd had their supper, and she was watching idly from the kitchen as he moulded balls of papier mâché and murmured to himself, 'This one's hydrogen, this one's helium, and this here's the methane molecule,' she would begin to think that she was worrying about nothing. After all, in his own way, he was enjoying himself. . . .

'Listening to you, though, makes me wonder—aren't you sort of egging him on?' the child's father remarked when they met. It had been a long time since she'd last seen him. She had never been the man's wife, nor lived with him. When Michie met him he was already another woman's husband and the father of that woman's child. Attempting to come between them, Michie had even given birth to a child of her own, but the man and his wife hadn't separated. Instead, he had stopped seeing Michie. They still met as the child's parents once every year or so, and went out, with him between them, to some place they thought he'd like. Michie would talk eagerly about the child all the while, for this was a precious chance to tell these things to someone who would listen.

This time they had gone to the haunted house at a downtown amusement park, and at the child's request had visited the hall of mirrors three times.

'You really think so? . . .' Michie inclined her head dubiously at the man's words.

'Yes, I do. I've told you so before.'

'Mmm, so you have. But wasn't he always different, really, ever since he was little? A baby's first words are meant to be things like "bye-bye", or "bow-wow", aren't they? Well, he did say "num-num", I'll grant him that—I suppose he couldn't get by without it. Otherwise he just wasn't into talking at all. I'd also try and get him to do those tricks that other people teach their babies, like flinging his arms up in the air when you give a cheer, or holding up one finger if somebody asked his age. Nothing doing. All I'd get was a great big smile. He had me worried, I can tell you. And then when he was nearly two, would you believe, he suddenly points at the ceiling and goes "light"? I was stunned. His next word after "num-num" was "light"! After that, it was "light, light" all the time. Well, at least I knew then I didn't have to worry about his talking anymore.'

Michie had begun to laugh as she remembered. The man, who of course had known this story all along, laughed too.

'Yes, I'll admit he's a bit eccentric.'

'What do you mean, "a bit"? He's very eccentric, really.'

'See what I mean? You sound proud of it, somehow. . . . Remember when you were pregnant, you'd get hysterical some-times and say nasty things to me about how the baby might be deformed, and what would I do then? So, after he was born, I figured maybe you went on saying the things you did just to bug me. That doesn't seem to be the whole story though.'

'I wonder. Not that there haven't been times when I've wanted to bug you. But . . . proud of it?'

'I suppose he does have his eccentric side, but he has a normal side as well, doesn't he? He looks okay to me.'

'Well, yes. He might not care when the teacher scolds him, but he does seem to like being praised.'

'And he has friends. . . .'

'Mmm, it looks as though he's made several friends.'

'Then isn't he a normal child? But you aren't willing to admit that, are you?'

'... Maybe not. I'm not sure. It's silly, but when he was about three or four, I sometimes felt awfully disappointed. Around that age, all of a sudden children start losing that baby look—they grow taller, and their cheeks firm up, right? And the same probably goes for what's in their heads too. So I'd be walking down the street, and I'd catch sight of the neighbours' kids playing and think, Oh no. I didn't want to accept that mine would turn out just like those other children, that he hadn't ever been any different, that he was in reality a growing child. I'd have to ask myself what's the matter with you, why is it such a letdown? Here I'd been raising a real child, and yet, all this time, maybe I hadn't quite believed he was real.'

'If that's so, it's terrible.'

'Of course it's terrible. But it does seem to be partly how I felt. I had him by myself, and I've raised him by myself because that was the only way. When I was pregnant, I couldn't hide the fact at my job. But my sister, she didn't find out till after he was born. And she still tends to hold back where he's concerned. Anyway, the thing is, I suppose at first I may have been thinking of him as a wonderful dream. A wonderful dream, pure and simple. I guess that's why I couldn't relax: What if I woke up from this dream that I had a child? . . . But here he is, in elementary school already, and it may have taken me a while, but even I can tell he's a real live person. Though maybe not very well brought up.'

'You haven't changed all that much, though, have you? How's he supposed to deal with a thing like that? The poor kid. Look, you will take care of him, won't you? Make sure he grows up right.'

'I am taking care of him, thank you very much. I go over his schoolwork with him because it's such a worry, and I try all kinds of things to stimulate his brain—letting him cook, and getting his friend's family from the country to take him out to their house. And that's not all.'

'Okay, okay. I'm sure you're doing your best. Just thought I'd mention it. . . .'

As the man merely handed over a reasonably large sum of money once a year and did nothing more, it was awkward for him to press the matter, however uneasy her attitude to the child was making him. Michie, too, was resigned to the nature of their relationship, but that was all the more reason she was concerned about what was troubling him. Even if he held back the words, he was still the only person who would get worked up before he knew it over the child that Michie was raising.

She really should be more careful, Michie told herself. It wouldn't hurt to be much, much stricter. She had to be more detached, for his sake, even if he hated her for it.

But was it as simple as that? She doubted whether everything would turn out happily-ever-after quite so easily.

In raising a child, doesn't every mother in fact cherish some sort of dream which may be totally absurd and have nothing to recommend it to the child? My mother, she thought, planted her own dreams in me, her daughter. Her admiration for Madame Curie, whose brilliant mind outshone even her husband's. Her dream of a boyish little girl wearing pants. Parents raise their children amidst all sorts of dreams. It makes no difference whether these are seemingly realistic or have a purely dreamlike quality. Everyone listens intently to their own fairy tales: Let her remain forever childlike and unspoiled, a sweet, modest wife, dependent on her husband and his large income. Or: All I ask is that he graduate from the right university and get a decent job.

Fantasies, of course. But we can't do without them. We need them if we're to have special feelings for the child born to us. Just how much could parents feel for their children, without fantasies? Children, too, discover their parents' bizarre fantasies working their way into their own bodies and, whether they rebel or consent, must come to acknowledge the connection. For if parents and children have a connection, this is surely it. Parents can only spin their self-indulgent dreams into their children.

Michie often remembered how she used to look at the man and marvel at what a strange, free-floating, wayward person he was. He wasn't merely wayward, naturally; he was also a good deal more assured than Michie herself when it came to social behaviour, and this had made all the difference in her situation. Even if it was only once a year, the fact that he offered his time and a certain amount of money for her child was, after all, something to be thankful for. Michie had never said a word to prompt him, and yet he didn't forget.

She knew that if she held no bad feelings towards the man now, it was because of his distance. The moment they got any closer, his wife and children would once again weigh on her mind; she would lose her equilibrium and resent, blame, and hurt him. Someone had told her she should count herself lucky because she'd been able to have the child, but she hadn't been so sure. She had wanted to watch the child grow with the man there day by day. But while watching him grow in the man's absence, since it couldn't be helped, she had ceased to think beyond the simple fact that the child was living here on earth. She wanted them to experience this life together; she couldn't turn away from the child. At some point, Michie's fantasy had begun to play like music.

There was a strange man. Michie was very attracted to him, and couldn't put him out of her mind. She never knew what he was thinking, or what his life revolved around. Floating free from the surface of the earth, with no past or future, he was gazing at its colours, the light of the sky, the sparkle of the water. Michie went on feeling for this man. And then, one day, these feelings took shape before her eyes. The shape of a child. He took after the man and had strange ways. They were father and child. Michie's feelings continued without pause. She never knew what he was thinking, this child, or what his life revolved around.

'I know *three* infinities,' the child announced to Michie.

'What are they?' she asked without turning her head. It was night, and she was taking in the washing hanging out on the balcony.

'Numbers, and mirrors, and space.'

'Ah, yes, that's right.'

She looked up at the sky. Only one or two stars were faintly visible in the sky of central Tokyo. She couldn't find the moon, either; perhaps she was looking in the wrong direction.

'It's cold. Hurry up and let's go inside,' the child said, hugging her waist. When Michie exhaled she could see her breath misting.

'Okay, then take this in.'

She tried to give him her armful of laundry.

'No-o, don't want to.'

The child darted away.

THE ELEPHANT VANISHES

Translated by Jay Rubin

When the elephant disappeared from our town's elephant house, I read about it in the newspaper. My alarm clock woke me that day, as always, at 6:13. I went to the kitchen, made coffee and toast, turned on the radio, spread the paper out on the kitchen table, and proceeded to munch and read. I'm one of those people who read the paper from beginning to end, in order, so it took me awhile to get to the article about the vanishing elephant. The front page was filled with stories of SDI and the trade friction with America, after which I plowed through the national news, international politics, economics, letters to the editor, book reviews, real-estate ads, sports reports, and finally, the regional news.

The elephant article was the lead story in the regional section. The unusually large headline caught my eye: ELEPHANT MISSING IN TOKYO SUBURB, and, beneath that, in type one size smaller, CITIZENS' FEARS MOUNT. SOME CALL FOR PROBE. There was a photo of policemen inspecting the empty elephant house. Without the elephant, something about the place seemed wrong. It looked bigger than it needed to be, blank and empty like some huge, dehydrated beast from which the innards had been plucked.

Brushing away my toast crumbs, I studied every line of the article. The elephant's absence had first been noticed at two o'clock on the afternoon of May 18—the day before—when men from the school-lunch company delivered their usual truckload of food (the elephant mostly ate leftovers from the lunches of children in the local elementary school). On the ground, still locked, lay the steel shackle that had been fastened to the elephant's hind leg, as though the elephant had slipped out of it. Nor was the elephant the only one missing. Also gone was its keeper, the man who had been in charge of the elephant's care and feeding from the start.

According to the article, the elephant and keeper had last been seen sometime after five o'clock the previous day (May 17) by a few pupils from the elementary school, who were visiting the elephant house, making crayon sketches. These pupils must have been the last to see the elephant, said the paper, since the keeper always closed the gate to the elephant enclosure when the six-o'clock siren blew.

There had been nothing unusual about either the elephant or its keeper at the time, according to the unanimous testimony of the pupils. The elephant had been standing where it always stood, in the middle of the enclosure, occasionally wagging its trunk from side to side or squinting its wrinkly eyes. It was such an awfully old elephant that its every move seemed a tremendous effort—so much so that people seeing it for the first time feared it might collapse at any moment and draw its final breath.

The elephant's age had led to its adoption by our town a year earlier. When financial problems caused the little private zoo on the edge of town to close its doors, a wildlife dealer found places for the other animals in zoos throughout the country. But all the zoos had plenty of elephants, apparently, and not one of them was willing to take in a feeble old thing that looked as if it might die of a heart attack at any moment. And so, after its companions were gone, the elephant stayed alone in the decaying zoo for nearly four months with nothing to do—not that it had had anything to do before.

This caused a lot of difficulty, both for the zoo and for the town. The zoo had sold its land to a developer, who was planning to put up a high-rise condo building, and the town had already issued him a permit. The longer the elephant problem remained unresolved, the more interest the developer had to pay for nothing. Still, simply killing the thing would have been out of the question. If it had been a spider monkey or a bat, they might have been able to get away with it, but the killing of an elephant would have been too hard to cover up, and if it ever came out afterward, the repercussions would have been tremendous. And so the various parties had met to deliberate on the matter, and they formulated an agreement on the disposition of the old elephant:

1. The town would take ownership of the elephant at no cost.

2. The developer would, without compensation, provide land for housing the elephant.

3. The zoo's former owners would be responsible for paying the keeper's wages.

I had had my own private interest in the elephant problem from the very outset, and I kept a scrapbook with every clipping I could find on it. I had even gone to hear the town council's debates on the matter, which is why I am able to give such a full and accurate account of the course of events. And while my account may prove somewhat lengthy, I have chosen to set it down here in case the handling of the elephant problem should bear directly upon the elephant's disappearance.

When the mayor finished negotiating the agreement—with its provision that the town would take charge of the elephant—a movement opposing the measure boiled up from within the ranks of the opposition party (whose very existence I had never imagined until then). 'Why must the town take ownership of the elephant?' they demanded of the mayor, and they raised the following points (sorry for all these lists, but I use them to make things easier to understand):

1. The elephant problem was a question for private enterprise— the zoo and the developer; there was no reason for the town to become involved.

2. Care and feeding costs would be too high.

3. What did the mayor intend to do about the security problem?

4. What merit would there be in the town's having its own elephant?

'The town has any number of responsibilities it should be taking care of before it gets into the business of keeping an elephant—sewer repair, the purchase of a new fire engine, etcetera,' the opposition group declared, and while they did not say it in so many words, they hinted at the possibility of some secret deal between the mayor and the developer.

In response, the mayor had this to say:

1. If the town permitted the construction of high-rise condos, its tax revenues would increase so dramatically that the cost of keeping an elephant would be insignificant by comparison; thus it made sense for the town to take on the care of this elephant.

2. The elephant was so old that it neither ate very much nor was likely to pose a danger to anyone.

3. When the elephant died, the town would take full possession of the land donated by the developer.

4. The elephant could become the town's symbol.

The long debate reached the conclusion that the town would take charge of the elephant after all. As an old, well-established residential suburb, the town boasted a relatively affluent citizenry, and its financial footing was sound. The adoption of a homeless elephant was a move that people could look upon favorably. People like old elephants better than sewers and fire engines.

I myself was all in favor of having the town care for the elephant. True, I was getting sick of high-rise condos, but I liked the idea of my town's owning an elephant.

A wooded area was cleared, and the elementary school's aging gym was moved there as an elephant house. The man who had served as the elephant's keeper for many years would come to live in the house with the elephant. The children's lunch scraps would serve as the elephant's feed. Finally, the elephant itself was carted in a trailer to its new home, there to live out its remaining years.

I joined the crowd at the elephant-house dedication ceremonies. Standing before the elephant, the mayor delivered a speech (on the town's development and the enrichment of its cultural facilities); one elementary-school pupil, representing the student body, stood up to read a composition ('Please live a long and healthy life, Mr Elephant'); there was a sketch contest (sketching the elephant thereafter became an integral component of the pupils' artistic education); and each of two young women in swaying dresses (neither of whom was especially good-looking) fed the elephant a bunch of bananas. The elephant endured these virtually meaningless (for the elephant, entirely meaningless) formalities with hardly a twitch, and it chomped on the bananas with a vacant stare. When it finished eating the bananas, everyone applauded.

On its right rear leg, the elephant wore a solid, heavy-looking steel cuff from which there stretched a thick chain perhaps thirty feet long, and this in turn was securely fastened to a concrete slab. Anyone could see what a sturdy anchor held the beast in place: The elephant could have struggled with all its might for a hundred years and never broken the thing.

I couldn't tell if the elephant was bothered by its shackle. On the surface, at least, it seemed all but unconscious of the enormous chunk of metal wrapped around its leg. It kept its blank gaze fixed on some indeterminate point in space, its ears and a few white hairs on its body waving gently in the breeze.

The elephant's keeper was a small, bony old man. It was hard to guess his age; he could have been in his early sixties or late seventies. He was one of those people whose appearance is no longer influenced by their age after they pass a certain point in life. His skin had the same darkly ruddy, sunburned look both summer and winter, his hair was stiff and short, his eyes were small. His face had no distinguishing characteristics, but his almost perfectly circular ears stuck out on either side with disturbing prominence.

He was not an unfriendly man. If someone spoke to him, he would reply, and he expressed himself clearly. If he wanted to he could be almost charming—though you always knew he was somewhat ill at ease. Generally, he remained a reticent, lonely-looking old man. He seemed to like the children who visited the elephant house, and he worked at being nice to them, but the children never really warmed to him.

The only one who did that was the elephant. The keeper lived in a small prefab room attached to the elephant house, and all day long he stayed with the elephant, attending to its needs. They had been together for more than ten years, and you could sense their closeness in every gesture and look. Whenever the elephant was standing there blankly and the keeper wanted it to move, all he had to do was stand next to the elephant, tap it on a front leg, and whisper something in its ear. Then, swaying its huge bulk, the elephant would go exactly where the keeper had indicated, take up its new position, and continue staring at a point in space.

On weekends, I would drop by the elephant house and study these operations, but I could never figure out the principle on which the keeper–elephant communication was based. Maybe the elephant understood a few simple words (it had certainly been living long enough), or perhaps it received its information through variations in the taps on its leg. Or possibly it had some special power resembling mental telepathy and could read the keeper's mind. I once asked the keeper how he gave his orders to the elephant, but the old man just smiled and said, 'We've been together a long time.'

And so a year went by. Then, without warning, the elephant vanished. One day it was there, and the next it had ceased to be.

I poured myself a second cup of coffee and read the story again from beginning to end. Actually, it was a pretty strange article—the kind that might excite Sherlock Holmes. 'Look at this, Watson,' he'd say, tapping his pipe. 'A very interesting article. Very interesting indeed.'

What gave the article its air of strangeness was the obvious confusion and bewilderment of the reporter. And this confusion and bewilderment clearly came from the absurdity of the situation itself. You could see how the reporter had struggled to find clever ways around the absurdity in order to write a 'normal' article. But the struggle had only driven his confusion and bewilderment to a hopeless extreme.

For example, the article used such expressions as 'the elephant escaped,' but if you looked at the entire piece it became obvious that the elephant had in no way 'escaped'. It had vanished into thin air. The reporter revealed his own conflicted state of mind by saying that a few 'details' remained 'unclear', but this was not a phenomenon that could be disposed of by using such ordinary terminology as 'details' or 'unclear', I felt.

First, there was the problem of the steel cuff that had been fastened to the elephant's leg. This had been found *still locked*. The most reasonable explanation for this would be that the keeper had unlocked the ring, removed it from the elephant's leg, *locked the ring again*, and run off with the elephant—a hypothesis to which the paper clung with desperate tenacity despite the fact that the keeper had no key! Only two keys existed, and they, for security's sake, were kept in locked safes, one in police headquarters and the other in the firehouse, both beyond the reach of the keeper—or of anyone else who might attempt to steal them. And even if someone had succeeded in stealing a key, there was no need whatever for that person to make a point of returning the key after using it. Yet the following morning both keys were found in their respective safes at the police and fire stations. Which brings us to the conclusion that the elephant pulled its leg out of that solid steel ring without the aid of a key—an absolute impossibility unless someone had sawed the foot off.

The second problem was the route of escape. The elephant house and grounds were surrounded by a massive fence nearly ten feet high. The question of security had been hotly debated in the town council, and the town had settled upon a system that might be considered somewhat excessive for keeping one old elephant. Heavy iron bars had been anchored in a thick concrete foundation (the cost of the fence was borne by the real-estate company), and there was only a single entrance, which was found locked from the inside. There was no way the elephant could have escaped from this fortresslike enclosure.

The third problem was elephant tracks. Directly behind the elephant enclosure was a steep hill, which the animal could not possibly have climbed, so even if we suppose that the elephant had somehow managed to pull its leg out of the steel ring and leap over the ten-foot-high fence, it would still have had to escape down the path to the front of the enclosure, and there was not a single mark anywhere in the soft earth of that path that could be seen as an elephant's footprint.

Riddled as it was with such perplexities and labored circumlocutions, the newspaper article as a whole left but one possible conclusion: The elephant had not escaped. It had vanished.

Needless to say, however, neither the newspaper nor the police nor the mayor was willing to admit—openly, at least—that the elephant had vanished. The police were continuing to investigate, their spokesman saying only that the elephant either 'was taken or was allowed to escape in a clever, deliberately calculated move. Because of the difficulty involved in hiding an elephant, it is only a matter of time till we solve the case.' To this optimistic assessment he added that they were planning to search the woods in the area with the aid of local hunters' clubs and sharpshooters from the national Self-Defense Force.

The mayor had held a news conference, in which he apologized for the inadequacy of the town's police resources. At the same time, he declared, 'Our elephant-security system is in no way inferior to similar facilities in any zoo in the country. Indeed, it is far stronger and far more fail-safe than the standard cage.' He also observed, 'This is a dangerous and senseless anti-social act of the most malicious kind, and we cannot allow it to go unpunished.'

As they had the year before, the opposition-party members of the town council made accusations. 'We intend to look into the political responsibility of the mayor; he has colluded with private enterprise in order to sell the townspeople a bill of goods on the solution of the elephant problem.'

One 'worried-looking' mother, thirty-seven, was interviewed by the paper. 'Now I'm afraid to let my children out to play,' she said.

The coverage included a detailed summary of the steps leading to the town's decision to adopt the elephant, an aerial sketch of the elephant house and grounds, and brief histories of both the elephant and the keeper who had vanished with it. The man, Noboru Watanabe, sixty-three, was from Tateyama, in Chiba Prefecture. He had worked for many years as a keeper in the mammalian section of the zoo, and 'had the complete trust of the zoo authorities, both for his abundant knowledge of these animals and for his warm sincere personality'. The elephant had been sent from East Africa twenty-two years earlier, but little was known about its exact age or its 'personality'. The report concluded with a request from the police for citizens of the town to come forward with any information they might have regarding the elephant.

I thought about this request for a while as I drank my second cup of coffee, but I decided not to call the police—both because I preferred not to come into contact with them if I could help it and because I felt the police would not believe what I had to tell them. What good would it do to talk to people like that, who would not even consider the possibility that the elephant had simply vanished?

I took my scrapbook down from the shelf, cut out the elephant article, and pasted it in. Then I washed the dishes and left for the office.

I watched the search on the seven o'clock news. There were hunters carrying large-bore rifles loaded with tranquilizer darts, Self-Defense Force troops, policemen, and firemen combing every square inch of the woods and hills in the immediate area as helicopters hovered overhead. Of course, we're talking about the kind of 'woods' and 'hills' you find in the suburbs outside Tokyo, so they didn't have an enormous area to cover. With that many people involved, a day should have been more than enough to do the job. And they weren't searching for some tiny homicidal maniac: They were after a huge African elephant. There was a limit to the number of places a thing like that could hide. But still they had not managed to find it. The chief of police appeared on the screen, saying, 'We intend to continue the search.' And the anchorman concluded the report, 'Who released the elephant, and how? Where have they hidden it? What was their motive? Everything remains shrouded in mystery.'

The search went on for several days, but the authorities were unable to discover a single clue to the elephant's whereabouts. I studied the newspaper reports, clipped them all, and pasted them in my scrapbook—including editorial cartoons on the subject. The album filled up quickly, and I had to buy another. Despite their enormous volume, the clippings contained not one fact of the kind that I was looking for. The reports were either pointless or off the mark: ELEPHANT STILL MISSING, GLOOM THICK IN SEARCH HQ, MOB BEHIND DISAPPEARANCE? And even articles like this became noticeably scarcer after a week had gone by, until there was virtually nothing. A few of the weekly magazines carried sensational stories—one even hired a psychic—but they had nothing to substantiate their wild headlines. It seemed that people were beginning to shove the elephant case into the large category of 'unsolvable mysteries'. The disappearance of one old elephant and one old elephant keeper would have no impact on the course of society. The earth would continue its monotonous rotations, politicians would continue issuing unreliable proclamations, people would continue yawning on their way to the office, children would continue studying for their college-entrance exams. Amid the endless surge and ebb of everyday life, interest in a missing elephant could not last forever. And so a number of unremarkable months went by, like a tired army marching past a window.

Whenever I had a spare moment, I would visit the house where the elephant no longer lived. A thick chain had been wrapped round and round the bars of the yard's iron gate, to keep people out. Peering inside, I could see that the elephant-house door had also been chained and locked, as though the police were trying to make up for having failed to find the elephant by multiplying the layers of security on the now-empty elephant house. The area was deserted, the previous crowds having been replaced by a flock of pigeons resting on the roof. No one took care of the grounds any longer, and thick green summer grass had sprung up there as if it had been waiting for this opportunity. The chain coiled around the door of the elephant house reminded me of a huge snake set to guard a ruined palace in a thick forest. A few short months without its elephant had given the place an air of doom and desolation that hung there like a huge, oppressive rain cloud.

I met her near the end of September. It had been raining that day from morning to night—the kind of soft, monotonous, misty rain that often falls at that time of year, washing away bit by bit the memories of summer burned into the earth. Coursing down the gutters, all those memories flowed into the sewers and rivers, to be carried to the deep, dark ocean.

We noticed each other at the party my company threw to launch its new advertising campaign. I work for the PR section of a major

manufacturer of electrical appliances, and at the time I was in charge
of publicity for a co-ordinated line of kitchen equipment, which was
scheduled to go on the market in time for the autumn-wedding and
winter-bonus seasons. My job was to negotiate with several women's magazines for tie-in articles—not the kind of work that takes
a great deal of intelligence, but I had to see to it that the articles they
wrote didn't smack of advertising. When magazines gave us publicity, we rewarded them by placing ads in their pages. They scratched
our backs, we scratched theirs.

As an editor of a magazine for young housewives, she had come
to the party for material for one of these 'articles'. I happened to be
in charge of showing her around, pointing out the features of the
colorful refrigerators and coffeemakers and microwave ovens and
juicers that a famous Italian designer had done for us.

'The most important point is unity,' I explained. 'Even the most
beautifully designed item dies if it is out of balance with its surroundings. Unity of design, unity of color, unity of function: This is
what today's *kit-chin* needs above all else. Research tells us that a
housewife spends the largest part of her day in the *kit-chin*. The *kit-
chin* is her workplace, her study, her living room. Which is why she
does all she can to make the *kit-chin* a pleasant place to be. It has
nothing to do with size. Whether it's large or small, one fundamen-
tal principle governs every successful *kit-chin*, and that principle is
unity. This is the concept underlying the design of our new series.
Look at this cooktop, for example. . . .'

She nodded and scribbled things in a small notebook, but it was
obvious that she had little interest in the material, nor did I have any
personal stake in our new cooktop. Both of us were doing our jobs.

'You know a lot about kitchens,' she said when I finished. She
used the Japanese word, without picking up on '*kit-chin*'.

'That's what I do for a living,' I answered with a professional
smile. 'Aside from that, though, I do like to cook. Nothing fancy,
but I cook for myself every day.'

'Still, I wonder if unity is all that necessary for a kitchen.'

'We say "*kit-chin*",' I advised her. 'No big deal, but the company
wants us to use the English.'

'Oh. Sorry. But still, I wonder. Is unity so important for a *kit-chin*?
What do *you* think?'

'My personal opinion? That doesn't come out until I take my
necktie off,' I said with a grin. 'But today I'll make an exception.

A kitchen probably *does* need a few things more than it needs unity. But those other elements are things you can't sell. And in this pragmatic world of ours, things you can't sell don't count for much.'

'*Is* the world such a pragmatic place?'

I took out a cigarette and lit it with my lighter.

'I don't know—the word just popped out,' I said. 'But it explains a lot. It makes work easier, too. You can play games with it, make up neat expressions: "essentially pragmatic", or "pragmatic in essence". If you look at things that way, you avoid all kinds of complicated problems.'

'What an interesting view!'

'Not really. It's what everybody thinks. Oh, by the way, we've got some pretty good champagne. Care to have some?'

'Thanks. I'd love to.'

As we chatted over champagne, we realized we had several mutual acquaintances. Since our part of the business world was not a very big pond, if you tossed in a few pebbles, one or two were bound to hit a mutual acquaintance. In addition, she and my kid sister happened to have graduated from the same university. With markers like this to follow, our conversation went along smoothly.

She was unmarried, and so was I. She was twenty-six, and I was thirty-one. She wore contact lenses, and I wore glasses. She praised my necktie, and I praised her jacket. We compared rents and complained about our jobs and salaries. In other words, we were beginning to like each other. She was an attractive woman, and not at all pushy. I stood there talking with her for a full twenty minutes, unable to discover a single reason not to think well of her.

As the party was breaking up, I invited her to join me in the hotel's cocktail lounge, where we settled in to continue our conversation. A soundless rain went on falling outside the lounge's panoramic window, the lights of the city sending blurry messages through the mist. A damp hush held sway over the nearly empty cocktail lounge. She ordered a frozen daiquiri and I had a Scotch on the rocks.

Sipping our drinks, we carried on the kind of conversation that a man and woman have in a bar when they have just met and are beginning to like each other. We talked about our college days, our tastes in music, sports, our daily routines.

Then I told her about the elephant. Exactly how this happened, I can't recall. Maybe we were talking about something having to do with animals, and that was the connection. Or maybe, unconsciously, I had been looking for someone—a good listener—to whom I could present my own, unique view on the elephant's disappearance. Or, then again, it might have been the liquor that got me talking.

In any case, the second the words left my mouth, I knew that I had brought up one of the least suitable topics I could have found for this occasion. No, I should never have mentioned the elephant. The topic was—what?—too complete, too closed.

I tried to hurry on to something else, but as luck would have it she was more interested than most in the case of the vanishing elephant, and once I admitted that I had seen the elephant many times she showered me with questions—what kind of elephant was it, how did I think it had escaped, what did it eat, wasn't it a danger to the community, and so forth.

I told her nothing more than what everybody knew from the news, but she seemed to sense constraint in my tone of voice. I had never been good at telling lies.

As if she had not noticed anything strange about my behavior, she sipped her second daiquiri and asked, 'Weren't you shocked when the elephant disappeared? It's not the kind of thing that somebody could have predicted.'

'No, probably not,' I said. I took a pretzel from the mound in the glass dish on our table, snapped it in two, and ate half. The waiter replaced our ashtray with an empty one.

She looked at me expectantly. I took out another cigarette and lit it. I had quit smoking three years earlier but had begun again when the elephant disappeared.

'Why "probably not"? You mean you could have predicted it?'

'No, of course I couldn't have predicted it,' I said with a smile. 'For an elephant to disappear all of a sudden one day—there's no precedent, no need, for such a thing to happen. It doesn't make any logical sense.'

'But still, your answer was very strange. When I said, "It's not the kind of thing that somebody could have predicted," you said, "No, probably not." Most people would have said, "You're right," or "Yeah, it's weird," or something. See what I mean?'

I sent a vague nod in her direction and raised my hand to call the waiter. A kind of tentative silence took hold as I waited for him to bring me my next Scotch.

'I'm finding this a little hard to grasp,' she said softly. 'You were

carrying on a perfectly normal conversation with me until a couple
of minutes ago—at least until the subject of the elephant came up.
Then something funny happened. I can't understand you anymore.
Something's wrong. Is it the elephant? Or are my ears playing tricks
on me?'

'There's nothing wrong with your ears,' I said.

'So then it's you. The problem's with you.'

I stuck my finger in my glass and stirred the ice. I like the sound
of ice in a whiskey glass.

'I wouldn't call it a "problem", exactly. It's not that big a deal.
I'm not hiding anything. I'm just not sure I can talk about it very
well, so I'm trying not to say anything at all. But you're right—it's
very strange.'

'What do you mean?'

It was no use: I'd have to tell her the story. I took one gulp of
whiskey and started.

'The thing is, I was probably the last one to see the elephant
before it disappeared. I saw it after seven o'clock on the evening of
May seventeenth, and they noticed it was gone on the afternoon of
the eighteenth. Nobody saw it in between because they lock the
elephant house at six.'

'I don't get it. If they closed the house at six, how did you see it
after seven?'

'There's a kind of cliff behind the elephant house. A steep hill on
private property, with no real roads. There's one spot, on the back
of the hill, where you can see into the elephant house. I'm probably
the only one who knows about it.'

I had found the spot purely by chance. Strolling through the area
one Sunday afternoon, I had lost my way and come out at the top
of the cliff. I found a little flat open patch, just big enough for a
person to stretch out in, and when I looked down through the
bushes, there was the elephant-house roof. Below the edge of the
roof was a fairly large vent opening, and through it I had a clear
view of the inside of the elephant house.

I made it a habit after that to visit the place every now and then
to look at the elephant when it was inside the house. If anyone had
asked me why I bothered doing such a thing, I wouldn't have had
a decent answer. I simply enjoyed watching the elephant during its
private time. There was nothing more to it than that. I couldn't see
the elephant when the house was dark inside, of course, but in the

early hours of the evening the keeper would have the lights on the whole time he was taking care of the elephant, which enabled me to study the scene in detail.

What struck me immediately when I saw the elephant and keeper alone together was the obvious liking they had for each other—something they never displayed when they were out before the public. Their affection was evident in every gesture. It almost seemed as if they stored away their emotions during the day, taking care not to let anyone notice them, and took them out at night when they could be alone. Which is not to say that they did anything different when they were by themselves inside. The elephant just stood there, as blank as ever, and the keeper would perform those tasks one would normally expect him to do as a keeper: scrubbing down the elephant with a deck broom, picking up the elephant's enormous droppings, cleaning up after the elephant ate. But there was no way to mistake the special warmth, the sense of trust, between them. While the keeper swept the floor, the elephant would wave its trunk and pat the keeper's back. I liked to watch the elephant doing that.

'Have you always been fond of elephants?' she asked. 'I mean, not just that particular elephant?'

'Hmm . . . come to think of it, I do like elephants,' I said. 'There's something about them that excites me. I guess I've always liked them. I wonder why.'

'And that day, too after the sun went down, I suppose you were up on the hill by yourself, looking at the elephant. May—what day was it?'

'The seventeenth. May seventeenth at seven p.m. The days were already very long by then, and the sky had a reddish glow, but the lights were on in the elephant house.'

'And was there anything unusual about the elephant or the keeper?'

'Well, there was and there wasn't. I can't say exactly. It's not as if they were standing right in front of me. I'm probably not the most reliable witness.'

'What did happen, exactly?'

I took a swallow of my now somewhat watery Scotch. The rain outside the windows was still coming down, no stronger or weaker than before, a static element in a landscape that would never change.

'Nothing happened, really. The elephant and the keeper were

doing what they always did—cleaning, eating, playing around with each other in that friendly way of theirs. It wasn't what they *did* that was different. It's the way they looked. Something about the balance between them.'

'The balance?'

'In size. Of their bodies. The elephant's and the keeper's. The balance seemed to have changed somewhat. I had the feeling that to some extent the difference between them had shrunk.'

She kept her gaze fixed on her daiquiri glass for a time. I could see that the ice had melted and that the water was working its way through the cocktail like a tiny ocean current.

'Meaning that the elephant had gotten smaller?'

'Or the keeper had gotten bigger. Or both simultaneously.'

'And you didn't tell this to the police?'

'No, of course not,' I said. 'I'm sure they wouldn't have believed me. And if I had told them I was watching the elephant from the cliff at a time like that, I'd have ended up as their number one suspect.'

'Still, are you *certain* that the balance between them had changed?'

'Probably. I can only say "probably". I don't have any proof, and as I keep saying, I was looking at them through the air vent. But I had looked at them like that I don't know how many times before, so it's hard for me to believe that I could make a mistake about something as basic as the relation of their sizes.'

In fact, I had wondered at the time whether my eyes were playing tricks on me. I had tried closing and opening them and shaking my head, but the elephant's size remained the same. It definitely looked as if it had shrunk—so much so that at first I thought the town might have got hold of a new, smaller elephant. But I hadn't heard anything to that effect, and I would never have missed any news reports about elephants. If this was not a new elephant, the only possible conclusion was that the old elephant had, for one reason or another, shrunk. As I watched, it became obvious to me that this smaller elephant had all the same gestures as the old one. It would stamp happily on the ground with its right foot while it was being washed, and with its now somewhat narrower trunk it would pat the keeper on the back.

It was a mysterious sight. Looking through the vent, I had the feeling that a different, chilling kind of time was flowing through the elephant house—but nowhere else. And it seemed to me, too, that the elephant and the keeper were gladly giving themselves over to this new order that was trying to envelop them—or that had already partially succeeded in enveloping them.

Altogether, I was probably watching the scene in the elephant house for less than a half hour. The lights went out at seven-thirty—much earlier than usual—and from that point on, everything was wrapped in darkness. I waited in my spot, hoping that the lights would go on again, but they never did. That was the last I saw of the elephant.

'So, then, you believe that the elephant kept shrinking until it was small enough to escape through the bars, or else that it simply dissolved into nothingness. Is that it?'

'I don't know,' I said. 'All I'm trying to do is recall what I saw with my own eyes, as accurately as possible. I'm hardly thinking about what happened after that. The visual image I have is so strong that, to be honest, it's practically impossible for me to go beyond it.'

That was all I could say about the elephant's disappearance. And just as I had feared, the story of the elephant was too particular, too complete in itself, to work as a topic of conversation between a young man and woman who had just met. A silence descended upon us after I had finished my tale. What subject could either of us bring up after a story about an elephant that had vanished—a story that offered virtually no openings for further discussion? She ran her finger around the edge of her cocktail glass, and I sat there reading and rereading the words stamped on my coaster. I never should have told her about the elephant. It was not the kind of story you could tell freely to anyone.

'When I was a little girl, our cat disappeared,' she offered after a long silence. 'But still, for a cat to disappear and for an elephant to disappear—those are two different stories.'

'Yeah, really. There's no comparison. Think of the size difference.'

Thirty minutes later, we were saying good-bye outside the hotel. She suddenly remembered that she had left her umbrella in the cocktail lounge, so I went up in the elevator and brought it down to her. It was a brick-red umbrella with a large handle.

'Thanks,' she said.

'Good night,' I said.

That was the last time I saw her. We talked once on the phone after that, about some details in her tie-in article. While we spoke,

I thought seriously about inviting her out for dinner, but I ended up not doing it. It just didn't seem to matter one way or the other.

I felt like this a lot after my experience with the vanishing elephant. I would begin to think I wanted to do something, but then I would become incapable of distinguishing between the probable results of doing it and of not doing it. I often get the feeling that things around me have lost their proper balance, though it could be that my perceptions are playing tricks on me. Some kind of balance inside me has broken down since the elephant affair, and maybe that causes external phenomena to strike my eye in a strange way. It's probably something in me.

I continue to sell refrigerators and toaster ovens and coffeemakers in the pragmatic world, based on after-images of memories I retain from that world. The more pragmatic I try to become, the more successfully I sell—our campaign has succeeded beyond our most optimistic forecasts—and the more people I succeed in selling myself to. That's probably because people are looking for a kind of unity in this *kit-chin* we know as the world. Unity of design. Unity of color. Unity of function.

The papers print almost nothing about the elephant anymore. People seem to have forgotten that their town once owned an elephant. The grass that took over the elephant enclosure has withered now, and the area has the feel of winter.

The elephant and keeper have vanished completely. They will never be coming back.

SHIMADA MASAHIKO (1961–   )

DESERT DOLPHIN

Translated by Kenneth L. Richard

A full moon, frigid and arousing. A night bright enough to outline
every red drop of blood rain. The astral clock marks midnight; I am
fatigued, my spirit a dank, dark forest. I have no definite memory of
what I have been doing, where I have been wandering, or even
which day or month it might be. I remember looking back up at the
moon, and the full orb of it sticking out a mauve, ashen tongue. I
am without family or ancestry. My past is nearly extinct. I recollect
meeting someone for the first time though it feels as though I have
known him forever, and on we talk until my voice grows hoarse.

'It's your turn to sing. Pick something.'
    Crooning to the karaoke, one hand in his pocket until this
moment, a middle-aged man now reaches over to tap the shoulder
of another man who perches alone on the next bar stool. The latter
sits rigidly erect, wearing a gray suit and a necktie with a pattern of
blue roses. His pallor makes his age indiscernible; he looks bewildered, as though he has been inadvertently snatched from a wonder-
world beyond the looking-glass and plunked down without warning
in this fetid karaoke bar.
    'I don't know. It's something about his eyes. Round like a puppy
dog's,' the middle-aged man's lady friend whispers, her voice as
fidgety as her body. The man's limpid eyes turn into flies, darting
here and there, alighting on nothing.
    'By the way, how long have you been sitting here? I'm a little
drunk. I didn't even notice you. Sing. Come on.' The words lolling
on the tip of her tongue, the long-haired woman nestles seductively
against the shoulder of the man who might be her lover, or her boss,
as though to make a pass at the unknown quantity with the puppy-
dog eyes. 'I know you from somewhere, but where? It was dark.
That's all I remember.'

Her shrill voice so grates on my ears that I turn around, intending to yell something offensive in response. And just then his big, round eyes meet mine. He seems somehow comfortable to me, familiar. His face is a strangely fascinating male version of a former lover's, which calls up feelings of anger, even embarrassment. At least this is my first impression. In fact, he was beginning his life on Earth the same way I had almost ten years earlier, blundering into this unknown cipher of a place, not letting on that there was anything out of the ordinary. My senses are so dulled by my long stretch of earth-bound existence that I am unable, at first glance, to penetrate his real identity. Had it not been for his song, we could have parted forever without having realized that we were of the same breed.

Puppy-dog Eyes suddenly looks ceiling-ward and begins to sing without a mike or recorded accompaniment. The melody is totally unfamiliar, yet everyone is drawn to it. So sweet is his voice that it plays on our senses as though plucking on the strings of a harp. Who would dream of hearing music fit for an opera house in a backwater bar? Heads cocked, we sit there in a state of acute aphasia, stunned by the song, the language, by the unknown nature of the singer. We have, without a doubt, had a wondrous aural experience, but I, for one, have no immediate realization of what has happened. I know only that my physical reaction precedes the mental. His voice reverberates to the depths of my organs, mainlining from my joints through my arteries, arousing a sensation that I have experienced before, but that now lies buried somewhere just beneath the deepest layer of my memory.

It has been ten years. Never would I have believed it! Not here! Instantly I am relieved of the tons of lead weights stuffed into every nook and cranny of my body. Instinctively, I grip the counter top. Otherwise, I feel, my body will burst through the roof of the bar and dance up into the sky.

'Something the matter?'

The madam behind the bar looks at me, smiling. I wouldn't expect you to understand, but, you see, I used to be able to fly. I circumnavigated Heaven with more skill than a sparrow, outflew even an F-14. And then ten years ago I was tried in the high court and exiled to Earth. Lead weights equivalent to the weight of ten trucks filled with gravel were forced down my throat until they glued themselves to my flesh. Then I was summarily pushed over the edge of the executioner's scaffold in the cumuli. I suspect the same thing has happened to him. The proof lies in the bumbershoot he is carrying even though there has been no rain. We are issued large umbrellas instead of parachutes, you see, and he had drifted down this very day and landed at a random spot on Earth. These are the days of our births. And me, I came into the world as a middle-aged man without a past.

'What a beauty of a voice! Never seen anyone here who can sing like that!'

The madam's words bring us out of our reverie. We applaud amid murmurs of 'Can't beat that!' and 'Is that what they call a Gregorian chant?'

I sit next to the man and buy him a whisky, thinking of how to get to the point. I am so overwhelmed the words stick in my throat. 'It hasn't been long since the set-down, has it? I knew it right away from the way you sang.'

'Incredible. How did you know?'

'My appearance has changed completely in the ten years I've been here. Don't let the way I look fool you. We're the same kind. You still have the aura of the other side about you.'

'I touched down just a while ago nearby, right in the middle of a bunch of people waiting in line.'

'You must mean the taxi-stand in front of the station. What brought you to this bar?'

'I walked due south until I just bumped into it. I mean, I still haven't a clue what I've become. Lucky for me to run into a veteran.'

From the moment we land, we take on the look of earthlings. In our original state, we are not put together in what you call a shape, so what we look like has a great deal to do with the earthlings who happen to be at the landing spot. We're what you'd call a mixed bag. He, for example, took on the average size, age, and height of those earthlings in the vicinity of the taxi-stand. His puppy-dog eyes are probably the by-product of a child or a dog among the sampling. Then again, I had puppy-dog eyes even before I was tinged by life on Earth.

When we touch down on Earth, we exiles are given the language as well as the shape of earthlings. Thenceforth, with these attributes as our only lifeline, we are obliged, above all else, to accommodate to earthly culture. Any special privileges we had in the other world are of no use here; our native intelligence dwindles until, in the end, it dies. Our innate bad habits, however, do not fade as easily. Intensely curious, we stick our noses into other people's affairs, committing to memory what is false as well as what is true, wandering the face of the earth with nothing better to do. And then, in a fleeting moment, we remember, you know, that once we were angels. It might be easier if we could just forget and get on with our lives.

'I'm an old-timer, yes, but I don't think I have any real advice to give you. That beautiful voice of yours may crack and the melody you sing may go flat, I fear. What you must do, at all costs, while you still have faculties left from the other life, is to decide on what you will do to stave off the eventual decay. At worst, you could end up being an average mortal.'

From the other side of the bar the madam grins, no longer able to conceal her utter astonishment. What's the matter, dear, don't you find our little joke amusing? I think to myself.

'I'd like to have a word with you alone.'

As I make my wish clear, the woman to his side with the shrieking voice begins to sing in a manner somewhere between a scream and a yelp of selfish delight. As we leave the bar, the madam turns and teases: 'Birds of a feather.'

Outside, the sound of bottles smashing, the whirr of taxis racing in low gear along narrow streets, the chorus of electronic beeps pouring from a video arcade, the laughter of a group of pub-crawlers, everyone making a noise, everyone a street urchin making sounds nobody cares to listen to. . . .

'Noisy place, isn't it, the world?'

'Not necessarily. It was pretty much the same in Heaven.'

'I wonder. Surely Heaven has a better sense of harmony, nothing near the random racket of Earth.'

'My ears must be deceiving me. These earthly sounds of yours are like beautiful chords.'

The din of the streets, a beautiful chord? He must be hearing the sounds of Earth with his heavenly apparatus intact, because in such ears even noise sounds like harmony. I had, without doubt, acquired a set of earthly ears. Were I to be allowed the sweet sounds of Heaven in my current state, I would complain that I had heard nothing of the ethereal melody. And why not? Heaven's music must fall as noise on earthly ears.

The line at the taxi-stand actively metabolizes and within five minutes we are in a car heading in the direction of my roost.

'Let me put you up tonight. I've got a million things you need to hear.'

'Asking as a young man to his mentor, what sort of earthling have you become?'

'Well, you might say I'm a loafer.'

As it speeds away from the city center, the taxi crosses several suspension bridges that look like strips pinched up from the Earth's skin, swerving past the cars ahead as though beset with a case of hiccups. Twenty minutes later, we stop just within the shadow of a huge wall.

'What's that?'

'The local residents call it Battleship Condo. My roost is lashed to the uppermost level, the twenty-first story.'

Like a scorpion who lives in a hole of one centimeter in diameter bored into the sands of a vast desert, all earthlings build boxes in which to live. At an appointed hour they leave the box, only to unfailingly return again. I can't help but feel sympathy for the likes of these creatures who toil without the slightest complaint about their lack of freedom. But now I share their lot. I shall live to the end of my days in the midst of the boredom of things repeating *ad nauseam*. When I first arrived from Heaven, I thought repetition was a torture to which I had been sentenced. The life of earthlings, from the standpoint of Heaven, seems like a factory grinding out suffering. A vicious, evil cycle! And yet, for a brief moment asleep in their coops, earthlings get a taste of Heaven.

'Hidden away in a tiny spot like this?' he remarks as soon as we enter the room.

'It's my home. In fact, it's on the luxurious side. There was a time when I slept in cardboard boxes. Do you know what a dream is? It's a phenomenon that can happen only on Earth, but it's the closest thing to Heaven earthlings can experience. It is the one time they can escape the vicious cycle that is Earth. This room is a place for dreaming. When earthlings dream, they are as free as air, yet with a purpose. Occasionally, they run into trouble. What you must do is build up a reserve of energy to face your next day of life on Earth.

From here on, you will be subjected to the ordeal of grappling with gravity.'

'I can certainly see your point. You know, this gravity thing is very tiring. I'm amazed at how they stand up to it.'

'They get tired too. It takes an awful lot of energy to go against gravity. This is why at night they return home to sleep—to forget about the rules of the Earth, to be angels that live in dreams, to fly away.'

I change into a dressing-gown, and loan him a sweat-shirt and trousers. I take a bottle of champagne from the refrigerator, open the window to the veranda, and pop the cork in an orgasmic burst. Filling the glasses to the brim with the bubbly champagne, I offer one to him. I raise the stem of my glass with my hand and gaze at the night sky through the effervescence.

'Look. The champagne bubbles turn into stars.'

'Strange effect this drink has. Ah, it's a full moon tonight.'

'Is it? Can you see all our friends falling?'

As we laugh, we look at each other squarely, searching for whatever trace remains of our angel natures.

'How old are you?'

'Forty-one. I fell into a group of middle-aged men and that was it. How old are you? Do you have a name yet?'

'No. I don't have an age, a name, or a nationality.'

'Be very careful when you choose. Once you've decided, you can't change it.'

'Do I have to decide for myself?'

'Of course. In most cases, no veteran is around to give advice. What sort of earthling do you want to be?'

'Anybody, as long as I have my music.'

'I might have known. You should make music your career. With your ear and your voice, you can't fail. Didn't you see how they reacted to you in the bar? Music, and dreaming, are the ties that bind Heaven and Earth.'

'To tell you the truth, I arranged my own fall. I wanted to hear what sort of sounds there were on Earth with my own ears.'

'Looking at the world through rose-colored glasses will get you nowhere.'

At heart I am half-frightened, half-astonished, that one of us would choose to come down to the planet to pursue some secret agenda. So he hadn't committed a crime, and his exile was his own idea of tourism and travel. Times had changed. I felt discredited. After all, I had been reduced to an earthling even while I was in Heaven. Once an angel without form, without a past, without age or name, is invested with a will and a memory and then sets to mouthing off in rational terms, well then, his angeldom ceases. Angels don't make pronouncements, they sing; they don't have regrets, they just are. The truth of the universe stems from a host of sounds, forms, lights, materials, and emanations, not to mention relativity. When one uses reason to discuss these things, their harmony suddenly collapses and chaos ensues. Evil spirits are the servants of chaos. An angel who, by his own will, lets those evil spirits in, will lose his freedom and can no longer live in exact accordance with the truth of the universe. This truth is so complex that it cannot be explained by angels or by God. That is why there is no other recourse than for angels and God to live as one with the universe. There is no time to waste on will or memory. An angel with a will or a memory is sick. Even God, in the same position, would go mad. God never makes pronouncements about truth; God is God precisely because the divine's position is to admonish those who make pronouncements. By the way, I have never heard the voice nor seen the shape of God. I've no interest in such things. It's fair to say that Heaven has a logic, and that logic deals with the satanic; to wit, Heaven was carved from the bitter experience of exorcising cycles of evil.

Earthlings sometimes ask, 'What is Heaven, anyway?'

A ridiculous question such as this requires an answer in a language even they can understand: 'It's like a sea. Angels are like dolphins who can't swim.'

It has been more my nature to be a terrestrial specialist in heavenly matters than to be a heavenly dolphin. The distance between Heaven and Earth is much shorter than it used to be, which may account for the appearance of one like myself. I understand the number of recently fallen angels is twenty times that of the Middle Ages. There are even some, I see, who take the plunge for the adventure of it.

From the moment I handed over my angelic abilities to the devil for cash, my life in Heaven became unbearably boring. I found myself wanting only to reformulate the truth of the universe through my own will and experience. What did I care whether this might be a mistake or a false premise? Quite the contrary. I felt that God and the angels would sit up and take notice of such a terrestrial, even demonic exegesis. I wanted to prove to them that it was arrogant to believe that the truth of the universe was immutable. This was the only way I could repay my debt to God. I did an excellent job of translating the truth of the universe using the terms of terrestrial logic. What I mean is that in Heaven I did a great service to earthlings through my exemplary instruction. And when I did make it down to Earth, I was finally able to come into my own as a teacher. In this sense, perhaps, I owe thanks to the grace of God for having been thrown out of Heaven.

Yet, the more logical my pronouncements, the less I was able to break down the walls of misunderstanding. Leading earthlings towards the truth was a hopeless task. The answer lay in identification, not in logic. Identification requires that one put oneself in the same position as the object of study. It took me five years to come to the realization that a fallen angel's work was not to enlighten, but to build a place where we could coexist—not through logic or through shows of competitive strength, but by constructing an imitation Heaven on Earth.

He may have been driven by curiosity to descend to the Earth, but I had no less curiosity than he. And I had a much more pronounced sense of mission. My many years involved in terrestrial research while in Heaven drew me to a final conclusion.

Sooner or later, Heaven falls to Earth.

I drag the shackles of gravity for this treasonous conviction of mine. Needless to say, this is a life sentence. The only way to lighten the sentence is to strive to become a superior earthling. The superior earthling is one who will hasten Heaven's fall.

'Are you okay?' he broke in. 'You seem sunk in thought.'

'Drink up. Alcohol is a liquid the more of which you drink, the more changed you become.'

'I see. You mean I should drink whenever I want to change myself into some other type of earthling. Point taken. I want to hear more about when you first landed on Earth.'

I close the window, sink deeply into the sofa, and shut my eyes. I came down to Earth on a night of a crescent moon. I remember the two horns of the crescent being painfully sharp.

'I didn't fall as you did, into the midst of an urban crowd. I landed in a completely unpopulated and nondescript bunch of scraggy trees, and clung like a spider-web to a branch, waiting for the earthlings to appear. One month and ten days passed. As you might imagine, I got cramps, but luckily I was not impatient. I found out later that I had been on a deserted island inhabited only by wild deer and monkeys. I was on the verge of becoming either a monkey or a deer. Had I fallen into the sea, I would have become one of the dolphins frolicking in the vicinity. When I think I almost became a dolphin! Dolphins are anathema to fishermen in that area. You see, they eat the same fish and squid as earthlings. With my luck, I would have been harpooned. Whereas dolphins in one culture may be the messengers of God, in Japan they're called "sea pigs". What I did was to jump into a fishing-boat that passed near the deserted island, and become a fisherman. There on the deck, mixed in with the freshly caught squid and sea bream, three dolphins lay covered in blood. It was horrible, like witnessing the remains of angels fallen into the sea. And here I was turning into the type of earthling who harpooned my former buddies.'

'Pretty ironic.'

'Don't be too smug. You were lucky, that's all.'

The boat that had left port with only four men returned with five fishermen on board, but neither the townspeople nor the fishermen questioned my presence. I had become, all of a sudden, a middle-aged man whom the village women called Umihiko, Prince of the Sea. I was forty-one then. Ten years later I am still forty-one. I shall be forty-one until I die.

'My lot was to be a single fisherman who took his lodgings in a local boarding-house. It's a stroke of luck you happened to alight in a crowd of complete strangers, so you have no name or occupation. I'd say you had no time to dawdle over what might be suitable. But you must be someone and the sooner the better.'

'I guess I'm very lucky.'

'Absolutely. You're no one and, best of all, you're young.'

I passed two months as Umihiko, renowned squid fisherman. I was, however, unable to slaughter dolphins. In time, I left the fishing village and wandered in search of a place where more earthlings gather. I had nothing in mind, no personal preferences. Had I been eighteen, it would have been a different matter, but how was an eternally middle-aged man to play the role of a dream-besotted youth? I wandered the streets, the image incarnate of either a homeless vagrant or an amnesiac. Policemen frequently questioned me about my occupation and I gave them my usual cover, which was that I was a migrant fisherman seeking work in the off-season.

I soon ran out of money and went to work for a transport company. With a body forged like armor by the fisherman's life, I was able to take on the physical labor of two men. As luck would have it, the transport company paid wages according to the number of packages carted. I was faithful to the earthly idea that laziness is the worst of sins. A sense of earthly enlightenment had not yet dawned on me, and so, with a sense of empty futility, I worked thirteen hours a day and made a hefty monthly salary. This was infinitely better than having to make a living murdering dolphins who might have been other fallen angels.

'Do you know what I mean by the word "money"? On Earth it is the most important thing after life itself.'

'You mean the printed paper with the faces and numbers that you can change for anything.'

'Correct. It has no value of its own, but it has the power to move earthlings to kill, to drive someone mad even. And no one is free from its want. When you have money, people credit you with any number of values, and your bonds to them are strong. What passes for a concept of love in Heaven is covered by the term "money" on Earth. I once thought that nothing could surpass becoming a wealthy man.'

I came to Tokyo a year later and investigated how money circulates. This is because I believed that understanding the money flow would instantly reveal the structure of the terrestrial world. I studied economics, sought work in places where money was most likely to be made and spent, jumping from job to job in securities, insurance, advertising, and so on. My white-collar period continued for the next five years. I may be fallen, but I was once an angel, so I far surpassed earthlings in the speed and sharpened response with which I adapted to the job. Wherever I worked I was known for being shrewd. I began by appearing to be one of the chronically unemployed, just pecking away at my word-processor in a corner. While on temporary status, I got a handle on the company's operating mechanisms so that I could easily make detailed new policy proposals. Quietly, I would put the first proposal on the section chief's desk. Three days later, I would submit another; on the fourth day, another. Usually, I became full-time after the first week.

My average monthly wage during this time was never less than five figures. Privately, I began to invest in stocks which turned out to be a huge success, until soon I owned two foreign cars and a condo in the middle of the city, and a listing in the high taxpayer bracket. On Earth, they call my kind of person a 'success'. As a matter of course, I began to be surrounded by women and other camp-followers. They believed that the world revolved around a god called money. I was anxious to know what notions they had about Heaven. I thought of seeing what sort of Heaven money could build. Well, almost invariably, they thought that being able to do nothing was what Heaven meant, and that if being idle got boring, one could liven things up by engaging in gluttony, violence, sex, drugs, and pretentious display. The pleasures they conceived were nothing but the cookie-cutter variety.

The self-made man is not all that different. He thinks idleness is the worst of sins, and that Heaven and Hell are two sides of the same coin. For him, Heaven and Hell are manifest on Earth, and which one he's living in depends on his state of mind. This is the realization I have come to after ten years on Earth.

I closed the chapter on my salaried life in its seventh year. For an angel, repetitiveness is unlucky. Do the same thing for too long, and people around you begin to suspect things. An angel must be in a constant process of change. At the very least, I needed to retain a semblance of pride in my former angeldom. In the eyes of an angel, then, life on Earth is an eternal nightmare. My pride and my memory as a former angel alone governed my conduct, I believed.

I turned to trying to explain to earthlings, in terms they could accept, what Heaven was like, and what sort of life angels led. In this role, people called me a priest, a scholar of religion, and a poet. If, through my teaching, most earthlings attained a clear image of Heaven, it would fall to Earth that much faster, I thought. And the more fallen angels there were, the closer the distance would become between Earth and Heaven.

I can never return to Heaven. For that very reason, I must drag Heaven down to Earth. God will perhaps say that it is only the revenge of a fallen angel. All I want, however, is to have my dream of a heavenly garden of fallen angels in this nightmare which is earthly life. Any angel in Heaven who has no need of dreams while up there would dream of the same ideal state as I do once he fell to Earth.

'What is going to happen when Heaven falls to Earth? What do you see in your dreams?' he asks, yawning.

I take three volumes from the shelf and hand them to him.

'I wrote these. The general information is there. Take them with you. But you needn't read them, because some day you will have the same dreams I do. It's nearly daybreak. You must be tired of hearing my old stories. I'll lend you my bed. Try to see what a dream is like.'

'What do I do to dream?'

I take him by the shoulders and lead him to the bed. The sheets are fresh.

'Lie down and close your eyes. Forget yourself and become one with the air and the darkness around you. I'll stay with you until you fall asleep. This is your first night on Earth. Sweet dreams!'

Despite my talk that night of the trials of getting on in life, I feel quite happy, as though a chunk of Heaven has fallen on my balcony. For the first time in a long while, I too want to take flight to a place beyond mere dreams. Once he falls asleep, I swallow a drug-soaked piece of paper and lie down on the couch. I am slightly tired, but I know I am not in for sleep.

Soon I feel a slight, sweetly scented breeze on my face. The force of the air grows steadily stronger, ruffling my hair and furling the hem of my dressing-gown. The window is closed. For some strange reason, the wind is coming from within the room. After a while, the air becomes tinged with pink until I can see it flow. It is coming from the room where he sleeps. The colored and scented air ebbs and flows as though breathing, colliding with the table and the walls to form complicated swirls. Suddenly, from under the couch a whirlwind twists up, burrowing its way up to my crotch and spiraling around my penis. The whirlwind grows until it fattens into a funnel which sucks the empty champagne bottle, the clock, books and lamps, cushions, and knick-knacks into its grip, finally reaching the table and the couch on which I lie, which is lifted into the air. My body starts to spin like a helicopter propeller, my penis as the pivot. I grab on to the flying curtains, make an attempt to open the window, but like the lashing tail of a whip, I am slapped to the floor and then to the ceiling. As I desperately try to push my hands towards the window, my body crashes through the glass and flies outside. I plummet down, still clutching a shred of curtain; then, just before impact, I'm swept up again and blown about like a fly making strange tracks in the night sky. Wait, I am not flying. It feels as though I am being sucked up somewhere by a giant straw drawn by a huge haphazard hand in a single twisting line.

Tossed back and forth, bumped here and there, my flesh and bones are whittled away like a yam being shaved in a grater. And then, when nothing is left but the two orbs of my eyes, I emerge from the straw into a vast, empty space. It seems as though I have been led from the darkness to a place immediately next to the sun. The blinding light feels as if it will melt my eyes.

'Hurry,' the sun cries.

I glance down and see a writhing sea. The white billows give birth to a succession of angels, angels too numerous to count. What looks to be the sea is in fact the sky. The billowing waves are actually angels falling like snow. I look up. I see a checkerboard pattern. It seems strangely like the grid of a congested metropolis. Countless angels are falling upward, emitting a faint light like the shredded curtains of the aurora borealis. Soon, as my transparent body is enveloped in the aurora's many layers, the weight of gravity presses down on me and with a monstrous speed I make my inverted descent.

A great boom, as though the entire world had turned into a drum, reverberates in the space around me. Autos, buildings, dogs, and men alike are all pulverized to chaotic bits which stab my body, still cloaked in the aurora. Emitting wan flashes of light, my body and the mysterious unnamed fragments dissolve into a mush, which is transformed into grains of brightly iridescent sand that fall and collect on the Earth.

The wind turns to a gale. As it blows the accumulated sand, a river is formed. And there I find not angels, not earthlings, not myself. A desert lies in every direction, and yet people and angels flow smoothly about as grains of sand. Sand shifts with the wind, collides, progresses and retreats, sometimes blending together, sometimes solidifying. And then the sound of flowing wind and sand turns into the ruckus of city streets and squares.

'Hey, man, have I got a woman for you!'

'Let's you and I go somewhere, baby, and make it together.'

'I'll blow your brains out, punk.'

'Are you Animal Baby? I come from Jill. Sell me the stuff.'

'Madame, you've dropped something.'

'I used to be a lawyer, but since I fried my brains with drugs, I've switched to being a comedian.'

'Are you there?'

From somewhere a familiar music rides the wind to my ears. Which tune is it?

'Sir, wake up!'

His face is before my eyes. Suddenly I find myself on the couch. Yes, I remember taking the drug and dozing off. It is already light outside.

'What time is it?'

'10:05. The music is on.'

I always set the radio timer for ten o'clock. At ten there is a re-broadcast of a program called 'The Universe of Music'.

'It's a favorite program of mine. Did you sleep well?'

'Yes, but I didn't find out what you mean by the word "dream". I seemed only to float in darkness.'

'I see. It's because your consciousness is still in Heaven. I had a dream about Heaven falling.'

'That must have been nice. I must thank you. I have to leave now.'

'You're going? You should stay for a while in my apartment. You're not a bother at all.'

'Thank you for offering. You've done it on your own. I ought to be able to do the same, trusting in my pride as a fallen angel. I will take these books you have written.'

'Have you decided on a name?'

'No, not yet.'

'Will you allow me to choose one for you?'

'I'd be very pleased.'

I affix my signature to the books I have given him and, after a moment's thought, write his name: Mr Sandy River. To his friends, the Dolphin.

'That's it. It's your stage name as a singer. How about eighteen?'

'Fine. Sandy River it is, age eighteen.'

'Wait a minute.'

I take a thick wad of cash from the desk drawer and give it to him along with four tabs of the drug I had taken during the night.

'Money makes the world go 'round, so they say. Nothing goes further than a little cash. And then there's this drug. When you get nostalgic for Heaven or just want to forget everything you're doing on Earth, take it. Just don't use it when someone else is around.'

'I can't thank you enough.'

'No need to thank me. I'm sure we'll meet again somewhere.'

His puppy-dog eyes filled with admiration, Dolphin leaves. I burrow into the bed where he has slept and inhale with my entire body the lingering aroma of his freshly fallen angeldom from the pillow and sheets. The faint perfume relaxes my whole body as nostalgia sweeps over me, and I think: Maybe Heaven is already falling to Earth.

I open the window and look up into the sky. It is cloudy. I see Dolphin's figure in the distance. Where is he planning to go? Why must I know all these things he doesn't? Better to be lost. Humanity finds its home in the labyrinth. Humanity has no destination. Come to think of it, I have forgotten to teach him about love. But with a face and voice like his, he will be pursued by women and gays. Being a rock star should suit him.

Somehow, the sounds of the neighborhood seem changed. What had resembled the rippled hissing of late-night TV static, this morning sounds like a thousand pipe organs in massed unison, all stops pulled as per a master score, now in chorus, now a cappella, creating a great symphony. Countless buildings visible from my balcony are resonating, perhaps with a melody unique to each.

DREAMING OF KIMCHEE

Translated by Ann Sherif

In just about every women's magazine you pick up, you'll find an article about extramarital affairs. The contents don't vary much:

Keep in mind that married men who have extramarital affairs rarely leave their wives to marry their lovers. If you can cope with that reality, then an affair with a married man may be just the thing for you. A woman is wise to regard such relationships as temporary, and something to learn from, rather than hoping for something more permanent.

I read dozens of those articles, but never took them to heart.

I didn't ransack the magazine stands trying to find magazines with 'men who cheat on their wives' articles. I just liked buying a magazine on the way home from work when I knew I would have enough time to read it, on the rare occasion when I got out of work at a decent hour. Could I help it that they always featured a 'loving a married man' article?

I relished those days when I had a few hours to relax at home. I wouldn't make a big deal about dinner, because I preferred to spend my time watching TV, or writing long-overdue letters to friends. Sometimes I'd just gab on the phone for an hour or so. Later in the evening, I'd never miss my soak in a hot bath, after which I'd jump into bed, ready to read my new magazine from cover to cover, including the obligatory blurb about the difficulties of getting involved with a married man. But I really just skimmed them without paying much attention, which is hard to believe, considering.

I adored the apartment I had then—my little castle, with a decorating job by yours truly. I chose every detail down to the towels in the bathroom. I looked for ages before I found dishes that I liked. Once ensconced inside my warm, safe haven, I forgot about everything, and even tried to banish work from my mind. And I looked forward to the nightly phone call from my boyfriend, at

10:00 p.m. sharp. Waiting for his call was part of my routine, even if I was too bushed to do much else.

I liked my life then. Those magazine articles didn't bother me at all, even the 'true confession' type, which were depressing and reeked of despair. I was so unaware that I could even resist the devastating pessimism of the trained professionals. I was in control. I'd sit there in my happy home, paging through my glossy magazines, until I found yet another article on the topic. I'd skim through it coolly, as if the subject didn't apply. When I was done reading, I'd take another bite of whatever cookie I was devouring that night, flip to the next page in the magazine, and forget all about it. Very odd, now that I think about it. It depresses me to recall my emotional state then.

Even though our love was strong and constant, we had our share of disagreements. I remember once we argued on the phone, and, after I'd slammed the receiver down, I swore to myself that I'd never talk to him again. And then there was the time when I had a conversation with his wife in person—that blew me away. But the most unbelievable thing was me in my wonderful, cozy, warm little room, watching TV, and sitting there reading articles about infidelity as if all the pain and doubt and uncertainty they talked about had absolutely nothing to do with me.

I can picture myself now, like someone I'd see through a window, a woman safe in a warm asylum. I would imagine that she needed a hug, though I'm not sure why, because ultimately no one can comfort her, not her lover, not her parents, and certainly not the present me, the victor.

'You really don't want to be reading articles like that,' I want to tell her. 'You pretend to be strong, but I know it hurts a lot.'

If there is a God, I bet She watches over us like that. Memories are energy, and if they aren't defused, they remain to haunt you. Of course God would worry, and hover around me, as I lay there leafing through my magazine, and shake me with an invisible hand.

'It's right here. Don't pretend you don't feel it,' She would yell, in a silent voice.

In the end, I married my lover. He left his wife and we got married.

The moment we met, I felt certain that he and I would spend some part of our lives together. There was no way around it. I didn't intuit the inevitability of our relationship, or will it into being. I simply knew it would happen. Our relationship came about naturally, without dreams or desire.

It wasn't as easy as I'm making it sound, of course. After all, I was in love with a married man, and sometimes the stress of the relationship hurt me tremendously. I'd get so sick of the whole thing that I'd feel like giving up. Every time we'd hit a snag, I'd find myself wondering why. We'll end up together eventually, so why all this backsliding? Sometimes it didn't even seem worth it, and I would stop trying, ready to give it all up. Gradually, though, I stopped holding back and just went with the flow. There was no point in resisting, because he and I were born into this world to be together.

I found out that only 5 per cent of couples like us end up getting married. I felt uncomfortable being made into a statistic like that, though, because I knew that we weren't just like every other couple.

Thinking about it now, I realize that a strange, invisible kind of pressure had taken control of me then, a pressure to conform. It's like when you go out to a restaurant with a group of friends and you plan to all split the bill evenly, you can't very well order a whole meal for yourself if everyone else is just having a cup of coffee. Just like you're obliged to go on company trips, even if you don't want to. Your superiors will look down on you if you don't. That's the way the world works.

Of course, it's natural for taxi-drivers who are working late at night to look for a fare with a long trip. If a single woman goes bar-hopping by herself, people conclude that she's loose. If you have lunch with a single guy from the office, the women you usually eat with get upset. All these things seem so trivial, yet the rules are hard and fast. It's weird. Just like it's strange how everyone automatically makes assumptions about people who are having affairs before they've heard the particulars. And then they feel like it's their place to judge the morality of those involved.

In my case, I promised myself that I would ignore what other people thought, and do what I needed to do for myself. And I realize now that I was waging a psychic battle with other things as well—and it wasn't just with him, his wife, and myself. It's the way society is now. You're not supposed to be by yourself. You get caught in the net, and you can feel it tugging at you as you try to get away from it, just as if you've walked into a spider's web. You struggle to free yourself, but you can't. It's in the air; there's no escape from this force, one so inferior to the life force, the energy within us. You can pretend to ignore it, but it still obscures your vision.

We'd been married for two years. We didn't have children, and I'd quit my job a year before. We had one cat and lived in a condo that we had bought together.

Every morning before he left for work, he'd promise to call if he'd be late getting home. Then he'd switch off the TV, and go. Silence filled up the apartment. My husband didn't eat breakfast, so I would usually still be in bed. I'd just lie there, quietly, watching him leave. When I heard him close the door behind him, a feeling of regret would flash through the room, and for a moment I would feel so lonesome. I could see the rays of morning sunlight shining across the dining room table and smell the coffee. The cat would wander into our bedroom, jump onto the bed, and curl up by my feet. As I gazed down at her, I'd drift off to sleep again.

At first, I wouldn't know where I was when I woke up. Sometimes I'd call my little sister's name.

'Kyon-chan? Are you there?'

During the last part of our 'affair', he would come to my apartment every night. We'd eat dinner together, have a couple of beers, and then go to bed. In the morning, he'd go off to work, and all that I had left were a couple pairs of his socks and some shirts, and his pillow next to mine. Eventually, I tired of this arrangement, and asked my sister if she wanted to share an apartment with me. She loved the idea, because it meant we'd be able to afford a bigger place by pooling our money.

Partly, I made the move to test our relationship, although I didn't relish the idea of hunting for hotel rooms where we could make love. If something like this would make our love go sour, then it wasn't meant to last anyway. But everything turned out to be fine, even when I didn't have a place of my own. Our future together seemed bright.

And I felt better, too, I'd been losing weight and was feeling down, but life with my sister agreed with me. She was like an ice pack when you have a fever, or a pot of bubbling stew and a soft cozy blanket on a cold winter day. I hadn't realized how stressed out I'd been.

We got along well, my sister and I. I'd wake up in the morning to hear her filling the teapot with fresh water for tea. She'd take charge and tell me what to do, like 'Get off your butt and go clean the bathroom.' One of my favorite things was to buy sweets from the bakery on my way home from work, so that she and I could spend time together having tea and talking about all the things that had happened that day. She always understood what was on my mind, but never tried to second-guess me. Plus, on my days off, I no longer had to spend the evening in front of the television watching variety shows all by myself.

I was starved for that kind of ordinary companionship and routine. A relationship with a married man totally lacks those aspects, of course, because he can get his creature comforts from his wife at home, if he wants to. That's one reason extramarital affairs are better avoided.

Every morning, I'd wake up and hear my sister bustling around in the next room. I'd just lie there half asleep, thinking about her, innocently, like a child. I knew that she would never do anything to hurt me. I felt absolutely safe with her. I could drift back to sleep without a care in the world, knowing that she'd be there when I woke up, and that she, at least, didn't have another home to go to. Her place was with me. My sister loved me as much as she loved her boyfriend, though in a sisterly way, and I knew that she would never cause me pain. Not like him, even though he loved me as much as he had loved his wife.

Most days, I'd eventually fall back asleep, nestled in my warm comforter, at peace with the world. Life was good.

That's why, after he got divorced, I wasn't exactly overjoyed when he asked me to marry him. Of course it made me happy that he had proposed to me, but I was finding life with my sister very comfortable. I might not have made it if I hadn't spent that time healing and trying to feel whole again. At the same time, I realized that I couldn't live with my sister for the rest of my life, and that's why I decided to take the leap into a new existence, one fraught with difficulty.

Our relationship had started out under rocky circumstances, and marriage itself did not alleviate all of the problems. For me, this meant that I was condemned to a role of eternal waiting, a state of anticipation of the day when the fatigue and tension implicit to our love would disappear.

To give a concrete example, something very strange would happen when he'd called to let me know that he'd be home late from work. By the time he'd phoned me, I'd usually already have dinner made, but I never spent much time on cooking anyway, so it didn't bother me that he wasn't going to eat at home. In fact, I couldn't believe how considerate he was. Not only would he keep me informed of his plans, he'd say, 'Instead of sitting at home by yourself, why don't you go and have dinner at your sister's?'

For a while after saying good-bye and hanging up, I'd be fine, but in less than half an hour I started to feel it, something like a chemical reaction, completely beyond my control. I would sit there staring into space, under the influence of this imperative to wait that filled the apartment like a mysterious vapor. Within a couple of hours, it had circulated throughout my body, and immobilized me completely. Eventually, I became impervious to everything around me, and couldn't respond to the sound of the telephone ringing, or recognize my books, the TV screen, the bath, anything, as if I had been enveloped in an impenetrable membrane. Only my mind was active, as all of the terrible possibilities visited me like evil spirits.

I longed for my old, simple life with my sister, when I could be myself completely. At the same time I had to remind myself that I had chosen to leave her, and to live with him as man and wife, but to no avail. I still felt just awful. What did work like a charm was chanting to myself, 'This is the way life is, and I can't change it.' I even tried saying it out loud, and somehow that made the clouds clear. I never spoke with my husband about it. There was no point talking. It was a really rough time for me.

The time I met his wife, she let me know the score in no uncertain terms. She's awfully harsh, I thought, with amazing nonchalance.

'In case it's never occurred to you, men who are unfaithful once are bound to cheat again. I promise you that's how he is. He can't resist.'

Could she possibly be right? I wondered. There's nothing for us to hold on to, no one we can keep forever as our own. Our souls are simply floating, anyway, waiting to be swept along with the current.

I remember her saying to me, 'I waited for him every day. Even after I found out about you, I was still waiting for him, every day, for months and months.'

She would also write me letters telling me about her many days of waiting. Even though I expected some pain from loving a married man, I had not anticipated how much it would actually tear me apart. At times, I felt tremendous sympathy for her, despite my position as adversary. After all, we loved the same man.

The last time I saw her, I felt overwhelmed by the weight of her pain. All she could do the whole time was complain about what a monster he was, and how much he had hurt her, but eventually my sympathy turned to anger. I said to her, 'You're obsessing. You've got to let go of him,' and without hesitation she raised her hand and slapped me hard across the face. The sting brought tears to my eyes.

It was the touch of her hand that had implanted the compulsion to wait for him in me, and eventually it spread throughout my body and grew, as if I'd been possessed by an alien. It sucked away all my energy, and the gauges in my body registered near empty.

How else could it have worked? From her point of view, I (Party A) stole her (Party B's) dreams and hopes for the future. (This is B's take on the situation, by the way, not mine. I think that no one individual possesses the power to alter the natural course of things. Besides, Party B is hardly guaranteed a happy future simply by remaining with her original partner.) So all the energy that Party B had been concentrating on her own future is now focused on Party A. If that energy becomes a negative force, then something like what happened between the two of us is inevitable. At least, that's how it looked to me, ever since she put her mark on me.

I worried, as all newlyweds do, that my new husband might fall in love with someone else, just as he had fallen in love with me. Then there was the additional twist to my fears. From early on, I realized that my daily life would be plagued with such anxiety, and I tried to avoid the pain of contemplating our future together.

Long ago, people would have said that I was possessed by evil spirits; now, we label it neurotic. I was suffering under the stress of her resentment. For my part, I saw it as the inevitable result of what I did. I altered the course, changed the plot. Of course, the spin-off from that glitch came to rest on me.

When I confessed my fears to friends, they would conclude that I just wasn't accustomed to married life. 'You're just exhausted from trying to learn to live with another person!' they'd say, or 'It takes a long time to adjust.' I admit, that was a large part of it, for me, and for him too, for that matter. He had been with his wife for a long time. Another aspect of it, I must confess, was that guilt needling at my conscience.

Then one day, when my exhaustion was at its peak, something happened. I was taking it easy, trying to fight off a cold and a headache. He had called to tell me that he wouldn't be home in time for dinner, but then appeared at a reasonable hour anyway.

A smile on his face, he fished inside his briefcase and pulled out a bag. Through the translucent plastic, I could see a jar with something bright orange in it.

'Look what somebody gave me!' he exclaimed.

'What is it?'

'It's kimchee, the spicy Korean pickles.'

'Somebody at work brought you kimchee?' I asked curiously. He handed the bag to me, and I could smell the spicy, luscious odor of cabbage and garlic.

'Oh, sorry, I thought I'd told you. I stopped in at the office this morning, but then I went over to Mr Endo's house and spend most of the day there. We needed some time together to discuss a design he's doing for us. Anyway, his wife made that kimchee. She's Korean, so it's the real thing.'

I knew that he was probably telling me the truth. If he were that good at making up complicated lies, he could have led a double life without ever having to marry me at all. But how was I to tell? He might be lying. He could have bought the kimchee at the store, and then just torn off the price tag. I could find out easily enough by looking at the package.

But I didn't inspect the bag or its contents because I hated the thought of stooping so low. If I let myself get carried away, and gave in to paranoia, I wouldn't be able to trust myself, much less my husband or anyone else.

'Thanks,' I said feebly, and my eyes averted, shoved the bag into the refrigerator. I could barely manage that.

My headache finally went away and I tried calling my sister to chase away my blues. I even took a leisurely bath, but nothing worked. I wasn't surprised when he asked, 'What's the matter? Is something bothering you?'

'No, everything's fine,' I replied, but I couldn't even manage a smile. I was like a faded flower, devoid of energy.

Later that evening, we sat down together in front of the TV with some beers and a dish of kimchee to nibble on. We chatted as we watched some silly program, and, at one point, he commented that I seemed under the weather lately. I tried denying it and claimed that I was just a bit worn out, that's all.

And then something amazing happened to me. I felt so clearly that I was changing inside, at that very moment, that I glanced at my watch to check the time. It was 10:15 p.m. To my utter astonishment, my head had cleared completely. I felt as if the fog that had been clouding my eyes had lifted. I don't know how it happened, but it occurred to me that such lucidity wasn't entirely new for me. Once, long before, I had been able to see clearly.

Or had it been that long ago? That was how I had felt when I first met him, as though I could relish each of the many flavors that life offers.

Love had given me energy and clarity of vision. Everything appeared vivid, down to the smallest detail, and I felt convinced that I could triumph over everything. To ensure my victory, and so as not to forget, I doted over every moment of our time together, and tried to absorb the details as if they were full of essential bits of information.

The bittersweet feeling of beautiful mornings when we made a date; the scent of the breeze during our brief times together; the steep slope of the street, down which we walked so fast, too fast. Glass, asphalt, mail-boxes, guardrails, fingernails. The display windows of department stores; sunlight reflected off the windows of tall buildings.

Those days, everything looked beautiful to me, and good. The things around me appeared distinct, their outlines graced by a fragrant presence. I could feel the excitement, that exhilaration deep inside. When I closed my eyes, I saw waves of energy swirling about, like patterns in a marble block.

Then I began to wonder what had just happened to me. Why had I been so overtaken by these sensations? Precisely at that moment, the phone rang. My husband answered it.

The call seemed to be for him so I gathered up the empty beer bottles and carried them into the kitchen. I felt refreshed, maybe even a little happy. Something was changing inside me. I decided to celebrate with another glass of beer. As I opened the refrigerator door, it struck me that I was very lucky woman. My future was secure, my marriage happy, and we even had our own space, a place we had chosen, just the two of us. I had the good fortune to have a roof over my head, a cozy place where I could make my bed. What on earth had been bothering me?

I could only faintly hear his side of the phone conversation from where I stood. I wondered whom he was talking with, and then felt pleasure in the fact that this question-mark no longer threatened me. Earlier that same day it would have been enough to bring me down.

I'll just ask him who called. It's no big deal. Maybe jealousy is an indication of a general lack of energy, rather than of problems in the relationship itself.

I heard him say good-bye as I carried the cold bottle of beer into the living room.

'Who was it?'

And he said the name of his ex-wife.

She had never called our place before, so I felt puzzled.

'Is something wrong?'

'Listen to this one. Remember I told you that she kept telling me that it was so unfair of me to leave her at this time in her life? "No man would want me at this age." Well, now she says that she's found a new husband, and he's younger than she is. They've got their marriage license already, and a new apartment and everything. She said that she hadn't been planning to tell me, but then she changed her mind.'

Suddenly, it all made sense to me. I know a coincidence when I see one, and this was no coincidence. Another line had converged to form a circle. Oddly, it felt so natural to me that I wasn't even surprised at how it had happened. A force, capable of liberating us from the burden of accumulated guilt, circled in to touch us that night.

'How are you doing?'

'Fine . . . relieved, actually, because now I feel like you and I can finally start our own life together,' he said. 'And I'm not saying that what we've had up to now hasn't been real. It's just that I couldn't stop feeling guilty about what I'd done.'

'I understand.'

Later, I realized why I'd felt so heady. It wasn't just because I'd been freed of the burden of negative feelings; I'd also come down with a fever. I decided to sleep on an ice-pack pillow.

'What smells in here?' he said from his side of the bed.

'Hmmm. I bet it's the kimchee.'

'So you think that we're the ones who smell, because we ate that stuff, huh?'

We both got up and sniffed about the room, trying to find the source of the smell.

'Oh, look,' I said. 'It's got to be my ice pack.'

He laughed.

'Yeah, you could smell it in the freezer too,' I said. After that, I tried wrapping a towel around the pack, but it still stank. Even so, I needed relief from the fever, so I decided to put up with the odor. We turned the lights off, and our bedroom smelled faintly of kimchee.

When I finally dozed off, I dreamed that I was strolling through a Korean market. The dream was brief, but quite vivid. In my one hand—I thought it was empty, but then I realized that I was holding someone else's hand. I looked up and saw my husband's face. And I remember seeing the bright sun, and all the goods in the market bathed in the sunlight, and the commotion, and the smell of garlic, and women with boldly drawn arched eyebrows. Red, green, pink, blue, in dazzling bright shades.

We were there to buy some kimchee. We saw big jars and barrels full of bright red pickles. He said that he wanted some special kind of kimchee. Let's go somewhere else to buy it, he said. Over that way.

And then reality broke into my dream; I had to pee. (Too much beer!) I sat up in bed, and felt my head. I was still feverish. When I got back from the bathroom, I could see well enough in the dark room to know that he was lying there with his eyes wide open.

'Having trouble getting to sleep?' I asked.

He replied drowsily, 'I just had a dream about kimchee. You and I were eating at a Korean barbecue restaurant.'

'That sounds like the dream I just had!'

'That smell goes right to your brain, doesn't it?'

'Unbelievable.'

We said good-night, and I lay down again. It felt good putting my feverish head down on the cool pillow, scented with kimchee. As I drifted off, I thought of our common dream, and the food, the odor, and the vibes in the room that had brought it about. Despite being bound as separate physical entities, we could share these aspects of daily life, and I knew that sharing, this kind of connection, was what constituted our life together.

I thought about the complications of what I'd been dealing with lately. And then I understood that actually it wasn't just the relationship—I had so much baggage from my childhood, from before I was born into this world, too. I understood that for the first time that night. And I knew it would always be that way, until we die. Even after we're dead.

But at last I had a chance to rest, after that long period of strain. I was tired and wanted to sleep. I felt that when I woke up the next morning, I would start anew. I would breathe fresh air, and start a day of entirely new experiences. It reminded me of the feelings I used to have when I was younger, like after a big test, or the night after a major school event. I'd always looked forward to waking up the next morning, when a fresh breeze would come to sweep through me, cleansing me. And when I opened my eyes at dawn, I'd feel a glow, a radiant white pearl. I hoped, nearly prayed, for that to happen again. That night, I believed with the same purity and innocence.

BIOGRAPHICAL NOTES

ABE KOBO (1924–93). Raised in colonial Manchuria. Trained as a doctor, but never practised. Created a rootless, Kafkaesque world through his novels, stories, and plays. *Beyond the Curve* (stories); *Woman in the Dunes*; etc.

AKUTAGAWA RYUNOSUKE (1892–1927). A literary craftsman who excelled at the short-story form, drawing much of his material from the distant past. His suicide is seen as marking the end of an era. *Rashomon and Other Stories*; *Hell Screen and Other Stories*; etc.

DAZAI OSAMU (1909–48). One of Japan's most popular writers, especially among young women. His novel *The Setting Sun* is a masterpiece of post-war fiction. *Crackling Mountains and Other Stories*; *Self Portraits* (stories); etc.

ENCHI FUMIKO (1905–86). Novelist, dramatist, and short-story writer. Like Tanizaki Jun'ichiro, she translated the *Tale of Genji* into modern Japanese. After an eye operation in 1973 her works, 'The Flower-Eating Crone' being one, were dictated to an amanuensis. *Masks*; *The Waiting Years*.

ENDO SHUSAKU (1923–96). Life-long Catholic who lived in France from 1950 to 1953. A prolific writer specializing in religious themes and the relationship between East and West, Endo is sometimes called 'Japan's Graham Greene'. *Silence*; *The Final Martyrs* (stories); etc.

HAYASHI FUMIKO (1903–51). A travelling peddler's daughter who worked nights in a factory to put herself through high school, Hayashi became one of Japan's most widely read novelists. 'The Accordion and the Fish Town' was her first published story.

HIGUCHI ICHIYO (1872–96). Fought poverty and ill health to become Japan's first great modern woman writer. Died of tuberculosis at the age of 24. *In the Shade of Spring Leaves* (stories).

HIRABAYASHI TAIKO (1905–72). One of the best writers to emerge from the Proletarian movement, she endured poverty, illness, and imprisonment for her political beliefs. 'Blind Chinese Soldiers' was published within months of the war's end, in 1946.

IBUSE MASUJI (1898–1993). Born near Hiroshima. His novel describing the effects of the atomic bomb dropped on that city, *Black Rain*, is one of post-war literature's great achievements. Ibuse's writing is characterized by its blend of pathos and humour. *Salamander and Other Stories*; *Castaways: Two Short Novels*; etc.

INOUE YASUSHI (1907–92). An extremely popular historical novelist whose works often centred around events in ancient China. *Lou-Lan and Other Stories*; *Tun-Huang*; etc.

Biographical Notes

KAIKO TAKESHI [Ken] (1930–89). Novelist and journalist. His experiences fending for his family as a teenager in the aftermath of the war and, later, while covering the Vietnam conflict in 1964–5, gave his writing a hard, often cynical edge. *Five Thousand Runaways* (stories); *Darkness in Summer*; etc.

KAJII MOTOJIRO (1901–32). Noted stylist whose poetic, autobiographical stories are considered classics of their genre. Succumbed to the tuberculosis described in 'Lemon', his best-known work.

KAWABATA YASUNARI (1899–1971). Won the Nobel Prize for Literature in 1970 for his strikingly visual and lyrical novels. 'The Izu Dancer', his best-known early work, appears here for the first time in unabridged translation. *House of the Sleeping Beauties and Other Stories*; *Snow Country*; *Sound of the Mountain*; etc.

KOJIMA NOBUO (1915–). Served in China during the Second World War. Most of his stories (although not 'The Rifle') are satirical, and written with a hard-edged, self-mocking humor.

KONO TAEKO (1926–). Like Tanizaki Jun'ichiro, one of her earliest influences, Kono's stories often use sado-masochistic themes to explore the inner reaches of the human psyche. *Toddler-hunting and Other Stories*.

KUNIKIDA DOPPO (1871–1908). A poet, short-story writer, and essayist who found his early inspiration in Christianity and the works of William Wordsworth. *River Mist and Other Stories*.

MISHIMA YUKIO (1925–70). A brilliant writer and critic whose dramatic suicide stunned his many readers in Japan and abroad. *Death in Midsummer and Other Stories*; *Confessions of a Mask*; *The Temple of the Golden Pavilion*; etc.

MIYAZAWA KENJI (1896–1933). A gentle, reclusive writer and poet who lived among farmers, and often wrote for children. Known for his unique cosmology, which combined modern science with animist and Buddhist beliefs. Although few of his works were published during his lifetime, he is widely read today. *Once and Forever* (stories); *The Night of the Milky Way Railroad* (novella); etc.

MORI OGAI (1862–1922). Studied medicine in Germany from 1884 to 1888, where he was exposed to European literature. Subsequently followed a dual career as a high-ranking military doctor and one of modern Japan's most important authors, translators, and critics. *Youth and Other Stories*; *The Historical Fiction of Mori Ogai*; etc.

MUKODA KUNIKO (1929–81). A television dramatist who turned to popular fiction mid-way through her career. Died in a plane crash. *The Name of the Flower* (stories).

MURAKAMI HARUKI (1949–). Best-selling novelist and translator of contemporary American literature. *The Elephant Vanishes* (stories); *A Wild Sheep Chase*; *The Hard-Boiled Wonderland and the End of the World*; etc.

Biographical Notes

NAGAI KAFU (1879–1959). After a youthful sojourn in the United States and France, Kafu immersed himself in the declining world of the geisha, the setting for most of his novels and stories. *Kafu the Scribbler* (stories); *During the Rains and Flowers in the Shade* (novellas); etc.

NAKAJIMA ATSUSHI (1909–42). Travelled widely in Asia and the South Pacific. Influences ranged from the Chinese classics to Robert Louis Stevenson.

NATSUME SOSEKI (1867–1916). A professor of English literature who gave up his academic career to become Japan's first great modern novelist. *Kokoro*; *Botchan*; *Sanshiro*; etc.

OE KENZABURO (1935–). Novelist, essayist, and a persistent critic of social injustice in Japan and abroad. Won the Nobel Prize for Literature in 1994. *Teach Us to Outgrow Our Madness* (stories); *A Personal Matter*; *The Silent Cry*; etc.

OKAMOTO KANOKO (1889–1939). Initially a poet who wrote in both the classic and modern styles. 'Portrait of an Old Geisha' is one of her best-known works of fiction.

SAKAGUCHI ANGO (1906–55). Essayist and short-story writer. His blackly sarcastic wit epitomized the sentiments of many in the post-war period, yet his essays in particular are still popular today.

SATOMI TON (1888–1983). Known for his finely crafted psychological stories and his advocacy of the kind of sensuality embodied in the kabuki actor in 'Blowfish'.

SHIGA NAOYA (1883–1971). A master stylist who excelled at the short-story form. Almost all of his fiction was 'autobiographical'. *Paper Door and Other Stories*; *A Dark Night's Passing*.

SHIMADA MASAHIKO (1961–). A prolific, often satirical novelist well-versed in literary theory and the Russian and English languages. *Dream Messenger*.

TANIZAKI JUN'ICHIRO (1886–1965). A master story-teller and stylist whose novels have influenced numerous writers in Japan and abroad. Translated the classic *Tale of Genji* into modern Japanese three times. *Seven Japanese Tales*; *The Makioka Sisters*; *The Diary of a Mad Old Man*; etc.

TSUSHIMA YUKO (1947–). One of the best writers of the post-war generation. Her experience as a single mother forms the basis for much of her fiction. Her father was the noted writer Dazai Osamu. *The Shooting Gallery and Other Stories*; *Child of Fortune*; etc.

YOKOMITSU RIICHI (1898–1947). An experimental writer and novelist whose works ranged from the modernist to the autobiographical. 'Spring Riding in a Carriage', for example, is based on the death of his first wife at the age of 20. *Love, and Other Stories of Yokomitsu Riichi*.

YOSHIMOTO BANANA (1964–). Best-selling writer whose novella *Kitchen* became a cult sensation in Japan and abroad. *Lizard* (stories); *N.P.*; etc.

Biographical Notes

YOSHIYUKI JUNNOSUKE (1924–94). In a detached and urbane style, his novels and stories portray life in the post-war water trade. *The Dark Room*.

Stories by most of the writers listed here have also appeared in one or more of the following twelve general anthologies:

Modern Japanese Literature, ed. Donald Keene (1956).

Modern Japanese Stories, ed. Ivan Morris (1962).

Contemporary Japanese Literature, ed. Howard Hibbett (1977).

Stories by Contemporary Women Writers, ed. Lippit and Selden (1983).

This Kind of Woman: Ten Short Stories by Japanese Women Writers: 1960–1976, ed. Tanaka and Hanson (1984).

The Showa Anthology: Modern Japanese Short Stories 1929–1984, ed. Gessel and Matsumoto (1985).

The Mother of Dreams and Other Stories, ed. Makoto Ueda (1986).

A Late Chrysanthemum: Twenty-One Stories from the Japanese, tr. Lane Dunlop (1986).

Monkey Brain Sushi, ed. Alfred Birnbaum (1991).

New Japanese Voices, ed. Helen Mitsios (1991).

Unmapped Territories: New Women's Fiction from Japan, ed. Yukiko Tanaka (1991).

Autumn Wind and Other Stories, tr. Lane Dunlop (1994).

FILMOGRAPHY

Japanese movies are an extraordinarily pleasant way of enhancing one's appreciation of Japanese literature. Thanks to the spread of audio-visual technology, they are also increasingly accessible. Although famous today, the Japanese cinema was virtually unknown in the West until the early 1950s, when films like Kurosawa Akira's *Rashomon* and Mizoguchi Kenji's *Sansho the Bailiff* played to astonished audiences at the Venice Film Festival, inaugurating what has been called the golden age of Japanese film. Since *Rashomon*, *Sansho*, and several other excellent movies are based on stories in this collection, and since a number of other translated works by the authors assembled here have been successfully adapted for the screen, I have appended this short list of eleven films for your pleasure and enjoyment. It is arranged in the order in which the authors appear in the Table of Contents.

Sansho the Bailiff (based on Mori Ogai's 'Sansho the Steward', in this collection): directed by Mizoguchi Kenji, 1954. Black and white. A cinematic classic of unsurpassed beauty by one of Japan's greatest film-makers.

Odd Obsession (based on Tanizaki Jun'ichiro's novel *The Key*): directed by Ichikawa Kon, 1959. Black and white. Like 'Aguri', examines the relationship between sexual obsession, life, and death. The novel is a prime example of Tanizaki's best work.

The Makioka Sisters (based on Tanizaki Jun'ichiro's novel of the same name): directed by Ichikawa Kon, 1983. Colour. An opulent adaptation of Tanizaki's celebrated masterpiece about a wealthy merchant family in decline, set in pre-war times. The endings of the film and novel are quite different.

Rashomon (based on two stories by Akutagawa Ryunosuke: 'In a Grove', in this collection, and 'Rashomon'): directed by Kurosawa Akira, 1950. Black and white. Won the Grand Prix at the 1951 Venice Film Festival, inaugurating the West's belated discovery of Japanese film. Perhaps the best-known and most influential of all Japanese movies.

Night of the Galactic Railroad (based on Miyazawa Kenji's novella of the same name): animation by Eguchi Marisuke, 1985 (original), 1995 (English version). A beautifully animated version of Miyazawa's most beloved work, which tells of a lonely boy who takes a train-ride through the stars.

Black Rain (based on Ibuse Masuji's novel of the same name): directed by Imamura Shohei, 1989. Black and white. A stylized, yet still hair-raising adaptation of Ibuse's masterpiece about the dropping of the atomic bomb on Hiroshima and its impact on one man and his family.

*The Dancing Girl of Izu (based on Kawabata Yasunari's 'The Izu Dancer', in this collection): directed by Gosho Heinosuke, 1933. Black and white. Silent. The first and best adaptation of Kawabata's beloved story, which has

served as a vehicle for launching the film careers of numerous young actresses.

*A Wandering Life (partially based on Hayashi Fumiko's 'The Accordion and the Fish Town', in this collection): directed by Naruse Mikio, 1962. Black and white. An adaptation of Hayashi's untranslated autobiographical novel of the same name, by a director who made six movies based on her work.

Woman in the Dunes (based on Abe Kobo's novel of the same name): directed by Teshigahara Hiroshi, 1964. Black and white. A cinematic *tour de force* about an urbanite who goes to the seashore to collect insects, only to be trapped in a sand pit with a local woman.

Conflagration (based on Mishima Yukio's *The Temple of the Golden Pavilion*): directed by Ichikawa Kon, 1958. Black and white. The story of a young priest obsessed with the transcendent beauty of an ancient Kyoto temple. One of Mishima's finest novels, rendered into a slow-paced, highly atmospheric film.

Kitchen (based on the novella by Yoshimoto Banana): directed by Morita Yoshimitsu, 1989. Colour. A coolly detached and stylized adaptation of Banana's contemporary classic about a girl who moves in with a young man and his mother, who was once his father.

*Indicates films which are especially difficult to obtain.

PUBLISHER'S ACKNOWLEDGEMENTS

Abe, Kobo, *The Bet* (*Kake*, 1960); from *Beyond the Curve* by Kobo Abe, translated by Juliet Winters Carpenter, published by Kodansha International Ltd. Original story *Kake* © 1960 Kobo Abe. Anthology copyright © 1991 by Kodansha International Ltd. Reprinted by permission. All rights reserved.

Akutagawa, Ryunosuke, *In a Grove* (*Yabu no Naka*, 1921); from *Rashomon and Other Stories*, translated by Takashi Kojima. Translation copyright 1952 by Liveright Publishing Corporation. Reprinted by permission of Liveright Publishing Corporation.

Dazai, Osamu, *Merry Christmas* (*Merii Kurisumasu*, 1946); from *Self Portraits* by Osamu Dazai, translated by Ralph F. McCarthy, published by Kodansha International Ltd. English translation copyright © 1991 by Kodansha International Ltd. Reprinted by permission. All rights reserved.

Enchi, Fumiko, *The Flower-Eating Crone* (*Hana-kui Uba*, 1974), © Fuke Motoko; English translation © 1997 Lucy North.

Endo, Shusaku, *Unzen* (*Unzen*, 1965); translated by Van Gessel (*Stained Glass Elegies*, 1984, courtesy of Peter Owen Ltd, London).

Hayashi, Fumiko, *The Accordion and the Fish Town* (*Fukin to Uo no Machi*, 1931), © Hayashi Fukue; translated by Janice Brown.

Hirabayashi, Taiko, *Blind Chinese Soldiers* (*Mo Chugoku Hei*, 1946); translated by Noriko Mizuta Lippit (*Japanese Women Writers: Twentieth Century Short Fiction*, 1991, pp. 41–5). Reprinted by permission from M. E. Sharpe, Inc., Armonk, NY.

Higuchi, Ichiyo, *Separate Ways* (*Wakare-Michi*, 1896); translated by Robert Danly (*In the Shade of Spring Leaves: The Life of Higuchi Ichiyo With Nine of Her Best Short Stories*). Copyright © 1981 by Robert Lyons Danly. Reprinted by permission of W. W. Norton & Company Inc.

Ibuse, Masuji, *Carp* (*Koi*, 1926); from *Salamander and Other Stories* by Masuji Ibuse, translated by John Bester, published by Kodansha International Ltd. English copyright © 1981 by Kodansha International Ltd. Reprinted by permission. All rights reserved.

Inoue, Yasushi, *Passage to Fudaraku* (*Fudaraku Tokaiki*, 1961); from *Lou-lan and Other Stories* by Yasushi Inoue, translated by James Araki, published by Kodansha International Ltd. English translation copyright © 1979 by Kodansha International Ltd. Reprinted by permission. All rights reserved.

Kaiko, Takeshi, *The Duel* (*Ketto*, 1968); from *Five Thousand Runaways*, Dodd, Mead & Co., 1987), reproduced by kind permission of the translator, Cecilia Segawa Seigle.

Publisher's Acknowledgements

Kajii, Motojiro, *Lemon* (*Remon*, 1925); translated by Robert Ulmer.

Kawabata, Yasunari, *The Izu Dancer* (*Izu no Odoriko*, 1925), © Kawabata Yasunari Kinenkai; translated by Edward Seidensticker.

Kojima, Nobuo, *The Rifle* (*Shoju*, 1952); translated by Lawrence Rogers (*Japan Quarterly*, xxxiv, Jan.–Mar. 1987).

Kono, Taeko, *Toddler-hunting* (*Yoji-gari*, 1965); translated by Lucy North (*Toddler-Hunting and Other Stories*, New Directions, 1996) reprinted by permission of New Directions Publishing Corporation.

Kunikida, Doppo, *The Bonfire* (*Takibi*, 1896); translated by Jay Rubin (*Monumenta Nipponica*, 25/1–2, 1970).

Mishima, Yukio, *Onnagata* (*Onnagata*, 1957); translated by Donald Keene (*Death in Midsummer and Other Stories*, Secker and Warburg, 1967), reprinted by permission of New Directions Publishing Corporation.

Miyazawa, Kenji, *The Bears of Nametoko* (*Nametokoyama no Kuma*, ?1927); from *Once and Forever: The Tales of Kenji Miyazawa*, translated by John Bester, published by Kodansha International Ltd. Copyright © 1993 by Kodansha International Ltd.

Mori, Ogai, *Sansho the Steward* (*Sansho Dayu*, 1915); translated by J. Thomas Rimer (*The Incident at Sakai and Other Stories*), University of Hawaii Press, 1977.

Mukoda, Kuniko, *Mr Carp* (*Koi-san*, 1985); reproduced from *The Name of the Flower: Stories by Kuniko Mukoda*, translated by Tomone Matsumoto (Berkeley, Stone Bridge Press, 1994).

Murakami, Haruki, *The Elephant Vanishes* (*Zo ga Shometsu Suru*, 1987); translated by Jay Rubin (*The Elephant Vanishes*, copyright © 1993 by Haruki Murakami. Reprinted by permission of Alfred A. Knopf Inc.).

Nagai, Kafu, *The Peony Garden* (*Botan no Kyaku*, 1909); reprinted from *Kafu the Scribbler: The Life and Times of Nagai Kafu, 1879–1959* by Edward Seidensticker with the permission of the publishers, Stanford University Press. © 1965 by Edward Seidensticker.

Nakashima, Ton, *The Expert* (*Meijin-den*); translated by Ivan Morris (*Encounter*, 10/5, May 1958).

Natsume, Soseki, *The Third Night* (*Daisan-ya*) from *Ten Nights of Dream* (*Yume Juya*, 1908); translated by Aiko Ito and Graeme Wilson (*Ten Nights of Dream, Hearing Things, The Heredity of Tastes*, Charles E. Tuttle Publishing Co. Inc., of Tokyo, Japan, 1974).

Oe, Kenzaburo, *Prize Stock* (*Shiiku*, 1958); from *Teach Us to Outgrow Our Madness*, published by Grove, 1977, English translation copyright © 1977 by John Nathan, reprinted by permission of Grove/Atlantic Inc.

Okamoto, Kanoko, *Portrait of an Old Geisha* (*Rokisho*, 1939); translated by Cody Poulton.

Publisher's Acknowledgements

Sakaguchi, Ango, *In The Forest, Under Cherries in Full Bloom (Sakura no Mori no Mankai no Shita*, 1947), © Sakaguchi Tsunao; translated by Jay Rubin.

Satomi, Ton, *Blowfish (Fugu*, 1913), © Yamakawa Shizuo; translated by Ted Goossen (*Descant 75*, Winter 1991–2).

Shiga, Naoya, *Night Fires (Takibi*, 1920), © Shiga Naokichi; translated by Ted Goossen.

Shimada, Masahiko, *Desert Dolphin (Sabaku no Iruka*, 1992), © Shimada Masahiko; translated by Kenneth Richard (*Descant 89*, Summer 1995).

Tanizaki, Jun'ichiro, *Aguri (Aoi Hana*, 1922); from *Seven Japanese Tales* by Junichiro Tanizaki, translated by H. Hibbett. Copyright © 1963 by Alfred A. Knopf Inc. Reprinted by permission of the publisher.

Tsushima, Yuko, *A Very Strange Enchanted Boy (Fushigi na Shonen*, 1985), © Tsushima Yuko; English translation by Geraldine Harcourt (*Descant 89*, Summer 1995), © Geraldine Harcourt.

Yokomitsu, Riichi, *Spring Riding in a Carriage (Haru wa Basha ni Notte*, 1926), translated by Dennis Keene ('*Love' and Other Stories of Yokomitsu Riichi*, University of Tokyo Press, 1974).

Yoshimoto, Banana, *Dreaming of Kimchee (Kimuchi no Yume*, 1992); from *Lizard*. Grove, 1995, English translation copyright © 1995 by Ann Sherif, reprinted by permission of Grove/Atlantic Inc.

Yoshiyuki, Junnosuke, *Three Policemen (Sannin no Keikan*); translated by Hugh Clarke (*Seven Stories of Modern Japan*, University of Sydney, 1991).

While every effort has been made to secure permission, we may have failed in a few cases to trace the copyright holder. We apologize for any apparent negligence.